WEY

P9-BJS-046

THINKING BIG

THINKING BIG

The Story of the
LOS ANGELES TIMES
Its Publishers and
Their Influence on
Southern California

ROBERT GOTTLIEB and IRENE WOLT

G. P. PUTNAM'S SONS, NEW YORK

Copyright © 1977 by Robert Gottlieb and Irene Wolt

All rights reserved. This book, or parts thereof, must not be reproduced in any form without permission. Published simultaneously in Canada by Longman Canada Limited, Toronto.

Library of Congress Cataloging in Publication Data

Gottlieb, Robert
　Thinking big.

　Includes bibliographical references and index.
　1. The Los Angeles Times.　I. Wolt, Irene,
joint author.　II. Title.
PN4899.C226L64　1977　　071'.94'94　　76–51847

SBN: 399–11766–0

PRINTED IN THE UNITED STATES OF AMERICA

Contents

Introduction

"What Southern California has done for the *Los Angeles Times,* and what the *Times* has done for Southern California, it would take a book to relate," wrote Los Angeles's literary pioneer Charles Lummis in 1900. More than three-quarters of a century later, those words ring truer than Lummis could have possibly imagined.

The story of the phenomenal expansion of Los Angeles and that of its leading establishment voice, the *Los Angeles Times,* have always been intimately related. The Chandler family, publishers of the *Times,* has always held a special place as the single most powerful family in Southern California because of its extensive investment and broad political clout in the region. Other newspapers and publishers have played roles in their city's history, but the extent to which the Chandlers and the *Times* held sway in Los Angeles was unique.

As the city changed, so did the newspaper and the family empire. From a small, undeveloped cattle town, Los Angeles became the second largest metropolitan region in the country. Once a parochial right-wing extension of the Chandler power, the *Los Angeles Times* is now frequently ranked among the five best papers in the country. The Chandler family's economic empire has been restructured into the multimedia conglomerate Times Mirror Company—the largest publisher in the nation—with newspaper, broadcast and cable, forest products, book publishing, and information service subsidiaries.

This transformation of the city. the newspaper, and the family holdings reflects the emergence of the modern megalopolis, the development of

7

monopolistic newspapers and corporations, and the overall institutionalization of power in the United States.

The story of the *Times* and its publishers is thus more than a history of one region. Los Angeles has come to represent a quintessential American quality, and the newspaper and its powerful owners have helped to shape the dominant culture of the city—its boosterism, its probusiness and expansionist outlook, and its celebration of bigness as a value in itself. Los Angeles, the *Times*, and the Chandlers have provided a model for the rest of the country.

This book is divided into four parts, corresponding to the eras of the *Times'* four different publishers and to four generations in the city's transformation. Urban history, journalism, economic analysis, and a biographical narrative with a cast of hundreds have been interwoven. Only in its entirety can the full story of the *Times*, its publishers, and Los Angeles be understood.

PART I

1881–1917

"A Great Big Boom"

THIS IS PURE GOLD!!!

SANTA ANA,

The Metropolis of Southern California's fairest valley,
Chief among Ten Thousand, Or the One
Altogether Lovely;
Beautiful! Busy!
Bustling! Booming!
The Town has the biggest kind of a
Big, big Boom.
A great Big Boom! And you
Can Accumulate Ducats by Investing!
—Ad in the *Los Angeles Times,* 1887

When the great real estate boom of 1887 exploded across the Southern California basin, it propelled Los Angeles forward along a route already mapped out by the town's leading businessmen. These frontier entrepreneurs—many only recently arrived from the East—looked with eagerness to the growth of their adopted city. Their arrival helped set in motion a chain of events which would dramatically transform the entire region.

Previously, in the years just prior to 1870, Los Angeles was little more than a dusty cattle town full of saloons and violence. Shootings and stabbings were so common that the town averaged a murder a day. With a

11

weak local government doing little to control the fighting and gambling, Los Angeles picked up a reputation as the toughest town in the country.

Cattle raising dominated the area's economy. Animals roamed the town's streets and grazed on the huge ranches which made up the "cow counties" of Southern California. The large cattle herds were owned by Spanish landholders, who controlled most of the wealth of the region.

In 1864 the lavish life-style of the Southern California cattle barons began to come to an end. The Great Drought, the worst in the region's history, drove cattle to their deaths and the cattle owners into debt. In order to settle their debts and pay their taxes, the owners had to relinquish parts of their extensive ranch holdings to land speculators.

The division of the ranches generated Southern California's first real estate boom. Land promoters broke down the large tracts and sold the plots to Anglo settlers. Immigration increased, provoking the formation of whole new settlements. Cheap land, fertile soil, and mild climate attracted aspiring farmers. A new epoch based on a farm economy was beginning to edge out the romantic era of the ranches.

The economic transformation made its presence felt in the city. Farm wagons and mule trains laden with silver from outlying mining sites replaced the old cattle herds. The downtown adobe structures gave way to new brick buildings. Los Angeles's first bank was established in 1868, its first fire company in 1871. A railroad linking the city with the port of San Pedro was constructed in 1868. Businesses flourished and multiplied. Even its lawless frontier reputation gave way as Los Angeles's new businessmen decided that a modicum of law and order was needed if their town was to continue to prosper.

The town's growth was ultimately dependent on the railroad. When the mighty Southern Pacific Railroad started laying tracks in Southern California, Los Angeles desperately wanted to be its southwestern terminal. Other Southern California towns, such as San Bernardino and San Diego, competed for the privilege. Fearing that their town would fail to grow if the railroad bypassed them, Los Angeles citizens voted to offer a subsidy to the Southern Pacific if it would build through the Tehachapi Mountains and come down into Los Angeles. The railroad owners, having made similar arrangements—and huge profits—with other townships, agreed. On September 5, 1876, an excited crowd cheered as D.D. Colton of the Southern Pacific hammered in the golden spike which connected the lines from Los Angeles to San Francisco.

The coming of the railroad opened new markets for Los Angeles's agricultural products. It also spurred new migration to the area, and new towns, such as Pasadena and Downey, formed along the railroad lines. The Southern Pacific, eager to sell its own lands and to build up areas along its tracks, aided the immigration by sending agents throughout the country to give lectures and to set up exhibits about its new territory. The population doubled within the decade.

Los Angeles's businessmen, aiming to attract even more immigrants, initiated a major propaganda campaign of their own. Books and pamphlets extolling the virtues of the area were distributed with an eye to the "frozen East." One newspaper, the *Herald,* was begun with the boosting of the region as one of its primary objectives. Each week the Los Angeles Chamber of Commerce sent out fifty copies of the *Herald* and other local papers to hotels and libraries throughout the country.

By the beginning of 1885, the *Los Angeles Times,* in the first of its annual midwinter booster editions, could boast of "the marvelous change" which had occurred in "the rough frontier settlements of fifteen years ago." The *Times* noted, "The wide cattle and sheep ranges, with nothing to indicate human habitation except the occasional crumbling adobe of the Spanish and Mexican cattle lords . . . have given place to numerous beautiful and thriving settlements with happy homes, schools, road facilities and all the other comforts of modern civilization."

Newspapers and business interests worked in tandem, launching campaigns to promote the climate, the agricultural possibilities, and the overall economic potential of the area. In 1885 the Southern California Immigration Association (SCIA) was set up under the direction of oilman Thomas Bard and *Los Angeles Times* partner H.H. Boyce to stage promotional exhibits around the country. SCIA events, such as the citrus fair it sponsored in Chicago, were accompanied by an ample supply of the *Times* and *Herald* booster editions.

In 1885 another incident occurred which greatly benefited the Southern California publicity campaign. A new railroad, a subsidiary of the Santa Fe lines, entered Los Angeles after defeating attempts of the Southern Pacific to keep the other railroad out of its Southern California territory. The two lines immediately began competing for customers. A highly publicized rate war took effect as each railroad tried to undersell the other by continuously lowering its fares. A ticket from the East Coast, which normally went for $125, went down to $95 in 1885, then to $45, and finally to a meager $25. In another much publicized maneuver, the railroads sold tickets from Kansas City for only one dollar.

By 1886 all the promotional efforts began to reach fruition. The Great Boom had begun. Their minds filled with images of the new Eden, thousands took advantage of the low train fares. Up to five trains a day steamed into the city carrying immigrants and land speculators. With hotels and rooming houses overflowing, people camped out in tents. Real estate values began to rise. An increased clamor for land prompted subsequent increases in its value, which in turn attracted a greater number of land speculators. Buying and selling of land rose to a fevered pitch.

Money and real estate changed hands faster than the sales could be recorded. Buyers, anxious to get first choice of lots before prices went up again, couldn't spare the time to look at sites. People didn't care what they bought as long as they thought they could sell it to someone else—at a higher price. Real estate values climbed to staggering heights, and scores of new "cities" sprang up overnight in the most inaccessible, rocky, and mountainous areas. One boom town, Border City, was later described by historian James Guinn as being "most easily accessible by means of balloon" and "as secure from hostile invasion as the homes of the cliff dwellers."

Los Angeles's boosters jubilantly spurred on the dealings. Newspapers were filled with real estate advertisements and pseudo news articles which let the reader know how he or she could take part in the buying. "Do not fail to read the advertisement of J.C. Bryan in the 'wants' columns of today's *Times*," led a *Los Angeles Times* news story headlined BARGAINS IN REAL ESTATE.

In June 1886 the *Times* had to add an extra page to hold all the real estate advertisements with their florid descriptions of the latest offerings: ESCONDIDO: THE PARADISE OF SOUTHERN CALIFORNIA, THE SUN-KISSED VALE OF THE SOUTH; GLENDALE, THE GEM OF ALL GEMS; MAKE YOUR FORTUNES—VERNONDALE. Others waxed poetic:

> Whittier! Whittier! Whittier! Beautiful Whittier,
> Whittier Queen of the Foothills and Crown of the San Gabriel
> Valley—No frosts. No winds in winter. Unobstructed ocean
> breezes in summer. Unprecedented views at all seasons. . . .

* * *

> Go wing thy flight from star to star
> From world to luminous world, as far
> As the universe spreads its flaming wall.
> Take all the pleasures of all the spheres
> And multiply each through endless years
> One winter at Vernon is worth them all.

Real estate promoters constantly had to find new gimmicks to attract buyers. Excursions were set up with all kinds of enticements. Brass bands, parades, and lotteries heralded the openings of new tracts. Free lunches were provided. Come-ons were extravagant:

> WHO IS THIS LUCKY MAN?
> This means you. Here is a little speculation that will discount anything in
> the market. Eighty-five acres of choice land, suitable for the successful

growing of strawberries of the finest kind, as well as any small fruit or vegetable in the town of Compton, has been subdivided into 16 tracts
. . . [which] will be distributed among the lucky purchasers of the 16 tickets
now for sale.

Such promoters as this one conveniently neglected to inform buyers of
the lack of water for the potential orchards and gardens. Hucksters and
fast-talkers resorted to anything that could sell a site. Rocky desert spots
were described in the most glowing terms. Ads for the boom town of Chicago Park pictured steamers chugging up the nearby San Gabriel River,
though the San Gabriel, like many desert "rivers," rarely held more than
a trickle of water. Other promoters hung oranges on Joshua trees in order
to pass off desert lots as citrus groves.

News and editorial policy of the newspapers complemented the frenzied ads. From the beginning the publishers encouraged the wild speculation. "Our city has taken a boom and the boom has come to stay," a
Times editorial boasted in early 1886. ". . . It is destined to be one of the
largest cities on the Pacific Slope." A few months later the paper predicted that Los Angeles would have a population of 100,000 within the next
five years.

The boom peaked in the summer of 1887. Within a three-month period
$38 million changed hands in real estate transactions—$100 million during
the year. The city's businesses were thriving. Bank holdings quadrupled.
Los Angeles's population, a meager 11,000 in 1881, jumped to 80,000.
Suddenly Los Angeles was a city of importance; overnight it had become
the second largest city on the West Coast. ". . . Los Angeles is growing
in no one direction alone, but in all directions," the *Times* noted. "Far
sighted capitalists have not been slow to perceive this and steadily in the
future, no less than in the past, the city's march will be to the northward
and the westward, no less than to the east and south. Los Angeles has ample room for the one hundred thousand people which a few years will see
here. She can provide homes and lands for them all." The *Herald* boasted
that the city could support a million people.

Los Angeles boosters predicted a permanent boom. "With a climate
which cannot be excelled in any portion of the state; with a rich and productive soil, to which almost every known plant takes kindly; with our ad-
vantagious [sic] location as a great depot for the neighboring Territories,
and with our numerous railway facilities . . . ; with constantly increasing manufacturers and the continued development of new resources;
what is there to hinder the continued growth and the future greatness of
this rapidly growing metropolis of the South?" the *Times* asked.

But little by little, buyers stopped buying. As the buying slowed down,
land values plummeted. Within months, the boom began to fall to pieces.

Whole towns disappeared; Sunset, Clearwater, Hyde Park, Chicago Park, Waterloo—altogether sixty-two platted townships—vanished into the desert. Real estate dealers and investors went bankrupt and quickly departed from the area.

Many Los Angeles boosters tried to ignore the collapse. "We've only Just Begun," a *Times* editorial asserted, and blamed "the conservative East" for not understanding the opportunities and the "daring and enterprise of the gigantic young West." "Southern California's 'boom' has just commenced," the *Times* continued, "and it will not subside until our rich territory is all occupied, our great ranches subdivided, and thousands of new homes have been planted throughout this section of the state. To those uncertain as to their future our advice is COME WEST, come to Southern California, the land of great opportunities. . . ."

By early 1888 the boom had become a thing of the past and the population began to drop at the rate of one thousand a month. The city tried to settle back into a semblance of normalcy, but the boom had left indelible marks on the landscape and consciousness of those who remained. Gone forever was the sleepy town and its "cow counties." In their place was the hustle-bustle of an instant city. "The boom," noted historian Glenn Dumke, "took the last step in the process of making California truly American."

The boom had given substance to an ideology which would endure for the next century. The city's business leaders—and the *Los Angeles Times*—had committed themselves to the vision of permanent expansion. "Nature has indeed done very much for this region, but man has ably seconded her efforts, and the result has been the 'boom'—a boom which is destined to stay and grow and spread until the whole of Southern California, from the Sierra to the sea, is one vast garden, dotted over with lovely homes. . . ," the *Times* prophesied.

Los Angeles did continue to grow, sprawling in all directions from the mountains to the sea. Always looking to its future as it expanded, the city quickly forgot its past. Each new flood of immigrants came with a different history. Only the future held them together—the American dream of a better life where anything seemed possible.

CHAPTER 1

"Destined to Do Big Things"

1. "A Walrus of a Fighter"

"Climate, real estate, and brass bands make a most intoxicating mixture here in California. There's nothing like it," Harrison Gray Otis wrote during the boom. Otis, as editor and publisher of the prospering *Los Angeles Times,* had ample reason to rejoice. Circulation of his newspaper had skyrocketed with the increase in population, and advertising revenues had poured in from businesses and land promoters. A boom-rich *Times* had purchased huge new steam presses and begun construction on a new three-story building.

But it was not monetary gains alone which excited the ambitious *Times* publisher. From the first days of his arrival in Southern California, Otis had envisioned a great future for the area, "a mightier Pacific empire, with a population numbering millions where now we see only thousands, and possessing a measure of wealth, civilization and power now inconceivable." Otis desperately wanted to be one of the "dauntless men" who would lay the foundations for that empire. With the flurry of the boom, his dream came one step closer to reality.

Otis had not thought that his home state of Ohio could offer him such opportunity. He was born in a small town near Marietta on February 10, 1837. His parents, Stephen and Sara Dyer Otis, named their son, the youngest of sixteen children, after the famous Massachusetts Senator Harrison Gray Otis. Stephen Otis was a native Vermonter who had arrived in 1800 at the age of sixteen in Ohio's Muskingum Valley. Sara Dyer Otis had come from Nova Scotia. The Otises were farmers, "staunch.

stalwart, intelligent, God-fearing people of the Methodist faith," as their son described them.

At the age of fourteen, Otis signed on as a printer's apprentice at the *Noble County Courier,* a newspaper edited by his older brother Charles. After five years of working in several printing shops, the young apprentice went on to take courses at Wetherby's Academy in Lowell, Ohio. From there he went to Columbus, Ohio, to continue his education at Granger's Commercial College and to work as a compositor at a book publisher. On September 11, 1859, the twenty-two-year-old student married Eliza Wetherby, the daughter of a wealthy woolen manufacturer. Upon graduating from Granger's, the young newlywed landed a job on the staff of the *Louisville (Ky.) Journal,* where he was exposed to Republican party politics. It was the era of the partisan press, when newspapers were deeply involved in party battles. In 1860 Otis became a delegate to the Republican National Convention.

Six months later fighting broke out at Fort Sumter, and Otis discovered war—politics by other means. The blond, blue-eyed Otis enlisted as a private in the Twelfth Ohio Volunteers Infantry Regiment on June 25, 1861. Otis took well to being a soldier. Within six months the twenty-four-year-old printer was promoted to first sergeant. Otis's aggressiveness, courage and ease at giving orders were well recognized by his superiors, and more promotions followed: in September 1862 he became a second lieutenant; in May 1863, a first lieutenant; in mid-1864, a captain.

On July 1, 1864, Otis was transferred to the Twenty-third Regiment of the Ohio Infantry, which was led by General William Rosecrans and Colonel Rutherford B. Hayes. Another future president, William McKinley, served under Captain Otis. These military ties would eventually prove very valuable for the young Ohioan.

In August 1865 Otis was discharged from the army. He had been wounded twice during his fifteen Civil War battles—at the Battle of Antietam in 1862 and, more severely, at Winchester, Virginia, in 1864. After recovering from the Winchester wound, Captain Otis was stationed as provost marshal at Harrisonburg, Virginia, where he handled paroles for Confederate soldiers and kept order in the area. Though discharged as a captain, Otis was awarded the brevet rank of lieutenant colonel "for gallant and meritorious services" upon the unsolicited recommendation of his commander, Rutherford B. Hayes.

After the war Otis returned to Marietta, where he took over a small newspaper and printing plant. But with his new military credentials, he had no desire to remain a small-town printer. In 1866 he attended two veterans' conventions and reestablished army connections. Within the year Otis became the official reporter for the Ohio House of Representatives. Soon after that he took the post of foreman for the Government Printing

Office in Washington, D.C., and, in 1871, with the help of Rutherford Hayes, Otis moved up to the U.S. Patent Office, where he remained until 1875. During his years in the government bureaucracy, Otis also edited the *Grand Army Journal,* the veterans' newspaper of the day, and wrote for the *Ohio Statesman.* He continued to attend veterans' conventions and Republican party affairs and by the 1870s had embraced the mainstream Republican ideology, an ideology which had gradually shifted from the radical libertarianism of the antislavery movement to the pro-business outlook of the large industrialists.

In 1874 Otis and his wife made a visit to California. The colonel was impressed with what he saw. "It more than fulfills my expectations," he wrote in the *Ohio Statesman.* "It is the fattest land I ever was in, by many degrees. Just enough has been done in the way of developing the wonderful, varied and rich resources of Southern California to show what are the mighty possibilities of the section."

Two years later ex-Ohioan Colonel W.W. Hollister, a prominent Republican whom Otis had met via mutual friends in California, offered the Civil War veteran the editorship and proprietorship of a new Santa Barbara newspaper which Hollister intended to finance. Otis accepted and in March of 1876 he, Eliza, and their three daughters moved west.

Otis quickly built a reputation in Santa Barbara as an ambitious businessman, ardent teetotaler, and crusading Republican. Within a matter of months, the editor of the new *Santa Barbara Press* was embroiled in politics. The 1876 national election was a tightly contested affair between Democrat Samuel Tilden and Otis's old army commander, Republican Rutherford B. Hayes. A Hayes victory would not only mean the triumph of the Republican party, but a direct line into the White House. The Santa Barbara editor lashed out at Tilden and the Democrats in a style of "personalized journalism" which would characterize his copy for the next forty years. The Democratic party was a "hardened hag," "a shameless old harlot" whose "polluting embrace" must be spurned, an Otis editorial warned a few days before the election.

After Hayes's victory Otis sent word through his former fellow officer William Rosecrans that he would like to be appointed marshal of California, a position with important military and political power. But California Senator Aaron Sargent, an ally of the mighty Southern Pacific Railroad, whose interests Otis had attacked in his Santa Barbara paper, blocked Otis's nomination. Two years later the *Press* editor did succeed in getting an appointment from President Hayes to the post of Special Agent of the Treasury Department for the Alaskan Seal Islands. Otis spent three years in the undeveloped North trying to control seal poaching and keep liquor out of the hands of the natives.

While Otis was in Alaska, his wife Eliza kept the *Santa Barbara Press* going. But the paper was on a downhill course. While home for a visit in the spring of 1879, Otis appealed to the businessmen of Santa Barbara, asking them for more ads. But Otis couldn't get the necessary ad revenue and decided to relinquish control of the paper as of March 1, 1880.

Otis had never really been happy in Santa Barbara. He didn't fit in with the local gentry who seemed content with their adequate income and small-town sensitivities. "Otis soon realized that Santa Barbara was too small a place in which to materialize his dreams," wrote Thomas Storke, the subsequent owner of the *Santa Barbara Press.* "He envisioned himself to be an empire builder, a big man destined to do big things."

The colonel had already given some thought to moving south to Los Angeles, a city which seemed more in tune with his ambitions. Otis visited Los Angeles in December 1881. While there he contributed a series of articles on Alaska to a fledgling newspaper, the *Los Angeles Times.* The newly established Republican *Times* had come into existence on December 4, 1881, founded by two Easterners, Nathan Cole, the debonair son of a wealthy St. Louis man, and Thomas Gardiner, the former editor of the *Sacramento Union.* Cole and Gardiner had made arrangements with the owners of a print shop to put out the new journal. The owners were already established in the newspaper business, having started the *Mirror,* their own advertising sheet, in 1873. But Cole and Gardiner were not so fortunate with their paper and within a few weeks were overrun with unpaid bills. They settled their printing debt by turning the newspaper over to the three print shop owners—Yarnell, Caystile, and Mathes—and promptly left town. *Mirror* editor C.J. Mathes became the editor of the *Times,* but soon after fell seriously ill. By the spring of 1882 both the *Times* and the *Mirror* were close to bankruptcy. Faced with the impending demise of their two newspapers, the owners searched desperately for an editor.

The timing was perfect for Harrison Gray Otis. In July 1882 he finished his stint in Alaska and took over the job of editor of the *Times* and the *Mirror* at a salary of fifteen dollars a week. Within a few weeks, the new editor mustered $1,000 in cash and $5,000 due from the Santa Barbara paper to buy a quarter share of the printing company. A year later, after the death of one of the original owners and the retirement of another, Otis and Eastern capitalist H.H. Boyce bought out the entire *Times* and *Mirror* properties. Following the purchase, the Times-Mirror Company was incorporated with $40,000 of Boyce's capital. Boyce, a former associate editor of the *Chicago Times* and a protégé of Stephen Douglas, became president of the new company.

Henry Boyce was, like Otis, an army colonel with numerous military contacts back East, a staunch Republican, and an avid booster of his adopted city. The new partners also had strong differences. Boyce was prolabor and anti-Chinese; Otis was antilabor and supported the use of cheap Chinese labor. Otis grew to despise his partner and considered him a lackey and a fool. The two owners jostled for control of the prospering *Times*. In March 1886 the conflict reached a showdown when the two men made a "buy-and-sell" agreement. Otis had either to buy out his partner or to sell his own interest on a stipulated day for a mutually agreed-upon price. Boyce was confident that Otis wouldn't be able to raise the sum, but Otis secretly arranged to borrow the necessary amount from a number of Los Angeles bankers and friends. To Boyce's surprise Otis appeared with the total.

Otis took full possession of the *Times* and Boyce went off with his money to start a newspaper of his own, the *Los Angeles Tribune*. The *Tribune* had a strongly prolabor and Republican orientation, and it provided heavy competition for the *Times*. The antagonism between the two men continued through the pages of their newspapers. Otis called "one-dollar Boyce" "a coarse and vulgar criminal" and labeled his paper the *Daily Morning Metropolitan Bellyache*, "the silly trombone, that pipes its feeble way." Boyce retaliated with a number of libel suits.

The fight with Boyce was only one of many for the pugnacious *Times* publisher. Otis's penchant for controversy led one antagonist to describe him as a "damned cuss, [who] doesn't seem to feel well unless he is in a row with someone." *Perseverance* and *manliness* were his bywords, and the colonel had no tolerance for those he considered too weak to meet such standards. The "old walrus of a fighter," as historian Remi Nadeau labeled Otis, infuriated many a foe. Friends, on the other hand, saw him as an admirable figure, quick to stand up for what he believed. "He was a man who . . . liked power," wrote local luminary Charles Lummis, an early *Times* editorial staff member. Angelenos, aware of Otis's increasing power, came to fear the aggressive, spirited *Times* publisher.

With ties in the state government and in Washington, Otis and the *Times* had gained a tremendous political influence by the 1890s. The paper had the backing and patronage of the local merchants. And both the newspaper and the print shop were pulling in sizable profits. Harrison Gray Otis had become one of the most influential men in Southern California.

When the Spanish-American War broke out in 1898, Otis yearned to get back into military life and requested a post from his old army mate, President William McKinley. On May 27, 1898, Otis was appointed Brigadier General of the United States Volunteers, but the choice caused an uproar, especially in northern California. Members of that area's National Guard, whom Otis had criticized in an editorial, claimed that the *Times* publisher "would make trouble among our soldiers in the field and at the front and would probably want to run things to suit himself, regardless of his superiors." The appointment was argued on the Senate floor, where opponents tried unsuccessfully to block the commission.

Otis was sworn in as brigadier general on June 11, 1898. The next day he was sent off to the Philippines, in charge of an expeditionary force. ". . . The call of the country, the sight of the flag and the sound of the bugle, are the only signals that I have required to summon me to the service in which I now am," he wrote home en route. In October the new general was transferred to the command of the first brigade of the Second Division of the Eighth Army Corps. The Spanish-American War had ended, and Otis's troops helped the Philippine forces to disarm the Spanish soldiers then preparing to leave the islands. But the U.S. troops had no intention of leaving, and after they defeated the Spanish they made plans to remain in the Philippines on a permanent basis. Otis defended the American position. "In the crisis which has come upon us and under the conditions which prevail today, we can do no less than go on with the task we have undertaken and carry the war to its logical completion," he wrote. "We must make Spain pay the cost of this business and as she has no money with which to pay, we will be compelled to take territory for indemnity."

In the course of his stay, Otis developed a paternalistic attitude toward the Filipinos. ". . . The Filipinos are without doubt incapable of governing themselves satisfactorily," he wrote to California Senator Stephen White. "The necessity of Uncle Sam holding on is obvious to me. . . . The local European business interests . . . certainly would aid cheerfully. . . . The average Filipino is not a bad fellow, nor wholly without merit or intelligence. He certainly has rights to be respected, and I believe that, properly managed, good can be got out of him, both for himself and for the country." The Filipinos, a *Times* editorial declared, would be "much freer and much more independent under the government which we shall give them, than . . . under independent government they could or would give themselves."

The Filipinos did not take well to the new American role. In February 1899 Filipino nationalists seized the city of Malolos and established a revolutionary government. Otis's attitude toward the Filipinos changed overnight. "These ignorant, misguided and bumptious natives . . . wantonly assailed the authority of the Republic," he angrily wrote.

Prior to the rebellion, Otis had asked to leave the islands to move on to "some more active field." The general had no desire to serve during peacetime, but, ironically, his regiment was caught right in the middle of the Filipino insurrection. For two months the Otis-led brigade, composed mainly of men from Montana, Pennsylvania, Kansas, and the Third U.S. Foot Artillery of the regular army, participated in most of the major campaigns against the Filipinos. The battles were fierce; one hundred of Otis's soldiers were killed or wounded. "The dead fell like soldiers at their posts of duty defending the laws of the Republic, and the wounded suffer that the flag may continue to float triumphant over territory fairly won by the national arms from a foreign foe," Otis proudly wrote to his commander in chief.

Within two months the uprising was quelled. Otis led the main force in the assault and victory in the decisive battle of Caloocan. The Filipinos lacked adequate arms and could not resist the constant shelling by the well-equipped American army. "The rebels were mowed down like grass," according to a *Los Angeles Express* article. "The slaughter of women and children was frightful," related an eyewitness, "the Americans burning and devastating all before them, conducting a war of extermination and shooting every Filipino."

From Caloocan, Otis's forces advanced northward toward the rebel capital. After five rough days, the brigade entered Malolos in the advance line. On March 30 the rebels were driven out, burning the town in their retreat to the countryside. For three years the disbanded rebels continued to fight a protracted guerrilla war against thousands of occupying American troops.

For Otis, though, the war was over. Two days after the fall of Malolos, he tendered his resignation, and on April 12 he was honorably discharged from the army. Otis was given a hero's welcome when he returned to California. Friend and foe lauded him for his successful military role. When he arrived home in Los Angeles, some 4,000 townspeople attended a rally in his honor.

Patriotism had become an all-pervasive concept for the *Times* publisher. "Teach the boy that inspiring lesson which cannot be too often nor too reverently taught—," Otis said in an address before local school teachers, "the lesson of love and respect for the flag, the matchless flag of the Union—that shining, blood-bought emblem of liberty and law within whose sacred folds are held the gathered hopes of humanity throughout the world."

Otis had become the compleat soldier. He named his homes the Bivouac and the Outpost, and his *Times* building, bolstered with solid granite, was specifically patterned after a fortress, with a large eagle—the new symbol of the *Times*—perched on the top. Implacable in his political and economic demands, Otis ruled over his paper like a military commander. He treated his staff, which he called his "phalanx," as a tightly disciplined brigade. During times of tension, such as major labor conflicts, Otis—with fifty rifles stored in a tower room and a case of loaded shotguns alongside the managing editor's desk—conducted military drills in the *Times* offices.

Any who opposed the general found themselves subject to sharp attack in the *Times*. Labor leaders were "corpse defacers," and reformers were cast off as "socialistic freaks." Otis was very clear about whom he liked and whom he didn't, and his derogatory epithets became notorious throughout the state. *Times* editor L.D. Hotchkiss wrote that "General Otis, like most of his notable contemporaries, was a believer in, and apostle of, personal journalism. Purely objective writing was frowned upon as 'weak and vacillating.' And if the General saw a news story or editorial in proof which he deemed worthy of amplification by a few personal touches, he never faltered."

Otis's politics and journalistic style made him dozens of enemies. To many he was a "fanatic," "a bully," "an unprincipled scoundrel," "intolerant, arrogant, . . . and vain," and "an arbitrary, dictatorial, brutal, egotistical man." Newspapers and magazine articles poked fun at his military egotism and love of titles.

One target of Otis's hyperbole, W. C. Brann, editor of the *Iconoclast*, gave Otis a taste of his own medicine. "I can wonder what will become of the *Times* editor when the breath leaves his feculent body and death stops the rattling of his abortive brain, for he is unfit for heaven and too foul for hell," Brann wrote. "He cannot be buried in the earth lest he provoke a pestilence, nor in the sea lest he poison the fish, nor swing in space like Mahomet's coffin lest the circling worlds, in trying to avoid contamination, crash together. . . ."

Otis brushed aside the attempts at verbal retaliation. His influence in the region became too firmly entrenched for him to have to worry about his antagonists. So strong was his hold over Los Angeles that some journalists mockingly referred to the city as "Otistown." Otis would live to see the realization of many of his goals — goals rigidly tied to his own ambitions and to an ideology based on expansionism and the notion that what was good for the men of capital was good for the community. With his fighting spirit and the leverage of the powerful *Times*, Otis acted as leader of those local forces of capital and left a mark on all areas of Los Angeles's development.

The early *Times*, former city editor Charles Lummis told the paper's employees in 1922, was essentially "the dominant personality of one man." Otis's character — his love for a fight, his loyalty to friends, his energy and ambitions, his persistence, his patriotism, and his probusiness conservative Republican outlook — played a large role in determining the shape of the *Times* in its formative years. The early paper cannot be understood without knowing the man. But the paper as an institution also had a life of its own.

2. The Paper

The first editions of the *Times*, in the months prior to Otis's arrival in Los Angeles, consisted of four pages six days a week. Page one had information of state and national interest, page two carried the editorials, page three concerned itself with matters of commerce, and the final page was devoted to local events. The tone was light and newsy.

The paper echoed the sentiments of the White Anglo population of the Southwestern community, with its antagonism toward the local Chinese community — "The Heathen Chinee" as a December 8, 1881, article described them. The paper warned of the city being overrun by Chinese immigrants. During the Yarnell, Caystile, and Mathes period, it joined a statewide campaign to pass a Chinese restriction bill. The *Times* accused Chinese wash houses of responsibility for the outbreak of "syphilitic sores" among "moral persons" and commented at one point "that so impure has become the Chinese nation as a whole that the custom of handshaking is unknown among them." Major crimes in California were attributed to its Chinese residents.

Despite the difficulties that beset the *Mirror* printers, the *Times*, under Mathes, had some success in picking up advertising. In April 1882 he enlarged the paper from seven to eight columns. By August, the time of Otis's arrival, the paper had reached nine columns.

While Mathes took care of the business end — until he was replaced by A.W. Francisco in May 1883, who, in turn, was succeeded by Henry Boyce five months later—Colonel Otis and his wife Eliza worked exceedingly hard to put out the paper. Eliza's poems and two columns, "The Saunterer" and "Susan Sunshine," became regular features. Eliza was also in charge of the religion, society, fashion, literature, drama, and "women's" sections. Otis wrote the editorials, most of the local news, and edited the telegraphic items from the wires and other papers.

The newspaper was first produced out of a twenty-by-thirty foot two-story building downtown on the corner of Temple and New High streets. The business office took up the ground floor; editorial offices, composing room, and the job printing plant were upstairs; and the pressroom was located in the basement. The first press was an old water-powered Potter drum cylinder, which turned out one side of 1,400 sheets an hour. The old equipment brought on a number of mishaps, such as when a small fish got into the supply pipe to the press and clogged up the motor.

In the fall of 1884, Otis made arrangements to increase his two-person editorial staff by 50 percent with the hiring of Charles Fletcher Lummis, who had written to Otis from Ohio of his plans to walk across the continent, contributing letters to the *Times* along the way. Otis promised Lummis a job at the *Times* when — and if — he arrived. Lummis, who coined the phrase "See America First," made the 3,507-mile walk from Cincinnati to Los Angeles at a rate of thirty to fifty miles a day. His lively accounts of his 4½-month journey, in which he described the hospitality of the Indians and Mexicans he met along the way, helped boost *Times* circulation to 2,700. Otis personally came out to meet Lummis on his arrival at the San Gabriel Mission on February 1, 1885. The traveler, Otis wrote, was dressed in "wellworn overalls, covering two pairs of pantaloons . . . a dusty white felt hat, with the skin of a rattlesnake for a band; a six shooter in his belt, and a staff in his hand."

The next day Lummis, already a town celebrity, became the *Times*'s first city editor and only member of its local news staff. "Every day he was at his desk an hour or two ahead of the required time," another early Timesman recalled, "and, before commencing his rounds, occupied himself in pasting in a big scrapbook and indexing every item of local news that had appeared in the paper that morning." In 1886, Lummis was sent to cover General Crook's battles with the Apaches as the *Times* war correspondent. A year after his return he suffered a paralyzing stroke from overwork and went to recuperate with Indians he had met in New Mexico. He recovered, but did not return to the *Times*.

Lummis later edited the cultural magazine *Land of Sunshine*. Through the magazine and the California Landmarks Club, which he organized in 1895, Lummis fought to preserve Southern California's missions and other landmarks and tried to secure appropriations and reservations for homeless Indians. Lummis authored some twenty books and also founded the Southwest Society and the Southwest Museum. Otis was a member of the Landmark Club's Advisory Board, an associate of the Southwest Museum, and a supporter of subsequent Lummis crusades.

William Spalding came on as telegraph editor and general assistant in May 1885. Spalding's task consisted of making sense of scrawled telegraph messages, writing heads and subheads, preparing a column of editorial briefs which appeared on the first page, reading proof, and holding copy for the Colonel so that he could read proof for advertisements and commercial matter. Spalding went on to become the *Times*'s city editor, manager of the printing and binding house, and the paper's editorial writer. He left the staff in 1893 to accept an appointment to the state's newly created Building and Loan Commission.

After Otis bought out Henry Boyce's half of the *Times* in April 1886, Spalding and journalist Albert McFarland purchased shares in the newly reorganized Times Mirror Company. McFarland, with his one-quarter interest, became vice-president and treasurer of the corporation, Otis became president and general manager, and Spalding acted as secretary.

"The motto of the now united proprietors," Otis wrote in an editorial announcement of the reorganization, "will be, PUSH THINGS!"

The great Southern California real estate boom soon gave substance to the *Times* slogan. The boom, spurred on by the paper, enabled the *Times* to expand dramatically. It increased to eight pages to pick up new ads and, with the extra revenue, began to publish seven days a week in response to a similar move by the *Tribune*. In May 1887, with the help of a loan, the *Times* moved to the corner of Fort and First streets into a larger, modern, newly equipped three-story brick and granite building which it had constructed for $50,000. The land had been purchased from the son of *Times* treasurer McFarland, who had offered extra inducements to the *Times* to take the corner lot of a larger piece of land he was subdividing.

A new Hoe perfecting press with a steam engine was purchased and installed in the basement, and new office furniture, type, and other equipment brought in for the rest of the offices. More new presses were installed in a short time, and in 1893 the *Times* became one of the first newspapers in the country to use the modern Mergenthaler linotype machines. Such technical improvements became a key feature of the *Times*'s development.

Several other new staff members helped shape the early *Times*. Harry Ellington Brook, who wrote pamphlets for the Chamber of Commerce and had established *Land of Sunshine* before it was taken over by Lummis, joined the *Times* as editorial writer in 1886. In March 1887 Frank X. Pfaffinger, a Bavarian cabinetmaker who attended Spalding's Commercial College in Kansas City, came to Los Angeles to be the *Times*'s bookkeeper. Pfaffinger stayed with the paper for more than fifty years, joining numerous family economic ventures and eventually becoming treasurer of Times Mirror and a member of its board of directors.

L. E. Mosher, author of the popular poem "The Stranded Bugle," also entered the firm in 1887 and soon became Otis's aide. When the *Times* editor was appointed general during the Spanish-American War he tried to secure a position for his friend, but Mosher's appointment as Otis's adjunct-general was held up, and he never got to join his boss. While Otis was away in the Philippines, Mosher took charge of the paper as managing editor and soon came into conflict with California Governor Henry Gage, an erstwhile Otis ally. When Otis returned, he and Mosher had a falling out over the matter, and Mosher left the *Times* to pursue a business career in New York. Mosher fared poorly there and returned to Los Angeles where he failed in business once again. On the morning of February 23, 1904, at his home in Santa Monica, Mosher shot himself in the mouth with a revolver. "After a third of a century of peace," Otis said at Mosher's funeral, "when the war cloud again lowered over the land, he wanted to go where he might once again hear the clang of sabers and the shriek of shell.''

The 1890s saw the entry of Harry Andrews, who rose to managing editor in 1906, and Hugh McDowell, who became editor of the *Times* magazine, which made its first appearance in the paper's Sunday edition. The magazine consisted of illustrated articles and syndicated features by popular writers like Jules Verne. While photographs first began to appear in Eastern papers by the 1880s, they were not seen in Los Angeles journals until the fall of 1892. Comics also made their first appearance in the late 1890s.

By 1900 the *Times*, according to a profile by Charles Lummis, had "grown to be the most profitable newspaper property not only in the city but in the whole West." The key to its growth was its advertising success. The paper carried more advertising than any other newspaper west of the Mississippi, more than all the San Francisco dailies put together. Very early on, the *Times* initiated a policy of doing everything possible to obtain the maximum number of ads. Rates were cheap, and salesmen used a variety of tactics to solicit ads — especially from real estate companies. Municipal reformer John R. Haynes labeled the *Times* policy "blackmail," recalling how a *Times* ad agent had informed a real estate salesman that *Times* attacks on him would cease if he advertised in the paper.

Quack medicine ads were also commonplace. "Ben-Yan Makes Men . . . Ben-Yan will cure Nervous Debility of every name form and nature . . . Ben-Yan absolutely cures all sexual depletion," an ad of January 1, 1889, noted. When a *Times* writer exposed the drug Peruna as nothing more than whiskey with some coloring, the ad was temporarily suspended. But when the clamor died down, the ad soon reappeared.

3. The Competition

The *Times*'s journalistic hegemony had always been crucial to Otis's ability to hold onto the leadership of Southern California's local establishment.

When Cole and Gardiner first established their Republican paper, Los Angeles had two newspapers, the *Herald* and the *Express*. The independent *Express* had been founded in 1871, and the Democratic *Herald* two years later. In 1886 Henry Boyce joined H. T. Payne and Edward Records to form the Republican *Tribune*.

The rivalry between the *Times* and the three other papers increased as the *Times* grew in power. Otis editorially condemned the publishers of the *Tribune*, *Express*, and *Herald* whenever those papers disagreed with the *Times* about an issue or posed any challenge to *Times* hegemony.

As with Boyce, the competition took on a personal dimension. Otis's rivalry with *Express* owner E. T. Earl became legendary. Earl, a wealthy fruit shipper, lived next door to Otis, and the two men had been good friends until Earl bought out the *Express* in 1901. With differing political outlooks and similar ambitions to be the most influential voice in the city, the two quickly became bitter enemies, refusing even to speak to each other. If one paper supported something, the other was almost certain to oppose it. "Almost every political issue in the city during the life of these antagonists," Albert Clodius wrote of the Earl/Otis antagonism, "became entangled with their personal rivalry and enmity."

When William Randolph Hearst started his Los Angeles *Examiner* in 1903, he too became subject to Otis's epithets. Hearst became the "Yellow Yawp" and *Examiner* reporters, "knockers." Attorney Earl Rogers recalled one instance when the *Examiner* scooped the *Times* with a front page story about a police shooting of some "unarmed citizens." Though the *Times* had no information on the situation it rushed out an extra accusing the *Examiner* of yellow journalism. In the following days, the *Examiner* continued to refer to the "police murder" story, while the *Times* identified it as the "yellow journalism case."

Times attacks on the *Herald* and its owner, oil man Wallace Hardison, who bought the paper in 1900, climaxed in a story on "Hardupson's" plans to marry a younger woman. The story drove the *Herald* owner to come after Otis, fists flying. Hardison — like Los Angeles publishers before and after him — hoped to surpass the *Times* as Los Angeles's number one paper. "That blankety-blank, Blank across the street," Hardison said of his rival, "thought we were going to run a one-horse paper and play second fiddle, but I tell you gentlemen, that we are going to play first violin in this orchestra." Hardison and Otis remained enemies, with the *Herald* publisher trying to undersell the *Times* without success. By early 1904, the oil man was prepared to sell his control of the business.

The progressive reputation of the *Herald*, a carryover from previous editors such as Charles Willard and former Timesman William Spalding, represented a potential threat to the *Times*. Otis had kept a watchful eye on events at the *Herald*, and after the *Herald* supported the Pullman workers in their bitter 1894 strike, Otis wrote to California Senator Stephen White, "I hope we will be able to secure the institution and put it in good hands." Three years later, in 1897, Otis wrote to White concerning indications that some of White's friends were thinking of investing in the *Herald*. Otis was interested, but wanted to help "without mixing up in it as an investor."

When word got out that Hardison was interested in selling his share in 1904, Otis decided to place the *Herald* in more secure hands: his own. Knowing that Hardison would never sell the paper directly to him, Otis contacted a Tacoma, Washington, publisher to act as his dummy. The

Washington man purchased 8,051 shares of the 10,000 outstanding shares of stock, and transferred them to Otto Brant at the Title Insurance and Trust Company, who held them for the *Times* publisher. Harrison Gray Otis became the secret publisher of the *Herald*.

Otis's secret purchase kept one of the most coveted prizes in the *Herald's* possession, its AP franchise, out of the hands of his competitors. More importantly, it put at his disposal a second newspaper with a progressive track record and a host of liberal writers. By exercising his hidden control, Otis could allow the *Herald* to maintain its position to the left of the *Times* except on those matters that Otis deemed essential to his own interests. To edit the *Herald*, Otis selected Thomas (T.E.) Gibbon, who was widely recognized within business circles for his allegiance to the progressive cause, though he also had intimate ties with Otis and Otis's son-in-law Harry Chandler. Although in political disagreement on a number of issues, Gibbon, willing to act as their broker on the *Herald*, worked closely with the *Times* owners on larger economic and business matters that affected them and the region as a whole.

Otis maintained his covert ownership for ten years without acknowledging or denying the persistent rumors concerning his hidden control. The *Herald* didn't always support *Times* candidates or *Times* positions, but it never strayed beyond a point that displeased the General. Dan Green, a young *Herald* reporter at the time, recalled how Otis forced his suspension in 1906 because of the General's dislike of a particular Green article.

" . . . Mr. Otis called the *Herald* his skeleton regiment," *Herald* writer Frank Wolfe testified at 1914 Congressional hearings, "and certainly he starved it to the point of being a skeleton." There was always a deficit at the *Herald*; keeping it barely above water suited the *Times*'s needs by preventing any serious competition from a healthy *Herald*, yet keeping it going meant that its readership would not desert to the *Examiner* or *Express*. The seriously crippled *Herald* was finally sold to Hearst's *Examiner* in 1911 on the condition that it be turned into an evening paper. Part of Otis and Hearst's motivation concerned the evening *Express*'s decision to break into the morning field with its own newly created *Los Angeles Tribune*. The elimination of the *Herald* allowed the *Times* to gear up for battle with E.T. Earl.

Much to the delight of Otis's foes, the sale of the *Herald* brought out into the open the ten-year secret ownership. "The *Times* has no explanation or apology to offer for having at times devoted some solicited aid and comfort, in the form of advances of money and materials, to keeping the *Herald* out of the clutch of Tobias Earl, who has been plotting for years to obtain possession of it and its Associated Press franchise," the *Times* noted in its defense. Earl's *Tribune* failed before long, and the *Times* maintained its primacy in the region.

Otis's *Times,* since its reorganization in 1886, had developed a clear and consistent policy. "That policy is the maintenance of the principles of the Republican party, the defense of liberty, law and public morals, and the up-building of the city and county of Los Angeles and the State of South California," the paper noted in its reorganization announcement. *Times* policy often resembled a crusade. It fought for—and won—licensing restrictions on saloons, construction of sewers, bonded improvements for the city, the establishment of a free harbor, the abolition of the closed shop, and a number of other causes for which it earned its reputation. The paper was explicit, its "advocacy" style straightforward, biting, and outspoken. Charles Lummis recalled an incident in the 1880s when he brought Otis proof that the *Times*-backed police chief was crooked. "But this," Otis answered, "is contrary to the policy of the paper."

Otis's *Times,* however, did earn a great deal of admiration from those who agreed with its positions. ". . . It has accomplished more in the way of making Los Angeles industrially independent and correspondingly prosperous today than any other influence," William Spalding wrote. Many local businessmen agreed.

The *Times* saw itself as the voice of Southern California, a promoter of business and an advocate of population growth and regional expansion. Otis equated Los Angeles's interests with those of the *Times* and acted on that belief. He desired to shape Los Angeles, and he and his papers had the political and economic power to do so.

CHAPTER 2

"Stand Fast, Stand Firm, Stand Sure, Stand True": Otis's Battle Against the Unions

1. Battle Preparation

On a summer day in 1890, Colonel Harrison Gray Otis prepared to face the enemy. Livid with anger, he stormed into the *Times* composing room. Otis raised a fist, banged it down, and bellowed at his union workers, "Every——man get out of here! And get out——quick!"

Otis's hostility toward the union had been building up for several years before the 1890 confrontation. His angry challenge marked the beginning of open warfare between employers and workers in Los Angeles. The struggle that followed would divide the whole city for the next two decades. It would culminate in the death of twenty-one *Times* workers and the establishment of one of the strongest antilabor environments in the country. In the process, Harrison Gray Otis and the *Los Angeles Times* would earn the reputation as the most powerful and persistent enemy of organized labor in America, a role of which Otis was intensely proud.

Otis had not always been opposed to organized labor. In 1856, as a young printer for the *Rock Island Courier*, he supported the union. Otis had demanded that the *Courier*'s editor sign a union shop agreement, and when the editor refused, Otis quit. Several years later, as a journeyman printer in the Government Printing Office in Washington, D.C., Otis joined the International Typographical Union (ITU)—the same union he would lock out of his shop in 1890. In later years, he referred to his ITU membership as a "folly of his youth."

In the early 1880s, when Otis became editor of the *Times*, union organization in Southern California was still very weak. Los Angeles was primarily agriculture-oriented with little manufacturing. The region was geographically isolated, separated from the rest of the state by mountains and deserts. The few unions that existed were chiefly locals not affiliated with the more powerful national labor organizations.

International Typographical Union Local #174, whose members worked in the printing trade, was an exception. The Los Angeles Typographical Union (LATU), the first labor organization to be chartered in Los Angeles, was strong and aggressive. The union formed the backbone of the city's labor movement through the turn of the century.

Local #174 was already firmly established at the *Times* when Otis took control of the paper, though workers who did the job printing for the company were not unionized. Only twelve days after Otis's arrival, the union printers announced their plans to unionize the unorganized printers from the job room. There was no management opposition. Otis, as a newcomer, was more concerned with setting his new business on a firm financial basis. Otis initially appeared friendly, though cautious, toward the union and even allowed the local to use the *Times* offices for its meetings. But within the year, hints of a less friendly outlook toward union activities began to appear in the newspaper. "It is to be hoped . . . that the temporary demand and the appearance of prosperity will not induce others of our tradesmen to join in a strike," a *Times* editorial commented after one of Los Angeles's earliest strikes had been settled.

In June 1883 Local #174 asked for preferential hiring of union members over nonunion men. Otis made no reply, but two months after the union request, the *Times* unexpectedly attacked a printers' strike in San Francisco and described unionism as "insufferable despotism." In response to the *Times* editorial, the LATU resolved to support the San Francisco printers. Before the week was out, Otis retaliated by firing union member A. E. Morrill, an assistant foreman, for alleged neglect of duty. Morrill and the union believed the discharge was based primarily on Morrill's union advocacy. The *Times* was declared to be a "rat-office," and union workers were immediately pulled out. The first printer's strike in Los Angeles had begun.

While publicly dismissing the matter as the work of "a few hot-headed boys in the *Times* office" who were "without any substantial grievance," Otis privately rejected any compromises presented by the union. The only way the strikers could be reinstated, Otis informed a union committee, would be to apply individually.

The striking printers saw Otis's actions as an attempt to oust the typographical union from his shop. "The *Times* stops not for trifles," Otis declared as he hired nonunion men in order to continue publishing. *Times* editorials were aimed at building public opposition to the union. Otis tried to foster a violent image of the strikers by having his friend, the chief of police, station officers to guard the nonunion workers as they entered and departed. But Otis's efforts were unsuccessful. Within a month, his nonunion replacements had dwindled away, and Otis found himself without enough men to put out his paper. On October 3 he agreed to rehire the fired union foreman on condition that he could still maintain an open shop, that is, one which allowed both union and nonunion workers. The union accepted the compromise and consolidated its position. Though Otis continued to call his establishment an open shop, it became a de facto union shop (one employing only union members) as typographical union members displaced non-union men. By the spring of 1884, the *Times* office was completely staffed by union workers.

In September 1886 the LATU received a report that the Times Mirror Company was discriminating against union employees in its job room. A union committee of three approached Otis with the request that he "square" the office, but Otis refused to "go back" on his nonunion workers. A few days later, Otis wrote to the LATU detailing wage and piecework rates and stipulating that the option to pay by day or piece be left to the management. The union demanded in turn that Colonel Otis pay union scale and employ only union workers. These demands were rejected by the *Times* publisher who stated, according to a union account, "that this union could not make laws for him" and insisted on maintaining the privilege of employing whomever he pleased. Otis was then notified that unless he squared the job office by that evening, the union workers would strike. On October 3 the *Times* publisher yielded to the unionization of the Times Mirror job office.

Otis and the union lived peacefully with one another through the boom years. In general, it was a favorable time for unions and employers alike. The influx of new people meant new homes to be constructed, new markets for local products, and new revenues for newspapers and other businesses. Though the *Times*'s coverage of strikes in other cities was largely negative, Los Angeles union demands for higher wages and better working conditions were met as a rule.

Otis had been very vulnerable to the union's demands during the boom. Construction on the new *Times* building had begun and money was owed on recently purchased large, expensive machinery. The *Times* had been awarded the 1887 city Great Register contract, a lucrative job that could be jeopardized by a strike in the print shop. In addition, Otis had to contend with the competition of Boyce's *Tribune*. The *Tribune* was friendly to labor, as were most of the city's residents, and Otis stood to lose many readers and advertisers to his rival if his antiunion sentiments went unchecked. In early 1888 the *Times* even ran a weekly column of "Notes and News from the Trades Unions," which detailed, in a fair manner, the activities of the local unions. ". . . All is peace and good will between labor and capital in the land of the orange and the vine," the column noted on January 23, 1888.

But the uneasy truce, like the boom which fostered it, was destined to come to an end. With the collapse of the boom, employers throughout the city looked to cut expenses. Wages were lowered in almost every industry and only the typographical union was strong enough to maintain existing salaries. When the city's newspaper owners suggested a wage reduction in August 1888, the typographical union refused to go along. Since the local had grown stronger during the boom, the publishers felt reluctant to challenge the decision.

Otis resented the LATU's independent power, and he began to formulate plans to counteract the union. Employer unity was crucial to these plans. When Boyce sold out his interest in the *Tribune*, Otis immediately gathered the other newspaper owners together to form a Newspaper Publishers Union.

On August 3, 1890, members of the new combine—Colonel Ayres of the *Herald*, Colonel Osborne of the *Express*, J.H. Morrow and C.F. Holder of the *Tribune*, and Colonel Otis and Albert McFarland of the *Times*—appeared before a union meeting to make a new request for a wage reduction, a 20 percent cut in the printers' earnings.

After the publishers departed, union discussion was intense and lengthy. A motion was made to reduce the salary scale; another was made to raise it. A communication from the San Diego Typographical Union settled the matter. The note from San Diego warned that a strikebreaking group of antiunion printers had informed the Los Angeles publishers of their readiness to provide all the workers they needed. After the San Diego communication was read to the meeting, the LATU members voted 67 to 10 to reject the proposed wage cut. In addition, the union demanded that the owners sign an agreement guaranteeing the present wage scale for another year. The newspaper owners were given twenty-four hours—until noon of August 5—to sign.

Otis and the other owners answered that "they could not yield to the unreasonable demands and arbitrary ultimatum of the union," nor would they negotiate with union representatives. The union set up a meeting for 4 P.M., August 5, to decide what action to take.

Before the union had a chance to meet and vote on whether or not to strike, Otis made a dramatic entrance into the *Times* print shop and ordered all his union workers out.

Otis's lockout made a strike inevitable. The union met and voted to strike all four papers.

The printers believed that Otis deliberately set out to get rid of the union. The *Times* publisher had already made plans to import nonunion printers to fill the places of the strikers well before the action occurred. Within days of the strike, members of the Printers Protective Fraternity (PPF), an antiunion group of professional strikebreakers based in Kansas City—the same group mentioned in the San Diego communication—arrived to run the strikers' machines. Negotiations had been carried out between Otis and the PPF before the wage reduction proposal was made. Once the strike appeared imminent, the *Times* publisher simply telegraphed for the men. These workers were then paid the same wages which the publishers had refused to the union, and they were given a one-year contract guarantee.

Thanks to the use of the PPF printers, the four dailies were able to continue publishing without missing a single issue. Otis described the organization, which banned strikes and boycotts and allowed owners and stockholders into its membership, as "a body of organized labor of the better sort," and encouraged the strikebreakers to move their headquarters to Los Angeles. The group eventually made their home in the *Times* building.

Despite the PPF aid and Otis's maneuvers, the *Tribune* and the *Express* pulled out of the publishers' compact. Only two days after the strike had begun, the two papers worked out a compromise with the union. In exchange for the reinstatement of the strikers and a closed shop, the union agreed to accept a small wage cut and forgo the one-year contract. Otis was outraged at the defection of the two publishers. "Had it not been for the unspeakable cowardice and the inexcusable treachery of our confreres of the *Tribune* and *Express*," he wrote to his friend Colonel H. H. Markham, "we might today be complete masters of the situation with the strikers minus a foothold in the town. As it is, the *Times* and the *Herald* stand together and will fight it out. Principle and manhood require it."

But within the next two months, the *Herald* deserted Otis as well. The *Times* management alone refused to compromise. Otis carried on the fight on his own. He lashed out at the strikers in the pages of the *Times*. Though the printers had shown unanimity in their actions, Otis described the strike leaders as a small group of "reckless and vicious" radicals who had tyrannically overruled the objections of the more fair-minded majority. Union demands were attacked, and union concessions were taken as "an admission that they have placed themselves in the wrong." "The desperate resort of a strike," Otis wrote, "was not invoked by the proprietors, nor was the crisis precipitated by them, but by the hasty, ill-advised and indefensible action of the men, who alone are responsible for the present state of affairs. . . ."

The 1890 strike, recognized by historians as "the most significant single event in the history of industrial relations in Los Angeles before 1910," marked the beginning of an intense labor-management conflict in Los Angeles. "Thus was begun the memorable struggle which was to shape the industrial future of a metropolis and to set an example for a whole country," a *Times* history recalled in 1929.

Otis saw the conflict in military terms. He was determined to fight to hold on to the exclusive control of his own business. The 1890 confrontation was the firing of the first cannon. The declaration of war was presented to the public. From then on, the contest could only escalate. Otis's goal would be transformed into a full-fledged crusade to banish the entire Los Angeles labor movement. Through the use of his political influence and the power of the *Times,* Otis set out to establish an environment which was hostile to unionism. "Its bitterness of attack," California historian Ira Cross wrote of the *Times* in the period after 1890, "has never been matched by any other newspaper in the United States or elsewhere."

The union printers "struck without cause" and "forced" him to hire other workers in their place, Otis argued in the columns of the *Times* and swore before a government commission twenty years later. Otis insisted that the strike was not brought on by the wage cut, but by the refusal of the owners to sign the union's "ultimatum," which he termed "a bludgeon shoved unceremoniously under the noses of the proprietors—an unreasonable demand, to which they could not possibly accede without forfeiting all self-respect."

Since Otis refused to negotiate, the printers desperately sought an effective tactic to force the *Times* publisher's hand. At the onset of the strike, they instituted a boycott against the paper. Angelenos were asked to stop buying the *Times,* and merchants were requested to withdraw their advertising. The printers tried to organize public support for the boycott by canvassing the city to discourage subscriptions, holding rallies, and publishing a list of *Times* advertisers under the ban. But the campaign had only sporadic success. Los Angeles's population growth created a constant source of new subscribers and customers for the boycotted businesses, and the union was not able to build a stable base of community support.

Otis reacted to the boycott with scorn and ridicule. "With unexampled folly and stupid mendacity, the strikers are feebly attempting a boycott . . . but their game will not work," a *Times* editorial scoffed. The device was described as "a cowardly, mean, un-American, assassin-like method of establishing a petty despotism." *Times* stories also attacked organizer M. McGlynn, a member of the San Francisco Federated Trades Union who had been sent in to manage the boycott campaign, as a "venal blackmailer" and a "professional agitator." Attempts by McGlynn and the union to meet with Otis were rebuffed.

In the fall of 1891, with the local typographical union penniless and disheartened, the Los Angeles Council of Labor made an effort to push negotiations by securing the support of the city's businessmen for a proposal of arbitration between the *Times* and the LATU. Otis rejected the proposal. "We do not recognize the existence of any differences which can properly form the subject of arbitration or compromise. . . ," Otis wrote in response to the offer. "In the first place, there is nothing to 'settle,' nothing to 'arbitrate,' nothing to 'compromise' between this office and its impotent enemies, the strikers and boycotters." As far as Otis was concerned, the strike was already over. He had won complete control over his business and had no need to negotiate.

Within a couple of days after Otis's refusal, the *Times* published a waiver signed by the same 120 businessmen who had endorsed the arbitration proposal. ". . . We did not mean to have our act construed as any improper interference in matters which do not concern us," the waiver stated. "We will neither advertise, nor refuse to advertise at the dictation of anybody. . . ."

The businessmen's reversal was crucial to Otis's objectives. He needed employer/advertiser unity as part of a larger class unity. The advertisers went along, unwilling to incur a *Times* attack; Otis, in turn, commended these "manly and independent merchants" for "righting themselves in an emphatic manner."

Despite increasing financial hardships, the typographical union continued the fight. A new statewide organization, the California Federation of Typographical Unions, promised full moral and financial support to the Los Angeles local. Contributions also arrived from the International office. The boycott was intensified, and other local unions threw in their support. Union members were fined if they patronized *Times* advertisers. New attempts were made to mediate the dispute, as the union appealed to persons influential enough, they hoped, to persuade Otis to become more tolerant of unionism. Union representatives approached Republican committees, and labor groups began to oppose *Times*-backed candidates in an attempt to get politicians to put pressure on Otis.

Finally, the unions found a tactic to bring the *Times* publisher to the negotiating table. The printers, with all of Los Angeles's organized labor behind them, decided to concentrate the *Times* boycott on a single advertiser, the People's Store, a large department store with a mostly working-class clientele. That boycott was so successful that the store's owner, D. A. Hamburger, was forced to act as an intermediary with Otis. For the first time since the beginning of the strike, Otis agreed to send a representative to meet with union delegates.

A conference between the typographical union and *Times* representatives was held on April 6, 1892. The resultant agreement stipulated that four union members would be immediately rehired. In exchange, Otis demanded the end of all boycotts and the cessation of the publication of the strikers' paper, the *Workman*. The terms of the conciliation required little concession on Otis's part: he didn't have to discharge the PPF men, he still had control of wages and hours, grievances would still be handled on an individual basis. But the union, after almost two years of generally ineffective struggle, saw the agreement as a victory. To get Otis to recognize the union was a triumph, and the *Times*'s representatives, led by Colonel J. A. Woodard, had indicated that gradual unionization of the *Times* shop would follow. The strike and boycott were ended the next day. The last issue of the *Workman* celebrated the termination of the conflict.

Otis rehired four union printers and went a step further by hiring a fifth, but, as one of the LATU officials later stated, "it [the union] did not know the man with whom they were dealing." Once the end of the boycott was secured, Otis never implemented the steps toward full unionization of his shop. The *Times* publisher, however, kept the union satisfied long enough to draw up long-term contracts with advertisers who might have been leery of the labor boycott. Within the first two months after the settlement, the *Times* laid off three PPF men, and Otis led a union committee to believe that more would follow shortly. But by the spring of the next year, with full unionization still not accomplished, the union began to question whether Otis was going to fulfill his pledge. The printers threatened to reinstitute the strike, whereupon Otis immediately hired another union man for his composing room, thus satisfying the union that he still intended to live up to the terms of the secret agreement. But between the spring and the fall, antiunion attacks multiplied in the pages of the *Times*. On September 24, 1893, a year and a half after the settlement, the LATU reported that the *Times* had only three union employees compared to seventeen PPF men. A motion was passed to call out those union men and renew the *Times* boycott. Otis was notified that a strike would be called unless the Times Company agreed to employ union men throughout its offices. When Otis made no reply, the LATU called its men out and the boycott was renewed.

The renewed boycott started out with a burst of energy. A county-wide Joint Boycott Committee had the participation of twenty-two Council of Labor unions, thirty-one lodges of the Farmers' Alliance, four Knights of Labor assemblies, five brotherhoods of railroad men, and four lodges of the Industrial Legion. The campaign had a short spurt of success in the spring of 1894 as evidenced by a decline in *Times* circulation figures and the reduction of its ad rates. But the success was short-lived.

2. The Pullman Strike

In the spring and summer of 1894, the polarization of forces in Los Angeles took a more dramatic turn. On May 11 of that year, workers for the Illinois-based Pullman Palace Car Company struck after receiving a large wage cut. The American Railway Union, with whom the Pullman employees had affiliated, subsequently called sympathy strikes against any railroad using Pullman cars. The action paralyzed the nation and deeply affected agriculturally oriented Los Angeles, where newly harvested perishable crops sat rotting for want of transportation. Street fights and disorders broke out through the city. After the issuance of a controversial federal injunction in early July, federal troops were sent out to keep order in several cities, including Los Angeles.

Public sympathy in California, with its long-standing hatred of the Southern Pacific Railroad, lay largely with the American Railway Union. Most of the state's newspapers supported the strike, and even the state militia in Sacramento refused to obey orders to disperse strikers. The *Times,* however, deplored the workers' actions and ran front page stories depicting scenes of violence and chaos. Bold headlines spoke of "Frenzied Mobs Raging at Chicago" and "Murderous Assaults . . . Made on Trainmen," and editorials strongly denounced the strike. "Certainly there can be no permanent surrender to the existing organized despotism. . . ," Otis urged on the second day of the strike. "To permit such an irrational and tyrannical movement as this to succeed would be to open the gates to anarchy and chaos." "The continuance [of the strike]," the *Times* publisher cautioned, "will threaten the very existence of the United States as a free country."

Eugene Debs, the leader of the American Railway Union, was accused of crimes ranging from murder to treason. "Debs and his buccaneering crew of lieutenants should be arrested before they have time to further inflame the minds of unthinking people and commit more overt acts. . . . The lines must be drawn. Let men who love their country and mean to support it take their stand and take it quick," Otis wrote.

So harsh were editorial and news attacks against the strike that union members began to concentrate their picketing around the Times Building rather than in the railway yards. Newsboys refused to handle the paper because of its coverage, and bundles of papers were seized and torn. The *Times* accused strikers of taking copies from news carriers as they came out of the building.

The strike was eventually undermined by court actions against its leaders and the intervention of federal troops. Debs and other union officials were arrested and charged with contempt of court and conspiracy to obstruct the mails and interstate commerce. Strikers were blacklisted by the railroad employers, and newly hired workers had to sign a statement disavowing any present or future connection with the union—a "proper course to adopt," according to a *Times* editorial.

On a visit to Los Angeles after the charges were dropped against him, Debs bitterly acknowledged Otis's role. "I have here a copy of the Los

Angeles Daily Liar, and I will now take up the lies one by one," Debs told a packed house. Debs challenged Otis, who was in the audience, to come forward and promised that if he couldn't prove the *Times* publisher a "monumental liar," he would give $1,000 to any charitable institution in California.

After the return to order following the Pullman strike, the Los Angeles labor movement set out to establish peaceful relations with the business forces who dominated the city. The *Times* boycott, rendered ineffective by the rise of a newly formed Otis-led Merchants' Association, which promised to protect members from losses, was dropped by the impoverished typographical union, and the Council of Labor participated in community events. The council was invited by the Merchants' Association to join in the planning of an 1896 city-wide fiesta, but *Times* reaction led the association to withdraw their invitation. Although several employers praised the unions' moderation, Otis continued his attacks against the typographical union and organized labor in general. Union members accused the *Times* publisher of "resorting to many nefarious schemes to carry out its ends," including the dispatching of PPF strikebreakers to other cities. "Recruits," the LATU noted in January 1896, "have been mustered here by the enemy for Tacoma, San Diego, Milwaukee. . . ."

By the end of May 1896, the union felt the need to tackle the *Times* once again. On May 26, the LATU, with the encouragement and support of the *Herald* and the *Express*, voted unanimously to reopen the *Times* boycott. In order to increase its resources in the fight, the Los Angeles Council of Labor affiliated with the national American Federation of Labor (AFL), and, for the first time, the *Los Angeles Times* was listed under the AFL "unfair" ban.

The combined efforts of the LATU, the Los Angeles Council of Labor, and the AFL brought some immediate success on the national political front. After the presidential election of Otis's army ally William McKinley in 1896, the Los Angeles unions had reason to believe that the *Times* publisher might receive a major political appointment. When the Council of Labor wrote to McKinley to explain its grievances against Otis, the new president defended his friend. But he also cautioned Otis. "I am sure you will appreciate that I do not desire to use any personal influence I may have with you, growing out of old friendship; and yet, I would not be frank with you," McKinley wrote to Otis, "if I did not say that it would give me great pleasure if you and the typographical union would settle your difference." Though Otis didn't change his policy, McKinley submitted Otis's name for the post of assistant secretary of war in early 1897. Angry telegrams were sent by the typographical union to protest the nomination, and union pressure, aided by the lobbying of other political opponents of the *Times* publisher, succeeded in killing the appointment.

". . . I would not change the attitude I have deliberately and successfully held for years past for the sake of securing any office on earth," Otis
remarked after the defeat.

Locally, the union was cheered by declines in the *Times* circulation
figures and its failure to win the county Great Register contract. "We un-
hesitatingly state that we believe that the 'old man' is hurt and that badly," a boycott committee reported to a LATU meeting of August 1896.
Union pressure also forced the city council to pass legislation requiring a
union label on all city printing. The measure was described by Otis as
"class legislation of the rankest kind," and the *Times* castigated those
councilmen who had voted for the proviso. With a new city council election coming up in three months, the *Times* threatened to oppose any incumbents still supporting the union label. Soon after the election, the new
council voted to annul the resolution.

The defeat of the union label proviso was a great disappointment to the
typographical union and resulted in their abandonment of the *Times* boycott once again. For the next several years, constantly faced with hostile
antiunion attacks from the *Times*, the union grew more and more despondent. At a time of increasing national business accommodation with
the conservative craft unionism of the American Federation of Labor,
Otis still called for "an end to the serfdom and tyranny of trades-unionism."

As the city's economy began to swing upward at the turn of the century, labor organizing, boosted by AFL assistance, began to build a new
base. Agreements were signed in many industries, but many union observers felt these accords were tenuous in the face of the constant harassment from the *Times*. As a counterpart to its continual antiunion editorial
assaults, the paper instituted its own training school for linotype operators. Students from the school did local work for rates far below those set
by the union and, as graduates, were available as potential strikebreakers.

On July 15, 1901, with the promise of help from forty-five unions, the
Council of Labor, the Printing Trades Council, the Building Trades Council, and the District Council of Carpenters, the Los Angeles Typographical Union voted unanimously to mount a new offensive against the *Times*.

A new organizer, Arthur A. Hay, was brought in from Syracuse, New
York, by the ITU to raise the level of leadership of the struggle. Hay
quickly infused new energy into the campaign. Cards defining labor's position were distributed to restaurants, barber shops, and other popular
gathering places. Ten thousand "I don't read the *Times*" lapel buttons
were printed. The homes of *Times* subscribers were canvassed to try to
induce them to cancel their subscriptions. Moving pictures and carica-
tures of General Otis were shown on busy street corners. The boycott on
the People's Store, still one of the *Times*'s biggest advertisers, was rein-

stituted. Union members and their supporters clogged Hamburger's store without buying anything and appealed to customers to go elsewhere. Stickers urging the boycotting of the People's Store and the *Times* were pasted all over the city. By the end of his first month in town, Hay was confident that the union would win "one of the greatest victories ever won by a local typographical union."

Otis met the new campaign with an editorial on the "renewal of the trade's disturbing and lawless boycott which proved such a nuisance— though an impotent nuisance—ten years ago." Within days after the boycott resumption; the *Times,* in an effort to win public sympathy, claimed to have discovered a union "plot" to "dictate terms to all industrial Los Angeles," whereby labor had intended, through a campaign of propaganda and terror, to unionize all of industry and displace all nonunion workers. The paper followed up the story with prominently displayed "exposures" of union leaders.

Otis's objective was no longer simply the defeat of the typographical union and its boycott. He was opposed to the entire organized labor movement. "This labor-union system is indeed a tyranny—one of the most monstrous tyrannies that the world has ever seen," a *Times* editorial commented. "As for the *Times,* we defy these bluffing shouting scavengers—these workingmen who do not work, but who fatten upon decaying commerce, despoil honest toil. . . . We denounce and condemn them, daring them to do their worst. The latest insolent and dictatorial boycott order directed at merchants is ample warrant for what we here assert."

With both the AFL and the ITU now sending aid to the local union, the printers' battle against the *Times* raged on through the next year. A great publicity campaign—inaugurated by a mass labor parade—kicked off the new year. Tensions ran high. Rumors circulated that Otis had armed his employees to fend off an imagined storming of the *Times* building.

Labor's varied tactics proved partially successful. The People's Store was strongly affected by the boycott—Hay noted a 25 percent drop-off in trade by the end of 1901. In May 1902 Hamburger offered to cut down his *Times* advertising in hopes of getting the boycott on his store lifted. If Otis hadn't been so powerful at that point, the union might well have been victorious. But Hamburger and the other businessmen felt that they needed the *Times* more than they needed an accommodation with labor.

Otis boasted of good business despite the boycott. His paper was still staffed by members of the PPF. Otis's ties with the group tightened and its official publication, the *Fraternity,* was filled with praise of the *Times* publisher. Otis showed his gratitude to the PPF men by naming one of his printing presses the Old Guard in their honor. The machine was adorned with the figure of an armored Roman soldier and capped by the *Times* motto, "Stand Fast, Stand Firm, Stand Sure, Stand True."

Otis had developed a consistent ideological framework for his opposition to unionism by this time. Every citizen, he wrote, had "the indisputable right . . . to pursue any lawful occupation of his choice . . . and to pursue it undisturbed by mere combinations of other workmen or other persons, no matter under what plausible guise they may act." Otis felt this principle was "vital to private and public liberty, vital to the prosperity and progress of the citizen and of the country, vital to the good of the industrial world, vital to the best interests of the Republic and all its citizens." It was, according to the *Times* publisher, a matter of "industrial freedom." "The question is, as it always has been," Otis wrote, "shall a citizen in this presumably free country—or a corporation— . . . be permitted to conduct his or their private (or public) business, without let or hindrance—to hire and discharge whom they please; to pay such wages as may be mutually agreed upon between employer and employee individually. . . ."

When questioned by a government commission as to how an employee under such a system could deal with a situation not to his liking, Otis noted that "any individual workman had the individual right to strike peacefully if he does not like his employment or his employer. I have never disputed that right whenever the striker feels moved to 'move on.'" An employee, according to Otis's logic, only had the prerogative of quitting. Any other kind of "strike" or organized action was viewed as a conspiracy. Otis abhorred the use of the strike, calling it "a great evil." "It retards progress," he testified. "It disturbs the industries. . . . It begets needless idleness; but worse than all, it harmfully affects the workman himself by throwing him out of employment, frequently against his will, annihilating his pay envelope and driving him and his family in too many cases to undeserving poverty and distress."

Otis's concern over labor was ultimately tied to his California boosterism. Manufacturers, he felt, would be drawn to Los Angeles if they thought they could run their businesses without the interference of labor unions. Otis knew the city needed a manufacturing base if the business community were to prosper, but the city had little to attract industry—no center of trade, no resources such as iron and coal, and its port was still in an incipient stage. Los Angeles could only offer its open shop industrial policy, with its cheap and permanent supply of nonunion labor, to attract interested manufacturers.

Otis subsumed all political matters under the overriding opposition to unions. The industrial question, Otis wrote to President Roosevelt in 1903, was the most "vital, burning question now before the country." The labor trust was viewed as "the greatest present menace to the peace of the country and to the rights of its citizens."

Business monopolies and capital trusts, on the other hand, were defended by the *Times* publisher. *Times* editorials constantly urged employers to stand together to put an end to unionism. "Where employers have associated themselves together, and have stood firmly by their agreements with one another, they have invariably won their fight," Otis stressed. "Let them have nothing whatever to do with the miserable disturbers who make it their business to stir up discord." Otis helped set up several such employer groups. The most important—and powerful—organization, described by historian John Caughey as "the biggest gun in Otis' artillery," was the mighty Merchants and Manufacturer's Association.

3. The M & M

In June 1896, on the suggestion of Harrison Gray Otis, the Merchants' Association and a new kindred Manufacturers' Association merged to form the Merchants and Manufacturers' Association (M&M). The M&M was initially set up to boost local products and further the interests of members' businesses, but, under Otis's leadership, the group developed a militant antiunion perspective.

In January 1903, with fear of a union victory in Los Angeles, the M&M stepped into the capital/labor conflict. The organization had pledged neutrality during the early *Times* boycotts, but the new boycott was having considerable effect. The People's Store, a member of the M&M, was losing a great deal of money, and the other businessmen feared its surrender, an action which might serve as a tremendous impetus to the unions. At an annual meeting in early 1903, the M&M declared its intention to back the *Times* and the People's Store. "We regret that these conditions exist today," M&M president Niles Pease told the meeting, "but we believe that it is the duty of the merchants to stand together in a controversy of this character, and to declare that an assault upon one is an assault upon all."

The M&M entry into the Los Angeles struggle marked the beginning of one of the most ruthless and systematic campaigns against organized labor in the history of the United States. With 80 percent of the city's firms subscribing, the combine wielded a tremendous amount of financial and political power. Immense sums of money were raised to further the group's antiunion goals. An "educational campaign" was initiated to instruct members and other citizens about the evils of unionism. Guards, spies, police protection, and strikebreakers were hired. Coercion—in the form of withheld bank loans, diverted orders, delayed payments, lack of supplies and raw materials, or the withholding of newspaper advertising space—were used on businessmen who refused to accept the M&M policy. M&M employers discharged union members or pressured them to leave the union in order to keep their jobs. Journalist Frederick Palmer, in an article in the January 1911 issue of *Hampton's Magazine,* described the organization as "without rival in its effective coherence, and example of the fast-bound cooperation of the banker, the employer, and the newspaper for selfish interests. . . . Otis has taught it strictly military principles. . . . always alert, is Otis with his daily newspaper ready to beat any laggard into line. It is not popular and it is not wise for a businessman to 'get in bad' with the 'M. and M.' ' "

The *Times* and the M&M effectively enforced a unity among the city's industrialists. "We are against the weak-kneed employer who, at the first sign of danger, surrenders his position to the assaults of lawless labor, in whatever guise it may come, and who fails to assert his indefeasible rights under the law to manage his own business in his own way," Otis wrote. Businessmen were so fearful of the M&M/*Times* power that, on one occasion, a company—the Senthouse Packing Company—got a court injunction to force the unions to remove its name from a union "fair" list.

On a national level, several employer organizations started to move toward an open shop strategy and took an active interest in the Los Angeles struggle. In 1903 the powerful National Association of Manufacturers (NAM) issued an open shop declaration and created the Citizen's Industrial Association—under the leadership of NAM president David M. Parry— specifically to fight organized labor.

Labor's national organization, the American Federation of Labor, was equally aware of the importance of the Los Angeles conflict and, at its 1903 convention, agreed to send a special organizer to Los Angeles so that "Otis and Parry and those of their kind shall be thwarted in their efforts to enslave that section of the country."

The antilabor employers, led by Otis, were intent on making Los Angeles a "model open-shop town." The *Times* publisher condemned even "recognition of the union, . . . [as] merely a euphemism for a form of oligarchical despotism, which if it could be put into practical realization, would destroy the liberty of every citizen, turning the most sacred of citizenship rights into an empty boast and a profanation," and he instructed employers on how to rid themselves of union influence. "Employers of labor in Los Angeles, having been thus forewarned," he wrote in a 1903 editorial, "should prepare for possible disturbances by quietly arranging with skilled workingmen in various parts of the country, whom they may, if necessary, summon at a moment's notice by telegraph, to take the place of their present employees, in case the latter should be persuaded to walk out and leave their work. The latter might then be notified to go about their business, and never to darken the doors of the establishment again. At the same time a watch should be kept over the weak and faithless, and all interlopers. Those who are found to be acting the part of the traitor and fomenting disturbance, should be weeded out, and replaced by men who believe in respecting and protecting the interests of their employer, as well as their own."

In the summer of 1902, Otis and Hamburger and some twenty-five other leading employers of the city banded together to form an Employers Association. The organization set up an Independent Labor Bureau to advertise throughout the East to attract new workers to Southern California. Scores of nonunion workers—potential strikebreakers—were continually lured into the city by booster campaigns. The *Times* promoted the project with frequent news stories and special editions with articles promising abundant employment at high wages. The Council of Labor tried to counteract the immigration by requesting the Los Angeles City Council to send notification to eastern cities denying the need of new workers. But the council, dominated by business interests, refused the request.

The employers also had an effective ally in the police department. As the struggle intensified, the police force began to operate as a private army for the M&M. Strikebreakers were deputized as special policemen. In August 1903 the city government put into use an ordinance which required police permits for street meetings. The labor movement tried to get the ordinance repealed and to oust Los Angeles's police chief, but the *Times* and M&M backed the chief and effectively quashed any possibility of an investigation.

The open shop forces were confident of their victory. Employer associations in each industry were rapidly converting their businesses to open shop conditions, and organized labor was in retreat. Throughout the year, Otis reiterated his belief that the open shop was here to stay. "The labor situation in Los Angeles presents the gratifying indication that the agitator and jawsmith is an inconsequential and a constantly lessening factor," Otis wrote in April 1903, "and that the great body of laboring men, union and nonunion, have too much horse-sense to be used as fools and catspaws by these delectable lilies of the field 'who toil not, neither do they spin,' except as they spin false tales into the ears of softheaded and willing dupes."

On July 4, 1903, several hundred of Los Angeles's businessmen presented Otis with a memorial in appreciation of his leadership of the open shop crusade. "Under your leadership," the inscription read, "the *Los Angeles Times* has fought and won a great victory for equal rights. . . . That the City of Los Angeles and environment are free from the tyranny of misguided agitators is chiefly due to the fearless advocacy of the rights of all men and the relentless condemnation of demagogues by the *Times*. . . . "

4. An Invitation to Hearst

The Los Angeles labor movement was still not ready to concede to the *Times*. As early as 1894, the typographical union had realized that "the only one great obstacle in our way has been that we have had no morning paper which we could offer to those who would willingly come out of the *Times*." In order for the boycott to be truly effective, the union reasoned, there had to be an equally attractive competitor to pick up those advertisers and subscribers willing to switch allegiance. The Los Angeles printers needed a prolabor newspaper on the scale of the *Times* operation. In 1901, the union had granted special favors to the *Herald* in the hopes that the paper would serve that function. But the *Herald* couldn't compete with the *Times*, and the printers decided to search elsewhere.

At the 1902 ITU convention, a resolution was unanimously adopted to discuss the possibility with newspaper publisher William Randolph Hearst of establishing a new daily paper in Los Angeles. Hearst expressed some interest in the idea and sent his San Francisco representative, Dent H. Robert, publisher of the *San Francisco Examiner*, to check out the city to the south. Equipment was installed within a few months. In exchange for the establishment of the newspaper and a five-year closed shop agreement, the unions guaranteed the Hearst operation forty to fifty thousand subscribers for a minimum of six months. By January 1903 the Council of Labor had begun to circulate subscription blanks; every union member in the city became a solicitor.

The first issue of Hearst's *Los Angeles Examiner,* filled with labor news, appeared on December 12, 1903. "TO LABOR AND CAPITAL WHAT JUSTLY BELONGS TO EACH . . . EQUAL RIGHTS TO ALL, PRIVILEGES FOR NONE," the front page exclaimed. "The *Examiner* will support with its whole power the proposition that labor is justified in demanding a fair share of the wealth it produces and its proportion of the country's prosperity," according to a front page policy statement. "Consequently, the *Examiner* will be the friend of the trades unions, and give them its energetic backing when their cause is just. . . . It shall be its endeavor to bring about better relations between Capital and Labor."

To Otis, Hearst's entrance was a declaration of war. While labor celebrated with a parade on publication of the first issue of the *Examiner,* Otis distributed weapons to his employees inside the *Times* building. A reporter who was in the *Times* office on the evening of the workers' parade, later testified that "shortly before the parade was to start they brought out bunches of Springfield rifles and ball and cartridges . . . capable of killing a man at a great distance."

"The fight is still on," Otis wrote a week after the *Examiner* first appeared. "If Los Angeles is to continue to grow; if we are to have civic order; if we are to go forward and not backward, we must continue to fight on, fight on, and on, and on." The arrival of the *Examiner,* the *Times* editorial concluded, would "array class against class" and "destroy the prosperity of Southern California." The *Examiner*, Otis wrote, was "an emissary of chaos."

Economic pressures on the new paper were as harsh as the *Times* editorial attacks. Otis had apparently let it be known that anyone who advertised in the *Examiner* would be refused space in the *Times*. Not wanting to incur the censure of Otis or the M&M, Los Angeles merchants were extremely reluctant to advertise in the Hearst paper. The *Examiner* also limited its own advertising base by refusing to accept ads from the People's Store, still a primary target of the labor boycott. Eight months after its momentous beginning, the *Examiner*'s business manager requested the typographical union to lift its boycott on the People's Store so that the paper could accept its advertising. At the union's insistence, a bitterly divided labor movement agreed to end the boycott.

The termination of the People's Store boycott was heralded as a great victory by the open shop forces. "The promoters of the *Los Angeles Examiner* entirely mistook the temper of this community," the *Times* commented. ". . . The laurels for the superb victory over the dangerous and desperate gang," the paper declared, "should go to the Hamburgers." Otis's son-in-law Harry Chandler was less modest. "There is one city in the United States where a strike has never been able to succeed; that city is Los Angeles. The reason . . . is because it has . . . the *Los Angeles Times*," he boasted before a convention of the Citizen's Industrial Association of America in February 1904.

"FEW LABOR STRIKES HERE," noted a headline for a 1904 midwinter article on the beginnings of manufacturing growth in Los Angeles. Industries were encouraged by the *Times* and the Chamber of Commerce to come to the area with the promise of "no danger of sudden shutdown" and "less risk of labor troubles."

In January 1904 the Los Angeles chapter of the Citizen's Alliance was set up, with Otis as chairman of its executive board and Felix J. Zeehandelaar of the M&M as its secretary. The organization, which was open to any citizen not a union member, developed an elaborate structure to support members subjected to strikes or boycotts. The *Times* gave appropriate attention to its announcements. By April of that year, the local association had 6,000 members, making it the strongest chapter in the country proportionate to the city's population.

The *Times*, the M&M, and the Citizen's Alliance worked closely together to make Los Angeles a completely open shop city. Antiunion activities became more overt; open shop declarations, lockouts, blacklists, discharge of union members, use of strikebreaking agencies, full financial help for struck firms, economic pressure on prounion employers, legislative lobbying, use of Mexican and black laborers as a reserve labor supply, and cancellation of union contracts were among the employer techniques. The labor movement fought back, but, except for an occasional success in the political arena, such as the 1904 recall of a pro-*Times* city councilman, it was constantly defeated. Of the fifty-one strikes recorded for Los Angeles in the years 1905 and 1906, forty-two were listed by the California Bureau of Labor Statistics as complete failures, four were considered partially successful, and only five were won by the unions.

The *Times* constantly portrayed unions as violent, dangerous organizations. "The object of the striking butchers . . . was to have the men driven off the grounds in order that the murdering thugs of the unions could get at them to kill, maim and otherwise work out upon them their inhuman vengeance," a *Times* story commented about an August 1904 strike. Employers who negotiated with unions were described as traitors.

San Francisco unions, among the most powerful in the country, were a constant target of the *Times*'s criticism. After the disastrous 1906 earthquake, the *Times* editorialized that "it was not a tenth part so serious in its results as the scourge of trade-union despotism which preceded it." A visit to Los Angeles by P. H. McCarthy, leader of San Francisco's building trades unions, brought forth an expressive example of the Otis style of journalism. "McCarthy is an industrial excrescence. He is a putrescent pustule which indicates a suppurating disease. He is a pest, and he radiates the germs of moral and industrial pestilence . . . and we say to him—Scat! Skidoo! 23! Git out! Keep out! Go back to your lair! Make yourself scarce! Make tracks! Skedaddle! Go home! Stay home! Stay shut! Bump-Thump-Slam-Bang!"

On January 2, 1906, as part of a nationwide push for the eight-hour day, Los Angeles's union printers, pressmen, and press feeders walked off their jobs. To head off the action, Otis, with the support of the Citizen's Alliance and the M&M, organized a militant Employing Printing Trades Alliance which had the participation of 95 percent of the city's printing firms. Otis hoped to parcel out his workers to replace striking union men from the other firms, but his plans were spoiled when twenty-five of his own workers, undercover union members, walked out, too. Though the printers had met with success throughout the other areas of the country, they could not completely secure an eight-hour day in Los Angeles. The general strike was called off in October 1906.

The *Times* publisher laid out the battle plans for the city's businessmen. Owners were urged not to reemploy strikers, "deserters" according to Otis. "The men who came to the relief of employers must be protected." Strike leaders should be "denied a job," and "blacklisted and their names posted in every place of employment as dangerous men who are not to be tolerated. . . ." It was a two-fold tactic; "Let the ring-leaders be driven from the community. . . . Let the strikebreaker be kept at his job."

In 1907 the *Times* claimed total victory for the open shop. "This city," the *Times* boasted, "is unique in having driven to bay the snarling pack of union labor wolves that have infested many other cities of the land and have snapped their red-seeking jaws over the fallen form of industrial freedom." As a testimonial to its own role, the Times Mirror Company put out a pamphlet, the "Story of the Distinct Victory over Militant and Despotic Trades-Unionism Won by the Los Angeles Times in a Sixteen Years Battle Showing the Virtue of Standing Fast."

The unions also gave the *Times* credit for the open shop success in Los Angeles. "Without question the *Los Angeles Times* is a hard proposition to proceed against," the typographers conceded at their 1907 convention. "Firmly entrenched in its position, enjoying a remarkable advertising patronage, reaching a clientele that is peculiarly susceptible to the anti-trade union views that it expresses, it can be easily seen that the movement to curtail its advertising patronage and limit its circulation is one that must proceed slowly. . . ." The national typographical union realized that it could not do battle alone and appealed to the American Federation of Labor for help. "The *Times* has succeeded in practically disrupting many of the unions of Los Angeles," an ITU resolution to the 1907 AFL convention noted, "and, unless strenuously opposed, will eventually make that city thoroughly non-union, thereby creating a breeding place for strikebreakers of all crafts and trades; . . . if unionism is crushed in Los Angeles, it will be but a short time before the same methods are applied to other cities. . . ."

The AFL convention responded in favor of the ITU resolution. For the first time in its history, the national federation voted to single out one locale for an intensive unionization campaign. Preparations were made to raise money for a "Los Angeles Fund" by levying a one cent tax on all AFL members.

Otis dismissed the ITU/AFL resolutions as "vain, idle, skyscraping, malicious, truculent and without any adequate excuse." Even before the AFL decision, a *Times* editorial had taunted, "Come on Hay! Come on Sam Gompers and your Federation of Labor! Come on, you smarting and scab-covered wretches, come on once more."

The M&M began preparations for the upcoming siege by setting up its own financial fund. Bolstered by the heavy flow of unemployed migrants who came to the city during the Panic of 1907, the M&M was able to withstand the AFL intervention. Dissension swept through the city's labor movement in the face of the consolidation of the open shop advocates. They were, as historian Grace Stimson described them, "the darkest days" that labor in Los Angeles had known.

The first decade of the twentieth century ended with the open-shoppers, led by the *Times,* in firm control of Los Angeles's economic policy.

The goal of developing the city into an open shop stronghold had been achieved. "Scab City," as Los Angeles came to be known, opened its antiunion arms to new industries attracted to the profitable arrangements of a cheap labor supply and the lack of union interference.

Journalists dubbed Los Angeles "Otistown of the Open Shop." Otis's fight with the typographical union had set the antiunion forces in motion, and his newspaper fanned the flames of the conflict. Through the use of the *Times* and the initiation of powerful "employer unions," Otis led the businessmen of the city, and his newspaper became their ideological spokesman.

It is hard to imagine what the course of labor in Los Angeles would have been without Otis's participation. "Organized labor would have found the battle easier without the *Times*," Stimson concluded. "The power of the press in influencing public opinion and in fostering a pet theory had been forcibly brought home to Los Angeles labor through bitter experience. The determination of Otis to fashion community thinking into a pattern of his own devising, and to make it reflect the antiunion principles on which his newspaper operated, was in its successful implementation the overshadowing influence which made Los Angeles an open-shop city."

With Los Angeles a secure open shop bastion, General Otis looked to the rest of the country. "The *Times* expects to be in the very forefront of the great national battle for industrial freedom which is surely destined to be fought out in this country within the next ten years," the paper predicted in 1909. Less than two years later, a dynamite blast would catapult Otis and his *Times* into the national limelight, transforming the battle in Los Angeles into one of the most important capital/labor conflicts in the country's history.

CHAPTER 3

"All for San Pedro"

1. The Murchison Letter

To win the endorsement of Harrison Gray Otis, a political candidate needed to have two qualifications: he had to be against organized labor, and he had to be a Republican. In terms of California politics, it also helped if he were against the railroad.

Since the Central Pacific had finished laying its tracks into California in 1869, it had built up a tight control of the economics and politics of the state, including the legislature, the courts, municipal and county governments, and many state, city, and county officials, in order to further its interests. The Central Pacific, later renamed the Southern Pacific (SP) held a virtual monopoly on the state's transportation system, dominated the press, and was the largest landholder in California. It dictated the political platforms of both parties and a large number of candidates on each party's slate.

Nearly from the moment he set foot in California, Otis and the railroad were politically at odds. Otis opposed the political and economic domination of the northern-California-based SP and supported attempts by Southern California Republican party forces to challenge that power. In 1877, as editor of the *Santa Barbara Press*, Otis unsuccessfully backed the anti-SP candidate T. R. Bard for the state senate. That same year the railroad, under Leland Stanford's leadership, blocked Otis's appointment as marshal of California.

After Otis became editor of the Republican *Los Angeles Times*, he be-

gan a stream of attacks against the SP's power. "It should declare," the
Times said of the 1882 state Republican Convention, "in language not
susceptible of a double interpretation, that it is the people, not the corporations, who own the State. The people, through the Convention,
should proclaim their determination that, while denying no just and lawful
privilege to the corporations, and invading no vested right of theirs, those
corporations shall be forced to let go their grip upon California's throat,
and be henceforth content with no more than their fair share of the pro-
ceeds of the common toil. No issue in State politics transcends in importance this burning one of anti-monopoly."

Otis quickly developed ties with other anti-SP political figures. These
included Civil War veteran Colonel Henry Markham, who won the state's
congressional seat for Southern California in 1884, and went on, thanks to
Times support, to become governor in 1890, and one of the leading Democrats in California, Stephen White.

White had done legal work for the Times Mirror Company shortly after
its incorporation in 1884, and was a personal friend of the *Times* editor as
well as his legal representative. In 1882 White was elected Los Angeles
district attorney. Four years later the ambitious young lawyer successfully ran for the state senate, and became its president in 1887. That same
year he became acting lieutenant governor on the death of Governor Bartlett. Though the *Times* opposed White's Democratic affiliations and endorsed his Republican opponents, it also praised him editorially as "an
honest man, a gentleman, and one of the brainiest men in the south country."

White came close to being supported by the strictly Republican *Times*.
When White ran for the U.S. Senate in 1893, his major Republican opponent, Representative Jeremiah Lynch, withdrew from the race shortly before the state legislature voted to select the new senator. The *Times* urged
Republican legislators to break precedent and support White, "a man of
known ability and character, who is big enough and broad enough to be
the Senator of the whole State."

Otis's relations within national Republican circles also aided his struggle in the state, where he was becoming the dominant Republican voice in
Southern California. An incident which occurred during the 1888 presidential campaign did much to strengthen Otis's position.

One of the key issues of the campaign between Democrat Grover
Cleveland and Republican Benjamin Harrison was the question of protective tariffs. The Republicans, who were tied to U.S. business and industrial interests, favored a strong tariff position and criticized the Democrats'
cry for "free trade". During the campaign, a Pomona farmer, who
claimed to be a loyal Englishman, sent a letter under the name Charles F.

Murchison to the British minister in the United States, Sir L.S. Sackville-West, requesting advice on how to vote. The British minister responded that it would be in England's interest to have the Democrats win.

The *Times* printed the letters on October 21, 1888. "The *Times* this morning," an editorial on that day noted, "is able to lay before its readers a document which goes a long way to substantiate the statements made by those Republican papers regarding the bond of brotherhood that exists between the British and the Democratic Party."

The letter produced an immediate storm which placed the *Times* in the national limelight. Otis capitalized on the situation. "Taken altogether," the paper boasted in an editorial shortly before the election, "the *Times* expose is undoubtedly the greatest journalistic sensation which this country has ever witnessed, judged by the far-reaching dissemination of its interest and the important consequence which will result from it." Los Angeles will replace Boston as the hub of the United States, "socially, climactically, and politically," the *Times* boasted.

The British minister was recalled for his political blunder, and Republican Benjamin Harrison won the presidential election. After the election, the *Times* revealed that a Pomona Republican of English grandparents, George Osgoodby, had been behind the scheme to entrap Sackville-West. He apparently wrote the letter and passed it on with the reply to Republican figures, including Otis.

Though some Democrats contended that Otis was the real mastermind, the *Times* publisher rejected any claims that the letters were a plot. The authorship of the letters, Otis wrote, must not be "unjustly fixed upon the National Republican Committee, the State or County Committee, or upon any individual Republican, save alone the real author George Osgoodby."

The Murchison letter, however, won Otis few favors from the new Republican in the White House. President Harrison, whom the *Times* portrayed as "mediocre" and a "chunky icicle," allied himself with the Southern Pacific forces and appointed an SP ally postmaster of Los Angeles. Otis, furious over the choice, wrote to Henry Markham about "the persistent efforts to fill these offices with personal enemies of mine."

Otis was able, despite the election of Democrat Grover Cleveland as president in 1892, to obtain a foothold in Washington to secure patronage for federal positions through Stephen White's successful bid for the U.S. Senate. In 1893 Otis had White intercede to retain Otis's nephew's proofreading position with the Public Printer's office, and numerous other political appointments were cleared through the *Times* publisher. The White/Otis alliance became, during the 1890s, central to the struggle against the Southern Pacific in Southern California, a struggle that would also involve Los Angeles's new Chamber of Commerce.

2. A Viable Port

Whereas, although Southern California is being settled and the land being improved with great rapidity, yet it is for the interest of this country and for the interest of every business man and owner of real estate here, that this settlement and development shall proceed as rapidly as possible, since with each settler who comes here, there is an increase to our markets and to our resources.

In the fall of 1888, that resolution was formulated by a five-man committee, consisting of four real estate men and Harrison Gray Otis, as part of an attempt by the city's business establishment to protect the interests of Los Angeles after the collapse of the boom. These men felt the need for a new permanent organization to replace the recently defunct Southern California Immigration Association, to stimulate expansion, and to market the city's products.

Colonel Otis formally introduced the motion to form the new organization. The resolution passed, and Los Angeles had a new Chamber of Commerce. Real estate owner Major E.W. Jones, an active leader in the old Board of Trade, was elected president, and Otis was chosen second vice-president.

Some local businessmen were skeptical of the new organization's attempts to revive the boom. "The sentiment was not uncommon," wrote Chamber of Commerce historian Charles Willard, "among many of those who had seen more than a decade on the coast that Southern California would never be able to support the great horde of people that had crowded into it, and that under no circumstances should any more be invited to come."

Those chamber officials committed to the idea of permanent expansion disagreed and sought to change the conditions that might make further growth difficult. Foremost in their minds was the need for a deep-water harbor.

Since the founding of the city of Los Angeles in 1781, fur traders, travelers, and immigrants had been making use of the natural harbor afforded by San Pedro Bay, twenty miles south of the city. Until the gold rush, San Pedro had been one of the most important shipping points on the West Coast. "It was the only port for a distance of eighty miles," Richard Dana wrote of San Pedro in 1835 in *Two Years Before the Mast*, "and about thirty miles in the interior was a fine plain country, filled with herds of cattle, in the center of which was the pueblo of Los Angeles—the largest town in California—and several of the largest missions; to all of which San Pedro was the seaport."

By 1869 the traffic between Los Angeles and San Pedro had reached such proportions that Los Angeles voters passed a bond to finance a twenty-three-mile-long public-owned railroad—the first railway in Southern California—between the two areas. The line was subsequently given to the Southern Pacific in 1876 as part of the city's deal to get the SP to make Los Angeles its southern terminal. At that time the San Pedro port consisted of an unprotected deep-water bay and an inner harbor accessible only to small craft. Large ships had to anchor in the outer areas, exposed to winds and storms, and transfer their cargo to smaller tugboats and lighters which could pass into the shallow inner harbor.

Los Angeles's boosters realized that to be a viable port the inner harbors needed to be dredged and a protective breakwater constructed for the outer area. In 1872 a small initial congressional appropriation was secured to deepen one of the channels.

The need for the harbor became more pressing with the announcement of the government's plans to help construct a canal across the Isthmus of Panama which would open up a new trade route for the West Coast. The new Los Angeles Chamber of Commerce immediately began to push for further congressional appropriations to develop the harbor. In the fall of 1889, the chamber helped organize an expedition of United States senators to the port. The group included California Senators Leland Stanford and George Hearst (father of William Randolph Hearst); Senator William Frye from Maine, chairman of the Rivers and Harbors Committee; Senator John P. Jones from Nevada; and several other officials. Any congressman visiting the coast had an open invitation to visit the harbor on a tour arranged by chamber representatives.

The Southern Pacific, which owned the monopoly San Pedro Railroad, was also interested in the San Pedro port, a position which created a temporary alliance with the formerly antagonistic Otis. In an interview with the *Los Angeles Times,* the Southern Pacific president, Senator Stanford, outlined his company's intentions to capitalize on the new port through its "Sunset Route" from Los Angeles to San Francisco, in the hope of making it the major transportation outlet for the commerce from Asian markets. The Southern Pacific also intended to build huge steamships to extend its role in the Asian trade. With Stanford and the SP working closely with the powerful Senator Frye, it appeared more than likely that San Pedro would receive the congressional funds necessary to begin the harbor construction.

In 1890 Congress authorized a special board of Army Engineers, headed by Colonel G.H. Mendell, to advise on a Southern California site for a deep-water harbor. The Mendell board report issued December 1891 favored San Pedro and recommended an appropriation of approximately three million dollars to begin necessary expansion work.

All the conditions for the construction of the San Pedro harbor appeared set. But in the year and a half that had elapsed between the inception of the Mendell board and the release of its report, the position of the Southern Pacific, unbeknownst to the Los Angeles businessmen, went through a major change.

In 1890 the Southern Pacific's monopoly over harbor land in San Pedro was about to be broken. That year, a syndicate of St. Louis capitalists incorporated the Los Angeles Terminal Railway Corporation, and began to buy up portions of unsubdivided land in Rancho San Pedro to the east of the SP holdings. The St. Louis businessmen planned to build a railroad from the Midwest to terminate in San Pedro. In 1891, the Terminal Railroad completed a section from Glendale, an area north of Los Angeles, to a point just opposite San Pedro.

The developments in San Pedro took place at the same time as an internal power struggle within the Southern Pacific. In April 1890, at a SP board of directors' meeting, Colis (C.P.) Huntington replaced Leland Stanford as president of the company, and issued a bitter public attack against his predecessor. Huntington, another of the railroad's Big Four, had represented the railroad's interest in Congress, and assumed much of the day-to-day leadership of the corporation.

Shortly after Huntington took control, he quietly began to buy and lease land in the Santa Monica area. Twenty-five miles up the coast from San Pedro, the community of Santa Monica had become a favorite beach resort of many inland residents of Southern California. In 1875 Nevada Senator John P. Jones, a Santa Monica landowner, in conjunction with several local businessmen, had constructed a 1,800-foot wharf and a railroad to connect the town to Los Angeles in the hopes of building Santa Monica into a commercial port. Just a few years after the Southern Pacific acquired its San Pedro railroad in 1876, it eliminated potential competition by also purchasing the Jones properties. The SP kept the Santa Monica wharf inactive while concentrating on San Pedro, though the possibility of developing a successful harbor there was geographically as feasible as at the San Pedro site, with the added advantage of being twenty-five miles closer to San Francisco.

When the Terminal Railway challenged the SP's monopoly in San Pedro, Huntington decided to put a halt to its San Pedro plans and instead construct a new port, Port Los Angeles, about two miles north of Santa Monica and its old wharf. Huntington's land ownership as well as the physical layout of the area, composed of steep cliffs which rose over the ocean, made it impossible for any competing railroad to lay tracks to the proposed new wharf.

In 1892 debate over the appropriations for San Pedro was held in the Senate's Rivers and Harbors Committee chaired by Senator Frye. While the committee was deliberating, William Hood, chief engineer of the

Southern Pacific, sent a telegram to Frye stating that the SP had abandoned its San Pedro pier because the area was too rocky for adequate supports. Hood informed the committee that the railroad planned to construct a new 4,500-foot wharf in Santa Monica.

The Hood telegram caught Los Angeles businessmen completely by surprise. The Frye committee postponed action on the appropriation and appointed a second committee of engineers, the Craighill board, to investigate the two sites.

The *Times* was outraged. "Is any individual or corporation to have a monopoly on this deep sea harbor when it is constructed?" a September 1892 editorial asked. "If it is found as the result of such an investigation that the Southern Pacific has taken in advance, a mortgage (death grip) on the forthcoming artificial harbor at Santa Monica, then we say let us not give any assistance to the scheme. On the contrary let us fight with all the self-respecting manhood we have. Better that the deep sea harbor be defeated altogether for the present, than that the government should be encouraged to appropriate $4 million or $5 million for the exclusive benefit of this already overgrown and too dictatorial corporation."

During hearings over the Santa Monica versus San Pedro site, the Huntington forces denied any monopolistic intentions. The SP claimed that any railroad competitor could build tracks, lease land, and build its own harbor, but railroad opponents pointed out the lack of space for any competing railroad. SP critics supported San Pedro since the Terminal Railroad Company provided a competitive rate structure and undermined the Southern Pacific's ability to dictate the terms of the port's development.

The Craighill report, released in October 1892, supported the San Pedro site. Senator Jones, who still maintained an interest in the Southern Pacific's Santa Monica holdings, was absent when the report was reviewed by the Frye committee, and asked that any vote on the matter be postponed. Frye, himself favorable to the Huntington interests, willingly obliged and held over the San Pedro appropriations issue to the next congressional session.

After the Hood telegram, a new antimonopoly coalition emerged in Los Angeles to fight for a "free harbor." A common opponent united traditional enemies: Democrats and Republicans, as well as the growing populist People's Party; most of the city's business interests; nearly the entire labor movement; and the *Los Angeles Times*. "It is indeed most encouraging to note," a *Times* editorial declared just a few months after the Pullman strike, "that in this matter the laboring element and the employers of labor are of one mind. This fact cannot fail to greatly lessen the probability of a recurrence of that unfortunate friction which has occasionally prevailed between the two classes in this city."

Otis and the *Times* played a leading role in the coalition, as did T.E. Gibbon, the lawyer for the Terminal Railroad group; Charles Willard, former secretary of the Chamber of Commerce and editor of the evening *Express* newspaper; and, after 1893, the junior senator from California, Stephen White.

When White arrived in Washington he found that the Southern Pacific had mobilized a great deal of congressional support for its position, and if it came to a vote, particularly in Senator Frye's committee—characterized by the *Times* as a "Star Chamber"—the Santa Monica/SP forces were likely to prevail. Through 1893 and 1894, deficit years for the federal budget, both sides maneuvered without forcing the issue to a vote, aware that any appropriation would be minimal. White and the San Pedro advocates attempted to influence the composition of the relevant congressional committees, and White himself quickly became a member of the Commerce Committee. White cautioned Otis and other local coalition members to tone down their attacks on the congressional allies of the SP for fear of alienating potential votes. The local forces fretted over White's tactics and wondered whether the senator's caution might indicate a willingness to compromise to SP demands.

SP forces, meanwhile, circulated a petition among Los Angeles Chamber of Commerce members asking for support of the Santa Monica harbor, and SP president Huntington made a personal appeal to chamber members: "I don't know for sure," Huntington told the local businessmen, "that I can get this money for Santa Monica; I think I can. But I know damned well that you shall never get a cent for that other place." If the chamber refused to give Santa Monica its support, Huntington threatened, he had the power " . . . to make the grass grow green in the streets of Los Angeles."

When more than a hundred members of the chamber signed Huntington's pro-Santa Monica petition, a *Times* editorial cried out, "Are the citizens of Los Angeles slaves and curs that they should permit themselves to be whipped into line by Colis P. Huntington? Is this a community of free and independent American citizens, or are we the vassals of a bandit, creatures open to bribery, slaves to a plutocratic master, who has neither bowels of compassion, common decency, nor an organ in his putrid carcass so great as his gall."

In April 1894 a vote was taken among chamber members over which site to endorse publicly: 328 backed San Pedro, and only 131 voted in favor of Santa Monica. After the chamber's San Pedro endorsement White, again urging Otis to moderate the language in his editorials, decided to make his move in the Senate. He tacked an amendment for a minimal $400,000 appropriation for inner harbor development at San Pedro on a rivers and harbors bill, hoping to ask for larger figures at a later session.

White's amendment passed through the Rivers and Harbors Committee without any protest from Huntington. But shortly after the vote, the wily SP president arranged a closed-door session between himself, SP engineers, and House committee members. At the meeting Huntington proposed a double appropriation: $400,000 for San Pedro to dredge its inner harbor and $3 million for Santa Monica to develop an outer deep-water harbor. The House backed Huntington's proposal, but White was able to postpone a final Senate vote by pointing out to his Senate colleagues that the House committee discussions had been held without any California congressmen present. White generated enough sympathy to stall a vote and prevent immediate adoption of the double appropriation.

Huntington's strategy threw the Los Angeles coalition into turmoil. The *Times* attacked the plan as a "cunningly devised trick of Huntington's to betray the people of this section to loot the United States Treasury for the benefit of the Southern Pacific Railroad." "The Southern Pacific is moving heaven and earth to confuse the harbor issue in the minds of the people," the *Times* later complained.

When the Los Angeles City Council, fearful that defeat of the double appropriation would mean no harbor at all, backed the Huntington proposal, the *Times* lashed out and demanded a retraction of the vote. "Citizens of Los Angeles are not in the humor just now," a *Times* editorial warned, "to put up with any double dealing. It is time that we should know who are for us and who are against us."

During the double appropriations controversy, the *Herald*, whose publisher, U.S. Senator Cornelius Cole, owned land in Santa Monica, came out in favor of the Santa Monica site. This stance prompted another angry editorial from the *Times* . "There have been, within a few days past, indications that the hidden hand of the railway company's old newspaper manipulation has resumed operation at the old stand."

In October 1895 some of the leaders of the local anti-monopoly coalition decided to form the Free Harbor League in order to battle for San Pedro. The bylaws of the new organization stated that its purpose was to "secure appropriations . . . [for] San Pedro which will be accessible to as many railways as may wish to come to the waterfront." "A FREE HARBOR FOR A FREE PEOPLE AT SAN PEDRO OR NONE AT ALL," a *Times* headline exclaimed.

Lumber merchant L.W. Blinn was chosen president of the league, banker W.D. Woolwine was selected secretary, and Harrison Gray Otis was named one of its two vice-presidents. Otis and three other members were selected to go to Washington to plead San Pedro's case before the Rivers and Harbors Committee.

Two months later, the coalition organized an enormous mass meeting attended by San Pedro backers ranging from, as a *Times* story put it, "day laborer to capitalist." The turnout and the enthusiasm inspired San Pedro advocates. "Up through the crowded thoroughfare they came," the *Times* proudly reported, "the Long Beach band at the head, shouting the yell designed for the occasion. 'S-A-N P-E-D-R-O, Free Harbor, Let the S.P. Go.' "

The battle intensified on the floor of the Senate. The Rivers and Harbors Committee—described by White as "a chattel personnel of the Railroad company"—added, on Huntington's request, a provision for Santa Monica outer harbor development. When White raised a fuss, the entire appropriation was eliminated, to be debated on the floor of the Senate. "I have been having a lively fight on the harbor issue," White wrote to San Pedro backer T.E. Gibbon on May 3, 1896. "I have never been through such an ordeal in my life."

Once on the Senate floor, White argued that the ultimate decision for site selection ought to be in the hands of an impartial board of engineers and that all appropriations ought to be determined according to the board's recommendations. It was a strong argument and the Senate backed the White proposal. A third board of engineers, called the Walker board after its chairman, Rear Admiral John G. Walker, was organized. It met in Los Angeles in December 1896.

"We are waiting for the verdict of the board," Otis wrote White two months later, "and when it is known and found to be right, the eagle on the Times Building will scream a scream which you will hear in your seat in the Senate."

The Walker board recommendations, released on March 3, 1897, strongly favored San Pedro; only one member, who had strong SP ties, dissented. " SAN PEDRO GETS THE DEEP WATER HARBOR," *Times* headlines celebrated. " AND UNCLE COLIS IS GIVEN THE MARBLE HEART ."

One obstacle still remained. The Senate had designated Secretary of War Russel A. Alger to oversee the collection of the bids to begin the harbor construction. Alger, a former senator from Michigan, was close to Huntington, and had spoken in favor of the Santa Monica site. It was clear that Huntington, through Alger, was trying to stall the San Pedro work. "Huntington is attempting to induce Alger not to let the contract for the San Pedro harbor," White anxiously wrote friends one week after the Walker recommendations.

Alger sat on the contract. To end the delays, Otis and other Free Harbor League members went to Otis's (and McKinley's) old military commander, General William S. Rosecrans, and urged him to write an open letter to the president. McKinley, Otis reasoned, could then forcefully demonstrate to his secretary of war "that he is trifling with law, committing an indignity against the law-making power, and unwarrantably ex-

ceeding his own authority by the course which he is now pursuing, and
that the best thing he can do is to retrace his steps and execute the law as
it stands."

While Alger delayed, Otis applied for the post of assistant secretary of
war, hoping to get on that "contemptible gang opposing me" and oversee
the completion of the harbor. But Otis's influential friends were unable to
secure him the position, and the combined opposition of Alger, Senator
Frye, and Huntington forced McKinley to withdraw the appointment.

"The fellow who goes to war must get used to fire and lots of it," Otis
wrote White in response to Frye's subsequent fight to block Otis's
appointment as brigadier general, "and under the circumstances I can
hardly expect to keep out of range of the Maine battery." Frye, according
to White, was vindictive because of a *Times* article which insinuated that
he had been hired to act as he did in the harbor matter. Ironically, Frye, as
president pro tem of the Senate, held the chair when Otis's appointment
came up. When he announced "confirmed," White wrote, "I looked at
him and a broad grin overspread his face; rather unusual for him, but he
appreciated the ludicrousness of the situation."

The Rosecrans letter, reprinted in the *Times* shortly after Otis's departure for the Philippines, and in other papers around the country, ultimately
broke Alger's resistance. The San Pedro bidding began in the spring of
1899. The anti-SP forces had their victory and the *Times* eagle—hooked
onto a giant whistle—let out its piercing cry.

On April 26 and 27, 1899, Los Angeles celebrated with a giant Free Harbor Jubilee as the first rocks were dumped in San Pedro Bay. The festivi-
ties began at the Chamber of Commerce where Charles Willard was honored and then moved over to the Times Building where an embedded
granite tablet commemorating "the effective service of the *Los Angeles
Times* in the contest for a Free Harbor at San Pedro" was unveiled. Otis's
son-in-law Harry Chandler spoke for the absent Otis. Chandler commented on the paper's alliance with "citizens of intelligence" who opposed
"selfishness and corporate greed."

"If the power and influence of the newspaper was absolutely necessary
to winning of the people's victory in the harbor controversy," Charles
Willard wrote of the *Times* role, "it is only fair to say that the controversy
formed one of the chief cornerstones of the *Times*' great financial and
journalistic success. Before the fight began, the circulation of the *Times*
was but little, if any more than that of any of the three competitors with
which it shared the daily field in Los Angeles. During the critical phases
of the contest subscribers flocked to it by the score and hundred. At the
close of the era . . . its circulation has more than that of all its competitors gathered together. . . . The *Times* subscriber, while he may speak

with regret of certain faults that he finds in it, if he is a resident of Los Angeles of ten years' standing, always closes with the remark, 'But it made a magnificent fight for the Harbor.' "

In April 1896, in the midst of the fight, a *Times* editorial spelled out clearly its principal interest in San Pedro. Growth for Los Angeles, the editorial commented, depended on three things: the Nicaragua—later the Panama—Canal to open up a new trade route; a deep-water harbor for the Pacific Coast; and the Salt Lake-to-San Pedro railroad to prevent the Southern Pacific from obtaining exclusive power over Southern California development. "The effect upon the growth of the city," the editorial concluded, "of the completion of any of these improvements would be most striking and should we be able to obtain them all, it is evident to the most superficial observer that no human agency could keep back the city from a career of astonishingly rapid progress toward the position which nature has evidently assigned her, as one of the largest cities of the United States, and probably the most important city on the Pacific Coast."

The *Times* and local business forces had scored a major victory over the railroad. The primary issue had been one of influence and control of the region. For many years, the Southern California "cow counties" had been virtually ignored by the state powers. But as the area began to develop in its own right with the advent of railroad connections and enormous population influxes, the state's northern-based railroad machine had stepped in to try to fill the role it had played up north. The SP's goals—to protect and expand its own interests—were not always compatible with those of Los Angeles, as defined by Otis and the local establishment. The local businessmen knew that a Southern Pacific monopoly had to be stopped, and the harbor fight became the battleground to determine who would control the southland. And those ten years of the San Pedro/Santa Monica struggle were, as Willard and many others continued to point out, the *Times*'s finest hours.

CHAPTER 4

"The Pestiferous Reformers"

And abruptly [he] saw again, in his imagination, the galloping monster, the terror of steel and steam, with its single eye, cyclopean, red, shooting from horizon to horizon; but saw it now as the symbol of a vast power, huge, terrible, flinging the echo of its thunder over all the reaches of the valley, leaving blood and destruction in its path; the leviathan, with tentacles of steel clutching into the soil, the soulless Force, the iron-hearted Power, the Monster, the Colossus, the Octopus.

—Frank Norris, *The Octopus*

1. The "Pharisaical Purifiers"

While Angelenos celebrated their victory over the Southern Pacific "octopus," other movements throughout the state began to challenge the railroad's monopoly over California's political parties. Support for such a crusade increased with the emergence of several reform-minded newspapers, primarily in the northern part of the state.

Otis's *Times*, in the period immediately following the harbor battle, continued to ally itself with Republicans who were independent of the SP machine, though the paper still supported railroad Republicans when the choice lay between a railroad Republican or an antirailroad Democrat. In 1900 Otis, who had become Mr. Republican in Southern California, and the anti-SP Republicans succeeded in electing Thomas Bard to the U.S. Senate. Two years later they backed Thomas Flint in the Republican gubernatorial primary against the SP-backed incumbent Henry Gage. George Pardee, a former Oakland mayor who had fought the SP over the issue of Oakland's wharf and had unsuccessfully opposed Gage four years earlier, also tried for the party's nomination. With the three big Republican papers in the state, the *San Francisco Call,* the *San Francisco Chronicle,* and the *Times,* attacking the incumbent, the Gage candidacy was in trouble. Rather than see the dangerous anti-SP candidate Thomas Flint win the nomination, the Southern Pacific political czar, William Herrin, worked out a deal to support the less threatening George Pardee. Pardee won the Republican nomination and, with Otis and the reformers as well as the SP supporting him, defeated his Democratic opponent in the general election.

With Pardee's victory, the *Times* developed a close relationship with the governor's office. *Times* Sacramento correspondent Edward F. Dishman became a political emissary to the governor and within the first weeks of the new administration took part in decisions on nearly every appointment affecting Southern California. Meanwhile, *Times* Washington correspondent Edward S. Little maintained an alliance and friendship with Senator Bard.

The *Times* strongly backed Bard for reelection in 1904. The paper announced its support of him on June 5 and honored him with a special four-page "Bard Edition" which coincided with the formation of "Bard Clubs" throughout the southland. But the railroad's candidate, Frank Flint, endorsed by Governor Pardee, defeated Bard in the primary. According to a biography of Bard, many Republicans who were not necessarily prorailroad had chosen Flint merely "to put Otis in his place." Flint then won the general election and went on to replace Bard in Washington. "The result is an outrage," Otis wrote to Bard.

Meanwhile, Los Angeles reformers prepared to challenge the Southern Pacific hold—through its local power broker Walter Parker—on the city administration. Many of the earliest efforts were led by John Randolph Haynes, a wealthy doctor whose patients included Harrison Gray Otis. Haynes believed that the first goal for social and political reform in Los Angeles was to take control of the government away from the Southern Pacific. Back in 1895 Haynes had organized the Direct Legislation League, a nonpartisan organization whose goal was to institute the initiative, the referendum, and the recall as a means of ousting the SP from power. The group hoped to incorporate those reforms into the city charter, and in 1898 it joined with the League for Better City Government, led by Charles Willard, and several other reform organizations in a bid to reform the old charter. But that attempt and a second one in 1900 were unsuccessful.

Otis's son-in-law Harry Chandler was among those elected to the 1900 Board of Freeholders, which attempted to introduce the reforms into the city charter. Though there were technical disagreements between Chandler and Haynes, Chandler and the *Times* backed the three-pronged proposal. The *Times* described the recall, the most radical of the three, as a "wise provision," though it also warned that the measure "might be subject to some abuse unless hedged about with some stringent safeguards."

But during the campaign to place the initiative, referendum, and recall on the ballot as charter amendments, the *Times* switched its position. Three and a half weeks before the vote, the paper had supported the amendments as "an effective check upon hasty, ill-advised and corrupt municipal legislation." But a week later the *Times* cited the opinion of an anonymous "prominent lawyer," who thought the amendments would be a great expense to the city, and an "open door to every agitator and socialist in the land." Both the *Herald* and the *Express* supported the measures and chastised the *Times* for trying to frighten the voters. On December 1, 1902, the three measures passed by a large majority.

Los Angeles was the first city in the United States to adopt the recall and it was the first to put it into use. A year and a half after the measures passed, the Los Angeles City Council came under attack for awarding the 1904 city advertising contract to the *Times*, though its bid had been 50 to 100 percent higher than those of the other papers. "It was a fair business proposition," the *Times* later claimed, citing its higher circulation and "better results." But many of the city's reformers were infuriated and the mayor refused to sign the agreement. The *Express* called for the recall of pro-*Times* councilmen, and a number of reformers went along with the idea. They decided to concentrate their test of the new amendment on J. P. Davenport, a councilman from a labor ward who had often displeased his constituents. "Not only did he 'take orders' from the *Times*," claimed the Los Angeles Typographical Union, one of the main sponsor's of Davenport's recall, "he would go after them."

A recall election was set for September 16, 1904. The recallers nominated Dr. Arthur Houghton, a prolabor candidate who was supported by the *Express*, the *Examiner*, and the *Record*. The *Times* and the local Republican machine backed Davenport, and the ostensibly radical *Herald* (by then owned by Otis) stayed neutral. The unions campaigned vigorously and won the election; Davenport became the first official ever to be recalled in a U.S. city. Two other councilmen who had backed the *Times* contract were also subsequently defeated, and the *Times* lost the printing contract for the next several years.

As a result of Haynes and other reformers' position on the recall, the *Times* began to break with its former allies, criticizing them as "pharisaical purifiers." In the 1905 mayoralty election, the *Times* backed the Southern Pacific candidate Owen McAleer against the incumbent, Mayor

Meredith Snyder, who had vetoed the *Times* contract. Snyder, whom the *Times* called an "artful dodger," lost the election.

The key target for the reformers, however, continued to be the Southern Pacific, which still controlled most of Los Angeles's public officials and continued in its attempt to dominate the harbor. The SP, which had merged its San Pedro holdings with those of Phineas Banning, the owner of large parcels of harbor land, had bought out its only competitor, the Terminal Railroad. The SP/Banning combination then purchased numerous San Pedro properties and franchises until they owned practically all the land around the inner harbor. The reformers, led by the *Examiner*, termed these acquisitions "illegal" and called for the municipal ownership of all harbor facilities. Although the *Times* noted that "the people of Los Angeles and Southern California must wage another warfare for a free harbor at San Pedro," it supported the SP/Banning company's right to acquire the San Pedro properties. Otis tried to work out a compromise between the two factions, but the reformers refused.

Antagonism towards the railroad reached an all-time high, as new, younger men took the leadership in the battle to oust the SP machine. Edward Dickson, the political editor of the *Los Angeles Express*, with publisher Earl's approval enlisted the aid of attorneys Russ Avery, Marshall Stimson, and Meyer Lissner and put together a new organization, the Non-Partisan Committee of 100. Neither Haynes nor Otis nor the labor unions were invited to its early meetings.

On July 9, 1906, the organization formed its own Non-Partisan City Central Committee, primarily composed of conservative Republicans. *Times* attorney W. J. Hunsaker had been persuaded to act as chairman in hopes of gaining the *Times*'s support. Lissner was elected secretary and R. J. Waters, a banker with political and financial ties to Otis, became the treasurer.

The committee had reason to believe it might receive Otis's support. Recent *Times* editorials had urged voters to take a nonpartisan position and had praised the ideals of the new organization. "The Committee of One Hundred promises to be one of the liveliest forces in one of the liveliest campaigns Los Angeles has ever gone through," a *Times* political columnist noted in early September 1906. In addition, the 100 Committee had not expressed any prolabor sentiments, and had selected real estate legal advisor Lee Gates, a personal friend of Otis and Harry Chandler who had repeatedly put forward Gates's name as a possible mayoral candidate in previous elections, as its choice for mayor on the nonpartisan ticket. "The honor of a nomination by a respectable body of citizens like the Non-Partisan City Central Committee adds to the strength of any candidate," the *Times* remarked of Gates's selection.

But a *Times*/Non-Partisan alliance never solidified. Otis, who had always held that the fight should be carried on within the Republican party, decided to oppose the reformers, labeling the nonpartisan leaders "adventurers" who lusted after power even more than the SP.

Many interpreted Otis's antagonisms as an outgrowth of his personal feud with *Express* owner E. T. Earl. Otis had apparently not been aware of the *Express*'s role in the nonpartisan campaign, and a *Times* political column in July noted that it had "stumbled on a report that Earl was expected to get in behind the nonpartisan group," even though Earl and Dickson were by then already deeply involved. Otis quickly began to resent the role of the *Express* as spokesman for the movement and felt slighted that he had not been invited to the initial planning sessions for the organization. At the same time, Otis and Chandler had become more closely aligned with the new head of the SP, Edward Henry (E.H.) Harriman, who had joined several Otis/Chandler land-buying syndicates.

Though it praised Gates as the 1906 campaign got under way, the *Times* decided to support Walter Parker's Republican party choice, Herbert Lindley. Also on the ballot were Democrat Arthur Harper and Public Ownership League candidate Stanley Wilson. The Public Ownership League, which was described by the *Times* as "an arch enemy of the city's peace and welfare," was a coalition of labor, socialist, and municipal ownership advocates which threatened the conservative Republicans. Its platform called for municipal ownership of both the Owens River water power plant and the electric railway to San Pedro, and fair wages for labor. The *Times*, the hard-line Republicans, and the nonpartisan group were all wary of the Public Ownership League, but none were willing to throw their support behind the other's candidate.

When neither Gates nor Lindley withdrew, the *Times* suggested an arbitration board decide between the two.

But the *Times'* suggestion, weighted as it was in favor of the regular Republican, only exacerbated the differences. According to Gates, Harry Chandler informed him that Lindley was willing to withdraw on the arbitrators' recommendation, but Chandler meanwhile requested from Gates a "conditional" letter of withdrawal. When Lindley refused to pull out and the nonpartisan committee voted against the arbitration proposal, Gates asked for his letter back. But Chandler kept it and published it. The *Times* then endorsed Lindley and made a personal attack on Gates and the reform leaders, accusing them of causing a schism in the Republican party and endangering the business interests of the city. The *Express*, in turn, accused the *Times* of aligning with the Southern Pacific, and from then on the two papers waged a continuous, bitter, name-calling battle.

During the campaign the *Express* held a straw poll on the candidates. The results, however, had to be judged by committee because of the large number of phony cards submitted. The *Express*, backed up by the sworn affadavit of a printer from the American Engraving Company, publicly accused Harry Chandler and the *Times* of being responsible for the thousands of forgeries.

The municipal election resulted in a victory for the Democratic candidate Arthur Harper. The *Times* and the nonpartisans both attributed the Harper victory to a last ditch effort by the SP machine to keep Gates from winning. Just days before the election, aware that Lindley had no chance, the railroad passed the word to Republican organizations to vote for Harper as the lesser of two evils. The *Express* blamed the *Times* for Gates's defeat, while the *Times* blamed the nonpartisans, but overall, the 1906 municipal elections demonstrated the strength of the anti-SP forces. Besides blocking Lindley's mayoralty bid, the nonpartisans won seventeen of the twenty-three other offices up for election, including four of the nine city councilmen.

2. The Lincoln-Roosevelt League

The *Times* stuck with the SP-linked Old Guard in the 1906 state elections as well. Otis had lost confidence in Governor Pardee, though Pardee claimed that he had "tried as hard as any man could to please that man [Otis]." Pardee had accommodated the *Times* on all but two matters: he couldn't go along with Otis's extreme antilabor position; and he reappointed Guy Barham, a Southern California Democrat who didn't line up with the *Times*, as state bank commissioner over the "unalterable" opposition of Otis. "This is certain," Pardee wrote of his political break. "No man can retain Otis' friendship and at the same time retain any spark of independent manhood."

The *Times* supported the Southern Pacific choice for governor for 1906, State Congressman James N. Gillett, a strong opponent of organized labor. Gillett won the Republican nomination and went on to oppose Democrat Theodore A. Bell, a militant antirailroad lawyer, in the general election. The *Times* actively campaigned for Gillett, while the *Express*, disgusted by the SP's control of the 1906 Republican state convention, threw its support to the Democrat. Bell, however, lost the backing of the Hearst newspapers when the newspaper magnate formed his own Independent League, which put forth its own prolabor anti-SP candidate. Gillet defeated Bell by a small margin.

The 1907 legislature appeared to be as dominated by the railroad as that of the year before. Two journalists covering the proceedings, Chester Rowell of the *Fresno Republican* and E. A. Dickson of the *Los Angeles Express*, were so angered with what they saw (three salaried railroad politicians, Rowell wrote, "visibly directed its proceedings") that they discussed the possibilities of setting up a statewide organization to challenge the Southern Pacific machine. Using the Los Angeles-based nonpartisan movement as its nucleus, Dickson arranged a meeting in Los Angeles for May 1907, which attracted muckraker Lincoln Steffens, ex-Governor Pardee, Lissner, Haynes, Stimson, and Avery. A subsequent statewide convention in Oakland drew ex-Senator Bard and Otis's attorney W. J. Hunsaker. The new group, pledged to support the reelection of President Theodore Roosevelt, adopted the name Lincoln-Roosevelt League of Republican Clubs, and put forth such aims as incorporation of the initiative, referendum, and recall; public utility rate regulation; workmen's compensation; and women's suffrage.

More than half of the state's newspapers supported the league, but the *Times* spoke out against the "pestiferous reformers," describing them as "chronic, professional busibodies . . . heady people who imagine they alone are right." The paper, maintaining that the Republican party and the SP machine were two "totally different entities," advocated the creation of "Taft Clubs" to detract from the Roosevelt-pledged league.

Once again the reformers tried to woo Otis. They backed William Hunsaker for Congress and delegated Marshall Stimson to try to secure the *Times* publisher's support. After sitting quietly while Stimson outlined the league's objectives, Otis bolted angrily from his chair, slammed down his fist, and directed a stream of curses against his rival publisher. "That man E.T. Earl," Otis proclaimed, "sent you here to bribe me by having my own attorney go to Congress. To hell with him. You never invited the *Times* to join the Lincoln-Roosevelt League." The league, Otis fumed, had excluded him and *Times* reporter Harry Carr from its early meetings, and had tried to sow mistrust between him and his attorney Hunsaker.

Otis continued to attack the Lincoln-Roosevelt League, describing it as a split in the Republican party. "A fraction, a small minority of the party is out in a vicious attempt to confuse the people and split the party," a *Times* editorial stated in early 1908. "These people are made up largely of renegade Democrats, Populists, and 'new lights' of all shades of flame. They did all the small mischief in their power to defeat the Republican ticket at the last state election, in a vain effort to elect one of their own radical clique Governor of the State." The *Times*, *Express* editor H.W. Brundige remarked, appeared "to have gone over bodily into the campaign of the southern Pacific railroad machine."

Otis and the *Times* had also gained the enmity of reformers in San Francisco, where a graft investigation under the direction of Special Prosecutor Francis Heney had begun to expose the corrupt Southern Pacific rule in that city. Political boss Abraham Reuf, the power behind the city's Union Labor administration, confessed to taking bribes and implicated both SP political leader William F. Herrin and Patrick Calhoun, the president of the United Railroad.

While Calhoun was under indictment, a strike was launched against his street railway company. A violent foe of unionism, Calhoun broke the strike by importing 1,200 strikebreakers and immediately became an anti-labor hero, winning the admiration of the state's antilabor conservatives, including Harrison Gray Otis. Heney's investigation team, led by detective William Burns, exposed a Calhoun/Otis arrangement to distribute copies of the *Times* that had been filled with attacks on the strikers. Heney accused Otis of "selling news columns" by accepting $15,000 from Calhoun for 20,000 copies of the *Times* earmarked for San Francisco. In addition, the *Times* had applied for low-cost mailing rates by claiming that the papers were being mailed to subscribers. But Heney demonstrated that the papers were sent in bulk to "safe" addresses furnished by the railroad, i.e., homes not traceable to any individual linked to the railroad, from where the SP company planned to send the papers in a sample mailing to unsolicited individuals. As the controversy became public, the Los Angeles postmaster asked the *Times* to pay the $3,000 difference between the two rates. The *Times* claimed that the papers had never been mailed out due to a mix-up by the railroads (the bulk of them still remained in the San Francisco post office) and got the $3,000 back. The unmailed papers were then sold by the *Times*—which had already received $15,000 from Calhoun for them—as waste.

Heney, who considered Otis "a fanatic upon labor unions," was encouraged to continue exposing Otis by Los Angeles reformer Haynes. "You will be doing the community, the State and the Nation a great good by showing the man up in his true colors before the world," Haynes wrote Heney.

The *Times* called the charges against it "too ridiculous to need denial," and attacked Heney as "ignorant of the law, violent in disposition, a bluffer by breeding and long practice. He is as tempestuous a blusterer as ever disgraced the practice of the law. He is a bundle of selfishness."

The paper also ridiculed Heney's investigations and the subsequent trials. When a prospective juror shot Heney in the courtroom, the *Times* was almost the only paper except for those owned by the railroad to continue to attack the wounded prosecutor: "We regret the elimination of Heney out of the case in the way in which it was done. But desirous of the good name of the State and the peace of San Francisco . . . we cannot help rejoicing."

Though the paper made some minor criticisms of E. H. Harriman's power, its owners had firmly aligned themselves with the Southern Pacific interests. "It is bandied about that the *Times* is a 'friend of the corporations,'" an editorial commented in July 1907. "Who are the corporations? the stockholders: Nearly every one of our neighbors on every respectable street in the city is interested in some way in some corporation.

The *Times* denounces the demagogic abuse of corporations simply because they are corporations and insists that they have the same fair play accorded to firms and individuals. The *Times* refuses to join in the anarchistic and hypocritical cry against rich men merely because they are rich."

After the Heney shooting, the San Francisco graft trials continued under the new prosecutor, Hiram Johnson. In the fall of 1908, Boss Reuf was found guilty and sentenced to fourteen years, but the jury deadlocked over Calhoun. The railroad man was ultimately acquitted in 1912. Despite this, the San Francisco graft trials had a tremendous impact on the movement seeking to break the SP's hold on the state government.

Otis, now firmly tied to the SP political apron strings, became one of the early victims of the reformers' efforts. In 1908 he was put forth as one of the Southern Pacific's choices for the four at-large delegates to the Republican National Convention. The labor unions, led by the typographers, raised a commotion against the nomination. "The selection of General Otis . . . would have been considered a direct affront and insult to union labor," Lincoln-Roosevelt leader Meyer Lissner later wrote to President William Howard Taft. The league put forth its own slate for at-large delegates, hoping that the union opposition to Otis might win it some much needed labor support. ". . . While the matter must be handled very gingerly and cautiously for fear of a boomerang," Lissner wrote to Dickson, "still there is probably nothing that will bring to us the cooperation of the union labor vote more than a knowledge on their part that Otis is backing the machine and fighting the Lincoln-Roosevelt League."

ITU organizer T. D. Fennesy, aided by Sacramento's trade councils, attended the state convention to try to defeat "Tyrant Otis's" election. Fennesy read a 173-foot-long protest petition with 180,645 signatures to the convention assembly. To Otis's great chagrin, he was the only SP nominee not to win, losing to the Lincoln-Roosevelt candidate by one vote. "I am sorry that Otis was so humiliated," former Senator Bard wrote to Chester Rowell, "for I have a personal high regard for the man, who was my earnest political friend, but I have to admit that his singular turning about and joining the enemy, that he has for many years antagonized, deserves some reprimand."

"It was worth going to Sacramento to defeat General Otis," Lissner wrote to an associate, "and the *Times* has been real good since then. It has forgotten all about Lissner and the Lincoln-Roosevelt League." But that August *Times* editorials preceding California state primaries once again denounced the league ticket. "The *Times* has never wavered in advocating every progressive movement for reform," an editorial noted, ". . . but at the same time it has refused to swallow panaceas." Voters were urged to "not be misled by any loud cry of a band of white-robed hypocrites hid in a cloud of dust of their own making."

Times editorials pictured the league as a new group of "brazen" bosses, headed by Lissner and Earl, who were working against the interests of California and the Republican party in their "thirst for power and for office." ". . . If you are merely following a new boss instead of the old one," *Times* readers were warned, "you are not forwarding the work of real reform by an inch. Indeed, the new boss, hungry and lean, is more to be feared than the old boss."

Otis expressed particular anger at the league leaders for labeling his paper an SP "harlot," and at their "pretension" of being the only ones opposed to the railroad. "The *Times* has been in the thick of this fight," an editorial said of the battle against the SP, "as it has been in all important contests in this community."

The Lincoln-Roosevelt ticket did not fare well in the election. The *Times* was gleeful about the defeat of "Boss Lissner" and "Boss Earl." "The disruptive organization," a post-election editorial suggested, ". . . has been put to rout. . . . It is the end." But it was far from the end.

3. *"What a Fine Way to Build up a City"*

The reformers had more success on the local level. In September 1908 Los Angeles assistant District Attorney Thomas Lee Woolwine testified before a grand jury about vice and general corruption in Mayor Harper's administration. Then when the mayor tried to appoint corrupt ex-machine councilman and chief of police Edward Kern to the Public Works Board instead of reappointing the popular James Anderson, a substantial protest developed. The public uproar, coupled with pressure from Otis (one rumor had it that Otis, who favored his close friend General Adna Chafee for the post, threatened to publish pictures of Mayor Harper and his friends with prostitutes) ultimately led Harper to withdraw Kern's name in favor of Chafee.

After the *Express* picked up on Woolwine's corruption charges against Harper, the mayor filed libel suits against Woolwine and publisher Earl. Woolwine was subsequently fired by his boss, machine-supported District Attorney John Fredericks, another close friend of the *Times*. The *Express* then began its own investigation into grand jury allegations of a Harper/ Kern syndicate that profited from various shady deals in the red-light district. While the *Express* called for a recall of the mayor, the *Herald* picked up on the charges in a series exposing the corrupt deals and Harper's ties to the SP.

The accusations, which the *Times* declared were the work of bitter "scheming politicians," were denied by Harper. But as the *Herald* and the *Express* kept up their campaign, a recall movement against Harper took shape. On January 20, 1901, a meeting took place under the auspices of the Municipal League, with the participation of the Dickson-led City Club—the successor to the Non-Partisan Committee—and the Chamber of Commerce. The M&M had been invited but refused to attend. A recall coalition emerged from the meeting. Petitions were circulated, and within two weeks enough signatures had been gathered to qualify for a special election. "What a fine way to build up a city!" A *Times* editorial complained, fearful of the impact on the city's reputation.

The *Times* thought the recallers were being unfair to Harper, and labeled their action "Hysteria Americana." The recall, a *Times* editorial proclaimed, was a "vicious, dangerous, unfair and unAmerican institution." "The device was unrecognized by the founders of the government and runs counter to the principles of the American constitution," the paper observed on another occasion, labeling it a month later "an offshoot of Socialism."

The *Examiner* and the *Evening News* also opposed the recall, and the Scripps-owned *Record*, which had initially supported the movement, changed its position because of labor's exclusion from the recall meetings. A businessmen's organization sponsored petitions against the recall while pro-Harper clubs formed throughout the city.

The recallers, under the aegis of Meyer Lissner's Good Government Organization, chose a seventy-year-old Scottish immigrant from Iowa, ex-Republican Supervisor George Alexander, as their candidate to replace Harper. Labor, which had been excluded from the recall activities, supported the Socialist candidate Fred Wheeler. The Republican Old Guard failed to nominate anybody.

The *Times* launched a new series of attacks on the manner of selection of the reform candidate. Calling their tactics "mobocracy," the paper pictured the recallers as a small minority clique wearing "pink socks" and "high hats" that wanted to impose their will on the city. "Fellow citizens of Los Angeles," a *Times* editorial implored, "this is America. We are living under a democratic-republican form of government. . . . Will you permit it to be a government of the classes, by the classes, and for the classes? Shall it be a government of a clique, by a clique, for a clique?

"We say not! And come what may, through obloquy or praise, facing defeat or victory. The *Times* must do its utmost that the government defined by Lincoln shall not be degraded into a government devised by Willard, Lissner, and Earl."

Alexander, depicted as a candidate who had to be roped into running after others declined, became the butt of numerous *Times* attacks. "Ha-ha! It is Uncle George Alexander," a *Times* news story declared at the announcement of his candidacy. Editorials were interspersed with anti-Alexander epithets and a sarcastic, fictitious serial by Harry Carr. "The

Sleuth in Search of a Recall Mayor,'' complete with cartoons, detailed the trials and tribulations of the recall newspaper editors' campaign to "torture" their victim "Uncle George Jelly-dander" to agree to become their candidate.

Though the paper ridiculed Alexander and opposed the recall, it did not endorse Democrat Harper. "The *Times* has never endorsed Harper and never will, although it will do all in its power to defeat the present recall game or any other," an editorial declared. "Would it not have been a good thing for the city if Dr. Lindley had been elected?" the paper constantly reminded its readers.

Shortly before the date set for recall, Harper resigned, and the anti-recall forces, led by the *Times*, unsuccessfully tried to get the upcoming election canceled. "Why a special recall election now?" the *Times* asked. "There is nobody to recall. we have a good mayor [referring to the interim head appointed by the City Council], one satisfactory to everybody but fanatics."

The Old Guard was in trouble. The election offered only two alternatives: an anti-SP reformer and a Socialist. Some conservatives threw their support to Alexander, identifying socialism as the greater threat, but the SP machine and many of those begrudging the reform group, went with the Socialist candidate. The *Times* announced that it couldn't support either one.

Good Government candidate George Alexander won the election by less than 2,000 votes. He immediately set out to clean up the city, reorganizing many branches of city government, appointing new commissioners to replace those who had resigned, and establishing new nonpartisan election rules.

The reformers still hoped to win the support of the *Times*. For his new police chief, Alexander selected Edward Dishman, the *Times*'s assistant city editor who had acted as liason with Governor Pardee seven years earlier. Dishman, whose main experience for the job came from his work as a police reporter, was clearly unsympathetic to reform and constantly fought with the police commissioners who had approved his appointment. The biggest disagreement centered on Dishman's reinstatement of Captain Thomas Broadhead, who had been previously indicted by the grand jury and subsequently acquitted. After the Police Commission, the Municipal League and others conducted their own investigation into the affair—belittled by the *Times*, which supported Broadhead—the captain was removed and subsequent appointments were passed on by the commission without Dishman's recommendations. Dishman himself was dismissed by the commission some months later, and eventually went on to become chief investigator for the California Corporation Commissioner.

Another *Times* friend also became a subject of controversy between the reformers and the Old Guard. Adjutant General Moses Sherman, who had come to Los Angeles with his brother-in-law Eli P. Clark in 1889, held extensive interests in real estate, public utilities, and the streetcar and interurban railways and was a close associate in many of Harry Chandler and General Otis's financial deals. In 1903 Sherman had been appointed to the Board of Water Commissioners. Harper reappointed him in 1909, but reform advocates raised the issue of Sherman's membership in a real estate syndicate that included Otis, Chandler, and E. H. Harriman, who could profit from Sherman's water board decisions. When the reformers demanded Sherman's resignation, the *Times* called the conflict-of-interest charge "nonsensical." The city attorney sent the matter to the courts, and Alexander, who felt Sherman should be ruled ineligible, asked the city council to remove him. A wary council sent the question back to the courts to leave the decision to the state attorney general. Sherman was eventually forced to resign.

Despite the new nonpartisan election rules, whereby candidates would be chosen by city-wide primary elections rather than nominating conventions, the SP-dominated Republican City Central Committee decided to hold, as the *Times* had suggested, an "advisory" city convention to nominate candidates for the upcoming municipal elections. The Old Guard chose George Smith as its favorite, but the *Times* only offered lukewarm support for the choice, admitting that the party could have picked a better slate if it hadn't been for the "newfangled laws." The paper endorsed Smith only a few days before the primaries as "the only way to save Los Angeles . . . from the grasp of the Earl-Lissner combination."

The reform Republican, incumbent Mayor Alexander, won a plurality, though not a majority, of the votes, and would have to face regular Republican Smith in the runoff election. The nine reform-oriented city council candidates also had the highest tallies in their primary race.

The reformers, who cited the ties between Smith and Walter Parker's Southern Pacific machine, attempted to portray the election as a clear-cut choice between the machine and the people's representative. Alexander had the support of the *Herald*, the *Express*, and even the reluctant *Record*. "The *Times* has put up its shutters and quit," a confident Willard wrote near the end of the campaign.

The reformers' confidence was well-founded. On December 7, 1909, the Good Government candidates won all the city's elective offices: mayor, treasurer, auditor, assessor, all nine council seats, and other subordinate posts. "We have met the enemy and they are ours. We put the Southern Pacific push to rout—horse, foot and dragons—in our city election," a jubilant Lissner wrote to Senator La Follette. "The *Times*," Willard noted, "takes it bitter hard."

Not completely satisfied with their routing of the SP in Los Angeles, the reformers looked to repeat their success on the state level. "The Republicans of Los Angeles are anxious to smash the Southern Pacific state machine just as they smashed it locally," the *Express* boasted a few days after the municipal victory.

The Lincoln-Roosevelt League had slowly been making headway in the state. The 1909 state legislature, in striking contrast to that of two years earlier, had put the SP machine on the defensive, but the large number of elected reformers were unable to pass the progressive measures they had introduced during the session. The next year was to prove the real turning point. That year the newly named Progressive party, the league's successor, chose former San Francisco Special Prosecutor Hiram Johnson, a leader of the state's progressive movement, to be its gubernatorial candidate.

The Southern Pacific machine couldn't decide which of two regular Republicans who had entered the race to support. Otis strongly favored a third candidate, former Assembly Speaker Philip Stanton.

Unlike previous years where candidates were chosen by nominating conventions, the gubernatorial candidates for 1910 would be chosen by the electorate in a primary election. For the first time party candidates could make their appeals directly to their constituencies. Johnson began his campaign six months before the primary by attacking the Southern Pacific's grip on the state.

"The railroad is practically out of politics," a *Times* editorial replied to Johnson's attacks. "It has been dead for years. There has not been a movement on the part of the bosses to elect or defeat any candidate here or elsewhere." The *Times* bitterly opposed Johnson, "the one man of the five Republican candidates upon whom the party cannot be united if he is nominated." The paper tried to link the Progressive candidate to his father, former Congressman Grove Johnson, an SP ally with whom Hiram had broken several years earlier over the SP issue. "Old Grove always knew where the meat was and young Hiram did not have to go to school to learn where the political plunder lay. . . ," a *Times* editorial declared. "When it comes to turning the crank or driving the machine a Johnson is sure to be to the fore. Hiram is to the new one what Daddy was to the old one." A cartoon two days earlier pictured an old Grove Johnson and a young Hiram sawing a log labeled "State Politics" with "SP tool" written on the saw. The caption read, "Like Father like Son."

The reformers worried about the effect of the *Times*'s attacks. "Despite the fact that it must realize that it can do little but discredit itself thereby," Los Angeles's progressives wrote of the *Times*, "it is continuing its policy of abuse of the reform leaders and coarse ridicule of the administration in general, relying, apparently, upon the belief that if untruths are pointed at sufficiently in the course of time some honest people will be misled into believing what it says. . . . The leaders in the reform movement, to a man, regard the *Times* as the most insidious individual foe with which they have to contend."

Lincoln-Roosevelt senatorial candidate John Works wrote to Chester Rowell that he could not "sit quietly by and say nothing when a newspaper like the *Los Angeles Times* is attacking me as it has been doing. . . ," but it was Hiram Johnson who gave the definitive retort to the *Times* jabs during a mass meeting held in Los Angeles's Simpson Auditorium. "What about Otis?" a voice from the audience called out, interrupting the candidate's talk. Johnson put down his prepared text, stepped forward, and delivered a scathing description of his antagonist.

"In the city from which I have come," Johnson roared, "we have drunk to the very dregs the cup of infamy; we have had vile officials; we have had rotten newspapers; we have had men who sold their birthright; we have dipped into every infamy; every form of wickedness has been ours in the past; every debased passion and every sin has flourished. But we have nothing so vile, nothing so low, nothing so debased, nothing so infamous in San Francisco, nor did we ever have, as Harrison Gray Otis. . . .

"He sits there in senile dementia, with gangrened heart and rotting brain, grimacing at every reform, chattering impotently at all things that are decent, frothing, fuming, violently gibbering, going down to his grave in snarling infamy. This man Otis is the one blot on the banner of Southern California; he is the bar sinister upon your escutcheon. My friends, he is the one thing that all California looks at, when, in looking at Southern California, they see anything that is disgraceful, depraved, corrupt, crooked and putrescent—that is Harrison Gray Otis."

Johnson won Southern California and the state in the primary election with almost 50 percent of the Republican votes, nearly 50,000 more than his runner-up. The results presented the *Times* owners with a difficult decision: support the "sorehead" Johnson or abandon the Republican party. The progressive forces had become the majority voice of California's Republican Party. Though the progressives had allied themselves more with business interests in their formative years, they now began to show signs of supporting certain labor movement demands. The progressive-influenced 1910 Republican state platform, adopted after the primary, recognized that "the wage earner has the same right to organize for the improvement of the conditions under which he labors that the capitalist has to use his capital in corporate enterprises." The progressive Republicans also hoped to pass an employer's liability act; to institute the initiative, recall, and referendum on the state level; as well as other progressive measures.

Such programs were abhorrent to Otis, who feared Johnson's prounion tendencies. "VIOLENT LABORITES ENDORSE JOHNSON—DECLARE HE HAS BEEN A 'TRUE FRIEND AND FAITHFUL ADVISER' IN THEIR MOVEMENT," a *Times* headline exclaimed just before the election.

But unlike the Southern Pacific, which campaigned openly for liberal Democratic candidate Theodore Bell, Otis could not endorse a Democrat. "Don't give up the ship," a *Times* editorial urged a few days before the election. "Owing to the working of the primary law by which the regular Republican vote was divided between three candidates for Governor, a minority of Republicans calling themselves insurgents seized the grand old ship in California and loaded a lot of populistic and some Democratic fads upon her deck. But because we do not like the new and strange and obnoxious cargo, let us not therefore abandon the old ship. . . . After the election the old and loyal crew will again take charge of the vessel and throw the noisome cargo overboard, and the mutinous insurgents will grow weary of their foolishness and return to duty."

Hiram Johnson won the election. "It was a big job to attempt to smash the machine of the interests," Meyer Lissner noted after the victory, "but it has been accomplished." The new administration heralded not only the end of SP domination but the beginning of a trend toward more progressive socially "humanitarian" legislation; observers of the 1911 legislature have called it everything from "astonishing" to "one of the finest administrations any state has ever enjoyed."

Johnson provided the cohesion necessary to bring about the progressive's objectives. His administration enacted the initiative, referendum, and recall measures, and, hoping to wipe out party lines, established a system of "cross-filing" whereby primary candidates could run for the nomination of different parties without having to list party affiliation on the primary ballot. Other reforms included the reorganization of private utility regulation with rate-fixing determined by the state; a water and power conservation act; the establishment of a railroad commission; a pure food act; the approval of women's suffrage; old age pensions; reorganization of the state's tax system; and some thirty-nine labor laws such as workmen's compensation, minimum wage requirements, and the eight-hour day for women. "God save the commonwealth," the *Times* cried out against the reform blitz.

Not all the new measures, however, had the support of the progressives. Many thought the recall should not extend to the judiciary, E. T. Earl opposed the eight-hour day for women, and Thomas Bard thought the reforms "are going too far and some of their policies are revolutionary." The progressives were most divided over a bill which called for the curbing of the use of injunctions in labor disputes. The senate passed the bill, although the Los Angeles progressives voted against it and Lissner begged Johnson not to sign it. The bill never made it past the assembly, and Johnson didn't intervene.

The split within the Republican party had left the *Times* and other Old Guard forces out in the cold. The *Times* was not about to make alliances with the administration, nor was Johnson about to allow any such accommodation. A story related by Judge James Harlan Pope, a *Times* reporter during the Johnson/Otis struggle, demonstrated the extent of the split. Sometime after the election, both Johnson and Otis attended the same large public meeting and Johnson happened to be standing near Otis. The General, dressed in his customary full military uniform, told an aide that he had never met Johnson and would like to. "There is a very prominent man here who has never met you and would like that pleasure," the aide asked the governor. "Certainly," Johnson replied, turning to extend his hand. But on discovering who the man was, Johnson loudly exclaimed: "What Otis? Never." General Otis responded with a military salute. "Your privilege, Governor" the general answered and retired from the scene.

The personal animosity between Johnson and the *Times* was to last another generation, influencing the course of California politics.

The victorious progressive movement had broken one uneasy coalition and replaced it with another. With its origins in the fight against the Southern Pacific over the harbor, the original reform coalition, which had included local business, professional, and working-class constituencies, focused on opposing the large monopoly-oriented corporation.

The ultimate defeat of the Southern Pacific machine had been a heady victory for the reform coalition despite the loss of Otis and the *Times* in the process. But as the progressives celebrated, a more devastating conflict appeared on the horizon. Confronted by a real threat to the nature of the system itself, the alliances would once again regroup.

CHAPTER 5

The Bombing of the Times Building

1. "Days of Common Peril"

By 1910 Los Angeles was the symbolic center of the nation's antiunion forces. "Among all her splendid material assets," Otis wrote of his city, "none is so valuable . . . as her possession of that priceless boon, industrial freedom." Many of the city's businessmen shared Otis's conviction that defeating organized labor was a precondition for economic growth.

The situation in San Francisco, perhaps the strongest union city in the country, provided a marked contrast to open shop Los Angeles. While Los Angeles industry expanded, San Francisco business, once larger than its southern counterpart, dwindled, as new enterprises, lured by lower wages, longer working hours, and fewer threats of strikes chose to settle in Los Angeles. San Francisco employers knew they had to equalize conditions in the two cities in order to compete; unless Los Angeles was organized, they warned their local labor movement, workers' salaries would be reduced to par with Los Angeles wages. The metal trade employers were the first to act on the threat when they refused to meet a union request for an eight-hour day as long as their southern competitors continued to profit from lower wages and longer hours.

In early 1910 San Francisco unionists met with Los Angeles labor leaders to plan a major drive to break the open shop rule in Los Angeles. Ten skilled organizers soon arrived in Los Angeles to begin the campaign.

The San Francisco intervention had come at a crucial moment. On May 19 Los Angeles brewery owners, attempting to undermine the only remaining closed shop industry in the city, announced that they would not renew the union's contract. The union immediately went out on strike and initiated a boycott on all Los Angeles beers.

The city's metal trade workers, dominated by the harshest employer's association in the region, soon followed. Aided by the support of the San Francisco organizers and a strong national union, the metal workers had formulated a contract and submitted it to their employers. Not one proprietor acknowledged the offer; Otis ally Fred Baker, owner of the Baker and Llewellyn Iron Works, later testified that he immediately threw it into the wastebasket. When the employers refused to negotiate, almost 1,500 metal trades workers walked out of twenty-five Los Angeles firms. It was the biggest strike Los Angeles had ever experienced. True to their word, the San Francisco metal trade owners put the eight-hour day into effect the day of the strike.

Both sides prepared for a long fight. While the M&M and the Founder's Association organized employer resistance, the statewide labor forces set up a General Campaign Strike Committee, headed by San Francisco organizers Olav Tveitmore and Andrew Gallagher, to plan strategy and bring funds from the north. For the first time in several years, Los Angeles's labor movement had its hopes awakened.

"These are days of common peril in Los Angeles. A foreign foe is at the gates and threatens all alike," a *Times* editorial noted of the renewal of activity. "This is a community . . . which will not tolerate picketing or interference by outsiders with the business of any man. We shall have peace here in the city of Los Angeles," the paper had affirmed three days earlier, "if every law-loving and law-abiding person in this city must arise and take matters into his own hands and secure the peace we are all intent upon."

The employers had ample financial reserves and, despite the animosity between Otis and the reformers, the support of the local government. The *Times* had advocated legislation against picketing and criticized the police for "catering" to strikers by their failure to arrest picketers. ". . . we warn you Eddie," a *Times* editorial threatened city prosecutor Guy Eddie for his upholding of the legal rights of the non-violent picketers, "that Los Angeles will not stand for your tactics." A month later in July 1910 the city council unanimously passed an ordinance which banned "picketing, carrying or displaying banners, signs, or transparencies, or speaking in public streets in a loud or unusual tone for certain purposes." Reform mayor Alexander signed the bill less than one hour after the vote.

The new law went into effect immediately. The strikers, however, continued to picket, and hundreds were arrested. "What had been a peaceful struggle," typographical union official Joseph Phillips wrote, ". . . became a reign of persecution and lawlessness, largely on the part of the police department and the district attorney's office, acting under instructions issued by the Merchant's and Manufacturers Association and its associated interests." Those that asked for jury trials were almost all acquitted, but the legal fees and cost of bail money added to the unions' financial problems.

The *Times* praised the actions of the police and the courts, and kept up a barrage of news and editorial attacks with headlines like UNION LABOR BREAKS BONES or BRUTAL HEADS IS THE ORDER, NOT ENOUGH BLOOD-SHED HERE FOR LABOR BOSSES.

Otis toured the city with a small cannon mounted on his car, while his paper called for "the forming of new resolutions to fight on and on and 'still some more' if it is necessary." "It is full time," another editorial stated, "to deal with these labor union wolves in such prompt and drastic fashion as will induce them to transfer their lawlessness and their murderous practices elsewhere, for the danger of tolerating them in Los Angeles is great and immediate."

Most Angelenos tended to side with the local labor movement, which, inspired by the renewed activity and subsequent rise in membership, had thrown all its resources into the struggle. Union members throughout the country followed the events. "You must make Los Angeles the battle ground where the victory of the Pacific Coast will be won," local Socialist attorney Job Harriman appealed to the AFL.

On September 25 the unions met to plan a mass parade to be held October 3 to protest the antipicketing ordinance. More than 25,000 people from throughout the state were expected. The State Labor Convention was also scheduled to convene in Los Angeles on that date and be addressed by Mayor Alexander and other city officials. On the thirtieth the breweries signed a contract with their unions. The Los Angeles labor movement, expecting more victories, looked confidently toward the future.

2. A Fire in the Night

At 1:07 A.M. on October 1, 1910, Los Angeles residents were awakened by an awesome roar which shook the whole city. At first many thought it was an earthquake. But the noise had actually come from the block of First and Broadway. The Los Angeles Times building had exploded. A second blast turned the entire structure into an inferno within seconds immediately after the first explosion. Thousands of spectators, many in their nightclothes, came out to look at the fire.

The initial blast had blown out a wall on the first floor, but most of the damage had been caused by the second blast and the fire. Tons of flammable ink stored in barrels in the alley behind the building had exploded at once. Heavy machinery had fallen and blocked the exits. The intensity of the rapidly spreading fire barred rescue work, and twenty-one of the hundred workers trapped inside perished. Total property damage was estimated at slightly over half a million dollars.

Neither Otis nor Harry Chandler had been in the building at the time. Otis was en route from Mexico, and Chandler, who usually worked until that hour, had been fetched from his office, shortly after midnight, by his wife.

The next morning, while firemen were still poking through the ashes, the *Times* printed a special one-page edition in its emergency auxiliary plant. "UNIONIST BOMB WRECKS THE TIMES," the headline blared. "They can kill our men and can wreck our buildings," proclaimed managing editor Harry Andrews in a page one editorial, "but by the God above they cannot kill the *Times.*"

Otis returned the next day and immediately blamed the disaster on his enemies. "O you anarchic scum," Otis wrote, "you cowardly murderers, you leeches upon honest labor, you midnight assassins, you whose hands are dripping with the innocent blood of your victims . . ." The *Times* news stories called the explosion "The Crime of the Century," "one of the worst atrocities in the history of the world."

Organized labor immediately denied Otis's accusations and offered sympathy and aid. The unions blamed the explosion on a faulty gas system in the building. *Times* employees had previously complained of gas fumes and the odor had been particularly strong the evening of the disaster. Other evidence, such as the absence of broken windows and the downward action of the explosion which left the walls intact, was cited as proof that it could not have been caused by dynamite. "It is inconceivable that a union man should have done this thing," AFL President Sam Gompers stated the day after the catastrophe. "The greatest enemies of our movement could not administer a blow so hurtful to our cause as would be such a stigma if men of organized labor were responsible for it."

Despite labor's denials the *Times* continued to attribute the event to labor agitators and suggested that San Francisco rather than Los Angeles-based unions were responsible. "Whether guilty or not, the labor unionists will have to be blamed for the crime" the *Times* quoted California Governor Gillett in a page one story, "as everything points to a desire to wipe out property and lives of those who have been fighting organized labor for years." A front page editorial in the *Examiner* on the day after the explosion also claimed that the explosion was no accident, while the *Express* suggested that the unions call off their strikes as evidence they have no sympathy for the "criminals."

The day after the disaster, explosives were discovered at the homes of Otis and Secretary Zeehandelaar of the M&M. The dynamite and alarm clock contraption found at Zeehandler's had not exploded, the "infernal machine" at Otis's went off just after police carried it out to the road. Laborites suggested the bombs were plants, that the dynamite was, as one labor paper put it, "placed there by agents of those who are eager to make the *Times* catastrophe appear to have been the work of the labor unions." Both bombs were discovered by police detective Tom Rico who had also allegedly "found" dynamite at two antiunion construction sites the previous month and had been involved in earlier antiradical investigations.

In the aftermath of the *Times* explosion, an antiunion fear campaign took hold in Los Angeles. Big firms increased their guards, and, at the urging of the M&M and Chamber of Commerce, the police force hired 100 new members. Police were encouraged to investigate and jail any "suspicious character," the brewery proprietors canceled their previously signed contracts, and the Founders and Employers Association refused to meet with a delegation from the metal trades union on the grounds that they weren't responsible leaders. The State Federation of Labor Convention, held on October 3, met without the scheduled appearance of Mayor Alexander or other representatives from the city government. "We were all regarded as a lot of dynamiters," one delegate recalled. "We couldn't even stand on the sidewalk in front of the building where we met."

The day after the explosion, Mayor Alexander had hired the famous detective William Burns who was in town to speak at a bankers' convention, hoping the appointment would reassure the unions of fair treatment because of Burns's role in the San Francisco graft trials. Neither Otis nor the M&M, however, were happy with Alexander's choice. "General Otis sent a vigorous protest to the mayor" Burns wrote to Hiram Johnson, "denouncing me and deriding the mayor for employing me, expressing his opinion of me and anticipating a failure."

The M&M hoped to offset Burns's role by hiring their own investigator, attorney Earl Rogers, who had opposed Burns at the San Francisco trials and had drafted the city's antipicketing ordinance. Rogers had already assumed union guilt. His daughter Adela Rogers St. John recalled that as they stood in front of the burning building, "Papa was talking to himself through clenched teeth. 'The murdering fiends,' he kept saying. 'The paranoiac assassins . . . They have to be chained like dogs that bite.' " Rogers, delegated as special district attorney, had a staff of assistants and $100,000 of M&M-raised funds to work with. District Attorney John D. Fredericks, in charge of the official investigation, collaborated with Rogers and was also given an "unusually large expense account" by the county board of supervisors.

After a week of investigation, official reports named dynamite or some other high-powered nitroglycerine product as the cause of the explosion. A committee of experts fixed the location of the dynamite as "Ink Alley," where, they surmised, the first explosion wrecked the gas mains, causing the fire. "The gas explosion theory," the *Times* announced the day of the report, "began and ended in malice."

But labor was not ready to give up the gas theory. Though most of the testimony at the coroner's jury identified dynamite as the cause, a telegraph operator testified that the gas had been so strong the night of the explosion that a man became sick and windows had to be opened. The California Federation of Labor appointed its own committee to investigate, but its efforts were hampered by Otis and city officials reluctant to grant permission to examine the damaged building. After four weeks of inquiries, the labor committee stated that dynamite could not have caused the explosion and attributed the disaster to gas based on the history of gas leaks and the type of damage done to the building.

The labor federation charged the *Times* with laying the foundation for another Haymarket case by attempting to pin the crime on unionists without evidence to back it up. The report pointed to Otis's criminal negligence as the real cause of the explosion and accused Detective Rico of planting the dynamite found at Otis's and Zeehandelaar's. "Dynamite has been 'found' before by detectives working in the interests of employers in time of strike," the report stated. "And time and time again it has been proved that the finders were the planters."

At the time of the explosion prospects for unionizing the city had never been brighter. Union sympathizers could not have blown up the building, the report argued, because they would know that "the incident would be joyfully seized upon as an excuse for inflaming the mind of the public against unions and unionism . . . [and] for bringing every available weapon into play to realize the ambition of General Otis—the extermination of the unions."

More militant unionists went even further and accused Otis outright of blowing up his own building, stating that antiunion forces had much more to gain by such an event than the unions. The existence of the *Times*'s auxiliary plant had shown that the General was prepared for such an occurrence, and, it was rumored, he already had plans for a new ten-story building. In addition, all the office accounts and records had been saved despite the rapid spread of the fire. ". . . The *Times* and its crowd of union-haters are themselves the instigators, if not the actual perpetrators of that crime and the murderers of the twenty human beings who perished as its victims," Eugene Debs wrote. "Was this a huge conspiracy against union labor in Los Angeles?" the *International Socialist Review* asked. "General Otis admits that he 'expected' the calamity. What led him to expect it and are his own hands clean?"

On October 27, a grand jury began secret hearings into the *Times* disaster with Earl Rogers—despite union protests—appointed special prosecutor. After twenty-five days of hearings that included the testimony of 174 witnesses, the grand jury issued secret indictments for a J. B. Bryson (alias Bryce), David Caplan, and Matthew A. Schmidt.

The credit for the unraveling of the case—later extensively recorded in books and magazines—is usually attributed to Detective Burns. The unexploded bomb from M&M Secretary Zeehandler's home, according to Burns, gave him his first lead. The dynamite, a particularly powerful type, was stamped with the name of a powder works in San Francisco, and Burns agents were able to obtain excellent descriptions of three men using the names J. B. Bryce, J. B. Leonard, and William Morris, who had bought 500 pounds of the special explosive. Tracing the movements of the three men, agents found the house where they had stayed, which apparently still contained ten large wooden boxes of dynamite, and an agency which had rented them a boat to transport the explosives. Leonard, subsequently identified as Matthew A. Schmidt, a former member of the Chicago woodworkers' union, and Morris, an alias for David Caplan, a San Francisco labor leader, had both lived in an anarchist colony in the state of Washington. Bryce's identity was not known.

Labor figures, many of whom had been questioned intensively, denounced the grand jury, calling it privately owned by the M&M, and dubbed Rogers the "persecuting attorney who used the refined torture of the grand jury room and the third degree." Even *Express* owner E. T. Earl wrote Hiram Johnson of the "malice and prejudice" evident in the jury's attitudes.

Strike activity continued despite the antiunion accusations, and workers at one photoengraving firm went out because their company produced the plates for the *Times* midwinter edition. In early November 1910, some 15,000 union sympathizers participated in a giant labor parade.

An editorial in the *Times* a few days after the grand jury indictments called for "Martial Law If Necessary." "A Vigilance Committee such as cleansed San Francisco half a century ago, and dangled the corpses of the leaders in crime from the windows of Fort Gunny bags will not be needed at this day," the editorial asserted, "for if the civil authorities prove unable to preserve the prosperity and lives of peaceful and law-abiding citizens from the thugs, there is such a thing as martial law."

Otis, now a national open shop hero, spoke up and down the coast affirming "union guilt." But his speeches were so harsh that they kindled suspicions that Otis might, indeed, have been in some way responsible for the explosions. "You hear talk," journalist Frederick Palmer wrote, "of the hateful baiting which breeds hate; of a man of power and position using his newspaper weapon with such venom in beating down his enemies that he created the elements which could find no voice except nitroglycerine to answer the dynamite of Otis' language."

3. McManigal's Confession

On Christmas Day, 1910, another explosion rocked Los Angeles. At 1:55 in the morning, an explosion of the notoriously antiunion Llewellyn Iron Works, still struck by the metal trade unions, injured a night watchman and caused $25,000 damage.

Burns merged his investigation of the *Times* bombing with the Llewellyn dynamiting, based on his previous assumption that the *Times* bombing and several others which had occurred around the country might be traced to the International Association of Bridge and Structural Iron Worker's Union (IBSIW), which had been locked in a bitter struggle with the powerful National Erectors Association (NEA). The NEA, the employer's association for the nation's five largest steel and iron erection companies (most notably United States Steel), had by 1910 brutally smashed every union in the industry except for the IBSIW. Hours were long, wages low, and dangers on the job so great that, according to testimony before a federal court, the average bridge and structural ironworker died before the age of thirty-four.

In May 1906 the NEA had publicly declared itself an open shop organization when it passed an explicitly antiunion constitution and appointed Walter Drew, known by union men as "the $12,000-a-year strikebreaker," to take charge of antiunion activities. The NEA maintained its own employment bureaus at which union men were blacklisted and set up a spy network within the ranks of the ironworkers.

The IBSIW, organized in 1896, was determined to resist the U.S. Steel-NEA combine, and, under the leadership of Frank Ryan, it, too, developed a reputation for militancy. After 1905 some 100 to 150 sites, according to NEA figures, fell prey to union dynamite. Though the IBSIW never acknowledged any connection to the explosions, many union sympathizers condoned the incidents, none of which caused any loss of life, as the union's last-ditch effort to save itself from annihilation by the NEA. Some union supporters attributed the destruction to "agents provocateurs," commonly used by belligerent open shop groups like the NEA. "When the use of dynamite in the strike situation was reported," Samuel Gompers wrote, "we knew the chances were that the responsibility lay with operatives in the services of the 'open shop' crowd."

Burns's agency had earlier been hired by one of the firms belonging to the NEA to investigate two explosions. Through those investigations, Burns agents began to follow a suspect later identified as Ortie McManigal. At the same time, the agents kept watch on IBSIW headquarters. Burns, allegedly struck by the similarities in the exploding devices used in both the NEA and *Times* cases, then began to link the two investigations.

Burns claimed to have established the ultimate connection after agents followed McManigal to Wisconsin, where he met a man who fit the description of J. B. Bryce, one of the suspects from the *Los Angeles Times* case. Burns agents disguised themselves as deer hunters and fraternized with the two men who were ostensibly on a hunting trip. An intoxicated Bryce was induced to talk at length, and the daughter of the boarding-house owner, on instructions from the agents, managed to get a picture of the suspect which was used to verify his identity by the San Francisco dynamite company and the boat rental agent.

Burns followed McManigal and Bryce—identified as James B. McNamara, the younger brother of the secretary of the IBSIW—hoping to obtain incriminating evidence on J. B.'s brother John J. (J. J.) McNamara and other higher-ups. In the hopes of wringing a confession out of McManigal, Burns set up an arrest of the two men. On April 12, 1911 Ortie and J. B. checked into a Detroit hotel, prepared to carry off another dynamiting job. When the police, accompanied by Burns's son, arrested them, McNamara and McManigal had in their possession a suitcase filled with fuse caps and all the other equipment necessary to detonate explosives. Burns needed to convince them to sign waivers to return to Chicago, so arresting agents charged the two with a trumped-up safecracking job. McNamara and McManigal then signed the waivers and were immediately whisked off to Chicago. En route J.B. caught on to the police's real motives.

In an effort to keep the arrests secret from John McNamara, the prisoners were held in the home of a Chicago police sergeant. "Arriving in Chicago," Burns wrote in his account, "we arranged so that we would not have to waste time in fighting habeas corpus proceedings and other obstacles that might be thrown in our way by representatives of the dynamiters." Various other subterfuges were used to allay any worries John McNamara might have had as to his brother's whereabouts.

Burns knew that he needed a confession from one of the defendants to implicate John McNamara. Ortie McManigal, already wanted for a previous charge of assault, seemed the likelier of the two prisoners to cooperate. Using a method described by one magazine writer as "psychological third degree," the detective convinced McManigal that even though he wasn't personally involved in the *Times* crime, he could still be convicted of murder under the conspiracy law. McManigal made a full confession.

According to McManigal's statement, the IBSIW had a "special organizational fund," chiefly under the direction of John McNamara, which was used to finance the jobs. J.B. McNamara and Ortie were the union's principal dynamiters. McManigal listed scores of jobs in which he had personally taken part, including the Llewellyn bombing.

In the confession, McManigal brought up the name of Herbert S. Hockin, an organizer for the IBSIW whom he described as ambitious and "wanting to do something" that might result in his election as an international officer of the union. Hockin, McManigal stated, had served as an undercover agent for William Burns and the NEA. Though Hockin later claimed to have turned informer because of the McNamara brothers' violent aims, McManigal noted that Hockin had one time put forth the idea of blowing up a bridge as a train crossed.

McManigal stated that Hockin was the first person to ask him, in 1907, to do a dynamiting job and that subsequent jobs were engineered by him. Until early 1910 Hockin was the only union person directly involved with McManigal. According to the confession, Hockin introduced McManigal to James B. McNamara in December 1909. Five months later Hockin and McManigal discussed a bombing with John McNamara—the first mention of J.J.'s involvement in the McManigal account. Two months after that meeting Ortie claimed that he discovered that Hockin had pocketed some money intended for the dynamiting and that he and J.J. had tried to lay a trap to catch Hockin at it. Soon after, Hockin's communications with the NEA allegedly began. Subsequently, McManigal asserted that he began to get his instructions directly from J.J. Though he never specifically accused J.J. of ordering the *Times* bombing, McManigal described how he went into J.J.'s office on the morning of the blast and found the union official reading the newspapers and smiling. " 'This will make them sit up and take notice,' " McManigal recalled J.J.'s words, " 'and that's what J.B. went out to the coast to do.' "

On the basis of the McManigal confession, Burns left Chicago for Indianapolis. The next day, with a contingent of policemen, he walked in on an executive meeting of the IBSIW and arrested John J. McNamara. McNamara was immediately rushed off to police court where the judge denied his request for counsel and okayed his extradition. In a matter of minutes, before supporters could appeal the extradition order, McManigal and the McNamara brothers were carried off to Los Angeles.

Soon after the arrests, Representative Victor Berger introduced a resolution in Congress calling for an investigation into John McNamara's seizure. Later congressional hearings revealed other irregularities. Although J.J. was not arrested until April 22, Burns had sent a telegram to the Los Angeles D.A.'s office on the fourteenth stating that McNamara was already being held. D.A. Fredericks then filed a statement of arrest with the governor to get the approval for extradition. This enabled Burns to carry it out within minutes of the actual arrest, instead of holding J.J. in the state where legal help would undoubtedly have intervened. An Indianapolis grand jury subsequently indicted Burns and nine other men, including Walter Drew of the NEA, for breach of the extradition law.

The illegal extradition contributed to the feeling that the arrests were part of a frame-up. Persons who knew John McNamara, a twenty-seven-year-old law school graduate, described him as a conservative man and could not believe he was involved. "No sane individual or organization would resort to anything of the kind under any circumstances," he had commented a few days after the explosion.

Organized labor saw the arrests as a plot to destroy the Bridge and Structural Ironworkers Union. The day after the arrests, eight international unions headquarted in Indianapolis set up a legal defense committee and urged the prosecution of those who abducted the arrested brothers.

On May 5, 1911, on the basis of Ortie McManigal's sworn statement, the Los Angeles grand jury issued twenty-one new indictments: one to McManigal for the Llewellyn bombings, one to John McNamara as a co-conspirator in that bombing; and nineteen others to James McNamara, Caplan, Schmidt, and sixteen fictitious "John Does" for the *Times* bombing. The McNamaras were arraigned before Judge Walter Bordwell that same day.

The day after the arraignment, the AFL issued "A Call to Labor" protesting the arrests. "The detective agency engaged in presenting these charges against the men of labor," the circular stated, "is well known to have no hesitancy or scruples in manufacturing evidence and charges against others." Gompers felt labor had a duty to defend the brothers, and, after conferring with the Legal Defense Committee who assured him there was no case against the McNamaras, agreed to let the AFL take over the administration and distribution of the defense funds.

Gompers personally appealed to Clarence Darrow to take on the case. Darrow, who had been approached before, refused; "I felt I had done my share of the fighting," he explained in his autobiography. But Gompers and numerous unions persistently urged him to save the brothers, and the AFL Executive Board offered him a $50,000 fee and $200,000 defense fund. Finally, on May 23, he reluctantly agreed to take the case.

Labor unions, convinced of a frame-up, voiced their support throughout the country. May Day, 1911, was proclaimed "McNamara Day," and demonstrations occurred all across the nation. In Los Angeles, 20,000 people marched by the jail chanting and carrying banners protesting the arrests.

A massive financial campaign was initiated by the AFL-inspired Ways and Means Committee to finance the defense. Christmas-seal type stamps were sold for a penny apiece; for a nickel one could buy a red, white, and blue "McNamara Brothers Not Guilty" button or one with a picture of John McNamara encircled by the words "Justice for the McNamaras." A movie detailed the plot against labor and J.J.'s kidnapping.

Gompers sent out circulars appealing to workers to contribute and protest the arrests. "The *Times* management," a July leaflet noted, "with its years of relentless warfare against humanity, fearing that its Belshazzar feast of organized labor's blood was about to be denied, redoubled its efforts and demanded that a sacrifice must be furnished that its unholy appetite might be appeased, specifying that some union workman or workmen must be supplied to assuage its unnatural and abnormal hunger."

Vociferous anti-McNamara denunciations were carried on not only by Otis and the *Times* but also by Detective Burns. Burns, who later characterized the McNamaras as "men who never did a day's honest work themselves and whose only occupation outside of licentious indulgence was the occupation of destruction and murder," was so outspoken in his accusations that the local Scripps paper, the *Record*, asked whether it was "possible for a labor leader to have a fair trial in the United States? Not surely if Detective Burns can help it! For this man who works for the Erector's Association (steel trust), for the American Banker's Association (money trust), for the Merchants and Manufacturers' Association of Los Angeles (organized labor-crushers), and for the *Los Angeles Times* (organ of capitalistic hate of the laboring class), seeks to convict the accused in the magazines and newspapers months before they go to trial to create a public opinion that will render possible no verdict save that of guilty."

The McNamara defense staff consisted of Darrow, Los Angeles Socialist attorney Job Harriman, ex-Judge Cyrus McNutt of Indiana, and two prominent local attorneys—Le Compte Davis, a conservative former assistant D.A., unsympathetic to labor or socialism, who was hired by Darrow for his knowledge of California law; and Joseph Scott, a well-known Catholic attorney. Both Davis and Scott had ties to Los Angeles establishment circles. Davis had even served as Otis's attorney. To head his investigative staff, Darrow employed John Harrington, an experienced investigator for the Chicago City Railway, and Bert Franklin, a former deputy sheriff and deputy U.S. marshal in Los Angeles.

Times protégé Fredericks directed the prosecution. Harry Chandler had talked at length about the possibility of employing another prosecutor outside the District Attorney's staff to be funded by money raised from the widows and orphans of the explosion victims, to offset the "mushy and sentimental talk" of the other side, as well as from larger contributions from other sources. Despite Fredericks's fear that it would appear "out of place" for employers and manufacturers to aid the prosecution, former U.S. Attorney Oscar Lawler was subsequently brought in to take a major role in the case. Neither the defense nor the public was aware of Lawler's employment. Earl Rogers, who had previously worked with defense counsel Le Compte Davis and who was a close friend of Timesman Harry Carr, also joined the prosecution team. National Erector Associa-

tion's Walter Drew—involved in all stages of the case from the investigation to the arrest to the trial—served as intermediary between Fredericks,
the U.S. attorney in Indianapolis, and the U.S. attorney general.

In the three months before the trial, the unions continued their fund-
raising activities to obtain the large sums of money necessary to carry on
the trial. Most progressive-minded citizens tended to believe in the brothers' innocence. "Save the McNamaras" banners hung from store windows, cars, barber poles, and porches, and rallies and torchlight parades
were held for the "Heroes of Labor." *Times* solicitors had discovered,
Harry Chandler wrote to Otis at the end of May, that "people are filled up
with the Socialistic and anarchistic idea that these men are innocent and
that Burns and the corporations have framed up a case on them."

The Socialist *Appeal to Reason*, featuring weekly progress reports on a
campaign to find out who besides Otis was really guilty of the crime, enjoyed dramatic circulation gains. "The conspiracy," Debs wrote in the
September 2 issue, "was hatched in Wall Street soon after the steel octopus was spawned. Morgan brought down his fist and hissed 'GOD DAMN
THEIR SOULS, THE UNIONS HAVE GOT TO BE WIPED OUT.' . . . If Morgan, Guggenheim and the steel trust, and Otis and the Merchants and
Manufacturers Association want red hell they can have it, but let them
take notice that when it comes the working class alone will not furnish all
the victims."

Demonstrations of support for the brothers were held on Labor Day,
designated as McNamara fund-raising day, as thousands paraded in the
streets. Fifteen thousand sympathizers, chanting their belief in the
McNamara's innocence, came out to hear Gompers speak in Philadelphia
on the day before the trial.

While labor demonstrated and collected funds, the defense and prosecution busily prepared their cases. The defense, using a model of the
Times building which Darrow intended to blow up in court, planned to
show that the building could have been destroyed by gas. Over six hundred detectives took part in preparing the prosecution's case. Though
more than four hundred witnesses were expected to testify, the D.A.'s
case essentially centered on one witness: Ortie McManigal.

Many found McManigal's story, which also alluded to plans to fire-
bomb Los Angeles, hard to believe. Defense investigators traveled all
over the country looking for holes in McManigal's statements. McManigal's wife and uncle, who felt that the confession had been made under
fear and threats from Burns, joined the defense and tried to convince Ortie to repudiate his statement. Mrs. McManigal complained of constant
harrassment by Burns' agents and the D.A.'s men, who threatened her
with a jail sentence and violence unless she corroborated her husband's
testimony. Instead, she publicly stated that her husband had agreed to

"confess" in exchange for immunity and a large share of the reward. In October Mrs. McManigal sued Ortie for divorce on grounds of extreme and repeated cruelty.

The prosecution alleged that evidence—union books, correspondence, and explosives seized from the ironworker's headquarters at the time of John McNamara's arrest and now in possession of an Indianapolis court—would corroborate Ortie's confession and prove McNamara's role in other IBSIW bombings. Fredericks had been unable to secure the cooperation of the Indiana authorities, Governor Johnson, or federal officials in getting hold of the material and he feared the defense would be more successful.

In desperation Otis and Lawler decided to appeal to President Taft, who was planning a visit to the West Coast. The two men set up an appointment with the President at the home of Taft's brother-in-law. Taft was hesitant at first, but Lawler and Otis spoke of the interests of justice and the "clarification" of the country's labor and capital problems. Lawler explained that the only means of protecting the evidence, was to call a federal grand jury in Indianapolis and impound the files. The next morning Attorney General Wickersham announced that grand jury proceedings had begun and federal officers had confiscated the union records from the vaults.

Some of the correspondence between Wickersham and his associates had been sent in code. Such undercover maneuvers became common practice for both the prosecution and defense, leery of leaks and spies from the other side. Defense witnesses complained of constant harassment while those of the prosecution were allegedly threatened and given money to leave town. One of the defense secretaries, an undercover Burns detective, made copies of everything so that the prosecution had up-to-date information on defense activities. A Burns man served lunch at the restaurant where Darrow ate, and Darrow's telegrams were stolen, his account books copied, and his telephone conversations bugged by a hidden dictaphone. Darrow, in turn, paid off a deputy from the D.A.'s office for information. Some of the private detectives played off defense and prosecution to such a degree that they received up to three separate salaries.

The prosecution also used a grand jury investigation into alleged influencing of witnesses as another important harassment weapon. Anyone helpful to the defense side, such as McManigal's wife and uncle, was hauled in and threatened, and even defense staff members were called to testify. When Darrow's aide John Harrington was cited for contempt after he refused to testify before the grand jury, the defense unsuccessfully filed a bias charge against Judge Bordwell for attempting to force a member of the defense team to answer questions about a trial in progress.

One week later, in early October, the McNamara trial opened. News correspondents from all over the country flocked to cover the event. The jury selection and the trial promised to be long and painstaking. The first three jurors didn't get sworn in until November 8.

While the jury selection proceeded, Los Angeles, on October 31, held its municipal primary election. To everyone's amazement, McNamara's attorney, Job Harriman, running as the Socialist party candidate, received the highest number of votes in the mayoralty race and Socialists came in first in eight of nine council races. Belief in the innocence of the McNamaras has been an integral part of his campaign. The runoff election, in which Harriman would face incumbent Mayor Alexander, was scheduled for December 5.

The *Times*, warning of a "dangerous conspiracy against the city's and the people's best interests," promised to do everything in its power to defeat Harriman. As a first step the paper threw its support to its one-time enemy George Alexander. The mayor was so surprised by Harriman's first-place margin and the threat of Socialist rule that he agreed to let the conservative Republicans run his campaign, promising to show any future plans to them in advance. The M&M, the Founders and Employers' Association, and others joined under the banner of a nonpartisan Citizen's Committee of One Hundred to try to defeat Harriman. Old-line Republicans, Democrats, Independents, and reformers all worked together in the campaign to keep Los Angeles from the socialists. ". . . If it were not for the menace of the lawless element," E.T. Earl wrote Hiram Johnson, "we would all laugh heartily at the idea of Otis and Hearst supporting the progressive movement locally."

Local labor, united politically for the first time, celebrated Harriman's success, and even the conservative AFL, which had previously refrained from supporting political candidates, unanimously passed a resolution to send greetings in support of Harriman.

4. The Plea

On December 1, four days before the runoff election, the McNamara prosecutors and their allies played their trump card to ward off the predicted Socialist victory. Few in Los Angeles would forget that day. Reporters in Judge Bordwell's court took their specially equipped places as usual, expecting a continuation of the tedious jury selection process. But inklings of something amiss cropped up at 10:45 A.M., when D.A. Fredericks requested an adjournment until the afternoon because of "grave matters." During the adjournment, Darrow, Davis, and Fredericks closeted themselves together, and the rumors began to fly.

That afternoon, the defense filed back in with both J.B. and J.J. McNamara, the latter not on trial yet. Both men appeared nervous and tired. Anticipation hung over the courtroom. "Your honor," Le Compte Davis announced, "we have concluded to withdraw the plea of not guilty, and have the defendant enter in this case a plea of guilty. . . ."

The announcement shook the courtroom. Word spread quickly to the outside as reporters sprang to their telephones. ". . . The public got the news, all in a flash. The human mind cannot change so suddenly," Lincoln Steffens recalled. The editor of the *Record* fainted at his desk. After the initial shock, members of the crowd outside the courtroom, angered at the apparent deception, tore off their McNamara buttons and ripped down their banners, calling Darrow and the McNamara brothers traitors. Many cried openly.

The press, especially those publications that had advanced the gas theory, tried to find out what had happened, but Fredericks refused to answer any questions. Darrow, described as "almost incoherent from fatigue," told reporters that "there was no way out of it." "To go on under such circumstances," he later stated to the press, "would have been madness." The evidence, Darrow told reporters, was too strong, and he knew the case was hopeless, so he had done the best thing and saved the two men's lives.

"The god that is still in Israel filled the souls of the dynamiters with a torment they could not bear," the *Times* announced on its page one story the next day. ". . . The muttered word 'yes' from the lips of these two men desperate and snatching at the little crumb of mercy that comes to the confessor was the end of a long tangled skein of crime."

Sentencing was set for December 5, election day. In court, D.A. Fredericks read James McNamara's confession: "It was my intention to injure the building and scare the owners. I did not intend to take the life of anyone. I sincerely regret these unfortunate men lost their lives. If the giving of my life would bring them back I would freely give it. . . ." James McNamara was sentenced to life imprisonment; John, who only pled guilty to the Llewellyn bombing, was given fifteen years.

The day the McNamaras were sentenced, Job Harriman lost at the polls by over 30,000 votes. Not one of the eight Socialist city council candidates won. "Yesterday, in the city of Los Angeles, God's people spoke," the *Times* proclaimed, "and the enemies of God stand confused. Scoffing, anarchistic Socialism has been crushed—as far as this city is concerned—with the same swift merciless annihilation that the heel of a giant crushed the head of a reptile. . . ."

The true story behind the startling change of pleas still remains a mystery, one that will probably never be entirely solved. The firsthand reports that exist, all filled with obvious exaggerations and half-truths, tend to contradict one another.

The most widely circulated account of how the settlement came about is that of muckraker Lincoln Steffens, who covered the trial for a syndicate of newspapers. The first suggestion of a plan to get Los Angeles's capitalist leaders to agree to a settlement had apparently been broached by Steffens while he and Darrow were visiting the ranch of newspaper publisher E.W. Scripps. Darrow, although pessimistic, allowed Steffens to proceed, with the understanding that the defense might repudiate him if his plan didn't work.

Steffens enlisted the aid of several progressive leaders, such as Meyer Lissner and Thomas Gibbon. He then went to see General Otis, but as the General was out, Steffens talked instead—by his own account—to Harry Chandler. Chandler agreed to help but cautioned against telling Otis until the whole plan had been set.

Chandler, who consulted nightly with D.A. Fredericks about his negotiations with Steffens, told the muckraker that the prosecution wanted stiffer terms than those originally proposed by Steffens. The D.A., under pressure from the NEA, insisted that the McNamaras plead guilty and serve prison time. The defense team, led by Darrow and Davis, decided to accept the prosecution's terms, but failed to inform Job Harriman, then busy campaigning for mayor, of the secret negotiations. Knowing a guilty plea would doom the Socialist's chances, they didn't have the heart to tell him.

The defense lawyers also had a problem convincing their clients to accept the plan. James McNamara initially agreed to plead guilty and take the punishment, but he refused to let his brother, with his high union position, implicate himself. The lawyers spent hours trying to change his mind. Finally, after an exhaustive session, and after Darrow had returned with assurances from Fredericks that James McNamara's accomplices would not be bothered as long as they stayed out of California, James agreed to Fredericks's conditions.

After the defense informed Fredericks, a secret meeting was held, attended by Chandler, Lissner, and the city's other leading Old Guard and progressive businessmen as well as Fredericks and Steffens. Fredericks's compromise terms were agreed to by all present.

Fredericks and Chandler spent Thanksgiving working out the logistics of the final terms with Le Compte Davis. The McNamaras were to plead guilty with no confessions; James would receive a life term and John ten years. The pursuit of other suspects was to be terminated; and a labor-capital conference would be held to settle the city's industrial conflicts. According to Steffens, the emphasis was on a "settlement"—a recognition of both labor and capital's "guilt"—rather than a confession.

But neither Steffens's "peaceful settlement" nor the terms of the compromise were carried out. James was given life, but John was given a fifteen rather than ten year sentence. Judge Bordwell contradicted the spirit of labor-capital rapprochement by harshly assailing the defendants and their crime in his sentencing remarks. A preliminary joint peace conference met in February 1912, but no meetings occurred afterward. And, to James's anger, other suspects were arrested, tried, and sent to the penitentiary three years later.

Though Steffens's version of events was widely accepted, many found parts of it, in the words of Adela Rogers St. John, a little "too hard to swallow," especially Steffens's contention that Otis had readily accepted the settlement. "General Otis, as expected," Harry Chandler wrote of the general's reaction on first learning of the negotiations, on the day of the plea, "became furious at the prosecution's plan. He stormed about, declaring, 'I want those sons-of-bitches to hang!' It was some time before he could be placated by the argument that it would be much better for his own cause if the trial were ended this way."

Defense attorney Le Compte Davis, a friend of both the D.A. and the judge, gave another account. Davis claimed he went to see Otis in late November to convince him of the possibility that the McNamaras might get off if the trial went through. After Davis convinced Otis that a confession would be sure to discredit labor, the *Times* publisher agreed to the "compromise."

Davis and Scott each claimed credit for having ultimately convinced the brothers to accept the plan. "Even though the McNamaras had killed all those people, I saved them from hanging," Davis recalled in 1958.

Still another version gives a large behind-the-scenes role to Otto F. Brant, manager of Title Insurance and Trust company and a close friend of Harry Chandler. Brant wrote that Chandler had called him a week before Thanksgiving to ask him to aid in settlement arrangements and that he had agreed to serve as a go-between with Fredericks.

Wherever the credit ultimately belongs, the arrangement, essentially worked out by a group of powerful industrialists, was a political settlement. The bargain, historian George Mowry noted, was "between capital and labor; not between the state and alleged criminals." Steffens, with his misplaced naivete had merely served as the unwitting tool of Fredericks, Otis, and the other employers.

Why then would the prosecution, with an apparently "iron clad and literally bombproof case against the McNamaras," as the *Times* own history of the case put it, agree to any bargain at all? "Not more than six men know all the facts and they have kept the secret well," the *Times* account declared. But a number of reasons clearly stand out.

No matter how ironclad the evidence, there was still a chance that a conviction might not have resulted given the state of public opinion at the time, Darrow's prowess as a lawyer, and, as E.T. Earl pointed out in a letter to Governor Johnson, D.A. Fredericks's lack of skill. Even if they had been convicted, the McNamaras would undoubtedly have appeared as martyrs, and sympathizers would have continued to believe in their innocence. "It was better," the *Times* history said, "in the view of the State, for them to proclaim their guilt with their own lips . . . than for the question always to remain in doubt."

A more important reason involved the timing of the upcoming mayoralty election with its probable Socialist victory. "Never in its history had Los Angeles [businessmen] been seized with such a panic of fear," Steffens wrote of the mood in Los Angeles at the time. Getting the McNamaras to plead guilty four days before the election was a master stroke for Otis, Chandler, and the business establishment. It not only undercut Job Harriman's chances, but regained the initiative in the ultimate struggle over who would control Los Angeles. The Socialists' defeat, combined with the fatal blow against the local labor movement, established business hegemony in the region for decades to come.

Lawler, Fredericks, and Judge Bordwell denied that any bargain had ever been made. They put forward another explanation for the sudden plea reversal. On November 29, just three days before the plea, police arrested defense investigator Bert Franklin for attempting to bribe a jury member. The arrest, it turned out, was only the first step toward the larger prosecution goal to get Clarence Darrow, the object of considerable hatred by the D.A.'s team.

Franklin's arrest had been set up by the police, who claimed they knew of the bribery attempt through former policeman and deputy sheriff George Lockwood, one of the two prospective jury members involved. Lockwood, according to the prosecutors, had informed his old friend the D.A. of the bribe offer, and the police then staked out the busy downtown street corner where the money was supposed to change hands.

Franklin ultimately pled guilty and implicated Darrow in his grand jury testimony. He received a suspended sentence and a fine equal to the amount of the bribe. The lack of punishment and Franklin's previous ties to Lockwood gave rise to speculation that Franklin, who had been a deputy U.S. marshal for five years just prior to working for Darrow, was in the employ of the district attorney at the time of his arrest.

Two separate indictments for bribery were issued against Darrow in February 1912. The first trial began in May. Fredericks, once again with the aid of the NEA, headed the prosecution, while Darrow hired his former opponent Earl Rogers to defend him. The defense planned to link the arrests to an overall conspiracy against the famed lawyer.

The trial was an emotional one. Prosecution and defense alike denounced each other's witnesses as liars and almost came to blows. Rogers tried to show the absurdity of the charges, pointing to Franklin's D.A.

ties, the use of a busy street corner for the paying of bribe money, the choice of unsympathetic jurors supposedly to be bribed, and the McNamara defense's awareness that they were being spied on.

Darrow's passionate and eloquent final address to the jury moved the jurors and audience to tears. "I am not on trial for having sought to bribe a man named Lockwood. . . ," Darrow said, "I am on trial because I have been a lover of the poor, a friend of the oppressed, because I have stood by labor for all of these years. . . . Men cannot lose all their heart, except by a surgical operation," he concluded, "and there are not here in Los Angeles twelve men without some heart. If there were they would have been in the employ of the District Attorney long ago."

After only thirty-four minutes, the jury returned a verdict of "not guilty." The crowds were hysterical; jurors embraced. Later that night Steffens threw a dinner celebration attended by Darrow, the judge, and the jury. "Darrow and his kind," the *Times* complained bitterly after the verdict, "have chosen their colors, and those colors are not the ensign of the republic. At a dinner given to Darrow by his anarchistic sympathizers, after this acquittal, the American flag was conspicuous by its absence. . . ."

Six months later Darrow's second trial, based on a different bribery charge, began. Darrow carried on his own defense after Rogers became ill and, despite warning from Rogers, made the *Times* bombing a major issue. An 8 to 4 vote for conviction resulted in a hung jury. Fredericks talked of retrying the case but dropped the idea after Darrow agreed to leave town and never practice law in California again.

5. Mysteries

The Darrow bribery indictments were only one part of the prosecution-NEA follow-up. Darrow, among others, suggested that they really wanted to get other higher-ups like AFL President Gompers. Burns in particular attacked Gompers in speeches throughout the country. According to the *Los Angeles Times* history of the case, Franklin had placed responsibility for the bribe on Gompers, and Darrow was informed that he would be let off if he furnished evidence against the AFL president.

On February 6, 1912, a federal grand jury in Indianapolis issued indictments for conspiracy to transport dynamite against fifty-four union leaders including Frank Ryan, president of the IBSIW; NEA-Burns informant Herbert Hockin, who had replaced John McNamara, as secretary of the union; the McNamara brothers; several California labor officials; and other IBSIW officers.

The trials began on October 1, 1912. McManigal served as the prosecution's chief witness, with further information supplied by Hockin, who described how he had procured explosives and hired the dynamiters. In addition, the prosecution produced union correspondence and records, mostly supplied by Hockin, allegedly describing eighty-nine dynamiting jobs.

The defense argued that the letters and other documents had been misinterpreted and that the government's overall case offered no concrete evidence. Despite their complaints, the judge continually referred to the defendants as dynamiters and murderers.

Thirty-eight of the forty men on trial were convicted, though some of the convictions were overturned by a higher court. McManigal received a suspended sentence and went on to testify against Schmidt and Caplan, who were arrested in February 1915 on the charge of first degree murder. After the trials McManigal disappeared quietly to Honduras. On his return, with a new identity, he was given a job as a watchman for Los Angeles County.

The Indianapolis trial brought on new attempts to implicate Samuel Gompers. One union official asserted that the prosecuting attorney, at Burn's insistence, promised immunity to him and other indicted men if they would testify that Gompers was involved.

Times editorials had compared the AFL leader to a "sleepy snake . . . [who] dresses in a long, greasy frock coat with a straw hat of ancient vintage jammed down over his scrofulous head." Just after the pleas, the paper published a fake picture of Gompers trampling an American flag; the photo then circulated among the nation's daily papers. Artists from the *Examiner* and an expert in Washington declared the picture a fraud, and the *St. Louis Republic* suggested that "most Americans who are acquainted with both institutions would rather trust the old flag to the American Federation of Labor than to the Otis crowd in Los Angeles."

But the national business-led campaign to intimidate Gompers and undermine tentative alliances that the AFL had made with Socialists and more militant trade unionists had succeeded. The AFL executives, frightened of the "dynamite" taint, quickly disassociated themselves from the McNamaras. "The McNamaras should not be spared. They should receive punishment commensurate with their crimes," AFL Secretary Frank Morrison declared as the AFL eagerly opened up its books and accounts to prove it had nothing to hide.

Though the AFL retreated, a number of noted citizens such as Judge Louis Brandeis questioned why the McNamaras felt that dynamite was the only recourse to improve workers' conditions. "If you want to judge John McNamara," Eugene Debs said after the trial, "you must first serve a month as a structural iron worker on a skyscraper, risking your life every minute to feed your wife and babies, then be discharged and blacklisted for joining a union."

The McNamara case, coupled with the decline of the Socialist and industrial union movements, led the AFL to turn away from its militant stance in an effort to build a more respectable public image and reconsolidate its conservative craft unionism traditions. Though the federation managed to increase its overall membership, it lost a certain working class esprit.

The effect of the McNamara events on the Los Angeles labor movement were devastating. The promising organizing campaign of 1910–1911, which had withstood the bombing and the arrests, came to a halt after the pleas. "As for me and mine," the *Times* boasted, "we stand vindicated in our quarter of a century stand for industrial freedom."

The city became more of an open shop bastion than ever. "The efforts of the misleaders of union labor to make Los Angeles a cringing suppliant at their feet have utterly failed," the *Times* noted at the new year. ". . . The effort to force the closed shop upon the employers of labor has been completely abandoned. Boycotting, picketing, and assaulting, and dynamiting are at an end. . . . Industrial freedom reigns supreme."

". . . I was dubious, and always will be until the last chapter is written, about the explosion of the *Times*" progressive Frances Noel testified during the 1913 congressional hearings to investigate labor conditions in the United States. That J.B. McNamara left the dynamite at the Times Building without the intention of causing harm to anybody, seems clear— though there are a few authors who still question even that act. But, the unforeseen gas explosions, and fires possibly caused by the neglected gas leaks in the building were the cause of the much greater destruction and death.

There are still questions about the nature of J. J. McNamara's involvement in the *Times* bombing and the other dynamitings. J. J. pled guilty to the Llewellyn bombing, but did not confess to that bombing or the *Times* dynamiting or any other incidents. An article by Socialist newspaperman George Shoaf who had met with J. J. after his release from prison, raised the possibility of J. J.'s innocence in connection with the *Times* explosion. The two planned to write a true story of the events around the *Times* bombing, but J. J. died before the work was begun.

The brothers' motivation for the plea clearly stemmed from their desire to protect each other from a possible death sentence and, according to later letters from a bitter J. B., due to the "compromise" agreement which stipulated that others would not be prosecuted. Darrow had put tremendous pressure on the two to change their plea and had kept them unaware of the massive movement that had sprung up in their defense. "If Jim and I had known what was taking place on the outside," J. J. later related to Shoaf, ". . . we would never have allowed ourselves to be coerced into confessing to the crime charged against us. . . . On the contrary, Darrow hinted that the situation was ominous . . . and that in the interest of public safety, it would be best if we acted on his advice." The brothers had hoped that the case would go to trial with Darrow stressing "the facts of the class struggle. . . . But Darrow and Steffens overruled us," J. J. stated, "and so we went to hell."

Darrow's motivation is a little more obscure. Historical accounts pictured him as a tired, worried man, fearful that his clients, whose guilt was evident to him for many months, would be sent to die. By relying strongly on Le Compte Davis, and later Earl Rogers, Darrow might unwittingly have served the interests of the Los Angeles business establishment, who were ready to do anything to keep the prolabor Socialist Job Harriman from becoming the next mayor of their city and the McNamaras from becoming martyrs to the cause of labor.

Major doubts concerning the credibility of the state's star witnesses also exist. There is a distinct possibility that Burns, who later founded the forerunner of the FBI, might have concocted Ortie McManigal's confession. The style and phrasing of Ortie's written account bears a striking resemblance—with almost identical phrases—to Burns's own narrative *The Masked War*. McManigal's book, like Burns's, calls for the purging of labor leaders, and on its frontispiece, where one might expect a picture of the author, is instead a picture of Burns—"the man," according to McManigal, "who secured the evidence to corroborate my confession."

Finally there is the curious and mysterious figure Herbert S. Hockin, the Burns-NEA informer, who replaced J. J. McNamara as secretary-treasurer of the IBSIW—that union later becoming one of the most conservative craft unions in the entire labor movement. Hockin had been in direct charge of the "dynamite gang," and it was he who procured much of the evidence used in the Indianapolis trial.

Hockin, according to McManigal's account, and substantiated by material in various federal records, was the man responsible for the dynamite jobs up through the summer of 1910. He allegedly became an informer in 1910 only a month before McManigal and J. J. were said to have discovered that fact. But even after the apparent discovery, Hockin continued to function as a union official; possibly, then, his double agent role was not known on October 1, 1910, the day of the *Times* bombing.

Given the accepted practice of the use of agents provocateurs by employer organizations, it is possible that Hockin could have served in such a capacity. The NEA, which used strongarm tactics, was in on all levels of the investigation, arrest, trial, and plea change arrangements. It is not implausible, given their long, bitter desire to destroy the one union which continued to fight them, that they could also have been directly involved in the dynamiting.

Second, given that Hockin was already an informer by mid-1910 and continued on with the union, he could have forewarned his NEA employers about the *Times* explosion, who in turn would have forewarned the *Times* owners. The dynamite placed there should not have done anything more serious than wreck the rear wall; the second deadly explosion occurred unforeseen as a result of the first explosion igniting the building's gas mains. The *Times* management—equipped with their auxiliary plant just in case of such an emergency—might have been willing to incur a little structural damage, paid for by insurance, in exchange for the destruction of the Los Angeles labor movement.

There is no direct evidence to substantiate such surmises—some of which are being raised here for the first time. They are only theoretical suggestions for a case that is still fraught with mysteries and unanswered questions. Only the results—so extraordinarily beneficial to Otis, Los Angeles's open shop employers, and the national NEA—are known.

"It will make you and your dear father-in-law, the strongest men in the country," Moses Sherman wrote of the plea change to Harry Chandler. Maybe not the country, but certainly Los Angeles.

CHAPTER 6

The Battle Goes On

1. That Damned Socialistic Thing

In the same December 1911 election in which Socialist Job Harriman was defeated, Los Angeles voters passed an initiative to set up a city-financed newspaper. The paper, to be published weekly under the direction of a Municipal Newspaper Commission, was directed to print without bias news items concerning Los Angeles and provide differing views of local controversies. In order not to become a sounding board for incumbents, the paper would avoid long interviews or statements by elected officials. The initiative called for a $36,000 yearly subsidy, with remaining costs to be made up through advertisements. Single copies would be given free to anyone who requested them, and home-delivered subscriptions cost 25¢ for six months.

The paper, called the *Municipal News*, immediately attracted a number of local and state newspaper people. A tremendous esprit existed among its staff, who were "the best newspapermen on the coast," according to veteran newspaper editor Frank Wolfe.

The *Municipal News* was an instant success. Thirty thousand copies were printed of the first issue; the number more than doubled for the second issue, and circulation continued to climb thereafter.

The paper immediately addressed itself to the most controversial topics in the city: the Owens River aqueduct; activities of the police, civil service, fire, and other city commissions; and questions being debated before the city council. It had a strong consumer-civic orientation, with one special issue, for example, devoted to an explanation of the city budget, describing "where city taxes go" and "what you get back." One of its news columns identified weekly price changes of various food items and "specials" on sale, and later expanded this coverage to include general price information on all merchandise. "It covered the news of the municipality better than any paper had ever covered it," Frank Wolfe claimed.

The initiative had provided for a full page, the "Party Politics Page," to be divided into columns allotted for each political party which had polled more than 3 percent of the vote in the previous election. Columns were thus available to the Republicans, Democrats, the Good Government Organization, the Socialist Party, and the Socialist Labor Party, which had just barely made the 3 percent figure. The Republicans, opposed to the allotment of two columns for the "reds," boycotted the paper, refusing to submit any material for the page. In the first three issues their column was blank, but the instant popularity of the *News* led the Republicans, still attempting to maintain an aloof posture, to submit quotations from speeches of East Coast Republican figures. The totality of the *News*'s conception and policy undoubtedly infuriated the *Times* and other papers as well.

The *News*'s advertising policy directly contradicted existing newspaper practices. While the *Times* took any kind of ad, the *Municipal News* refused specific classes of ads such as fraud, patent medicine, attorneys, loan sharks, clairvoyants, bogus employment agencies, and false news items ("readers"). "Advertising—the right kind of advertising has a genuine value to a reader . . . ," the paper announced in an October 1912 editorial. "This advertising is best exemplified in a classified mercantile department that the *Municipal News* has established as a permanent feature on Page 3. Here inch advertising items, brief, to the point, have for every reader a news value. Each advertisement is equal in interest and importance to any like amount of space throughout the city's newspaper." The paper's ad policy reflected its strong "consumer" orientation.

Many of the large stores and markets placed ads in the growing paper, to the displeasure of the *Times* management. "Every dollar that damned socialistic thing gets is a dollar out of the *Times* till," Otis exclaimed.

The *Times* publisher, according to Frank Wolfe, "sent agents to various advertisers to notify them that if they continued to advertise in this paper they would be boycotted, black-listed, and put out of business. . . . Advertisers were cajoled, browbeaten, and blackmailed until nearly all left the paper." In addition distribution agents from other papers physically ganged up on *Municipal News* agents to keep the paper off the streets, preventing large-scale distribution in residential areas.

Finally, the anti-*News* forces placed a special amendment on the ballot to kill the funding for the *News*. The amendment's wording was confusing. A yes vote opposed continuation of the paper; a no vote favored it.

With two-thirds fewer voters casting ballots than in the earlier election which had established the paper, the *Times* and its allies managed to win the election.

Its funding eliminated, the *News* had to close. Its last issue appeared on April 9, 1913. The *Times* said of its rival that day, "The *Municipal News* is a municipal failure . . . It was a convenient dumping ground for the money of the taxpayers."

In its brief life, the *News*, a unique experiment in journalistic history, attracted a great deal of attention among newspaper people and municipal reformers throughout the country. It anticipated a number of journalistic tendencies that came into their own a half century later. The death of the *Municipal News*, which solidified the *Times*'s influence in Los Angeles, was, as Frank Wolfe lamented, "a triumph of reaction."

2. San Diego Skirmishes

"While God gives me life, I will go on with my work and person for my self-imposed task as best I can," Otis wrote in early 1912. "I will stand by the flag, swear by it, and if need be die for it. I will continue to worship the American Eagle and look up to him as the symbol of liberty." As he passed his seventieth birthday, Harrison Gray Otis still had a lot of fight left. Though his son-in-law had taken on most of the day-to-day work at the *Times*, Otis continued to play an active role at the paper and in political affairs. The old general was still feared and respected by Angelenos and *Times* staff.

Just as the *Times* eagle survived the 1910 bombing "unscathed," the paper's power and reputation was considerably strengthened by events following the bombing. Los Angeles became more open shop than ever, and employers looked to the *Times* for leadership in maintaining that policy.

The *Times*'s belligerent attitude toward unionism and political reform became more pronounced than ever, and some of the remedies it suggested bordered on the violent. "And soon — it has begun already —," a *Times* opinion piece noted in 1911, "the plain citizens of every country will form a combine. Its object will be the suppression of sedition and anarchy in the persons of the professional agitators. . . . The first thing the Plain Citizens Combine will accomplish is the Quiet Removal of these gentlemen. They won't be blown up; they will just quietly disappear from human ken. With the itch removed the great disease of unrest will soon be cured. . . ."

Though the *California Outlook* magazine dismissed the editorial as another instance of the paper merely making "an ass of itself," the emergence of such a combine did occur in San Diego the following year. Since

1906 San Diego had been the home of a chapter of the International Workers of the World (IWW), also known as the Wobblies, whose fight for "one big union" had won them the enmity of both employers and the more conservative AFL craft unions.

A key Wobbly tactic in San Diego was to have supporters speak out on street corners and other public areas in an attempt to publicize the issue of free speech. Just after the *Times* printed its "Plain Citizens Combine" piece, Otis and M&M secretary Zeehandelaar spoke at a businessmen's conference in San Diego and called for the city to limit those free speech rights. Soon afterward the local merchants, frightened by the ogre of radical unionism after the McNamara pleas, petitioned the San Diego Common Council to prohibit street speeches within the downtown district of the city. Despite a counter-petition signed by four times as many names, the council unanimously passed such an ordinance.

Immediately afterward, a Free Speech League was set up with the participation of the IWW, the Socialist party, local AFL unions, and a local evangelist. A protest parade took place in early February 1912, and free speech proponents continued to violate the ordinance, resulting in massive arrests. "The I Won't Workers of San Diego have organized a Free Speech League," the *Times* noted. "They are against everything free except labor but they are against work under all conditions. If they went in for more action and less gab they might come nearer realizing the satisfaction that lies in a full dinner pail."

The situation quickly escalated. Nearly 300 people were arrested. Conditions in prison were substandard, many prisoners were denied water, beds, or toilet facilities. Some complained of being kicked and beaten by the police. Legal counsel was not made available, and bails were excessively high. When a protest meeting was held in front of the jail to demand better treatment for prisoners, the gathering was dispersed with fire hoses.

The city, egged on by the local press owned by sugar king John D. Spreckels, was in a state of hysteria. The Wobblies had sent out a call for recruits to replace those arrested, and hundreds of supporters responded from all over the country. Speakers continued to make their "soap box stand," claiming that thousands more would come if the arrests went on. The police chief in turn ordered a general round up of all "male vagrants" in an effort to keep the newcomers away.

As trials began, the *San Diego Evening Tribune*, one of the two Spreckels papers, urged stiff punishments. "Hanging is none too good for them and they would be much better dead for they are absolutely useless in the human economy; they are waste material of creation and should be drained off in the sewer of oblivion there to rot in cold obstruction like any other excrement," the *Tribune* said.

The arrests and harsh treatment did not stop the free speech forces. New people kept arriving, the jails overflowed, and the prisoners sang and showed high spirits. Within a couple of weeks after the *Tribune* editorial, some of the paper's followers devised a system to relieve the overcrowding in the jails and avoid the costly and time-consuming trials. Prisoners were taken from the jail in the middle of the night by "citizens groups," brought to the outskirts of the city, and beaten and abandoned, their lives threatened if they ever returned to San Diego. Eventually, the free speech "violators" weren't even booked; police just picked them up, held them until midnight, and then turned them over to the vigilantes. An IWW song described the situation:

> In that town called San Diego when the workers
>   try to talk
> The cops will smash them with a say and tell 'em
>   "take a walk."
> They throw them in a bull pen, and they feed them
>   rotten beans
> And they call that "law and order" in that city, so
>   it seems.
>
> They're clubbing fellow working men who dare their
>   thoughts express;
> And if old Otis has his way, there's sure to be a
>   mess
> So swell this army working men and show them
>   what we'll do
> When all the sons of toil unite in *One Big Union*
>   true.

The vigilante citizen's committee actions had the approval and participation of the police and the town's leading businessmen. Stories of vigilante actions were legion; deportations became more elaborate as free speechers were forced to sing the Star Spangled Banner, kiss the flag, or engage in other "patriotic" rituals, and were sometimes forced to run a gauntlet of up to sixty men after which they were dropped naked in the middle of the cold desert night.

After the editor of the *San Diego Herald* (a non-Spreckels independent paper which provided fair coverage to the free speech forces) was kidnaped from his home, complaints were registered with Governor Johnson. Johnson commissioned Harris Weinstock to investigate the situation. Weinstock held three days of public hearings in San Diego, which were boycotted by local officials, and released a report that, although not favoring the IWW, denounced the tactics used against them. The special commissioner likened the conditions to Czarist Russia, and suggested that the state attorney general be ordered to start criminal proceedings.

In turn, San Diego public and business officials sent telegrams to the U.S. attorney general alleging threats against the lives of city officials and describing a Wobbly plot to cross the Mexican border and take over Baja California.

Though the U.S. attorney for Southern California backed the San Diego businessmen, U.S. Attorney General Wickersham felt that it was up to the state to preserve order. But an Otis-Spreckels-led committee of 500 put pressure on President Taft, insisting on the existence of a nationwide IWW conspiracy to overthrow the U.S. government which would begin in Southern California. The attorney general ultimately caved in and authorized the U.S. attorney to lay the matter before a grand jury.

The hearings were held in Los Angeles in the spring of 1912. On July 5, the day before the grand jury was to end its term, the U.S. attorney announced that the grand jury was ready to issue indictments. But neither Wickersham nor Taft saw proof of any imminent uprising; the evidence, Wickersham wrote, was "too vague." Despite a telegram from Otis (which he signed under a code name "Boanerges") urging the immediate issuance of indictments, Taft refused to act. No indictments were handed down.

That fall, the California Old Guard decided to try again. In early September Otis and California Republican National Committeeman F.W. Estabrook sent private detective Charles De Lacour to Washington to tell of alleged military preparations for revolution then in progress in Southern California. Two days later Taft, again reversing course, told Wickersham to proceed with the matter and set up a special grand jury to issue possible indictments. "There is not any doubt," Taft wrote, "that that corner of the country is a basis for most of the anarchists and industrial world workers, and for all the lawless flotsam and jetsam that proximity to the Mexican border thrusts into those two cities of San Diego and Los Angeles. We ought to take decided action." But Taft's recommendation was never acted upon, as the second special grand jury failed to issue any indictments.

3. Bull Moose

The San Diego free speech issue exemplified the divisions that cut through the Republican party in California and nationwide. In 1912 the country had appeared to be moving to the left. The Socialist party had swept to victory in hundreds of local elections throughout the nation, and its presidential candidate, Eugene Debs, threatened to be a major candidate in the 1912 presidential campaign. The *Times* and its choice for president, incumbent Taft, were well aware of the Socialist threat and decried the state and nation's leftward political shift.

The alliance between Taft and Otis, originating when Taft served in Theodore Roosevelt's cabinet, had grown during Taft's presidency. The two exchanged gifts, and Otis had been appointed by Taft in 1910 to a three-man commission representing the U.S. at the Mexican independence centennial celebration.

As Roosevelt's choice to succeed him in 1908, Taft had won the support of the California Lincoln-Roosevelt League. But the progressives had become increasingly alienated as Taft moved to the right and identified with Otis and other conservative, big business interests. In mid-1911 Taft denounced the California progressives. As the Taft Republicans became more conservative, the progressive "insurgent wing" of the party looked to their champion, former President Theodore Roosevelt, to be their candidate for the 1912 presidential nomination.

By 1912 Otis and Roosevelt had broken politically. Roosevelt described the *Times* publisher as "a consistent enemy of every movement for social and economic betterment." Otis, in turn, spoke of Roosevelt as "Teddy the Terrible," a "subordinate devil in the lower regions, a cleaner of cuspidors in Tophet."

Otis and the *Times* led the Taft forces in California during a highly emotional campaign for the May 14 primary. But the Roosevelt delegate slate won all but two of the state's Republican delegate seats in the primary. However, the California delegation, along with other progressive delegations, lost contested seats at the tense and bitter national convention. Outraged at the "steamroller" rulings of the convention's Taft-dominated committee, the Roosevelt delegates, led by Hiram Johnson, stormed out of the convention.

The next day, the contingent of 344 delegates who had walked out with Johnson founded the Progressive "Bull-Moose" Party. The California Progressives became its leaders, and Hiram Johnson, who chaired the national organizing committee, was selected by Roosevelt as his Vice-Presidential running mate.

The *Times*, furious at the defection of the Progressives, described them as "coiling and hissing and seething with the virus of anarchy." "The movement that you head," an editorial addressed the Bull-Moose leaders "is overripe, it is overrotten." The garbage barrel is the proper place for it . . . ."

The paper strongly backed Taft and printed every day the same poem on its editorial page entitled "Attitude of this Journal":

> For the country and the flag
> For the Constitution and the Courts
> For upholding the honour of the army and navy
> For orderly liberty under law
> For an ocean-to-ocean highway;
> For true freedom in the industries
> For unshackled labor, nation wide
> FOR PRESIDENT TAFT
>
> And against his allied antagonists
> Against political fads, freaks, and frenzy
> Against the Big Noise and the Big Stick
> Against the new fangled judicial recall
> Against free trade and free soup
> Against union conspiracy and misrule
> Against the un-American closed shop . . .

By election day the Taft forces were clearly in trouble. The *Times* kept on promoting the candidate, on election day running a page one headline, VOTE REPUBLICAN TODAY! VOTE TAFT!, with the warning, "Roosevelt Would Wipe Out Civil War Victory." But both Taft and Roosevelt (and Debs, who came in fourth, polling a surprising one million votes) lost to Democrat Woodrow Wilson. "No political occurence, within the recollection of a long life," Otis wrote to Taft's secretary after the election, "has ever produced in my mind such a profound regret. . . ."

Though Roosevelt trailed Taft nationwide, the California Progressives had managed to maintain control of the state's Republican party apparatus. Otis, now without links to Washington or Sacramento, complained of the "primary infamy" which allowed those "without real sympathy with the Republican Party . . . [to] hold the balance of power in its control." ". . . It's a shameful situation," the *Times* moaned, asking, "How long, O Lord. How long?"

As Otis and Taft commiserated on the "tammanyian of Johnson" and hoped "for the suppression of hypocrisy and the restoration of sanity in California," Governor Johnson announced his decision to run for reelection in 1914. The Times actively supported as his opponent in the Republican Primary District Attorney John Fredericks, despite the disapproval of his candidacy by the state's other nonprogressive Republican forces and Fredericks own farcical attempt to "avoid the tag of the *Los Angeles Times*." Moses Sherman, who kept in constant contact both with Harry Chandler and Fredericks, counted himself as "the largest individual contributor" to the Fredericks campaign.

Johnson, however, defeated Fredericks easily, winning a majority in both Los Angeles and San Francisco and becoming the first California governor to be elected to two consecutive four-year terms.

But the Progressives were not so successful in other parts of the country and their defeats led to a motion to disband the Bull-Moose Party and return to the Republican fold. Roosevelt's attacks on Woodrow Wilson's policies began to sound more and more like those of the Old Guard, but Otis would still have nothing to do with the man. "If there is any one political end more necessary to achieve than another," Otis wrote to Taft, "it is the utter defeat and extinguishment of the extraordinary aspirations of Theodore Roosevelt, the man who is a positive menace to the country."

By 1916 the Progressives decided to work with the regular Republicans, seeking unity through the nomination of Hiram Johnson as Republican vice-presidential candidate. They proposed holding their own convention which would put forth the same slate as the Republicans. Several Republican leaders, including Taft, endorsed unity and expressed the hope that the Republicans would select a candidate the Progressives could support. Taft wrote Otis explaining his desire not to make it difficult for the Progressives to come back to the party, but Otis still begrudged them the 1912 defeat and did not want the Republicans to reunify with this "progressive disturbing element." "There is no reason or excuse for it," Otis wrote Taft. "*It has in it the element of danger* and no element of victory."

"Republicans welcome to their ranks all men without distinction of race, color, or previous condition of servitude to Hiram Johnson," a *Times* editorial in March 1916 noted. "Whenever a crook . . . or any member of the Johnson plunderbund shall make an appearance at a Republican Club banquet, let us receive him courteously, welcome him warmly, and tell the steward to keep his eye on the spoons."

Otis worried that the less conservative Republicans were making deals with the Progressives behind his back. In May 1916 he wrote to Frances Keesling about a rumor that Keesling intended to make a bargain to divide up the California Republican delegation between the regular Republicans and the Progressives. "The *Los Angeles Times*," Otis wrote in opposition to seating Progressive delegates, "is supporting the Republican cause, pure and unadulterated."

As Otis fretted, the Republican and Progressive conventions began simultaneously in Chicago. When the two groups could not work out an agreement, the Progressives finally nominated Theodore Roosevelt. A few minutes later the Republicans nominated Charles Evans Hughes, a candidate the Progressives probably would have agreed to support. When Roosevelt declined in favor of Hughes, the Progressives were left without a candidate or a bargaining position. Ultimately, a number of Progressives decided to support Hughes, though the party as a whole refused to make the endorsement.

Hiram Johnson, now a candidate for the Republican nomination for senator, agreed to support Hughes in return for the support of the regular Republicans in his own senatorial campaign. But the California Old Guard continued to attack Johnson and worked to defeat him in the primary. Two regular Republicans had entered the race: Los Angeles banker Willis H. Booth, supported by the Southern Pacific's William Crocker, and Judge Walter Bordwell. The regulars maneuvered among themselves to eliminate one of the two candidates. Otis, on Taft's advice, urged Booth's withdrawal, but instead Crocker and Keesling convinced Bordwell to drop out.

A Charles Evans Hughes campaign visit to California highlighted the divisions within the party. The visit was arranged by the regulars (primarily Crocker and Keesling) who wanted to keep Hughes from any show of support for Johnson. Hughes's campaign manager, receiving conflicting reports on the "lack of cooperation" of the state's Republicans, urged the regulars to "harmonize all differences. . . . Particular attention has been called," he wrote to Crocker, "to the attitudes of the *Los Angeles Times*. . . ."

In Los Angeles, Progressive pressure guaranteed the presence of some Progressives on Hughes's reception committee. Chester Rowell wrote to Theodore Roosevelt of the irony of the "farcical love feast with E.T. Earl and Harrison Gray Otis in the front line of the reception committee." Hughes stayed the night at Otis's home and was accompanied throughout his California tour by Crocker or Keesling. The regulars viewed the trip more as a boost to the anti-Johnson campaign than a presidential trip, hoping that by disassociating Hughes from Johnson, the senatorial candidate might lose Republican votes.

As it turned out, Johnson lost nothing by the Hughes snub, but it possibly cost Hughes the presidency. While California voters sent Johnson to the Senate, Hughes lost the state to Wilson and California's thirteen electoral votes tipped the balance in favor of the Democrats.

A number of historians have pointed to one specific incident as the reason for Hughes's California loss. While simultaneously campaigning in Long Beach, California, Johnson and Hughes coincidentally stayed at the same hotel. Hughes made no recognition of the governor, which Johnson took as a personal affront. When Hughes lost the election, Otis railed at Johnson's treachery. The day after the election, the *Times* printed a page one editorial, signed by Otis, accusing Johnson and the Progressives of having sold out the Republican party, implying that the Johnson forces had made a deal with the Democrats to support Wilson in exchange for Democrat backing for Johnson.

The Progressives suggested that Otis, Crocker, and Keesling were the major guilty parties. The *Times*, according to an account by Chester Rowell, "at the very outset of the presidential campaign assigned its most experienced and accomplished professional liar, S. Fred Hogue — late chief prostitute of Patrick Calhoun's journalistic brothel — to instill malicious suicidal poison in the minds of the innocents who were then in charge of the Republican Party in California." Rowell counted Crocker and Keesling among the "innocents." These three—Otis/Hogue in malice, Keesling in something too contemptibly petty to rise to the dignity of malice, and Crocker in gullible innocence — took Charles E. Hughes prisoner at the state line of California and reduced him from a presidential candidate to the mere stalking horse of their treacherous man-hunt against Governor Johnson."

Keesling, though he put a large part of the blame on Chester Rowell, felt that the conflict was brought about by "an ill-advised attack on the part of the *Los Angeles Times*" who "by reason of their vindictiveness, accomplished the defeat of Hughes."

Otis, later accounts revealed, might have been personally behind the plan to keep Hughes away from Johnson. Hughes's Los Angeles arrangements had been organized by a close Otis ally — described by Rowell as Otis's "personal henchman" — who had written to Keesling of his plan to send a group of twelve to fifteen regular Republicans, including Fredericks, to the California border to meet Hughes and prevent any contact with the Progressives. Although the deception succeeded, it is also clear that Hughes's lack of decisiveness might have ultimately cost him the election.

4. A *"Permanent Peace"*

With World War I raging across the ocean and uprisings occurring to the south in Mexico, the issues of war and peace dominated Otis's thoughts in his last year. When he was not working on the *Times*'s illustrated weekly magazine—his last chore at the paper—he devoted time to the development of a "Plan for Ending Wars." He had first broached the subject in a letter to President Taft in June 1910. "Peace is a good thing, and we need it in our business," Otis wrote. "In fact, it is so good a thing that the American people ought to determine to have it, even if they have to fight for it."

Otis's proposal, developed over several years of correspondence with Taft, called for an International Alliance of Nations to make military and legal compact with each other agreeing not to go to war among themselves. "Bellicose and cocky nations" not in the organization who threatened the peace would be crushed by the more powerful compact nations. Such a plan, Otis hoped, could result in the "forced cessation of war." The plan did not call for disarmament; in fact, it suggested an increase in military expenditures of alliance countries in order to maintain their position of power over the other nations and suppress "domestic insurrection and revolution."

Otis published his World Peace Plan in a series that ran in the *Times* in May 1915, and sent copies in English and French to every official foreign government representative in Washington. He insisted that he had developed the cure to the world's problems and was determined to have his plan acted on, but he died before he could see his dream realized.

On July 30, 1917, while eating breakfast in bed at the home of his daughter, Marian Otis Chandler, Harrison Gray Otis died. Just before passing away, Otis murmured "I am gone." He was eighty years old.

A year before he died, Otis had deeded his Wilshire Boulevard home, the Bivouac, to Los Angeles County, to be used as a center for art and music. After the county picked up an option on the adjoining Earl estate, it began construction on a school for the arts, which was eventually called the Otis Art Institute.

Otis left a political testament for his daughter and son-in-law which called for the maintenance of his militaristic traditions, hostility toward organized labor, and a continuation of his conservative, pro-business outlook. "Stand Fast, Stand Firm, Stand Sure, Stand True," Otis wrote —the words that had become the *Times* insignia during his reign as publisher.

The Otis slogan was also inscribed on a monument to the *Times*'s publisher commissioned after his death by a group of downtown business and professional men. The huge statue portrayed Otis attired in his army outfit, his arm raised and finger pointing as if to lead his troops onward. On one side of Otis stood a bronze soldier and on the other a newsboy, representing the two facets of his life. "The two great passions of his life," *Times* writer John M'Groarty wrote the day after the General's death, "were the flag of his country, and Los Angeles, the city of his adoption. . . . The city itself is his monument."

PART II

1917 – 1941

"The Richest Man in Southern California"

"If Harry Chandler had the same moral shrewdness and character as his commercial intelligence," county supervisor John Anson Ford said of his long-time opponent, "Los Angeles would now be the finest city in America."

The eldest of four children, Harry Chandler was born in May 1864 to New England farmers Moses Knight Chandler and Emma Jane Little. He grew up in the small town of Landaff, New Hampshire. As a boy, he delivered papers in the area, but early on he showed signs of restless ambition. "He thinks big," his parents had told their neighbors.

Young Chandler went to Hanover, New Hampshire, in the fall of 1882 to attend Dartmouth college, but he never began his studies. When several students challenged the freshman-to-be to dive into an ice-covered vat of starch in a nearby factory, Chandler took the dare and jumped in. He immediately developed a case of pneumonia and a hemorrhage of the lungs. Doctors told Chandler he might not have long to live and advised him to try the dry and warm climate of Southern California and hope for the best.

In 1883 Chandler arrived in Los Angeles with little money, a bad cough, and no idea of what lay ahead. He found a room near The Plaza at a cheap boardinghouse and started to look for work. After other lodgers, fearful of possible contagion, complained of his cough, Harry, still jobless, was evicted from his lodgings. For days he wandered aimlessly around Los Angeles, feeling sick and rejected. One afternoon, while looking in shop windows, a photograph of a child with a soft, round, almost perfectly proportioned face—the portrait of the ideal American boy in post Civil War

America—caught his eye. As a boy, Chandler had been photographed a number of times because of his features. Looking closer at the picture, he recognized himself. He felt it was a sign that his fortunes were about to change.

Soon afterward Harry met a woman whose husband suffered from the same type of lung problem. The man, a Dr. Nichols, welcomed Chandler to his farm on the southern edge of the San Fernando Valley, in the area now called the Cahuenga Pass. The young New Englander, camping out in a tent, broke horses and picked fruit in exchange for a share of the crops. Chandler sold his fruit to the threshing crew at a nearby ranch, part of the huge 50,000 acre Van Nuys/Lankershim property in the San Fernando Valley. When the ranch supervisors discovered Chandler's profitable business, a foreman accused the twenty-year-old New Englander of selling liquor to his workers. Chandler was about to be escorted off the property when he spied ranch owner J.B. Van Nuys on horseback with several associates. Chandler appealed to Van Nuys and convinced him to allow him to continue his business.

Within the year Harry Chandler accumulated $3,000. He decided to return to Dartmouth for the fall term. But within two days after returning East he started hemorrhaging again, and he returned to Southern California, this time to stay for good.

The next year Chandler found a job as a clerk in the circulation department of the *Los Angeles Times*. He quickly advanced to become supervisor of a delivery route for some 1,400 subscribers. Chandler soon recognized the crucial importance of an effective circulation system for a newspaper in preautomobile Los Angeles. In later years Chandler proudly boasted that when the Los Angeles River flooded after a terrible storm he had delivered papers by rowboat to keep customers happy and hold the route intact.

Newspaper distribution was then largely handled by independent contractors, and Chandler soon decided to go into the distribution business for himself. He purchased several routes, not only of the *Times* but also for other Los Angeles papers. "Through a friend, I secretly bought the circulation routes of the *Herald*, entirely unknown of course to my ex-partner," Chandler wrote of the 1890 period. "Then I hired a big tallyho and one day shipped off the entire *Herald* circulation and carrier crew in the San Bernardino mountains for a five-day holiday. When the time came to distribute the *Herald*, there weren't any boys to do it, and the confusion was so great for the next few days that *The Times* put on a subscription campaign and got about half the subscribers of the *Herald*."

Chandler used the distribution monopoly he had acquired in his secret purchase of the *Herald* route to kill the *Time*'s main competition, the morning *Tribune*, then owned by Otis's arch-rival, Colonel Henry Boyce.

"My scheme was to starve out the *Tribune*," Chandler boasted. "With two of the three morning paper distribution systems under my control, it would be simple to play them together against the *Tribune*. If a *Times* subscriber quit, we could swing him to the *Herald*, whereas he might have gone to the *Tribune* if left alone. If a *Herald* subscriber quit we could swing him to the *Times*."

The *Tribune* folded soon after. Acting swiftly and secretly through a third party, Chandler bought the *Tribune* plant, its machinery, subscription lists, and circulation routes for very little money. He then approached Otis, who had heard of the secret buyer and worried about the potential new competitor.

"Can you find out," Otis asked the distribution man, "who bought the *Tribune* in?" "I think I can," Chandler answered. "The press I understand was taken back by the manufacturer, but the rest of the equipment was purchased by a speculator." "Find him," Otis instructed, "and we'll make a deal with him." "I won't have to go far," Chandler replied. "As a matter of fact, I bought it myself." Soon after, young Chandler became the *Times*'s circulation manager. As he rose in the hierarchy, he also began to court the General's daughter.

Chandler's first wife, Magdalena Schlador, the daughter of a Berlin merchant whom he had married in 1888, had died shortly after the birth of their second child in 1892. Two years later Chandler married Marion Otis, one of the *Times* publisher's three daughters. It was a June wedding, and not long after, Harry Chandler was appointed business manager of the *Times*.

The thirty-year-old Chandler now began to look into real estate throughout Southern California and farther south in Baja, Mexico. Systematically Chandler organized a number of syndicates among the town's leading bankers, railroad men, industrialists, and real estate entrepreneurs. By World War I, Chandler had created the largest real estate network in the state.

Chandler became the consummate maneuverer, packaging deals, investing in a diverse range of businesses, and providing political and economic leadership for the local business establishment. He was a political conservative, having changed his Democratic party affiliation in 1896 after the presidential campaign of William Jennings Bryan adopted a number of populist causes. Chandler pursued the antilabor, open shop policies of his father-in-law, writing with his wife after Otis's death: "*The Times* will continue to be THE TIMES—*The Times* of General Otis, *The Times* that he made. Men may die, but influences do not."

Unlike the General, however, Chandler was extremely adept at behind the scenes activities. Chandler was not a "true believer" like Otis and could easily discard ideological positions if other objectives warranted it.

Success in business matters provided the framework for Chandler's plans and his means were determined by those goals. Political or social objectives were either extensions of, or subservient to, Chandler's goals of creating an economic empire and developing a united business establishment in pursuit of overall Southern California expansion.

Chandler continued to use one of General Otis's early *Times* features—the Midwinter—as a major promotional event in which the entire local establishment participated. "The Los Angeles Chamber of Commerce and all of us are doing all we can to have this Midwinter number sent all over the United States," Chandler's colleague Moses Sherman wrote to another local businessman about the 1915 Midwinter. Each businessman purchased several hundred dollars worth of Midwinters and arranged with the Chamber of Commerce to distribute them across the country in an effort to keep the Los Angeles boom going and attract capital to the region. "Every good citizen with money who is brought to Southern California to live, through the Midwinter *Times*," Sherman continued in his letter, "helps you and helps me." Chandler felt he had a mission to develop the community—a mission built around his pursuit of more power, more land, more industry, more "things," as Carey McWilliams put it. Chandler's economic strategy centered around the idea of population growth stimulating economic activity and, most especially, real estate values, through suburban development. When a temporary lull in Southern California immigration occurred during and immediately after World War I, Chandler worried that the decrease in tourism might have been partially responsible. Local hotel owners charging high winter rates to make up for slack summer tourism had driven people away, the Chamber of Commerce complained. Chandler decided to intercede. He set up a meeting with the hotel owners and local businessmen. Out of the discussions came the idea for the All Year Club, an organization specifically designed to encourage year round tourism and permanent immigration. The hotel owners contributed the initial funds for the organization. Afterward, the business group arranged for the county board of supervisors to give funds to the organization in the public interest. Each year the businessmen who served as directors of the All Year Club hosted a luncheon for the supervisors at the elite California Club and each year the county earmarked larger and larger appropriations to keep the club going. In this manner the county, Supervisor John Anson Ford later pointed out, subsidized new industries and real estate development and contributed to the overall strategy defined by Chandler and his associates. The subsidies lasted over thirty-five years, until the late 1950s, when the county supervisors finally stopped the payments.

The All Year Club, with Chandler its leading director, launched a massive promotional campaign in the 1920s which fostered Southern California's image as the land of the "boosters." "Southern California is America's ideal Summer as well as Winter Resort," read an announcement on *Times* stationery, which ran the summer months' "average mean temperature" bordering the letterhead.

Chandler designed a *Times* "Make a Friend for California" contest, under which businessmen urged their employees to send letters throughout the country advising people to settle in Los Angeles. Chandler provided a kit complete with a mimeographed sheet of facts and figures and a sample letter. The best booster letter received an award.

Boosterism by the 1920's had, in the language of the *Times,* become synonymous with Americanism. The *Times* sponsored a number of essay contests, not only on the *Times* itself ("Why the *Times* is Number 1" was the theme of one contest), but also on how America was best, and what Americanism really meant.

Harry Chandler had become the most important member of Southern California's probusiness establishment. He operated in a whirlwind of activity, joining over fifty boards of directors, setting up numerous dummy corporations and secret trusts, providing investment capital for a number of budding Los Angeles enterprises, and acting as the leading promoter of the region. The Los Angeles Realty Board voted Chandler its "Most Useful Citizen Award," and he became the subject of numerous profiles including ones in the *New York Times* and the *Saturday Evening Post.* "He is mixed up in so many ventures," the *Post* remarked, "that nobody, with the possible exception of himself, has ever been able to count them."

Chandler organized his famous $1,000-a-plate luncheons, to which various businessmen came expecting to provide money for one or another Chandler-backed activity. "All businessmen, heads of stores, heads of banks, that sort of thing," local merchant Neil Petree recalled, "naturally knew Mr. Chandler. . . . Sooner or later you'd hear from him." At the luncheons, "he [Chandler]," his son-in-law Earle Crowe wrote, "talked with the persuasiveness that men in Los Angeles later learned to dread and admire."

While he promoted Los Angeles and took leadership in the local establishment, Harry Chandler became an enormously wealthy man. Estimates of his fortune ranged from a low of $200 million to a high of over a half a billion dollars; the *Times* newsroom had it that he was the eleventh richest man in the world. This was characteristic of the attitude summed up by Chandler's bitterest enemy, Hiram Johnson, who called the Timesman "probably the richest man in Southern California, perhaps in all the West." So many of his promotions were disguised investments, so much of his real estate constantly shifted in value, and so many of his investments were conducted through other parties such as associate Moses Sherman or through his sons and nephews, that it was almost impossible to trace the extent of the Chandler empire. Reformer John Randolph Haynes was particularly perturbed to learn from one of his sources in the IRS that Chandler paid only $2,000 a year in taxes in the early 1920s.

By nature secretive, Chandler, on his deathbed, is said to have ordered the destruction of his and General Otis's papers. He lived in a modest way, gaining a reputation as something of a skinflint. Though not strongly religious—he was a Congregationalist and a Mason—he abstained from alcohol, backed organizations like the Salvation Army, and lived very much in the style of a man who had made his money and knew more about how to invest it than spend it.

The 1920s, when his economic activity reached its zenith, was his decade. A conservative, strait-laced man, tall and imposing in appearance in contrast to his soft-featured baby face, he displayed throughout his life a reserved manner. But behind the scenes he was a tempest, gladly rubbing shoulders with the roughest and meanest provocateurs, police spies, and speculators, who also comprised his circle. He became the man most responsible for molding the distinctive character of Southern California. In the minds of the realtors and promoters, he was Los Angeles's most useful citizen.

CHAPTER 7

The Owens Valley Water War

1. "If You Don't Get the Water, You Won't Need It"

In Southern California water has been the essential prerequisite for growth. With water, the semiarid coastal plain has been transformed into a rich agricultural region. But there has always been a problem of supply; available water sources throughout the southwest have been limited. "With the progress of civilization," the superintendent of Los Angeles' water department, William Mulholland, noted in 1902, "first the Mission, then the Pueblo, and finally, the advent of the American, the importance of the water supply was emphasized by the marked way in which the relative growth of each town was measured by the greater or less abundance of this life-giving element."

Before the turn of the century, the water supply for Los Angeles primarily came from "zanjas," a complex series of irrigating ditches set up to divert water from the natural bed of the underground Los Angeles River. The zanja source was more than sufficient in the era before the boom, but the massive migrations of the late 1880s threatened to tax the area's limited resources if they continued. When the population began to level off at around 100,000 during the 1890s, several accounts showed that the Los Angeles River supply was more than adequate, capable of serving a population of 220,000 to 300,000 by conservative estimates. "It is evident that the possibilities of the future are ample to meet all requirements . . . ," the boosting *Los Angeles Times* reassured alarmists in the midst of a protracted dry spell in 1899. "There is no need for precipitancy of action, there being no pressing need for immediate extension of irrigation works.''

To expansionists like the *Times's* owners, a stable population and defined urban boundaries were unacceptable. The boom, with its rapid subdivisions of large unirrigated lands, had provided an early model for land development and population growth. Subdivision, besides offering enormous profits for investors, meant greater population, which, in turn, meant a thriving city. But more population necessitated more water.

The issue concerned many in the town's power structure. Their first step was to put the old Los Angeles Water Company, a privately owned operation, into the hands of the city, where it would be run by the new board of Water Commissioners. The agreement between the city and the water company had been worked out by former city engineer Fred Eaton, a recently retired mayor who had been strongly supported by the *Times*. Eaton, who took a special interest in water matters, had the aid of close friends, engineers J.B. Lippincott and Bill Mulholland, in the final transaction. Mulholland became superintendent of the new municipally owned company, the position he had occupied with the old water company, and Eaton was named consulting engineer of the new Water Board. Board members included banker J.M. Elliot, who had spoken of the need for more water for Los Angeles, and Harry Chandler's friend and intimate business associate streetcar owner Moses Sherman, an influential political figure among the Republican Old Guard.

Mulholland had an epigram: "If you don't get the water, you won't need it." "He knew," Lippincott later said of his friend, "that the available water supply of Southern California was the measure of and limit of its growth."

Growth also meant settlement and subdivision in the unpopulated fringe areas of the region, such as the San Fernando Valley, twenty miles to the north of Los Angeles. "Doubtless these lands," Mulholland commented in one of his annual reports to the water commissioners, "if irrigated, would soon become densely populated suburban additions to a Greater Los Angeles."

The Board of Water Commissioners' main concern was to find a new water supply to support the kind of expansion envisioned by Los Angeles's business leaders. Supplies from the immediate areas near Los Angeles, as detailed by Mulholland's first three reports and the U.S. Geological Survey (which had begun to search for new water sources for Los Angeles as early as 1900) were eventually ruled out, since those areas were "commercially and politically" linked to a Greater Los Angeles and their water was necessary for large scale regional expansion. Fred Eaton promoted another possibility to meet the requirements for growth. It concerned lands two hundred miles northeast of Los Angeles, well beyond the city's potentially expanding perimeters in a valley that rested below the High Sierras near the California/Nevada border.

The Owens Valley, centrally located in California's Inyo County and populated by small farmers and sheepherders, was, at the turn of the century, largely unirrigated land. Most of the valley's 256,000 acres were semidesert, but the irrigated and cultivated land along the Owens River which passed through the center of the valley was rich and lush with corn, hard grains, and apple crops.

In 1902 the U.S. Congress, backed by the Theodore Roosevelt administration, created the Bureau of Land Reclamation to sponsor land development, particularly for the Southwest. J.B. Lippincott, who had done extensive work for both the Los Angeles city government and local businessmen, was appointed the bureau's supervising engineer for California. Though Lippincott joined the Federal Reclamation Service, he still maintained his status as a consultant for Los Angeles and its business organizations, advising the Board of Water Commissioners on its plans to expand Los Angeles's water supply.

In June 1903 Lippincott and Reclamation Service engineer J.C. Clausen undertook a surveying expedition to the Owens Valley. Clausen immediately envisioned a major reclamation project to capture the spill from the Owens River and use the reclaimed waters for thousands of acres of Inyo land. Once the reclaimed waters were available, the Owens Valley could become open to homesteading and small farm development. Clausen filed a report and urged that all public lands in the area be withdrawn and reserved for possible reclamation and reservoir uses. The government approached farmers about relinquishing their water rights. Almost all, having heard the rumors concerning the government's plan to develop the valley, obliged; 90 percent of the holders of water rights did so within the year.

Through the spring and fall of 1904 Clausen began pushing for the acquisition of key Inyo lands, especially the 22,000 acre Rickey Ranch, strategically located along the Owens River. But Lippincott stalled and postponed action. While holding off Clausen and assuring the Owens farmers — "socially" as he later testified — of the possibility of the reclamation project, Lippincott by February 1904 was preparing his boss, the head of the California Reclamation Service, for "a possibility of our [the Reclamation Service] not constructing the Owens Valley project, but of our stepping aside in favor of the city of Los Angeles."

Fred Eaton, who had already purchased some land in Inyo County, claimed the idea of using Owens Valley water for Los Angeles originated with him. Eaton foresaw an aqueduct, beginning at the Owens River, travelling 230 miles south, over two mountain chains, to terminate in Los Angeles. The costs might be enormous, but Los Angeles's business interests, fully committed to the notion of rapid and large scale expansion, would undoubtedly provide the political muscle to insure such a project's approval.

Furthermore, unbeknownst to others, a small land syndicate of some of the most powerful men in Southern California had taken an option on one of the biggest farms in the San Fernando Valley. A three-year option on the 16,000-acre Porter ranch had been purchased for $50,000 in October 1903. The syndicate included General Otis of the *Times*, E.H. Harriman of the Southern Pacific, some title men and bankers, E.T. Earl of the *Express*, and Moses Sherman of the Water Board. These businessmen did not intend to farm the land, but inclined instead toward suburbanization and subdivision. San Fernando development, they knew, would require a tremendous volume of water. No existing supply could meet such needs, but the 200-mile aqueduct project of their political ally and associate Fred Eaton could.

In 1904 the three water men, Eaton, Mulholland, and Lippincott, took trips to Owens Valley. Lippincott, though he had done his surveys of the Owens River in the name of the Reclamation Service, was reimbursed over $5,000 by the city of Los Angeles, on whose payroll he still remained. In August 1904 Eaton and Lippincott took what they later called a "camping trip" through Inyo County. The next month, William Mulholland, the Irish-born water superintendent for Los Angeles — the "water warrior" as he was later called — also made an expedition to Inyo to judge the feasibility of Eaton's aqueduct idea for the Los Angeles Water Board.

Soon after Mulholland's return, on November 28, 1904, the syndicate which had purchased the option on the Porter Ranch incorporated as the San Fernando Mission Land Company. Fully aware of Water Board plans for Owens Valley, thanks to Moses Sherman's membership in both the syndicate and the Water Board, it picked up the option to buy four months later. The price was $500,000—$150,000 down in cash, the rest to be paid by issuing bonds. George Porter, the original owner of the ranch (brother-in-law of former *Mirror* print shop owner Tom Caystile) was included in the new syndicate. "I can't tell you what's in the wind," Harry Chandler told an associate he hoped to get involved in the syndicate, "but there's a big hen on, and there'll be a boom in the valley when the deal is put through that will boost real estate up there, sure."

That winter Eaton returned to the Owens Valley to purchase additional lands, including the large Rickey Ranch. Eaton, saying nothing of his ties with Los Angeles, represented himself as a federal government man to some of the Owens farmers. In May 1905 Eaton sold the Rickey lands to the Los Angeles Water Board for the identical price he had paid, though he kept the ranch's 4,400-plus head of cattle. Eaton also asked for and secured a $10-a-day retainer for the time spent on each transaction.

On July 28, 1905, J.B. Lippincott brought up the matter of the original Owens Valley reclamation project before the California Reclamation Service. Though bitterly opposed by Clausen, Lippincott received the support of reclamation chief F.H. Newell to suspend all Reclamation Service activity for the Owens Valley and leave the area for the city of Los Angeles.

Lippincott's actions prepared the way for the next step in the Water Board's plans, to make public the proposal. During the winter of 1904–1905, Los Angeles's water commissioners had informed the city's newspaper publishers of the Owens Valley aqueduct idea, asking them to keep the subject secret until the completion of the Inyo land purchases. On July 29, 1905, one day after the Reclamation Service's decision, the *Los Angeles Times* violated the pledge and broke the story. The water campaign was on.

2. *"Bright Days in The San Fernando Valley"*

"TITANIC PROJECT TO GIVE CITY A RIVER," headlined the *Times* story, whose lead spoke of "the greatest scheme for water development ever attempted on the American continent." The *Times* praised Eaton and Lippincott and the water commissioners, and tied the aqueduct project to the potential for growth. Not only would Los Angeles expand, the *Times* predicted, but that expansion could now proceed in the San Fernando Valley — "a golden message," it noted, for the San Fernando landowners. "The farming lands of the [San Fernando] valley," the *Times* stated in a July 29 editorial, "will reap as great a blessing from this glorious water enterprise as will the dwellers within the city's gates. Let all the people say 'Amen!'"

Within a matter of weeks the Los Angeles City Council authorized a special election for September 7, less than a month away, to approve a $1.5-million bond to begin work on the aqueduct. Only prolabor Councilman Arthur Houghton dissented. For the next several weeks the *Times* carried on a daily campaign to convince Angelenos of the necessity and benefits of the project. "With this water problem out of the way," the *Times* told its readers on August 11, "the growth of Los Angeles will leap forward as never before. Adjacent towns will soon be knocking at our doors for admission in order to secure the benefits to be derived from our never-failing supply of life-giving water, and Greater Los Angeles will become a magnificent reality."

The *Times* used its own outside "technical experts," men like William Mulholland and *Times* writer Allen Kelley. "Los Angeles has arrived very close to the limit of her growth fixed by the supply of water obtainable this side of the mountains," Kelley wrote. "What the consequence of a series of drought years or failure of the Los Angeles rivulet from any cause would be, any property owner in Los Angeles can figure out readily for himself.''

Drought scares had in fact been stirred up. "Facts relating to water development," the *Times* warned the second day after the aqueduct announcement, "which have been kept secrets lest they create a panic are now freely discussed." But panic was precisely what the *Times* and its allies helped create. IF LOS ANGELES DOES NOT GET OWENS WATER NOW SHE NEVER WILL NEED IT, Mulholland was quoted by the *Times* on August 18. On September 1 he warned that Los Angeles might run out of water within a few weeks if current consumption rates were continued.

The apparently radical *Herald*, then secretly controlled by Otis, echoed the *Times*'s prodevelopment stance. "Three hundred thousand population for Los Angeles," a *Herald* editorial proclaimed four days before the election, "that is the 'war cry' of the *Herald*. . . . Following the announcement that the Los Angeles water nightmare is a thing of the past, thousands of people in the east who have been held back by misgivings will come to Los Angeles for permanent homes, bringing millions of dollars for investment." If the bonds didn't pass, the *Herald* warned, "building would come to a standstill; lack of employment would force workers to leave the city. . . .''

Besides the *Times* and the working-class-oriented *Herald*, the *Los Angeles Express*, with its audience of progressive-minded businessmen and professionals, praised the aqueduct proposal. Readers of the three papers were unaware of the San Fernando Valley syndicate membership and its potential profits for the papers' owners.

On August 24 Hearst's *Los Angeles Examiner*, the only paper which had expressed reservations about the plan, came out with a lead news story exposing the activities of the San Fernando Mission Land Company. The article revealed, through a diligent search of the public recorder's office, who had purchased what land and when. "That these persons [Otis, Harriman, Earl, Sherman, et al.] are moved by self-interest in the matter does not, of course, show that the project itself is bad," the next day's article cautioned, "but it DOES weaken the force of what they urge, since the motive impelling them is merely mercenary.''

Over the next several days, enormous pressure was brought to bear on the *Examiner* and its editor Henry Lowenthal. Although the Hearst paper had modified its views since its origins as the voice of Los Angeles labor, it still occasionally opposed the local business forces. Lowenthal later testified how advertisers threatened to withdraw their revenue. When Lowenthal raised objections to the plan at a meeting where Mulholland outlined the proaqueduct position, he was denounced as an "anarchist." Finally, a week before the election, and only six days after the syndicate story, William Randolph Hearst made a personal visit and met with the local business establishment. The profit-minded, increasingly conservative

Hearst quickly ordered the *Examiner* to change its position and endorse the bonds. For the next day's edition Hearst himself wrote the page one editorial under the head, THE CITY MUST HAVE WATER. The newspaper consensus was complete.

The central issue in the aqueduct election was the future of the San Fernando Valley. "To take more water for the city from the underground reservoir," *Times* writer Allen Kelley noted, "would stop the growth of the surrounding country, . . . [and] set a limit to the growth of Los Angeles." That surrounding country meant the San Fernando Valley. "It is certain," Kelley wrote in the *Times* during the campaign, "that after the basin shall have been filled to the saturation point [with Owens Valley water], more water than Los Angeles needs will come through the conduit and may be diverted into canals and used for irrigating in the San Fernando Valley."

San Fernando ranchers had previously been denied access to Los Angeles River water, thus preventing subdivision and urbanization of the valley. But with the Owens aqueduct, the city of Los Angeles and the San Fernando developers had ample water for their respective needs. Subdivision and suburbanization were the key concerns of the San Fernando Mission Land Company, and after the *Examiner* attacked the syndicate for those "mercenary ends," the *Times* defensively answered that the syndicate would only use Owens water "should they require more."

While the *Times* tried to defuse the *Examiner* charges, the syndicate undertook a massive advertising campaign to explain the relationship between future San Fernando land development and Owens water. In tones reminiscent of the 1887 boom ads, the syndicate announced the sale of small subdivided lots in San Fernando. "Have a Contract for a Lot in your Pocket When the Big Bonds are Voted," urged one *Times* ad three days before the election. "An ideal suburb of Los Angeles," another syndicate ad announced in promoting "Pacoima," its first major subdivision. "Pacoima Will Feel the First Benefits of the Owens River Water and Every Purchaser Investing Now Will Reap the Fruits of His Wisdom in Gratifying Profits." On the day before the election a syndicate ad promised that the price on every unsold lot would rise 10 percent the next day if the water bonds carried.

A week before the vote a committee of representatives from both progressive and right-wing business factions came back from the Owens Valley with a strong endorsement of the aqueduct. Labor also backed the measure, responding to the aqueduct booster's promise of "More Water, More Wages." "It is not too much to say," the *Times* editorialized on election eve, "that every person who votes in the negative on Friday night will be placing himself in the attitude of an *enemy of the city* and will be opposing its progress and prosperity."

With just a handful of opponents and no serious organized opposition,

Los Angeles voters went to the polls on September 7. Those who turned out—less than half the number of voters who cast ballots in the municipal elections in 1904—voted overwhelmingly (a margin of 10,693 to 754) for the bonds.

"It's a GO, The Bonds Are Carried," syndicate ads exclaimed the next day; "Now for Pacoima, watch us grow."

The *Times* was equally exuberant. "MAGNIFICENT CHORUS OF VOTERS SHOUTS FOR OWENS RIVER PROJECT," its full page headline read. "Los Angeles joyously announces to the world that she has just begun to grow" an editorial jubilantly proclaimed. "Water made Southern California; water is the vital element of growth in all the communities of this land of Sunshine."

"Truly the Lord has been good to Southern California," Mayor McAleer commented when he first set his eyes on the Owens River water. But Inyo County residents had a different reaction. On August 3, 1905, the *Inyo Register* first broke word of Los Angeles's plan. "LOS ANGELES PLOTS DESTRUCTION," the *Register* proclaimed in its headlines. "WOULD TAKE OWENS RIVER, LAY LANDS WASTE, RUIN PEOPLE, HOMES AND COMMUNITIES." Inyo's fears had substance. "Do not go to Inyo County," Bill Mulholland told an acquaintance. "We are going to turn that country dry."

Owens residents began to organize opposition. Independence land registrar S.W. Austin, husband of Inyo's novelist Mary Austin, wrote to President Roosevelt: "The settlement of this large and now arid area will prove of far greater value to California and the contiguous parts of Nevada than the supplying of the city of Los Angeles with water. . . . In justice to the people here," Austin pleaded to Roosevelt, do not "abandon the Owens River project."

Austin and several members of the Reclamation Service filed complaints with the secretary of the interior about engineer Lippincott for his double role on the Owens Valley matters as representative of the U.S. government and employee of the Los Angeles Board of Water Commissioners. After the secretary ordered an investigation, Lippincott was suspended from duty. He then took the job of number two man, under Bill Mulholland, in the construction of the aqueduct where, in addition to his consultations, he acted as patronage dispenser for jobs and influence.

Through 1905 and 1906 the people in Inyo attempted to block aqueduct construction. Their strongest argument centered on the Los Angeles Water Board's underlying motivation to use the water for speculative purposes for the San Fernando Valley subdivisions, and as a means of attracting a much larger population to the city. "The real purpose of the whole undertaking," Inyo resident W.A. Chalfant wrote, "was not the alleged city need, put forward as an excuse, but the diverting of Owens River from its natural watershed and from use on the lands which so much needed it, to areas in the vicinity of Los Angeles for irrigation and speculative purposes.''

"Los Angeles wants something she has not for a population that has not arrived," an Inyo pamphlet asserted, "and has endeavored to get it by means that have neither justice nor good civics to recommend them.''

In Washington, California Congressman Sylvester Smith, who represented the Inyo area, tried to add an amendment to a right of way bill needed by Los Angeles to begin aqueduct construction. Smith argued that the Owens water could be shared between the city of Los Angeles and Owens Valley. Los Angeles engineers, Smith pointed out, had spoken in terms of 2,500 inches of supplemental water flow as an ample supply for the city's domestic needs, even anticipating population growth up through at least 1925. The Owens watershed, on the other hand, could provide at least 10,000 inches of water flow. Smith's amendment called for primary allotments to owners of vested rights in Inyo; then 10,000 inches for Los Angeles's domestic purposes (four times Lippincott's estimate of existing needs); then for irrigation in Owens Valley; and finally, any remaining surplus to go to Los Angeles, for whatever use it chose.

The *Times* blasted Congressman Smith for his efforts. "He [Smith] is the man" an editorial declared, ". . . who had the impudence to declare that he would permit the city to take from Owens Valley only so much water as he deemed necessary for domestic use.''

Pro-Los Angeles advocates in Congress, led by California Senator Frank Flint, opposed any interference with Los Angeles's use of the Owens water. Flint argued on the basis of the greatest good for the greatest number, insisting that Los Angeles had the right to use the water for outlying irrigation in the San Fernando Valley. With the right of way bill under increasing opposition, Flint took his case to Theodore Roosevelt. A conference between the president and Mulholland and other Los Angeles representatives took place in June 1906. Mindful of the political clout of the Los Angeles business establishment, Roosevelt not only endorsed the aqueduct but supported Los Angeles's demand that it use the water as it saw fit, including for outlying irrigation. Five days later the right of way bill passed Congress without Smith's amendment. "The government held Owens Valley," W.A. Chalfant bitterly concluded, "while Los Angeles skinned it.''

The Los Angeles Water Board still had one further obstacle to overcome. After the Bureau of Land Reclamation, under Lippincott's proddings, dropped its Inyo project in favor of Los Angeles, a number of farmers and ranchers prepared to lay claim to the restored public lands which had been withdrawn for reclamation. The Los Angeles Water

Board, fearing future disputes over water rights, once again looked to the federal government for help. The head of the U.S. Forest Service, Gifford Pinchot, a "warm personal friend" of Los Angeles City Attorney and aqueduct board official W.B. Matthews, responded by extending the boundaries of the Sierra Forest Preserve through much of the Owens Valley, thus closing off all public land within the "preserve" from homesteading. The land, which the government labelled "forest," "included square leagues covered with grass and sagebrush," according to Chalfant, "where the only trees within any reasonable distance were those that had been planted by settlers." The Forest Service held the land until such time as Los Angeles could monopolize all claims on the property. Five years later, the Taft administration rescinded Pinchot's order and the water board laid claim to the lands.

Though Angelenos had approved the $1.5-million bond to purchase Inyo lands and water rights, additional money for major financing of the project still had to be raised. A second referendum for a $23-million bond was called in 1907. Once again, a united business coalition strongly backed the measure. The small Socialist party provided some opposition, but the major attack against the project came from the *Los Angeles Daily News*. The *News*, begun in 1906 by local progressive Samuel T. Clover, was not unfriendly to the local business forces, and Harry Chandler had even approached Clover to invest in the San Fernando syndicate.

By the time the second aqueduct election got under way, Clover, who didn't join the syndicate, had become a strong opponent of the project. Clover hired his own "experts," who reported that Owens water might not be fit for drinking or other domestic purposes because of a high alkaline level acquired by its lengthy traveling. The *Times* retorted by labeling Clover "Alkaline Sammy" and disregarded *News*'s claims. Clover's strongest argument, however, remained the charge against the San Fernando land syndicate and its speculative activities.

In the midst of the campaign, Mayor A.C. Harper, a strong booster of the aqueduct, asked Otis to help repudiate the syndicate accusations. On May 22, 1907, Otis answered with an open letter to the mayor, reproduced in the *Times* two days later. Otis stated that he had sold his interest in the San Fernando Mission Land company in February 1905, well before any discussion of the aqueduct became public. "The charge that either myself or the *Los Angeles Times* have been influenced in our advocacy of the Owens River project by private interest therefore falls to the ground," Otis wrote in his inimitable style. "I repudiate the false and foolish allegations of the knockers and 'defy the alligators' whether these crustaceans inhabit the alkaline water of Owens lake or merely bivouac-dry for the time being in the hostile camps of the knockers in Los Angeles."

That evening the *News* replied, gleefully pointing out that an August 23,

1906 *Times* editorial (a short box in the "Pen Points" editorial column) had stated that "the general manager of the *Times* holds a small interest" in the syndicate lands. The *News*, however, had little power to stop the water coalition. The second bond issue also passed by a large margin and Sam Clover went out of business.

Major construction on the aqueduct got under way in 1908 and was plagued from the outset by cost overruns and problems in financing the water bonds. Controversies also continued to flare over syndicate land speculations, and one of the first acts of the reform administration which came to power in 1909 was to remove syndicate member Moses Sherman from the Board of Water Commissioners.

Just before his removal, Sherman joined Harry Chandler, San Fernando Mission Land Company president L. C. Brand, Hollywood subdivider H. J. Whitley, and Otto Brant of Title Insurance and Trust company in the biggest real estate deal ever made in Southern California. The new syndicate, called the Los Angeles Suburban Homes Company, purchased 47,500 acres in the San Fernando Valley, acquiring the land from the Los Angeles Farm and Milling Company, the corporate child of San Fernando's Lankershim and Van Nuys interests, for $2.5 million. Wheat farmer James Lankershim had originally purchased the ranch in 1869 from former California Governor Pio Pico. On Lankershim's death in 1882, the ranch was taken over by a former employee, Isaac Van Nuys. With his health starting to deteriorate in 1909, Van Nuys was open to Chandler's notion of a major subdivision of the old San Fernando wheat and barley ranch. Van Nuys sold his land, the largest undivided piece of property in Los Angeles County, and joined the new Los Angeles Suburban Homes syndicate.

The two syndicate tracts encompassed nearly the entire San Fernando Valley from the present sites of Burbank on the east to Tarzana on the west. The Tarzana subdivision had originally been part of General Otis's "Mil Flores" estate carved out of the Los Angeles Suburban Homes purchase, and the 540-acre tract was later sold to Edgar Rice Burroughs, the author of the Tarzan books.

The syndicates subdivided the huge tracts into small plots in the hope that townships would spring up and boost the value of each new "suburban" lot. Chandler personally held onto large portions of both subdivided and unsubdivided lots, usually the choicest, most valuable real estate. On part of his land, he helped construct and lavishly decorate Van Nuys Boulevard, the major thoroughfare which was soon worth several million dollars alone.

By the time construction on the aqueduct was finished, the two syndicate operations had become multi-million-dollar operations. Estimates on syndicate profits have varied greatly, but by using an index provided by the testimony of E. T. Earl in 1912, one can reasonably project that the first syndicate's profits (the San Fernando Mission Land Company) were in the range from $5 to $7.5 million. Profits from the second syndicate, the Los Angeles Suburban Homes subdivision, were much higher. One estimate in the 1930s, citing a jump in land values on the subdivided plots from $20 to $2,000 an acre, put syndicate profits in the range of $100 million. In addition, the original syndicate owners still held the most valuable real estate in the subdivision. The profits from the two syndicates established the basis for the enormous Chandler fortune which was used to dominate Southern California for the next three generations.

3. The Fight Over Surplus

By 1911, shortly before completion of the aqueduct, the growing awareness of the massive San Fernando Valley syndicates' profits contributed to another stronger challenge within Los Angeles to the assumptions and goals of the city's real estate kings. Los Angeles in 1911 was dominated by a mood of reform. Socialist Job Harriman, whose party's campaign had criticized the aqueduct, had come in first in the primary election for mayor. The Socialists accused syndicate members, in league with city officials and city water engineers, of fostering a "gigantic plan" creating a "fake water famine and frightening the people into building an aqueduct" in order to irrigate syndicate lands and make fortunes for its owners. In spite of the 1905 claims of water shortages, the Los Angeles River by 1911 (once the rains had fallen) had nearly doubled its supply; it was then estimated that the local supply could adequately serve the needs of a population of one million people.

The Socialists also opposed indiscriminate population expansion, seeing it as a capitalist strategy to preserve an available cheap labor supply and an open shop city. Socialists, the labor movement, and a number of businessmen in the progressive coalition, advocated controlled growth for the city. The key to the future, the Socialists declared, lay in the disposition of the aqueduct water.

The Socialists lost in the 1911 general election, but the issue continued to dominate the news. In 1912 Angelenos voted to set up the Aqueduct Investigation Board to look into the origins of the aqueduct, the charges surrounding the San Fernando syndicates, and the construction and financing of the project. A five-person committee held extensive hearings in the spring and summer of 1912. Most major participants testified. The board's seven-volume report, released in August 1912, included some dramatic conclusions. Los Angeles's available water supply, the report stated, had never been fully developed and the supply in surrounding areas had never been thoroughly investigated. Though no specific criminal charges were alleged, the report did note that the initial discussions on the aqueduct plans which included city officials—most notably Moses Sherman—took place within a time frame that clearly allowed the San Fernando syndicate to use that information in order to make its land purchases and reap the profits. The report further stated that the site for the terminal reservoir, at "great advantage to the land syndicate" had been changed to the head of the San Fernando Valley.

The Aqueduct Investigation Board's report created enormous controversy, though the *Times* downplayed its findings. In later, more conservative times, the Water Board's successor, the Department of Water and Power, confiscated all but one copy of the report.

As the aqueduct neared completion, the water board revealed that it had a serious problem deciding how to dispose of the *surplus* water once the aqueduct was completed. Two plans evolved. One, sponsored by the *Times* and its business allies, called for the disposition of the surplus water through annexation; that is, the water could be used by a community only if it was legally a part of Los Angeles city.

The Socialists and their supporters came up with an alternate plan, called the Graham plan after its author, W. C. Graham. The Graham plan, embodying the notion of controlled growth, called for competitive distribution of the water according to higher or lower grade of use. Cost would rise according to the type of use; water used to irrigate and subdivide new territories, for example, would cost much more than water for existing domestic uses within the city. The Graham plan, as opposed to the annexation proposal, would increase revenues for Los Angeles and actively discourage water use for purposes of speculation and subdivision.

In 1912 antisyndicate forces were clearly on the ascendance and the citizens of Los Angeles, won over by the attacks on the syndicate, initially backed the Graham plan by a more than two-to-one margin. Even William Mulholland criticized the syndicate rationale. "Instead of being developed as agricultural lands," Mulholland was quoted in September 1912, "the property has been subdivided into town lots, and small rich men's country estates at prohibitive values, which will result in keeping the land from being developed until we have enough people to settle there. The capitalists have stolen the unearned increment for the next twenty years. . . ." Mulholland's aberration, however, was only momentary, and he ended up actively backing the annexation proposal.

The 1913 mayoralty election proved to be the climax of eight years of fighting over the aqueduct. After losing narrowly in the primary, the Socialists backed independent Henry (H.H.) Rose, who had favored the Graham proposal. The *Times* backed Rose's runoff opponent, John Shenk. When the votes were counted, Rose, a former police judge, emerged the victor.

Once in office, the new mayor soon showed signs of a change of heart. He took a trip to the Owens Valley where he met with Mulholland. "Criticism of the aqueduct," Rose said the day he returned, "so far as I have been able to determine, is captious." Rose appointed his own "annexation commission" to study the possibility of disposing the water through expanding the city limits. "Annexation and consolidation will give Los Angeles official standing as the metropolis of the Pacific Coast," the commission reported. "Wherever the aqueduct water is placed—be it north, south, east, or west—there the greatest development of the future will be found, and that development should be a part of, and help constitute the Greater Los Angeles that is to be."

The aqueduct was finally completed on November 4, 1913, and the first waters flowed down into the San Fernando Valley. William Mulholland, in the ceremonies at the aqueduct base, uttered his famous words, "There it is! Take it!" ". . . A great river has been turned from its course," a *Times* editorial commented the next day, "a course that it followed since the hand of God raised the mountains and laid the oceans in their places on the morn of creation—and brought down to serve the people of Los Angeles who are here today, and the millions more who are to come tomorrow, and tomorrow, and tomorrow."

As the water flowed down, residents of Los Argeles, San Fernando, and dozens of other suburban townships went to the polls to decide on annexation proposals. The campaign by the proannexation forces, led by Los Angeles realtors, utilized a wide array of tactics. In suburban areas, realtors often created "water scare" environments reminiscent of the 1905 election. In one instance, bottles of evil-smelling water, labeled as if they came from the local water distributor, were placed on resident doorsteps with the note, "This is the water you drink."

Annexation forces won almost every election. In 1915 San Fernando, an area more than twice the size of Los Angeles, was annexed, increasing the city's size from 100 to 275 square miles. By 1928 sixty-two cities, communities, and townships had voted to become part of Los Angeles. Los Angeles, after thirteen years of annexation, quadrupled in size.

"Annexation, as the price of water," historian Vincent Ostrom wrote, "was the means of building Greater Los Angeles." Water fed the push for growth, and more growth created the need for more water.

"Yourself and the *Los Angeles Times* have been so conspicuously devoted to the successful upbuilding of Southern California," one of Harry Chandler's associates wrote to the *Times* publisher shortly after the last of the annexation campaigns, "that with an adequate water supply (and climate, oil, natural gas, electric power) all the fundamentals would be at hand to make it possible to create in Los Angeles County, the largest center of population which the world has ever known."

4. *"Dry Ditches"*

The Owens Valley attempted to survive. Owens residents had managed to keep their lands productive by constructing a series of ditches off the Owens River. But due to a light snowfall in the Sierras in the winter of 1921, the streams that came down from the mountains in the spring of 1922 had a subnormal flow, lowering the amount of water that reached both Inyo and Los Angeles lands.

Los Angeles of 1922 was in the midst of its largest boom ever. The city's population had passed the one-million mark, and the town's businessmen, led by Harry Chandler, had organized the county-financed All Year Club to attract more people. The city, however, was experiencing a sustained drought.

While water engineers led by William Mulholland explored the possibility of a future water supply several hundred miles east at the Colorado River, the city's water department decided to take away the limited supply still remaining in the tributary streams and ditches of the Owens Valley. Though the Owens residents had set up an irrigation district to act against Los Angeles, the city's water officials had the power and money. Los Angeles officials found a couple of local residents who were willing to sell their land and act as Los Angeles's agents in covertly buying up other properties. Los Angeles began to purchase a number of plots adjacent to the ditches. Inyo residents, ready to sell because of Los Angeles water department induced depressed land prices, had hoped to get loans for improvements either from the federal or state government. But officials were unwilling to help until land values stabilized, and Los Angeles's speculative activities prevented the market from reaching any kind of equilibrium. With their newly purchased land, Los Angeles officials diverted the streams and ditches back into the river and on to the aqueduct.

On learning of Los Angeles's actions, Owens residents sent armed guards down to one of the canals to prevent the diversion. On November 16, 1924, at ten in the morning, a number of Owens residents gathered at the aqueduct spillway at the Alabama Hills, four miles north of the town of Long Pine, to take control of the aqueduct opening. They opened the gates of the aqueduct and allowed the water to spill back into the Owens River, reversing its flow to Los Angeles.

The gates were kept open for four days. The act was enormously popular, with 500 to 800 people participating. All business activity in the main town of Bishop came to a halt. "If I'm not on the job, you'll find me at the Alabama Spillway," read a sign hung in the center of Main Street.

The protest, with Owens residents threatening to stay through the winter, brought the issue to the front pages of the state's newspapers. Even the *Times* commented sympathetically. "It is to be remembered," the paper editorialized on November 18, "that these farmers are not anarchists nor bomb throwers but, in the main, honest, earnest, hard-working American citizens who look upon Los Angeles as an octopus about to strangle out their lives. They have put themselves hopelessly in the wrong by taking the law into their own hands, but that is not to say that there has not been a measure of justice on their side of the argument—so long as it remained an argument and not an appeal to dynamite and force. . . . There must be no civil war in Southern California," the *Times* warned.

On the fourth day of the protest, Inyo's largest bank owner, W.W. Watterson, returned to the valley after extensive negotiations with local Los Angeles bankers. Watterson asked the Owens residents to end the protest on a pledge by Los Angeles banker J.A. Graves that the Los Angeles Clearing House, the banks' trade organization, would mediate fairly between Los Angeles and Inyo. The Owens residents returned to their homes, but the mediation never took place.

In May 1926, after unsuccessfully pleading their case in Sacramento, several Owens residents turned to dynamite, blasting a ten-foot hole in the concrete conduit about a mile north of the Alabama Hills spillway. Through the year, dynamiters struck several wells in the vicinity of Big Pine and Bishop. In May 1927, a group kidnaped guards and cut telephone lines to prevent communication with Los Angeles after blowing out the No Name siphon. A few days later, 600 reservists were assembled at the central police station in Los Angeles and a detachment of 100 armed men, with orders to shoot to kill anyone near the aqueduct, went to Owens Valley to guard the aqueduct.

Using information provided by a single informer, the federal government indicted six Owens Valley men on conspiracy charges in 1927. When they came to trial the judge dismissed the case on grounds that the informer had told contradictory tales. Just before the judge issued his directed verdict, Owens Valley residents took out full page newspaper ads throughout the state headlined WE WHO ARE ABOUT TO DIE.

With conspiracy trials, armed vigilantes, price manipulations, and the political hostility of the Los Angeles establishment, Owens residents felt harassed at every turn. "Probably in all Western history," Cornelius Vanderbilt wrote in the *Reno Journal*, "there has not been a more flagrant example of one part of the country, politically and financially powerful, destroying a weaker section. And doing it without regard to obligations, moral or financial."

The final blow came on August 4, 1927, when W.W. Watterson and his brother Mark closed the doors to their banks. The wealth of the region—the farmer's savings and mortgages—were in the Watterson banks. The failure had been "brought about by the past four years of destructive work carried on by the city of Los Angeles," according to a notice the Wattersons posted on the bank doors. But several days later the brothers were charged with thirty-six counts of fraud and embezzlement. After they pled guilty to the charges, the Owens resistance lost its remaining momentum.

The fight was over. Many more Owens residents sold their land to the city, and in 1930 a more moderate Department of Water and Power President Harlan Palmer negotiated an equitable settlement with the remaining farmers in the valley. After a $38.8-million bond issue was passed that year and the DWP completed the last land purchases, the city of Los Angeles owned 95 percent of the Owens Valley, including title to property in the townships of Laws, Big Pine, Long Pine, Independence, and Bishop. Owens Valley became a desert—a man-made desert.

"Ten years ago," Will Rogers wrote in 1932, "this was a wonderful valley with one quarter of a million acres of fruit and alfalfa. But Los Angeles had to have more water for its Chamber of Commerce to drink more toasts to its growth, more water to dilute its orange juice, and more water for its geraniums to delight the tourists, while the giant cottonwoods have died. So, now, this is the valley of desolation."

On March 12, 1928, only months after Los Angeles's final victory over Owens Valley, the San Francisquito Dam, constructed to hold aqueduct waters, broke, sending its waters into the northern San Fernando Valley. More than four hundred people were killed. At a hearing over the dam break, William Mulholland was asked if the dam foundation would be affected by water. Mulholland replied that it would not. But then, with the courtroom hushed, the plaintiff's lawyer produced a rock from the dam's foundation. When he dropped it into a glass of aqueduct water, it broke apart. Owens Valley had its fitting epitaph.

CHAPTER 8

The Empire Builder

1. "A Real Estate Conspiracy"

The single activity that established Harry Chandler's power within local ruling circles was his real estate speculation. "Chandler's land operations," a *Saturday Evening Post* writer said in 1926, "are of a sort to leave the ordinary real estate investor calling weakly for the smelling salts." Chandler and his business associates' land manipulations and promotions determined the character of Southern California development. Unlike the promoters of the first boom, Chandler carefully organized each speculative activity, drawing in the most powerful members of the establishment and laying the groundwork for further expansion. He took the real estate speculator of the nineteenth century and turned him into a modern industrialist.

At the heart of Harry Chandler's real estate strategy was his use of syndicates. "It's not what you go into, it's whom you go into a venture with," Chandler had once told his son Norman. In order to make a subdivision successful, the organization needed the cooperation of various political and business interests. It needed bankers to finance each step of the operation and provide loans to the new settlers, newspaper owners to create the attendant hoopla to generate interest in the new subdivisions, political figures who could help on a broad range of questions from water supply to annexation possibilities, title insurers and other real estate men to take the lead in attracting future residents, and railroad men and utilities owners to provide streetcar service and electricity to the new townships.

When the Huntington interests—owners of both streetcar lines and utility companies—merged with the Kerckhoff interests to form Southern California Edison, a near-monopoly in utilities, the *Times* praised the merger, linking it to real estate development. " 'Los Angeles, a city from the mountains to the sea!' " the editorial exclaimed, "rapidly is becoming the Southern California slogan, and along with the annexation of Hollywood, San Pedro, and Wilmington, the Huntington interests are helping to pave the way for other valuable acquisitions, for wherever the Huntington railways extend their lines, the Huntington electric and gas companies are preparing to furnish fuel and light."

Because of its size, the syndicate could also undertake much larger acquisitions and subdivisions than could individual investors. For example, when the Los Angeles Suburban Homes Company purchased the Lankershim lands, although the sale price was $2.5 million, each member of the thirty-person Chandler-organized syndicate put up only $25,000 as down payment, with the rest to be paid in yearly installments. Those thirty syndicate members then had options to buy land from the syndicate before it was offered to the public. Those first lots were the most valuable lots since some land was better suited for subdivision than other land. Thus, members had two advantages: a relatively small initial investment, and first option on the choice lots in the proposed subdivision.

The syndicates were essential to the entire process of suburbanization in the Los Angeles basin. Syndicate members provided small amounts of capital to create the beginnings of a township—for banks, hotels, the city hall, street paving, electricity, etc. But, as soon as settlers arrived and a township was incorporated, the residents were obliged to raise money to complete construction and pay back the syndicate's initial investment.

Working closely with businessmen, particularly large employers, the real estate men created the proper conditions for settlement by low-income, working-class residents. "We have received great assistance from the employers," real estate speculator Edwin Janss testified before a government commission in 1914, "because in many instances the wage earner would inquire from them relative to owning a home, buying a lot, and they have practically always encouraged it, and, in fact, in some instances, they have even advanced the first payment."

Los Angeles boosters actively promoted Los Angeles as the city with more wage earning home owners than any other city in the country. But many of the new suburban homes, Janss admitted, were little more than shacks of two-room frame construction, and although payments frequently lasted up to seven years, families were often unable to maintain them. Keying the policy to the open shop notion, employers were able to utilize the real estate situation to their benefit as their employees, constantly worried about mortgages and home upkeep, feared risking their jobs.

When one of the largest builders and subdividers faced the prospect of going under because of a temporary housing slump in 1913, Chandler and his business allies stepped in to take over the company. Bankruptcy, they felt, would hurt "the reputation of the city should such a widely advertised company pass into the hands of a receiver. . . ." "Strong hands," the company's annual report noted, "were needed to uphold the company in its hour of trial."

Organized labor and the Socialist party actively opposed Los Angeles real estate speculation and suburbanization. "Inviting enormous amounts of population to a community helter skelter, that is, creating an abnormal condition of influx to a community," labor advocate Frances Noel testified, "does not benefit that community. That a gradual growth, sane, rational, according to the natural resources of a given locality is far better than abnormal condition of growth."

By World War I real estate, according to one observer, had become "our chief stock in trade in Los Angeles." The city had almost five thousand real estate agents, that number dramatically increasing in the rampant expansion of the 1920s. In the period from 1921 to 1928, the height of Los Angeles's second great boom, real estate speculators created 3,233 subdivisions, embracing 49,608 acres and 246,612 building lots. "With all the outdoors to operate in," one Bank of America official noted, "subdividers clustered around Los Angeles as if drawn by a magnet. Zigzagging roads up hillsides, they sliced the precipitous slopes into pocket-handkerchief 'parcels', as if land were California's scarcest commodity."

"It's a . . . real estate conspiracy," Socialist newspaperman Frank Wolfe exclaimed, and Chandler was the chief real estate conspirator. "From the mountains to the sea" was the *Times* slogan for Los Angeles, as the region became a collection of town sites interspersed with farm land and semidesert uninhabited territory. Those who came to settle ranged from elderly retirees hoping to live the rest of their lives in warmth and comfort, to working-class families looking to buy their own home in the "land of milk and honey," to middle-class speculators and promoters who hoped to make a quick buck. "They have no organized connection with one another," novelist Upton Sinclair bitterly wrote of an expanding Los Angeles. "Each is an individual desiring to live his own life, and to be protected in his own little privileges. The community is thus a parasite upon the great industrial centers of other parts of America. It is smug and self-satisfied making the sacredness of property the first and last article of its creed. . . . Its social life is display, its intellectual life is 'boosting,' and its politics are run by Chambers of Commerce and Real Estate Exchanges."

2. Hooray for Hollywood

At the turn of the century, Chandler's friend Moses Sherman, then heavily involved in the streetcar business, decided to build a rail line to an unsettled rural area northwest of downtown Los Angeles. Sherman and local realtor Hobart J. Whitley incorporated the Los Angeles Pacific Boulevard and Development Company, planning to subdivide the land and create a number of town sites to provide potential commuters for Sherman's streetcars. In order to make their plans operational, the two men turned to Harry Chandler, and with his help organized a syndicate which attracted political and financial establishment figures such as General Otis, bankers Herman Hellman and O.T. Johnson, and the powerful Judge Bicknell. "These names," wrote local historian Edwin O. Palmer, "ranking high in Los Angeles finance, made a rare combination of capital, railroad and newspaper interests for real estate development."

In order to expand the syndicate, Whitley, Sherman, and Chandler offered up to one-fourth of each town site at practically giveaway prices. They arranged expeditions to the site complete with bands, picnics, and fast-talking promoters. They even hung "sold" signs on several of the half-finished buildings and lots.

On Chandler's suggestion the syndicate constructed a hotel as the centerpiece of the main town site in order to give the area a more substantial urban feel. According to a story told by an old-time local resident, one day while the hotel was being completed, a man riding a bike and carrying holly berries passed by and suggested to Chandler that the *Times* business manager call the building the Hollywood Hotel after the munificent holly berry patches surrounding the town site. By 1903 the new township of Hollywood had become a reality.

For several years, the subdivision maintained a modest growth rate similar to those of several other suburban developments in the region. But by 1910 Los Angeles, with its warm dry climate perfect for outdoor on location filming, had attracted a different group of settlers. As several production companies of the budding movie industry settled in the Hollywood town site, the subdivision became a national curiosity.

While the movie industry settled in, Chandler's land holdings in the Hollywood area increased. Through several dummy or family-related companies such as Chandis Securities and the Clark and Sherman Land Company, as well as through his Trust number S–5975 held by the Title Insurance and Trust Company, Chandler picked up sizeable amounts of agricultural land throughout the area. His subdivisions aided in the expansion of the existing town site to the north and west of the original site. Chandler also developed economic ties to the growing movie industry, leasing buildings which later became studio properties and providing loans and investment capital for productions. Chandler and Sherman, who secretly held the mortgage on Mack Sennett's well-known mansion, generally tried to keep their economic activities as much in the background as possible. When money to finance movie productions became scarce in the 1920s, Chandler and bankers Motley Flint and A.P. Giannini helped out. Their efforts helped guarantee the survival of Warner Brothers.

The *Times* became the first major newspaper to promote actively the motion picture business. It created a special section called "The Preview" to carry Hollywood news and hired the nation's first gossip columnist, Grace Kingsley, who produced a regular column called "Stella, the Star Gazer."

The austere and conservative Chandler, however, was upset with the series of sex scandals, such as the famous Fatty Arbuckle affair, that rocked the industry in the early 1920s and resulted in a boycott of movies by the Catholic Church's Legion of Decency. With the industry in crisis, Chandler sent one of his top reporters, Chapin Hall, to tour the country to enlist the aid of other newspaper publishers to support—and clean up— the industry. Chandler invited more than forty newspaper critics, at *Times* expense, to come out and investigate Hollywood firsthand. He worked behind the scenes with industry figures to bring in ex-Postmaster General Will Hays to head the Motion Picture Producers Association and create a morals code for industry productions.

Chandler eventually cut back on *Times* coverage of the industry, and in the late 1920s the paper lost its leadership to Hearst's *Examiner*. The *Times* let Grace Kingsley go, and, in the early 1930's, Hearst filled the vacuum for Hollywood gossip with Louella Parsons. When the *Times* hired Hedda Hopper in 1938, the paper once again effectively challenged Hearstian dominance.

3. The Land Baron

In 1911 another Chandler-led syndicate purchased 300,000 acres of sprawling ranch land in Los Angeles and Kern counties. The property, known as the Ranchos Tejon, extended several miles south from the Tehachapi Mountains into the area just south of Bakersfield. The massive sheep ranch had been consolidated by former U.S. Indian Commissioner Edward Beale from Mexican land grants which, in turn, had been seized earlier in the century from the native Indian population.

The seventy-member Tejon Ranch syndicate (which included Chandler, Otis, and their friend Moses Sherman; Otto Brant and William Allen of the Title Insurance and Trust Company; utilities man W.G. Kerckhoff; *Times* treasurer Frank X. Pfaffinger; Max Ihmsen, publisher of Hearst's *Los Angeles Examiner*; and T.E. Gibbon, former Free Harbor advocate and close business ally of the Chandler interests) paid $1.5 million in cash, the balance to be paid by a mortgage for the same amount. Several other businessmen, including Harvey Firestone of the tire family and the Van Nuys interests, joined later on.

Soon after the purchase, California's State Highway Commission began deliberations over a proposed interstate highway between Los Angeles and Bakersfield. Two routes were under consideration: one passed directly through the syndicate lands, and the other went through the Antelope Valley to the east of the ranch. The Tejon route was thirty-five miles shorter, but forty miles of it ran through rugged, mountainous terrain prone to washouts and heavier snowfall. Further, the more extensive development along the Antelope Valley pass potentially meant more traffic along that route. The Tejon route, opponents argued, would only be traveled by tourists and agricultural concerns. Bakersfield and Antelope Valley residents argued for the Antelope Valley route, while an organized pressure campaign led by the Automobile Club, the M & M, and the Chamber of Commerce—many of whose directors belonged to the Chandler/Tejon syndicate—lobbied for the Tejon Pass route.

When the commission decided to go with the Tejon route in spite of its potential extra costs and the dissatisfaction of valley residents, the *San Francisco Bulletin* attacked the decision, claiming Chandler's influence was responsible. The *Bulletin* printed a statement by a landowner who claimed that Chandler and Otto Brant had suggested integrating his property north of Tejon into the syndicate's territory, in order to benefit from a probable increase in value when the proposed highway went through. Chandler denied the allegation. The Tejon route was built and the syndicate land soon acquired the name of the "right of way" ranch.

The first several years of ranch operation did not bring the immediate returns that a number of syndicate members—primarily small businessmen attracted by the promise of instant riches—had envisioned. Mortgage payments were beyond the capacity of several investors, and in 1916 Chandler and Sherman began to buy out their shares, Chandler using capital from the Times Mirror company to increase his holdings.

Around the same time as Chandler began to buy out syndicate investors, another group of people whose lives had been affected by the Tejon purchase began to agitate. The ranch area had been the ancestral home for the Tejon Indians, a large number of whom still lived there at the same time of the syndicate purchase. Within three years of the purchase, the federal government began to receive complaints from the Indians about their treatment by the syndicate. The new owners, who used several Tejon Indians as laborers around the ranch, required the Indian group to pay rent for their land, and had initiated a suit in Tehachapi Superior Court to eject them from the ranch.

The federal government wanted the syndicate to sell or donate a large plot of land for the Indians, but Chandler refused. "Mr. Chandler," special assistant to the attorney general A.H. Fraser wrote in 1920 about the *Times* publisher, "is accustomed to having his own way and is doubtless unwilling that the Indians should be securely and permanently established on the ranch."

". . . If you had a hundredth part as much experience in the cattle business as you have in the law," Chandler answered Fraser, "you would at once realize that what you suggest would be impossible. It is hard to believe that there is to be a consolidation of the forces of our government to reverse the law under which we purchased our property in order that one bad Indian and one half-breed Mexican can collect a little graft money from the good Indians and live without work themselves. We claim that the Indians on the Tejon Ranch are clean, industrious, well-paid and happy."

In November, 1920, the Department of Justice filed suit against the syndicate to force it to give a stretch of ranchland to be used as a permanent residence for the Tejon Indians. The Tejon owners argued that the government had no foundation for their suit and that it was politically motivated because of *Times* opposition to the Wilson administration. The syndicate successfully appealed to the Supreme Court, which dismissed the case on the basis of the Indians' failure to have presented their claim before the appropriate body, the Private Land Claims Commission. "This decision," Fraser sadly wrote in 1924, "will hardly shine as a brilliant star in the court's judicial crown."

Evicting the Indians, however, didn't help ranch economics as the depression put a squeeze on the ranch's financing. Chandler arranged with Sherman's former secretary Arnold Haskell, who had taken on a major role in the ranch operations after Sherman's death, to develop new sources of financing by incorporating the ranch and issuing new stock. On February 14, 1936, the Tejon Ranch Company was legally incorporated with the Chandler family and the Times Mirror Company its major stockholders.

The Tejon property also served a social and family function. Chandler frequently took guests out to the ranch to conduct business deals and entertain them in the pleasant rural surroundings. The Chandler children spent time on the Tejon land, and Norman Chandler worked as a ranch hand during his summers as a teenager.

Tejon was just one of several ranch retreats. In 1926 Chandler purchased the 350,000-acre Vermejo Ranch near the Colorado/New Mexico border and turned the property into a "sporting club for the rich," a place where Los Angeles businessmen could come to relax, fish, hunt, and make deals. Chandler also purchased the Three Brothers Ranch in Pomona, so that his sons, as he described it, "could learn the joy of sweaty toil." He was also involved in the subdivision of Ramona Acres, east of Los Angeles; had interests in the Diamond Bar Ranch; purchased some beach property at Dana Point, south of Long Beach; and had extensive holdings in the Imperial Valley. By the 1930s Harry Chandler owned more than two million acres in ranches, agricultural property, cattle and cotton operations, and suburban land. He had become California's premier land baron, an American version of the state's earlier establishment figure, the Spanish don.

One of Chandler's more curious real estate ventures concerned William Randolph Hearst. In the crisis days of March 1933, Hearst, in need of quick cash, tried to borrow $600,000 from the local U.S. National Bank, offering his property at San Simeon as collateral. When payment was delayed because of Roosevelt's bank holiday (instituted to forestall massive bank failures threatening the country) Harry Chandler, a major stockholder and director in the bank, offered to put up the $600,000 himself. Hearst immediately agreed. When the loan came due a few years later, the Hearst interests had problems meeting the payments. Chandler thought of foreclosing, but after a visit to the ominous castle, decided to extend the loan.

In the summer of 1936 Chandler organized his last major syndicate. In the name of the Rancho Santa Anita Corporation, Chandler and associates purchased what remained of the Lucky Baldwin ranch in the area called Arcadia, east of Los Angeles. In a complex series of transactions, the Chandler syndicate purchased the valuable 1,300 acres with its historic buildings on July 1, and three months later made the Chandler holding company, the Chandler-Sherman Corporation, trustee over the property after it had made a $450,000 loan at 7½% interest to the Rancho Santa Anita syndicate.

The syndicate then sold nearly one-fifth of the property to the Los Angeles Turf Club, a syndicate operation involving local real estate people and Hollywood investors such as Hal Roach. The Turf Club had built a racetrack on another portion of the Baldwin property it had purchased a few years earlier, just after the California Legislature had legalized racing. The Turf Club syndicate had also been involved in the acquisition and development of Lake Arrowhead on the California/Nevada border.

A San Francisco dentist, Charles Strub, owner of the San Francisco Seals baseball club, had been brought in to head the track operations, and quickly established a good working relationship with Chandler. The *Times*, which had always had a strong anti-gambling bias in its news and editorials, now found itself on the side of the horses. The paper began consistently to oppose increases in racing taxes and even sponsored a *Times* charity day at the track. Its top reporter, Kyle Palmer, was put on the Turf Club payroll, and the Los Angeles Police Department sent thirty-five of its officers free of charge for guard duty at the track.

The racetrack thrived. Within a year of its purchase of the Baldwin property, the Rancho Santa Anita syndicate had begun to subdivide their suburban tract. The corporation organized a medium-priced Santa Anita Village in 1937, followed by the more exclusive Santa Anita Gardens and Colorado Oaks projects. The syndicate promoted new shopping centers and residential developments with a total project investment of $40 million. By the 1950s, the once rural territory associated with the famed Lucky Baldwin had been almost completely transformed into yet another Southern California urban landscape.

4. Downtown Space

Chandler was also a major "downtown power." *Times* interests in the downtown area dated back to the 1887 boom, when Otis acquired holdings by cashing in on loans made to pay for advertisements and by taking part in a few investments. At the turn of the century the *Times* downtown property centered around the Times Building and City Hall at First and Broadway in what is today the northern section of downtown. As speculators began to push the downtown center southward in the late 1890s, the *Times* opposed the move.

By 1909, Otis and Chandler began to diversify their downtown holdings with real estate purchases on the southern rim at Ninth and Broadway. Within ten years, Chandler, working closely with Moses Sherman and realtors William May Garland and Robert Rowan, had picked up numerous parcels throughout the southern and northern sections of downtown, including the mortgage on the Los Angeles Athletic Club, land to the west in a section known as Griffith Park, and the area around General Otis's old home, the Bivouac, adjacent to Westlake (later MacArthur) Park. Chandler owned office buildings, empty lots (kept for speculative purposes), movie theaters, (the big Orpheum Theater among others), and leased property to such diverse operations as Douglas Aircraft, the Lasky Famous Players movie studio, and the Salvation Army.

For a number of years Chandler was actively involved in the debate over the need and eventual location of a central Union Station terminal. Chandler wanted a station built in the northern end of downtown adjacent to his own holdings, but other interests—including some downtown powers and the reform-minded Municipal League—were opposed to a new station and disagreed with the location, given the southward shift of downtown. The Municipal League suggested an improvement of the city's interurban transportation service instead. The Southern Pacific railroad, which wanted to maintain its existing depot, also broke with the *Times* on the Union Station issue, in spite of its generally close relationship to the Chandler interests.

By the mid 1920s, traffic in Los Angeles's center city had become congested as streetcars and automobiles blocked each other. To relieve the downtown traffic, the SP proposed creating an elevated system which would rely on its existing terminus. The SP proposal, which would have meant, in effect, the scuttling of the new terminal plans, was actively opposed by the *Times*. Two measures proposing elevated structures instead of the Union Station were placed on the ballot. All the major newspapers except the *Times* and the majority of the city's business forces lined up with the SP. These "dirty, deafening, hideous" structures, the paper warned of the elevateds, "depreciate appallingly the section of the city through which they run." In contrast, a *Times* news story pointed out, "Los Angeles' dream of a great downtown beauty spot of civic splendor is coming true" with the Union Station/Civic Center development.

Revivalist Aimee Semple McPherson, just back from the Holy Land, echoed the *Times* in a radio appeal during the last week of the campaign. "Los Angeles has ever been a city of beauty, a place of refuge where tired men and women from all over the world have come seeking retreat," she cried out. "They left the noise, dirt, unsightliness, gloom and danger of the elevateds to come to our fair city where there is peace, quiet and comfort. . . . Rise up," Sister Aimee proclaimed, "[and do] not let this horrible menace be slipped over." In the nip and tuck election, Angelenos voted to defeat the elevated-train proposal, thus removing a major obstacle in the path of the Union Station plans.

The development of a new Civic Center was intimately tied to the Union Station plans, although its location was still to be determined. One set of plans called for a center to go up on First and Broadway where the Times Building stood. A decision by city officials favoring that location went through in 1929. The *Times* initially opposed the selection, fearful that the sale of their building would bring less money than would construction of the Civic Center adjacent to the site. The *Times* soon worked out an agreement with the public officials. "Rather than stand longer in the way of the Civic Center's progress," the paper said of its apparently magnanimous gesture, "the *Times* reluctantly yielded and expressed its willingness to accept the award of any fair board of appraisal."

As negotiations began in 1931, *Times* opponents suspected a deal favoring the *Times*. The *Times*, they discovered, had already acquired a site for a new building a block away on First and Spring and had prepared to sell the old building to begin construction on its new home. Further, they were appalled at the $1.8 million that the supervisor's appraisal board had awarded the *Times*.

Municipal reformers, led by the Minute Men and the Municipal League, voiced opposition to the deal, organized a petition drive that collected 25,000 signatures, and ultimately brought the *Times*/county agreement into the courts. In January 1933 Judge George Scovel ruled that the sale price should be lowered to $1.02 million. The differing appraisals partly resulted from the estimates of the old equipment in the building. The *Times* had hoped to use the opportunity to invest in new machinery, in effect, to subsidize the new capital investment with the sale of its old machinery, though the latter had been independently appraised as having only junk value.

Still not satisfied, the supervisors hired another appraiser, who set a new price at $600,000, one third the original figure. Municipal League officials pointed out that a comparison on the value of the buildings adjacent to the *Times* property at First and Broadway made even the new appraisal figure high, since those values at 1930 figures hovered around $500,000 and prices on Broadway had been falling in the depression years.

Under pressure from the municipal organizations, the city attorney instituted proceedings to abandon the sale altogether. Although the lower courts upheld the city, the state Supreme Court ordered the case retried.

Harry Chandler decided it was time to "compromise" and offered to sell the building at $1.6 million, which created a new round of protests. "Are you going to stand idly by," one reform newspaper warned, "and let Harry Chandler raid the public treasury for $1.6 million for the purchase of the old 'TIMES' property which is worth only $600,000 at a time when thousands of taxpayers are hungry and the city is almost bankrupt?" But in spite of the public clamor the city administration, with its back to the wall and still prone to Chandler influence, agreed.

While the *Times* publicly called for compromise, it sent its top political reporter Al Nathan into the police department's subversive files seeking information on the opponents of the *Times* building sale. The *Times* then attacked its enemies as "reds" and "radicals." "From the *Times* standpoint, it is better to contend that the only people who oppose the *Times* grab are radicals!" the *Hollywood Citizen News*, a major opponent, editorialized in May 1934. "The people of this city have seen for years the *Times* defend those in public office who beat the government to the demands of the greedy interests. . . . When the facts are faced," the *News* concluded, "then the *Times* defense amounts to nothing but further evidence of its willingness to outrage a public from which it has gathered millions of profits."

While the fight over the sale of the *Times* building raged, construction began on the new Union Station a few blocks northeast from the Times— far removed from the southward-shifting center of downtown. As station construction uprooted the old Chinatown community, creating a possible loss of tourist trade, one of the town's leading society ladies, Mrs. Christine Sterling, took up the cause of locating a new Chinatown adjacent to her other tourist center concept of an "Old Mexico" on Olvera Street, just west of Union Station.

Mrs. Sterling and Chandler, who immediately supported the proposal, hit it off from the start. The society matron praised Chandler for keeping "faith with the finer things of life," as Chandler organized one of his famous luncheons to raise money—$39,000 altogether—for the projects.

The *Times* also provided extensive news coverage and support, as *Times* writer John Steven McGroarty launched a public campaign for Olvera Street with an article entitled "The Plaza Beautiful" in the fall of 1926. "She knows what bait to use when she goes fishing," McGroarty wrote of the project backer. "A woman whose ulterior object is the achievement of beauty but who realizes that in this day and generation romance can live only if it can be made to pay."

McGroarty's piece was soon followed by a series of articles by editor Ralph Trueblood and Chandler's daugher Connie, among others. With the extraordinary publicity, Sterling was able to raise the necessary funds for the project with regular monthly contributions provided by the *Times* and the Chamber of Commerce. Police Chief Davis provided free prison labor for construction, and in 1933 Olvera Street opened to the public. The less publicized new Chinatown also opened, despite the objections of a number of Chinese residents who had settled several blocks away, thus creating two "Chinatowns." As a tourist attraction, Olvera Street and the new Chinatown helped Chandler's overall plan to see the north side of downtown, with its Civic Center, Union Station, and *Los Angeles Times* building, gain in prestige and real estate value.

"The best interests of Los Angeles are paramount to the *Times*," Harry Chandler wrote as the *Times* moved into its new building, a move subsidized by the sale of its old one. "They have always been. The city and this newspaper have grown up together. With humility, those in charge of its conduct realized that it grew because it was, in a certain sense, the voice of a lusty, energetic, progressive community. That it prospered because it echoed the call of a triumphant pioneer spirit."

5. The Industrial Base

Chandler knew that in order to continue expanding, Los Angeles had to develop an industrial base. In the period immediately following World War I, he and his business associates systematically began to seek out large Eastern industrial enterprises which might bring their plants to sunny Southern California where favorable climatic conditions helped lower building costs and allowed outdoor work activities.

Chandler immediately recognized the importance of the budding automobile industry. As his first major objective, he set out to attract rubber companies to locate in Los Angeles. In February 1919, Chandler and Sherman hosted a luncheon for Colonel Colt, chairman of the board of

U.S. Rubber. Three months later Chandler hosted another luncheon at the Los Angeles Athletic Club for Frank Seiberling of the Goodyear Tire and Rubber company. Seiberling proposed establishing two plants, one for rubber and one for the manufacture of cotton cloth for tires.

He suggested that if Chandler's group underwrite his plant development by investing $6 million in stock for the rubber plant and $1.5 million for the cotton company, Goodyear would settle in Los Angeles and would create a local board of directors to operate it with board members to include Chandler and his associates—banker J.F. Sartori, insurance man Lee Phillips, and lawyer Henry W.O.K. Melveny.

On July 16, 1919, at a Chamber of Commerce luncheon, the Goodyear man reviewed his plans and the reasons for his decision to settle in Los Angeles. He stressed four themes: cheap fuel, cheap power, an adequate supply of fresh water, and most important, the cherished commodity of "free American [open shop] labor." Seiberling's speech, according to the next days' *Times*, "brought 500 business men to their feet with cheers of applause." Three days later, the *Times* announced that Goodyear would settle in Los Angeles, marking "the opening page of a new chapter in the industrial history of Los Angeles."

One of Chandler's most inspired investments was in the newly developed aircraft industry. In 1919 Chandler gave one of his top reporters, Bill Henry, a year's leave of absence to work with Glenn Martin, a Cleveland, Ohio, aircraft manufacturer. Chandler was interested in the budding aircraft companies, but had been unwilling up to then to underwrite production facilities in Southern California. Henry met Martin's young associate Donald Douglas in Cleveland and together the two men decided to try to set Douglas up on his own in Los Angeles. Henry returned to the city in the winter of 1919–1920 and told Harry Chandler of Douglas's plans. "All the other wealthy men swear by him," he wrote, "and when anybody wants to put something over in the way of a promotion scheme they always run up against the proposition that 'Allright, I'll take some stock in it if Harry Chandler OK's the proposition!'"

Henry was optimistic after his talk with Chandler. "Now, I'm convinced that the thing will go," Henry wrote to Douglas, urging him to come west immediately.

By 1922, Douglas had successfully arranged, with Chandler's help, to get $15,000 in initial capital. Chandler had written out a check for the first $1,500 and given Douglas a list of nine other people to see. As Henry had predicted, once Chandler was in, other investors quickly joined.

Within the year Douglas Aircraft became an important Los Angeles business, and the city had the beginnings of an aerospace industry. Chandler, Sherman, and William May Garland leased a large plot to Douglas in 1924 for $42,000 a year for the new company's factory.

Another Chandler syndicate in the 1920s with banker Henry Robinson and realtor Garland created a local air transport company, Western Air Express, in hopes of making Los Angeles competitive with San Francisco, and help boost the city in its quest for recognition and business. Western quickly became a major airline for the West Coast, with passenger service between Los Angeles and Salt Lake City, San Francisco, Texas via Kansas City, and other routes to Cheyenne and Denver. The company also engaged in airmail service, owned airports in South Pasadena and Pueblo Colorado, had a fleet of twenty-two airplanes and a gross annual income of $3 million.

When Herbert Hoover was elected president in 1928, he appointed his campaign manager, Walter Brown, as U.S. postmaster general. Brown, realizing that airmail would soon become a major form of postal delivery, decided to reorganize existing facilities along monopolistic lines. Brown wanted to divide air lanes into two or three east-west zones with a single air transport company serving the post office in each zone.

For the western zone monopoly, Brown chose Transcontinental Air Transport Company (TAT), an Eastern combine dominated by the Mellon family and Pennsylvania Railroad interests and dubbed the "Lindbergh Line" because Charles Lindbergh had lent his name for company promotions. TAT had attempted to merge with the well-run and profitable Western Air Express, but Western management, which felt TAT "was poorly conceived and wastefully managed," had resisted. But TAT continued to pressure the smaller company. In June 1929 it organized a combination air and railroad service between New York and Los Angeles, and even the postmaster himself intervened to push the merger.

Finally Western executives went to Chandler and Garland, both Western directors and stockholders and close political allies of Herbert Hoover. The Western executives were told to chance a merger though it might hurt their own investments, and "not do anything to embarass the President." Soon after, Herbert Hoover, Jr., the president's son, was named chief engineer of Western Air Express, and the merger went through. A new corporate entity, Transcontinental and Western Air, known today as TWA, was formed. As part of the arrangement, Western sold its Los Angeles-to-Dallas route to American Airlines (another large Mellon combine) at a considerable loss for Western. TWA picked up the western postal monopoly, and went on to become one of the largest airlines in the world.

Chandler's Western investment might not have paid off in economic terms, but it reinforced an important political relationship that aided Chandler's activities. One of these activities centered around the oil industry. Southern California oil production first developed after E.L. Doheny discovered oil in the region in 1892. By 1899 wells were producing up to 4 million barrels a year; ten years later that figure had jumped to 58 million barrels. Most of the drilling was undertaken by a number of local operators, including Lyman Stewart, who organized the Union Oil company, Doheny and his interests, and, as was to be expected, Harry Chandler.

Chandler organized several syndicates to drill for oil throughout the Southern California basin. Several companies were tied into Chandler-related oil interests, including Sherman Oil, Puente Oil (a consolidation of Chandler's Pico Oil Company and Puente, an old-time company which had discovered oil on Rancho El Puente in the eastern edge of the rim), and several smaller companies primarily organized by Chandler's close ally Max Whittier. Though Chandler had close relations with the Union Oil people, the major local company (*Times*-backed Senator Thomas Bard had been one of Union's founders), a degree of competitive rivalry on oil matters still existed.

In 1914 a British syndicate purchased a block of Union Oil stock in an effort to gain entry into the American market but decided soon after to divest themselves of their interest by selling it to a group of New York financiers headed by Percy Rockefeller, nephew of John D. The New York group organized a holding company in 1919 called Union of Delaware. The company's assets were the 26.7 percent of Union of California it owned.

At this point Royal Dutch Shell, which had been looking for an American arm, decided to make a bid for control of Union of California. Shell joined with the Rockefeller group to form the Shell-Union Oil Company, in which it hoped to take over Union of California. As part of this maneuver, Shell-Union decided to acquire a Southern California base and link its interests with those of Harry Chandler and his allies. Shell purchased several local companies, including Puente Oil, while Chandler and Sherman each purchased $150,000 of Union of Delaware stock. With its 26.7 percent of Union of California stock, the Shell interests maneuvered to get Harry Chandler and banker J.E. Fishburn on the Union of California board of directors.

Union of California fought the Shell/Chandler takeover. Union Chairman Lyman Stewart created Union Oil Associates, a holding company for stock in Union of California, and began a public campaign urging Union stockholders to transfer voting control of their stock to the new holding company to resist the foreign takeover. Most of the local newspapers supported Stewart's move. "Every stockholder owes it to his pocketbook, to California, and to the nation to keep the American flag flying over California oil fields," the *Los Angeles Express* commented. Only the *Times* disagreed, editorializing that Eastern capital ought to be encouraged to invest in Southern California.

Stewart's holding company managed to acquire 54.7 percent of Union of California's stock, and the Shell interests, recognizing defeat, sold their Union of Delaware shares back to Union of California at a handsome profit. Chandler was defeated but came out well ahead economically.

Harry Chandler had long recognized the relationship of economic success to political influence. Soon after World War I, he and Sherman, along with their associate Harry Haldeman, each invested $100,000 in the Yosemite National Park Company, owned by both northern and Southern California businessmen, which held the concession rights in Yosemite Park. Chandler, Sherman, and Haldeman joined the board of directors and took an active role in the company. One of Chandler's goals was to develop and further alliances between businessmen in the two regions.

The company, which hoped to stimulate tourism in the park, was in direct competition with the Yosemite Curry Company. In 1925 the two companies undertook merger talks. Since the park had been put under the protection of the Department of the Interior in 1906 to prevent its exploitation by private interests, such a merger was controversial. But Chandler used his contacts with the Republican administration in Washington to arrange a dinner for the secretary of the interior when the latter passed through Los Angeles in the spring of 1925. The dinner went smoothly, and the secretary arranged a "reorganization" which set up a new Yosemite Park and Curry Company, with Chandler a major stockholder and director. The company quickly extended its influence by picking up the stage line from Fresno to Sequoia. The Interior Department contracted with the new company to handle all services within the park. The Park and Curry Company felt that promotion ought to be linked to development; over the years it built shopping centers, hotels, and other tourist-related buildings. "A lot of people complain that there is not much to do except look at the scenery and camp," one company official explained. "We are going to give the people what they want."

By the 1930s Harry Chandler had added major interests in a range of manufacturing, industrial, and tourist-related companies to his extensive real estate holdings. In the 1920s, he and Sherman invested in a clothing manufacturing company, Bond Great West Clothing, as part of the never ending strategy of attracting new industry to the region while turning a profit. Chandler also was involved in new publishing efforts (Times-Mirror Press, which printed the phone books, election ballots, and auto club maps; Pacific Coast Salesbook Company; and the American Engraving Company), the insurance business (Mortgage Guarantee Company), hotels (the Biltmore and the Ambassador), and countless major buildings sprinkled throughout the region, many of which were owned by the Chandler-related Central Investment Corporation. He had become, as one writer put it, "Southern California's modern Midas."

6. Hawaii

Harry Chandler was not simply a Los Angeles booster/businessman; he also kept on the lookout for interests which could unite his local power base with other regional businesses. Eventually Chandler looked to the west, out over the Pacific Ocean to Hawaii.

"The annexation of the Hawaiian Islands," the *Times* had commented, after President McKinley signed the annexation into law in 1898, "will figure in history as an important event for it marks the commencement of a new era in the history of this great nation." Annexation also marked the end of attempts by Hawaiian residents to keep control of Hawaii out of the hands of profit-seeking American planters.

By 1898 Hawaiian land ownership had become centralized in a few American hands. The islands' economy was based on a single crop, sugar, that took up four-fifths of Hawaii's arable land and was its chief and most profitable export. The islands' large landowners had already linked up with the San Francisco-based Matson Navigation shipping firm as their main export vehicle to the States. Economic and political power on the islands was then centralized in the hands of five corporations known as the "Big Five," who controlled the banking and credit system and much of the sugar and pineapple trade.

Other interests attempted to establish a power base outside the Big Five. The most significant attempt evolved around the Dillingham brothers, who, recognizing Matson's lock on the San Francisco connection, desperately needed a trade route for their products and looked to Los Angeles's budding shipping industry to find it.

Prior to World War I, with the San Pedro harbor only recently completed, few ships came to Los Angeles. The city lacked both the industrial base and shipping facilities to compete with the highly developed port of San Francisco. To develop their harbor, the Los Angeles business establishment, including Chandler, successfully proposed annexation of San Pedro to Los Angeles in 1909, after incorporating a narrow, shoestrip corridor between downtown Los Angeles and the harbor twenty miles to the south.

With the advent of World War I, Chandler, Sherman, and their ally Fred Baker set up a new syndicate to construct and refinish government ships for the war. Organized as the Los Angeles Shipping and Drydock Corporation, the company, along with a second Chandler-initiated company, the Ralph Chandler (named after Harry's nephew) Shipbuilding Company, held an effective monopoly over early shipyard activities in the region. The war provided a lucrative business as the two companies—employing thousands of construction and longshore workers—built nineteen vessels. When the war ended, a U.S. Shipping Board contract with the company to build ten more hulls was canceled. Despite the cancellation, the government paid Chandler's company $670,000, including $31,000 in plant improvement cost already incurred. The payment later came under fire in a congressional investigation of corruption in the Shipping Board.

In 1920 Chandler decided to expand his shipping activities by creating a steamship syndicate, the Los Angeles Steamship Company (LASSCO), which incorporated with a capital stock of $5 million held by seven partners: Harry Chandler, Ralph Chandler, Sherman, Baker, Max Whittier, and two prominent lawyers, Erle Leaf and Frank Seaver. The company immediately put in a bid for two ships, the *Yale* and the *Harvard*, which had been put up for auction by the Navy Department. LASSCO beat out a New Orleans company bid of $1.7 million by $55,000, but it put down only a 25 percent downpayment, with the rest to be paid in yearly installments at 4½% interest, beginning in 1923.

The successful bid portended other things to come. Republican Warren Harding's administration had numerous ties with the Southern California business establishment, and the U.S. Shipping Board in particular had intimate ties to the Chandler interests which Chandler and Sherman were prepared to use. LASSCO's general manager A.J. Frey was appointed director of operations of the Shipping Board, and the board's president, Albert Lasker, was, as Sherman put it, a "great friend" of Chandler's and *Los Angeles Times*'s Washington representative, Robert Armstrong. Armstrong, who became assistant secretary of LASSCO and had political connections to the Harding, Coolidge, and Hoover administrations, proved to be an effective lobbyist on shipping matters. His activities, for example, enabled LASSCO to postpone payments on the *Harvard* and *Yale* for nearly a decade until the Chandler operation was merged into a larger combine.

While Armstrong pleaded poverty in regard to the *Harvard* and *Yale* payments, he also began negotiations on behalf of Chandler and Sherman to purchase a former German passenger ship named the *Aelous*—confiscated during the war by the Navy—from the U.S. government. Armstrong urged Lasker to allow LASSCO to operate the ship until such time as bids were opened. By July 1923, when advertisements for the bid were placed, LASSCO had already started to use the *Aelous*—renamed the *City of Los Angeles*. In order to see the ship, bidders had to make an appointment with LASSCO to make sure the boat was in Los Angeles Harbor instead of on its regular run. After the two-week period for bids ended, the Shipping Board announced that only one bid had been received. LASSCO purchased the ship at less than one-third the vessel's original price—a figure equal to an estimate of the boat's value *when sold as scrap.*

After the bid was accepted, Armstrong, who told Sherman that he had saved them at least $50,000, wrote to Los Angeles seeking an increase in salary and some money for "services." LASSCO's board voted to give Armstrong a $1,000 gift and $100 a month on the condition that he get an extension for the *Harvard* and *Yale* debt. Armstrong not only got the extension but also helped postpone payments of back taxes to the government on the Ralph Chandler Shipbuilding Company after Chandler and Sherman decided to close it down. Armstrong frequently received gifts from his bosses, including free steamship trips to Hawaii and a pair of Arabian horses from the Tejon Ranch.

In 1922 a U.S. Senate investigation began to look into the alleged corruption of the board. One of the important charges centered around the *Aeolus* sale. But though Lasker resigned his post, the Shipping Board affair receded in the face of the breaking scandals concerning Teapot Dome.

Just as LASSCO service was getting under way, the company had made its first contacts with the Dillingham interests. The two groups explored a Los Angeles-Hawaii route which could challenge the Big Five/Matson link from the islands to San Francisco. Los Angeles Chamber of Commerce president (former D.A. and later Congressman) John Fredericks was enlisted to plead the case for establishing a Hawaii-Los Angeles route before the Shipping Board, and the helpful Albert Lasker agreed to the link. In the fall of 1923, LASSCO sent its luxury liner, the *City of Honolulu*, on its maiden voyage to the islands.

Though the Chandlers had remodeled the *City of Honolulu* the ship was structurally unsound. On the return leg of its first run to the islands, a fire broke out, and, unable to control the blaze, the captain gave the order to abandon ship. The passengers were lowered in lifeboats to the accompaniment of the ship's orchestra and were picked up by a U.S. Army transport, en route to San Francisco. A San Francisco press party came out to welcome the army ship as it approached San Francisco Bay and, on discovering the story of the L.A. boat, prepared to file stories mocking LASSCO's attempt "to interfere with San Francisco's traditional supremacy in the Pacific," as one passenger described it.

Before the transport reached harbor, one of the passengers from the *City Of Honolulu*, a local realtor and Chandler associate William Paul Whitsett, sent a wire to Chandler explaining the situation and the potential bad press LASSCO faced once the ship arrived. Chandler immediately sent a message to his friend Secretary of War Weeks, who ordered the army ship to reverse course and head down the coast to Los Angeles. "On board there was almost a mutiny," Whitsett recalled, describing the reaction of the sailors to the orders. "Friends and relatives by the hundreds were waiting anxiously at the San Francisco docks to welcome their kin and loved ones." Two days later the transport docked in Los Angeles.

Meanwhile Chandler and Dillingham systematically began to integrate their interests. The Dillingham brothers invested several hundred thousand dollars in LASSCO, and Chandler and his associates invested heavily in the Dillingham companies in Hawaii. LASSCO purchased 40 percent of the stock in the B.F. Dillingham Building Company, which had constructed a major Honolulu office building complex, with Chandler, Sherman, and Whittier providing a $245,000 loan to LASSCO to help finance the purchase. The Chandler group also took shares in the Dillingham-controlled Honolulu Land Trust Co., Cebu Sugar Co., and other sugar holdings in the Philippines and tried to arrange loans through the Pacific Mutual Life Insurance Company for Dillingham's Hawaiian development. Armstrong in Washington provided necessary political ties to the Republican administration and in exchange asked to be appointed Washington lobbyist for the Hawaiian Chamber of Commerce at a $400-a-month fee. Chandler and Sherman did their best to cultivate Hawaii's Governor Farrington, who had been appointed by the "Matson crowd," as Sherman put it. "We must be sure and please the Governor (He can do a lot for us)," Sherman wrote to Armstrong.

Both the Chandler and Dillingham interests launched major compaigns in Los Angeles and Hawaii to promote tourism. The *Times* devoted whole sections of its booster Midwinters to praising Hawaii. Once regular service between Los Angeles and the islands was instituted, the service broke the San Francisco monopoly over both trade and passenger travel. In 1927 LASSCO surpassed Matson in the number of visitors it brought to Honolulu.

After some initial hostility from Matson, the huge San Francisco company decided that the increased traffic to Hawaii actually benefited the company in the long run by its expansion of Hawaiian/U.S. relations. Dillingham, in turn, established much closer relations to the Big Five and began to be referred to as the Little Sixth.

In 1930 Matson approached the Chandler interests to suggest a possible merger. An agreement was reached on October 14. But unknown to Matson, LASSCO was in serious financial trouble. Passenger traffic in 1930 had declined by one-third, and freight traffic was also down. LASSCO had badly overextended itself financially, particularly through the reconditioning of the *City of Honolulu* in 1926, and had been juggling funds between its owners and the company. As early as 1922 Sherman had described LASSCO as a very poor investment; he had always insisted that he and Chandler had organized it "to help build up Los Angeles." Indeed, with a minimum of cash and a maximum of political maneuvering, Chandler and Sherman had accomplished their goal of cracking the San Francisco shipping monopoly. Eventually they even received a favorable return on their investment through the Matson merger.

The merger pleased all parties. Matson wanted a Los Angeles base and a more secure monopoly over Hawaiian trade, and the merged company could now shift its headquarters to an expanding Los Angeles and eliminate effective competition. Ralph Chandler was named Matson vice-president and later became a director of the San Francisco-based Crocker Citizen's Bank. The Chandlers received a considerable amount of Matson stock.

By the late 1930s Harry Chandler had become a legend in his own time. Based in a city that at the turn of the century didn't even claim to be a junior partner to East Coast economic interests, he systematically built an economic empire. "If General Otis was the architect of the *Times* and the coincident growth of Southern California," Chandler intimate Kyle Palmer commented at a *Times* commemorative event, "Harry Chandler was the builder." *

---

*See pages 396-397 for chart giving Harry Chandler's economic interests.

CHAPTER 9

Intervention in Mexico

1. The C–M Ranch

At the turn of the century, political and economic conditions in Mexico, with its dependence on foreign capital, provided an ideal situation for the spawning of another Chandler syndicate. Since 1876 the country had been governed by General Jose de la Cruz Porfirio Diaz. Don Porfirio's iron rule encouraged foreign investors, which the general felt was the best way to convert the country from a semifeudal to a modern industrial nation.

At the time Diaz took office, large areas of Mexican land by tradition belonged to the Indian villages. The Diaz regime, viewing this a burden holding back progress, developed a policy of taking over those "national lands" and assigning them as concessions to favored individuals. Under laws during the 1880s and 1890s, individuals receiving concessions were to "colonize" the lands by selling them to foreign investors. " . . . It thus came about that a small number of foreign companies had free reign to roam the country and examine the titles of all property owners in Mexico," historian Frank Tannenbaum wrote. "The companies were allowed to retain one third of all the 'national' lands they discovered, and to purchase the rest at [a] pittance."

German, English, and American buyers picked up millions of acres of Mexican land; 20 percent of the country's land soon belonged to foreigners. Among the first purchasers was the Hearst family, which acquired— for twenty cents an acre—a 200,000 acre tract. Besides owning much of the land, the foreigners—mostly Americans—laid claim to mines, manufacturing plants, banks, oil lands and refineries, public utilities, and almost all the nation's railways. The country had, according to Tannenbaum, "become the 'catspaw', the tail of the foreign capitalistic kite."

The Diaz regime resorted to repressive measures against those who disagreed with its policies. Elections were a farce; the press was controlled; protests led to execution, imprisonment, or exile; and the courts leaned over backwards to protect the foreign interests.

In 1898 Harry Chandler took a trip to Baja California, the peninsula of Mexico which extends south from California. Chandler wanted to investigate some land being offered for sale by General Guillermo Andrade, a Diaz supporter who had served as Mexican Consul in Los Angeles. Andrade had acquired a large tract for less than ten cents an acre from President Diaz several years earlier. Chandler expressed his interest in the land by paying $3,000 for a three year option to buy the territory at sixty cents an acre.

In August 1902 Chandler organized the California-Mexico Land and Cattle Company with a capital stock of $2 million. Three months later the new syndicate incorporated in Mexico as the Colorado River Land Company, S.A. The directors and major stockholders in the two companies included Chandler, General Otis, *Times* official Albert McFarland, Frank Pfaffinger, Moses Sherman, and Otto Brant and three other officials of Title Insurance and Trust Company.

In the spring of 1904 the company began to exercise its option. Its first acquisition was 230,000 acres of the Andrade estate, described by the son of syndicate member Otto Brant as "the biggest cash purchase ever made in Mexico up til that time." About a month after the original Andrade purchase the syndicate acquired a 10,000-acre tract from the Mexican Irrigation Company, then followed the purchase of 135,907 acres known as the Mountain Land Tract or Cocopah Lands, another 450,000 acres from a group of Petaluma and San Francisco buyers, and an undivided half-interest in another 40,000-acre tract which Andrade had earlier sold to other investors.

Though major decisions about the operation were made by the company's board of directors, the day-to-day affairs of the immense ranch —over 860,000 acres of Mexican land—were under the direction of the resident general manager William K. Bowker. A tough man with a reputation as a colorful character, Bowker also became a member of the syndicate.

One thousand acres of land in California's Imperial Valley had been purchased simultaneously with the Mexican acquisitions by a syndicate composed of Chandler, Sherman, Pfaffinger, Brant, and Allen. "As soon as they'd decided—found they were going to get the Mexican side—they began to look for land on the American side so it would work back and forth," Brant's son noted.

The Mexican and Imperial Valley lands became known as the C-M

(California-Mexico Land and Cattle Company) Ranch. Many of the Imperial Valley residents viewed Otis and other C-M absentee owners with bitterness. "The corporation," oldtimer Gordon Stuart recalled, "showed no signs of having a heart, not a trace." Others, however, looked forward to the annual barbecue which the ranch sponsored as part of its horse and mule sale. People from all over the valley attended. "There was a glamour associated with the big Mexican ranch," engineer Walter Packard remembered, "and the barbecue that was hard to ignore."

Though separate ranch headquarters existed on both sides of the border, the two territories were treated as one. Policies set on the Mexican side determined those for the Imperial Valley lands, as the border was virtually nonexistent. Still, the syndicate realized that it depended on favorable relations with the Mexican government.

From the outset C-M managers maintained influence with the Diaz administration. Chandler and Sherman had both met with the Mexican president, and emissaries from the ranch were occasionally sent to Mexico City to make sure their interests were taken care of and "to stir things up" if necessary, as Sherman put it. In return, the *Times* printed pro-Diaz stories.

Chandler and Otis also used their ties to the U.S. government to their advantage. After the syndicate's initial purchase, Otis had written to President Roosevelt to ask "just consideration" of the federal government in protecting his Mexican interests, and in 1910 President Taft appointed General Otis to represent the U.S. at Mexico's centennial celebration.

" MASSES NOW TAKE INTEREST IN THE GOVERNMENT AS NEVER BEFORE KNOWN " a July 3, 1910, *Times* headline proclaimed about Mexico under Diaz. Just a few months later, a full scale revolution broke out against the government. Three major figures emerged from the uprisings: Francisco Madero, son of a wealthy landowning family, who represented the professional and capitalist anti-Diaz forces; Pancho Villa, leader of the northern peasant movement; and Emiliano Zapata, who led the peasant movement in the south. In May 1911 President Diaz, beseiged by the three revolutionary groupings, resigned. After the fighting died down, Francesco Madero took power and was subsequently elected president.

The *Times* expressed hostility to the revolution. "He brought order out of chaos," the paper said of Diaz. "If he has been a despot," another *Times* editorial commented, "he has been a wise and benevolent despot. Railroads and factories and foundries have been built, mines have been opened, over $1 billion of American capital has been brought in. . . . "

"The triumph of the insurrectos," a *Times* editorial noted while Diaz was still in power, "would be a triumph of advanced socialism. The property of foreigners and of the wealthy class of Mexicans would be confiscated. Americans would be driven out and while thousands of Mexicans would be relieved from peonage, they would go out of the frying pan of industrial slavery into the fires of enforced idleness, homelessness, and hunger.'' Otis wrote to Taft, ''that nothing short of the prompt suppression of the insurrection will serve to save the day, not only for the welfare of our sister republic, but also for the interests of thousands of Americans residing in Mexico and the millions of American money invested there. . . . Should the worst come to the worst, it would be sound and justifiable policy on the part of the United States to intervene by force for the protection of American citizens and interests in Mexico and for the sustaining of President Diaz in power.''

2. The Baja Rebellion

Otis's desire for American intervention was increased by events in Baja California, the seat of the C-M ranch. In the winter of 1910–1911, an anti-Diaz armed insurrection led by the Mexican Liberal Party spread across the northern half of the province. The Liberals, a mixture of socialists, anarchists, and Wobblies, called for distribution of Baja's land, 78 percent of which was then under foreign ownership, to Mexican peasants. The party was headed by two brothers, Ricardo and Enrique Magon, who had been living in exile in Los Angeles.

For several months, battles between the Diaz forces and the Magonistas raged through Mexicali, Ensenada, and Tijuana. ''BANDITS SACK MEXICALI ACROSS STATE LINE—MOTLEY REVOLUTIONIST BAND IN POSSESSION OF MEXICALI,'' a *Times* headline noted in January 1911. A few days later, as the Liberal party ''army'' moved west from Mexicali, a *Times* page one story with the head HOBOS AND CRIMINALS FLOCK TO STANDARD OF INSURGENTS continued to assail the rebels. ''The chicken thief band now numbers about 200,'' the *Times* story began. ''Most of the revolutionists are either Mexican criminals or mongrel Americans who have good reasons for not risking their presence again on American soil.''

As the rebels continued to fight, *Times* attacks became so hostile that the *Imperial Valley Press* accused the Los Angeles paper of being the ''worst offender of truth and decency in its border reports.'' The Mexican insurrectionists, a *Times* editorial alleged, were made up of the same kind of people responsible for Los Angeles's recent strike wave. ''The apostles of disorder,'' the *Times* called them, ''the missionaries of unrest, the jawsmiths of closed-shop unionism, the haters of honest industry, the acquisionists of other people's property, the enviers of other people's prosperity, the brawlers, the larcenists, the dynamiters, the I.W.W.'s and the friends of raising the devil generally are flocking to the standards of Absalom. The air is incarnadined and made mephitic with their presence.''

While the paper kept up its campaign, Otis and Chandler worked to try to get military help from their friends in the federal government. In February Otis wrote to Secretary of the Interior Ballinger and to the State Department urging military action against the Baja rebels.

The Taft administration was prepared to protect a partially constructed canal system, designed to bring Colorado River water to California's Imperial Valley. The canal work had been contracted in the name of the Colorado River Land Company, with funds estimated by Chandler to be $1 million and supervision provided by the U.S. government.

Only a few days after the Magonista uprising, the U.S. government requested protection for the canal construction area from the Diaz government and sent Brigadier General Tasker H. Bliss to check on conditions in the Imperial Valley. Otis, who had known Bliss in the Philippines, traveled to the border with him to present his views on the situation. "This class of people, " Bliss wrote to the war department, "ardently desire the intervention of the United States to put a stop to the insurrectionary movement in Southern California before it gathers headway."

But many in Los Angeles and the Imperial Valley did not share Otis's sentiments. "The majority of Americans . . . were sympathetic to the rebels," according to Lowell Blaisdell's extensive account of the Baja events. Several newspapers during the early days of the campaign also favored the Liberal party insurgents. Mass rallies held in Los Angeles in support of the Magonistas prompted an angry reaction from the *Times* which called the participants "conspirators . . . who are openly aiding the Mexican rabble."

Harry Chandler, in a May 1911 letter to Otis, noted that a "majority of residents," of the Imperial Valley were aiding the Baja insurgents. "There is an unfortunate, and, I think amazingly disloyal and stupid sympathy existing in the Imperial Valley for the insurrecto cause," Otis wrote to Taft. "They are a bad lot," Otis continued, referring to the Baja rebels, "who ought to be exterminated in the interests of right, peace and order, and for the protection of honest citizens on both sides of the line."

But Bliss decided against intervention and rejected Otis's proposal that U.S. troops establish a three-mile martial law zone along the border. "It is a great shame that these scoundrels are permitted to hover on the border, to secretely cross and recross for their own wicked purposes, and to jeopardize the peace and the interests of citizens of both countries," Otis wrote to Taft, continuing to urge intervention. "The socialistic American leaders of the insurrection . . ." Otis went on, "openly boast that they intend to seize and divide up among themselves the real property of the California-Mexico Land and Cattle Company."

As the rebel troops began to "requisition" food, horses, and other supplies from the C-M ranch, Otis and Chandler appealed to the Mexican government for aid. The Diaz government officially—though "privately," as Otis put it—authorized the Colorado River Land Company to organize a "police force" of its own to protect its property and the canals. The Mexican government also informed Otis at the end of March 1911 that some five hundred Mexican soldiers armed with machine guns were on their way to Mexicali. "It appears that there is a God in Israel who utters the Spanish tongue with a strong Mexican accent," Otis wrote to Taft on the arrival of the troops. "The danger in Lower California is dispelled." C-M men were quickly enlisted as guides and scouts for the federales.

But Otis's happiness was short-lived, as the federales failed to follow through on their initial victories. "The insurgents are getting fresh recruits very rapidly," C-M manager Bowker wrote to Chandler. "They come on every train and get across the line in the night. They are also securing more ammunition and arms daily . . . if this foolishness is allowed to go on much longer you can depend upon the C-M co. losing every animal and all improvements on the Mexican side." Three days later Bowker informed Chandler of insurgent raids on three of their camps, and the announcement by a rebel leader that "the insurgents intended to hit the C-M ranch and hit them hard from now on." "We have plenty of horses, cattle and provisions—enough to feed a thousand men for many months," an IWW appeal for more men declared, "and you bet we are not living on coffee and doughnuts either, but living on the fat of the (what used to be) Otis and other ranches . . ."

As the situation deteriorated, Otis went to Washington to lobby. "The situation at Mexicali and throughout the Mexican end of the Imperial Valley is much worse than at any time before," Chandler wrote to Otis in Washington. "Unless we can get relief our ten-thousand-acre alfalfa field will die from lack of water and our company will be up against more than a quarter-million-dollar loss." Otis phoned Taft to fill him in on the situation, but the president was still unwilling to intervene.

After Diaz resigned, Chandler wired the new president, Francesco Madero, urging him to send troops immediately to suppress the "band of outlaws" in Baja. Chandler and the *Times* played upon the ideological divisions between Madero and the Magonistas and helped spread the notion that the Baja rebels intended to take over the peninsula and secede from the rest of Mexico. Chandler told Madero of threats to dynamite the Imperial Valley Canal, and described the insurgents as "almost entirely American anarchists and criminals" who claimed they were "going to make of that portion of Mexico an independent country."

The rumors of secession from Mexico spread throughout both Mexico and the U.S. and were used with telling effect to generate hostility towards the Baja revolutionaries. "The ultimate scheme," Otis had written Taft, "is to establish a socialistic republic in Lower California, cutting loose from both the United States and Mexico, and attempting to set up a Socialistic heaven of their own."

While Chandler warned Madero of secession, he privately toyed with the notion of annexation of Baja by the United States. "I am hoping," Chandler wrote to Otis in 1911, "that before the Mexican affairs are entirely settled and back to normal, that some way will be found for the United States to take over Lower California, and hope that your talk with the Secretary and the president will set the ball rolling and that it will not stop until the purchase is an accomplished fact."

Unaware of Otis and Chandler's attempt to convince the Taft government to take over Baja, Madero, after Taft granted permission for the Mexican federales to pass over American territory, agreed to send troops to put down the Magonista rebellion. By early June, with Madero's military advisor Benjamin Viljoen en route to Mexicali, the Magonistas prepared to law down their arms in the C-M area. The arrival of the Madero federales brought to an end a campaign already marked by discord among the Magonistas. Skirmishes continued through the summer, but after pressure from American socialists and Magon's older brother Juan Sarabia, a converted Maderista, the Magon forces finally surrendered.

In June 1911 a Los Angeles grand jury indicted Ricardo and Enrique Flores Magon and other rebel leaders for violating United States neutrality laws. Their trial was held a year later, shortly after the McNamara confessions. After a two week proceeding the Magon brothers were found guilty and sentenced to the maximum one year and eleven months in federal prison.

The failure of the Magonista rebellion in Baja paralleled developments in the rest of Mexico. In February 1913 Madero was assassinated by agents of Victoriano Huerta, who, with the foreknowledge of the American embassy, seized control of the government and proclaimed the end of the revolution.

The Huerta regime, which shared some of Diaz's politics of alliance with foreign interests, was a godsend to American investors, and the *Times* praised Huerta as " . . . the one man who had the Diaz quality of knowing how to deal with [Mexico's] semibarbarous population."

Political and military struggles continued, however, in opposition to Huerta. Villa and Zapata took up arms again and a third force under Venustiano Carranza, governor of the state of Coahuila joined the attack. The renewed disturbances reawakened the fears of both American investors and southwestern farmers, anxious about possible raids by Mexican "bandits" or damage to the Mexico-located irrigation system, almost the sole source of water for Imperial County ranches. Scores of telegrams arrived at the governor's office requesting national guard troops, ammunition, neutralization of the Colorado delta territory, and protection of the canal system.

As the new civil war raged, anti-Huerta forces made the C-M ranch a target, and in one instance the C-M managers had the aid of Huertista troops to recapture several horses stolen from the ranch.

In July 1914 Huerta was forced to resign, but Carranza and Villa forces continued to battle each other. While Villa retreated to the north, Carranza moved his new government to Vera Cruz. In January 1915, in a bid for popular support against Villa, Carranza issued the Agrarian Law. Despite its failure to challenge the essential structure of property rights, as the first political pronouncement to recognize the demands for land, it gave hope to the peasantry. The edict called for splitting large landholdings into smaller properties and returning them to the villages, but did not specify implementation.

Just two days after the Carranza agrarian reform decree, *Los Angeles Times* correspondent George Addison Hughes advised readers of the situation and called for U.S. intervention, under the page one headline UNITED STATES MUST INTERVENE TO SAVE MEXICO FROM HERSELF. "Intervention in Mexico is inevitable," the story began. "Many Mexicans secretly desire it . . . because the United States must save Mexico from herself and to save her from herself we must fight her."

"What the *Times* stands for and what the *Times* has always stood for in regard to Mexico," an editorial spelled out a few days later, "is cooperative intervention by the United States and other powers."

As the Villa forces continued to hold the north, Imperial Valley farmers stepped up their call for military protection for their Mexican canals. After a series of Villa attacks in New Mexico in 1916, President Woodrow Wilson sent 15,000 U.S. troops to "pursue the bandits." "Villa is a savage a little higher in type than Geronimo or Sitting Bull," *Times* power Harry Carr wrote in 1916. ". . . He has taught the peon class of the country to substitute looting and robbery for honest work. He has become an idol with the lower classes by robbing the rich and distributing easy money among the poor."

The new civil war also extended into Baja. In the fall of 1914, Balthazar Aviles took over as governor of the province. While publicly professing allegiance to Villa, Aviles actually sided with the landowners. After only three months, Aviles was ousted by Colonel Esteban Cantu and fled to San Diego.

Cantu's allegiances were not clear at first. He spoke of abolishing the export duty on cotton, a measure favorable to the large cotton-producing ranches such as C-M, but he also criticized the use of "alien labor"— mostly Japanese and Chinese—on the foreign-owned ranches.

The American interests feared Cantu would move in a more radical direction, given the mood in Mexico. When several Mexican farmers tried to seize C-M lands after the passage of the Agrarian Law in January in order to create communal farming units (*ejidos*), the C-M's owners decided to take matters into their own hands, and mobilized arms and men to protect their ranch.

A short time earlier a meeting had taken place in Los Angeles between Harry Chandler, Aviles, and B.J. Viljoen, Madero's military advisor who had led the expedition to Baja and who now served as assistant general manager of the C-M ranch. A week later, Viljoen, under Chandler's direction, gave Aviles $5,000 to use to recruit an army to overthrow Cantu.

The plot collapsed when two of Aviles's early recruits—Manuel Brassell, the brother of a *Times* employee, and J.N. Fernandez—informed U.S. officials about the plan. The government launched a formal investigation.

On February 19, 1915, Harry Chandler, Walter Bowker, B.J. Viljoen, Balthazar Aviles, Geronimo Sandoval (Aviles's associate serving as Villa's Mexican consul in San Diego), Challey Guzman (a Mexican real estate agent), and two other men were indicted by a U.S. grand jury for "conspiracy to organize a revolution against Colonel Cantu, the military governor of Lower California, an adherent of President Carranza."

The evidence against Chandler consisted primarily of the grand jury testimony of attorney Adolphe Danziger. Aviles had told Danziger that Chandler and Viljoen had given him money for an attempt to regain control of Lower California by military means. Danziger subsequently learned that C-M had placed guns and ammunition at Aviles's disposal, as well as a sixty-ton steamer to transport men from San Pedro and San Diego. Aviles had then asked Danziger to act as middleman in obtaining more money from Chandler to pay off a Carranza officer who would help the invaders take Tijuana. Danziger talked to Chandler who confirmed his own involvement. "There is no reliance on these greasers," Chandler allegedly told Danziger. "Aviles told me some months ago," Chandler went on, "that if he had $5,000 he would organize an army of his own people at San Diego and march on Tijuana. I gave him the $5,000 and he promised faithfully that he would set about at once, and now he wants more money. I want to have nothing to do with him."

The grand jury testimony of Nicholas Zugg, a former military engineer for Madero's army, corroborated Chandler and C-M's participation in the plot. According to Zugg, there existed a map of a new empire, one of whose states was named "Otis" which was to be created out of existing Mexican territory.

At the hearings, held before Chandler ally Judge Benjamin Bledsoe, Chandler and the others entered not guilty pleas. The *Times* publisher told the press that the C-M ranch always refrained from attempting to influence Mexican political affairs. Though he admitted in an affidavit that he had paid money to Aviles, Chandler claimed it had been "either for taxes past due by our company or for export duties for cattle."

A trial was scheduled for November 1915, but the defense, over government objections, was able to postpone its opening five times. One delay stemmed from a Chandler plea of illness—he had a sinus condition.

The trial finally began on May 28, 1917, more than two years after the indictments, with the Justice Department expressing concern as to the makeup of the jury venire, half of whom were well-known *Times* advertisers. Of the seventy-five veniremen, forty were officers of corporations and members of the establishment California Club. The judge suggested that the prosecutors were "unduly apprehensive about the situation."

The defendants moved for dismissal of the charges on the technical grounds that the indictment did not precisely subscribe to the language of the law. The Neutrality Act only banned attempts to enter into military agreement with an *existing* government. Since Aviles was not then a representative of a legitimate government, Chandler's lawyers argued, the defendants could not have violated the law as alleged in the indictment. Judge Bledsoe agreed with the argument and directed the jury to return a verdict of not guilty for all the parties.

The government failed to reindict. The prosecution felt that witness Nicholas Zugg, who had served three months in jail for contempt after calling the judge a "judicial prostitute" and was subsequently sent to Folsom Penitentiary for passing bad checks, would no longer be credible. And Adolph Danziger, the prosecution's star witness, had a change of heart and denied having written the letter used in the first indictment, nor could he remember anything about the events to which he had previously testified. Danziger, the assistant U.S. attorney sadly noted had "probably been influenced by some of the defendants. . . ."

3. Cantu and Cloth

As it turned out, Chandler's support for a coup in Baja was unnecessary. Soon after Cantu became governor, he made peace with Chandler and the American investors. "I realize what great pursuits have been attained by fostering agricultural pursuits in my country," Cantu had declared in early January 1915," and I certainly shall aid in developing the land rather than imposing a tax on such a valuable asset as cotton."

While battles raged throughout the rest of Mexico, Cantu developed a little kingdom of his own, closely linked to the American dollar—"an oasis of perfect peace in bloody Mexico," wrote Harry Carr. "Baja California was said to be the only country in the world that had a foreign money for a standard," recalled Gordon Stuart. "Only United States dollars were recognized by Cantu. Mexican money was unstable, and Cantu would have none of it." Cantu conducted Baja's trade with the United States rather than the rest of Mexico and paid his soldiers in American money. Most of the soldiers' money got back to Cantu in the form of taxes, and the governor also pulled in large sums of money from vice concessions, run primarily by American operators.

"Naturally," a memo from American consul Walter Boyle noted, "Governor Cantu living on the Border knows the value of American political support, the value of American newspapers who do not mention his various grafts and enormous incomes from Vice concessions that draw their revenues from the American side." The strongest of his political supporters, Boyle observed, was probably Harry Chandler, who was in "a position to deal directly with Governor Cantu exchanging much desired newspaper propaganda and the influence his newspaper can bring to bear at Washington, for protection and consideration of his holdings in Mexico."

Chandler also acted as Cantu's agent in investing the governor's money. In May 1918, Chandler and Sherman "lent" $15,000 to a close friend of Cantu's, and a month later the C-M ranch paid off the debt. In other cases the bribery was more subtle. While the American government opposed Cantu's tax of five dollars a month on bonded mules and tried to get it removed, Chandler associate J.S. Dodds was put in charge of collecting the tax. Of the five dollars collected, only one dollar went to the Baja government. The other four, according to the U.S. consul in Mexicali, was divided "between Governor Cantu and the officers on the 'inside'. . . . The presumption is that this arrangement was made because in the first place the local Americans seeing that the Chandler interests were profiting in the tax would become convinced of the futility of trying to seek redress through Washington, and in the second place because these interests could be used to justify the tax if redress was sought in the United States."

While Cantu, who had declared himself neutral in Mexico's civil war, worked out his arrangements with Chandler and the American landowners, he incurred the wrath of the Villa and Carranza forces. As early as January 13, 1915, a Villa representative demanded that the Baja governor step down in his favor. When Cantu subsequently made his peace with the Villa forces, Carranza envoy Enrique Cota launched an attack, calling the governor a captive of American interests.

Finally in early 1917 Carranza consolidated his power. Cantu hinted at secession. "Lower California will be separated from the Mexican Republic," the Mexican consul in Los Angeles warned Mexican government officials in January 1918. "Its government with Cantu at the head, will declare in favor of the allies and will be recognized as an independent state by the government of this country [the U.S.]."

The American government, now at war, and the *Times* were concerned that Carranza's Mexico might seek an alliance with Germany. "We will seek no spoils of territory," a *Times* editorial declared in April 1917. "Of course if Mexico shall be mad enough to offer her territory as a base for German military operations against us, we will be compelled to guard our frontier by moving it down to the south line of Chihuahua, Sonora, and Lower California. Wherever American valor shall plant the American flag, there the flag shall stay."

Mexico's new Constitution of 1917 increased Chandler's enthusiasm for Baja's secession or for American intervention. This revolutionary document extended the 1915 Agrarian Law. Under Article 27, the government declared its right to expropriate foreign-owned land and foreign-dominated concessions. The creation of government-owned ejidos granting Mexicans small plots of large village-farms was suggested as an interim measure to return the land to the people.

Since the 1910 uprising, the C-M ranch, preparing for possible expropriation, had geared its agricultural policies toward immediate profits instead of long-range development, which would have required large capital investment. Much of the land was never developed, and the major crop on the cultivated portions was cotton, which yielded immediate profits but also exhausted the soil. Most of the cotton was grown after 1910; previously cattle and other livestock had been the main source of income.

In 1916, the C-M ranch harvested 26,623 acres of cotton—$2.1 million worth. Within a few years a total of 92,975 acres had been planted in cotton, bringing in $28 million. The ranch also produced thousands of tons of cottonseed and cottonseed oil. *The New York Times* described the C-M set-up as "the largest cotton growing enterprise under a single management in the world." The Chandler interests also held substantial control of the Compania Industrial Jabonera del Pacifica, S.C.L., which acquired the ranch's cotton gins.

Some eight thousand Mexican laborers worked the C-M fields. Many were employed by tenants, who leased portions of the land from the company, such as the Phoenix Beef Co., which rented 1,000 acres. A large number of the tenant farmers were Asians, primarily Chinese, who were alloted parcels ranging from 50 to 1,000 acres. Because of the tenant employment system, employee dissatisfaction was often directed at the renters rather than the owners of the ranch. Interracial hostilities, exacerbated by wage and working condition differentials between American, Asian, and Mexican laborers, became common on the ranch.

By 1918, 72,000 acres of C-M property were leased. Two-thirds of that acreage was in cotton. Rents varied from one dollar an acre for uncultivated land to ten dollars an acre for developed areas. The system was highly advantageous for the syndicate owners. "Uncultivated land was given up, through a certain quota, for only a year; at the end of that time the client who had cleared it and worked it, paid for this land ten times more rent" wrote historian Pablo Martinez.

Besides gaining revenue from rental income, the company also profited by financing loans to the small farmers. Imperial Valley farmer Gordon Stuart recalled that Chinese farmers were charged 50 percent a year on money borrowed to operate their ranchlands. The Colorado River Land Company also owned substantial shares of two banks in Calexico, on the American side of the border, and was also involved with the Mercantile Bank of Mexicali. Sherman and Chandler each mantained $150,000 on deposit and jointly subscribed $25,000 when the bank was reorganized and its capital increased. Tenants also financed their plots by selling their crops to the Jabonera del Pacifico company.

Despite the provisions of the 1917 Constitution, expropriation of foreign-owned land did not occur right away. "Article XXVII is still a part of the Mexican constitution but its rights have been softened by recent legislation," a *Times* editorial noted in 1923 in commenting favorably on Mexico's new head, General Obregon. "American companies engaged in legitimate enterprise in Mexico have not been hampered or robbed. The government has sought to encourage the investment of foreign capital in productive enterprises by protecting the property of foreigners and making their taxes as light as the efficient function of government will permit."

The *Times* had developed a comfortable relationship with Obregon, who had seized control of the country after a military coup in 1921. Obregon, the paper noted, "is not one of those demagogues who seek to curry favor at home by arousing enmities abroad." Sherman and Chandler made frequent visits to Mexico, and on one occasion Sherman wrote of meeting Obregon in Nogales and going in his private car to a barbecue. "He generally gets what he goes after," Sherman said of Chandler after the latter made another visit to Mexico in 1924. That year, the *Times* publisher persuaded the Mexican government to lower duties on the transportation of cotton across the border and got a contract for the CRLC to build a railroad connecting Baja and the United States, for which Obregon would provide one-half the costs.

The Obregon government also accomodated American interests by meeting specific demands of the U.S. government, including a nonretroactive interpretation of the 1917 Constitution to exempt landholdings such as the C-M ranch purchased prior to the constitution's enactment. In 1924, in exchange for a nonretroactive payment policy, Chandler renounced claims totaling $750,000 against the Mexican government for alleged damages resulting from the revolution.

Warm relations also continued between the C-M owners and Baja's government. Though Cantu was finally ousted in 1920, many of his policies were continued by his successors. "Harry Clark [the C-M manager in the 1920s] said that he saw the new governor," Sherman wrote to Chandler shortly after Cantu was replaced, "also he likes the new man and he hopes he will be all-o.k." The next year Clark and Chandler took the governor to the San Fernando Fair. "Everything about him seemed good. He seems to like Harry Clark very much" Sherman wrote. The same letter informed Chandler that the new governor had taken a cut in salary from his former career in banking and expected some help from his American friends.

Chandler also attempted to use his influence with the American government. Through Washington correspondent Robert Armstrong, the *Times* publisher tried to convince President Hoover to make an official request for a change in Article 27 of the Mexican Constitution. "He suggests in effect," the State Department wrote to Hoover, "that you take some steps looking to changes in the Mexican law so that Americans can invest there with less difficulty and greater safety, particularly in stock ownership."

Amicable relations continued with Obregon's successor, Enrique Calles. Though the new president publicly favored a retroactive interpretation of Article 27 and sponsored an antialien land law, he compromised with American interests, agreeing to enforce expropriation gradually and pay satisfactory compensation.

The C-M owners, faced with harassment by squatters, future expropriation, and all sorts of financial impositions, began to consider liquidating their interests. In 1917 a Japanese syndicate, according to Chandler, had offered $50 million for the Mexican lands, but the State Department interceded and stopped negotiations while the war was on. A group represented by a Toronto, Canada, agent also considered the land but did not come to an agreement. After these deals fell through, the C-M owners decided to try to deal with the Calles government, and by the early 1930s a tentative agreement had been reached to purchase the ranch for between ten and twelve million dollars. But this agreement, too, was never consummated, thanks to increasing anti-American sentiments.

In 1932 the Mexican government confiscated 55,000 acres of C-M land, claiming defective title. Two years later General Lazarus Cardenas came to power and ended all trace of pro-American policy.

Cardenas's land reform program developed into a policy of "colonization," in which foreign landowners yielded their land to Mexicans in exchange for an equivalent compensation. The C-M owners, therefore, tried to avoid direct expropriation by setting up their own private colonization program. "In view of the communistic trend of the country," Sherman's successor Arnold Haskell wrote in 1936, "we may never collect from the colonists." The ranch, with government approval coming in April 1936, began to sell tracts of developed land to Mexican citizens for about eight dollars an acre, offering a twenty-year payment plan. By 1937 311 colonists had bought 35,000 acres, though few could meet the annual payments.

The company's land distribution program was, however, inaccessible to the poor tenants. So in January 1937, 400 rural laborers responded by seizing the C-M lands as well as those of other foreign owners throughout Baja. The squatters planted the Mexican flag and refused to move until their petitions were heard. Within hours of the land seizures, C-M managers and tenant/owners appealed to Baja Governor Rafael Navarro Cortina to move against the squatters. Cortina responded immediately, and when the squatters refused to leave, troops came and arrested scores of people.

The syndicate intended to continue its colonization program, but government expropriations in 1937 and 1938 changed their plans. C-M land expropriated by the Mexican government was subsequently sold—with ranch owners and colonists, whose lands were mistakenly included at first, in opposition—for a price barely one tenth of the C-M price. Again Chandler tried to sell his land at a bigger profit, attempting to work out an exchange system with Mexicans living in Los Angeles. Property in the United States held by Mexican nationals was exchanged at two and one-half times its value in C-M acreage. Many Mexicans living in and around Los Angeles participated by exchanging their tiny plots of Los Angeles real estate in order to return to their homeland.

The Chandlers then provided "virtually 100 percent financing" to allow the repatriated Mexicans to develop their new land. This financing was accomplished through Chandler-linked Anderson, Clayton and Co. (new owners of the Jabonera del Pacifica), the Chandler-Sherman Corporation (a corporation created solely for various Chandler deals), and several banks in Calexico and Mexicali. By the late 1920s, Chandler had sold most of his Baja and Imperial Valley banking investments, but in order to deal with the new situation he returned to the banking business by either buying up or reorganizing some of his old banking concerns.

Within eighteen months after the beginning of the government's colonization program 180,000 acres had been returned to Mexican hands. With settlements proceeding rapidly, the Cardenas government increased its expropriation activities. Chandler made a deal for his unseized C-M land—considerable amounts of which he still owned in the early 1940s—with W.O. Jenkins, an American serving as Mexican consular agent in Pueblo, Mexico. In return for the Baja land and its bank, finance company, and cottonseed oil mills, Jenkins exchanged improved business property in Los Angeles worth more than $1.5 million.

Chandler, however, insisted he had not gotten sufficient payment for his expropriated land and decided to get a ruling from the U.S. courts, which might give him extra clout before a Mexican Mixed Claims Commission. On March 11, 1938, the Superior Court of Los Angeles County ruled that the Chandler syndicate's Baja lands were worth $3.9 million or about $120 an acre, allowing for land with "cultivation and improvements." The Mexican government claimed that the land should sell for one-quarter of that amount. Chandler also claimed an additional $1.63 million was owed him as interest.

The dispute went before a new American/Mexican Claims Commission set up in the early 1940s. Just weeks before he died, Chandler sent a letter to California Attorney General Bob Kenny outlining the C-M situation. Up to September 1944, the Mexican government, through the Mixed Claims Commission, had paid him $838,000, but the *Times* publisher wanted more. In the late 1940s, several years after Harry Chandler's death, with a conservative government in power in Mexico, the matter was finally settled.

The total ultimately received by the Chandlers included $3.75 million for compensation, $1.5 million worth of Jenkins property, and countless small plots in Southern California from the exchange program. In 1904 Chandler's syndicate had paid under $500,000 for the C-M land. After four decades they had cultivated only one-fourth of their property, yet by 1950 their descendants had received the equivalent of $5.25 million plus unaccountable Los Angeles property for that acreage—plus the profits extracted from the land in the forty-year period.

The Chandler involvement in Mexico stands as a classic case of foreign profiteering in an underdeveloped country. As major landholders in a country with a majority rural population and through their political and financial ties, the C-M/CRLC syndicate wielded enormous power with the Baja and Mexican governments. Such influence was multiplied through Otis and Chandler's use of the *Los Angeles Times* news stories and editorials to promote causes that aided their Mexican interests and bitterly attack those movements which attempted to seize the massive C-M ranch to return the land to Mexico's landless peasants.

4. The Imperial Valley

Before he retired from his position as superintendent of Los Angeles's Water Department, William Mulholland once again had called for a new water supply: the Owens Valley watershed was no longer sufficient, Mulholland argued, because of Los Angeles's accelerated growth. Though Mulholland and other water officials had estimated in 1905 that the Owens aqueduct would be more than sufficient until the end of the century, "if not for all time," they now spoke of the urgent need—less than two decades later—for a new supply and a new aqueduct. Mulholland looked now to the Colorado, the great river of the West which flowed down to the Mexican border.

Since the turn of the century, Colorado River water had been used to irrigate the farmlands of the Imperial Valley. The first construction cut into the river eight miles south of Yuma, Arizona, in 1900, but soil conditions and other problems forced construction to move further and further south, into what later became the C-M lands.

In 1906 the Colorado River broke through its banks and flooded the Imperial Valley, creating financial ruin for farmers and the irrigation company. In 1910 the federal government, under pressure from Harrison Gray Otis and Imperial Valley residents who feared another flood, sought to resolve the Colorado River problem. "SITUATION OF LOWER COLORADO EXCEEDINGLY SERIOUS," Otis telegrammed President Taft. "UNLESS QUICK RELIEF CAN BE HAD THOUSANDS OF PEOPLE AND MILLIONS IN LAND VALUES WILL BE JEOPARDIZED." The Taft administration responded by funding a twenty-five-mile levee and dam on C-M land, which was constructed by army engineers under the aegis of the C-M/Chandler syndicate. A treaty with the Mexican government stipulated that 50 percent of the water taken from the Colorado would be used in Mexico; in effect, on lands controlled by the Chandler syndicate. During water shortages one bitter Imperial Valley resident recalled that the C-M "would help themselves to the water while the ranchers north of their border saw their crops dry up."

State and federal representatives continued to hold discussions on the use of the Colorado River by the states bordering the river. In 1922 a federal Colorado River Commission, chaired by Herbert Hoover, worked on an agreement. Harry Chandler and C-M representative J.C. Allison insisted that such an agreement was unnecessary since there was enough water to meet all needs, but government officials disagreed, and their efforts resulted in a Colorado River Compact ratified by six states, including California.

After the compact was signed, a federal Bureau of Reclamation proposal authorizing the federal government to build and operate a power generator and high water storage facility on the Colorado River near Boulder, Colorado, was embodied in a bill in Congress sponsored by California Representative Philip Swing and Senator Hiram Johnson. The Swing-Johnson bill also specified that waters to irrigate the Imperial Valley would be brought to the valley via an "All-American Canal" that would provide no water for Mexican land.

The Swing-Johnson plan was enormously popular in Southern California, but it also caused intense political controversies regarding the allocation of water, its use as a source of electric power, public versus private ownership of the power source, and the restrictions of the "All-American Canal." All these issues directly affected Harry Chandler and the *Times* and he made major efforts to influence each one.

Chandler vigorously opposed the Swing-Johnson bill and favored an alternate plan to provide a low flood-control dam with power generating facilities under private ownership. The *Times* and the Chandler-backed private power companies led the opposition to the Swing-Johnson bill.

In August 1921 the public ownership forces, including Socialists, trade unionists, and progressive businessmen, had organized as the Public Power League. The private interest lobby set up their own group, the People's Economy League. Chandler and the *Times* gave the private interests strong backing, especially when the issue came to a head in the 1925 mayoralty race between incumbent George Cryer and *Times*-backed Judge Benjamin Bledsoe. After Cryer rode the issue to victory, Los Angeles's Water Department and Power Bureau merged to form a municipally owned Department of Water and Power to control the water and power supply for the city. The DWP exhibited a probusiness, proexpansion outlook in offering cheap rates for industrial and business users and low rates—cheaper than its private counterparts—for consumers.

The second issue for Chandler was the All-American Canal, first proposed by Chandler's long-time enemy Hiram Johnson, who hoped to create a canal at the U.S./Mexican border which could divert waters from the Colorado to the American side of the border rather than letting it flow naturally into Baja. All-American Canal advocates combined arguments of national chauvinism with populist and anti-big business appeals primarily directed against Chandler and the C-M ranch. While Imperial Valley ranchers had to pay eight dollars an acre foot for Colorado water, Chandler only paid eighty-six cents on the Mexican side of the border.

On May 7, 1924, Chandler appeared before the Arid Lands Committee of the House of Representatives to testify about the All-American Canal. He said he opposed the canal, but not because he had Mexican lands. "I am only opposed to the All-American Canal," Chandler testified, "because I have considerable land holding on the American side. We have figured that the All-American Canal would put such a burden on that land as to make the land valueless for farming." Chandler thought the idea, which involved "prohibitive costs," was "impracticable from an economic standpoint."

While debate continued in Congress, Chandler, with the *Times* and the C-M ranch, mobilized to defeat the canal amendment. "BOULDER DAM BILL MIRAGE," a *Times* headline cried in 1925. The ranch issued a series of pamphlets on the subject, complaining in one that taxes on Chandler land holdings would be doubled if the legislation went through.

Johnson continued to defend his bill and bitterly attack his opponent, calling Chandler's position an act that did "injury of Americans and of the country to which he should yield grateful allegiance."

When the Boulder Dam bill passed in Congress in December 1928 after two defeats, Johnson's canal amendment passed along with it. Even after the act was passed, Chandler still fought the canal. In the fall of 1931 he sent a letter to the Interior Department suggesting that they proceed with the utmost caution on the canal, since, Chandler asserted, it would reduce Imperial Valley farmers to ruin by imposing an unbearable financial debt on them, result in overproduction of food products, and jeopardize prior water rights in the area.

In spite of his defeats, Chandler, having sold most of his Mexican lands by the time Boulder Dam was completed, could be pleased with the overall project. The new water and power supplies from the Colorado, Chandler noted, would insure "the development of the whole Pacific Southwest territory—a region of tremendous possibilities—a new empire growing and developing faster than any other part of America." By the 1920s, Chandler's "Los Angeles First" philosophy had been expanded to include the entire Southern California region from the Arizona border on the east to Mexico on the south.

Chandler, who had maintained close ties with numerous interests in the outlying communities of the Southern California basin, quickly began to promote the notion of region-wide use of the Colorado to promote region-wide growth through an aqueduct that would bring its waters to the Southland. Through annexation, the local establishment had used Owens Valley water to create Greater Los Angeles. With the Colorado, the goal shifted to the creation of a supra-agency for the entire region. "The communities of Southern California are all members of the same big family," the *Times* commented, after Los Angeles first applied for the Colorado waters. "What we do for them we do for ourselves. As they grow stronger and richer and happier, so do we grow in like proposition."

As an Imperial Valley investor, Chandler benefited from the Boulder Dam act *and* the canal provision. He owned banks, buildings, and lots in the Imperial Valley towns of Calexico, Niland, and Calipatria, and rented land to other farmers and companies. Chandler, Sherman, and C-M manager Bowker took over a dominant role in the Imperial Valley Farm Lands Association, a selling agency which had belonged to the Southern Pacific. After the association bought 45,000 acres of land from the SP some Imperial Valley settlers brought suit hoping to prevent subdivision and price-gouging and asking that the lands be sold to settlers at a fixed price. The suits were dismissed by Chandler's friend Judge Benjamin Bledsoe on the grounds that there was "no cause of action."

Finally, with the *Times* pushing the idea of Southland unity, Los Angeles and several adjacent cities voted to create a Metropolitan Water

District (MWD) to supervise Southern California's interest in the Colorado waters and any future water supply serving the region. Set up in 1928, the MWD's first chairman, William Paul Whitsett, a former Chandler-associated realtor from San Fernando days, sounded the now time-honored Southern California cry: new water supplies feed future population growth and economic expansion. "They say a man is just as old as his arteries," Whitsett told the Rotary Club soon after assuming MWD leadership. "I say a city on the desert has ceased to grow and is starting to decay when its aqueducts fail to carry to it an ever-increasing, unfailing supply of water—its lifeblood of wealth and growth." Whitsett predicted the Colorado supply would cause Los Angeles to double its population within ten years. "This is the new Babylon on its way," Whitsett's biographer quoted him, "one vast city between Santa Barbara and San Diego."

That was the kind of talk the *Times* knew best. "Today the work of conserving water for future needs goes on," a Times Midwinter proclaimed as construction on the Colorado aqueduct got under way, "looking forward to the day when the Los Angeles basin will be the home of from seven to ten million people."

Ultimately, Chandler came out ahead in all areas. He had cashed in his Mexican lands for a comfortable profit; thanks to the Colorado, his Imperial Valley land benefited; and, once again, Los Angeles had more water to feed its endless quest for expansion.

CHAPTER 10

THE RED MENACE

1. Bolsheviks at Home and Abroad

Harry Chandler's *Times*, quick to attack Mexican revolutionaries, also denounced the uprisings which, during and after World War I, threatened to sweep through Europe. The events in Russia in 1917 demonstrated to American businessmen where such revolt might lead. *Times* coverage reacted with scare headlines—RED TERROR RIPS SILESIA; REDS KILL OFF PEASANTS, BOLSHEVIKI DESTROY SCHOOLS IN SIBERIA.

But Chandler, unlike General Otis, would readily discard ideological positions if an economic objective warranted it. On October 22, 1920, the Bolshevik government, so assailed by the *Times*, signed a sixty-year lease with an American mining and oil engineer named Washington B. Vanderlip to develop the Russian oil and coal fields in Kamchatka in northeast Siberia. Vanderlip, a distant cousin of Frank B. Vanderlip of the First National Bank in New York, had conveyed the impression to Lenin and his ministers that he represented a powerful American syndicate, which quite possibly involved Republican presidential candidate Warren Harding.

Three days after the signing of the lease, the *Los Angeles Times* ran a page one story about the Vanderlip agreement, mentioning that about "25 businessmen, all of them reputed to be wealthy and several of them rated as multimillionaires, are associated with Mr. Vanderlip." The next day a little box in the back of the paper listed the syndicate members, headed by Harry Chandler and including Chandler's closest business associates such as oil men Max Whittier, William Stewart, and E.L. Doheny, and financiers J.F. Sartori and Lee Phillips. In its story, the *Times* quoted Vanderlip — who became known as the "Khan of Kamchatka" — commenting favorably on Lenin and the Russians.

While the *Times* played down the syndicate, Hearst's *Examiner* had a field day. "CHANDLER DENIES HE IS A BOLSHEVIK FISCAL AGENT," one *Examiner* headline proclaimed, quoting Chandler statements that he knew very little about the whole matter since his syndicate had only provided funds for Vanderlip but was unaware of the terms of any deal that Vanderlip might have arranged.

Chandler's position greatly amused his political antagonists. "Imagine the Los Angeles 'Times' and J.F. Sartori in alliance with Nickolai Lenin," Hiram Johnson wrote to Meyer Lissner. "What a sermon there is in the transaction and how it demonstrates what we have so often said of these people. They prate about the 'Reds,' they talk of the horror of Bolshevism, they would draw and quarter every man of liberal tendencies, and yet, when they can turn a dollar and make a little profit, they will deal with anything or anybody."

Some rubbed it in. "By the way Harry," municipal reformer John Haynes wrote to Chandler, "when I asked you, while sitting by your side at a luncheon not long ago, how you could conscientiously enter into a business deal with Lenin, a man you had been daily denouncing as a blood thirsty fiend desirous of destroying all property rights throughout the world—with the color mounting to your face—you said you had entered into this deal for patriotic motives. Oh Harry, what an arrant humbug you are. For after the news of the concession became known your paper gave a whole page or more convincing the people what a fine fellow Lenin really is—Oh Harry what a ranting humbug you are."

When the Kamchatka concession failed to win approval, the *Times* went back to its condemnation of the Bolsheviks. "We can make honorably no compromise with criminals," an April 1922 editorial announced, arguing against U.S. recognition of the Soviet Union, "and it would be to sully our national honor to send representatives of our government to sit about a conference table with those representing a government guilty of a thousand crimes against justice and humanity."

While the *Times* assailed the foreign "Bolsheviki," it reserved its harshest, most consistent anti-Red campaigns for its domestic enemies. During the period after World War I, a time of inflation, unemployment, and great unrest the *Times* found many "Reds." There were general strikes in Seattle and Portland; a strike by the Boston Police Department, walkouts by longshoremen, carpenters, telephone operators, stockyard employees; and the Great Steel Strike of 1919–1920. Employers saw "Red" behind every strike, as the Red tag became a convenient way to consolidate the business establishment's resistance to socialists, labor unions, and reformers.

Attorney General A. Mitchell Palmer, a businessman close to the National Association of Manufacturers, in an attempt to destroy the country's radical movements, extended—with the aid of his assistant J. Edgar Hoover—the Red scare campaigns through his infamous nighttime raids in 1919 and 1920, which rounded up an estimated 10,000 men and women in cities all over the United States. The *Times* strongly supported the Palmer raid arrests, calling them "evidence of a widespread plot to sovietize the government and industries of the country."

Los Angeles, however, the *Times* declared, is "freer from the menace of Bolshevism than any other city of equal population in the United States." But just days after its editorial, IWW organizers arrived in the city to organize workers in Southern California's orange groves. "BOLSHEVIST CONSPIRACY BARED," cried a three-column *Times* headline, as the paper immediately launched into a systematic attack against the Wobblies, constantly alluding to them as "Russians" and undesirables who only worked a few hours a week. The proof of the "conspiracy," the *Times* claimed, was available in government files that identified the citrus organizing as "directed and financed from New York by the Bolshevist or Russian section of the IWW." The paper also ran numerous accounts on alleged sabotage, though the police were never able to back up the paper's accusations.

The continuous scurrilous characterization of the Wobblies—"young Russian men and women with bobbed hair in the approved Bolshevik Washington Square manner," as one article described them—by the area's most powerful newspaper had its effect. A strong anti-IWW sentiment developed, which ultimately manifested itself in an outbreak of vigilantism. What was needed, one anti-IWW leader declared, was the "mailed fist the late General Harrison Gray Otis would have used." The vigilantes gave the Wobblies an ultimatum to leave town, loaded them on trucks, threw their furniture into the street, and escorted them to the city limits of Los Angeles, where many were arrested for disturbing the peace. The Wobblies eventually abandoned their orange grove efforts.

Los Angeles businessmen, still concerned about future organizing attempts by the IWW, decided to insure themselves through protective legislation. A group of conservative Southern California businessmen, organized as the Commercial Federation, pressured state authorities to move against the radicals. State legislators responded by passing the California Criminal Syndicalism Act.

The act, specifically aimed at the IWW, defined criminal syndicalism as anything which advocated the commission of crime, sabotage, force, violence, or terrorism to effect changes in the industrial or political order. Anyone who even circulated literature or belonged to a group which advocated such beliefs would be subject to felony charges, punishable by one to fourteen years in prison. Mere membership in a group like the IWW was thus grounds for arrest.

Other states had passed similar laws between 1917 and 1920, but none were used with such vehemence as California's. "A veritable witch hunt was inaugurated," ACLU President Clinton Taft recalled, "and kept up for five years." Over five hundred people, primarily IWW members, were arrested on syndicalism charges, with more than one hundred ultimately going to jail—all without proof they had committed any overt acts. The policy, as George West wrote in the *Nation*, was clearly designed to dispose of any labor unrest. In the climate of the postwar anti-Red hysteria, Los Angeles employers were able to employ what West called "legal terrorism" to accomplish their antilabor goals.

In the fall of 1919, the anti-IWW campaign gathered momentum in the Los Angeles area. In early October, while the *Times* drummed up support with a series of news stories playing up the apparently destructive nature of the IWW, police stormed the local IWW hall and arrested several Wobblies. *Times* headlines the next morning proclaimed a WAR OF EXTERMINATION based on Los Angeles police chief George Home's promise that the Wobblies and "all their kind" would be driven out of Los Angeles. "The time has come to strike and the whole force of the police and the district attorney will be used to combat the working of the Reds who are attempting to gain a foothold in this city . . . ," the *Times* quoted Home. "Today the cleanup has started and will continue until the last of their number have been placed behind bars or driven out of the state."

Despite the stories of IWW violence and sabotage, convictions under the new criminal syndicalism law were too few for some of the business establishment. The American Legion, hoping to remedy the situation, set up a "Law and Order" committee to work with the police, and warned the attorney general that its "future activities . . . in dealing with the IWW would not be confined to the adoption of resolutions and verbal attacks." After the group organized a "military" branch, representatives met with District Attorney Woolwine, Mayor Snyder, Chief of Police Home, the sheriff, and a Department of Justice official to work out an unofficial alliance that included arrangements for deputizing the Legionnaires.

That same evening, twenty-five men disrupted a meeting at IWW headquarters. Four persons were hospitalized and five IWW members were arrested for inciting to riot. While the American Legion received congratulatory notes after the occurrence, the *Times* story on the event noted that there was "no clue" as to the identity of the raiders.

Three days later, fifteen legionnaires were sworn in as special deputies, and Buron Fitts, one of the leaders of the California Legion, was made special district attorney. Later, the police established an "anarchist and bomb squad," forerunner of the infamous "Red Squad," to gather evidence against the IWW. Then the Los Angeles City Council passed a "Red Flag Law" which made display of any flag or banner or symbol of opposition to organized government a felony. The law was quickly overturned.

The liaison between the American Legion, the police, and the city's business leaders—with the cooperation of the AFL—soon succeeded in undermining IWW strength in the city. The Palmer raids contributed to driving the IWW underground throughout the country. In 1920 Mayor Snyder praised the Legionnaires for their part in ridding Los Angeles of the IWW "nuisance."

2. The American Plan and the B.A.F.

The methods that worked so well in destroying the radical movements were also applied against the regular labor movement and its sympathizers, as well as against any liberal political movement. A well-organized campaign against trade unions developed out of a national network of open shop organizations, many of which sprang up overnight after World War I, which gathered in Chicago in January 1921. The basic strategy—officially adopted in the name of the "American Plan"—was to equate the open shop with Americanism, while labeling unionism and the closed shop "un-American" and equating every demand for better pay, shorter hours, or regulation of child labor as the first stage of a Communist takeover.

The American Plan involved a lot more than just propaganda. In the name of protecting the American way, employer organizations made frequent use of strongarm measures such as the discharge of union members, the blacklist, the "yellow dog" contract (under which a worker was forced to sign a statement as a condition of employment that he or she would not join a union), professional strikebreakers, company unions, and outright violence. "To the employer," a *Times* editorial declared, "the American Plan guarantees the right to run his business on sound economic principles free from dictation by unionite overlords."

By 1920 the wave of strikes that had swept the country the previous year had diminished dramatically. By the end of the decade strikes were almost nonexistent. Wages were down, as industrial activity sped ahead. Even closed shop San Francisco began to shift toward open shop conditions.

In open-shop towns like Los Angeles, the reduction of union activity was only a matter of degree. The Los Angeles M & M stepped up its campaign to defeat the few gains realized by labor during the war, and new industries joined the open shop ranks. The major struggles of the early

1920s in southern California, such as those in the movie studios and the Kern County oil fields, ended in defeat for the unions.

Open shop employers also had the aid of a new organization—the Better America Federation (BAF). BAF, under its previous name, the Commercial Federation, had organized to combat socialism, Bolshevism, the IWW, trade unions, and the Progressive party, all of whom were seen as closely related. The group claimed credit for the passage and implementation of the California syndicalism law.

Shortly after the war, the group, headquartered in Los Angeles, adopted the name of the Better America Federation. Under the leadership of its chairman, Harry Haldeman, it became the political arm of the antiradical, antilabor, antiprogressive forces in the state. Haldeman, the city's leading pipe and plumbing supplier, was involved in a number of Chandler-related activities including the Yosemite Park and Curry Company and the Beverly Wilshire Investment Company. His son and Harry Chandler's son Norman became close friends (and his grandson, H.R. Haldeman, developed a reputation of his own as Richard Nixon's chief of staff). Though Chandler himself never joined the BAF's Board of Directors, his closest business and political friends, such as Eli Clark, his lawyer Oscar Lawler, Fred Baker (of National Erector Association and Chandler shipbuilding ties) and Henry Robinson of the First National Bank, were among BAF's founders and leaders.

"Its purpose," a BAF newsletter described the organization, "is to sound a cry of warning whenever it detects the presence and influence of the radical-socialist in the government, the church, the workshop, the home. These institutions must all be protected and kept pure from the taint of radicalism; for they are the institutions to which is entrusted the duty of making better Americans." ". . . the Reds have as many disguises as the traditional Prince of Darkness," noted a newsletter piece on "The Red Plot to Seize the Churches."

BAF put out "educational" materials against labor demands such as the eight-hour day, the minimum wage, and other social welfare legislation. "The open shop," pamphlets cried, "is the American way."

"The Better America Federation, which is really a camouflaged open-shop group, is affecting organization throughout the state," Progressive party member Katherine Phillips Edson wrote in 1920. "They . . . are trying to make it appear that every man who joins a trade union is both an anarchist and a socialist, and at the same they are subtly undermining the social welfare legislation inaugurated by Johnson."

The BAF attacks ranged through every sector of society in its attempt to undermine any progressive activity. The group denounced teachers and professors "who have infected our boys and girls with the poisonous psychology of revolution"; they also kept watch over newspaper editors "who have prostituted their columns to the propaganda of the 'reds'" and who "have taught the masses that the possession of wealth is a crime." Enlisting the aid of student informers, BAF organized a spy network to identify students and teachers guilty of "subversive-sounding" remarks. The group then exerted pressure on the school administration to keep teachers in line and on local employers to refuse summer jobs to students unless they changed their political outlook.

Basic to the ideological onslaught was the BAF effort to elect candidates who shared its point of view. In Los Angeles, the Republican-oriented BAF worked through its political front, the Association for the Betterment of Public Service, a group of one hundred county businessmen that had formed at the suggestion of the *Times* in the hope of "saving" the state from the progressives. Since Hiram Johnson's 1910 victory, political differences between the northern and southern parts of the state had widened considerably, with the south becoming increasingly conservative. "We have the whole campaign blocked in Southern California by the activities of an organization camouflaged under the name of the Better America Federation," Katherine Phillips wrote to a friend "It is a powerful group of non-union employers. They have large money interests back of them and they are controlling public opinion through the press; are putting their stamp of approval on candidates for the legislature and congress and even the judges are crawling to their chairman Mr. Harry Haldeman, and explaining why they make the decisions they do. It seems the ultimate debasement of Southern California and you could never believe it was at one time the seat of the Progressive movement of this state."

The key struggle was over control of the state government, which was in the hands of the Progressives. In 1918, former Los Angeles Mayor and Congressman William Stephens—appointed lieutenant Governor by Johnson in 1917—won the gubernatorial election. Though Stephens had viciously attacked the IWW, he continued some of the progressive policies initiated by Johnson. His sponsorship of the King Tax Bill, which called for increased taxes for corporations and private utilities to eliminate the state's treasury deficit, especially created conflict with the state's large corporate interests. The fight over the tax bill was described as "one of the most acrimonious parliamentary struggles in California annals."

As Stephens sought to win support for the measure by touring the state, Chandler assigned his political reporter Kyle Palmer, recently hired away from the *Express*, to follow the governor and report on his activities. "The administration's corporation-baiting junket is political in its inspiration and seeks among other things to lay a foundation for a campaign to re-elect Governor Stephens two years hence," Palmer wrote in one of a series of articles attacking the governor and the tax bill.

Both sides prepared for assembly debate of the tax bill, with the *Times* via Palmer and the Better America Federation attempting to influence assembly votes. The efforts were successful—as the bill fell short of the necessary two-thirds margin; and a bitter pro-King state senator accused BAF of trying to take over the state government.

With the defeat of the King tax measure following hard on the heels of Warren Harding's presidential victory in 1920, Republican conservatives, led in the south by Harry Chandler and the *Times* and in the north by Michael de Young of the *San Francisco Chronicle* and Joseph Knowland of the *Oakland Tribune*, set their sights on defeating Stephens in the 1922 gubernatorial election. In preparation, Chandler and his associates in 1921 organized the Lincoln Republican Club in an effort to win back control of the Republican party from the Progressives. Chandler, Henry Robinson, Harry Haldeman, former Assembly Speaker Phil Stanton, Edward Dickson of the *Los Angeles Express* (whose paper had turned increasingly conservative), and Pasadena banker John Willis Baer sat on the group's board of directors.

The Chandler/Young/Knowland newspaper triumvirate, supported by the corporations that had fought the King tax bill, backed former State Treasurer Friend Richardson for governor. With Kyle Palmer playing an active role in the campaign—"more active than any other newspaperman in the state" according to Assemblyman Elmer Bromley—Richardson won the election. After the conservatives returned to Sacramento, progressive programs were cut back, the budget cut, and the progressive trend reversed.

Friend Richardson also proved to be a friend of the Chandler interests, granting patronage to the Chandler/Sherman group, as in the appointment of Sherman's secretary R.W. Priestly as Los Angeles County notary public. Despite the support of the Chandler/Sherman forces, Richardson, whose administration had earned the enmity of organized labor and progressives, lost in his bid for reelection to the Progressive/Republican candidate C.C. Young.

The Chandler interests also had Hiram Johnson to contend with, as Chandler and Johnson remained bitter enemies. Attacks on Chandler were an essential component of Johnson's successful reelection strategy in 1922; and Chandler, Sherman, and Eli Clark picked up half the campaign debts of Johnson's opponent, Charles Moore.

Johnson also irritated the *Times* by running against Chandler-backed candidates in Republican presidential primaries in California. In the 1920 campaign Chandler became statewide treasurer of the Hoover for President Clubs. Johnson also entered the race, campaigning on his antipathy to the League of Nations, a stand which lost him the backing of many progressives. Johnson's "Americanism" helped him pick up support from a number of arch-conservatives, including de Young, Knowland, and William Crocker. Though Johnson defeated Hoover in the primary, he failed, for the first time in his career, to poll a majority in Southern California, and eventually he lost the nomination to Ohio Senator Warren Harding.

Johnson tried again in 1924. Though Chandler still had close ties to Herbert Hoover, the local conservative establishment rallied behind Calvin Coolidge (who had become president after Harding's death) as the strongest candidate. William May Garland headed the campaign in Southern California and Chandler and Sherman aided the fund-raising. Coolidge had succeeded in avoiding being touched by the Teapot Dome and Shipping Board scandals which had rocked the Harding administration, and his appeal reached out to those eager to maintain the status quo. "The business of America is business," Coolidge proclaimed, and California's Republican voters responded two-to-one in his favor.

"HIRAM JOHNSON DEFEATED, REAPS HIS CROP OF VENOM AND HATRED," headlined the *Times* the day after the election. The tone of the news story clearly recalled the intensity of the Otis/Johnson rivalry. "And so Hiram Johnson goes howling and foaming into political oblivion," the article began. "It is the end of the most amazing career in the history of California. A career stained by treachery, cruelty, and chicanery. A career in which double-dealing went hand in hand with insensate violence and brutality. . . . Where he could not bulldoze, Johnson manipulated by political sleight-of-hand. Where trickery failed him, he plunged in with a knotted club and walked over the corpses with bloody boots. He was a born mob leader—a whooper—a howler—a roarer."

While Chandler did not live to see Johnson ousted from the Senate, he did see his friends elected to the White House. In 1928 Herbert Hoover, helped by the campaign and fund-raising efforts of *Times* political correspondents Kyle Palmer and Robert Armstrong, won the Republican nomination and the presidency. Chandler called Hoover's victory "an epochal one in the country's history." Hoover's election marked the culmination of Chandler's efforts to gain control of the California Republican party. Hoover's presidency was marked by extremely close relations between the White House and the *Times*, and Chandler's influence, exercised through his Washington surrogate Armstrong, was at its greatest ever.

3. Liberty Hill

In the spring of 1923, *Times*-backed candidates occupied the White House, the governor's office, and the Southern California congressional seat (the occupant was John D. Fredericks, who, Sherman claimed, "owed his election to the *Times*") and the mayor's office. More important to Chandler, the city had an acceptable police chief, former Detective-Sergeant Louis Oaks, who had been appointed by Cryer in April 1922.

A friendly police chief was essential to Chandler and BAF goals in Los Angeles. More than one mayor, opposed in a campaign by the *Times*, made his peace with Chandler by appointing a chief to the publisher's liking. Police cooperation was crucial to the implementation of antiunion, antiradical policies. By 1921 the department had thrown a major share of its resources into those activities. In April 1921, after BAF pressure on the city council to allocate extra funds, the Los Angeles Police Department (LAPD) officially announced the formation of a new undercover squad designed to combat radicalism. A few months later, a police "hobo squad" began a series of "antivagrancy" sweeps, rousting hundreds of homeless men asleep at the Midnight Mission soup kitchen and the local YMCA. Despite *Times* praise of the police arrests, public pressure forced the abandonment of such tactics.

A year later, more extensive raids began. As *Times* stories hinted that the IWW, then involved in a controversy in Portland, Oregon, was planning to move to Los Angeles, the police department began to round up local IWW members. The police action prompted a call to other Wobblies to come to Los Angeles to protest the criminal syndicalism law being used to imprison members and to stand up for free speech.

The new IWW effort centered around the harbor area in San Pedro. As arrests increased, newcomers kept arriving, and businessmen and shipowners began to panic. By the spring of 1923, IWW concentration in the area had reached a high point, and the group had focused its efforts on organizing the longshoremen and other maritime workers. On April 25, their effort culminated in a strike.

The demands of the "Great San Pedro Strike(s)" included: repeal of the Criminal Syndicalism Law and release of all IWW members imprisoned under it, recognition of the Marine Transport Workers Union, a minimum wage for seamen, abolishment of the Shipowners Association employment office, the granting of a worker's hiring hall, and other benefits for longshoremen and harbor workers. The strike had wide support. Many sailors refused to unload the ships, and the docks soon became tied up.

The *Times* initially played down the strike. "SHIPS NOT HAMPERED, IWW STRIKE IS FIZZLING," the paper's headlines declared the first day of the strike. Subsequent headlines continued the same theme; PORT STRIKE WAVERING, I.W.W. PORT STRIKE FAILS: SHIPPING CONDITIONS VIRTUALLY NORMAL, REDS CONFIDENCE OOZING: PORT LEADERS ADMIT WALKOUT IS COLLAPSING. Though the official *Times* history of labor conflicts in Los Angeles, written in 1929, claimed that there had been "no appreciable slowing up of business," M&M President Rice said the strike resulted in an "almost complete tie-up." According to the IWW paper the only two ships able to make regular trips between San Francisco and Los Angeles were the Chandler-owned *Harvard* and *Yale*.

The local businessmen, especially the lumber barons who made the most use of the port, refused to negotiate with the strikers. Pressure was exerted on the police to break the strike, while the *Times*, playing up the theme of IWW violence, claimed it had discovered a plot by the strikers to try to take the law into their own hands and run Los Angeles Harbor as they saw fit. Two hundred fifty men were added to the police force and imported strikebreakers began to arrive. "The time for action," District Attorney Keyes declared on May 10, ". . . has come."

The expanded police force soon began a series of mass arrests; hundreds of men were pulled in off the streets or from their homes and jailed. Fifty at a time were packed into a single jail tank without ventilation or heat, and many were beaten. Several got pneumonia. Meetings of strikers were not allowed; even those held on private property were disrupted by the police. Those who protested the arrests or handed out literature were arrested as well. In fact, people found near the harbor faced arrest unless they could prove that they weren't IWW members.

The *Times* called the drive "the greatest in the history of constituted authority against the IWW trouble makers" and continually egged on the police actions. Reports of alleged IWW threats and sabotage plots appeared often, and any tragedy in the vicinity of San Pedro was linked to the IWW. Editorials talked of REDS AT THE HARBOR and questioned the strikers' patriotism.

Los Angeles's liberal community protested the unconstitutional treatment of the San Pedro strikers. A campaign led by the recently organized Southern California chapter of the American Civil Liberties Union (ACLU) tried to get the criminal syndicalism law repealed. The *Times* responded by publishing an FBI report which described the ACLU as the defense branch of the IWW. Wealthy women who aided with bail money were attacked by the *Times*, which called them "women parlor Bolsheviks of the intellectual pink type," citing shipping men who claimed the women had prolonged the strike.

Figures like writer Upton Sinclair came to express their sympathy and support. Sinclair had informed Mayor Cryer and Chief Oaks of his intention to speak at a meeting to be held at a small tract of privately owned land that had been dubbed "Liberty Hill." While reading his speech, which consisted of the Bill of Rights, Sinclair was arrested. Chief Oaks declared that Sinclair would not be allowed to read any of "that constitutional stuff." Three other Wobbly supporters were arrested—the first had been reading the Declaration of Independence, the second had started to say, "We have not come here to incite to violence," and the third had merely remarked, "This is a most delightful climate." No reprimands were made against the police who had held Sinclair and the others incommunicado until their release on a writ of habeas corpus.

Over seven hundred people were arrested, more than the city's jails could hold. Local businessmen, with the support of the *Times*, urged the immediate construction of a stockade in Griffith Park to hold the "subversives." "The challenge to ordered government has been given, and it must be met," the *Times* editors wrote, ". . . stockades and forced labor are a good remedy for IWW terrorism."

The M&M and the Shipowners Association handed down an ultimatum that the "IWW must leave the harbor and the seamen and longshoremen must go back to their jobs at once," or strikebreakers would take over their jobs. Vigorous police work and a crusading *Times*, coupled with the thousand strikebreakers brought in to operate the harbor, finally succeeded in breaking the strikes.

But the Wobblies continued to stay on in San Pedro, where they faced another round of vigilantism. On June 14, 1924, a mob composed of 150 San Pedro businessmen, off-duty policemen, and sailors, armed with clubs, axes, and pipes, interrupted a program in the IWW hall, attacked and destroyed everything in sight. Several men, women, and children were injured, and numerous Wobbly leaders were seized, thrown into a truck, and driven to a desolate canyon where they were tarred, feathered, and beaten. The hall was systematically wrecked and a huge bonfire made of the broken furniture.

The newspapers almost unanimously excused the actions of the mob, with the *Times* blaming it on an alleged Wobbly celebration over a disastrous naval explosion, which had killed forty-eight sailors a few days earlier. Follow-up articles and headlines made it appear that the "IWW riots" had been caused by, rather than directed against, the Wobblies, and news articles warned of "reds' threat of reprisals." A sign hung over the wrecked IWW hall feebly tried to counter the paper's accusations: "No member of the IWW has ever, in word, act or thought, cast any slurring remarks upon the victims of the terrible naval disaster, or has in any way threatened to dynamite the morgue. The daily press is using these slanderous lies to incite violence." Though victims identified some of the raiders, no indictments were issued, and the raids continued. By the winter of 1926, the Wobblies, who had dubbed the *Los Angeles Times* "the bitterest newspaper foe of union labor west of the *Wall Street Journal*," had totally disappeared from the Los Angeles area.

4. Harry Calls Him Ben

Police Chief Oaks might have successfully dealt with radicals and labor unions, but his laxness about the city's widespread vice operations was not pleasing to the Chandler-dominated power structure. Vice had been an issue in local politics since 1919, when mayors and police chiefs, each pledging "reform," were subject to rapid turnover as new scandals continued to be uncovered. Chandler's strategy was to downplay the scandals in exchange for a voice in the administration and an antilabor police chief. Only after Los Angeles—which proclaimed itself the "White Spot of America," free of radicals, labor unrest, vice, and crime—picked up a national reputation as the most crime-ridden, scandalous city in the country, did the establishment decide to intervene.

The 1919 affair involved one of the *Times*'s top reporters, city hall man Horace Carr, who served as mayor Frederick Woodman's most influential advisor. A county grand jury indicted Woodman, Carr, and some vice operators, for arranging to open a section of the city to gambling, prostitution, and liquor. Carr received immunity and testified against the mayor, who denied any knowledge of Carr's misdeeds. Woodman, defended by John Fredericks and supported by the *Times*, was acquitted.

Though Woodman ran for reelection with *Times* backing, he lost to ex-mayor Meridith Snyder, who had incurred Chandler's wrath because of his friendliness to the municipal power advocates. Snyder's police chief George Home was embroiled in a new set of scandals and every paper but the *Times*, which was still concerned about the city's reputation, exploited the issue. Snyder lost his bid for reelection to a relative unknown, George Cryer, who, oddly enough, had been backed by labor, the *Times*, Old Guard Republicans, and Southern California Edison (because of Cryer's anti–public ownership stance). Snyder accused Cryer of being Chandler's deputy because of the *Times*'s role in the new mayor's victory.

During the Cryer administration, subject to its fair share of vice and corruption charges as well, business and civic leaders like Harry Chandler began to take a greater interest in the crime problem and its effects on the city's image. "Business has continued to flow in this direction," a *Times* editorial noted in the spring of 1923, "very largely for the reason that this community has always been a place where law and order were supreme. . . ." Los Angeles's Community Development Association (CDA), an alliance of the city's key businessmen under the leadership of BAF leaders Haldeman and Harry Lee Martin and newspaper representatives including Chandler and *Times* editor Ralph Trueblood, set up its own crime commission in the hope of protecting the good name of Los Angeles. The commission had the backing of the city's daily newspapers, the Chamber of Commerce, and the M&M and utilized the organization and records of the BAF.

After Mayor's Cryer's reelection in 1923—again with *Times* backing—the CDA and Chandler began to express dissatisfaction with the continuing vice charges. Responding to the political pressure, Cryer ousted Chief Oaks and replaced him with August Vollmer, a famed criminologist and police reformer from Berkeley. Vollmer, with the support of the crime commission, the Municipal League, and the BAF, immediately clamped down on the department and its links with vice operations. But Cryer's manager, Kent Parrot, called the "de facto mayor" by the *Los Angeles Record*, was not happy about Vollmer. Parrot, "a swaggering, more or less insolent and altogether colorful personality [of] imposing physique and magnetism," as the *Times* described him, basically ran the city, much to Chandler's chagrin. Parrot, the mayor, and the D.A. all wanted to see Vollmer ousted, but the crime commission wanted him to stay. D.A. Keyes called the crime commission an "oligarchy of great wealth," charging that Harry Chandler controlled it and hoped to use it as his means of influencing city officials. Parrot agreed; as a profile in the *Record* put it, Parrot had two obsessions: to break up the crime commission and "to place tacks in spots where he thinks that Harry Chandler, publisher of the *Times*, is apt to sit down."

The Parrot group won out, and Vollmer was replaced with Parrot's friend Lee Heath. It was a direct affront to the *Times*. As a member of the crime commission, Chandler tried to get Cryer to remove Heath, but the mayor, nearly reduced to tears and exhaustion, according to one report, refused. Cryer, according to *Times* editor Trueblood, was "a great disappointment." As the 1925 election neared, the *Times* cast about for a new candidate, eventually settling on federal Judge Benjamin Bledsoe, who had ruled favorably on Chandler's Mexican affairs, and was known for his antilabor bias and ease in handing down labor injunctions.

Parrot, in anticipation of such opposition, had built his own political power base among public power advocates, organized labor, and gambling and vice interests, and had pulled in large campaign contributions through his protection of criminal operations.

The key issue of the campaign proved to be public ownership of the city's utilities. "Keep Cryer, Protect Your Water and Power" became one of the mayor's campaign slogans, as Bledsoe's pro–private ownership position led many reform-minded groups and individuals to side reluctantly with the vice-ridden Cryer regime.

The Chandler/Bledsoe relationship also became an important factor in the campaign. A cartoon in the *Record* showed a pompous and stuffy Judge Bledsoe on a court bench, holding a gavel, with Harry Chandler standing familiarly by his side. The caption read: "Harry Calls Him Ben." The cartoon became an instant success, as the Cryer campaign printed it up on thousands of posters that were placed all over the city.

The *Times* tried to counter the effect of the cartoon by putting out its own front page drawing showing a smiling judge with the caption "Everybody Calls Him Ben," but the damage had already been done.

"Shall we reelect Boss Parrot?" the paper asked, as its pages overflowed with pro-Bledsoe pieces, praising his "notable public record" as compared to "the dilatory and vacillating attitude of Mr. Cryer during his two terms in office.'' The day before the election, page one of the *Times* local section carried a long Bledsoe statement, ''What I Propose to Do as Mayor of Los Angeles,'' referring to the ''business principles'' to which Bledsoe would devote his administration. But between the ''Harry Calls Him Ben'' and ''Injunction Ben Must Go'' slogans, the *Times* had a lot to overcome, and Chandler's candidate lost by 15,000 votes.

''Regardless of all that has gone before, however,'' the *Times* said after Cryer's reelection, ''Mr. Cryer has been retained in office and should receive the support of all good citizens in all that he does for the benefit and welfare of the city. He shall receive such support from the *Times*.'' Cryer, despite some anti-Chandler appointments and political positions, did try to keep the peace with the *Times*. In 1926 the mayor appointed James Davis—described by Los Angeles reporter Harold Story as ''a burly, dictatorial, somewhat sadistic, bitterly anti-labor man who saw Communist influence behind every telephone pole . . .''—to be the new police chief Three hundred local establishment figures, including Chandler, Guy Barham of the Hearst press, William Garland, and Louis B. Mayer turned out at a celebration to honor the new chief.

Davis fostered the growth of the ''Red Squad''—the intelligence bureau of the metropolitan division which collected information on radical organizations and individuals, prepared intelligence reports to ''enlighten'' the public mind and keep public officials aware, and kept watch over public meetings, picketing, and demonstrations. The Red Squad was under the direction of Captain William ''Red'' Hynes, whose career as an undercover agent began with his infiltration of the IWW in 1922, and his double-agent role during the San Pedro strikes. ''He created so darn much disturbance,'' businessman W.P. Story said of Hynes's role in San Pedro, ''that they [the union people] were in a fight all the time and couldn't do anything.''

The squad functioned as a separate unit from the rest of the police force and maintained a close relationship with the city's business establishment. Its headquarters were in the Chamber of Commerce building, and Hynes frequently appeared with BAF leaders at public appearances. While the Red Squad acted as the foot soldiers, the BAF worked out the political strategy, the M&M worked out the economic tactics, and the *Times* provided the ideological/inspirational support. The four worked hand-in-hand, with Harry Chandler helping to link them together. Chandler, for example, served on the Ways and Means Committee of the M&M, which concentrated on the maintenance of open shop conditions in Los Angeles, and also served, with six other men, on the Open Shop Committee of the American Newspaper Publishers Association, which supplied nonunion strikebreakers for struck papers throughout the country.

Besides the police, Chandler could rely on a business-oriented county government, including the sheriff, superior court judges who could prosecute labor organizers and issue injunctions, county assessors who set taxes on real estate holdings, and an immensely powerful board of supervisors. "There was no single influence in Los Angeles as powerful as Chandler and the interests he represented," a radical newspaper remarked.

That power, however, was not in full control on the city level. In 1925 and 1926 prolabor candidates won several contested council seats and other city offices, but the following year a political uproar, spurred on by the *Times*, over shady pre-election tactics of labor official J.W. Buzzell resulted in the defeat of local prolabor candidates. Chandler also helped remove his one significant opponent in county government, District Attorney Asa Keyes, through a scandal involving the Julian Petroleum Company. The company had received some unorthodox "investments" by several of the city's bankers, MGM head Louis Mayer, and BAF leader Harry Haldeman. When Julian crashed in May 1927, just after some of the large investors had scrambled out with their profits intact, an investigation was launched by the county grand jury that led to indictments of Haldeman, Mayer, Cecil B. DeMille, and the bankers. Due to little effort by D.A. Keyes, the jury acquitted the first defendants, and Keyes then dismissed charges against the others. An astonished public questioned the D.A.'s integrity, and a secret grand jury finally met and issued an indictment for bribery against the county prosecutor.

The evidence which led to Keyes's indictment was first revealed in the *Times*. The stunning public exposure—which the pro-Keyes Hearst newspapers had previously declined to print—led to a confession by one of the participants. Keyes subsequently resigned, was found guilty and sent to San Quentin. His replacement, *Times*-backed Legionnaire Buron Fitts, helped establish complete Chandler hegemony on the county level.

The Keyes affair had an unintended negative consequence for the *Times*, since John Porter, the foreman of the grand jury which had indicted the D.A., went on, despite *Times* opposition, to win the 1929 mayoral election. Cryer, who had lost all his earlier backers, including organized labor and the municipal ownership advocates, had withdrawn early in the race. Organized labor and the *Daily News* had supported the president of the city council, William G. Bonelli, who pledged to reform the police department. Though some of the municipal ownership forces had thrown their support to Bonelli, others backed Porter, the choice of the *Los Angeles Record*. The *Times* endorsed the senior officer of the American Legion, John R. Quinn. Though *Times*-backed candidates did well for other city races, Quinn came in third. The *Times* didn't endorse either candidate in the runoff, which was won by Porter.

The new mayor's initial appointments came from the ranks of organized labor and public power groups. Even more distressful to the *Times* was a move to oust chief of police Davis. In October 1929 the city police commission officially charged the chief with incompetence and neglect of duty. The *Times*, whose power once again appeared to be circumscribed, attacked the "Dump Davis" movement as a horrendous conspiracy and filled its pages with praise for the chief. In December Davis was demoted to deputy chief in charge of the traffic bureau.

Though there had been numerous ups and downs between the *Times* and the city's mayors, D.A.s, or City Councils, Harry Chandler came out of the 1920s with his power as great as ever. He had always maintained enough influence in the city to keep the key policies such as the open shop intact. He could count on a friendly police department, county government, and much of the local, state, and national political infrastructure to further his ends and enhance his influence. His methods to maintain and extend that power, some of which developed out of the Red scare environment of the postwar period, flourished in the standpat, conservative temper of the 1920s. But as the decade ended, Chandler's methods, used with such success in the previous decade, were about to face their severest test.

CHAPTER 11

The EPIC Challenge

1. The Depression

"Know this: if you apologize for and defend the Communist, or Socialist, or IWW, or Anarchist, in the United States of America or elsewhere, you look to us exactly like them," the BAF announced in its April 26, 1929, bulletin. "You blat about free speech; you are jolly well going to get it from us. . . . We give notice that we shall continue to shoot at this accursed target; and if any mewling apologists get between us and the target, they shall *ipso facto* be considered our enemy."

The BAF proclamation signified a new phase of the old Red scare strategy, as large-scale unemployment marked the beginning of the depression, with its hunger marches and social unrest undercutting the peaceful prosperity which the country's businesses had enjoyed for the past decade.

The depression exposed the 1920s Los Angeles boom cycle, where the entire credit-based structure of easy money and financial and real estate speculation collapsed. Some of the city's largest manufacturing and financial institutions went bankrupt and/or were reorganized, including Richfield Oil, Pacific Mutual Life Insurance Company, the U.S. National Bank, and the Mortgage Guarantee Insurance Corporation. Tens of thousands of workers were thrown out of work.

To conservative businessmen like Harry Chandler, the large-scale unemployment created the conditions that made "the red prophet's job . . . easy. His work is half done for him already. Idleness is still the devil's workshop and his wholesale product is anarchy." Chandler and his allies—Los Angeles's guardians of "Americanism": the BAF, the M&M, the Red Squad and the *Times*—prepared to meet the new challenge. They immediately brought pressure to bear on the new reform mayor concerning his choice for chief of police.

Mayor Porter's alliance with the reformers had proved to be short-lived. His appointments to the water and power board began to lean more towards private ownership interests, but the key shift was his choice for police chief Roy "Strongarm Dick" Steckel, a former Tennessee steel-worker known for his rough handling of prisoners as a vice squad officer in Chinatown. Under Steckel, the Red Squad continued to flourish, and a new reign of terror was initiated against radicals. Meetings and demonstrations became an open invitation for "Red" Hynes and his squad to barge in, beating and arresting anyone in their way. They broke up ACLU forums and protest rallies and threatened hall owners who allowed the use of their buildings. "The policy of this department," the *Times* quoted Hynes, ". . . has been concerned mainly with the protection of the rights, privileges, and interests of the vast majority of the law-abiding citizens of Los Angeles, and not with protecting any asserted rights of known enemies of our government or with their fantastic and hair-splitting free speech rights." "Los Angeles Police," a well-known criminologist commented, " . . . express a theory of law enforcement more openly opposed to the constitution than any I had yet encountered."

To its critics, Hynes's Red Squad reeked of "cossackism" as it continued to prevent public discussions, raid and wreck radical headquarters, halt the distribution of literature, enter individual homes without search warrants, and arrest anyone it considered "suspicious." "Suppose it is against the law, is that any good reason why it shouldn't be done?" Chief Steckel asked.

Rejecting citizen complaints as a matter of course, the *Times*, the mayor, and the police commissioners backed Steckel. "The more the police beat them up and wreck their headquarters, the better," Police Commissioner Mark Pierce declared. "Communists have no constitutional rights and I won't listen to anyone who defends them." When a delegation of representatives from church groups, the Los Angeles Bar Association, and the Municipal League came to complain to the mayor, Porter turned the accusations around, declaring that the delegation was supporting a plot to overthrow the U.S. government.

It was a dangerous time to be open-minded in Southern California. The Los Angeles Board of Education, for example, attempted to discourage "radical" thinking by its students or teachers, using a "good citizenship" test as a prerequisite for high school graduation, with any tinge of Communist-oriented answers resulting in the denial of a diploma. Pressure was applied on teachers who leaned too far toward a radical approach, and tenure could be denied on the basis of "criminal syndicalism" in thought or deed. An investigation looking into alleged "parlor Pinks" among Los Angeles Public Library personnel took note of books on Russia on display and a talk in the library on Soviet theater.

By 1932 the Southern California Methodist Minister's Conference voiced fears that the Red Squad embodied the vanguard of fascism in the city. The next year, Los Angeles citizens, tired of Porter's Red Squad and his continuing vice connections, voted to replace the incumbent mayor with former county supervisor and city councilman Frank Shaw. Shaw, who had directed the county's unemployment relief program and established a prolabor reputation, had the support of the liberal/labor/municipal power coalition, radicals, the Ku Klux Klan, and the Hearst papers. Porter's support came from the private power interests, some underworld figures, a few diehard prohibitionists, and the *Times.*

Immediately after coming to power, Shaw began to make good on his promises to create a "New Deal for Los Angeles." He appointed a prolabor commissioner to the Bureau of Public Works, a new police commission, and frequently followed the suggestions of reformer John Haynes concerning other appointments. The Red Squad was cut back and the mayor cooperated with the city's unions, which were then enjoying a sudden resurgence in response to the recent passage of the National Industrial Recovery Act (NIRA), with its famous Section 7a granting unions the right to organize.

In Los Angeles, after the NIRA was signed into law, thousands of new members joined the unions in a matter of weeks. By the spring of 1934 a strike wave had spread throughout the state. Celery and berry pickers walked off their jobs, a protracted garment workers' strike began in October 1933, furniture workers, millinery workers, meat packers, the movie studios, and the relief workers at the Department of Charities all went out over issues of recognition or wages. Twelve major strikes, each involving more than a hundred employees, occurred in Los Angeles in 1933, and eighteen more in 1934. In May 1934 a seamen and longshoremen's walkout tied up the entire Pacific Coast and led to the historic general strike in San Francisco. Unions had transformed overnight from defensive to offensive organizations. To the participants in the struggles, it seemed like the beginning of a social revolution.

"The strike in San Francisco is not correctly described by the phrase 'general strike,' " the *Times* warned. "What is actually in progress there is an insurrection, a Communist-inspired and led revolt against organized government."

For Chandler, much of the blame lay with the new president, who had created policies which, according to the *Times* publisher, resembled "the antics of a Mad Hatter." "Judging from numerous of Roosevelt's utterances and many of his policies, he is hopeless," Chandler wrote to Clara

Burdette in 1934. "How he manages to maintain his prestige and following is more than I can understand in the face of all the impractical asinine practices that he has thrust upon us."

The *Times* publicly tried to convey the impression that the economic crisis was primarily a state of mind, and not so substantial that it required major structural changes to provide remedies. "Much of the depression is psychological," a *Times* editorial declared.

The problem of unemployment, Chandler wrote, could be dealt with simply by creating what he called a "new division of available work." His proposal, introduced into the *Congressional Record* by California Senator Samuel Shortridge, suggested lowering the work week to only five or less days a week at six or seven hours per day. "Such a readjustment," Chandler argued, "necessarily would involve a corresponding readjustment of pay, in order that no inequitable burden be placed upon industry." Thus, Chandler reasoned, more jobs would be available without cutting into industry's profits, as those workers already employed would take a pay cut commensurate to their work reduction. Unemployment insurance, on the other hand, Chandler declared, would be a bad mistake, describing it as a "dole system" that might take away the worker's motivation to work.

"In times of Depression, prepare for prosperity," the *Times* put forth as the slogan for Southern California.

2. *"I, Governor of California"*

But neither the Depression nor the insurgent movements would go away. By the fall of 1933, the entire country was in turmoil. Unemployment continued to climb and bread lines began to form in the nation's urban centers. Los Angeles County, with more than 300,000 unemployed, seemed ready for a different kind of message than the booster talk of the town's establishment.

The political insurgencies and radical challenges of the early years of the Depression were basically *extraparlimentary*—outside the electoral arena. Both Socialists and Communists ran candidates for president in 1932, but neither amounted to serious campaigns.

The Roosevelt victory in 1932 and the early months of the New Deal appeared to open the Democratic party to new constituencies and social programs, and the radical movement divided on the question of whether to attack or coalesce with the New Dealers. A number of candidates, espousing economic and social reform programs and stealing some of the thunder from the left, filed as "Roosevelt Democrats" in the 1934 election. In California, the left-leaning Roosevelt followers joined under the banner of the Democratic candidate for governor, Socialist writer Upton Sinclair.

Sinclair, the author of *The Jungle* and numerous popular tracts and novels, had lived in Southern California since World War I. He had constantly battled with the local business establishment, particularly Harry Chandler and the *Times*—described by Sinclair as the "fountainhead of so much unloveliness in California life." During the Red scare period after the war, the *Times* launched a campaign to send the writer to jail. For the *Times*, Upton Sinclair had become the symbol of Southern California radicalism. He supported municipal ownership, free transportation, the free speech rights of the IWW, and numerous social programs that the *Times* opposed.

One of Sinclair's constant arguments with the Socialist party leadership stemmed from his desire to make the Socialist program concrete and fully "American." Like the Communist left, the Socialists were constantly linked by press attacks to the Soviet Union and "Bolshevism." Their inability to communicate their programs and ideas effectively further isolated them from an already-prejudiced antiradical public.

The radical movement had been extremely effective in organizing around single issues, such as unemployment and union representation, but Sinclair wanted to reach a mass audience around a multi-issue program that could speak to both the problems of the system and how to remedy them. The best way to get his message across, he decided, was as a statewide candidate—not as a Socialist, where he might effectively be shut out from serious consideration, but as a Democrat, a party which had little organizational cohesiveness or "boss-run" traditions in California.

On September 1, 1933, Sinclair went down to the registrar of voters to change his registration from Socialist to Democrat. Within a matter of weeks he announced his candidacy for governor and issued a pamphlet entitled "I, Governor of California, and How I Ended Poverty." The campaign's slogan, "End Poverty In California," led to its "EPIC" nickname.

The EPIC program called for the creation of state authorities to run California's idle factories and untilled farms and to distribute the goods produced to feed, house, and clothe the previously unemployed Californians who would work the land and factories. Colonies or communes with their own exchange system would be set up in the factories and farms, making the whole operation self-sufficient. Though the EPIC proposal did not mention "Socialism," it directly attacked the capitalist system for maintaining unused factories during times of large-scale unemployment and having land lie fallow while people starved. Under the slogan "production for use," EPIC proposed what radicals called a transitional program toward socialism, where the public sector, run by the people who worked within it, competed with the existing private sector. "EPIC was going to be like a rising river," according to Sinclair speeches. "It would cut into the banks of private enterprise and wash away the whole private enterprise system, so that ultimately you would have nothing but EPIC colonies."

Californians bought and read the EPIC pamphlet by the thousands. The sales, which eventually reached the one million mark, provided a substantial base for campaign funds. EPIC clubs sprang up overnight; more than eight hundred were organized throughout the state. The EPICS, as they were called, began their own newspaper, which quickly reached a circulation of several hundred thousand; one issue run shortly before the election, reached more than two million. The neighborhood clubs organized in each assembly district printed their own local issue-related inserts for the newspaper, and club members became an army of newspaper distributors. Within six months EPIC had become the most important mass movement in California.

The campaign embodied inspirational as well as highly practical politics. As a movement, it began to merge its efforts with the large number of self-help cooperatives that had developed in the early 1930s—before the advent of social programs such as unemployment insurance, food stamps, or welfare aid. Poor, unemployed, and many working people banded together in cooperatives for improvised exchange systems; a poor farmer who had some surplus produce, for instance, might exchange his food for hand-made clothing produced by other members of the cooperatives. The self-help cooperatives were receptive to the EPIC notion of "public colonies," which were controlled by participants and provided services and amenities for members. For a socially and economically devastated country, the EPIC program created a real basis for hope.

EPIC was also colorful and exciting, with a premium on membership participation. When a group of unemployed actors formed an EPIC troupe, Sinclair wrote a campaign play for them entitled "Depression Island." The play became part of the standard repertoire of EPIC campaign events and led to the signing of several volunteers on the spot at each performance. By the summer of 1934, EPIC had seized the imagination of thousands of Angelenos and other Californians.

3. The Campaign

Several candidates entered the Democratic race, but it wasn't until shortly before the June primary that any of them began to take the EPIC candidacy seriously. The leading contender was George Creel, a former Socialist who had moved rapidly to the right during World War I after being named to head the propaganda arm of the Office of War Information. A second candidate, Justus Wardell, attacked Sinclair as a tool of the Communists, although both the Communist and Socialist parties had attacked Sinclair for his decision to run as a Democrat.

None of the candidates could match the organization and political esprit of the EPIC campaign. Sinclair won the primary, doing better in Los Angeles than the rest of the state. Los Angeles had shifted the Democratic party so far to the left, Creel complained after the primary, that "Hiram Johnson in comparison looks like a hidebound conservative. Northern California offered no problem, for the hard-headed hard-working native sons and daughters were in a majority," Creel added, "but when I crossed into Southern California, it was like plunging into darkest Africa without gun bearers."

Republican Frank Merriam, an uninspiring candidate, opposed Sinclair in the general election. Merriam, a close *Times* ally, had been former Speaker of the Assembly and had run successfully for lieutenant governor in 1930. When Governor James "Sunny Jim" Rolph died in 1933, Merriam was propelled into the governor's chair.

The Republican party had, prior to 1934, been much stronger organizationally, financially, and in numbers of registered voters than the Democrats—Republicans held a three-to-one edge in party registration in 1930. But business circles feared that the growing momentum of the EPIC campaign, combined with the antiestablishment sentiment throughout California, might tip the scales in favor of Sinclair.

After the primary, these business forces prepared to use any means necessary to defeat this "spectre of socialism." Under Harry Chandler's initiative, a Los Angeles business group held a war council at the California Club, the informal headquarters of the local elite. Included were not only the conservative wing of the establishment—such individuals as Chandler, Chamber of Commerce President Byron Hanna, Pacific Mutual Life Insurance Company's Asa Call, and Gibson, Dunn and Crutcher lawyer Sam Haskins—but also representatives of the progressive wing of the Republican party. The group knew it had a difficult candidate to sell, one who was capable of making mistakes if left to his own devices. They decided to centralize all fund-raising and expenditure decisions for the campaign under the charge of the group's chairman, C.C. Teague, and its secretary, Asa Call. Through business contacts, the group was able to raise an enormous sum for the campaign—estimates have ranged from several hundred thousand to ten million dollars.

The committee hired the advertising firm of Lord and Thomas—the first time an ad agency was used in an electoral campaign—to develop campaign imagery. The ad men developed a strategy of attacking Sinclair while minimizing Merriam's role. "Hold your nose and vote for Merriam," became one of the unspoken slogans, much to the discomfort of the Republican candidate. "A hell of a lot of money is being spent," Merriam told Asa Call, "and it's all about what a stinker Upton Sinclair is. But there's nothing about me." "You're a tough guy to sell and we're going to do it our way,'' Call dryly replied. ''We're going to continue to say that Upton Sinclair is a no-good-son-of-a-bitch, and we're going to spend a lot of money for that. In the last ten days of the campaign we'll promote you with billboards with your name all over the place. That's what we have planned, and that's that.''

The election generated one of the most incredible and ingenious media campaigns in American history. The newspaper triumvirate of the *Los Angeles Times, Oakland Tribune*, and *San Francisco Chronicle* organized a media blitz to discredit EPIC in every way possible. The *Times* outdid all the other newspapers in its attempt to undermine the Sinclair effort. In an October 5 editorial, ''Stand Up and Be Counted,'' the *Times* declared that the election was no longer politics, it was war. ''Underneath the sheep's clothing of pleasing euphemisms is the same red wolf of radicalism and destructive doctrines that Sinclair has preached for thirty years,'' the *Times* warned, ''and which, given the opportunity, he has scores of times pledged himself in writing to carry out.''

To prove its point about Sinclair's ''thirty years'' of radicalism, the *Times* created its famous ''boxes'': little sidebars with headings concerning Sinclair positions—''Sinclair on Marriage,'' ''Sinclair on Religion,'' ''Sinclair on Disabled War Veterans,'' etc.—quoting passages from his writings. Invariably, the quotes were taken out of context, distorting the meaning and intention of the passages. Sometimes the *Times* would use one of Sinclair's novels, failing to distinguish between a fictional writing and a nonfiction essay. Thus, in the ''Sinclair on Marriage'' box, the *Times* quoted from Sinclair's novel *Love's Pilgrimmage* describing the wonders of free love. But the character quoted was someone who— characterized by Sinclair as ''naif and foolish''—did not represent the author's point of view.

Ellipses were also frequently used to distort meanings. One passage had the quote: ''We are moving toward a new American revolution. . . . We have to get rid of the Capitalist system.'' The ellipse had substituted for: ''That does not mean riot and tumult, as our enemies try to represent.'' The actual passage then continued with favorable quotes from Sam Adams, George Washington, and Abraham Lincoln.

In a region where religious fundamentalism had deep roots, the cumulative effects of the antireligion, antimarriage statements, coupled with distortions concerning Sinclair's politics, were enormous, and undoubtedly strengthened the conviction among *Times* readers that Sinclair was an ''extremist'' of the worst sort.

The most successful anti-EPIC *Times* ploy was its famous California immigration story. At a Sinclair press conference in late September, the EPIC candidate had been asked if his plan would have the effect of causing many unemployed to come to California. Sinclair laughed and replied,

"I told Mr. Hopkins [the Federal Relief Administrator] that if I am elected, half the unemployed of the United States will come to California, and
he will have to make plans to take care of them." Sinclair—talking "seriously," as he put it—then went on to comment that it actually wasn't a
joking matter, since California's warm climate made large-scale immigration a real possibility. As the press was leaving, a *Los Angeles Times* reporter told a colleague (who passed it on to the EPICS) that he would
write a story on how Sinclair had said that half the country's unemployed
would come to California if he were elected. "But you know he didn't
mean it," the second reporter exclaimed. "Maybe he didn't mean it," the
Times writer rejoined, "but he said it, and that's what my paper wants."

The following day, the *Times* ran a banner headline: HEAVY RUSH OF
IDLE SEEN BY SINCLAIR—TRANSIENT FLOOD EXPECTED—DEMOCRATIC
CANDIDATE CITES PROSPECT IN EVENT OF HIS WINNING ELECTION. "If
I'm elected Governor, I expect one half the unemployed in the United
States will hop the first freight for California," Upton Sinclair, Socialist-
Democratic gubernatorial candidate said here today," the lead began. A
Times editorial in the same issue raised the spectre of *five million* unem-
ployed entering California after the election. The story was picked up by
the other newspapers and became the single most effective campaign de-
vice used against EPIC.

Lord and Thomas produced several radio programs devoted to the
theme, with two hobo characters aboard a freight train talking of the good
things in store for them in the advent of Sinclair's election. Simultaneously, the tightly controlled Merriam campaign issued thousands of leaflets
and put up 2,000 billboards reading, " 'If I Am Elected Governor, I expect one half the unemployed in the U.S. will hop the first freight to California,' Upton Sinclair, September 26, 1934. MORE COMPETITION
FOR YOUR JOB."

The effect was devastating. The idea that thousands, if not millions, of
unemployed would enter the state to compete for the scarce work available helped induce the panic atmosphere that the *Times*/Lord and Thomas
group had been trying to create. Sinclair and the EPICS could do little to
counteract the impact: They had no access to the established press, little
money to do counter advertising, and could only rely on their own
media—the EPIC paper and leaflets—to protest the inaccuracy. "A lie
can travel halfway round the earth," Sinclair sadly cited a Mark Twain
proverb, "while the truth is putting on its boots." The EPIC paper cited a
California Tourists Association official's statement that *fewer* people settled in California during 1934 than the previous year. The EPIC paper also
pointed out that the Los Angeles County Board of Supervisors continued
to allocate funds—$166,667 in 1934—to the All Year Club for purposes of
encouraging people to settle in Los Angeles.

Several months before the election, *Times* political writer Kyle Palmer was "loaned" to the Hollywood industry to work under Motion Picture Industry Association head Will Hays. Palmer, under the official title "public relations director of the Motion Picture Producers Association," helped organize the movie industry's participation in the campaign.

To start with, studio workers earning over $100 a week were assessed one day's wages to contribute to a fund earmarked for the election. The assessment financed the production of several movie "newsreels" which the studio heads sent to all the theaters in the state.

Movie audiences in 1934 were enormous, and films had the power to reach great numbers of people. The studios, which controlled the distribution outlets, could force theater owners sympathetic to EPIC to play the newsreels under threat of losing the main feature.

One newsreel pictured a raggedy mob scene as an announcer explained that crowds of unemployed were waiting at the border in the hope of getting into California because of the possible Sinclair victory. Though the EPIC newspaper pointed out that the crowd scenes were actually footage from other movies, almost all the major newspapers in the state failed to pick up this information.

Another set of newsreels showed a "roving interviewer" talking to average Californians about the election. In one sequence, the interviewer approached an elderly lady, sitting on her front porch in her rocking chair. "For whom are you voting?" the interviewer asks. "I'm voting for Governor Merriam," the lady replies. "Why, mother?" he asks. "Because I want to save my little home," she answers. "It's all I have left in this world."

In another sequence, the interviewer approached a shaggy man with bristling Russian whiskers and a menacing look in his eye. "For whom are you voting?" the interviewer asks. "Vy, I am foting for Seenclair," replies the bewhiskered man. "Why?" asks the interviewer. "Vell," the man answers, "his system vorked vell in Russia, vy can't it vork here?"

By the end of the campaign the entire business establishment had been mobilized. The Chamber of Commerce had set up a publicity corps. The May Company department store had held a meeting of all of its workers and insisted they all wear Merriam buttons, threatening that if Sinclair won, the store would immediately be forced to close. Banks, insurance companies. and other large corporations sent notices to their stockholders, stating that a Sinclair victory meant disaster.

"Sinclair, lifelong socialist, associate and collaborator of radicals," the *Times* declared in a front page editorial shortly before the election, "admirer, defender, and self-proclaimed instructor of Communist Russia, proposes to sovietize California and destroy her businesses and industries by confiscatory taxation and the competition of land and factory communes. Having done this he would patch their ruins together as 'public enterprise' under a system of state socialism.''

In spite of the incredible establishment-led effort, Sinclair came close to victory. Most of the votes for a third candidate, Progressive Raymond Haight—programmatically much closer to the EPICS than to the Republicans—undoubtedly would have gone to Sinclair. The combined Sinclair and Haight vote—879,537 for Sinclair, and 302,519 for Haight—was larger than Merriam's final total of 1,138,620. Sinclair had even carried a majority in Los Angles County.

For the establishment, Sinclair's defeat represented only a partial victory. Numerous EPICS were elected to the assembly and Congress. Culbert Olson, running for the state senate in a district representing all of Los Angeles, won the race with EPIC backing, and John Anson Ford was elected to the Los Angeles County Board of Supervisors. The Democratic party, thanks to the EPIC campaign, was transformed from minority status into the largest party in the state, with a two-to-one edge in registered voters by 1938.

Carey McWilliams, in his classic *Southern California: An Island on the Land*, described the impact of the Depression on Angelenos and the lasting effect of EPIC. ''Years after the campaign was over,'' McWilliams wrote, ''I used to see, in my travels about the state as Commissioner of Housing and Immigration, New Economy barber shops, EPIC cafes, and Plenty-for-All stores in the most remote and inaccessible communities in California. I have seen the slogans of the EPIC campaign painted on rocks in the desert, carved on trees in the forests, and scrawled on the walls of labor camps in the San Joaquin Valley. So swiftly had the depression engulfed thousands upon thousands of middle-class elements in California, that people thought nothing of enlisting in the campaign of an internationally famous Socialist, selling his pamphlets and books, and preaching the doctrine 'production for use.' Five years previously, these same people . . . would no more have voted for Sinclair than they would have voted for Satan himself.''

California—and Los Angeles—would never be the same again.

CHAPTER 12

"A New Deal for Los Angeles"

4. The Labor Offensive

The EPIC insurgency coincided with the dramatic revival of organized labor activities in Los Angeles following the passage of the federal NIRA law under the new Roosevelt administration. "The situation under the New Deal is so fraught with labor unionism, that it seems to me the open shop hereabouts is seriously threatened," a Chamber of Commerce memo noted in March 1934. The Chamber, with the *Times* and the M&M, urged businessmen to resist demands for union recognition, despite the NIRA law.

In Los Angeles, as in other cities, members of the National Labor Relations Board (NLRB) set up to enforce the act and deal with grievances, were drawn from open shop ranks and worked closely with the open shop forces. In Los Angeles, the local board shared facilities in the Chamber of Commerce building.

On July 5, 1935, President Roosevelt signed into law a bill introduced by Senator Robert Wagner of New York aimed to correct the faults of the NIRA. The law strengthened the powers of the National Labor Relations Board and guaranteed employees the right to organize and bargain collectively, without employer interference. Calling the act "subversive," the Los Angeles Chamber of Commerce, along with the *Times* and the M&M, opposed it and other laws, such as the Federal Social Security Act and State Unemployment. While their lawyers attempted to have the law declared unconstitutional, open shop employers continued to defy NLRB rulings that went against them.

Organized labor, after the bill's passage, launched a major challenge against employer resistance in Los Angeles. Successful organizing drives, many led by the newly formed Congress of Industrial Organizations (CIO), took place in 1935 and 1936, and membership increased dramatically. The *Times* described the new campaign as "the greatest drive in fifty years to unionize and subjugate" the city.

Open shop interests were on the defensive. The M&M reopened their placement bureau and initiated an antiunion publicity campaign with extensive *Times* participation. Several open shop articles appeared in the paper in conjunction with the M&M program, and editorials warned against the activities of union leaders.

The more reactionary members of the M&M pressed for action beyond the publicity. In the summer of 1936, a five-man committee, which included Ralph Chandler, met to deal with the situation. On their recommendation, a "special Secret Advisory Committee" was set up, which eventually matured into an M&M executive committee. Ralph Chandler became vice-president of the committee, which had the task of reorganizing the M&M to be more effective in its fight with the unions. The reorganization led to the resignation of the M&M's general manager, Edgar Perry, who opposed the shift in policy along more "militant anti-labor lines," believing it to be in violation of the new Wagner Act.

The M&M reorganization broke down into five major areas: "molding of public opinion in support of the principles of the Association . . . through cooperation of the law enforcement, legislative, and administrative branches of city and county government"; furnishing employers with guards covertly paid for and supervised by the M&M; promoting the passage of legislation favorable to business and defeating unfavorable legislation; maintaining the M&M employment office; and increasing M&M membership. The new M&M recommendations also suggested that employers raise wages to union scale in order to offset wage demands, and that they accept and even initiate collective bargaining, but through their own "company unions."

The Los Angeles Chamber of Commerce, veering sharply from its former progressive self, closely allied itself with the M&M and its fight to preserve the open shop. A chamber committee in charge of the task included the seventy-year-old Harry Chandler, whose usual modus operandi was behind the scenes. Chandler's views were frequently solicited, and he appeared as guest of honor at M&M or Chamber events. The younger open shop advocates appreciated and made use of the *Times*. It was not unusual for an open shop meeting to be held in the *Times* auditorium.

Through 1936 and 1937, the *Times*/M&M/Chamber group kept a close eye on industries which might have otherwise attempted to deal with the unions. Each kept the other informed, and the three worked out mutual programs to deal with different situations. Employer Associations were set up in threatened industries under the auspices of the M&M. Undercover detectives and private guards were hired. The association benefited from police protection and Red Squad intelligence operations, with employers covering "expenditures." Pressure was applied to employers who rejected membership in the association.

The open shoppers strategy had considerable success. Many industrial groups—including dairy employers, bakers, candy manufacturers, and dress manufacturers—organized to meet the union drives. By controlling suppliers, retail outlets, and other economic channels, the M&M could maneuver most employers into signing agreements with their respective associations. Only two industries presented major problems for the open shop proponents: the truckers and the marine workers.

Since the 1934 maritime strike, the longshoremen's fight for better conditions, under the radical and militant leadership of Harry Bridges, had turned into a bitter, protracted battle. Several short, sudden strikes and work stoppages in 1935 culminated in a major strike in October 1936. Thirty-seven thousand longshoremen and other maritime workers—5,000 in Los Angeles Harbor—walked out along the Pacific Coast after their contract ran out. The Los Angeles M&M had been involved in the struggle even before the strike call when a three-person committee, including Ralph Chandler, now vice-president of Matson Navigation, met with San Francisco ship owners to discuss the "critical waterfront situation." Reporting on the situation to the board and implementing its policy, Chandler was the pivotal figure within the M&M on maritime matters.

As Ralph Chandler worked out arrangements with the M&M placement bureau to send in strikebreakers, *Times* editorials cried out against the high cost of the strike and FDR's failure to intervene while the state government continued to pay relief to the strikers' families. In January 1937 Harry Chandler set up a luncheon—with the guest list supplied by the M&M—to discuss the problems resulting from the strike.

But Chandler's efforts could not stop the momentum of the strike. On February 4, 1937, the employers caved in and offered satisfactory terms for their workers. A year later, the longshoremen's contract was negotiated without employer resistance.

The open shop forces also failed to stop the unionization of the trucking industry in 1936. When the Teamsters Union, revitalized under Seattle's Dave Beck, the union's western region head, sent organizers to Southern California, the *Times* and the M&M responded with alarm. *Times* articles attacked the union by linking it to racketeers and accusing members of terrorizing nonunion workers. The M&M used its standard techniques of hiring guards and undercover agents, supplying strikebreakers, and enlisting the aid of the local city administration and the police Red Squad.

The M&M saw the Teamsters' drive as the "first move in subjugating this city to their domination. . . . The union situation in our city is more serious at present than it has been at any time in the past." Chandler and the open shop groups feared that Los Angeles would turn into another Seattle, where Dave Beck and the unions held considerable sway. To Chandler, Seattle was "a plague spot to be avoided by industries seeking a Pacific Coast location" because of its union domination. *Times* editorials condemning the Teamsters were accompanied by daily front page comparisons and attacks on Seattle.

The *Times*'s harsh treatment of that city prompted the chairman of the board of Seattle's First National Bank to write Harry Chandler in protest.

"Would you have Los Angeles follow Seattle," Chandler answered the Seattle banker, "in selling its birthright for a soured mass of pottage of 'labor peace?' Keep your Mr. Beck at home—or at least, away from Los Angeles," Chandler concluded, "and then we will, in friendliness to your city, cease publication of these Seattle dispatches."

Just before Christmas, 1937, the Teamsters extended their campaign to cover drivers for the Los Angeles department stores, particularly at the May Company. "DAVE BECK IS TRYING TO KILL SANTA CLAUS," *Times* headlines declared, as the paper ran full-page May company ads.

A few months later, the union became involved in a labor dispute with dairy distributors after employers protested a contract renewal with their drivers. The *Times* prepared the public for a possible strike. "Milk Now Vital Food of Infants," the paper noted. "Davebeckism now seeks to impose closed-shop tribute on every bottle of milk distributed in Los Angeles County. Today milk. Tomorrow—what?" *Times* scare tactics continued. "Some of the drivers who have refused to join the Beck union have reported that in some instances when they left milk on doorsteps or other exposed places the milk had been uncapped and fouled with cigarette butts and dirty sticks," the paper later alleged. Housewives were also warned that they might find poison in their milk.

Despite the *Times* campaigns, the truckers succeeded in almost complete unionization of the industry.

The Teamsters' success, and the subsequent Supreme Court ruling upholding the constitutionality of the NIRA, spurred on other organizing campaigns. As the balance began to shift in favor of the unions, the M&M and Chamber of Commerce held a number of joint sessions to formulate strategy for retaining the old system. Out of these meetings, a new group, Southern Californians Inc. (SCI), was formed.

The SCI, publicly launched in December 1937, functioned as a broad front to coordinate the numerous open shop interests. One of its first concerns was to pass an ordinance to regulate picketing. When the mayor vetoed the ordinance after its passage by the city council, the open shop forces prepared an initiative for the 1938 city ballot. Designated Proposition #1, the bill, which virtually outlawed picketing, received a majority of the vote, though the *Times* was the only daily which openly endorsed it.

SCI attorneys participated in the enforcement of the new law by sitting in on hearings and aiding in the prosecution of violators. With *Times* backing the SCI also tried to get a similar law passed on the state level. Though the SCI disbursed enormous sums of money in support of the measure, the proposed law had strong opposition and failed to pass.

Five days after the state election, *Times* troubleshooter Kyle Palmer, who had been invited to early SCI/M&M meetings, was appointed head of the SCI's public information committee. He was subsequently elected to the group's executive committee. Ralph Chandler sat on the group's board of directors from its inception—at the same time as he sat on the M&M board. In March 1939 he was also elected to its executive committee. Harry Chandler's links were less official; he had an open invitation to attend all meetings through a unanimous vote of the executive committee. When Paul Shoup of the Southern Pacific took on the job as president of SCI in June 1938 at a salary of $3,500 a month, one of his first meetings was with Chandler. In July 1939 an executive committee meeting responding to a move for consolidation of the SCI and the M&M concluded that Harry Chandler should be asked to call a meeting of the two boards in his office regarding the possible merger.

Meanwhile, other open shop groups organized to offset the growing labor upsurge. One of these proclaimed to have arisen spontaneously, but had actually been hatched in the offices of Harry Chandler. The *Times* publisher had invited Byron Hanna of the chamber and SCI and Sam Haskins of the M&M to hear a plan presented by Mrs. Edwin Selwyn, former organizer of a Seattle-based "Women of Washington against Dave Beck" group. She and Chandler proposed to create a similar organization of women in Los Angeles. Chandler favored Mrs. Selwyn to head the new group, but Byron Hanna wanted Mrs. Bessie Ochs, owner of a rattan factory in China. Ochs, who had previously lectured to women's groups under M&M auspices, was hired.

In September 1937 The Neutral Thousands (TNT), with the slogan "Truth, not terror," was born. The group quickly claimed a membership of over a hundred thousand but many of the names, it later turned out, had been copied from telephone directories and direct-mail catalogues. Records also claimed funding from voluntary subscriptions, though almost 90 percent of the income actually came from the SCI, who cooperated closely with the new group.

Under the cover of neutrality, TNT, with its major emphasis on publicity, tried to appeal to women as consumers. The group issued a mimeographed newspaper and broadcast several radio series, including a show entitled "California Caravan," consisting of a commentary by Mrs. Ochs and a reading of *Los Angeles Times* clippings. Another radio series offered dramatizations dealing with gangsterism and violence in the unions.

TNT developed a strategy for setting up independent company unions. By portraying itself as "neutral," the group could qualify as an impartial organization under the Wagner Act. With the aid of two male organizers, TNT created at least thirty company unions at the request of employers within a few months. "There are literally several hundred firms in Los Angeles today who never make a move among employees, change of employment, addition of workers, etc., without first consulting our organization," Mrs. Ochs boasted.

In 1939, the SCI decided that the company union organizing service was the only TNT activity worth supporting. The service was reorganized as the Employers Advisory Service, and TNT was subsequently disbanded.

Another women's "consumer" group, the Women of the Pacific, launched in 1938, was even more intimately tied to the *Los Angeles Times*. Harry Chandler's ally, Mrs. Edwin Selwyn, headed up the new, explicitly open shop group. The *Times* served as the most important publicity medium for Women of the Pacific. Some labor groups identified it, in fact, as nothing more than a front for the paper. A campaign in the *Times* editorial columns entitled "Industrial Freedom—or Slavery" was keyed to the launching of the group, and editorials often appeared urging financial support or membership.

"The people of Los Angeles would be in bondage today were it not for two men," Mrs. Selwyn replied in kind. ". . . One of these was the late Harrison Gray Otis. The other is Harry Chandler. Their great newspaper, the *Times*, has stood as a rock-ribbed bulwark against every onrushing torrent that has menaced present stability and future greatness of Los Angeles and all Southern California."

Marion Otis Chandler was among those who gave small personal donations to Women of the Pacific, but the largest contributions came from companies involved in labor disputes. The organization attempted to encourage patronage of struck firms and worked on a campaign to place a state-wide initiative restricting labor unions on the ballot. Despite urgent *Times* editorials, the measure, thought of as too extreme even by the TNT and SCI, failed to secure enough signatures.

All the open shop forces, by and large, complemented each other's work. Employer associations looked after individual industries, the M&M provided strikebreakers and other "services," TNT and Women of the Pacific put out publicity and tried to reach women in the community, the Employer Advisory Service set up company unions, the SCI raised and dispersed funds to support the antilabor activities, and the *Times* served as the ideological mentor for them all.

2. The Slow Machine

The momentum established by EPIC and the labor movement also spilled over into Los Angeles's local political scene. Within a year after the 1934 EPIC defeat, several of the city's labor, progressive, and radical organizations coalesced to form the United Organization for Progressive Political Action (UOPPA). "The issue of radicalism versus common sense is more to the fore . . . than in any preceding municipal election or since Job Harriman ran for mayor as a Socialist," a *Times* editorial warned, in response to the new coalition's slate of city council candidates. Three UOPPA candidates won election to the council. The next year the coalition set its sights on challenging *Times* ally District Attorney Buron Fitts.

Since he replaced Asa Keyes in 1928, Fitts had been, in the words of UOPPA figure Reuben Borough, a "crony and pet" of the *Times*. Chandler's top troubleshooter Al Nathan, along with A.M. Rochlein, who served the same function for Hearst's *Examiner*, had stayed in constant contact with Fitts, keeping his misdoings quiet in exchange for his loyalty.

Some of the city's progressive forces threw their support to reformer Harlan Palmer, editor of the *Hollywood Citizen News*, to run against Fitts in 1936. The *Times* did everything it could to ensure Fitts's victory: It praised the D.A. for keeping the city the "White Spot," it attacked Palmer as the "common scold of the country," and its political reporter Kyle Palmer helped raise funds for the campaign. Fitts, endorsed by the conservative AFL labor council (the CIO backed Palmer) and the Hearst papers, also had financial support from the underworld. Palmer ran a close race but lost.

The following year, the one-time EPICS and other groups from UOPPA regrouped as a Coordinating Council of Progessive Groups. "This aggregation of political extremists," as the *Times* portrayed the coalition, planned to run a campaign against the incumbent mayor of Los Angeles, Frank Shaw. Though Shaw had made good on his prolabor, proreform promises when he first came to power in 1933, he soon did an about-face.

Many blamed the *Times*, which had kept up its attacks on Shaw after his victory, for the change. According to some reports, the paper kept a file on Shaw which included photographs of checks to him from the Los Angeles underworld and proof that he was not a bona fide American citizen. Shaw made his peace with Harry Chandler; soon after the election, he worked out a "gentleman's agreement" with the *Times* by reappointing *Times* favorite James Davis as chief of police.

A year later, according to one critic, the *Times* was "bossing" Mayor Shaw and would "eventually break him." Shaw appointed former key *Times* reporter Ray Jones as his first field secretary, and the mayor cooperated with the *Times* on the sale of its building to the city.

Most importantly, Shaw allowed the *Times* labor policy to have the upper hand again. The police still remained the key to the *Times*/business strategy. Chief Hynes returned from limbo status and his Red Squad resumed its harassing tactics. In several instances police had the use of tear gas guns and projectiles supplies by companies expecting labor struggles. The most notable of these confrontations occurred during the bitter and violent Los Angeles Railway strike of November 1934. A special force of some six hundred police patrolled the railyards, and Hynes took a leave of absence to advise the railway employers—for a fee of over $7,000. Besides providing *Times* support for the railway employers, Chandler personally participated in strike-breaking activities. He started a fund to provide Christmas turkeys for employees who stayed on the job—a "scab turkey" fund as the *Citizen* dubbed it.

Police Chief Davis also had *Times* backing for his infamous "Bum Blockade" of 1936. Responding to the Chamber of Commerce and other business-related groups, who were outraged at the number of depression migrants coming to look for work in the Golden State, Davis sent 136 officers to the California border entry points to turn back anyone trying to enter the state without funds. Davis also recommended the deportation of migrant families to relieve the state's welfare system and his radio broadcasts asked Los Angeles housewives to report beggars to the police.

The "bum blockade" continued for several months, despite the protests of neighboring states and a court ruling which declared the police actions illegal. "The Attorney General may succeed in proving Chief Davis legally in the wrong," a *Times* editorial pointed out. "It was up to somebody to do something and Chief Davis did it. He may get licked but it will take some time to do it. In that interval a lot of undesirables can be turned back and a lot more discouraged from even starting in this direction." The new immigrants, the *Times* complained, had produced an "army of imported criminals" and transformed the state into a "paradise for radicals and troublemakers." If Davis's reaction was an outrage, the *Times* cried out, "LET'S HAVE MORE OUTRAGES."

As Shaw/Davis policies accommodated the *Times*'s concerns, the paper once again ignored the ties between vice interests and the municipal administration. Chandler's about-face support of the mayor and his profits from the questionable *Times* Building deal led reformers to lump the *Times* publisher together with the underworld figures behind the city government.

Once again reformers took up the crusade to clean up the city. A semi-secret group known as the Minutemen carried out an investigation of the city's graft situation and pressured the state supreme court and county grand jury to look into the matter. The grand jury, under Judge Fletcher Bowron uncovered several corrupt arrangements involving the Shaw administration, but its findings were ignored by D.A. Fitts and indictments never materialized.

The anticrime forces lined up with the EPIC-oriented groups to support liberal supervisor John Anson Ford to defeat Mayor Shaw in the 1937 election. Ford's candidacy pushed the city's business establishment into action. Under the initiation of Chamber of Commerce head Byron Hanna, a behind-the-scenes coalition with an executive committee including the *Times*'s Kyle Palmer, and Asa Call and Sam Haskins of the M&M formed to take leadership of Shaw's reelection campaign. Ralph Chandler served on the finance committee.

Shaw was backed by all the large daily newspapers except for the *Hollywood Citizen News*. In marked contrast to its 1933 position, the *Times* became the loudest pro-Shaw voice, praising him and insisting that none of the corruption charges against him had been sustained. *Times* editorials criticized Ford's inexperience and his ties to the city's radicals. "The mayoralty race," the *Times* declared on election day, "is not difficult. It rests between a tried official, Mayor Shaw, who has demonstrated his capacity, and a relative unknown with an unimpressive record as supervisor, and a political record of extreme variability . . . who has received the endorsement of the CIO as well as the communistic elements."

Ford lost, but by only 25,000 votes. He blamed the newspaper attacks for his defeat. After his victory, Shaw's campaign manager wrote to the city's newspapers thanking them for their support. Harry Chandler received special mention. "The support of the *Times*," he wrote to Chandler, "was valuable not alone because of the prestige of your newspaper, but because of the subtle and intelligent manner in which the story was handled. The voter is in a curious mood in these latter days and the direct method of approach is not always successful in a campaign. Your Mr. Cleave Jones [*Times* political reporter] cooperated with us very discretely [sic] and the result was that the material carried in the *Times* was most effective."

"The *Los Angeles Times* has praised crooks in office and if people believed that publication, they would believe that we had a good reputation. But multitudes throughout the country have always looked upon Los Angeles as having one of the most corrupt of all city governments," a *Holly-*

wood Citizen News editorial proclaimed, with its eye on the new Shaw administration. Reformers, refusing to accept the *Times* image of a scandal-free city, continued their attempts to expose and eradicate the rampant corruption linked to all levels of city and county government.

Clifford Clinton, whose parents worked for the Salvation Army, was one of those determined to clean up the city. In 1936 County Supervisor John Anson Ford had requested that Clinton, the owner of Clinton's Cafeteria, look into complaints about food services at County General Hospital. Clinton's own cafeteria had gained a local reputation during the depression when it fed thousands of needy diners for a nickel or less. His report, which noted the high quality of the doctors' food and the low-grade, spoiled food served to patients, stirred up quite a row. Clinton's Cafeteria soon became subject to harrassment through sanitary inspections calling for expensive changes, increased taxes, refusal of permits, and complaints of food poisoning. Despite the harrassment, Clinton went on, at Ford's recommendation, to serve on the 1937 county grand jury, where he initiated an investigation into graft and corruption that stretched beyond the county hospital kitchens.

Since the majority of grand jury members were Shaw supporters, Clinton did much of the investigating on his own. He accumulated a long list of gambling joints and prostitution houses which operated against the law, and sought to prove the links between them and the Shaw government. When the grand jury failed to follow up on the charges, Clinton set up the Citizens' Independent Vice Investigating Committee (CIVIC), whose backers included three of the grand jurors, Municipal League Secretary Reuben Borough, and Harlan Palmer, whose *Citizen News* published Clinton's findings.

The *Times* and the Hearst papers, on the other hand, ridiculed and belittled Clinton's efforts. When Clinton's house was bombed after he exposed Shaw administration kickbacks to the jury foreman, *Times* coverage—predominantly based on an interview with Chief Davis—suggested that the bombing was a publicity stunt for Clinton.

The 1937 grand jury's final report, which cited Clinton's evidence as entirely unfounded and unverifiable, was editorially applauded by the *Times*. The Clinton jury faction decided to countermand the report by distributing its own minority report, which outlined the relationship between the Shaw administration and the city's racketeers. The *Times* attacked the minority report as an irresponsible attempt to smear city officials to further Clinton's political ambitions.

Three weeks after the release of the minority report, Harry Raymond, a CIVIC investigator who had been scheduled to testify about campaign contributions to Shaw from the gambling syndicate, stepped on the starter of his car and set off an explosion which left him hospitalized in critical condition. The overt nature of the bombing shocked the city. The daily press immediately began to change its attitude toward the Shaw administration. Even D.A. Fitts, sensitive to the rapid political shifts generated by the bombing, began to criticize Shaw and called for a grand jury investigation into the matter. Only the *Times* failed to see what the uproar was all about. After the incident the paper gave prominent news space to Shaw and Davis, who denied any involvement on the part of the Los Angeles Police.

Though an investigation by Police Chief Davis apparently failed to show any involvement by the Red Squad, D.A. Fitts, taking personal charge of the investigation, found that Davis's subordinate, Red Squad investigator Earl T. Kynette, had been surveilling Raymond for several months, that Raymond's phone had been tapped, and that a peddler who had heard incriminating information was beaten by Kynette to keep him from talking.

On June 16, 1938, Kynette and another LAPD officer were convicted of setting explosives in Raymond's car and were subsequently sentenced to prison. Under pressure, Davis abolished the intelligence squad a few days after the conviction. The *Daily News*, among others, held Shaw and Davis responsible, and called for the dismissal of the police chief. "The intelligence squad should be abolished," the *Times* reluctantly agreed, "but Kynette's superiors are not to blame for his derelictions." The paper continued to support Shaw and Davis.

The bombing had spurred the reform groups to set up the Federation for Civic Betterment—a coalition which included churches, labor groups, and CIVIC—to consider the steps necessary to recall Mayor Shaw. The Kynette conviction hastened the process by convincing many Angelenos to sign the recall petitions. The *Times* ridiculed the recall movement as ineffective and Communist-led. "Mayor Shaw was reelected less than a year ago and by an emphatic majority of Los Angeles voters. If anything has happened since to justify so sweeping a reversal of that popular verdict as this recall seeks, it has not become public."

With the recall election scheduled for September 16, a mass meeting of the Federation for Civic Betterment convened to find a candidate to run against Shaw. Supervisor Ford, the almost unanimous first choice, declined to run. Feeling Ford was too liberal, Clinton leaned toward Superior Court Judge Fletcher Bowron, while some radical members wanted progressive assemblyman Sam Yorty. Rather than split the vote, the radical faction—led by Don Healy of the CIO's Labor's Non-Partisan League—decided to support Bowron, who reluctantly agreed to run.

Bowron had a lot going for him. His conservative background, which included six years as a reporter for the Hearst press and a position as executive secretary to Republican governor Richardson, offset any potential

Red-baiting. He was a Republican who appealed both to open shop businessmen and organized labor. Faced with the tarnished reputation of Los Angeles, which had been characterized by U.S. Attorney General Frank Murphy as "one of the most corrupt, graft-ridden cities in the United States," M&M President Elmer Howlett, along with a number of establishment figures, endorsed Bowron.

Every newspaper but the *Times* favored the recall candidate. The *Times* pictured Bowron as an "honest reformer who has become the unwitting dupe of the CIO, the Communists, and certain crackpot reformers." But it was an uneasy position for the paper, which was also greatly disturbed by the city's adverse publicity. Its support of Shaw was weak and attacks on Bowron were kept to a minimum—only two editorials referred to him directly. *Times* reporters Chic Hanson and Ross Marshall theorized that M&M's Howlett might have asked the *Times* to go easy in its attacks on Bowron and the recall movement. In exchange the conservative Clinton went easy on criticizing the *Times*. "I believe that Harry Chandler sincerely desires to use his power and his publication to build a finer Los Angeles," Clinton stated in a July radio broadcast. "But this man is—permitting only partial truths to be told. I firmly believe that this effort to present but part of the truth is well meant in that Mr. Chandler feels he is protecting the community—first from unnecessary scandal—and second from inroads by Communists. But his attitude will assist in bringing about these conditions rather than preventing them." Shaw's unofficial campaign manager, Harold Story, postulated that Clinton must also have convinced Chandler and Hearst that the conservative Bowron wouldn't greatly upset the political and economic status quo in Los Angeles. According to reporter Hanson and reformer Harlan Palmer, Chandler felt sure that Bowron would retain police chief Davis and the Red Squad if he were elected.

Shaw expressed bitterness at the halfhearted *Times* support. A pro-Shaw scandal sheet aimed at working-class voters, entitled the *Progressive Digest* charged that Clinton, characterized as a vicious reactionary employer, had made a deal with Chandler to keep on Chief Davis and the Red Squad if Bowron won. Shaw theorized that the *Times* became distrustful of him because of his admiration and support of FDR.

The *Times* Election Day editorial endorsed Shaw—but without the fervor of earlier crusades. The editorial mildly praised Shaw's "efficient and economic administration," then chided Bowron for his backers—"the radical labor agitators and Communists"—and described him as "untrustworthy."

Shaw had become completely isolated. Bowron won a landslide victory, with almost twice as many votes as Shaw. It was the largest plurality given any Los Angeles mayor, and the first time a mayor had been successfully recalled in any American city. Shaw and *Times* reporters Chic Hanson and Cleave Jones believed that the *Times* policy of only lukewarm support had played a large part in the election results.

3. End of an Era

"One thing I want to make clear," Bowron told his supporters on election night. "Harry will never call me Fletch." Any hopes of Chandler's that he might work out a compromise with the new mayor were soon dashed. "Just because Chandler has sixty million dollars on the newspaper is no sign he can run this town," Bowron noted after his victory. "He wants the kind of government he can control directly or indirectly. He can't control me, and if he attacks me, I'm not going to take it lying down."

Though by no means a radical, Bowron nevertheless represented a change of priorities and a realignment of the powers in the city. His nomination of radical Reuben Borough to the Board of Public Works, a move which greatly displeased the *Times*, augured well for those changes. One of his earliest and most important acts was to abolish the Red Squad and remove Chief Davis. Red Hynes was sent to a post in West Los Angeles, and Davis went off to head the protection unit for Douglas Aircraft. Bowron also opposed the local antipicketing ordinance, though he pledged to enforce it as long as it remained the law.

Bowron's victory coincided with other events that signified the end of Los Angeles's blatant antiunion environment. *Times* attacks and the numerous open shop fronts of the late thirties had not been able to stop the imminent triumph of the union movement. "Not since the *Times* Building was dynamited by the closed shop union terrorists twenty-eight years ago and twenty-one employees murdered, have the people of Southern California been in such danger as confronts them now," a *Times* editorial had warned in early 1938.

The old-style fear tactics no longer sufficed. Labor leaders, fed up with the continuous SCI/M&M resistance, requested the Senate's La Follette committee, charged with investigating violations of the labor act, to come to Los Angeles to look into the situation. The proceedings, held in January 1940, brought out into the open the wide variety of illegal tactics used by the open shop groups. As a result of the hearings, the company union/Employer Advisory Service ended, the SCI dissolved, and the M&M, ordered to cease its interference in labor disputes, closed its employment agency.

The momentum that had taken off with the 1934 EPIC campaign, the vibrant labor activities of the depression years, and the 1938 city recall election culminated in the state wide elections of 1938. Opposing incumbent

Governor Frank Merriam—recognized even by the Chandlers as a weak candidate—was Los Angeles's State Senator Culbert Olson, who had been elected as an EPIC candidate in 1934.

The *Times* brought back the Red scare tactics that had been successful in the previous gubernatorial election against EPIC. One editorial asserted that Olson's election would "throw open the schoolhouses to Communist meetings, promote sit-down strikes and otherwise turn the industries of California over to Harry Bridges and the CIO." Olson and his running mate for lieutenant governor Assemblyman Ellis Patterson, the paper charged, had been "assigned to Communist duty in the legislature . . . to direct the radical bloc in the two houses and secure the passage of Communist-inspired legislation."

But here too the tactics proved to be outdated. A massive political shift had occurred in California since the beginning of the Depression: the Democrats, once relegated to minority status, now far outnumbered Republican voters in the state. More importantly, the social revolution embodied in the labor movement and the flourishing of radical ideas in the arts and the media had made Californians more receptive to concepts which challenged the status quo. More and more Californians became attracted to what Carey McWilliams characterized as "the politics of utopia." On election day, Olson and Patterson swept to power, and former EPIC candidate Sheridan Downey was elected United States senator.

The victories that occurred during the 1930's exhilarated the liberal and radical forces, previously isolated and fragmented during the counter-revolutionary period of the "Red Menace" and the Better America Federation. "The air is fresh here," a California observer wrote in the early forties, "but the real twang in it is the foretaste of coming change. That really makes men's nostrils flare, and their eyes look round."

CHAPTER 13

Crime Waves, High Powers, and Union "Gorillas"

1. Times Fundamentalism

Los Angeles, Harry Chandler's *Times* had often reminded its readers, was the "White Spot of America," blessed by the absence of crime and labor unrest. The message appealed to those middle-class Angelenos of the 1920s and 1930s who identified with the paper's Midwinters, its Monday morning religious sermon reprints, its weather reports on the "storms back east," its "oil news" and "shipping news," its Southland provincialism, and its constant barrage of antiradical, antiunion reports.

The *Times* was a fundamentalist newspaper. It backed prohibition and vigorously attacked the "wet" Al Smith in 1928. Chandler had even proposed "that newspapers favoring prohibition organize a cooperative news bureau to mould public opinion toward its support." The *Times* editorial page, as Upton Sinclair liked to remark, would often break "into a spiritual ecstasy of its own," and its news file gave ample space to the city's latest religious fad. When Aimee Semple McPherson opened her Angelus Temple in 1923, the *Times* heralded Los Angeles's new evangelist. Like the other papers in town, the *Times* loved Aimee for her news value. When the evangelist disappeared in the ocean near Ocean Park beach in 1926, the *Times* carried lengthy page one stories for several weeks.

Kidnappings, disappearances, and homicides filled the newspapers of the 1920s, and the *Times* was no exception. As elections were frequently won or lost on the basis of crime conditions, the paper was also apt to use "crime" for political purposes. When pro-Chandler administrations reigned, the paper downplayed the city's law and order problems, but if a city official displeased the *Times* publisher, the paper suddenly discovered that the city was overrun by criminals.

Since the police department had always been the most crucial institution to the Chandlers, the *Times* kept a careful eye over appointments and firings of police chiefs as well as captains and heads of divisions. When the Cryer administration dismissed Chief of Detectives George K. Home, a Chandler ally, in October 1924, the *Times* took after Cryer, with the warning that the firing, which "crippled and demoralized" personnel, was coming at the worst possible moment "for what bids fair to be the worst winter in the city's history from the standpoint of violent crime," an editorial declared.

Launching one of its famous crusades to prove its dire predictions, the *Times* instituted a new column on the front page of the second (local news) section, with a picture of a clock and the caption, "In the last 24 hours—Is Los Angeles getting the police protection to which it is entitled?" Under the clock were the reports of the city's "criminal activities" for the previous twenty-four hours.

The Clock became a daily feature complementing a series of adjoining *Times* stories on "Burglary Wave on Increase" or "Crime Wave Sweeps On." "Emboldened by the apparent inability of the police to check the prevalent crime wave, thugs and bandits operating in various sections of the city late Sunday night and early yesterday morning, added a series of assaults to a long list of depredations," a November 10 story proclaimed.

Suddenly, after less than a month of the campaign, the Clock was dropped. George Home had been restored to his post as Chief of Detectives four days earlier. Crime, according to the paper, had subsided despite police statistics to the contrary.

When the *Times* was not attacking Reds or Wobblies or giving elaborate details of crime, scandal, and gossip news, it was actively boosting itself, its city, and its overall "Americanism" ideology. In the early 1920s, Chandler placed state editor Burton Smith and editorial writer Randolph Leigh at the service of the Southern California Citizens Committee, a Chandler-sponsored Chamber of Commerce offshoot. Smith and Leigh helped devise an essay contest on "Americanism" for college students, with a first prize of $1,500.

The contest became an immediate success, and Chandler decided to transform the operation onto the national level with the involvement of prestigious political personalities and a first prize award presentation to be held in Washington, D.C. He solicited the aid of other newspaper editors and turned to political friends such as William Howard Taft, Calvin Coolidge, and Herbert Hoover to help promote the affair. The newspapers provided enormous publicity and strong chauvinist appeals on behalf of the contest. Chandler's opponents, however, questioning the *Times* publisher's motivations, worried about the event. "Everything possible should be done," Progressive State Superintendent of Public Information Will Wood wrote to a friend, "to eliminate the possibility of partisan propaganda in the contest."

The 1920s *Times* was a proud, self-satisfied reflection of an emergent Southern California, celebrating what the paper called "the era of business stability." Supporting the open shop, the Better America Federation and the M&M, the paper was integral to the pro-business mood that dominated the town. Boosting Los Angeles meant boosting the *Times*: in addition to the Americanism contest, the paper also created a "Why the *Times* is Number One" competition with a $1,000 first prize.

The *Times* tried to give shape to the region by defining its values as Los Angeles's values. The paper linked its future with what it called the "triumphant pioneer spirit" of the largest city in California.

2. High Powers

By the 1920s Chandler had created a special category of favorites among *Times* reporters and editors. Alternately known within the *Times* as "pets" or "high powers," these chosen individuals acted as Chandler agents or troubleshooters to help him maintain his enormous power. In the area of straight newsgathering, Chandler's high powers acted as intelligence agents, often in conjunction with police intelligence units.

Al Nathan was the highest power of them all. He came to the *Times* when he was twenty years old to work as a police reporter. Within ten years he had risen up the organization to become Chandler's number-one troubleshooter.

A quiet, confident, neatly dressed man—a "smoothie" as one reporter recalled—Nathan was never very visible around the *Times*. Though he kept the "reporter" label, his byline appeared infrequently, and he reported to no one except old man Chandler. In the space of two decades he became so instrumental to Chandler affairs that he received more than one and a half times the official salary of the executive editor of the paper. "Al Nathan," several *Times* reporters pointed out, "was Mr. Chandler's 'fixer.'"

Nathan's troubleshooting took in a wide range of activities. During the 1923 San Pedro strike, Nathan and his young protégé (later editor) L. D. Hotchkiss went down to San Pedro, not to write stories—the *Times* had a regular man on the "shipping" beat—but to investigate the situation in order to protect Chandler's extensive shipping holdings. During the fight over the sale of the Times Building, Nathan communicated with the police department's Red Squad in seeking out information concerning the opponents to the deal. Nathan helped Chandler on other real estate matters and investigated libel suits or other court-related situations involving Chandler and the *Times.*

In the twenties, Nathan paired up with another effective troubleshooter Al (A.M.) Rochlein. "They were the Gold Dust Twins," reporter Nadine Bickmore recalled, and the two seemed to be behind every covert operation involving Chandler. One former Timesman characterized them as "Chandler's Hunt and Liddy."

Nathan, despite his political and economic activities, remained in spirit a crime reporter, a "specialist in crime news" as a *Times* obituary/editorial put it. He worked behind the scenes on most of the major murder stories of the period. By the late 1930s, Nathan began to recede from active duty and started training younger men to take his place. By World War II, his era, like Harry Chandler's, was coming to an end. His old associate Rochlein went to Hearst's *Examiner.* Six months after Chandler died in 1944, Al Nathan, his top troubleshooter, also passed on.

While Nathan took care of business in Southern California, *Times* Washington correspondent Robert B. Armstrong actively looked after the Chandler interests on the national level. Armstrong's clout rose with the coming to power of the Republican administrations in the 1920s. Armstrong had been Warren Harding's publicity manager during the 1920 election. During the Harding and Coolidge years, he often served as go-between for California Republicans who wanted to see the president.

But it was with Herbert Hoover that Armstrong played his most decisive role. Armstrong, according to Herbert Hoover's California campaign manager Ralph Arnold, was the man "to whom our Hoover organizations owe more than to any other man for political guidance and publicity support. . . . Robert Armstrong was not only Washington correspondent of the *Los Angeles Times,* he was representative and counselor for our Hoover organization in the Capitol." During the 1928 presidential campaign, Armstrong became one of Hoover's top aides.

As Chandler's representative in Washington, Armstrong took care of lobbying needs, and the cable flow between Los Angeles and Washington had a great deal more to do with Chandler's economic affairs than with Armstrong's newspaper responsibilities. Armstrong's value in getting things done in Washington was recognized by Chandler and Sherman, and they were quick to reciprocate. "There is so little I can do for you in return for your kindness to me," Sherman wrote, after paying the costs to move Armstrong's furniture to Washington. When Armstrong considered a job offer with the U.S. Mint in 1923, Chandler, Sherman, and Herbert Hoover argued strongly against it. Two days after letting Armstrong know they wanted him to refuse the U.S. Mint job, Sherman sent Armstrong $1,000 as "a small showing of my appreciation of your kindness to me and mine."

"This wonderful man," as Sherman loved to call him, helped in countless other ways: procuring hotel arrangements for any of the Chandlers traveling to Washington, passing on Chandler gifts to various important Washington figures, and keeping his eye on and advising California's Republican delegation. He was, as the number one national "high power," a full-bodied extension of the Chandler influence. He finally retired in 1932, shortly before the Democrats took over the White House.

While Armstrong was the number one national man, Kyle Palmer played a similar role on the state level. Palmer had worked as a reporter for E.T. Earl's *Evening Express* before coming to the *Times* in 1919. He headed up the *Times*'s Sacramento bureau and organized it along the same lobbying lines as Armstrong's Washington. In the 1930s, after Armstrong's departure Palmer had become, as Sherman called him, "Mr. Chandler's confidential man in politics," assuming the top troubleshooting role on both the state and national level. Like Nathan, he effectively trained a number of assistants, most notably Chester "Chic" Hanson. As Nathan and Armstrong began their decline, Kyle Palmer, by the late 1930s, reached the height of his power.

While Al Nathan handled the covert side of the Chandler operation and Armstrong and Palmer its political and lobbying, Harry Carr, "the grumpy little fat man," as one *Times* reporter characterized him, embodied the "lighter" newspaper side. Carr started with the *Times* at twenty covering areas as diverse as sports and Washington and foreign news, until he eventually became the *Times* regular columnist, "The Lancer."

By World War I, Carr was an established member of the *Times* hierarchy. Like his bosses, Carr expressed the Los Angeles booster philosophy. He covered stories—such as the International Highway, or a favorable profile of Baja Governor Esteban Cantu—that could promote Chandler causes and allies. After Chandler got involved in the motion picture business, Carr handled public relations for Mack Sennett (with whom Chandler had some financial dealings), took a job briefly at Paramount Pictures, and became executive writer and supervisor of scripts for D.W. Griffith, Cecil B. De Mille, Sennett, Jesse Lasky, and several others.

Carr's replacement, Bill Henry, maintained Carr's tradition through the 1940s and 50s. Like Carr, Henry was best remembered for his regular column—entitled "By the Way"—which somewhat casually promoted an ever-expanding Los Angeles.

Until his death in 1926, Harry Andrews had served as the *Times* managing editor. Andrews, who became an officer in two of Chandler's land companies, was the last of the irascible oldtimers from General Otis's era.

Yet the new *Times* editors—Harry Chandler's stern and foreboding assistants—also ran the *Times* with an iron hand. Andrews's successor was Ralph Trueblood, a slight, pale man who ran the paper until his death in 1934. "Everyone was scared of him," reporter Phil Scheuer recalled of Trueblood, and Kyle Palmer remembered him with a sense of awe.

During Harry Chandler's reign, the *Times* became a classic example of the newspaper as a servant of its publisher's interests, with both editorial writers and news reporters reflecting the publisher's viewpoint in their writings. Reporter Bill Dredge, who got his start as a stringer in the San Fernando Valley in the 1930s, recalled going out to cover a big strike on a chicken farm in the valley. Dredge interviewed both parties in the strike and wrote an impartial story. Soon after, Dredge received a call from his immediate superior, state editor Ed Ainsworth, telling him to come to the *Times*. "There's only one way to cover a union story," Ainsworth told his reporter, rebuking him for his impartiality, "and that's the *Times* way." Dredge and countless other *Times* reporters learned to anticipate that "*Times* way."

3. Wars and Accommodation

The chief competition to the *Times* throughout Harry Chandler's reign was Hearst's morning *Examiner*. But it was a strange kind of competition, encompassing one part war and one part accommodation. As early as 1912, Chandler had made efforts to include *Examiner* publisher Max Ihmsen in some of his real estate deals. And the *Examiner* largely abandoned its prolabor, semiradical origins. Although it remained the "out" paper with the establishment, occasionally making cause with public ownership and labor forces, the *Examiner* was not essentially an antiestablishment journal.

Most of the battles were fought over circulation through the 1920s, with strongarm tactics constantly employed by both sides. Fights broke out over control of newsstands and blocks where newsboys would peddle the morning paper. The *Times* distribution organization, one *Times* worker recalled, consisted of "thugs" who would go out to beat *Examiner* newsboys in the fight for circulation turf. The head of circulation developed a reputation as a tough character. When complaints were registered, Harry Chandler dismissed them. "Obviously," he wrote to an acquaintance, "we can be depended upon to be arraigned upon the side of law, order, and decency in our business operations."

Another competition with the *Examiner* was maintaining ad revenue leadership. The *Times* proudly printed its overall figures for the previous year at the beginning of each January, pointing out how it continued to lead in volume of national advertising. The *Times* still continued its policy of accepting all kinds of ads, even when an advertiser's credit rating could not be determined. Thus the business office became a de facto collection agency, with employees sent out to track down overdue debtors.

If the *Times* competed with the *Examiner*, it warred on its more liberal rivals, the *Los Angeles Record*, and the second *Los Angeles Daily News*. The *Record*, an old Scripps afternoon paper, operated in the best tradition of muckraking and investigation in Los Angeles journalism. When the Owens Valley farmers waged their last desperate struggle, the *Record* was the only Los Angeles paper to take up their cause. When the Teapot Dome scandal became a major national issue, involving local oilman E. H. Doheny, among others, only the *Record* gave the story substantial page one play. But in the early 1930s the *Record* went through a major upheaval when two of E. W. Scripps's grandsons took over the paper and fired its editor Henry Briggs. The new publishers soon found readership on the decline. In 1935 the newspaper closed down operations and sold its remaining assets to the *Daily News*.

The second *Daily News* (unrelated to Sam Clover's short-lived paper) was founded by Cornelius Vanderbilt, Jr., the son of the commodore of railroad fame. Vanderbilt, the black sheep of the family because of his somewhat liberal political ideas, had come to California to try his hand at journalism. On arriving in Los Angeles, he went to see Harry Chandler and asked if he could buy time on the *Times* printing presses. Chandler, hostile to the idea of a new newspaper, refused, warning Vanderbilt, "You'll never make a go of it. Los Angeles is in no need of another newspaper."

Vanderbilt, however, with some capital of his own, was able to convince bankers to lend him the rest. Employing a racy tabloid format that appealed to working class readers, his *Daily News* began with a flourish in 1923 and immediately took after Chandler and other establishment figures. According to Vanderbilt, a consortium led by Hearst and Chandler began to employ "intimidation and bribery, then fists and clubs" against *Daily News* newsboys, much in the manner of the attacks against the *Municipal News* ten years earlier. The attacks led Vanderbilt's financial backers to call their loans, and in 1926 the young publisher gave up on the operation. Chandler, with Young from the *Examiner* and Dickson from the *Express*, offered $150,000 for the paper with the stipulation that the operation be abandoned. Vanderbilt refused, and, instead, the paper passed into the hands of a syndicate headed by Times Mirror Printing and Binding employee Manchester Boddy.

During the depression Boddy, who had not previously expressed radical opinions, became attracted to the cause of "technocracy"—one of a handful of utopian movements that spread throughout Southern California in the early 1930s. Boddy filled the pages of the *News* with technocracy items and events, but when the paper was forced to choose between the utopian-oriented gubernatorial candidacy of Upton Sinclair and that of the business-oriented Frank Merriam, the *News* endorsed Merriam. When Boddy went out on a limb to support reform candidate Harlan Palmer for district attorney against Buron Fitts in 1936, several large advertisers withdrew from the paper. Although the *News* maintained a liberal Democratic position through the thirties and forties, the policy of economic intimidation by the business establishment kept the paper from going too far in its support of radical or labor-oriented causes.

Meanwhile, the once fiery *Express*, the organ of the progressive movement under E.T. Earl, had become a full-fledged member of the conservative establishment. The paper's publisher, Edward Dickson, joined forces with Chandler and his allies in support of issues such as transportation, antisyndicalism legislation, and the need for population expansion, and even helped organize various conservative Republican movements to combat progressive influence throughout the state. In 1931 the *Express*, no longer having a distinctive audience of its own, folded and was absorbed by Hearst's afternoon paper, the *Herald*.

The *Times*, too, had constituency problems. In the 1920s and 30s the paper defined its readership as "intermediate circulation," meaning a range from lower-middle to upper-income readers. Thus, it found itself in a bind in its competition with the *Examiner* as it tried to provide both the yellow journalism of crime, sex, and gossip of the mass papers, and national, international, and business news of the class papers. By the 1930s, the *Times* found itself losing the circulation war with Hearst's *Examiner* and afternoon *Herald-Express*, seemingly caught between both worlds, unable to make up its mind about which kind of look it wanted to project.

Harry Chandler, at seventy, gradually had begun to hand over some of the newspaper functions to his oldest son and heir apparent, Norman. Then, with the *Times* in trouble in the early Depression days, Harry Chandler brought in, at Norman's urging, a "newspaper doctor," Colonel Vissniski, an efficiency expert from Chicago. Vissniski became a terror to the staff, who resented him, not only because of the firings he initiated, but also because his cost-cutting frequently involved such trifling items as orders not to change typewriter ribbons or the monitoring of staff phone calls to make sure they were business-related. Yet Vissniski, with Norman Chandler's help, was eventually able to shift the *Times* towards a mass audience operation. Columns were widened, a picture page was established, and the typeface was enlarged. As the old era closed, with Harry Chandler's retirement in 1941, Norman Chandler was able to assume the helm of what he hoped would be a more modern-looking *Times*.

Though competition still existed in Los Angeles, by the late 1930s it

was, at best, politically muted. Even the Hearst papers provided little political and issue-oriented competition, as William Randolph Hearst took
his papers down an extraordinary road of admiration for Hitler, antivivi-
section campaigns, and anticommunism. Hearst and the other publishers
seemed to have abandoned all hope of ever breaking the Chandler hegemony.

4. *"Probation for Gorillas?"*

In the late 1930s, the antilabor *Times* ironically found itself in court as
codefendant with one of the country's most militant labor leaders. The
case grew out of a jurisdictional dispute and strike involving Harry
Bridges's International Longshore Worker's Union. After an injunction
was issued against union picketing, an angry Bridges fired off a furious
telegram to Labor Secretary Frances Perkins, denouncing the judge's action. The *Times* printed the text of the Bridges telegram and editorially
praised the judge who had issued the injunction.

With events threatening to escalate, the judge enlisted the Los Angeles
Bar Association to take Bridges to court on contempt charges because his
public remarks had been made before a hearing on the injunction had
been held. In June 1938 a bar committee decided to take both Bridges *and*
the *Times* to court for contempt citings, since the *Times* had also printed
material concerning other court cases while they were still in process. The
first *Times* editorial mentioned by the Bar (there were five in all) had commended the conviction of twenty-two sit-down strikers the day before
sentencing was to be pronounced. Another *Times* editorial entitled "Pro-
bation for Gorillas?" had opposed clemency for two Teamsters Union
members convicted of assault and recommended that the judge make
"examples" of the two men.

A number of local prolabor and radical groups and individuals came to
the support of Bridges and the *Times*. But at first *Times* lawyers were cold
toward the Bridges defense team, headed by ACLU counsel Al Wirin.
"Though they never said I should disappear" Wirin recalled, "if ice could
speak that's what they would have said." When Wirin informed *Times*
lawyers of his intention to cite a case which involved the free speech
rights of a member of the Communist party, *Times* lawyer A.B. Cosgrove
replied that the *Times* could never use such a citing in its defense.

The superior court found Bridges and the *Times* guilty of contempt. In
1941 the case came up on appeal before the U.S. Supreme Court, under
the heading *Bridges v. California / Times Mirror Co. v. Superior Court of
California*. This time Cosgrove, who finally used the Communist party-
related citation, worked in harmony with the Bridges defense team. In a 5

to 4 decision, with Justice Black delivering the majority opinion, the court reversed the earlier ruling and upheld Bridges and the *Times* in what has come to be recognized as a major victory for freedom of speech and freedom of the press. "The assumption that respect for the judiciary can be won by shielding judges from published criticism wrongly appraises the character of American public opinion," Black wrote in his decision. "For it is a prized American privilege to speak one's mind, although not always with perfect good taste, on all public institutions. And an enforced silence, however limited, solely in the name of preserving the dignity of the bench, would probably engender resentment, suspicion, and contempt much more than it would enhance respect."

The next year, the *Times* won its first Pulitzer Prize for meritorious service on the basis of the Bridges/Times Mirror court victory. But, as chief counsel Cosgrove later told ACLU counsel Wirin, the *Times* management found it embarrassing to have the case's formal legal citing referred to as "*Bridges v. California*." The case and the Pulitzer Prize would later be referred to by in-house company historian James Bassett as the old *Times*'s finest hour.

The *Times* could use all the prestige it could get. Only a couple of years before the Bridges decision, the *Times* had suffered one of its worst indignities. In 1937, Leo Rosten published a book-length study of the attitudes and perspectives of the major Washington newspaper correspondents. In the course of his research Rosten asked the ninety-three correspondents he interviewed to rate the "least fair and reliable" ten newspapers in the country. The results, published in a chart, ranked the *Los Angeles Times* as the "third worst," trailing only the Hearst papers and the *Chicago Tribune*.

Rosten's *The Washington Correspondents*'s poll undoubtedly helped precipitate some of the first actions taken by Norman Chandler as he began to assume day-to-day management of the *Times*. The days of the old Wobbly-hating, Bolshevist-stomping, small-town transplanted booster were coming to an end. Norman Chandler saw that changes would have to be made, not so much to the paper's substance, as to its image. The old attitudes and attacks no longer worked. Harry Chandler's political allies, such as the M&M and Better America Federation had either disbanded or gone into retreat. The *Times* no longer seemed to wield the influence it had in the days of Harry's $1,000-a-plate luncheons.

Los Angeles was changing, emerging from its fundamentalist period: its days of water conspiracies and antilabor plots, of religious revivals and hammer murders, of Wobblies, EPICS, and Better America Federations. In its place was developing a new, sprawling Los Angeles—a modern metropolis with freeways and smog and the new, powerhouse anticommunism of Howard Hughes and Richard Nixon—a city ready to inherit Harry Chandler's legacies.

On September 23, 1944, Harry Chandler died of a coronary thrombosis. He was eighty years old. He left a detailed trust arrangement to pass on his vast fortune to the new generation of Chandlers. Not wanting to let others know how he had achieved his fortune and power, he had told his children that he didn't want any family or newspaper history published. Without files, without correspondence, with no records of the vast majority of his extraordinary economic activities, the "Yankee Trader" slipped away to a shrouded history.

PART III

1941–1960

"Principles Don't Change"

"When Harry Chandler ran the *Times* . . . he believed in what he believed in, and he put it in the paper," Los Angeles businessman Ernie Loebbecke recalled. "When Norman Chandler ran the paper, the great thing he did, in my judgment, was having an establishment point of view, a Republican point of view: what's good for Los Angeles is good for everybody in it, including the *Times.*"

Though he had four older sisters, Norman Chandler—Harry Chandler's eldest son, born in 1899—seemed destined from birth to continue the Chandler succession at the *Times,* and oversee the vast economic empire his father had created. Norman's early life was a strange mixture of upper-class trappings and middle-class penny-pinching. "Rich boys who get spoiled don't ever develop the determination to stay with the job," he later noted. As a youth his parents—who had never paid him an allowance—expected him to earn whatever money he needed. Yet his family's wealth was very visible. His father, for example, had installed the first private swimming pool in the community in which the Chandlers lived.

While attending Hollywood High School, part of the class of 1917, Norman became good friends with Harry "Bud" Haldeman, Jr., the son of the chairman of the Better American Federation. Norman went on to Stanford, where he developed ties with a number of individuals, such as Goodwin Knight and John McCone, who would later constitute the Southern California establishment. At Stanford Norman dated an attractive young woman named Dorothy Buffum, know to her friends as "Buff."

Dorothy Buffum was three years old when her family moved to the town of Long Beach in 1904. Her father and uncle, who had run a store in Lafayette, Illinois, purchased Long Beach's major department store, "Schilling Brothers," and changed its name to "Buffums." Long Beach was then a quiet, small (population 5,000) community of retired middle-class Midwesterners. Buffum's sales increased as Long Beach's growth paralleled that of Los Angeles. The Buffums became influential members of the Long Beach establishment, and Charles Abel Buffum, Dorothy's father, served as the city's mayor.

In 1919 Buff entered Stanford, where she devoted herself to the campus social life and won the campus queen title. She met the handsome, wealthy Norman Chandler, and they began to date regularly, seeing each other frequently during the summers when the newspaper heir delivered papers as part of his father's systematic training program. "I had an old Model-T," Norman recalled, "and I'd pick up the papers at 2 A.M., wrap them, deliver them, and collect from some four hundred homes. . . . After I'd caught a little sleep and gone out to take care of any complaints, I'd head on down to Long Beach, sleep on the sand all day, take Dorothy to dinner, and get back home to milk the cow."

Married in 1922, Dorothy and Norman honeymooned on the Hawaiian Islands, sailing on a Chandler-owned steamship. When they returned to the States, the Chandlers took an apartment in Hollywood. Norman, starting as a clerk in the circulation department, began his formal training at the *Times*. He learned much about the business and production end of the paper by spending time in the circulation, advertising, and promotion departments. Though his sister Connie Chandler took a job as a general assignment reporter and later married *Times* financial editor Earle Crowe, young Norman was more concerned with the corporate aspects of newspapering and steered clear of the editorial side.

Like other young men of wealthy families, Norman began to socialize with the town's young elite. He joined an organization called the Economic Roundtable, which was set up in 1925. The group met periodically at the exclusive University Club to listen to speakers who discussed general political and economic topics of interest to the future establishment. Members included Bud Haldeman, Al Robbins (whose sister Betty married Haldeman), John McCone, lawyer Frederick Warren Williamson (who would soon marry Norman's sister Ruth Chandler), Reese Taylor (the future president of Union Oil), Preston Hotchkis (Pacific Mutual Life Insurance Company and heir of the Bixby Ranch), and local business leader Emerson Spear (whose son would marry Norman Chandler's daughter). The Roundtable provided a comfortable and privileged setting in which a new generation of Los Angeles businessmen could create the social ties that would last for decades and form the basis of future Los Angeles upper-crust society.

In 1926 Dorothy Chandler gave birth to a daughter, Camilla, and the family moved to larger quarters in Pasadena. Two years later she had a son, Otis. Dorothy felt hemmed in by Pasadena, by the strait-laced, tight-fisted elder Chandlers, and by the general ambience of Los Angeles's upper class. "I was not interested in the social life of Pasadena or in joining the bridge-playing," she recalled. "I knew it was not for me. I was still that little girl, believing when I woke up each day that life was running too fast." She always felt that she didn't quite belong to the Chandler family. "I was accepted as long as I stayed in the traditional patterns. But if I went outside . . ."

By 1932, after ten years of marriage, Dorothy Chandler reached the emotional breaking point. "I had begun to doubt myself, to feel there was something wrong with me," she recalled thirty years later. She decided to commit herself to a private psychiatric residence in Pasadena run by Dr. Josephine Jackson. Dorothy lived on the grounds for more than six months, returning home for a visit once a week. Through pyschiatric help, she was able to feel more in touch with herself, and she decided to make her peace with the Chandlers. "They're the way they are," she said of Norman's parents, and hoped that they would accept her and her desire to make her mark.

With the children in school and Norman increasingly occupied with the paper, Dorothy looked for an outlet for her energies. She went to work as a volunteer at Children's Hospital in Los Angeles. Instead of limiting herself to one specific program or to fund-raising activity, she decided to get involved in the institution as a whole. She advised on personnel matters and made reports to the hospital's management on how to upgrade conditions and improve output.

During the war years, with Norman's blessing Dorothy decided to play a role at the *Times*. She set up her own office and had a small apartment up on the top floor of the *Times* building. She became responsible for the paper's corporate image, an intangible which in Dorothy's hands became a specific means of determining direction and goals. She assumed control over the women's pages and turned the society coverage into the most widely read among the Los Angeles elite.

Norman had difficulty understanding his wife's ambitions. So many things came easily to the young, amiable, good-looking Chandler. In the late 1920s, for instance, he had been invited, because of his social connections, to join the insurance firm of Emmet, Gillis, and Lee. Norman's "job" was to open the doors—to set up appointments among his friends in the Los Angeles upper-class circles. The company had immediate success, and when one of the partners left, Norman became a full partner in the renamed firm of Emmet and Chandler. The venture, its profits split fifty-fifty, eventually became a multi-million-dollar business.

Norman also took over some of his father's numerous economic involvements. He became vice-president of the Beverly-Wilshire Investment Company, a real estate firm that included his brother-in-law Fred Williamson and his friend Bud Haldeman. He became treasurer of the family-run Los Angeles Steamship Company, headed by cousin Ralph Chandler, and took over his father's directorship in the Farmer's and Merchant's Bank. He also took the titular leadership of several of the family holding companies, and, in 1935, after his father organized the Chandler trusts to divide Times Mirror stock among his eight children, Norman was delegated to look after the Chandler economic empire.

During the Depression years, Norman had begun to assume control over the operation of the *Times.* In 1929 he had been named assistant to the publisher, but not until efficiency expert Colonel Vissinski made his report in the early 1930s did Norman get a chance to take full responsibility. "Department heads were old, tired," Norman recalled of the period. "We needed younger people, more aggressive people. Times were changing. We needed to keep the *Times* abreast of change."

In 1934 Norman, as the new assistant general manager of the paper, started actively to give direction to the paper's management. Conscious of the loss of circulation leadership to the *Examiner,* he pushed the paper to become more competitive by being more readable, widening the columns, using more pictures and bolder headlines. Unlike his father, Norman rarely "put the paper to bed," working until its final printing stage, nor did he take much day-to-day interest in the paper.

Norman also essentially kept himself removed from routine operational decisions. He was a delegator, as one of his business friends put it, and left most of his decisions to surrogates. Politically, he shared his father's hatred of the labor and radical movements. In the 1930s he participated in the various campaigns by the Chamber of Commerce and the Merchants and Manufacturers' Association to defeat union efforts to organize Los Angeles.

Norman also became a confirmed anticommunist. *Times* news columns and editorials preached an anticommunism as virulent as that of the Hearst press.

Spending most of his time on economic matters, Norman developed the company's major expansion program in the period after World War II. He became a director of several major national corporations, including Kaiser Steel (actively encouraged by the *Times* to set up its Southern California Fontana plant), Safeway Stores, Dresser Industries in Texas, the Santa Fe Railroad, and Pan American Airways. He was a member of the Lost

Angels camp of the Bohemian Club, an outrageous once-a-year gathering in a northern California setting, where the national establishment rubbed shoulders in two weeks of rituals and theater.

By the time his father died in 1944, Norman Chandler, popular among his social peers for his easygoing manner, had become a major figure in the Southern California establishment. No one, however, pictured Norman "leading the troops," as business associate Herbert Allen recalled. He preferred to be out on the golf course or riding horses in his Tejon Ranch. He was a third-generation aristocrat, and his few ambitions reflected that fact.

Norman's wife made up for his own lack of drive. By the late forties Buff had become a power at the *Times* and was taking an active interest in the cultural affairs of the city, as well as keeping on top of internal corporate matters. In the late 1920s, she had expressed the hope that Harry and Marian Chandler—Norman's parents—would not try "to change or destroy me, nor was I going to change or destroy them." Yet, ironically, of all the younger Chandlers, only Buff, a Chandler by marriage, seemed to have the real feel of power that Harry Chandler had so skillfully developed.

When the Hollywood Bowl, beset by a financial crisis, closed down during its opening week in 1951, Dorothy Chandler was named chairman of an emergency committee . That appointment started her extraordinary career in the world of cultural politics. Buff's plan to save the Bowl included closing it down temporarily, and then building up concern in the community through stories in the *Times* and the other newspapers, culminating in a "Save the Bowl" fundraising event.

Buff used the power of her name and her paper to mobilize Los Angeles's business establishment. She approached downtown businessman Neil Petree for help. After a two-week series of free performances to encourage emergency contributions, the Bowl was back on its feet. Buff solicited Petree to become permanent chairman of the Bowl committee and provide strong business backing.

Buff's work in the world of music had political overtones as well. In 1955, while visiting Russia with her husband, Buff proposed to the Russian Ministry of Culture the possibility of bringing the Bolshoi Ballet and Moiseyev Dancers to Los Angeles.

On returning to the States, Buff began to promote the idea of cultural exchange with Russia. Though a number of right-wing local business leaders (who called the idea of such an exchange "unpatriotic and unwise") pressured Bowl directors to veto the project, Buff and her ally Z. Wayne Griffin, who had assumed the Bowl presidency, convinced a majority of the directors to give their support.

When the Moiseyevs came to town in 1958, there were pickets at each performance and Griffin received almost two thousand letters a week. Some key business leaders, Griffin recalled, talked as if they wanted to blow up the Bowl. But the Russian dancers played to a packed house each night.

By the mid-1950s Dorothy Chandler's influence was felt throughout the *Times.* Sports editor Paul Zimmerman recalled an incident when Dorothy, who had worked closely with the county supervisors over efforts to build a Music Center in Los Angeles, took him to task. With clearance and support from Norman Chandler, Zimmerman had done a column on the conflict between Supervisor Kenneth Hahn and Mayor Norris Poulson over the use of public funds to build a sports stadium. That evening Zimmerman, hosting an Olympics Star Night in Los Angeles, passed Norman and Buff's table. "That was a nasty column you wrote about Kenny Hahn," Buff said. Norman, who had earlier commended the piece, looked the other way. The next morning an angry Zimmerman went in to see editor Hotchkiss. Zimmerman explained what had happened and remarked, "I guess I'm in deep trouble with Buff." "Son," Hotch replied, "the line forms in the rear."

Dorothy enjoyed telling a story about her influence with Norman. During the 1952 Republican national convention, Norman preferred Taft but Dorothy wanted Eisenhower. Neither would budge. Finally Dorothy announced that she would resort to her last method—sex. As one family member recalled it, she told her husband they couldn't sleep together until he changed his mind. Though Norman denied that was the reason, the *Times* backed Eisenhower.

By the mid-1950s the business elite began to realize that Dorothy, rather than Norman, had become the most important power at the *Times.* In 1954 she was appointed by Governor Goodwin Knight to the state Board of Regents and two years later was named by President Eisenhower to serve on the United States Committee on Education Beyond the High School. As a woman, she was frequently confronted with problems that men with power never had to face. In her first two years as regent she suffered the indignity of having to miss the after-meeting sessions held at the all-male upper-class clubs, such as San Francisco's Pacific Union. "Next time we have a Regent's session," Buff suggested in a letter to regent John Neylan, "please do not ask all of my favorite men friends to dinner at the Pacific Union Club because that means that I cannot join them . . . even if invited."

Still, Dorothy Chandler pulled away from the implication of feminism, preferring, for example, to be identified as *Mrs. Norman* Chandler. "I've earned my achievements by what I as a woman have done," she told one journalist. "But to say I'm a women's libber and I want equal this and equal that is wrong. Sure I've had to work hard at being accepted, but to talk about this competition with males all the time—I can't understand it."

While Dorothy maneuvered and organized, Norman became the embodiment of the *Times*, the Chandlers, and Los Angeles of the 1940s and 1950s: anti-Communist, conservative, content, celebrating the American way. He also became the personification of the Southern California Old Guard. "The readers know where the *Times* stands," he wrote in a signed column in 1959. "They began to see as the newspaper came of age, that the news buttressed its opinions. Their confidence is rooted in the news columns." "Principles Don't Change," Norman noted in the early sixties. "The *Times* basic philosophies—supporting the Republican Party and free enterprise—[are] basic philosophies that we stick by."

Norman Chandler was a man of his generation; an upper-class Angeleno who viewed conservative politics and the business ethic as the wellspring of American life. With the advent of the Cold War, as erstwhile Eastern liberals accommodated with these men of the Southern California right, the Southern California ideology became for nearly a decade *the* American ideology.

By the 1950s, the *Times* stood at the peak of its power in Los Angeles. But the land was changing. A major social and economic upheaval had begun to strike at the very roots of the *Times*'s ideology. When the time came for change, Buff, who covertly held the power of the *Times* empire, would be prepared to act.

CHAPTER 14

Big Red Dies

"Black Monday," as July 26, 1943 came to be known, marked the fourth time that summer that the city had been attacked by dense black air. "With the entire downtown area engulfed by a low-hanging cloud of acrid smoke yesterday morning," the *Times* front page story began, "city health and police authorities began investigations to determine the source of the latest 'gas attack' that left thousands of Angelenos with irritated eyes, noses and throats. . . .

"Visibility was cut to less than three blocks in some sections of the business district," the article went on. "Office workers found the noxious fumes almost unbearable."

"A lot of guessing is going on as to the cause of a sudden smoke, or haze, nuisance in Los Angeles," the *Times* commented editorially. Although the problem of the pollution had been identified by local health authorities as far back as 1906, the distinct shift in the type and quantity of the pollution had begun with those "gas attacks" of 1943. The city's health officer, George Uhl, was quoted by the *Times* as blaming the "Black Monday" attack on increased industrial activity and vehicle traffic in the city, but nobody was prepared to slow down industrial production nor limit the number of automobiles entering the center city. The gas attacks continued. Along with the freeway and the vast, uncontrolled industrial infrastructure which had changed the face of the city, Los Angeles had another, new, permanent, addition: the smoky, foggy nuisance that came to be called "smog."

1. A Transportation Nexus

"The economy of Los Angeles is rubber tired," Fletcher Bowron had once remarked. Harry Chandler, as a charter member of the Southern California Automobile Club and a director of the organization for more than thirty years, played the single most important role in having that come to pass. Chandler worked closely with Automobile Club President Fred Baker and with Frank Miller of Riverside, who lobbied for the "Good Roads" movement, the first expression of California's famed highway lobby. Chandler envisioned an interstate highway system that would run down the coast into Mexico, through Chandler's Baja lands, and into Central America, to create what Chandler and friends called an "Intercontinental Highway."

Even in the period before World War I, when the auto was more novelty than industry, Chandler had foreseen the advantage of the automobile system in the suburbanization of Southern California. Chandler's Los Angeles Suburban Homes Company in the San Fernando valley made a major effort to develop wide boulevards and streetways—primitive highways—to accommodate both the auto and the streetcar. He was successful in the construction of an interstate highway connecting Bakersfield and points north with Los Angeles—a highway which conveniently passed through Chandler's Tejon "Right of Way" Ranch.

Chandler and his business allies saw the development of the automobile as a complementary system to the city's massive rail and interurban network. Chandler had numerous ties to the streetcar interests. His close colleague Moses Sherman had set up Southern California's first interurban systems, which he sold to Henry Huntington in 1901. Huntington, a nephew of the SP's Colis P. Huntington and frequent syndicate partner of Chandler, was committed to the expansion of the region through the interurban streetcar empire he established. Huntington's streetcar lines, like Sherman's before him, laid tracks to link up new subdivided communities—where Huntington had frequently purchased land—to the central city. The practice gave Los Angeles a vast rail system, the largest in the country. In the peak years in the twenties and early thirties, the network encompassed 1,000 miles of track and 700 route miles of service.

In 1911 Huntington's system was bought out by the Southern Pacific railroad, which had finally decided to join with Los Angeles's booster businessmen. Huntington maintained a smaller company, the Los Angeles Railway Company, which he called the "yellow cars," in contrast to the SP subsidiary Pacific Electric Railroad's "Big Red" cars. Chandler strongly advocated the use of the Big Red and Los Angeles Railway systems. He fought against any efforts to put the interurbans under city ownership and applauded the railway's aid in developing a Greater Los Angeles. He kept up friendly economic and political relations with the giant Southern Pacific and its Pacific Electric subsidiary.

Soon after World War I, Chandler began to promote the rapid development of the automobile system as the *primary* transportation system for Southern California. He lent "high power" reporter Bill Henry to the Automobile Club to reorganize and edit the Auto Club's periodical. In the *Times* Chandler launched a new section called the "Pink Sheet," a Sunday supplement devoted exclusively to automobile news—in effect a publicity arm of the budding automobile industry.

Chandler had several economic investments tied to the automobile. He sat on the local board of Goodyear Tire and Rubber Company, in recognition of his role in bringing Goodyear to Los Angeles. He had road construction interests, including Western Construction Company, which he partly owned, and major investments in the Southern California Rock and Gravel Company and Consolidated Rock Products Company (Conrock), on whose board Harry's son Harrison Chandler sat. Chandler also developed controlling interests in several local oil companies and had worked with the Royal Dutch Shell interests in their attempt to gain stock control of Union Oil company, the largest of the locals. By the early 1920s, Harry Chandler had an economic interest in every related aspect of the automobile operation except the production of the automobile itself.

By the spring of 1919, the rapid growth of automobile traffic, competing for space with the city's interurbans, created a massive tie-up in downtown Los Angeles. The *Times* proposed a street-widening program, the development of "good roads," and, in a cautious, yet significant suggestion, talked of the automobile's right of way over the interurban system.

As the traffic problem worsened in the 1920s, the city council initiated a downtown parking ban to allow more space for streetcar operations. The *Times* attacked the parking ban as bad for business. "MOTOR CARS ARE ESSENTIAL," a *Times* headline declared. "Two weeks of no parking proves that business can't do without them." The council action, an editorial complained, "has merely deprived motorists of the rights of citizens and taxpayers."

To ensure "rights" for motorists, Chandler and his associates set up the Major Highways Committee (MHC), an autonomous subcommittee of the Traffic Commission of the City of Los Angeles. By assessing each member $1,000, the MHC financed a committee of engineering services, headed by Auto Club consulting engineer J.B. Lippincott, of Owens Valley fame. The MHC funds, coming from both public and private sources and completely controlled by its businessmen members, went toward the promotion of an overall "Major Traffic Street Plan," which centered around a street-widening program to speed up automobile flow. The MHC introduced a charter amendment, strongly backed by the *Times*, to create a "Major Traffic Street Plan Fund," based on property tax assessments, that would be exclusively controlled by the MHC. The bond issue passed—the only one to do so in 1927—"due to the frank publicity of the newspapers," MHC member Edward Dickson wrote.

The MHC also worked with the state legislature to pass favorable legislation that created a street-widening/highway fund, permitted the city to overcome homeowner objections to street widening, and allowed the MHC to file property condemnation suits.

The *Times* praised the MHC's efforts. "The completion of this great street plan," the paper quoted one realtor, ". . . . will act as a magnet to draw people from all over the world at an even greater rate than in the past. And, as it is estimated that each new individual is worth to a community a $1,500 increase per person in real estate values, you can readily understand what this constant influx of people must mean to the value of our real estate holdings."

The automobile was fast becoming king. "In Southern California," the *Times* proudly proclaimed in 1934, "it was the *Times* that was first and foremost in a campaign for good intercity, intercounty, and interstate highways." When the first gasoline tax bill—providing a one-cent a gallon tax for highway construction purposes—passed in 1927, the *Times* pointed out that "no element, possibly, has contributed to the fame and welfare of California than her good roads." The state then had 1.6 million registered cars, the *Times* happily noted, far more than any other state in the country. "At a tremendous rate," another *Times* article exclaimed in 1933, "the wild virgin areas of Southern California are being broken down to the uses of progress and yielding up their beauties to the motoring public."

As congested traffic conditions downtown slowed up service, and the Southern Pacific moved increasingly away from passenger lines toward the more profitable freight delivery, the interurban system began to decline. Throughout the 1920s socialist and progressive movements made major efforts to halt the deterioration by trying to place the railroads into municipal hands, but the *Times*, in alliance with the Southern Pacific, bitterly opposed any such proposals. In 1920 the paper led the attack against a progressive-backed initiative which called for public ownership of the lines between Pasadena and Los Angeles. It Red-baited the effort, and took pleasure when the initiative went down to defeat in the antiradical upsurge following World War I. "Faddists are Rebuked," the *Times* proclaimed, insisting that only a privately run system was viable.

Los Angeles Railway's call for a fare increase in 1926 from five to seven cents spurred the call for municipal ownership once again. Since the railroads, already receiving large subsidies, claimed they couldn't make money off the passenger service, the progressives argued that the city ought to operate the streetcars to make possible a cheaper fare structure and improved service without having to subsidize a private operation.

When Henry Huntington died the following year, the city attempted to purchase his Los Angeles Railway system. But the attorney for the estate, Albert Crutcher, delayed the transaction and successfully took the case to court to prevent public ownership.

A conspiracy of General Motors (GM) and several other companies provided the *coup de grace* for the transit system's deterioration. In 1936, a consortium of corporations, including General Motors, Standard of California, Firestone Tire and Rubber, B.F. Phillips Petroleum, and Mack Manufacturing company, organized a company called National City Lines (NCL). NCL was in the business of converting existing electric rail systems—trolleys and streetcars—to motorized buses. Each of the companies bought substantial amounts of NCL stock, and, in turn, NCL purchased buses from GM, tires from Firestone, and oil from Standard and Phillips.

In 1937, the Southern California Auto Club issued a major report calling for the displacement of the interurban system with buses and cars. A report by the club-sponsored Citizens Transportation Committee, composed of key local businessmen and executives of the Pacific Electric and Los Angeles Railway Company, backed the Auto Club proposals. "Our local lines must realize that we are well along in a period of transition," committee strategist Henry Keller, an Auto Club executive and Chandler associate, commented, "and they must accommodate themselves to it by doing what other like companies are doing all over the world, by substituting rubber for rails."

In 1938, NCL set up a West Coast affiliate called the Pacific City Lines (PCL), which immediately began to buy up the Los Angeles Railway system. PCL allowed the system to continue its downward course and removed cars from operation, which caused long waiting periods between rides. "We always say," the local manager of the operation stated in 1947, "people sitting down pay the driver's wages; people standing up pay operating costs; people hanging outside in the numbers—that's the profit."

But the primary operation of PCL was its conversion of the electric system to buses. PCL was always able to secure approval from the Public Utilities Department to tear up the tracks and convert the system—a process undoubtedly helped by the constant shuttling of personnel between the company and the regulatory agency.

As conversion proceeded, *Times* management and other local businessmen gave the PCL operation its blessing. The Hearst *Herald-Express*, however, with a working-class readership who used the interurban system, publicized the community efforts to stop the conversions, and frequently ran front page stories on city council hearings and proceedings of the Utility Board. When the Justice Department brought conspiracy charges against the General Motors consortium in 1947 for the violation of antitrust laws, the *Herald-Express* gave banner headlines to the story. Though the executives were later found guilty, their punishment was confined to a one-dollar fine and no jail terms. The *Times* gave little or no coverage to the proceedings and the indictments. The remarks of the PCL general manager or business officials who supported the conversion when a public hearing was held were cited instead.

The only significant organized force opposed to the conversion was the railroad unions. When PCL or the Southern Pacific proposed abandonment of rail lines, union head Hugh Wilkins organized community campaigns with town hall meetings, flyers, and speakers to mobilize support to save the interurbans. Wilkins argued that peoples' transportation needs could be effectively met through a rail and bus feeder system. The union also called for the development of a "rail on the freeway" system, with tracks in the center or the side of the freeways to alleviate the already congested freeway automobile traffic and to help resolve the "right of way" problem involved in any major new construction. Tracks and costs, the union argued, could come out of the gasoline tax earmarked for highway funds. The Auto Club and its allies bitterly attacked the "rail on the freeway" proposal and its funding suggestion, in particular.

Wilkins and the union fought against impossible odds. They failed to establish a coalition of radical and liberal forces—both on the defensive during the beginnings of the Cold War in the late 1940s—around the issue. Though some community efforts resulted in forestalling displacement, the PCL strategy ultimately paid off. The intentional reduction of service and lack of repairs aroused resentment of long waits and noisy, loud, and sometimes dangerous high-speed trains. More and more, buses displaced the streetcars, and the myth of the Southern Californian's preference for his or her auto over rapid transit began to take hold. Wilkins, up for re-election in his local, was attacked for failing to pay attention to bread and butter issues while putting so much effort into saving rapid transit. After he was defeated, the union withdrew from the campaign. Full rail displacement and abandoned lines soon followed.

Throughout this period the *Times* maintained its hostility to rapid transit proposals. "The Transit Authority really ought to give up its fanciful plans for a vast rapid-transit system," the paper editorialized in 1958. The paper's opposition centered on three related variables: that municipal ownership was bad, that the automobile and freeways were preferable systems ("our love affair with the freeway system," as Norman Chandler characterized the *Times* attitude), and that the financing of rapid transit must be completely divorced from the sacrosanct gasoline tax fund for highway construction.

By 1963, when the last of the Big Reds terminated, Los Angeles had become a city without trains or streetcars.

2. *"Our Once Celebrated Air"*

In October 1946 the *Los Angeles Times* launched a program to "bring the sun back to the city." "The recent rain washed the once-celebrated air of Los Angeles and gave Southern California an unaccustomed view of an object known as the sun," *Times* staffer Ed Ainsworth wrote, in the first of a series of antismog articles. "For years now the sun has become something of a mystery here. Presumably it was rising and setting as the almanac indicated it should. But through the pall of 'smog' which settled over Los Angeles in 1943 and has persisted with exasperating firmness ever since, it hardly ever was visible to the naked eye."

The *Times* campaign continued through the fall and into the following year. Ainsworth's research indicated that the smog might have multiple causes: rubber plants, trucks, incinerators, possibly gas emissions: it was a 'systems-wide' problem, according to later language. The *Times* hired its own independent technical expert to come to study the problem and to write about it in the paper.

In December 1946 the *Times* set up a "*Times* Smog Advisory Committee," headed by the former president of the Union Pacific Railroad. The committee included among its fourteen members the heads of Southern California Edison, the Auto Club, and the All Year Club. The committee sponsored efforts to pass legislation which would set up a supervisory body to deal with the problem. Opposition came from the industries most identified at the time with smog—oil refineries, lumbering interests, and the diesel railroads.

Without a successful resolution, the *Times* complained, Los Angeles might lose its ability to continue to attract people and expand the city. On October 14, 1947, the paper proudly hailed the "climax" of its campaign, when the county Board of Supervisors set up a unified Air Pollution Control District (APCD) for the county.

In its first turbulent years, the regulatory agency took after resistant oil refineries in an attempt to remove sulfur from the air. The APCD leadership that survived the battles with the oil companies, in particular Robert Chass and his assistant Robert Lunche, were able to maintain close relations with the proexpansionist Board of Supervisors and other powers within the region. The growth issue compounded the pollution problem, since more people and industry meant more industrial pollutants and cars.

Through the 1950s and 60s the APCD and its friends, trying to identify particular components of the problem in order to come up with technical solutions, refused to look at the overall problem of growth itself. Though the smog got worse, the APCD, in tune with the scientific mystique of the period, when technology appeared to offer unlimited resources for resolving any conceivable environmental problem, continued to talk in optimistic terms. Smog became a political football, with politicians and technicians identifying one or another root cause. After the conflict with the oil companies in the late forties, APCD officials led by Chass moved away from identifying industrial causes to placing the blame on the automobile. In 1956 the APCD identified automobiles as the major contributor to smog. "Industry and refineries are no longer the big villains of smogmaking" the *Times* reported. "Somewhere there is the last nail to Old Man Smog's coffin," the *Times* quoted APCD head S. Smith Griswold, "and we're going to find it and end him forever."

Old Man Smog did not go away, and the problem was not so easily isolated. Industrial pollution, the automobile emissions, population increases, land use patterns were all clearly factors. While the *Times* had led the drive the for the APCD, it had also maintained its pro-growth philosophy. But others in Southern California had questioned the logic of continuous growth and booster objectives. In 1940, a major study by planners, transportation experts, architects, and other urbanologists, released under the title *Los Angeles: Preface to a Master Plan*, argued strongly that further population growth in Los Angeles would be harmful. "Expansion has doubtless been too great and too fast," planner Clarence Dykstra wrote, "with the result that the present physical city must pay the price of over speculation. . . . We have been living under the assumption of continuous growth, and it now proves to be a slender reed upon which to lean."

The *Times* and its allies had become leaders of the campaign to fight smog—their main worry stemming from the fact that the smog was interfering with the continuous growth of the region—that very growth which contributed to the smog in the first place.

The *Times* acknowledged the problems but scoffed at the criticisms. Its vision of unlimited expansion, which continued through the 1940s and 50s during Los Angeles's last great boom, was one of permanent expansion. "Los Angeles is destined to be the headquarters town of the largest city-complex the world has ever known or dreamed of, well before the year 2000," a *Times* Midwinter exclaimed in 1961. "Imperial Rome was built five square miles in its glory; Greater London fills 725 square miles. The metropolis of the Pacific Littoral that we are building will contain thousands of square miles, the home of 22 million by 1970, of 35 million two decades later. The area from Santa Monica to Riverside and San Bernardino, it is predicted, will be built solidly within a decade, and still the city will spread. . . ."

The vision of growth, for the *Times* and its owners and friends, had been intricately bound up with the automobile. By 1933 the *Times* had identified Los Angeles as the "Motoring City," and that notion became integral to the *Times* philosophy. "In Los Angeles, as elsewhere," the *Times* editorialized in 1959, "the new highway program is adding momentum to the revolutionary dispersal and urbanization of American life . . . . Southern California is eating its cake and having it too. For the scenery ringing all the changes and thrills, from the height of Mount Whitney to the depth of Death Valley, is still there, knit together for the pleasure of everyone by a highway system that grows and grows and the largest automobile population in the world."

The death of the Big Red streetcars, the emergence of smog, the permanent boom, and the triumph of the automobile, all turned out to be part of the same Southern California package.

CHAPTER 15

Running City Hall

1. "The Ringmaster's Whip"

"Carlton Williams was an activist. He did more than cover the news at City Hall, he moved it," recalled PR man and Williams intimate Herb Baus. "He was," remarked City Councilman George Cronk, "Mr. Big in city politics."

In the 1930s Al Nathan, the most powerful reporter at the *Times*, took police reporter Carlton Williams under his wing. Williams, who had been with the *Times* since 1916, became Nathan's protégé and learned the ways to utilize the vast powers of the paper. He often joined Nathan in visits to Harry Chandler's Vermejo Club in Colorado, where the senior Chandler wined and dined the most powerful men in the country.

Williams had loved his police beat. He had been a "front page" journalist at a time when the crime reporter was as much a part of the action as the criminals and detectives. In the forties Williams took over the city hall beat and started to apply the lessons he'd learned from Nathan. Williams held court at election time, interviewing prospective candidates and deciding—with Norman Chandler's almost automatic approval—which ones the *Times* would support. Each election day the *Times* printed a full-page ballot complete with markings, which its readers took into the voting booth. No other paper or organization came close to its power, and in many elections, particularly local races with traditionally lower voter turnouts, the *Times* endorsement became tantamount to victory in Republican primaries and a solid advantage in nonpartisan races.

Williams became the expert hatchetman and power-broker and the most visible expression of the political muscle of the paper. "I saw the nodding and I saw the naying, you know," the one-time lobbyist for the Los Angeles Police Department (and later police chief) Ed Davis recalled. Williams, Davis noted, would walk past each city council member in Council Chambers, nodding or shaking his head, lining up his votes.

Other stories about Williams and his power abounded. In a 1953 mayoralty election, an anti-*Times* candidate attacked Williams for running city council affairs by standing in the back of the Council Chambers during vote counts with his thumb pointed up or down, while conservative council members looked to him for signals. The story was repeated and soon became something of a legend. Some of the council members close to the *Times* denied any specific instructions, but, as City Councilman Cronk put it "Carlton felt he owned part of City Hall."

2. *"Our Son of a Bitch"*

Williams, known for outlandish actions, frequently enraged one of his opponents, Councilman Karl Rundberg. One day Rundberg stood up on the Council floor and complained of Williams's parading through the Council telling members how to vote. If Williams continued, Rundberg declared, he ought to wear a ringmaster's uniform and carry a whip.

When Carlton Williams first began his city hall beat, the *Times* had just come out, bloody and bruised, from the recall election of 1938. The paper tried to ignore the loss and held its breath when Fletcher Bowron took office. The new mayor had abolished the police Red Squad, opposed the *Times*-backed antipicketing ordinance, and recommended repeal of the handbill ordinance, which had been used to arrest labor organizers engaged in leafletting. In addition, he appointed a number of liberal and radical commissioners whose efforts furthered the goals of the progressive movements.

The old recall coalition held together for the 1941 election and Bowron was reelected over *Times*-backed conservative councilman Stephen Cunningham. Shortly afterward the mood began to change. A number of businessmen decided that hostility toward the mayor ought to be replaced with an accommodationist policy that might wean the mayor away from his more radical backers.

With the United States's entrance into World War II, a new political and economic dynamic in the city emerged. Large sections of the radical community, led by the Communist party, adopted a "win the war" perspective which coincided with a nationwide "no-strike" pledge and a class-wide coalition set up by the Roosevelt administration. Several Communists and radicals were appointed to federal and local governmental bodies, where they worked closely with the same people who had red-baited them just months before. In the face of the generally conciliatory attitude of the left, some radicals within the Bowron administration found themselves increasingly isolated in their attempts to develop new, controversial measures in their departments.

Once the radical momentum waned, Bowron began to break with many of his previous allies. In 1944, he selected a Chamber of Commerce committeeman for a crucial post in the Department of Water and Power, over the opposition of the municipal ownership movement and the local electrical workers union. When a union raise was denied, the electrical workers went out on strike in spite of the "no-strike" pledge, and Bowron was forced to settle on the union's term. Future DWP appointments shifted back to promunicipal ownership advocates.

When Bowron ran for his second full term in 1945, his only significant opposition was former recall leader Clifford Clinton. Bowron, with class-wide backing from the Left and the CIO, to the *Los Angeles Times* and the business communty, easily won reelection.

Police actions against strikers at Los Angeles's General Motors plant in 1946 further estranged the mayor from his old allies. Police Commissioner Van Griffith, in opposition to the rest of the police commission, called for an open hearing into the charges of "police brutality." Under increasing business pressure, Bowron removed Van Griffith from the commission. That same year, police were used as strikebreakers in a Newspaper Guild strike at the Hearst *Herald-Express*. Bowron claimed ignorance, but a skeptical CIO accused the mayor of issuing the orders to the police for their use of tear gas, nightsticks, and blackjacks in harrassing the pickets.

The quiet resignation of radical Public Works Commissioner Reuben Borough after Bowron's reelection in 1945 symbolized the death of the old coalition. As Carlton Williams later confided in one of the pro-Times Council members about Bowron, "He's our son of a bitch."

In the 1949 election, city engineer Lloyd Aldrich opposed Bowron, attacking him for his antilabor police actions. Supported once again by a unified business community and the *Los Angeles Times*, the mayor, by a small margin, was reelected to a third term.

3. The Housing Fight

In 1950 the Bowron/business establishment accommodation came to an end. The basis of the conflict originated in a law passed by Congress in 1949 which allowed local governments to terminate rent controls established during the war. Los Angeles, like other large urban centers which experienced an enormous housing shortage after the war, was very concerned with the housing issue. Controversy over the law quickly developed. Landlord lobbies, pressing hard for decontrol, won the backing of major business forces, including the *Times* and their City Council allies, while those opposed to decontrol—the labor movement, civil rights organizations, and citizens groups—organized a Los Angeles Tenants Council. On July 28, 1950, the city council held hearings on the subject. Under tremendous political pressure, council members passed a decontrol measure. According to federal statutes, decontrol could only be put into effect with the approval of Federal Housing Expeditor Tishe Woods. Citing the council's failure to hold adequate public hearings, Woods decided to reject decontrol for Los Angeles. Woods also noted that a housing shortage seemed to exist in the city, necessitating some form of control. The *Times* blasted Woods's decision, calling the housing official a "Tin-Pot Dictator." Two months later new federal legislation made the issue moot by lifting all housing controls.

In the 1951 councilmanic elections, the *Times* made the decontrol vote a key to its endorsement. A disunited labor movement was unable to stop the *Times* slate from coming to power. The decontrol issue, however, had marked only the first round of a protracted fight on housing questions in Los Angeles.

For more than forty years Los Angeles business forces had made the single-unit dwelling the cornerstone of their housing perspective. Working-class families were encouraged to move into suburban districts in small fabricated homes under financing occasionally provided for by their employers. "Los Angeles has more home-owning working men than any other city in the country" the *Times* proudly proclaimed in the 1920s. With a home and a car, the *Times* and its business allies reasoned, working people would stay away from radical or union activities.

As the population of the city increased, so did its housing problems. During Bowron's first term, he went after and received federal grants to begin construction on several thousand low-cost housing units throughout the city. When the Title I Housing Act was passed in 1949, Bowron, under urging from labor and tenant groups, signed a contract with the federal government to construct 10,000 more public housing units. Los Angeles became the first city in the country to qualify under the new act.

But the *Times* and the real estate interests, particularly those absentee landlords who owned property in Bunker Hill—a large section on the western edge of downtown that Bowron hoped to redevelop with low cost public housing—launched a massive attack against the idea of public housing. The realtor/business alliance distributed pamphlets with headings such as BOWRON ADMINISTRATION MOVING PEOPLE VIA GESTAPO HOUSING AUTHORITY and created organizations under such names as "The Committee Against Socialist Housing." "Government-owned tenement housing . . ." one pamphlet proclaimed, "would infringe the rights of the people by destroying the freedom of private ownership . . . [and] would accomplish the major step to Communism.''

The *Times* attacked the public housing coalition and the mayor's appointed Housing Authority, which had begun to implement the plans. "The Housing Authority bureaucracy, gerrymandering low rents in the 10,000 projected units, could almost sway the city," the *Times* complained in one editorial. "The power to control a man's home is coupled here with the authority to give him something for nothing, and that adds up to a tremendous primal influence.''

Once again under pressure, the city council brought the issue up for a vote, despite the fact that money had already been expended and any action to stop construction at this stage would result in a lawsuit from the federal government. The council, which had earlier approved the plan 14 to 1, voted 8 to 7 to keep the project. Carlton Williams continued to exert all the pressure he could muster. A week later Councilman Harold Harby, a longtime labor ally, changed his vote against the measure. Public housing advocates charged that the *Times* had threatened to run a well-financed opponent against Harby if the councilman didn't switch. Harby, though, argued that his sudden transfer of allegiance had ideological motivations. The public housing, he claimed to have suddenly realized, would be on vacant land, and thus would not involve any "slum clearance." "When you remove the slum clearance element from public housing," the *Times* cited Harby, "there is nothing much left but Socialism." With Harby's switch, the council voted 8 to 7 against the project.

After the vote Mayor Bowron issued a fourteen-page report upholding the need for public housing and attacking its critics. Bowron observed that his opposition labeled federal subsidies for the poor "socialistic," but didn't level the same judgment against federal subsidies for businessmen.

Even though the state supreme court ruled that the city could not defer on its contractual obligations with the federal government, the city council decided to submit the question to a public vote. Both sides mobilized for the campaign. The *Times*/business alliance, under Carlton Williams's leadership, linked public housing to socialism and called the proposition "The Socialist Public Housing Measure." The coalition issued pamphlets emphasizing costs, and telling taxpayers they would be required to "pay a part of somebody else's rent for the next 40 years." With the election taking place at the height of the Cold War, the anti-Communist campaign succeeded; the no vote prevailed by a wide margin. Although the election was nonbinding, Bowron's continued backing of public housing made it appear that he was defying the public will; yet any attempt to abandon the project would be subject to legal intervention.

After the referendum, the anti–public housing forces, with their eye on the mayoralty elections a year later, decided to break the stalemate by utilizing the red-baiting tactics that had begun to flourish once again in the early 1950s. Their main target was the Housing Authority and, in particular, its public relations officer, Frank Wilkinson. Wilkinson, whose politics had been well known when he was appointed—with tacit business approval during the "classwide" coalitions of the second World War—had become a special mark for Police Chief William Parker. Parker, a strong anti-Communist and opponent of public housing, had reactivated the old anti-radical intelligence operations reminiscent of Red Hynes.

After Wilkinson publicly pointed out that a particular slum area mentioned in the police chief's testimony to back up his argument against public housing was in reality an uninhabited area of land cleared by the Housing Authority, Parker brought Mayor Bowron a police file showing Wilkinson's left-wing ties. The mayor—an old family friend of the Wilkinsons—threw the folder in the trash. Parker, furious and vowing to get both Wilkinson and Bowron, leaked the contents of the file to some slum landlords who faced the Housing Authority in an eminent domain proceeding. When Wilkinson came up to testify at the proceeding, he was asked—in 1950s style—about his organizational affiliations. Wilkinson refused to answer and the press, led by the *Times*, had a field day. With the pressure mounting, the Housing Authority fired the beleagured Wilkinson.

4. *"Two Armies"*

"I've never seen a hotter fight, before or since," Herb Baus recalled of the public housing debate. "It was a very emotional thing. It was like two armies preparing for the battle, and our army felt Bowron had to go."

The *Times*/business alliance had thought of finding a new candidate to run against Bowron since the initial fight around decontrol. Small meetings of the most powerful of the local elite, including Norman Chandler, Asa Call, and Lin Beebe, met around the question. Conservative Councilman George Cronk was solicited, as was Congressman Glenn Lipscomb, but both declined. Finally, at one meeting, the name of Congressman Norris Poulson came up. Though not a strong campaigner, Poulson had effectively served Los Angeles business interests in his position on the congressional committee that dealt with the Colorado River matter. In addition, he opposed public housing and supported the antilabor Taft-Hartley law. The small group of the business elite decided that Norman Chandler—who had the best rapport with Poulson—ought to sound him out on a possible candidacy. On December 26, 1952, Chandler wrote to Poulson that the *Times* publisher, Asa Call, Neil Petree, Lin Beebe, and four other businessmen had met and decided they wanted Poulson to run for mayor. Chandler promised the congressman that campaign funds would be made available, the mayor's salary would be increased, and that the mayor was also "entitled to strut around in a car (Cadillac) and chauffeur supplied by the city."

Poulson, assured of financial and *Times* campaign backing, and pleased with the potential financial benefits—especially the Cadillac—as he later remarked in an interview, agreed to run. Carlton Williams convinced retiring Councilman George Cronk to serve as Poulson's campaign manager, and the freewheeling Williams became—along with Cronk and public relations man Herb Baus—overall campaign strategist, speech writer, and media tactician. Howard Hughes's man in Los Angeles Noah Dietrich provided $20,000 for campaign billboards.

Having lost the referendum on public housing, the Bowron forces knew they were in trouble. With his back to the wall, Bowron attempted to revive elements of his 1938 recall coalition with an attack against the Chandlers and the *Los Angeles Times* as the cornerstone of his campaign.

In a series of radio and television speeches, Bowron told Los Angeles voters that his opponent's selection was "an attempt by a small, immensely wealthy, incredibly powerful group to force you to elect as your mayor a man who will do their bidding, not yours. . . . They mean to do this," Bowron (appearing on that particular program with backer Ronald Reagan) went on, "by using their newspaper—the *Los Angeles Times*—as they have been using it—to misrepresent the facts, to suppress the news, to convince you that falsehoods are the truth, that the truth is false, that black is white."

Both Norman Chandler and Lin Beebe were singled out as "absentee landords" seeking to seize political control of the city.

Bowron also took after Carlton Williams, telling of his lobbying power and his alleged thumbs up/thumbs down activities at the city council. With Williams's "ruthless use of the power of his paper," and his ties to campaign manager George Cronk, Bowron warned, a Poulson victory would mean a new power base running city hall. "If the syndicate wins this election," he appealed in a TV speech, "we will have a triple-play combination in Los Angeles—Chandler to Williams to Cronk to Poulson—with the *Los Angeles Times* backstopping to cover my opponent's inevitable errors."

As the election neared, Bowron supporters tried to present their point concerning *Times* influence dramatically, by issuing flyers with a drawing of Poulson climbing a ladder up City Hall holding a sign reading "Los Angeles Times," Down below stood Norman Chandler, with his thumbs up, saying, "I've had that sign in storage since '38, Norrie."

The *Times* blasted Bowron from the outset of the campaign. "Mayor

Bowron used to be a good mayor and the *Times* frequently said so," the paper commented in an early editorial. "But something has happened to him. He has grown crochety and dictatorial. He has put his personal quarrels ahead of the city's business."

The *Times* publisher, in a series of page one editorials, issued a counterattack to Bowron's anti-Chandler radio and TV speeches. "The *Times* and I have personally been made the target of one of the most venal and vicious attacks in the history of local politics. Mayor Bowron, in campaigning for reelection, has stooped to practices I believed not possible of a man of his standing. . . . The *Times* will not stoop to dignify his dishonest charges by refuting them. Its answer is the place the *Times* holds in this community."

"If Mayor Bowron were in possession of all his faculties, this newspaper might resent the vicious but childish attack made on it by [him]," another page one editorial, entitled "Fletcher Blows a Fuse," commented. The *Times* compared Bowron's "slander of the Chandler family" to "the anarchists who bombed the Times Building 43 years ago."

For the *Times*, the election had become a crusade. Making the attack against public housing the key to their coverage, the *Times* linked Bowron to "convicted Communists" and "left wingers." "The public housing program brought him to bed with some characters who were dubious indeed," one *Times* editorial noted. "And he did not detach himself from them even when he was given the evidence of Red connections."

The Red-baiting reached its climax a few days before the election, when the House Subcommittee on Government Operations—similar in purpose to the Un-American Activities committees—came to town to investigate the Housing Authority on invitation of the *Times* allies on the city council. In televised hearings, with star witness William Parker recalling Bowron's action on the Wilkinson dossier, the House committee hammered at the theme of alleged Communist infiltration in Bowron's Housing Authority.

In the final three weeks before the election, the *Times* provided Poulson with 1,019 column inches of news space to 219 for Bowron. Bowron might have hoped for even less space, since mention of him was hardly favorable. Stories included: "San Fernando Valley Group Raps Bowron," "Dope Spread Blamed on [Bowron] Committee System," "Engineer Calls Bowron an Inept Administrator," "Bowron Tactics Target of Three Democrats," "Council Investigates Letter Backing Bowron."

With campaign literature written by Carlton Williams, strategy and tactics developed by the Williams/Cronk/Baus triumvirate, and daily appeals in the *Los Angeles Times* to vote "Yes for Poulson and No to Public Housing," the Poulson campaign hoped for an easy victory. But despite the *Times*'s characterization of Bowron as a "snarling, frenzied rabble-rouser mouthing untruths,'' Bowron's attacks on the Chandler paper touched a chord for many voters. From a three-to-two margin against public housing in 1952, Bowron began to chip away at his opponent's lead. But the last-minute Red-baiting—the televised hearings shown and reshown those last days before the vote—took the wind out of the charge, and Poulson came to power by a small margin.

5. *Saboba Hot Springs*

The night following the election, Carlton Williams set up a small dinner party at a fancy restaurant to celebrate the victory. Attending were Carlton and his wife, the Cronks, the Bauses, and the Poulsons. It was a fitting celebration. Not only had Williams helped run the campaign, but the day Norris Poulson entered City Hall, Carlton Williams moved in with him to become chief of staff and surrogate mayor.

Times power at city hall reached its height during the Poulson administration. Appointments, programs, legislation, budgetary matters—literally every substantial aspect of mayoral jurisdiction—found its sanction or initiation at the *Times*. Poulson, not an aggressive man, was honored and charmed by the occasional attentions he received from the powerful Chandlers. Norman assured the new mayor that the *Times* had no intention of running his office, and wanted instead a relationship of mutual interest to prevail.

"I never took orders . . . [but] I knew what they stood for,'' Poulson remarked about the *Times* in his autobiography. But the paper, through Carlton Williams and editor L.D. Hotchkiss, did intervene with Poulson on a day-to-day basis. Police lobbyist Ed Davis recalled that whenever he wanted to get something from city hall he first went to see Hotchkiss. If Hotchkiss went along, Davis discovered, he would get backing from the mayor as well. Almost every time he walked into the mayor's office after a previous session with Hotchkiss, Davis recalled, "Carlton Williams would walk out and he'd give me a big wink. . . . I learned to interpret this that Carl had gone in and everything's ok baby; you know everything Hotch [Hotchkiss] said we were going to do would be done.''

The chairman of the State and Local Government Committee of the Los Angeles Chamber of Commerce, Lin Beebe, also wielded a great deal of power over the new mayor. "He [Beebe] had a committee that he ran with an iron hand, and their recommendations were tantamount to city hall approval,'' Davis recalled of Beebe. "The men on that committee represented the biggest law firms, some of the biggest corporations—it was downtown power.''

James Lin Beebe, former president of the Chamber of Commerce and a senior partner in the O'Melveny & Myers law firm, was Mr. Big in the city. Beebe had founded and run the State and Local Government Committee since 1932. Beebe, through O'Melveny & Myers, often wrote the city's bond offerings and could thereby determine how the city spent and administered funds.

Beebe and Williams worked closely with Poulson and the council as well as with City Administrative Officer (CAO) Sam Leask, Jr. The CAO post had been created through a 1951 charter amendment first proposed by a task force on Los Angeles's fiscal operations—which included Lin Beebe—to reorganize city government. Leask had been vice-president of the May Company and J.W. Robinson department stores and had participated in many of the business organizations and clubs in the city. Working closely with Beebe and Williams, Leask sometimes made decisions that bypassed Poulson.

The city officials and their business advisors institutionalized their relationship with a semiannual trek to Saboba Hot Springs, a small desert resort community not far from Los Angeles. Twice a year Beebe and Williams, with Beebe's aide George Gose, hosted a delegation of Los Angeles city officials including Leask, Poulson, and their closest advisors. Leask would bring a tentative rough draft of the city's budget or other major administrative report, and Beebe and Williams and the others would go over it point by point. "The meeting was all business," one of the participants recalled, "there was no monkeying around." The Saboba meetings became the most striking example of business/*Times* domination of city hall.

The issue of housing and urban redevelopment continued to predominate during the Poulson years. Shortly after the new mayor took office, the *Times* proclaimed that it was "proud of its part in crying the alarm against this creeping Socialism and in supporting the Mayor who found the way to stop the creep." Poulson immediately cut back on the public housing plans already under contract with the Federal Government, working out a compromise whereby 5,700 of the proposed 10,000 units were dropped. The city absorbed a major loss, which included thousands of dollars worth of architectural and engineering drawings and abandoned land that had already been cleared at taxpayers' expense. The federal government also lost approximately $4.4 million already spent on the project.

At the very moment that plans for public housing were dropped, another set of plans for one of the designated housing areas—Bunker Hill—began to emerge. Once a well-to-do community, dotted with mansions of the city's doctors, lawyers, and merchants during the 1800s, the area had become a slum half a century later. After World War I, the large mansions had been turned into rooming houses for transients, pensioners, and derelicts. By the 1930s and 40s Bunker Hill residents—poor Mexican-Americans and whites—lived there in crowded facilities. But to many, Bunker Hill was the most attractive of Los Angeles's poor neighborhoods. A feeling of neighborliness existed throughout the community; its steep incline, which eliminated large-scale automobile traffic, had helped keep its many trees and gardens intact.

To the city's businessmen, Bunker Hill—in close proximity to Los Angeles's downtown—was an obstacle to development. The current condition of the neighborhood, one realtor noted in 1929, was "a barrier to progress in the business district of Los Angeles, preventing the natural expansion westward."

The Housing Authority—supported by the community's residents and the public housing coalition—had hoped to develop large-scale low-cost integrated public housing on the northern end of the hill, with apartment units that could upgrade the neighborhood but keep its current population intact.

The downtown business/anti-public housing forces instead wanted to clear the land and the current population to make way for high income housing, upper-class cultural institutions, and skyscraper office buildings.

In November 1954, after the Bunker Hill public housing had been dropped, the pro-*Times* city council voted to ask the federal government for $33 million to help subsidize Bunker Hill redevelopment—a plan that the *Times* and the large realtors wholeheartedly approved. Mexican-American City Councilman Edward Roybal, who represented the Bunker Hill constituents, was bitter. "Approval of the new Bunker Hill project was not a signal for heads to roll," Roybal wrote, contrasting the reaction to redevelopment with that toward public housing. "No billboards blossomed with propaganda legends; no property owners were organized to march on the City Hall; no voters were urged to refuse to pay another man's rent. No editorials alerted the city to 'creeping Socialism,' and not a single congressional investigator was called in."

The redevelopment plan contained substantial tax benefits for the real estate developers and landlords who most strongly—with the *Times*—pushed the plan. "In effect, they are being handed a seventeen-million-dollar tax subsidy," one of Roybal's advisors wrote to him. "This is the Public Housing Authority story all over again, except under public housing the tenant gets the subsidy—under Redevelopment the subsidy goes to the landlord."

Bunker Hill residents fought the plan through the courts, but the redevelopers' actions were upheld. In the spring of 1961 the first piece of redeveloped Bunker Hill property changed ownership. The old mansions, with their intricate towers and Victorian facades, were leveled. The Angel's Flight rail incline that brought commuters to and from downtown was torn down. The small shacks that housed the people of Bunker Hill were turned to rubble. In their place rose massive corporate structures such as the Security Pacific Bank building, the Music Center complex, and two luxury apartment twins called the Bunker Hill Towers.

6. Take Me Out for the Ball Game

Just north of Bunker Hill lies Chavez Ravine, an area of more than a hundred acres of rolling hills, only partially urbanized, inhabited primarily by poor Mexican-Americans. Like Bunker Hill, the Ravine, with its existing vacant land and proximity to downtown, was to have been a site for a public housing project. By the time Poulson came into office, Chavez Ravine residents, promised first priority in the new low-cost housing, had been almost entirely cleared from the area. When the Chavez Ravine project was also abandoned, the city-boosting business leaders soon found an ideal use for the site.

Sometime in the winter of 1956, City Councilwoman Roz Wyman had a hunch, as she put it, that the owner of the Brooklyn Dodgers baseball team, Walter O'Malley, might be open to moving his franchise to Los Angeles. Wyman, a Democrat whose husband had emerged as the leading power-broker in his party, had been opposed by the *Times* in her first election try in the early 1950s. After working with Dorothy Chandler on one of her cultural activities, Wyman became friends with Buff's son Otis Chandler and eventually received the *Times* Woman of the Year award, as well as the paper's endorsement in later election tries.

After Wyman approached Poulson, Leask, and several other officials, the group flew down to the Dodgers' winter headquarters in Vero Beach, Florida, to talk to O'Malley. The idea of a baseball stadium in Chavez Ravine had already been explored, thanks in part to a secret $5,000 survey grant from Howard Hughes. Leask, among others, felt the Ravine would be impossible to develop and that costs, as the survey pointed out, would be exorbitant. To their surprise, O'Malley was not only interested in Los Angeles, but in the Chavez Ravine site.

With the help of local business power, Harold "Chad" McLellan, the group worked out a deal with O'Malley. Besides turning over the Chavez Ravine land, the city was to contribute $2 million for grading the site and another $2.7 million from the state gas fund to be used for building access roads. In return, the Dodgers, who had decided to play in an interim ballpark until the new stadium was built, would set aside forty acres of Chavez Ravine land for recreational purposes.

Opposition to the deal immediately developed. Some of the opponents, such as C. Arnholt Smith, the San Diego businessman who owned the minor league San Diego Padres baseball team, were clearly motivated by economic interests. Others, like Councilman John Holland, argued against the giveaway of the land to O'Malley. The most significant opposition came from the residents of Chavez Ravine and their City Councilman Edward Roybal. Roybal insisted that they were not opposed to the Dodgers' coming to Los Angeles, but only to the deal that virtually gave away the Chavez Ravine land. In order that a stadium and access roads be constructed, poor residents would have to give up their homes in one of the few low-income neighborhoods with immediate access to downtown. Roybal and others initiated a referendum for the city voters which called for a renegotiation of the contract. A new contract, they hoped, could grant the city a percentage of the gate, rental fees, and other revenues, as well as use of the stadium when the Dodgers were not playing.

With early indications pointing to a possible victory for the proponents of renegotiation, the city's business forces once more swung into action. They suggested that the referendum was actually a vote against baseball and that the city had to "honor" its contracts. The *Times* and Hearst's *Examiner,* soliciting coverage from their sports writers during the campaign, gave major support to the original deal.

On the Friday before Election Day, Walter O'Malley telephoned Richard Moore, president of the Chandler-owned TV station KTTV. The two brainstormed about possible last-minute tactics, and Moore eventually came up with the idea of a telethon. KTTV cameras went out to the airport to film the Dodgers team, which had just arrived from a tough series with the Chicago Cubs. Several of the players were interviewed, and the telethon became a celebration and affirmation of baseball. The show aired twice before the election. The Chavez Ravine stadium advocates won by a scant 25,000 margin.

Ill feelings in the community still prevailed, and when the remaining Chavez Ravine tenants began to be evicted, some, like the Arechigas family, put up a fight. Television coverage of the event turned the eviction into a *cause célèbre.* The *Times* fumed over the intervention of the new medium. "The television pictures—wonderful action pictures—were the answer to the demagogue's prayer," an editorial declared. "With such pictures, facts would only spoil the effects."

The Arechigas eviction storm died down when it was discovered that the family—not quite as poor and desperate as TV had made them out to be—also owned two other small houses. But the evictions had stirred a response among many Angelenos, and the affair would come back to haunt Poulson and his backers when the mayor came up for reelection a few years later.

The last years of the decade saw for the first time in twenty years the incipient signs of diminishing *Times* power—touched off by the Chavez Ravine storm. Carlton Williams had lobbied hard on the Chavez Ravine matter, and he was increasingly under attack for his tactics. His nemesis, Councilman Rundberg, blasted Williams on the council floor, brought his charges about Williams's influence up on a TV program, and even went to Norman Chandler to complain. The new editor of the *Times*, Nick Williams, didn't care for Carlton Williams's style, and the *Times* city hall correspondent began to experience a lessening of his power to use the paper to browbeat politicians. "There's a big power struggle going on at the *Times*," Carlton Williams confided to Poulson, "and its outcome might determine my future."

Both Poulson and Williams, in their own ways, symbolized the two modes of surrogate power that gave the *Times* and its friends a hold for so many years over Los Angeles. As they faded, the *Times* would have to look elsewhere for new forms of power.

CHAPTER 16

Republican Fortunes

1. The Little Governor

He was the most powerful "high power" of them all. Kyle Palmer, a diminutive man with a sharp wit, had secured a reputation for political infighting and influence that was second to none at the *Times*. In 1939, in honor of his work and his power, the "Little Governor," as he was called, was named a director of the Chamber of Commerce.

"One cannot overstate Kyle Palmer's influence," former Nixon aide Bob Finch said of the *Times* political editor. "He took the lead in a pretelevision era in which the press and the *Times*, and Palmer's role within the *Times*, was dominant, when combined with the relatively weak role of political parties in California." *Times* Washington bureau chief (and later aide to Gerald Ford) Robert Hartmann called Palmer "an organizer, a manipulator. Anyone who wanted to run for office had to clear it with Kyle."

Palmer, aware of the importance of the press, worked closely to select and endorse candidates and to create political issues with some of the other major Republican newspapers in the state—Knowland's *Oakland Tribune* and De Young's *San Francisco Chronicle*, as well as the Ridders and the Copleys, smaller newspaper chain owners.

"His power," Finch remarked of Palmer, "was a double power of the broker who influenced and made politicians' careers and the political editor with the clout of the *Times* endorsement." Palmer would interview various candidates and judge their electability and willingness to pursue a political life in accord with the *Times*/business ideology.

With Asa Call, "Mr. Big in California politics," Palmer developed the

271

Republican party's large donor fund-raising apparatus. Call, Palmer, and a few others, including Norman Chandler's brother-in-law John J. Garland, organized an informal network of conservative money men who were willing to contribute large amounts of money for particular candidates or issues based on the recommendations of Call and Palmer. The informal network, which was separate from the smaller, contribution-based United Republican Finance Committee, thus had the power to make or break a candidate by either creating or drying up funds. The money men then could determine what issues the candidate ought to run on and, once in office, what positions he or she ought to take.

Through the 1940s and 50s Palmer maneuvered within the Republican party structure to get his closest allies elected to the highest party posts. In 1947, for instance, Palmer helped McIntyre Faries get the post of National Committeeman for California Republicans. Bob Finch, a Republican county chairman in this period, recalled how he talked with Palmer on a daily basis about which party official would be successful and what internal fights or maneuvers were occurring. Palmer developed a highly centralized information network which allowed him to evaluate, predict, and influence the careers of any Republican elected to county, state or federal office. The system relied primarily on the media and fund-raising apparatus instead of the traditional "party boss" system of patronage. Within the Republican party—a relatively weak infrastructure without an extensive constituent base or highly motivated cadre—Palmer, as power-broker/fund-raiser/political editor, could create spectacular careers overnight. The California Republicans became a party of kingpins, and Kyle Palmer was the man who made the kings.

One of the top political reporters for Hearst's *Examiner,* Alan Williams, recalled an incident in the late 1940s that illustrates the extent of the Palmer influence. Williams, who considered himself something of a hotshot reporter at the time, went down to Union Station one day to catch former President Herbert Hoover's arrival. When the train pulled in, Williams managed to elbow his way through the huge crowd to walk next to Hoover. The former president was in a rush, and Williams had to sprint alongside in order to ask questions and take notes. After Williams persisted, the former president reluctantly answered a few of the reporter's questions. Williams, pleased with his "exclusive," thought he had a damned good story, but the next morning when he picked up a copy of the rival *Times*, his heart sank. There in the *Times* was a long interview with the former president written by Kyle Palmer, an interview, Williams later found out, that had been conducted at Palmer's house, where the former President was rushing from the train station.

Palmer had his own office in the Times Building, and he frequently conducted his business with politicians and party officials seated at his desk.

Former *Times* reporter Fred Chase recalled how one time he had entered the political editor's office to discuss some business and saw Palmer gesturing and berating a man seated opposite him. Palmer, sounding as if he were scolding a little child, continued in spite of Chase's presence. When he finished, the man stood up to leave, and Chase realized it was California Governor Goodwin Knight. No Eastern political reporter, Theodore White observed, rivaled Palmer in local clout.

Palmer's influence extended to the different industry associations, whose lobbyists often came to see the "Little Governor" to discuss issues and candidates in coming elections. The lobbyists almost invariably passed on the Timesman's recommendations to the industry chiefs. Palmer had become a political interpreter for an entire class.

Palmer also knew a great deal about the ins and outs of the California Democrats. He was a friend of Democratic National Committeeman Paul Ziffren; the two frequently lunched together and traded information. Ties with Ziffren strengthened Palmer's ability to predict, and, therefore, influence. In one instance, Palmer foresaw more than a year in advance the emergence of Sam Yorty as the Democratic choice for the Senate in 1954.

Palmer's influence was greatest at a time during the 1940s and 50s when California Republican fortunes were at their peak. Earl Warren, William Knowland, Richard Nixon, and Goodwin Knight—any one of whom might successfully run for the presidency—were all national figures. Yet the astute Palmer understood that in many ways the Republican fortunes were deceptive, as grass-roots Democratic organizing took hold in the mid-1950s while Republican powerhouse figures dabbled in presidential politics.

Kyle Palmer was ultimately a man of the media, a maker of images. One of his most successful political image manipulations involved the "nonpartisan" portrait of one of the most popular Republican politicians in California history.

2. Mr. Nonpartisan

Earl Warren, the son of a Swedish teamster, was a most extraordinary politician. He was a political oddity: part reactionary, part progressive, and at all times a tremendous vote-getter. As an officeholder in California, in the context of his right-wing California backers and the inner circle of the Republican party, Warren was a conservative. Once freed from his former supporters in his position as Chief Justice, he actively pursued a liberal, interventionist role for the Supreme Court that made the Warren Court respected and admired by the justice's former opponents and detested by anti-Communist Republican party regulars.

Warren first came to the attention of the state's two most influential newspapermen and Republican powers, Joe Knowland of the *Oakland Tribune* and Harry Chandler of the *Los Angeles Times*, around the time of his victory for the post of district attorney of Alameda County, in northern California, in the early years of the Depression. Unlike most Republicans in the 1930s, Warren, who projected himself as a low-key, proficient, nonpartisan official interested in getting the job done, did not seem to fit the label of spokesman for the rich. Though some of his actions as D.A. were controversial and subject to attack by liberal and labor critics, he managed to avoid the reactionary Republican caricature that FDR had so successfully exploited in Depression days. His antilabor activities, however, were sufficient to meet the political criteria of his new, wealthy backers.

In 1938, after incumbent California Attorney General U.S. Webb announced he would retire, Warren entered the race, cross-filing in all three parties—Republican, Democratic, and Progressive. The cross-filing system was ideally suited to Warren's style. Since 1934 the Democrats had been the state's majority party, holding a three-to-two edge in registration. In order to maintain their influence, Republican power-brokers led by Asa Call formed a new organization in 1936, the California Republican Assembly, whose main function was to endorse Republicans in the primary. The CRA endorsement made clear which candidate was receiving the unofficial party endorsement—without technically breaking the primary laws. Afterwards, Republican party workers could rally around that candidate, making it difficult for another Republican to undertake a primary challenge. The unofficially endorsed candidate, no longer worried about his chances in his own party's primary, could then cross-file in the Democratic party. Republicans, with greater funds and a public relations apparatus, occasionally won Democratic primaries, but even if the cross-filed Republicans lost, they might still effectively cripple their Democratic opponents by polling a large percentage of the Democratic vote.

Warren, who had successfully developed a nonpartisan image as Alameda D.A., used it and his strong financial backing to his advantage. He presented himself as someone who "passed" as a Democrat, someone above the party fray, a man of moderation in turbulent times. "Support the man, not the party" became a Warren trademark.

Yet Warren was just as much an extension of the Kyle Palmers and Asa Calls as any other Republican in that period. In 1934, attacking Upton Sinclair and the EPICS, he called for "nonpartisan unity to destroy the spectre of socialism." He remained strongly hostile to labor and radical movements and sponsored an antisabotage bill that included a curtailment of a union's right to picket or strike. He refused to recommend clemency for three labor organizers imprisoned on a murder charge, a *cause célèbre* in labor's ranks. And he helped guide a "hot cargo" bill through the state legislature which banned secondary strikes and boycotts.

Warren's nonpartisan appeal swept him to victory in all three 1938 primaries, precluding a runoff in the general election against a Democratic opponent. Four years later Warren ran for governor, cross-filing against Democratic incumbent Culbert Olson. Olson, who had come to power as a strong left-liberal candidate in 1938, had moved to the right and alienated large sections of his own party through his inept administration. Republican power-brokers had also undermined Olson's programs by organizing a legislative coalition called the "economy bloc," composed of conservative Democratic and Republican legislators, who blocked much of Olson's legislation in the name of fiscal responsibility.

With Olson under siege and the advent of the war eliminating many of the political conditions that had brought the New Deal constituency to power, Republican chances seemed promising. Under Kyle Palmer's urging, Warren announced his candidacy and put the finishing touches on his nonpartisan strategy. Olson was depicted as a man of controversy, fighting the legislature, in conflict within his own party. Warren, on the other hand, under Palmer's guidance, projected himself as a man of unity, who could bring the state together in wartime. Warren easily won the Republican primary and pulled an impressive 45 percent of the vote in the Democratic primary. Warren swept to power in a landslide. His election was, according to the *Times*, "the best political news California has had in a generation."

The nonpolitical cooperative spirit strategy, conjured up through the political genius of Kyle Palmer, had been ostensibly embraced by the *Times*, the most intensely partisan newspaper in the state. It was an extraordinary performance. The new governor maintained a studied ambivalence for three terms in office, maintaining his progressive nonpartisan image through public health legislation; a veto of some of the more virulent anti-Communist legislation sponsored by State Senator Jack Tenney; liberalization of old-age benefits, unemployment insurance, and workmen's compensation; and his strong working relationship with one of the most popular Democratic politicians in the state, Bob Kenny. But Earl Warren continued to be the representative of the most reactionary business group in the country. "These diehards," Carey McWilliams wrote of the California establishment in 1943, "were used to the ruthless methods of the Open Shop, the Red Squad, and the Labor Frame-Up. . . . But with the EPIC campaign of 1934, the popular front campaign of 1938 [which elected Culbert Olson], the spectacular rise of the powerful pension-plan movements and the increased strength of organized labor, the smarter elements realized that ruthlessness must be eliminated in favor of cunning, that slickness must replace brazenness, and that dizzily conducted public relations must take the place of the old knock-their-teeth-out campaign. Nowadays such bastions of reaction as the Merchants and Manufacturers Association of Los Angeles have been virtually eliminated. They have long since been replaced by the slickest streamlined front that big business has been able to create anywhere in the United States. Earl Warren is the front man for this machine." As one Democratic candidate, frustrated by the Warren nonpartisan magic, stated: "He *was* a right-wing Republican; he didn't *seem* like it, he *was*."

The 1940s saw the beginnings of the use of political public relations in election campaigns. In California, probusiness publicists, such as Baus and Roos in Los Angeles and Whitaker and Baxter statewide, handled all the major political campaigns, creating the various techniques that could elect "the man, not the party." California, McWilliams wrote, was "Government by Whitaker and Baxter."

The period also showed the first signs of a major readjustment of the relationship of business forces to labor. Many of the major industries that came to settle in Southern California during World War II had granted union charters to their employees without the preliminary of an organizing campaign. In turn, the unions acted as effective disciplinarians in imposing the "no-strike" pledge and pushing high productivity goals.

Not all the Southern California business elite accepted the accommodation with labor so easily. Though the *Times,* under Kyle Palmer's leadership, promoted the concept of "nonpartisanship," it still had trouble parting with the idea of the open shop. In 1944, under the leadership of the former SCI head, Southern Pacific's Paul Shoup (then heading the M&M), an "Employment Initiative Amendment," popularly known as the Right to Work measure, was put on the ballot in hopes of legislating away the closed shop. The proposition gave employers the right to hire nonunion labor in a shop which already had a union contract. A coalition of Southern California business groups, with backing from the *Times,* supported the amendment, but for the first time a serious split in business ranks occurred. Many of the aerospace executives who spearheaded the top-down unionization of industry in Los Angeles refused to contribute to the M&M war chest and the San Francisco Chamber of Commerce actually opposed the measure. Earl Warren and Fletcher Bowron were among those who decided to oppose the initiative. The "right to work" was defeated by a three-to-two margin.

The end of the war saw a reversal of the accommodationist trend. As Cold War politics provided an effective weapon in Republican/business ranks for breaking the back of the enlarged power of the labor movement and radical advances within the Democratic party, a different type of Republican candidate emerged—a tough-talking anti-Communist riding the wave of political reaction spawned by McCarthyism. The model for the new candidate was a young Whittier lawyer, who became the new political face of the Southern California establishment.

3. *"We Stand by Nixon"*

The candidate had passed his first hurdle. He had impressed the group of businessmen, the Committee of 100, who had wanted a candidate to defeat Jerry Voorhis, the Democratic congressman, one-time Socialist and EPIC, who had been the model for the naive and idealistic politician of the movie *Mr. Smith Goes to Washington*. The *Times*, always having disliked Voorhis, commented in one editorial, "Again and again Horace Jerry Voorhis has shown his complete subservience to every whim of the New Deal."

All the young Republican needed was the blessing of the *Times* and the approval of its political editor. The Whittier lawyer had a great deal going for him. One of his backers was David Faries, a close associate of Kyle Palmer; another was John Jewett Garland, married to a Chandler and also a Palmer intimate. Richard Nixon emerged from his meetings with the backing of the Committee of 100, Kyle Palmer, and the *Times*—and the 1946 Republican nomination for Congress in the thirteenth congressional district locked up. It was the beginning of an auspicious relationship.

Nixon's Senate try against Helen Gahagan Douglas in 1950 was undoubtedly the most important campaign in his California political career. Nixon, who had defeated Voorhis and was easily reelected in 1948, had been tagged by the Republican power-brokers as one of the brightest stars in the party, a man who could effectively utilize the anti-Communist tactic to win elections. As Asa Call started to collect funds for the 1950 race, Kyle Palmer began to sound the drums for the two-time congressman. A group of twenty Southern California businessmen put up the first $20,000 for his Senate race. Murray Chotiner, who had managed both the Earl Warren and Bill Knowland campaigns, became a key figure in the Nixon entourage.

While Nixon had a relatively easy time of it in his primary, the Democrats waged a bitter and bloody battle that would rub off on the general election. The liberal candidate, Los Angeles Congresswoman Helen Gahagan Douglas, backed by the labor movement and the old New Deal coalition, had antagonized the oil and agribusiness interests through her support of federal regulation of offshore oil and support of a 160-acre limit for use of federal reclaimed waters. Manchester Boddy, the publisher of Los Angeles's only Democratic paper, the *Los Angeles Daily News*, opposed her in the primary. Boddy, then a strong anti-Communist conservative, backed by Democratic oil men Edwin Pauley and John Elliot, opposed Douglas on the oil and agribusiness issues. But his sharpest attack was based on the issue of communism. A Douglas victory, Boddy stated, would allow "a small minority of red-hots to establish a beachhead on which to launch a Communist attack on the United States."

Douglas won the primary, but Boddy's attacks were immediately picked up and elaborated on by Republican candidate Nixon. With Chotiner's guidance, the Nixon campaign labelled Douglas the "Pink Lady" and issued an infamous "Pink Sheet," which compared Douglas's voting record to that of radical congressman Vito Marcantonio. Douglas invented the epithet "Tricky Dick" for her opponent, but it didn't stop the Republican candidate. She's "pink right down to her underpants," Nixon charged. The remark was characteristic of the tenor of his campaign right up to Election Day.

For the *Times*, the election had become the cutting edge of Cold War politics. California, an editorial commented, is "the only state where Communism becomes the main issue." Though the *Times* made references to its "young, forward-looking, aggressive and able" Republican candidate, the paper reserved its fire for Douglas. "She is the darling of the Hollywood parlor pinks and Reds," an editorial proclaimed a few days before the election.

"The election of Representative Nixon," another editorial dramatically concluded, "will be seen by the nation as a sign that the State of California wholeheartedly opposes Communism." The *Times* gave the Republican candidate three times as much space as Douglas and printed eight photographs of Nixon and his wife to none for the Democratic candidate. Nixon's victory was the triumph of the new 1950s politics, and the paper heralded its significance.

Richard Nixon had become a power within the state. He was enormously ambitious, ready to seize each opportunity that came by. He sensed that the open-ended 1952 Republican Presidential Convention would be ideal for improving his fortunes. The two front-runners were Dwight Eisenhower, with strong backing from the Republican East Coast establishment, and conservative Senator Robert Taft. California Governor Warren, a favorite-son candidate, was a long shot if the convention deadlocked.

As the train pulled out of Los Angeles on the way to the convention site in Chicago, Nixon—whose relations with Warren were already strained—lined up some of Warren's California delegates to work his game. On a crucial procedural matter, Nixon swung his California bloc to support Eisenhower; the maneuver provided the momentum that swept the general to victory. Many of the Warren delegates, and more importantly, Kyle Palmer, harshly criticized Nixon's tactics. "Honorable men," Palmer wrote, "don't stab their friends—or enemies—in the back." But Nixon was able to neutralize the antagonisms when he received the Republican vice-presidential nomination. Not since Herbert Hoover had there been a Californian in the White House, and the *Times* and their allies welcomed the opportunity.

Through the first months of the campaign, the *Times* enthusiastically supported the Republican ticket by providing nearly double the column inches and number of stories than for the Democrats. The Stevenson campaign in Southern California was so outraged by the behavior of the *Times* that they took ten minutes of a weekly half-hour radio show they had purchased to answer what they considered *Times* distortions. One of the most famous incidents in the campaign coverage was the August 5 photograph of an Eisenhower speech before the Veterans of Foreign Wars at the 100,000 seat Los Angeles Coliseum. Though only 16,000 people showed up, the *Times* angled the photograph to make the Coliseum appear filled, providing no information to the contrary.

The Chandlers loaned one of their star reporters, Jim Bassett, to work as Nixon's campaign press secretary. Bassett, along with aides Chotiner and Bill Rogers, advised the candidate on policy and tactics.

Less than two months before the end of the campaign, the *New York Post* broke a story about an $18,000 personal fund set up for vice-presidential candidate Nixon by some of his Southern California backers. The Democrats seized the issue and demanded that Nixon be dropped from the ticket. While the issue raged for several days, Eisenhower seriously considered the move. With his back to the wall, Nixon decided to appear on television to explain the circumstances of the gift and plead for sympathy.

The *Times* ran a front page "We Stand By Nixon" editorial the day of his TV appearance. "The personal tragedy of an upright man sacrificed unjustly to satisfy the clamor stirred by the cunning objectives of his political enemies would by no means be as deplorable as would be the loss to the public of a career genuinely dedicated to the public interest," the *Times* editorial appealed to Nixon's constituency.

Bassett and the others worked on the "Checkers" speech, but it was Nixon's television genius that pulled off the event. The next day the *Times* devoted its entire front page to favorable coverage of Nixon. "DRAMATIC PLEA STIRS NATION," one headline read; "DOCUMENTS SHOW NIXON BLAMELESS," according to another. A third headline told the paper's readers "HOW TO DIRECT MESSAGES TO GOP CHIEFS." Nixon's obvious sincerity," the lead article began, "loosed a flood of response from all America . . . He spoke from his heart and mind rather than a transcript."

Dick Nixon survived "Checkers" and went to Washington as part of the massive Eisenhower landslide. The *Times*, ecstatic, talked of a new era, one already foreseen in the "Pink Lady" victory. "We have just come through a political period," a postelection editorial noted, "in which the manipulators of the national government, after enlarging their powers beyond anything older Americans ever dreamed of, set about destroying the American belief in growth and progress. These manipulators conceived of the citizens as a kind of vegetable to be watered and manured with the various implements of the welfare state. . . . But they were stopped before it was too late."

With Nixon in Washington, the scars caused by the '52 "stab in the back" were forgiven or overlooked. Nixon continued to turn to Kyle Palmer for advice, and Bassett stayed on in varying capacities. He headed the P.R. effort for the Republican National Committee in 1954 and returned to work for Nixon in 1956—serving, in effect, as the vice-president's campaign manager. In Nixon's 1960 presidential run, Bassett became one of the three key aides to work on policy matters and general strategy.

During the 1956 election, *Los Angeles Times* coverage, one magazine pointed out, appeared to be of Nixon, rather than of Eisenhower and Nixon. Nixon, as a *Times* favorite, continued to adorn both editorial and news copy throughout the decade. In the eyes of the *Times*, he had become a statesman—a man of wisdom and stature. "As distinguished from the hypercritical and broad generalizations of Stevenson," a *Times* editorial noted during the 1958 campaign, "Nixon's remarks for the most part were directed to the factual and realistic conditions facing not only the embattled political parties but the country as a whole."

In 1958, it appeared that the fortunes of the California Republican party were still climbing in Washington and Sacramento. California Republicans occupied the vice-presidency, the two U.S. Senate seats, and the office of the chief justice of the Supreme Court. But Kyle Palmer, perhaps more responsible than any other individual for this star-studded success, still worried about his party's future.

4. Party Dogfights

The son of the founder and owner of the *Oakland Tribune*, William Fife Knowland, a key backer of Earl Warren, had been appointed by Governor Warren to fill out Hiram Johnson's remaining term in the U.S. Senate after Johnson's death in 1945. After Knowland's term expired the next year, he ran for his seat against Democratic opponent Will Rogers, Jr., a unity candidate supported by both liberal and conservative factions within the badly splintered Democratic Party, as well as by both wings of the labor movement, the AFL and the CIO. The *Times* attempted to attack and isolate Rogers as a candidate of the left. Whenever the paper discussed Rogers's backers, his support from the more conservative AFL Central Labor Council was not mentioned. When the AFL complained, *Times* assistant managing editor Bill Holden replied, "It may be necessary in our campaign to defeat Mr. Rogers, to refer to him occasionally as endorsed by CIO-PAC, feeling that this is one of the effective means of bringing about his defeat." Rogers immediately protested, calling Holden's statement "a major un-American act by a great metropolitan daily."

Knowland engaged in the strong public relations-oriented political campaign so successfully used by Earl Warren and numerous other Republicans. He defeated Rogers in '46. In his race for reelection in 1952, he cross-filed, winning both the Democratic and Republican primaries with a total victory margin of one million votes.

In 1953–1954 when the Republicans became the majority party in the Senate, Knowland served as Senate Majority Leader. The senator, strong-willed, ambitious, and stubborn, considered himself a principled conservative, particularly on matters concerning labor, and felt supremely confident not only in the rightness of his position but in its popularity as well.

Blending strong anti-Communist and prointerventionist politics, Knowland became the leader of the Senate's "Taiwan Bloc," expressing hostility to the new Communist government in China and endorsing John Foster Dulles's aggressive foreign policy in Asia. Knowland, as part of the "Vietnam Lobby," helped engineer crucial backing for Ngo Dinh Diem in the first years after the Indochina settlement in Geneva in 1954.

On the strength of his principles and his popularity, Knowland envisioned a possible presidential nomination when Eisenhower stepped down. But Knowland the politician also realized that he could only become a serious contender if he had the California delegation behind him. The major difficulty, as he saw it, was that the party's infrastructure was far more bound up with Sacramento than with Washington. As governor, Knowland would have far more party clout than as senator. But a Republican already sat in the State House.

Lieutenant Governor Goodwin "Goodie" Knight had succeeded to the governorship in 1953 when the new Republican administration in Washington named his predecessor, Earl Warren, as the new chief justice of the Supreme Court. Knight, a former Stanford classmate of Norman Chandler, had been a conservative superior court judge, first appointed to the bench by Governor Merriam in 1935. He already had friendly ties to Kyle Palmer and the *Times* when he successfully ran for lieutenant governor in the Warren sweep of 1946. Staking out a position to the right of Warren, Knight quickly became one of the prominently mentioned Republican figures in the late 1940s.

After 1952, Warren, Nixon, and Knowland each tried to build an independent political base in order to prepare for a 1956 or 1960 run for the presidency. Before Warren's Supreme Court appointment, Knight again began to make inquiries about a possible run for the governor's post. But Kyle Palmer warned his friend. "I am getting a lot of letters from various individuals who seem to feel that Warren, Knowland and Nixon aren't doing too well with each other," Palmer wrote Knight in the summer of 1953. "Please my friend, please, keep out of any dog fights between those three. Keep friendly with everybody!!!!" Palmer also tried to discourage Knight from opposing Warren in the '54 primaries. "If you and Warren run against each other," Palmer wrote, "you will set the stage for a Democratic governor and U.S. senator." ("Keep this letter" Palmer added "just in case I need proof of being a prophet.")

As new governor, Knight, following Warren's footsteps, attempted to build a broader constituency and a milder nonpartisan form of politics in order to keep the governor's post. In the '54 race, Knight, strongly backed by the *Times*, won by a substantial margin over liberal Democrat Richard Graves.

In a first step toward building his own political base within the party, Knight pushed for the election of Howard Ahmanson as state chairman of the Finance Committee of the California Republican party, a position then held by Asa Call. Ahmanson, the president of Home Savings and Loan, had hitched up with Goodwin Knight when Knight was lieutenant governor, becoming, as one of Ahmanson's associates put it, the man "who picked up the tab." Ahmanson was Knight's bankroller, providing, along with several other Savings and Loan executives, major financial support for his campaigns. With him as party finance chairman, Knight's group would be in a major position to exercise control over Republican affairs. Ahmanson got the position.

The Old Guard, angry at Knight's ambitions, became furious when the governor, in seeking to expand his political base, started to make overtures to organized labor. "The spectacle of a Republican Governor of California kowtowing to labor union officials is a shameful one," the *Times* declared, as they launched an attack against Knight in the summer of 1955. After George Meany praised Knight at a meeting in San Diego in October 1956, a Kyle Palmer column warned the governor about his failure to make the distinction between collaring support of working-class votes à la Warren, and making alliances with trade union leaders. The governor, the *Times* warned, "is losing the respect of many who formerly believed in him." His actions, the paper complained, had revealed him "as a typical opportunist. The road of the political opportunist," the paper concluded, "is a dead-end street."

The three forces—Nixon, Knight, and Knowland—each attempting to secure a major role within the California delegation—came into direct conflict during the 1956 Republican National Convention. It took a last-minute effort by Los Angeles Mayor Norris Poulson to calm things down and to work out an effective compromise. The *Times*, though politically closest to Bill Knowland, was caught in the divisions. Kyle Palmer worried about Senator Knowland's occasional ideological forays and political stubborness, was mindful of Vice-President Nixon's power and access to the national political machinery, and still had doubts about Goodwin Knight's popularity and political base. When Ahmanson had a heart attack in the mid-1950s and was forced to resign his party posts, Knight lost his opportunity to create an effective alternative financial/power base.

While the Republican stars maneuvered, the Democrats organized. In 1950, conservative Democratic oil man John Elliot took a major step toward breaking the Republican monopoly on statewide elections by organizing a petition drive to place a measure on the ballot to eliminate cross-filing. The Republican legislature, sensing defeat, put up a compromise measure which allowed cross-filing but required party identification next to each candidate's name. Though the Elliott measure was narrowly defeated in the 1952 elections, the Republican compromise easily passed.

Within two years, Democratic membership clubs began to spring up around the state to serve the same function as the old California Republican Assembly in endorsing a candidate for the primary. With the club endorsement and the required party label on the ballot, the power of the Republicans to cross-file effectively was severely undermined. The party clubs, the California Democratic Council (CDC) became popular grassroots instruments for reaching the large, unorganized Democratic electorate, who still maintained a heavy registration edge over the Republicans. In 1956 not one Republican successfully cross-filed.

Pat Brown was the only Democrat to win a statewide election—for Attorney General in 1950. Brown, a former Republican, had modeled his electoral strategies in the Earl Warren mold. He appeared as a reasonable, nonideological Democrat who could also work well with Republicans. Four years later, Brown repeated Earl Warren's versatile cross-filing trick and won reelection in both the Republican and Democratic primaries.

As the 1958 election neared, Pat Brown, with a united and strengthened Democratic party behind him, decided to make a run for the governorship. The Republicans, on the other hand, were in a state of disarray. William Knowland had set off a chain reaction within party ranks with his announcement that he would not be a candidate for reelection to the Senate in 1958. The *Times* editorial the day after the announcement correctly speculated that the Majority Leader, in preparation for a bid for the presidency in 1960, had decided his first step was a run for the governor's spot in 1958.

Knowland decided to link his governor's race with a major offensive against the labor movement through a "right to work" initiative. Both Kyle Palmer and Asa Call worried that such an initiative might create an enormous backlash against Knowland. The two power-brokers, working behind the scenes, convinced several state legislators to agree to try to pass similar legislation—which would not require a popular vote—after the 1958 election. Call and Palmer then held a meeting with Knowland in Call's office. The two men tried to convince Knowland not to file the petitions, explaining that "right to work" could be accomplished without a popular vote. Though there were only a few people in the room, Knowland puffed out his chest, stepped forward, and started to make a speech. "The working man is entitled to the right to work," Knowland insisted. He stated that he had decided to make the initiative the main plank in his campaign. "File the petitions!" Knowland dramatically declared.

To run for governor, Knowland had to convince Goodie Knight, with national pretensions of his own, to step down and run for Knowland's Senate seat instead. For more than six months Knight refused to cede, and a bitter primary fight seemed inevitable. In August 1957 Knight announced his intention to run for reelection as governor and to take on William Knowland. The *Times* quickly declared in favor of Knowland, warning that "union labor bosses" who backed Knight in the past might send their members to register Republican to defeat labor's enemy.

The *Times*—paralleling Kyle Palmer's 1953 prediction of disaster from a Republican primary battle—dreaded the confrontation. The week of his announcement Norman and Buff, one Chandler intimate recalled, were constantly on the phone trying to change Knight's mind, and failing that, to pressure him into dropping out. Vice-President Nixon also tried to persuade Knight. If he ran for the Senate, Nixon told the governor, Eisenhower would give his personal blessings, but if he ran for governor, he'd get a cold shoulder.

Finally, Kyle Palmer used his ultimate power. He let it be known that if Knight persisted, he would lose his financial backing. Knight didn't believe it. After his closest financial advisors pleaded with Knight to withdraw, the governor phoned Palmer demanding to know what was happening. Palmer replied that Knight's funds had dried up. When Knight's chief financial backer verified Palmer's statement, Knight furiously phoned a couple of the money men he had thought were already committed, only to receive the same answers—no money. Knight got back on the phone with Palmer, who told him that if he ran for the Senate the funds would become available again. On November 6, Knight announced his decision to run for the U.S. Senate.

"Fundamentally the reason Governor Knight decided to run for Senator next year was his conviction that he could not defeat U.S. Senator

William F. Knowland in the Republican gubernatorial primaries . . . ,''
Palmer coyly wrote a few days later. "If there was any 'pressure' on the
Governor to take the step which, however unpalatable, appeared to be a
sensible one, it came solely from his own thinking and, from all I know,
with the approval of those who have his best interests at heart."

The campaign was set. On one side was Knowland and the *Times*, treat-
ing the election as an ideological crusade, a last effort to keep the labor-
inspired Democratic tide from engulfing the state. On the other side was
Pat Brown, who in the face of the *Times*/Knowland antilabor onslaught,
fit the image of a man of moderation in the face of Republican extremism.

It was the last great political crusade for the *Times*. Day after day pro-
Knowland, anti-Brown stories, cartoons, and editorials filled the paper as
the polls pointed to a major Democratic victory. The Democratic candidate, the *Times* declared, would inevitably become a "tool of the labor
bosses." "It's Got to Be Knowland," a series of page one editorials told
its readers. "California is verging toward government by a coalition of
union bosses and the Americans for Democratic Action who are almost as
far left as the foul line through third base," one editorial warned. "William F. Knowland is the only man with the nerves and staying power to
prevent the catastrophe."

On Election Day William Knowland and his cherished right to work
were both defeated by a margin of one million votes. In 1952 Knowland
had won reelection by the largest margin in California history; six years
later he suffered its worst defeat. Knight, too—with only lukewarm backing from the *Times*, and without Palmer's promised campaign funds—
went down to defeat, losing to Clare Engle, a popular "moderate" Democratic congressman, by a commanding 400,000 votes.

The *Times* puzzled over the incredible loss the day after the election.
"Californians are prosperous. Californians are owners of property. They
should by all the rules be conservative," the paper theorized.

The fifties were coming to an end. The tactics of anticommunism had
begun to outlive their usefulness. Kyle Palmer, who had run the campaigns that had kept the *Times*/business alliance in power for two decades, was now an old man, with just a few years more to live. The political mentor, the guiding hand of both Warren nonpartisanship and Nixon
Red-baiting, couldn't shake the gloomy political mood that had settled
over the entire paper. His friend Bill Knowland was ready to drop out of
politics. Though Asa Call was still active, the finely tuned Republican machine that Palmer and his paper had been so effective in creating seemed
wobbly at best. Only one man had pulled through untouched, and it was
to him, Richard Nixon, that Republican eyes would turn to ward off their
most bitter and conclusive defeat.

CHAPTER 17

Winning The Poker Game

1. Industrial Los Angeles

Los Angeles was a changing city after World War II. Industrial production had taken off with the war's geometric growth in the aerospace industry and the settlement of the first major steel plant at the rim of the Southern California basin. Returning veterans crowded into the expanding region looking for jobs and hoping to enjoy the famed Los Angeles sunshine and easy life. Experiencing its most dramatic growth ever, Los Angeles became by 1950 the third largest city in the country.

The new migrants were different from earlier Los Angeles settlers. In the twenties Los Angeles's immigrants had generally been middle-class professionals, small shopkeepers, get-rich-quick speculators, or elderly retirees. During the thirties, dust bowl farmers had come looking for agricultural or industrial work. With the new industries of the forties came an influx of industrial workers.

The new settlers were sprinkled throughout the region. The peculiar nature of the Los Angeles sprawl, the development of the automobile as the primary means of transportation, and the county tax structure that allowed industries to settle in outlying locations designed to meet their tax needs—places named City of Commerce or City of Industry—contributed to the emergence of several industrial centers throughout the basin. In less than a decade, the sixty-mile Southern California basin stretch—what had once been predominantly agricultural land—became thoroughly urbanized. The character of the city seemed to change overnight.

The new industrial workers and their families differed from the usual *Times* constituency. The Chandlers doubted whether the *Times*, with its strict Republicanism, probusiness appeal, and upper-class pretensions

286

could ever attract such an audience. The attempt during World War II to expand the *Times* base—to create what the advertising men called a "class" and "mass" paper—had at best been only partially successful. Circulation had increased, but the class composition of its readers had not effectively changed. "You can't get mass circulation by slapping the people in the face," one *Times* observer noted of the antilabor newspaper. By the end of the war, the Chandlers had decided on a different strategy: to create a new daily newspaper for Los Angeles. We needed a paper, Norman Chandler later remarked, that would "appeal to the new elements of our population more than the *Times*."

The prospect, with its prohibitive costs, was risky. No new daily newspaper had formed in a major metropolitan area since 1941. Los Angeles then had four newspapers: the *Times* with its Republican "class" audience; Hearst's morning *Examiner*, generally appealing to a less affluent audience; Hearst's afternoon *Herald-Express*, a racy right-wing tabloid offering the Hearstian formula of anti-vivesection, anticommunism, sex crime, big photos, and bold headlines; and the more liberal Democratic *Daily News*, a twenty-four-hour edition directly appealing to a working-class audience. Chandler feared that the *Herald-Express* and *Daily News* would pick up the new industrial working-class constituency, cause a loss in the *Times* circulation percentage, and possibly diminish the *Times's* political influence. *Times* advertising revenue, however, would likely remain constant, since more expensive department stores, such as Bullock's, had and would continue to keep 95 percent of their ads in the upper-middle-class *Times*.

There was also a personal motivation behind the notion of a new newspaper. "It was to be Norman's big contribution to the empire built by his father and grandfather," a Chandler associate remarked. Norman Chandler's economic expansion program, initiated after the war, already included the purchase of television station KTTV and a joint investment with the Mormon Church for forest lands and pulp and paper companies in Oregon.

A key to the economics of the new paper investment was its tax write-off possibilities, which would allow the Chandlers to absorb major losses in the initial operation. The new paper could then effectively challenge its competition, for even if it didn't succeed as a money-maker, it could still force its competition out of business or help create a realignment of the newspaper operations in the city. Even if the new paper failed, the *Times* could gain, and if the paper succeeded, its profits would be an additional benefit.

In August 1948 Norman Chandler announced that his Times Mirror Company would launch a second Los Angeles daily, to be called the *Los Angeles Mirror* in honor of the weekly supplement that had predated the

Times. The *Mirror*, to be housed in a building extension to the *Times* headquarters on First and Spring, would be an afternoon tabloid—a looser, breezier paper than the *Times*—that would appeal directly to a working-class audience. After the announcement, the J. Walter Thompson advertising agency was enlisted for an intensive one-month promotional campaign, with inserts in all the Southern California dailies and suburban papers.

On October 11 the first issue of the *Mirror* rolled off the presses. Norman Chandler issued two editorial instructions for the paper: "One, not to favor communism in any way. Two, not to print anything that couldn't go into the American home."

Though several *Times* reporters were sent over to the *Mirror*, most of the management was hired from outside. The *Mirror*'s publisher, Virgil Pinkley, had been the UP bureau chief for Europe. Several UP staffers came along with him. The new managing editor, Ed Murray, perhaps the single most important editor in the early years of the *Mirror*, had been former UP manager in Italy, and Murray's assistant managing editor, Philip Ault, had been UP bureau chief in London. "High power" *Times* reporter—later Nixon aide—Jim Bassett was sent in as the *Mirror*'s chief political writer.

The new management team, with Murray providing the day-to-day leadership, tried to create a brash and irreverent "hot tabloid," where editors were ready to tear up the edition for a late-breaking story. In its first ten weeks, the paper proposed five ostensibly hard-hitting civic campaigns attacking loan sharks, the black market in baby adoptions, and the presumption that alcoholism was a crime and not a disease, as well as endorsing actions to clean up the city and bring about better housing. In March 1949 the classified ad department allowed personalized notices to run, further spicing up the paper. Though the *Mirror* was not exceptional in its gimmicks and use of "sex, crime, and slaughter," as one tabloid critic put it, it quickly dawned on Norman Chandler that he had created something quite risqué in Chandler terms.

When circulation didn't rise to its expected levels after only six weeks of operation, Chandler sent the *Times* city editor, Hugh "Bud" Lewis, over to supervise the paper. Lewis tried to keep up the tabloid spirit by launching more gossip features and circulation stunts, such as a $100,000 reward to *Mirror* readers who could solve twenty local murders described in the paper. Lewis, the Chandler troubleshooter, came in to tinker around, perhaps change format or content, to make sure that the paper kept its Chandler bearings.

Kyle Palmer's political influence carried over to the *Mirror*. Endorsements rarely differed from those of the *Times*. "The *Mirror* never was anything but a Republican paper in spite of what it pretended, and I don't

Harrison Gray Otis, first publisher of the Los Angeles *Times*, and founder of the dynasty. *(Photo: Sherman Foundation)*

General Otis after his return from the Philippines.

The young Harry Chandler, second *Times* publisher, who organized the economic base of the family power. *(Photo: Sherman Foundation)*

The Mirror Book Bindery, the first office of the Los Angeles *Times. (Photo: Title Insurance and Trust)*

Hollywood Boulevard, 1900. Moses Sherman, Harry Chandler's trusted aide and colleague is at the wheel, and A. Hammel, the sheriff of Los Angeles, is his passenger. *(Photo: Title Insurance and Trust)*

The Los Angeles Times Building after it was dynamited the morning of October 1, 1910. *(Photo: Title Insurance and Trust)*

The McNamara defense team. *From left to right*: James B. (J.B.) McNamara, Clarence Darrow, Joseph Scott, and LeCompte Davis.

McNamara prosecutor John D. Fredericks, Los Angeles District Attorney and close ally of Harry Chandler.

The McNamara Brothers, John J. (J.J.) and James B. (J.B.) McNamara, in their cell, awaiting trial.

Opening of the Los Angeles Aqueduct. First waters are flowing into the San Fernando Valley. *(Photo: Title Insurance and Trust)*

L.A.'s Water Warriors in the Owens Valley. *Left to right:* John R. Freeman, Joseph Schuyler, J.B. Lippincott, Fred Stearns, and William Mulholland.

Los Angeles *Times* Old Timers. Standing in the center, hands in pockets, is Harry Chandler. On his right is *Times* treasurer Frank X. Pfaffinger. Harry's three sons, Harrison Chandler, Norman Chandler, and Philip Chandler are in top row, second, third, and fourth from the right, respectively. The dapper man reclining on the ground is Leo Altman, head of advertising. *(Photo: Title Insurance and Trust)*

Los Angeles Times Building 1926.

Harry Chandler and his son Norman at the opening of the new Los Angeles Times building 1934.

Frank Shaw, mayor of Los Angeles, 1933-38. He was recalled after the dynamiting of the car of investigator Harry Raymond was linked to the police "red squad."

Earl Warren (then California Attorney General) and Los Angeles Mayor Fletcher Bowron.

Hiram Johnson, leader of the Progressive movement, whose "snarling infamy" attack on Harrison Gray Otis stands as one of the most famous philippics of all times.

"Cops with a Pencil." *From right to left: Times* reporters Carlton Williams and Albert Nathan with a local Los Angeles underworld figure. *(Photo: private collection of Mrs. Carlton Williams)*

Times high power Harry Carr.

From left to right: Norman Chandler, Philip Chandler, and *Times* managing editor L. D. Hotchkiss at an AP convention. *(Photo: Wide World Photos)*

Nick Williams, Los Angeles *Times* editor 1958-71. Played the key role in the paper's transition from a right-wing, cold-war-oriented publication to today's more prestigious nationally recognized journal.

Dorothy Buffum Chandler standing under her portrait at the Los Angeles Music Center, talking to local business power Charles Ducommun. "Buffie," as she is known, is the widow of the third *Times* publisher (Norman Chandler). She has played a dominant role in the transformaton of the *Times*,

Carlton Williams at Mayor Norris Poulson's desk, circa 1955. Williams' own caption to the photo reads: "Now, Norrie, as I was saying . . ." *(Photo: private collection of Mrs. Carlton Williams)*

Norman and Otis Chandler at the Biltmore in April 1960, when Otis was named fourth *Times* publisher. *(Photo: Wide World Photos)*

From right to left: Dorothy Chandler, Mayor Tom Bradley and his wife Ethel Bradley, and Music Center official William Severens. *(Photo: Otto Rothschild)*

Franklin Murphy, UCLA's cor-
porate-minded chancellor, who
became Times Mirror chairman
of the board in 1968.

William Thomas, the son of a
Midwest banker who made his
way through the *Times* ranks to
become editor in 1971.

Jean Sharley Taylor, Los Angeles *Times* associate editor in charge of the software sections, who follows editor Thomas' lead in promoting "life-style" journalism.

Anthony Day, Los Angeles *Times* editor of the editorial page.

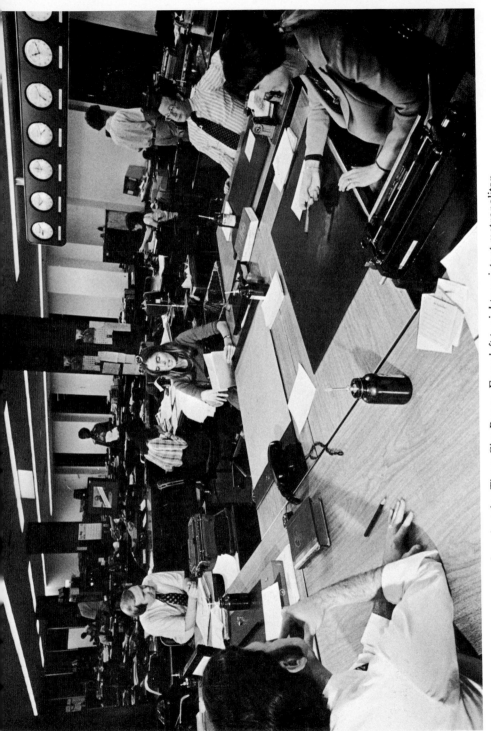

Los Angeles *Times* City Room. *From left to right:* assistant metropolitan editor Lee Dye, *Times* reporter Bill Farr, KCET-TV producer Nancy Salter, *Times* reporters Ken Reich and Narda Zacchino.

think anybody ever thought differently," Bud Lewis remarked to *Editor & Publisher*. In Nixon's 1950 race against Helen Gahagan Douglas, the *Mirror* tried to avoid some of the more outlandish views and editorializing that appeared in the *Times*, but it still endorsed Nixon. While the *Times* talked of the Hollywood "parlor pinks," the *Mirror* kept a low-key approach, commenting favorably on Nixon's "experience," "integrity," and "fearless leadership." In one of its rare differences over politics with the *Times*, the *Mirror* supported the pre-convention candidacy of Dwight Eisenhower over Robert Taft for the 1952 Republican presidential nomination—an endorsement which paralleled Dorothy Chandler's position rather than her husband's.

Dorothy Chandler, in fact, looked after the *Mirror* as a special project. The two-face strategy fit nicely into her developing priorities in cultural politics and the shift away from the rabid anticommunism of the period. Whatever autonomy the *Mirror* managed to maintain might well have been a function of differing family positions and interests.

2. *"Saloon Empire"*

William George Bonelli—"Big Bill"—was one of the most powerful politicians in Southern California in the period after the war. A rancher and former government professor, Bonelli started out in politics in the late 1920s as a reform-minded progressive and ran unsuccessfully for mayor, without *Times* support. By 1934 Bonelli made his peace with the *Times*/Republican establishment and endorsed Governor Merriam for election against Upton Sinclair and the EPICS. In 1938 Merriam appointed him to a vacancy on the State Board of Equalization to represent the fourth district extending south from Santa Barbara to the Mexican border.

The enormously powerful Board of Equalization supervised the state tax assessments and, among its other duties, assigned and regulated liquor licenses. Creating a power base from his position on the Board, Bonelli enjoyed all the favoritism and lucrative possibilities that came with the job.

Bonelli, a master at the use of cross-filing and campaign misinformation, ran for reelection four times between the 1940s and 50s, each time with the support of the *Times*. In his race against Ernest Debs in 1950, the Republican Bonelli cross-filed and, according to Debs, paid off several individuals to enter the Democratic primary. Bonelli and Kyle Palmer then teamed up in the general election to do what Debs later called "a hatchet job like you've never seen before." Their campaign spread false statements and implied that Debs was a socialist because of his name.

Though Bonelli was consistently endorsed for reelection by the *Times*, the paper was undoubtedly uncomfortable with the persistent accusations that Bonelli was tied into Southern California organized crime circles. Bonelli had been investigated by the Governor's Crime Commission and had appeared before the Kefauver anticrime hearings in 1951. Though the Kefauver committee had questioned him carefully on his ties, the astute and articulate Bonelli managed to parry all questions.

Bonelli failed to dispel the accusations. It became an open secret that in order to get a liquor license in Southern California, "arrangements" had to be made with the board member. Both Earl Warren and Attorney General Pat Brown considered Bonelli far too powerful to initiate any kind of criminal investigation, but for any newspaper willing to take it on, the situation provided a made-to-order *big story*.

Art White was the closest thing the *Mirror* had to an investigative journalist. On one of his first major assignments, a series on the "B-girl" operations in Los Angeles, White had come across material pointing to possible kickbacks in the granting of liquor licenses that involved Bonelli. Convinced that he had a major story, White went to managing editor Ed Murray to ask for some time to nail down and prove the corruption. After Murray okayed the project, White went up and down the state to interview officials and look through public records. He eventually uncovered a systematic case of influence-peddling, whereby licenses were granted for properties—such as vacant lots, empty stores, "hideous Main Street dives," and "fronts for known criminals"—and then passed on to the black market, where they could be sold at exorbitant prices.

Managing Editor Murray and Jim Bassett went over White's story word for word to make sure he had an airtight case. Murray made a decision *not* to clear with the Chandlers, but instead to take the heat after the fact.

The first of eight stories ran on October 5, 1953—complete with a front page picture of Bonelli—under the headline BONELLI'S SALOON EMPIRE: SHAME OF CALIFORNIA. "This is the fabulous, frightening story of a czar with a simple name of Bill," White began in his lead. "At 58, with the ruddy face of a wind-whipped rancher (which he is) and the coldly shrewd eyes of a master politician (which he also is) William G. Bonelli rules the liquor traffic of eight southland counties." White detailed his findings by blending information culled from his investigations with descriptions of the "dread mafia" and other evil forces linked to the Board of Equalization member.

"Bad trouble is brewing in Southern California. It arises from the antics of a sordid, sinister element operating within the confines of an otherwise legitimate business, the alcoholic beverages trade," declared an editor's note which ran as a sidebar to the White piece. Calling the series "a long-overdue, badly needed crusade against a malignant cancer in the liquor industry," the *Mirror* editorial that day proclaimed its exposé was "in the public interest" and "in full knowledge of risks involved."

The *Mirror* articles came as a bombshell. Bonelli reacted angrily and wanted the Chandlers to repudiate the *Mirror* staff. When Chandler refused, Bonelli decided to retaliate. Just thirteen days after the *Mirror* series ended, the Board of Equalization rejected Chandler's appeal of assessments on his paper's national advertising revenue. Soon after, Bonelli announced he was switching his registration from Republican to Democrat, a decision he claimed was based on the role of the Chandlers in Los Angeles. "The picture of this scheming Chandler family," Bonelli told reporters, "owning and controlling a half-billion-dollar empire, with its $50-million-a-year income, is frightening. All forms of business are invaded competitively by this hungry and cunning group."

Bonelli also approached a liberal newspaperman and author, Leo Katcher, about ghost writing a Bonelli book on the Chandlers. He gave Katcher just six weeks to whip together a completed version based on a rough, unpublished manuscript on the *Times* Bonelli had recently purchased, and a few tidbits that Bonelli passed on about his early political relations with the Chandlers. "Both the Chandlers and Bonelli knew where each other's bodies were buried, " Katcher recalled, "and I felt that Bonelli had decided not to tell all that he had to tell." Working as rapidly as he could, relying mostly on secondary sources and substituting with rhetoric what was lacking in hard information, Katcher met the six-week deadline.

Soon afterward, Katcher's ghost-written book *Billion Dollar Blackjack* was released under Bonelli's name. Bonelli himself printed 20,000 copies simultaneously in cloth and paper. The book was an immediate success, and sold out in a few weeks. According to Katcher, a dummy corporation bought several thousand copies.

Bonelli, meanwhile, was indicted on charges of violating the State Election Code. While the grand jury met, Bonelli left for Mexico, where he stayed until his death fifteen years later. With no word from Bonelli, *Billion Dollar Blackjack* never had a second printing, and the book became an underground classic, kept in the special collections of libraries.

For the *Mirror*, it was a great breakthrough. They had undertaken what White called the "finest newspaper investigation that had ever occurred in L.A." and had done so without explicit Chandler approval. Though managing editor Murray had a number of problems with the Chandlers over the early direction of the paper, for the *Mirror*'s first five or six years Murray basically preserved its autonomy. "Norman discussed it with me, contending forthrightly that we were cheapening whatever high professional intent we may have had by sensationalizing our presentation with screaming headlines, lurid color, and horsey illustrations," Murray wrote. "As I always did, I tried to convince him that the *Mirror* was not the good grey *Los Angeles Times*. Norman did not insist that I tone down or change direction on the Bonelli campaign, and, of course, I didn't."

3. Death of the Daily News

Chandler's toleration might have come in response to the *Mirror*'s successful role in hurting the competition, particularly the liberal *News*. The *Mirror*'s entrance in 1948 had badly wounded the *News* by cutting into its circulation and advertising revenues. Though the *Herald-Express* and *News* both raised their street sale price to seven cents just before the *Mirror*'s arrival, the new Chandler enterprise was launched at a price of five cents. The *Mirror* didn't go up to seven cents until three years later, when the other two tabloids were forced to raise their price to ten cents.

By the late 1940s, the *News* had lost much of the independent and feisty spirit it had developed in previous years, as its crusty publisher Manchester Boddy moved increasingly to the right. By 1950 the paper, according to one of its staffers, had "abandoned its liberalism." When a story reached the desk about an issue like police brutality, the editors, who had once attacked such topics with vigor, now said, "Let's see what the *Times* does first." Disgruntled *News* staffers began to describe their boss as "the liberal newspaper publisher who leads liberals up alleys and then clubs them to death."

After Boddy retired in 1950, at a time when the afternoon papers, especially the *News*, were in serious trouble in automobile-oriented Los Angeles, his number two man, Robert Smith, the new publisher, was barely able to keep the paper alive. In 1953, when San Diego Congressman Clinton McKinnon purchased the financially troubled *News*, the paper's loyal staff hoped for a revival. But McKinnon never really made an attempt. A short time later, when a broker by the name of Albert Zugsmith made an offer for the *News*, McKinnon expressed some interest. Other offers came in, including one from radio station owner Robert Straus of New York City. McKinnon arranged to give Straus an option to buy at $50,000, and the staff once again hoped that the paper would be saved.

As Christmas approached, *News* employees offered to hold off back-salary claims and the labor movement organized a subscription drive to keep the paper going. But two days after the Straus offer, Zugsmith worked out a new deal with McKinnon, offering him $275,000 for the paper's name, goodwill, and features. Zugsmith revealed that he represented the Chandler interests. The *News* assets now belonged to the rival *Times*. Chandler also agreed to pay McKinnon $125,000 for "personal services," whereby the former *News* publisher would devote four weeks to securing *News* subscribers to the *Times*, and thereafter write an occasional column for the *Mirror*. The deal, closed on Christmas Day, 1954, left Los Angeles without a Democratic paper.

As the *News* closed its doors, serious problems began to plague the *Mirror* staff. Whatever autonomy had existed there was largely a result of Ed Murray's persistent and often courageous attitude. Murray's attempt to steer a middle course during the public housing fight caused Carlton Williams to blow his stack, and Norman Chandler to register complaints with his managing editor because of *Mirror* "bias" on the issue. Murray, deciding to answer directly, put together a scrapbook of clippings, which ranged from the violently opposed *Times* to the pro-public housing *Daily News*. As the *Mirror* clips clearly presented an example of journalistic "balance," Chandler backed down from his charge.

But for every instance of a Bonelli exposé or public housing news story, there were dozens of examples of Chandler intervention. "As things turned out," Murray commented in retrospect, "Chandler was questioning Pinkley's judgment and autonomy almost from the beginning of actual publication. Bud Lewis continued to shuttle back and forth between the two papers, expressing his dislike for the *Mirror*'s more racy approach and telling the editors that the paper ought to more resemble the *Times*."

By 1954 the center of the conflict concerned format. The Chandlers, according to Murray, "never really had any stomach for a gutty tabloid." In 1954, under Lewis's supervision, the *Mirror*, contrary to Murray's and Pinkley's approach, was changed to a standard eight column format. Murray saw the shift as a "grand mistake . . . transforming a hot tabloid into an anemic, non-character standard size paper." Others on the *Mirror* desk agreed.

The managing editor, holding on to whatever independence the paper could still muster, tried to keep the *Mirror* staff together. He assigned reporter Paul Weeks to do a story on Los Angeles's black community, then practically invisible to Los Angeles newspaper readers because of lack of coverage. Less than two years later Murray launched "zone" editions —once a week special sections—as a means to develop community-by-community coverage in an expanding Southern California. Murray was particularly wedded to the zone idea as a means to investigate and report stories in the burgeoning suburban market. The *Mirror*, as a metropolitan newspaper with no ties to any of the particular outlying communities, and, therefore, independent of any of the special interests there, was in an enviable position to go out and develop such stories. Under the charge of city editor Hank Osborne, the *Mirror* extended its hit-'em-hard crime-busting attitude toward communities which had up to then seen only the ad-oriented news of the weekly throwaways. But the zones didn't last. Before the year ended they were dropped for their failure to conform to the *Times* conservative news and format standards. Ironically, the *Times*, utilizing the zone idea for its own purposes, transformed Murray's "no-special interests" notion into an effective medium for local advertisers.

In October 1957 the Chandlers moved in to take full control of the *Mirror*. Pinkley, who had never exerted any effective leadership in his nine years as publisher, was fired, and Bud Lewis was named in his place. Otis Chandler, named assistant to the *Mirror* publisher, reported to the *Times* Board of Directors on the various economic options regarding the *Mirror*'s future. New format changes were immediately instituted, the picture page was dropped, as were the zones, and Lewis planned to eliminate some of the long features that had become a *Mirror* trademark. "From now on we are going to take a hard look at the content," Lewis vowed. "The Tower," as *Mirror* staffers called the *Times*, was taking over.

For the next three years Murray tried to keep a discouraged staff from leaving, but the handwriting seemed clear as meetings of upper *Times* management and the Times Mirror Board of Directors continued to discuss the options of the paper.

In the summer of 1960, the Chandlers made their final shakeup. Two desk men from the *Houston Post*, Arthur Laro and Jack Donahue, were appointed executive editor and assistant managing editor respectively. "The Texans," as *Mirror* staff called the new management, had few illusions about their role. Donahue kept a cartoon of himself seated at his desk with a hatchet on top. When Laro immediately began to institute changes, Murray realized he was finally being forced out. Laro called him in and said he couldn't get hold of the paper while Murray was still there. Murray offered to resign on the spot. The relieved Texans made the announcement a few days later. With Murray—the heart of the paper's autonomy, a reporter's editor, most trusted by the staff—departed, there were no pretenses left at the *Mirror*. It was a *Times* operation, with Laro and Donahue serving a caretaker function until the final decision to close down could be made. On January 5, 1962, the *Mirror* ceased to publish.

The *Mirror* never really had a chance to survive. It never got the opportunity to establish a format or character that could create a regular and loyal audience. Afternoon tabloids were hard-pressed in the evolving suburban-oriented newspaper market, and the death of rapid transit in Los Angeles only exacerbated their problems. Though *Mirror* losses were great they were only fifty-cents-on-the-dollar losses because of the tax write-off. For the Chandlers, the decision to stop publishing the *Mirror* was not entirely economic, but was a result of the paper's brashness and independence. Kyle Palmer's two-faced strategy might have sounded good in theory, but it became a nuisance when put into practice by the enterprising Murray and his staff.

The *Mirror* did fulfill its ultimate purpose—dealing with the competition. It had helped to drive the *Daily News* out of business, and it had provided a tremendous competitive wedge against Hearst's *Herald-Express*. When the deals were finally concluded in 1962, the Chandlers remained with a morning monopoly for the *Times*, leaving the afternoon field for Hearst's financially troubled amalgam the *Herald-Examiner*. "The Chandlers won the poker game," Murray remarked. The *Mirror*, in the end, had been nothing more than a chip to raise the stakes.

CHAPTER 18

Cold War Journalism

1. Relocation Camp

The Japanese attack of Pearl Harbor, which opened the door for Los Angeles's massive industrial expansion and urbanization, also brought out a renewed racial hostility from the white Southern California population. Antiforeign/nativist movements had deep roots in the area. Since the 1860s the state's labor movement and small farmers, threatened by massive immigrations of cheap Asian and Mexican labor, had reacted with prejudice and attempts at exclusion. General Otis's and Harry Chandler's *Times* had expressed an ambivalent position on the question, but tended to go along with the dominant mood, except when basic labor questions were involved.

Japanese and Mexican labor, extensively used on Chandler agricultural holdings, was essential to Chandler's overall strategy for control and profits. Chandler had attacked various racist-inspired moves to limit land ownership—the 1913 Alien Land Law, for instance—or to restrict immigration. While the Hearst press raged against the Japanese in the debate over a 1920 exclusion initiative, Chandler defended his Japanese tenants. "Although they represent the highest efficiency in farming," Chandler wrote on July 1, 1920, "this act would practically forbid them to till the land." Chandler favored some restrictions on Mexican immigration, but recommended the use of seasonal labor for California agriculture. "The Mexicans do not come here to live, they do not come here to mix," Chandler testified before a House committee in 1930. "We have not any cross-breeding with the Mexican people—never did. They do not mingle. They keep to themselves. That is the safety of it."

By the late 1930s, as first- and second-generation Japanese and Mexi-can-Americans entered the job market, questions concerning immigration were replaced by the urban-based social and economic problems of accul-turation and discrimination. With the outbreak of the war, some of the old tensions found new expression, and the Los Angeles press, led by the Hearst papers and the *Times*, contributed to one of the region's most shameful periods.

Within a month after the Pearl Harbor attack, California's press began a systematic campaign to evacuate all Japanese-Americans in California and the rest of the country into "relocation" camps for the duration of the war. The *Times* at first was hesitant. "Many of our Japanese," a Janu-ary 23, 1942, editorial commented, "whether born here or not, are fully loyal and deserve sympathy rather than suspicion. Others, in both catego-ries, hold to a foreign allegiance and are dangerous, at least potentially. To be sure it would sometimes stump an expert to tell which is which and mistakes, if made, should be made on the side of caution."

Five days later, as pressure mounted on the White House to issue relo-cation orders, the *Times* changed to a firm evacuation position. "The rig-ors of war," the paper insisted, "demand proper detention of Japanese and their immediate removal from the most acute danger spots."

Times headlines through February tried to tie battle stories together with the evacuation issue. A headline reporting on the fighting in the Pacific, for instance, would carry a subhead referring to items on the relo-cation front. Scare stories appeared daily, and the *Times* reverted to items from its morgue to conjure up images of potential sabotage. A February 1, 1942, article, for instance, referred to a 1934 letter by the Japanese con-sulate inquiring about Los Angeles's water system.

That same month the House Un-American Activities Committee, with extensive coverage from the *Times*, came to California to investigate al-leged Japanese-American subversion. Ten percent of the paper's total news hole was turned over to the question of relocation.

In the third week of February, the Roosevelt administration finally yielded to the heated campaign and prescribed military areas for the relo-cation. "The Hearst publications and the *Los Angeles Times* kept up a drumfire of editorials, columns, and slanted news stories," head of the War Relocation Authority, Dillon Myer, commented, "that pressured officials and caused the public generally to become fearful and emotional regarding the alleged dangers in their midst."

Though authorities revealed that not a single act of military sabotage had occurred, either before or after Pearl Harbor, the Japanese-American evacuation proceeded. Ninety thousand Japanese-Americans in Califor-nia were uprooted from their homes and farms to live for more than three years in concentration camps such as Manzanar in the Owens Valley. Jap-anese-American economic losses ran up into the millions of dollars. "It is expected that ultimately there won't be a parcel of Jap-owned real estate in Los Angeles," the *Times* commented after more than $5 million in Japanese property was auctioned off in the city. With the removal of the Japanese farmers, Los Angeles's wholesale produce market became chaotic.

The economic dislocation was so severe that some politicians, including Democratic Governor Culbert Olson, timidly suggested the release of some evacuees for farm work. But Olson's opponent, Earl Warren, lashed out at the proposal and made Olson's soft-on-Japanese-Americans stance a theme in his campaign. At the height of the press scare several months earlier, Warren had identified the absence of any sabotage up to then as an attempt to create "a false sense of security."

Through 1942 and 1943, the *Times* kept up its attacks against the "soft-headed" thinking that called for the disbandment of the concentration camps. A series of headlines through the year kept Angelenos aroused and on edge: DISTRICT ATTORNEY SEES BLOODSHED IF JAPS RETURN; ARIZONA FEARS RIOTING IF JAPS SETTLE THERE; SERVICEMEN VOW TO KILL NIPS; RIOTING PREDICTED IN EVENT JAPS RETURN. "As a race the Japanese have made for themselves a record for conscienceless treachery unsurpassed in history," the *Times* editorialized on April 22, 1942, and the next day came back to the same theme. "Once or twice since Pearl Harbor," the editorial remarked, "the *Times* has likened the Japanese to rattlesnakes. This is to apologize to the rattlesnakes."

Hardly a voice had been raised in opposition to the *Times*/Hearst campaign. Many of the state's liberal and progressive Democrats like Lieutenant Governor Ellis Patterson accepted the sabotage argument. A few critics, such as writer Carey McWilliams, the ACLU, and State Attorney General Bob Kenny, attacked the evacuation program as racist, but the "win the war" coalition, with its racial overtones regarding the war in the Pacific, prevailed.

2. Zoot Suit

Only a few weeks after the Japanese evacuation orders, the *Times* and the Hearst press initiated another racial campaign. All through the spring and summer of 1942, the papers, referring to "greasers," "pachucos" (youth gangs), and "zoot suiters," raised the cry of spreading Mexican-American juvenile delinquency. The paper's coverage of the Mexican-American community, one study showed, had shifted from "fiesta" and "old California culture" stories, glorifying a mythical past, to negative accounts of the zoot suit symbol.

Zoot suits were a stylized costume originally designed for fast "jitterbug" dancing, with tight trouser cuffs, widened coat shoulders, and heavy shoes. The men wore duck-tailed haircuts, and the women short black skirts, long black stockings, and a sweater. Though Anglo and black youths also wore zoot suits, their widespread use among Mexican-American youths created an identity for the young Mexicans.

On a Saturday night in August 1942, a young Mexican-American was discovered unconscious at a roadside near an open reservoir in the east side of Los Angeles called the Sleepy Lagoon. When the youth, an apparent gang-fight victim, died without regaining consciousness, the police decided to use the opportunity to conduct massive sweeps throughout the Mexican-American neighborhoods. They set up roadblocks and checked each automobile that passed through the community, arresting anyone they considered suspicious. The police brought in 300 Mexican-American youths. They paraded their prisoners in an improvised line-up for any robbery or mugging victim who could be induced to come down to the station. Police also arrested twenty-three Mexican-Americans from the raids on the charge of murdering the young man found by the reservoir.

The case, dubbed the "Sleepy Lagoon" murder, was splashed across the front pages for the next several months. Though there were no eye-witnesses to the alleged murder nor any proof that a murder rather than an accident had occurred, the press had a field day detailing the "crime" as the trial began. Demonstrating marked hostility toward the defendants, the presiding judge did not allow them to sit or confer with their defense attorneys on grounds of insufficient seating space. At one point the judge refused to inform a witness of his rights, commenting "I can't take the time." The assistant District Attorney instructed the jailer that the defendants ."not be allowed haircuts or changes of clothing on the ground that their 'distinctive' appearance had to be maintained for purposes of identification." In the course of the trial, the D.A. pointed to their unkempt appearance as evidence of guilt.

The Sleepy Lagoon defendants never had a chance. Seventeen of the men on trial were found guilty and sent to jail. Finally, two years after the trial had begun, the U.S. District Court of Appeals threw out the guilty verdict and rebuked the trial judge. After two years in prison, the defendants returned home.

During the Sleepy Lagoon trial's intense press campaign, a representative from the Office of War Information, fearful of offending America's war ally, had met with the editors from the *Times* and the Hearst press to urge them to drop the word "Mexican" when discussing gang violence. The newspapers agreed, but the stories only shifted gear slightly as the term "zoot suiter" replaced "Mexican."

A number of servicemen stationed at Los Angeles's large naval and marine bases, were bored and easily influenced by press campaigns and prevailing community temper. On the night of June 3, 1943, several sailors, claiming they had been set upon by Mexican youths over the Anglos' flir-

tations with some Mexican-American women, went through the barrios
with rocks, sticks, and clubs, beating up any zoot suiter they could find.
When some Mexican-American youths from a local club left a police station after a meeting to discuss the incident, they were attacked by waiting
sailors. Instead of protecting the youths, the police later sent out their
own "vengeance squad," which swooped down the edge of downtown
looking for suspicious zooters.

Many of the sailors perceived the action of the vengeance squad as a
signal to continue. Over the next several nights, large groups of sailors,
traveling in commandeered taxicabs, patrolled the barrios, beating up any
Mexican-American they came across. "Is this a pogrom?" a terrified old
Jewish woman who lived in one of the barrios asked her neighbor.

By the third evening, soldiers and marines had joined the sailors and
together marched through downtown Los Angeles and into the east side,
four abreast, attacking anyone in their path. The police followed at a distance, arresting, not the servicemen, but the badly beaten Mexicans. At
one corner, an eyewitness, Anglo publisher Al Waxman, wrote, "a Mexican mother cried out, 'Don't take my boy, he did nothing. He's only
fifteen years old. Don't take him.' She was struck across the jaw with a
nightstick and almost dropped the two-and-a-half-year-old baby that was
clinging in her arms."

Times coverage declared that the zoot suiters had learned a lesson in
their fight with the servicemen. "Those gamin dandies, the zoot suiters,"
a *Times* news story commented, "learned a great moral lesson from servicemen"; those "wearers of the garish costume that has become the
hallmark of juvenile delinquency," the article went on, had been "un-
frocked."

After the Mexican ambassador to the United States lodged a complaint
with the Roosevelt administration, the State Department intervened by
asking the Los Angeles newspapers to tone down their language. The
Times responded by denying the riots were racially motivated: "When
trouble arose through the depredations of the youth gangs attired in zoot
suits, it was their weird dress and not their race which resulted in difficulties. That is a simple truth which no amount of propaganda will change."

One week after the zoot suit riots ended, Eleanor Roosevelt issued a
statement deploring "the attitudes towards Mexicans in California." The
Times and its business allies in the Chamber of Commerce replied with
strong denials. "Mrs. Roosevelt Blindly Stirs Race Discord," a *Times*
editorial proclaimed.

A commission appointed by Governor Warren after the riots discounted any significant rise in Mexican-American juvenile delinquency and
criticized the role of the press in creating the kind of environment which
made the riots possible.

But the *Times* was unrepentant. Convinced that the "zoot suit problem" was not a racial one, the paper continued throughout the war years, to carry the most blatantly racist copy on Mexican-Americans and Japanese Americans ever to appear in its pages. Like the Hearst press, the paper constantly sought out to unmask "the enemy within." When the war was over, the enemy no longer became identified by the color of his skin, but by the nature of his politics.

3. The Red Menace—Round Two

"The hopes are now bound up with Mr. Churchill's observation at Fulton," the *Times* remarked of Winston Churchill's March 1946 "Iron Curtain" speech, "that the Russians despise weakness and admire strength." From Fulton—the official inauguration of the Cold War—until the early 1960s, the *Times* overflowed with anti-communist articles, sidebars, editorials, and page one headlines. As many as twenty anti-Communist stories appeared *daily*. "Both editorially and in its news columns, the paper seemed concerned with Communism to the point of obsession," one academic researcher noted.

The *Times* strongly endorsed the actions of Joe McCarthy and his allies of the House Un-American Activities Committee. "He speaks softly and carries the big stick of logic," one *Times* news story commented about the Wisconsin senator. When HUAC held hearings in Los Angeles, the *Times* praised the committee's efforts, and in a *news* story editorialized harshly against the "venemous testimony" of one hostile witness, lawyer Ben Margolis.

One of HUAC's casualties was a *Times* proofreader, Bernard Burton. Burton was a former staff member of the Communist party's publications, the *People's World* and *The Daily Worker*. Having left the party in opposition to the Russian invasion of Hungary in 1956, Burton had applied for a proofreader's job at the *Times*, instead of a reporter or editor's position, in hopes that his past would not be investigated. For his previous employment he had listed the print shop that published the Communist publication.

After a U.S. marshall handed *Times* lawyers a subpoena requiring Burton to appear before the HUAC committee, *Times* management called the employee in. Burton told them that he intended to testify freely about himself and his own activities, but would refuse to answer questions concerning any former colleagues. The *Times* fired him on the basis that he hadn't given a complete employment record when he had applied for the job. Off the record his supervisor told Burton that the *Times* had to fire him; it could not face explaining the presence of a one-time card-carrying member in its ranks.

The Cold War strategy of post–World War II was as much an attempt to undermine the liberal/left coalitions that had dominated American politics in the era of the New Deal—paralleling BAF's attacks against the Progressives in the 1920s—as an attempt to destroy the radical left. "Suckers Always Pay in the End," the *Times* warned liberals. "Some of them are unthinking, sentimental people, a soft touch for the tap from the Communist front organizations. Their hearts bleed easily."

But even at the height of the anti-Communist barrage, an imperceptible shift, inspired by Dorothy Chandler, began to occur. Buff was concerned with the image of Los Angeles and her newspaper in the eyes of the world. By the late 1950s, the East Coast establishment press and politicians had begun to consider anti-Communist fundamentalism as slightly outré. When Nikita Khrushchev toured the country in 1959, that establishment urged Americans to be polite. When the Soviet premier got in a shouting match with Los Angeles Mayor Norris Poulson, a Buff-inspired *Times* editorial gently rebuked the display. "We said in the beginning that Premier Khrushchev's visit could be useful to the United States," the editorial noted, "but since Americans have had a little time to reflect about the impending visit, they have developed all the jitters of a bride who is cooking her first dinner for company. Their anxieties, one way or the other, don't do them credit."

4. Timesmen

Loyal Durant Hotchkiss, generally known around the paper as "Hotch," was a short man, terribly conscious of his height. When someone went in to see Hotch, according to one of the unspoken rules of the *Times*, he immediately headed for the couch and sat down. Though Hotchkiss was generally quiet and reserved, he was also capable of unleashing a mean temper, sometimes at the slightest cause.

Born and raised in Iowa, Hotchkiss often gave staffers a break on discovering that they grew up there as well. Hotch came over to the *Times* in 1922, after a desk job at Hearst's *Examiner*, and within a year was assigned coverage of the San Pedro Harbor strike under *Times* top journalist Al Nathan. In 1926, Hotchkiss, aided by Nathan, became city editor and rose to assistant managing editor seven years later. When managing editor Trueblood died in 1934, Hotchkiss took over the number one desk position. While Kyle Palmer ran the political side, Norman Chandler left Hotchkiss to take charge of the overall news operation, making many of the day-to-day decisions about the paper.

Hotchkiss symbolized the mood of the forties and fifties *Times*, a stuffy, conservative, strait-laced operation, far removed from the feisty atmosphere of the *Front Page*. Former staffers described the paper as "lackluster" and "gray." Spitoons were situated between reporters' desks; wearing a coat and tie was *de rigueur;* and staffers were expected to be prompt.

Hotchkiss's number one assistant, city editor Hugh Alban "Bud" Lewis, also a short man, had a potbelly, a penchant for dressing up, and an enormous ego. The staff had little respect for Lewis's journalistic skills. Lewis frequently rewarded his favorite reporters and punished those who defied him. But Lewis knew how to promote himself with the paper's publisher. "Norman Chandler regarded Bud Lewis with special respect, complete trust, and warm friendship," *Mirror* managing editor Ed Murray remarked of Lewis, "He could do no wrong."

While Lewis remained Chandler's favorite, editor Hotchkiss, after one famous incident, lost some of his earlier esteem. Though he was married and as *Times* editor was the symbol of conservative decorum, Hotchkiss had carried on a secret love affair with the secretary of the Los Angeles Newspaper Association, Jerrine Hicks. When Hotchkiss ended the relationship, Hicks, distraught, swallowed a handful of sleeping pills before Hotchkiss could stop her. Hicks died en route to the hospital.

Though Hearst's *Examiner* printed a page one item with information including Hotchkiss's presence, the *Times* editor managed to weather the incident. But his standing with the Chandlers had been severely diminished. As soon as he turned 65, he was retired, though others such as Kyle Palmer continued to work beyond that official retirement age. Hotchkiss's retirement, without the awareness of the people involved, prepared the groundwork for a changeover at the *Times*.

Nick Boddie Williams, after twenty-seven years on the desk and more than ten years overseeing many of the day-to-day tasks in putting out the paper, became Hotchkiss's replacement. The young Williams got his first taste of newspapering as an office boy for the *Dallas Morning News*. He later worked for the *Fort Worth Star Telegram* and the *Nashville Tennessean*. In 1931 he arrived in Los Angeles and took a job as copy editor at the *Times*. Slowly he worked his way through the desk bureaucracy, becoming telegraph editor, picture editor, makeup editor, news editor, assistant managing editor, managing editor, and on Hotchkiss's retirement, the new number one man in the *Times* hierarchy.

A diminutive man, with none of the braggadocio of Bud Lewis nor the stuffiness and conservatism of a Hotchkiss, the new editor was well liked by many of the staff. Some thought that Williams, less out-spokenly reactionary than many of the other deskmen, was a closet Democrat. The new *Times* editor explained in later years that, although he had once been a *Southern* Democrat, he found the transition to *Times* Republicanism not so painful. "I might not have been quite so conservative as some of the Chandlers," Williams recalled, ". . . but in any case I was still a Republican."

Without a word to anyone, Williams began to hatch some plans. He

knew, however, that he wasn't proceeding completely in a vacuum. Soon
after Williams's new appointment, Dorothy Chandler approached the
Times editor. "She asked if I knew why the *Times* had been named the
third worst newspaper in the country," Williams recalled, referring to
Leo Rosten's poll. "I took it as a signal," Williams concluded.

The signal meant change, any kind of change to transform the *Times*'s
conservatism, biased journalism, and rock-ribbed Republican philosophy. Williams began slowly, cautiously, without any direct order from
above, by maneuvering internally, shifting around some staff, and hoping
that the few new staff he could hire might move the paper in a different
direction. He had no strategy as such; no real conception of what the
Times ought to be, only a sense of what he didn't like of the old *Times*.

Williams's first move was to bring Taylor Trumbo, the only Timesman
from the old school who had any real news experience, out of retirement
to be a transitional managing editor. Next he began to cut back on the
number of staffers assigned to the traditional beats, in hopes of freeing
some reporters for new features. Since there were no increases in editorial funds, expenses for a story had to be kept to a minimum. Williams
knew that ultimately the *Times* could only make fundamental changes if
the Chandlers were willing to part with some of their immediate profits to
use as reinvested capital.

One of his new men, Dick Mathison, the new religion editor, embodied
the Williams transition perspective of 1958–1959. "The old paper was like
an insurance office," Mathison complained, "dull, with that don't rock
the paper atmosphere. It was a provincial paper in a metropolitan area."

Mathison discovered that some of the strongest taboos were a function
of the self-censorship that the staff had derived over the years in inter-
preting and anticipating *Times* conservatism. Mathison decided to do a
story on a right-wing fundamentalist minister, Dr. James Fifield, who had
allied himself with the then secret John Birch Society. Staffers felt Mathison was treading on dangerous waters, since rumor had it that Fifield had
some backing from the number two Chandler in the hierarchy, Norman's
younger brother Philip. Mathison, however, went ahead with his story—a
straightforward account of the minister's beliefs and political philosophy.
Mathison never heard a word from editor Williams.

For Nick Williams, the key to any change revolved around the power-
brokering function of the *Times* surrogates. Williams secretly detested
the surrogates' role and was deeply embarrassed by Carlton Williams's
heavy-handed flaunting of the *Times* power at city hall. The increasing attacks against Carlton Williams in 1958 and '59 only made the *Times* editor
more determined to cut back or remove that power altogether. But editor
Williams couldn't move without full backing from the top, and in 1959 no
one quite knew what the Chandler policy would be.

Nick Williams had little idea how extensive his changeover would become. New forces were at play in the late 1950s, but they were barely detectable at the time: a new politics was emerging; new social forces would erupt within a couple of years and new economic realities would force the Chandler family to reevaluate the position of its newspaper and the rest of the family assets.

The fifties, which started with an anti-Communist reaction, ended on a note of apathy and a curious dialectic of Doris Day movies and the beatnik movement. For the *Times*, in spite of Nick Williams's tentative steps, it appeared that what had brought the Chandlers to the pinnacle of their power would always be. That assumption would soon be proven wrong.

CHAPTER 19

The Politics of Culture

1. GLAPI

"Critics of Los Angeles and Southern California, and they are legion," a 1950 *Times* editorial proclaimed, "can no longer refute the census figures. Already we are one of the biggest cities in the world and we are still growing. But the *Times* has said before and will say again that bigness isn't necessarily greatness. Greatness requires the kind of civic pride and long-range vision which, in years past, brought to this community railroads, a sure water supply, a busy harbor, diversified agriculture, industrial prosperity, airports, freeways, homes, parks, schools and churches. Now Los Angeles needs a civic auditorium and music center. Faced with the facts, the critics of Los Angeles have to fall back on the old insinuation that we have no culture, that nothing really important ever happens here, that there is no metropolitan 'feeling' to the town, that we are a mere collection of suburbs in search of a city. Of course they are wrong. We know that. We like it here."

The rapid suburbanization of the Southern California basin that had begun with the subdivisions of the Los Angeles Suburban Homes Company and other Chandler-related enterprises had now come back to haunt the local business establishment. Downtown Los Angeles was in trouble. Rapid transit had seriously deteriorated and the new freeway systems that attempted to bring commuters from the outlying communities around the basin were already congested. The downtown stores, fearful of the suburban competition, had opened chain stores throughout the region. While

306

these branch stores profited, they inevitably hurt the performance of the parent store downtown.

Downtown needed help—revival, as some businessmen called it. "The city has to have a center to it, you have to have a hub like a wheel. If you let the hub deteriorate, you haven't got much to be suburban to," remarked Neil Petree, head of Barker Brothers furniture store and president of the Downtown Businessmen's Association in the mid 1940s. Petree and about twenty-five of the key downtown businessmen began to meet to discuss ways to revitalize downtown without hurting the expansion in the suburban areas, in which most of the businessmen also held interests.

The informal discussions resulted in a decision to create a new organization, outside the existing business associations such as the Chamber of Commerce, which would push the idea that upgrading downtown benefited the entire region. Leadership of the new organization, named the Greater Los Angeles Plans Incorporated (GLAPI)—included men such as Petree, Asa Call, Norman Chandler, and P.J. Winant of Bullock's Department Store who came from the small group of downtown business executives. Its initial funds consisted of assessments from each corporation that subscribed to the organization.

The first step in GLAPI's strategy to change downtown was the creation of an Opera House and Convention Center. "We didn't have a cultural center in Los Angeles," Petree recalled. Los Angeles opera-goers had been forced to depend on visiting performances of the San Francisco Opera for their local music.

In the late 1940s, GLAPI purchased several parcels of land, including a twenty-six-acre plot in the Bunker Hill area, for possible construction sites. GLAPI decided, with the aid of Lin Beebe, to put up a bond in the 1951 municipal elections to raise money for initial construction of an Opera House. "Los Angeles Resumes the Large Outlook," a *Times* editorial proclaimed in support of GLAPI plans. "The old spirit of accomplishment resurges." With Asa Call chairing GLAPI's election effort, business forces hoped for an easy victory, but the bonds failed to win the necessary two-thirds majority.

GLAPI leaders decided a second bond offering ought to include an Auditorium and Sports Arena in order to attract a larger vote. But Los Angeles voters, in the midst of the stormy 1953 mayoralty race between Poulson and Bowron, once again failed to pass the financing measures. The next year GLAPI forces established a new organization, Forward Los Angeles, and presented each of the three goals—Opera House, Convention Center, and Sports Arena—as separate items. For the third and last time, the GLAPI bonds went down to defeat.

The business group continued to meet to formulate a new plan that would bypass the need for public approval for financing. Some of the GLAPI leaders tentatively raised the possibility of a "lease/lease-back arrangement," whereby the county Board of Supervisors would provide initial support from the county employee pension fund, with matching private donations, to finance the construction of the buildings, garages, parking structures, etc. Once the construction was completed, the county could lease back each of the buildings and parking structures. The corporation that ran the operation could then issue nontaxable bonds—bonds that did not need voter approval—using lease money to advertise the bonds. The method was a controversial one—"some men saying that they know better than the public," as George Gose characterized it. Lin Beebe, who handled bond matters for the city, was called on to work out the legal details for the arrangement. Beebe was at first hesitant about the method, but eventually went along.

Two conditions had to be met for the plan to succeed: the supervisors had to approve the idea and release the pension fund money, and a general political environment had to be created to give the project "civic" respectability. The supervisors wanted reassurance that the private fund-raising would be large enough to equal the county money. The package was complete when the plan encompassed the construction of a music center to house the Los Angeles Philharmonic. The next step was to start the fund-raising.

2. The Music Center Drive

Dorothy Chandler's work on the Hollywood Bowl had "woken her up," as one of her associates remarked. She had all the necessary tools for becoming the leading fund-raiser in the city. She was a Chandler, had control of the society pages of the *Times*, and had the allegiance of dozens of society women who favored the idea of a prestigious new cultural center and who had time on their hands. Many of Dorothy's society aides had been recipients of the *Times* Woman of the Year awards, an extraordinarily successful device Buff had invented to gain loyal ties and win leadership within society's ranks. The awards were given to women at lavish ceremonies which were displayed across the pages of the *Times*.

Under Dorothy Chandler's leadership, *Times* Woman of the Year winners Grace Salvatori (the wife of a wealthy oil man) and Evelyn Bancroft joined Charlie Jones of Richfield Oil to plan a kickoff event, which came to be known as the Eldorado Party, for the Music Center drive.

Tickets for the event, held at the Ambassador Hotel, cost $50 a person. Several entertainers, including Dinah Shore and Danny Kaye, performed, and a Cadillac Eldorado was raffled. The more than six hundred people that attended helped contribute $400,000.

The Music Center campaign had begun, but it didn't go as fast as hoped. Many of those who contributed at the Eldorado event came from the old Los Angeles elite—the merchants, lawyers, bankers, and industrialists that constituted Los Angeles's business establishment. Dorothy Chandler knew there were limits in fund-raising within that group, where no one individual might be willing to give a large sum of money.

The campaign had stalled, and Buff needed a breakthrough badly. Following a hunch, as she later put it, she decided to take a Sunday drive to Orange County to talk to Irvine Ranch owner Myford Irvine. Irvine's ranch—some 93,000 acres—was located in an area that had been largely unpopulated and unsubdivided before World War II. In the 1950s Irvine began to subdivide the property and open it up to private development.

Buff had not been personally involved with the Irvines, but hoped to inspire Myford with her ideas. "I told him I had a dream," Buff recalled, "and if I could say I had a half a million dollars I could really feel I might bring it about. He [Myford Irvine] thereupon asked his treasurer to draw up a check for $100,000."

Less than a month after her visit, Myford Irvine was shot to death in mysterious circumstances, which police ruled a suicide. Before his death Irvine had been heard to remark that he was sitting on a keg of dynamite and needed a huge sum of money. Some reporters covering the case speculated about the gambling connections, but a later investigation by the Orange County D.A. maintained the suicide theory.

But Buff had already followed up on Irvine's contribution. During Christmas week she called her friend Grace Salvatori to tell her to get ready for a new push. In March she approached the Board of Supervisors and pledged to raise an immediate $4 million by private subscription to get the construction under way. She also proposed a new site for the center a few blocks west of the Civic Center and the Times Building, adjacent to some Times Mirror property on Grand Street. The site had originally been intended for the new Department of Water and Power building, but with the supervisors' backing Buff managed to get the lot for the center, and have the DWP building pushed one block farther west.

With the Irvine contribution providing new momentum, Buff systematically began to organize her fund-raising drive. She set up a small office by the swimming pool at her house in Hancock Park and began to survey and study her targets. "I prospected," she remarked. "I read the paper to see who was giving the big parties. I had my antennae out. Few refused to see me." "Many thought she was ruthless in her approach to raising funds for the Music Center," a *Town and Country* article said, describing her efforts. "There were complaints that she would frequently call hosts away from their dinner tables when she knew they were entertaining an affluent guest to see if the large donation she wanted from the individual had been obtained."

Her base of power continued to be the *Times*. Potential donors who spent an hour with her might talk for fifty minutes about their opinion of the *Times*, almost as a precondition for giving their money. Buff patiently heard each one through. The *Times* was also directly enlisted in the campaign. News articles, such as one headlined ON-TO-VICTORY DRIVE SET FOR MUSIC CENTER, appeared with forms for contributions.

Buff by now had become a serious political force in her own right. In the late fifties the Chamber of Commerce set up a committee to oversee the Music Center question and asked Asa Call to chair it in an attempt to offset Dorothy Chandler's growing power. The committee included Call, Buff, Charlie Jones, Charles Ducommun from the chamber, Bob Hastings from the Civic Light Opera Association, Lin Beebe, and Franklin Payne, the publisher of the *Examiner*. Call, with his enormous political muscle, was able to get most of the supervisors to agree to the lease/lease-back arrangement, but Buff was the one able to win the support of liberal supervisor John Anson Ford, a longtime establishment critic. The Chandlers offered to sell the county some of their Lucky Baldwin Arcadia land for the development of an arboretum, a cherished John Anson Ford goal.

Buff became an all-purpose organizer. She put together a Blue Ribbon 400 Committee of society matrons and wealthy newcomers with a task of fund-raising one thousand people for $1,000 donations. She turned to Hollywood, which had lived on the fringes of Los Angeles's old wealth, to raise funds from stars, producers, and studio heads. She managed to obtain the movie *Cleopatra* for an opening night benefit at $250 a ticket.

"A fund-raiser," Buff explained, "should be at various times a psychiatrist, a psychologist, a marriage counselor, and even a sort of family doctor. You have to know the family situation at all times. Divorce, illness, death—or just a routine change in the family situation—can inhibit contribution." Her little office became the complete fund-raising center, with her society allies running in and out to report. Even the *Times* astrologer was on call to help construct astrological charts for prospective donors. Dorothy Chandler was becoming the best informed, and perhaps most powerful, individual within the Los Angeles upper-class social galaxy.

Pursuing the Myford Irvine strategy, Dorothy Chandler began to look toward a new constituency. "The city was fragmented . . . ," Buff realized. "There was Hollywood, and there was downtown, and they didn't know who the others were. The older people (those active in civic affairs) were getting tired. Their sons and daughters were not stimulated to pick it up. New business was coming into the area. New money. Many new people. . . . I decided it would be done on an individual basis—never any meetings in clubs of the so-called Establishment—in my house or somebody else's house, or in little private dining rooms, everyone accepted on the same basis." *Town and Country* ironically paraphrased Buff's approach: "The Music Center would be for the people. . . . Society must integrate!"

Buff met with Gene and Roz Wyman and their friends to discuss the Music Center. Gene Wyman, a powerful lawyer within wealthy Jewish circles—the Hillcrest Country Club set—was a key fundraiser/power-broker in the Democratic party. City councilwoman Roz Wyman had led the fight in favor of the Chavez Ravine development. The Wymans told Chandler that the Hillcrest group was reluctant to get involved in the Music Center fundraising since it appeared to be an old elite affair. After all, the Wymans contended, Jews were still excluded from the California Club and Jonathan Club and clearly not welcome in the old established society. But Buff, with her new approach, got the Wymans and all their rich friends enthusiastically involved.

Still $300,000 short of her $4 million goal and fearing a reversal in momentum, Buff scheduled a meeting with her fund-raising committee to take place at Perino's, an upper-crust restaurant. When she arrived at Perino's, Buff noticed two oil men, Democrats Sam Mosher and Ed Pauley, both fringe members of the old elite. Buff approached Pauley and began to give a pitch to her long-standing friend, talking of patriotism, Los Angeles chauvinism, civic pride, and social duty. Pauley wrote out a check for $125,000 on the spot. Turning to Mosher and feeding off the rivalry between the two oil men, Buff managed to procure another $125,000.

Some of Buff's old blueblood acquaintances started to take offense at her reckless definition of the new upper-class social milieu. She became a Trojan Horse symbol, undermining the old Los Angeles society's foundations. "Los Angeles society is much like the frog that wanted to inflate himself bigger than the bull," Hedda Hopper scornfully complained of Buff's approach. "Outside our city's limits, its 'society' doesn't mean much primarily because our standard isn't 'Who are you?' but 'How much have you got?' "

One of the important sources of new wealth in Southern California after World War II came from the growing savings and loan industry. Savings and loan banks provided loans and development money for real estate construction and housing projects and sponsored scores of new suburban developments. Howard Ahmanson's Home Savings and Loan, based in Los Angeles, had made him an extremely wealthy man. He was scornfully dubbed "The Pink Republican" by Old Guard opponents such as Asa Call during Ahmanson's tenure as Goodwin Knight's money man.

The S&L man had contributed to Barry Goldwater's campaign in 1964 to shake off his pink label. Like others of the new rich, Ahmanson yearned for recognition and respectability.

Mark Taper, who entered the mortage banking business in 1941, also sought out a place in Los Angeles society. Having made his fortune by the mid-1950s by financing suburban housing, he organized his own American Savings and Loan bank. By the late fifties Taper had become a fierce and bitter rival of the wealthier and more powerful Ahmanson.

Approaching him during the Christmas season in 1961, Buff emphasized to Taper, who considered himself a maverick, that a new, resourceful, experimental theater—one of three components proposed for the Music Center complex—would offer a major opportunity for the advancement of culture in Los Angeles. But the cautious Taper wanted to know more. "It took a lot of luncheons," Buff remarked. "I'll tell you, Mark was a difficult man, but I really liked him. . . . It was two years before I had his commitment."

The arrangement that Buff finally nailed down with Taper had three key provisions. Taper would have a permanent box seat adjacent to the Chandlers' box, the theatre would be named in his honor, and he would have veto power over the naming of the other two buildings in the Music Center complex. In turn, Taper donated over $1 million to Buff's own organizational creation, The Center for Performing Arts Council, which served as a conduit for the funds for the Music Center construction.

The use of the Performing Arts Council as a forwarding device symbolized the jockeying for cultural/political domination of the Music Center project that had peaked by the early 1960s. Chandler and her new rich allies were widely resented by the Old Guard faction, who competed against them. The key to the Old Guard's cultural power was the Los Angeles Civic Light Opera Association, which had arranged for some of the out-of-town performances of various opera companies in the forties and fifties. The organization received substantial contributions from its old Los Angeles elite "guarantors" in the form of annual pledges. Other Dorothy Chandler-led cultural organizations, such as the Southern California Symphony, were poor cousins when it came to financial backing. Buff created the Center for the Performing Arts Council to challenge the pre-eminence of the old Light Opera group. The Taper contribution was a major coup.

While working on the Taper contribution, Buff also approached Taper's S&L nemesis, Howard Ahmanson. "You've got to play one against the other," she commented. "You've got to know when to push and when to shove. It took a lot of talking, a lot of understanding, a lot of listening to their personal lives. One wanted to give as much as the other." Ahmanson, not to be outdone by Taper's pledge, offered more than $1 million to the Performing Arts Council for a large theater hall. And Buff, in turn, agreed to Ahmanson's condition to name the building after him.

Meanwhile, on March 13, 1962, after Asa Call and his committee had worked out the final leasing arrangements with the county Board of Supervisors, the articles creating the Music Center legal structure were signed. More than thirteen million dollars in bonds were issued and sold by the Music Center Lease Company, which oversaw the construction and lease-back arrangements. Buff's funds, which now approached close to $10 million, combined with county pension money, was enough to set construction on all three buildings—a music pavillion, a large-scale theater and a smaller theater—into high gear.

When Jacques Lipchitz was commissioned to do a sculpture of a peace offering for the Music Pavillion, everyone assumed the building would be named "A Memorial to Peace." But Buff's allies campaigned to name the building the "Dorothy Chandler Pavillion" in recognition of her fundraising. Though some of the Old Guard felt resentful, there were no objections. Nor did anyone oppose naming the smaller theater the "Mark Taper Forum" in consideration of Taper's million-dollar contribution. But the Old Guard went into an uproar over the idea of an "Ahmanson Theater."

Howard Ahmanson, the new rich "upstart" who had supplanted Asa Call as finance chairman in the fifties, had not won favor with Los Angeles's old elite. Pleas went out to Taper to exercise his veto power to stop the name. As the issue was about to come before the supervisors, Taper sent word to Asa Call and Old Guard forces that he'd use the veto. But at the eleventh hour, Buff approached Taper to ask him to waive the veto "in the name of the effort," as Taper recalled. If Ahmanson withdrew his money, plans for the building might have to be halted. Buff's pleas, Taper claimed, led him to drop his opposition to the name. The Old Guard, especially Asa Call, suspected other reasons for Taper's cooperation. One prevalent rumor concerned a possible scandal regarding S&L lobbying activities tied to Bobby Baker, LBJ's aide who was about to be indicted. Asa Call—the grand old man of power-brokering—and his allies had been bested.

Buff enlisted the aid of Walt Disney for one last campaign: The Buck Bag. Disney designed and manufactured a special shopping bag to be used to solicit $1 contributions from as many Angelenos as possible. Mark Taper pledged $500,000 to match funds brought in by the buck campaign.

It was the last stretch. The buildings were almost completed and the Buff-originated Center for Performing Arts Council began to use its funds in preparation for future theater and musical performances. The rest was simply a matter of waiting for opening night.

* * *

3. The Mehta Interlude

Rising to power in the music world in the fifties,Buff became vice-chairman of the Los Angeles Symphony board. She had differences with both conductor Alfred Wallenstein, who left Los Angeles in 1956, and his replacement, Edward Van Beinum, whom Buff found "too independent."

By late 1960, choices for a new permanent Los Angeles conductor after the death of Edward Van Beinum, had narrowed down to Georg Solti and George Steinberg of the Pittsburgh Symphony Orchestra. Though the board's general manager George Kuyper favored Steinberg, Chandler decided that Solti was the better choice, and her clout with the board prevailed. Solti, Kuyper, Chandler, and Henry Duque, chairman of the Symphony Association, worked out a contract that provided for Solti's services for thirteen weeks of the year.

There was friction between Solti and Chandler from the start. At a reception to honor the new conductor following his opening-night concert, the Chandler-directed Symphony Board decided to include a presentation by the Austrian Consul General of a "Gold Insignia of Honor for Meritorious Services to the Republic of Austria" to Dorothy Chandler, who upstaged the new conductor at the reception. The *Times* news story the next day gave more than twice the space to the Insignia presentation than to Solti's part in the event.

As Solti took on his job with the symphony, he began to look for an assistant conductor to handle his tasks for those weeks he'd be out of the city. He arranged to listen to several young conductors, including a twenty-six-year-old Indian from Bombay, Zubin Mehta. Solti, immediately impressed by Mehta, tried to get his services, only to discover that the young Indian had only limited time available, since he had just arranged a contract with the Montreal Symphony Orchestra.

Solti's next choice was an assistant to Leonard Bernstein in New York, but Buff successfully pushed to postpone negotiations until a management report by Chandler advisors, McKinsey and Company, could be completed. The McKinsey group considered the question of combining the affairs of the orchestra, the Hollywood Bowl and the Music Center—and its findings could affect the role of the assistant conductor.

In January 1961 Zubin Mehta pinch-hit as guest conductor for the symphony when Fritz Reiner cancelled his engagement because of ill health. The young Indian's opening night performance was, as George Kuypers put it, "A smashing success with audiences and orchestra." "The women just swooned," music critic Goldberg remarked on the reaction of Dorothy Chandler and the society women around her.

Overnight, Mehta became a sex symbol, a musical superstar. "His personality engulfs you," Kuypers recalled. At an "emergency" executive committee meeting of the board, called to discuss "the subject of the Associate Conductor," Buff proposed that Mehta be offered the assistant position and insisted that arrangements be completed before he left Los Angeles. The board acted on Chandler's urging, though Solti, obviously expecting to have final say on the choice of his assistant, was out of town. Some of Buff's advisors warned of future difficulties, but Chandler wanted Mehta and was determined to have her way.

After Chandler and Mehta worked out an agreement, Buff sent a telegram to Solti (then in Europe): GOOD FORTUNE FOR YOU. THIS AFTERNOON EXECUTIVE CABINET APPROVED YOUR NUMBER ONE SELECTION MEHTA AS ASSOCIATE CONDUCTOR. She then tried to follow up with a phone call to Solti but never reached him.

A few days later Buff and Norman went to South America. After they left, all hell broke loose. A dispatch in the *New York Times* implied that Mehta was to share responsibilities with Solti as co-conductor, and the *Chicago Tribune* noted ironically that Solti would be interested to discover that "Mehta has just been named conductor of the orchestra." The European papers also carried the story.

Solti, amazed and infuriated, registered strong complaints in a series of phone calls and telegrams, and then through his lawyer. "This is ruining my reputation," he told friends, "hiring this boy without my consent." Solti's lawyer finally proposed to the board that it—and Chandler—could save face by cancelling the Mehta contract. If not, Solti would resign. "It was a precarious moment," in Buff's career, music critic Goldberg recalled, surmising that she might well have lost if the Music Center had not already been under construction. The symphony board, though, backed Chandler. Calling the board's decision a "serious breach of contract," Solti resigned.

On April 3, 1961, the *Examiner's* music critic Patterson Greene blasted Chandler and the board's actions. "Is the Philharmonic Orchestra of Los Angeles a civic enterprise, drawing upon the public for support, or is it a private enterprise, dictatorially controlled? . . . The whole story amounts to a high-handed maneuvering of a civic enterprise that gave no consideration to the citizens who are asked annually to support it . . . . The City of Los Angeles," Greene concluded, "has been trapped once again into artistic mediocrity."

As the Solti affair heated up, *Times* music critic Albert Goldberg tried to steer clear of the dispute. "I need to be protected," he pleaded with his editor Nick Williams, who downplayed the importance of the Solti affair, but pledged to keep Goldberg from being forced to take sides. As the *Examiner* attacks intensified, Williams decided the *Times* needed to respond and, keeping his word to Goldberg, he wrote his own reply to Greene's polemics. Williams speculated that the anti-Chandler attacks might have been generated out of envy of the *Times*'s circulation lead over the Hearst papers. "Criticism," Williams wrote "I know is the price that those who lead must pay. But when criticism inspired by corporate envy ravages the purposes of selfless volunteers, then in my opinion it becomes deplorable and a degradation of the ethics of the newspaper publishing profession."

Buff came out of the affair injured but not mortally wounded. Six weeks after Solti's departure she was reelected president of the Southern California Symphony Association and given a standing vote of confidence. At the association meeting she called for the creation of a standing committee of five to seek out a new conductor. That committee soon after recommended, with the board's approval, that Zubin Mehta be the new conductor of the Los Angeles Symphony Orchestra.

4. Opening Night

Dorothy Chandler had succeeded beyond anyone's wildest expectations. "When they are not flinging epithets at one another's credentials, the various social factions [in Los Angeles] are championing their own leaders. One woman's name crops up again and again. She is Mrs. Norman Chandler, the feared and revered wife of the president of the Times Mirror Company," *New York Times* society writer Charlotte Curtis remarked. "I wanted my symphony to have a home," Curtis quoted Buff.

"In a dazzle of diamonds and décolletage, with cinema stars, celebrities, and just plain millionaires on hand," as *Time* magazine described it, the Music Center opened on December 6, 1964. *Time* put Buff on its cover, and she received laurels and recognition throughout the country. "Just think," Bob Hope joked at the ceremonies, "all the money for this beautiful center was raised by voluntary contributions—voluntary, that is, when Buff stopped twisting your arm so you could sign the check." A sign board designed for the occasion hung over the building. "Los Angeles thanks you Mrs. Chandler," the billboard read, "for our new Music Center."

With a pavillion named in her honor, a full-sized portrait inside the center, and the leadership of her Performing Arts Council and Blue Ribbon 400, Dorothy Chandler had become the most powerful figure in Los Angeles society. "It is rare in life that you can say that one person did it," Roz Wyman remarked. "She did it."

What she did, to the acclaim of downtown business, was not appreciated by everyone. Like New York's Lincoln Center, which was also completed in 1964, the multi-million-dollar project had necessitated the removal of a poor community to make way for a cultural center endowed by and serving the expensive tastes of the well-to-do. Further, by the time the Music Center was completed, $13.7 million in county pension fund money had been spent by utilizing a leasing system that had bypassed public approval.

The Music Center never had been a project limited to music. It was initially conceived as part of the business establishment's objective of revitalizing downtown and creating the social conditions for upper-class recognition around the country. The Center gave Dorothy Chandler a major opportunity to help transform her city's image and the relations of power by redefining the nature of the establishment. By opening society's doors to the new rich and other formerly excluded social groups such as the Hillcrest set, Chandler created a more flexible and viable framework for Los Angeles's establishment. Her cultural politics laid the foundation for a changing *Times* to adjust to a changing city. More than any of the Chandlers, she recognized that an expanded elite provided the only means to maintain power. Dorothy Chandler became the link, the continuity, between the old and the new *Times*.

PART IV

1960–1976

Most Likely To Succeed

1. The Changeover

The late fifties was a deceptive period in America: a period of apparent calm before the social dislocations of the next decade. Even at the *Times*, beneath its proper, conservative tone, trouble was brewing. The Chandlers were not a united family, and jealousies were rife. The family feud was deepening. At the heart of the matter lay the prerogatives of power: who would control the *Times*, and what would be the shape of power in Los Angeles?

Dorothy Chandler still had much to overcome. In a society where positions of power were almost exclusively occupied by men, Buff had assumed a leadership role in the Music Center, an institution which meant a great deal to powerful Angelenos. Her rise with the development of the Music Center paralleled her increasing intervention in the affairs of the *Times*.

Buff's role at the *Times* was disliked by some staff members who complained about her activities, but dared not defy her power. When actress Dame Judith Anderson, noted for her performance of Lady Macbeth, received a *Times* award in the early 1960s, *Times* staffers wrote underneath a bulletin board picture of Anderson, "Who is the real Lady Macbeth?"

To many in the family, Buff was a usurper and not a true Chandler. Her European-style salons, advocacy of cultural exchanges with the Russians, and casual attitude toward the new rich, Democrats, Jews, and actors ruffled her family antagonists, as well as many in the old Los Angeles establishment.

321

That discontent had its political counterpart. A radical right, a group which had long tasted power and took the premises of the Cold War as faith, now increasingly felt alienated from the national ruling circles. For years the radical right had found strength in *Times* news articles and editorials, which reinforced its perception of the battle of Free Enterprise against Communism. The *Times* was its information bible, a means by which the Southern California upper-class recognized itself and its politics.

For the Eastern elite the Cold War ideology had served its purpose by uprooting the left-leaning liberalism of the New Deal and its labor allies, but by 1958 the terms of the ideology had begun to shift as Russian/U.S. relations stabilized. The radical right, unable to accept the beginnings of détente, felt like outcasts. Two different politics and two different attitudes towards the *Times* had taken shape. On one side was Buff and her son Otis and their vision of a modern paper and contemporary city; on the other was Philip and Alberta Chandler, who feared the liberal-cum-communist menace that was eating away at the fabric of society. Alberta and Buff had long been rivals, but only recently had the dispute taken on a political dimension. Norman, whose leadership was accepted by both sides, was in the middle, never one for trouble and reluctant to treat the squabble as a split. Though sharing the Cold War language of his brother and sister-in-law, he did nothing to prevent Buff's increasing interest and role in the operation of the *Times*.

An uneasy peace reigned until 1958. That year, while touring the Hawaiian Islands, Norman Chandler came down with a serious illness. The family thought he might be close to death. If the *Times* publisher died, he'd be succeeded at the top by his brother Philip, then second in command. The line of succession at the *Times* had previously seemed firm: Norman would relinquish the publisher's post after his retirement and hand over the title to his son Otis, who would have completed a lengthy training program similar to the one Norman went through. But in 1958 Otis still had several more years of training ahead of him. With Philip in power, even temporarily, all of Buff's calculations might blow up in her face. There was no time to lose.

Buff first approached *Times* editor L.D. Hotchkiss and asked if he would assume the publisher's post. "Don't involve me in family affairs," Hotchkiss told his boss' wife. He wanted to continue his job as editor. With one avenue closed, other help was sought. A short while later, Buff retained the service of McKinsey and Company, the management consulting firm. McKinsey was asked to prepare an organizational study and field report on general Times Mirror operations, including the matter of succession. McKinsey suggested that the Times Mirror Chief Executive

Officer have at least a fifteen-year tenure in order to achieve maximum corporate stability; ipso facto eliminating Philip Chandler, then aged fifty-one, given the company policy on retirement at age sixty-five.

Bringing in McKinsey meant more than a family power play. It meant, as it turned out, a transformation of the business. The McKinsey people spoke of diversification, the "synergistic company," of going public—new concepts that the once staid family operation would soon adopt. McKinsey argued that major company changes required that Norman, now fully recovered from his Hawaiian illness, assume command of over-all Times Mirror affairs, and step down as publisher of the *Times* newspaper. Otis would advance to the publisher's post a few years earlier than anticipated. The plans were made in secret and a date in April 1960 was chosen.

The invitation read: "Come to the Biltmore Bowl auditorium April 11 for an announcement of great importance." The cream of the California elite—governors and county supervisors, industrialists and bankers, publishers and editors, several hundred in all—came to the packed luncheon. Nearly everyone, even high Times Mirror executives, was unaware of what was in store.

With everyone seated, Norman Chandler approached the podium. He spoke of the great *Times* traditions and of his father and grandfather, who had created their paper in the image of their city and built a city in the image of their paper. Heads nodded approvingly as Chandler boasted of the power and accomplishments of the *Times* and its heritage.

Then Norman turned toward his son: "I hereby appoint, effective as of this minute, Otis Chandler to the position of publisher of the *Los Angeles Times*, the fourth in its seventy-nine-year history." The *Times* quoted the senior Chandler the next day: "I say to you—you are assuming a sacred trust and grave responsibilities. I have the utmost confidence that you will never falter in fulfilling these obligations. This trust is dearer than life itself."

There was dead silence. Then, as the *Times* article described it, Otis Chandler, flushed and almost out of breath, stepped to a microphone and, to break the tension, uttered just one word: 'Wow!' He added that if he were putting the shot, he could do seventy feet, and if trying the high jump, at least eight feet.

It was an incredibly embarrassing moment. There was some coughing and some shuffling in seats. Otis continued in a more serious vein, according to the *Times* article, and began to talk of the deeds of his father and the accomplishments of the *Times*.

The climax to the two years of maneuvering had come; Buff's will had been done.

2. Most Likely To Succeed

"With this sudden changing of the guard," Otis Chandler wrote in the *Times* his first day as publisher, "some may ponder what this means to their favorite newspaper. No changes are in the offing. A continuation of the successful *Times* format of an unbiased, informed and responsible press is in order." A week later Chandler told *Time* magazine that he intended to do a lot of listening about the paper's policy. "I don't want to open my mouth in front of the wise men," Chandler said, "until I know what I'm doing it for." It was an inauspicious beginning for a new era, but Chandler correctly pinpointed the fact that in the spring of 1960 the paper was the same as ever. The *Times* was, as always, dominated by anti-Communist politics, local boosting, crime news, and wire copy. Kyle Palmer still occupied the political editor's chair and Carlton Williams was busily preparing to reelect Mayor Poulson to his third term. Advertising lineage was up and the *Times* management continued to explore the ways in which it might ultimately establish a secure monopoly for its paper in Los Angeles.

Otis Chandler was thirty-two years old the day he became publisher. The younger of two children, Otis grew up in the foothills of Pasadena. During the war years, Otis attended Philips Academy in Andover, Massachusetts. After graduation in 1946, he came back to the West Coast to begin college at Stanford which was the surrogate Ivy League for wealthy Californians and many of Otis's relatives numbered among its alumni. In keeping with his expected training, Otis majored in business, economics, and journalism, but his first love was elsewhere. Even before college Otis had become a sports enthusiast with skills in track and field, weightlifting, swimming, and surfing. In college he became the consummate athlete, a high-level performer who broke records on various teams. Otis Chandler became Stanford's premier shot putter and his great ambition was to perform in the Olympics, a dream which was never fulfilled because of injuries.

The celebration of the "outdoor life," so prominent in the pages of the climate-boosting *Times*, preoccupied Otis, the big-game hunter, surfer, and weight-lifter. The blond, 6' 3" boyish-looking man inherited the shy reserve and good looks of his father and his grandfather's baby face.

It was natural that young Chandler would be attracted to Marilyn Brant: a Southern Californian at Stanford, a woman with the same class background and associations, in fact, a granddaughter of Otto Brant of Title Insurance and Trust company, Harry Chandler's real estate companion in countless syndicates. Marilyn, or "Missie" as she came to be known, also shared Otis's love of sports and the outdoors, his preoccupation for physical fitness, and his ambitions. On June 18, 1951, Otis Chandler and Marilyn Brant were married. Within a year Missie gave birth to a son, the first of five children with whom they shared their active outdoor values.

In spite of the sports enthusiasm and Olympic hopes, Otis Chandler would ultimately, his parents reasoned, come home to the *Times*. In 1953, after a short stint in the Air Force as an officer during the Korean War, Chandler began his *Times* training program. He served as an apprentice pressman, and then went through the mechanical and electrical shops, the mail room, engraving, transportation, and all the advertising departments. Unlike his father, Otis spent fourteen months as a general assignment reporter (eleven months at the *Times* and three months at the *Mirror*). When the *Mirror* went through a management shakeup in 1957, Otis was sent over as assistant to the president to begin some executive training. In late 1958, when Buff began to make her moves, Otis was made marketing manager at the *Times*.

During the training period everyone at the *Times* was aware that the next Chandler in line for the top was making his way through the paper. Staffers were polite and friendly, but Otis was awkward with the employees and kept aloof.

One day, while Otis was working general assignment at the *Mirror*, he went down to his locker and saw several of the staff hanging around, drinking, and talking. One of the reporters started rambling on about how wonderful it would be if there existed a paper that never pulled its punches. Everybody started speaking about serving the public and its right to know. "That's what it's all about," one of the reporters sighed. Otis, who had stood apart several lockers down during the entire conversation, finally intervened with the declaration that the real purpose of a newspaper was "to make money."

Making money was the name of the game at the *Times*. In 1960 the paper had become one of the most profitable in the country.

When Otis Chandler assumed the publisher's spot in April 1960, there was no developed strategy for change. Otis's first desire was to be acknowledged as the great publisher of the best newspaper of the United States, and failing that, the publisher of the second best newspaper after the *New York Times*. A great newspaper is possible, Otis's advisors explained, but only through large infusions of capital. The more money spent, the better the newspaper. Nick Williams, with his long experience in the organization, argued that the *Times* needed a new format, a new staff, and a new product, especially one geared toward making the *Times* a national newspaper. Such a product, Williams argued, would have its payoff with increased ad revenue.

No longer a parochial sheet, the new *Los Angeles Times* would merge into the spirit of Kennedy's New Frontier. To make the *Times* nationally prominent would mean national prominence for the Chandlers and, for Otis, a break with those "old men" of the California Club that ran the affairs of Southern California. Otis never cared for the social milieu of the Los Angeles upper class. His own friends came from different circles. Otis and the Old Guard became so distant that several of the local businessmen would mutter they could hardly remember the last time they saw young Otis at the club.

"When I was chairman of the Convention Center committee, I wanted to get some editorial support from the *Times*," downtown businessman Neil Petree related, " . . . I had to go through a lot of formalities, go through a committee and all that sort of thing, when [in the past] you didn't bother with anything like that. You just ran into Norman, you just called them up, and said, 'are you going to the meeting, we need some help on this,' and they said yes or no and that was that. The *Times* has gotten pretty big now."

The new *Times* publisher wanted to put a new face on an old empire but he had no idea where to start. Otis had to rely on his advisors, particularly editor Nick Williams, to formulate the ideas and draw out the implications. Chandler had never been considered a heavyweight thinker, but Williams found young Otis accessible and willing. Change was a delicate operation, for every political and financial shift inevitably produced its counterreaction. Nick Williams became a master of soothing words and careful guidance. The *Times* editor, who, in turn, relied on his assistants, put together a conceptual framework revolving around the idea of a daily newsmagazine, which would fight off the competition of television and serve a "supercity" from the desert to the sea with an upgraded product that had a strong dose of expertise and a big expense account.

The idea of a daily newsmagazine had grown out of several related factors: the success of *Time* and *Newsweek*, the emergence of television as an effective headline and fast-breaking-news service, and the movement within journalism to explain events as well as report them. The circulation growth of *Time* and *Newsweek* was attributed to the growing middle class of college students and graduates who had jobs in skilled professional and technical areas. Many of the weekly magazine readers lived in suburban neighborhoods and got their local, community news from the suburban papers.

In 1959, *Printer's Ink,* an important trade publication, published a survey of the Los Angeles market which dealt with the suburban question. The magazine suggested that the population in Los Angeles was finally beginning to stabilize after years of rapid expansion. Los Angeles, the publication suggested, was not a single city, but a region of suburb-cities, each nearly self-contained with a separate mayor, school system, and tax base. This suburban character was the essential characteristic of the mar-

ket, and advertisers were counseled to reorient their message to the growing middle-class sophistication of the suburbs. These readers and viewers
were not interested in "inner city" news (crime, sensationalism, wed-
dings, and sex) but wanted regional, national, and international news. The
new suburban papers, which by 1960 included thirty-three dailies in
Southern California, took care of the local news. It was clear that new
market needs called for a changing *Times*.

The problem was magnified by the increasingly prominent role of television. Newspapers had relied on fast-breaking stories, lots of pictures,
and vivid writing to hold and increase their circulation figures. Television
was changing the terms of the industry. Yellow journalism would have to
give way to a grayer, more complex product in order to maintain its readership base.

The political basis for the shift away from the old-style journalism dated back to the early 1950s and Senator Joe McCarthy's manipulation of
the press for his own objectives. The Senator had timed his press announcements just prior to newspaper deadline so that even his wildest un-
substantiated charges got prominent display. Locked into its schedule and
format, the press became a conduit for McCarthy and an extension of his
power.

The political criticism of the press's performance concerning McCarthy
turned into an overall critique of deadline journalism. Journalists began to
toy with the idea of explaining events, of developing what was known in
the trade as "background." The rules of objectivity were still to be observed: that is, the reporter could not draw conclusions unless he or she
did so in the form of comments from a news source. But reporters fought
for the practice of explaining how an event happened and why.

The suburban reader constituted the new audience for this changing
newspaper. In Southern California, the geographical boundaries of the
suburban sprawl coincided with what had once defined the physical
spread of Chandler interests: from Santa Barbara on the north to the
Mexican border on the south, and from Arizona on the east to the Pacific
Ocean on the west. "In the not too distant future," Otis Chandler told
Time magazine in 1960, "the city will stretch from Santa Barbara to San
Diego. By the time that supercity is in existence, there will, I suspect, be
only one metropolitan morning paper and one metropolitan evening paper
to serve it. There will of course be area publications serving everything
from new subdivisions to cities like Santa Barbara or San Diego. But
there is going to be only one dominant central newspaper—and that's going to be the *Los Angeles Times*."

The Chandlers related the supercity concept to the educational and
technological sophistication that had come to Southern California. "Los
Angeles was becoming an important center of thought," Chandler

testified in a legal deposition in December 1965, "[with] the growth of our universities, the growth of our so-called research and development agencies, such things as the Rand Corporation, the continued development of the aerospace and electronics industries, the cultural development of Los Angeles. All of these things were coming about and developing rapidly in 1960, and Nick Williams and I were planning the editorial changes in what we felt the *Times* should be, and the group to which it should appeal in the future."

Beyond all else the *Times* publisher wanted prestige: national recognition for his paper, for himself and his family, and for his city. He wanted to be thought of as big league, with a top ten newspaper and business connections. Though he sometimes scorned the local Old Guard, Otis still sought out new business ties, joining the board of directors of Western Airlines in 1964, Union Bank in 1966, and Pan Am in 1970. By 1970 Otis Chandler would also sit on the boards of TRW, the Tejon Ranch, the Associated Press, Emmet and Chandler insurance company, and GeoTek Resources Fund, and he would rise to the vice-chairman's spot in the family's Times Mirror Company. He had holdings in oil, real estate, agribusiness, and publishing, and income from three trust funds.

Otis Chandler came to power in the period of the modern corporation and corporate-oriented liberal politics of a Robert McNamara and Nelson Rockefeller. He took part in company matters just as Times Mirror entered the brave new world of conglomeration, diversification, and corporate upgrading.

The Chandler maxim "think big" summed up Otis's contribution to the Chandler lineage. The young publisher was a big man with a big ambition: a child of monopoly who was used to having his way.

CHAPTER 20

Taking Off

1. The First Period

When Frank McCulloch and Nick Williams first met in 1958, Williams took a liking to the tough, hard-nosed ex-Marine who had worked his way up to become *Time* magazine's West Coast bureau chief.

Williams mentioned to McCulloch that some changes might soon be taking place at the *Times*, and if an opening arose he'd like McCulloch to consider a job. McCulloch replied that he'd seriously keep it in mind. A new relationship had begun—one that, perhaps more than any other at the paper, symbolized the commitments and the limitations of the changeover at the *Times*.

McCulloch knew the paper and the family. He had been assigned the *Time* cover story on the Chandlers in 1957, and his profile of power was well received by the family. McCulloch followed Nick Williams's progress closely. Under the surface of the stodgy, reactionary *Times*, Frank McCulloch sensed the possibilities of which journalists forever dream: the rare opportunity to influence the transformation of a newspaper. Nick Williams wanted the *Times* to change, but neither he nor his assistants had the skills required to bring about that change. Those who had risen within the ranks of the *Times* did so more because of their social grace, conservative outlook, and mechanical desk skills, than because of any reportorial talents. Williams himself had come up through those ranks, and he knew he needed a reporter's editor to provide inspiration and journalistic leadership for the paper.

The pressure and momentum for change from below could be chan-

329

neled through Williams, who would slow down or halt anything that got out of hand. The wily editor would work back and forth as a mediator between publisher and staff. He would coax and soothe the Chandlers with an economic rationale for change and check a boisterous staff.

Nick Williams decided to create two managing editor's posts—a day managing editor, in charge of the local staff and political coverage, and a night managing editor to run the desk operation and the bureaus. Williams would reach into the ranks of the old-timers for his desk man, but he knew he had to go outside the organization to find his day man, the reporter's editor. In the fall of 1960, Nick Williams approached Frank McCulloch with a firm offer for a job, and the *Time* man accepted.

McCulloch brought to the paper a new spirit which generated fierce loyalty and inspired journalism. "The only good reporter is one in motion," he advised his staff, and he was on the run more than anyone else, as he tried to push the paper as fast as he could.

Williams and McCulloch's first hurdle was the composition of the staff, who conformed to the slow pace and quiet conservatism of the paper. Nick Williams convinced his boss that the way to gain prestige and recognition was through a new hiring policy. With Otis's approval the *Times* embarked on a massive campaign to attract a new staff, primarily from the newsweeklies such as *Time, Newsweek, Business Week,* and *U.S. News and World Report.* High salaries were offered, and the word spread that the *Times* was ready to change. In January 1962 forty new staff were picked up from the defunct *Los Angeles Examiner* and *Los Angeles Mirror.* For the first time in *Times* history, wholesale firings occurred to make way for the new group. The dramatic facelift changed the character of the paper overnight. Within five years an almost entirely new organization had been hired outright and many of the old-timers had either retired or resigned.

A new mood began to take hold. "Frank McCulloch's leadership was infectious," commented *Times* reporter Jack Tobin. "People could hardly wait to get to work. McCulloch experimented with long detailed series, such as a fourteen-county business survey and an extensive study of the black and Mexican-American communities. The paper allocated travel money and expense accounts for the first time. When the idea for a new series came up, McCulloch would give a pep talk and keep the energy level high. The process of change, however, was given its most dramatic boost when the *New York Times* decided to come West and give the Chandlers a competitive scare.

2. Making Dreams Come True

"The idea" according to the *New York Times* correspondent Gladwyn Hill, "was inevitable:" the *New York Times* would go national. For years, the New York executives had closely followed the career of the profitable *Wall Street Journal*, which, along with the *Christian Science Monitor*, was the only publication resembling a national newspaper in the country. The *New York Times* had the staff, expertise, and prestige to match the *Journal* effort to cover national news in multiple editions.

In 1961, the Sulzbergers decided to take a giant step toward that goal by making plans to publish a western edition of the *New York Times*. The Los Angeles market, third largest in the country, was essential to the whole operation.

In the fall of 1961 the New Yorkers contacted the post office to work out delivery arrangements. They withdrew the *New York Times* wire service from all West Coast clients, including the *Los Angeles Times*. They also began to make some discreet—and not so discreet—inquiries about the availability of reporters, advertising salesmen, and other personnel they'd need to start the operation. *New York Times* general manager Andy Fisher informed Otis Chandler of the New York paper's intentions, and Otis's reply was curt: "I indicated," Otis later testified, "that we were not in sympathy with the *New York Times* attempt to become a national newspaper."

The Chandlers were quick to react. Shortly after the *New York Times* wire service was withdrawn, the Chandlers set up a syndicated news service with the *Washington Post*. The wire service would immediately bolster the weak national and international coverage in the *Los Angeles Times* and help make the Los Angeles paper more competitive with the New York attempt.

While the Chandlers strategized and fretted, Frank McCulloch and Nick Williams and many of the *Times* staff rubbed their hands in anticipation. As competition, the western edition hardly represented much of a threat, without a local base, and with only limited ability to attract local advertisers. To compete with the *New York Times* in terms of product, however, would enormously help those pushing for change. McCulloch could go to his bosses with an idea or suggestion about what the *Los Angeles Times* needed and then compare the coverage with the best paper in the country.

Nick Williams felt the same way as McCulloch. Though the plans for change were already on the drawing boards, as Otis Chandler frequently pointed out, they could still have been rejected. "Those plans," Williams commented, "would likely have been implemented anyway, though one can never be sure. What the *New York Times* attempt did was to certainly speed things up quite a bit, and that's no small accomplishment."

But the western edition, launched in October 1962, was, as McCulloch had accurately predicted, plagued with problems from the outset. The New York management, wanting the edition to be as uniform as possible with the New York paper, made little effort to expand local California coverage. Ideas filtered down from New York, instead of being initiated by the California staff, and the western edition became nothing more than a thin version of its New York counterpart. It was difficult for the New York executives to shake the notion that a New York story was of local, and not national, interest. In the western edition, New York still dominated.

Advertising and distribution problems added to the difficulties. The western edition never developed its own sales force. Though it attracted national ads, it couldn't get anywhere in the local market. Newspapers are preeminently a local medium, and the edition desperately needed the local merchants. But the advertisers wouldn't buy. The local *New York Times* sales representative felt hampered every step of the way. Even those local merchants who might have been willing to advertise were frightened away by what the New York sales rep thought were warnings from the *Los Angeles Times* that any ad appearing in the western edition would not appear in the *Los Angeles Times*.

All through 1963 the edition struggled to keep its head above water. An initial circulation of 100,000 fell within eight months to 71,000. In spite of a small upturn in the winter, the edition continued to lose money.

When the edition went $2 million in the red, the Sulzbergers decided to end the experiment, barely fifteen months after it began. Though they had made a large initial investment, the New York executives assumed that the edition could return a profit from its first day of operation. Without taking the substantial risk of loss of revenues for several years, the *New York Times* western edition never became anything but the ghost of competition.

To this day, many Angelenos attribute the changes in the *Los Angeles Times* to the *New York Times*'s move west. Publisher Chandler is particularly sensitive on the subject and whenever it comes up is quick to point out that the changes were already in the works well before the *New York Times* made its move. "We did nothing—and I repeat nothing," Otis angrily testified three years after the western edition had folded, "to change the *Times* or change the *Times* schedule or spend more money because the *New York Times* was coming." The whole matter of the timetable had become for Otis a point of honor. But for his editors and his staff, the edition had made a real difference.

3. Going National

The changeover meant new faces in Washington, Paris, Asia, and throughout the world, as well as in Los Angeles. The old Washington bureau, under the gruff and headstrong conservative, Bob Hartmann, immediately sensed trouble with the new regime.

The Los Angeles editors worried that the Hartmann bureau lacked the prestige and clout necessary to compete in Washington. Williams and his assistants in Los Angeles requested a new improved Washington bureau product, with greater emphasis on background and features.

The problem was compounded with the initiation of the *Washington Post/L.A. Times* news service. The *Post*, with its large home-based Washington staff, could easily outdo Hartmann's small operation. By late 1962 *Post* bylines from Washington started to appear within the *Los Angeles Times* on a regular basis. *Times* editors began to request more California-oriented stories from their own bureau to complement the *Post* material. Hartmann flew to Los Angeles to complain to the senior Chandlers, who told him to speak to their son. Otis at first wanted to fire Hartmann on the spot, but decided to give the bureau chief an out: a job at a new foreign bureau either in Bonn or Rome. Hartmann reluctantly chose Rome and brooded for three months. He missed Washington and was convinced there was no future in foreign coverage. After a thirty-year career, Bob Hartmann quit the paper and returned to his old haunts. Contacting an old congressional friend from Michigan, he signed on as Jerry Ford's assistant. Eleven years later Hartmann would follow his boss into the Oval Office of the White House.

With Hartmann gone, Nick Williams decided to approach one of the most respected journalists in Washington about the bureau chief opening. Williams spoke to Robert Donovan, one of the sharpest and most experienced correspondents then in Washington. With his expansive charm, the silver-haired Donovan could disarm the most cold-blooded sources. As head of the New York *Herald Tribune*'s Washington bureau, Donovan was a strong writer, who excelled in analytic and interpretive pieces about Washington and national and international affairs. He tended to be politically conservative, somewhat in the style of Walter Lippman. His greatest strength lay in his ability to bring together and give leadership to a loyal and energetic staff. Bob Donovan would be, if Williams succeeded in wooing him away from the *Tribune*, a major *Times* plum.

In the spring of 1963, the New York *Herald-Tribune* was in financial trouble and the Washington group tried to ignore the rumors about the *Tribune* going down. Williams, who knew the situation at the *Tribune*, asked if Donovan was interested in working for the *Times*. After some correspondence, Donovan began to consider the offer more seriously. Maybe, Donovan thought, he could bring New York journalistic ideals out to California.

For Donovan, New York ideals meant such concepts as "mixed file," "take outs," and "interpretive journalism," that is, writing in depth, with analysis, and with some attempt at explaining the whys and wherefore of an event. While this form of journalism was practiced by the New York papers, most newspapers around the country were still locked into the traditional wire-oriented standards of who, what, where, and how journalism. A change at the *Los Angeles Times* might have a significant impact on national journalism. The challenge appealed to Donovan. *Times* management discovered Donovan to be a tough and shrewd bargainer. The old pro insisted on complete freedom in selecting his own staff and running the bureau. He made a pitch for a "dream bureau," knowing full well that any such staff would be enormously expensive. But Donovan pushed hard and got the money he asked for—in amounts that took the breath away from old-timers who remembered the days of the hassle over carfare to the Ventura County Fair. Negotiations were completed by late fall.

Tripling the size of the bureau, Donovan organized an initial crew of nine. Donovan's appointment stirred the *Times* staff to great hopes. At last the *Times* had a nationally prominent group of reporters to bring attention to the paper.

Despite the whirlwind of change and activity at the paper, the spirit of the old *Times* was tenacious. The Old Guard had retreated, but looked for leadership from night managing editor Frank Haven. Haven, a big, lumbering man who began his career as sports editor of the *San Diego Sun*, came to the *Times* in 1941 as a copy editor. Antagonistic to the feisty brand of journalism Frank McCulloch represented, Haven was resilient enough to realize that his future lay with the feature-oriented journalism and daily newsmagazine framework that would soon come to dominate the *Times*.

In the early sixties Haven became the champion of the desk men, the news and copy editors who chopped up the stories that McCulloch's people handed in. The desk still had power. It wrote the headlines, edited copy and determined how a story would be played. It controlled all night operations. Haven and the desk men still set the overall tone of the paper.

The *Times* had become a two-way street; commited to change, but with a built-in force for counterrevolution. In between stood Nick Williams; a mediator and negotiator who maneuvered his paper between continuity and change. Each new journalistic event at the *Times* became a juggling act with different forces contending for power. Ironically, the news story that began it all, that put the question of change in focus, came right back to the family and its feuds.

4. The Birchers Are Coming

"On a wintry day a little over two years ago, a dozen men gathered in Indianapolis at the invitation of a retired Massachusetts candy manufacturer Robert Welch. . . .

"These men weren't exactly sure why they were there, except that they all shared the same concern over the menace of international communism, its influence in America and the fate of this nation.

"For two full days they listened to Robert Welch set forth his views of the problem and what he thought should be done about it. Out of that meeting of Dec. 8 and 9, 1958, came the John Birch Society."

With those words, written by reporter Gene Blake, the *Times* began, on March 5, 1961, a careful, controlled five-part report on the activities of the John Birch Society. Since their founding, the Birchers had mushroomed to a membership of several thousand in Southern California and a national membership of nearly 100,000. The JBS constituency included upper-class and upper-middle-class professionals and business executives, many of whom had been the backbone of the conservative tendency within the Republican party. Their politics had matured in the postwar period of McCarthyism and the Cold War and they identified locally with the antilabor, antiradical politics of William Knowland and the 1958 *Los Angeles Times*. The Birchers organized against what they considered communist infiltration in Hollywood, the schools, the church, the universities, and newspapers. JBS groups initiated letter-writing campaigns, circulated petitions, leafletted, and put direct pressure on business leaders to support their programs.

Times editor Nick Williams was one of those who felt the Bircher pressure. Williams, who disliked the heavy-handed anticommunism of the group, decided that the Bircher attack against the chief justice of the Supreme Court—the campaign to "impeach Earl Warren"—might be used to turn the pressure around. One day Williams approached the senior Chandlers, who were long-standing friends of the former California governor. The *Times* editor facetiously asked the Chandlers if they thought Earl Warren was a communist. "Earl Warren a communist," Norman Chandler exclaimed, "why that's the most ridiculous thing I ever heard."

The *Times* became a special target for Bircher pressure. "On three separate occasions in 1960–1961," Nick Williams wrote Santa Barbara publisher Tom Storke, "the *Los Angeles Times* became the target for a very heavy barrage of mail containing the same exhortation. The last of these barrages featured a demand for the impeachment of Chief Justice Warren. Earlier the barrages had demanded that Pres. Eisenhower not attend a summit conference scheduled with Khrushchev—and that if he did attend, that he not return; and that the *Times* keep any news of Khrushchev's visit to the U.N. off its front page, on the threat of subscription cancellations. With each barrage, the mail became more and more abusive, not only of the primary targets but of the *Times* itself."

With the issue building, Williams decided to do a profile of the society. He assigned the story to Gene Blake, an old-timer who had covered some of the top murder trials of the fifties. Blake was somewhat more liberal in outlook than most of the older staff, but Williams was more concerned that Blake, with his background as a courtroom reporter, could create the appearance of strict objectivity in the tone and style of the writing. No matter what Blake came up with, the *Times* editor knew it would be controversial.

Blake got hold of a copy of the society's *Blue Book*, a 182-page manual which outlined the group's political objectives and organizational goals, from another *Times* reporter. Dwight Eisenhower and Earl Warren were communist agents, the manual suggested, and even Dick Nixon came under suspicion. Welch's analysis of Communists in high places seemed extraordinarily paranoid to Gene Blake. Bircher anticommunism, calling for a renewed and highly organized McCarthyism, clashed with the conservative consensus of the Eisenhower years and the liberalism of the New Frontier. Blake was appalled at the Bircher perspective, but he was determined to maintain a fair and objective stance throughout his research. He contacted local Bircher leaders and arranged for their interviews. The JBS leadership was cooperative and hoped for favorable treatment from their old friend the *Times*. But Blake asked disturbing questions. The Birchers, recently subject to an attack which would win the *Santa Barbara News-Press* a Pulitzer, were wary about the changes taking place at the *Times*.

Having been burned in Santa Barbara, the Birchers held a special meeting of their National Council to make conditions for their cooperation with the *Times*. The Birchers asked to see Blake's material, but the *Times* reporter agreed to show the Birchers only those portions that contained direct quotations.

On Sunday, March 5, 1961, the first of Blake's five articles appeared, under the heading THE JOHN BIRCH SOCIETY: WHAT ARE ITS PURPOSES?

For all its controversy, the *Times* JBS series today reads like a cautious profile. The damage came from quotes of Bircher members and publications. Blake had no need to editorialize. Unlike many pre-1960 stories, the articles were careful to not take a position.

After the first article appeared, many rank-and-file Birchers called up the *Times*. "They were more confused than angry," Williams remembered, but by the third or fourth piece the unfriendly nature of the series became clear. Everyone wondered what the Chandlers would say and awaited the Sunday editorial.

Nick Williams selected chief editorial writer Kerby Ramsdell, a strong conservative who could criticize the Birchers from a conservative's perspective, to write the editorial. After Ramsdell finished a rough first draft, Williams, anticipating trouble from the family, cautiously approached his publisher, under whose by-line the editorial would appear. But Otis complained that it wasn't strong enough. A "tougher" editorial appeared with the publisher's blessing, on March 12, 1961, under the heading "Peril to Conservatives."

"With all honorable Americans," the editorial began, "this newspaper looks with disgust and dread upon the godless materialism and blood-soaked tyranny of the Communist conspiracy." The editorial went on to criticize the Bircher member "who abandons all the rules by which he has lived his decent life, and adopts instead the techniques and rules of conspiracy to fight Communists in Communist fashion? If the John Birchers follow the program of their leader, they will bring our institutions into question exactly as the Communists try to do. They will sow distrust, and aggravate disputes, and they will weaken the very strong case for conservatives. . . . The *Times* believes implicitly in the conservative philosophy . . . ," the editorial concluded. "But the *Times* does not believe that the argument for conservatism can be won—and we do believe it can be won—by smearing as enemies and traitors those with whom we sometimes disagree. Subversion, whether of the left or the right, is still subversion."

The editorial generated immediate and strong reactions. The *Times* was deluged with letters, phone calls, subscription cancellations, and various retaliatory threats from Bircher sympathizers. For the first time since the free speech case of 1941, the *Times* was applauded by liberals and moderates. Richard Nixon and the *New York Times* added their words of praise. But the Chandlers knew their historical constituency on the right was increasingly attracted to Bircher politics.

The problem was far from abstract for Nick Williams and Otis Chandler. As Gene Blake had discovered—and avoided in his articles—two of the most prominent Bircher members in Southern California were Philip Chandler, the executive vice-president of the Times Mirror Company and the number two man in the family hierarchy, and his wife, Alberta Williamson Chandler.

Philip and Alberta Chandler had become disenchanted with the *Times*. For more than two years they had been outmaneuevered in the family power shuffle by Dorothy Chandler. They mistrusted Otis Chandler and thought he lacked the ability to distinguish between right (conservative) and wrong (liberal/radicals). They felt the great historical traditions of the *Times* were being undermined by a politically leftward drift engineered by the crafty Nick Williams and radical Frank McCulloch. In their alienation, they became attracted to the politics of the John Birch Society. Their house in Pasadena was used for an invitation-only seminar for Robert Welch, and they aided the Bircher cause with all their clout. The Philip Chandlers were the most prestigious and powerful Bircher advocates in Los Angeles.

By the end of March, the Birchers threatened a systematic campaign of pressure against the *Times*, with special pressure on advertisers to withdraw their advertising. Otis and his parents had not expected the intensity of the attack. "My mail," Otis wrote, "continues to be explosive as well as staggering in quantity on the John Birch subject. When will it ever end?" *Times* management (also fearful that the society was preparing to file a lawsuit) became increasingly jittery as the ferocity of the campaign mounted, but Williams and McCulloch were convinced the pressure was bound to fail. "Where could the advertisers go?" McCulloch rhetorically asked. In a matter of days, most of the advertisers had come back. For every cancelled subscription, a new one appeared to take its place.

The most effective attack against the *Times* was the implication that the paper had failed to prescribe effective methods to fight communism as an alternative to Bircher methods. Maybe, several readers complained, the *Times* isn't really anti-communist after all?

The *Times* management scrambled for a position. In one column, Nick Williams suggested a "positive attitude" as an alternative—doing fine American activities, such as attending Kiwanis or church meetings, and voting for the person of your choice. "Shifting some of your money from repetitious political pamphlets to Girl Scout cookies will do more for your country," Williams advised.

Otis Chandler was a bit more defensive. "Putting aside for a moment the debate on what are the best means of successfully combatting communism," Otis wrote on March 19, "certainly one of the most salutary effects of our discussion of the John Birch Society was to cause public awareness of and awakening to the threat of communism everywhere."

To protect its anti-Communist flank, the *Times* over the next several days readopted its most militant and reactionary anti-Communist tone, reminiscent of the fifties. When the state Un-American Activities Committee issued a report soon after the Bircher series, the *Times* editorially offered a public thanks to the committee. "The report," the editorial concluded, "is an adequate answer to the clamor that un-American activities committees should be abolished, either at the state or national level. Until everybody can detect a Communist operative by his style or smell, such publishing committees will be necessary."

Anticommunism spread to the news pages as well. When Fred Schwartz and his Christian anti-Communist Crusade came to town for a giant rally at the Sports Arena and a week-long seminar on communism, his activities were extensively covered by the paper, and the Chandler TV station KTTV broadcast Schwartz's seminars live. After the broadcasts, Richfield Oil, which had sponsored the event, began to receive the patronage of the large anti-Communist constituency in Southern California, and for weeks Richfield gas stations had long lines of cars waiting to buy gas.

The family feud now focused on Philip Chandler's pro-Bircher position. At the November 29, 1961 board of director's meeting, the issue came to a head. Item #7 on the agenda, "Changes in Executive Responsibilities," called for Philip's resignation. The resolution passed without comment, and Philip Chandler walked out, never to return to a position within the company.

Otis Chandler's break with the Birchers was not strictly motivated by a defined political position. The *Times* publisher did not have a clear liberal perspective in 1961. Before the *Times* JBS series Otis wrote to Thomas Storke, publisher of the *Santa Barbara News-Press*, about problems with the society: "We are also getting a little fed up with the John Birch Society and their 'head in the sand' attitude toward modern day problems." "Head in the sand," "out of date," "unmodern" were all concepts more in line with Otis's critique of the Birchers than "totalitarian" or "extreme right wing" or "anti-Communist." Otis Chandler considered himself an anti-Communist conservative, though he was attracted to the feeling of "modernity" implicit in the mood of the New Frontier, its advocacy of youth, and reliance on technology to solve problems. The Birchers and most of the local power structure seemed wedded to an antimodern, antiyouth outlook. The JBS was one more example of the old image of Southern California, an image the new *Times* now wanted to counteract.

Ultimately, the most profound impact of the Bircher series was its effect on local journalists. "By God, when I saw that series, my eyes popped," reporter Don Neff recalled, "and I realized that this was going to be a serious newspaper."

Before the Bircher series, *Times* reporters had always anticipated management's right-wing politics. Now, the anticipatory writing and editing began to loosen up and some contradictory signals appeared. The greatest contradictions were caused by McCulloch, "the skinhead liberal," as some affectionately called him. McCulloch's most subversive idea was that the function of the newspaper was to report the news no matter where it might lead.

5. The Teamsters' Pension Fund

Frank McCulloch loved to probe, to sniff out stories that nobody else would touch. He knew Los Angeles was a town bursting with tales of power and corruption, but its newspapers never went after the big guys and crooks. The *Times* had always been far removed from the world of rough-and-tumble journalism, and, for such a large staff, had practically no experience in the ways of investigation.

McCulloch decided to experiment. He looked to Jack Tobin, a tough, feisty ex-marine, who had been a sportswriter and later city hall correspondent for the *Mirror*. When McCulloch came to the *Times*, Tobin abruptly left his city hall beat at the *Mirror* and came over as well.

"I want you to do something for me," McCulloch told Tobin one day. "Find out who owns the Santa Monica Mountains. I'll bet there's a story there somewhere." The Santa Monica Mountains were one of the few remaining low-density, unsubdivided areas within the city of Los Angeles. Recent speculative buying there mostly went through fictitious names or dummy corporations, and McCulloch suspected that something fishy was going on at the Planning Commission involving some recent zoning decisions.

"Where do I start?" Tobin asked his boss. "Is there anyone here who has experience searching real estate records?"

"You're on your own," McCulloch told his reporter. "Come back in three weeks and let me know what you've found." To spend three weeks on a story without any assurances that something would turn up was unprecedented at the *Times*. Tobin looked at his managing editor questioningly, but McCulloch insisted.

The former sportswriter went to the tax assessor's office, but he had little idea on how to proceed. "Grantees, grantors, it was all mumbo jumbo to me," Tobin recalled. With help from the county recorder's office, he learned to work his way methodically through ownership records. It was tedious and slow and after three weeks Tobin had little to show. "Keep on it," McCulloch advised.

One name, Gordon Campbell, continued to show up. Coincidentally, Tobin knew a Gordon Campbell, a former football coach, from his sportswriting days. He got together with his old contact to ask if he knew who owned the Santa Monica Mountains. "Funny thing, I've been trying to find that out myself for my clients," Campbell declared. He gave Tobin a list of every owner of every parcel of land in the Santa Monica Mountains. Working with one central list, Tobin, who had already plowed through thousands of real estate transactions, could compare names and single out any that seemed interesting. One company, Lantan Park, which went under various other names, was involved in dozens of transactions with a strange assortment of companies including one called the Central State Southeast/Southwest Pension Funds. Tobin thought that Central State might be a fund for retired teachers and wondered what a pension fund was doing buying land and making deals in the Santa Monica Mountains. Neither McCulloch nor anyone else at the *Times* had ever heard of this curious pension fund.

Looking through the microfiche at the assessor's office, Tobin discovered that in several loans, the principal trustee for the Central State fund on various deeds of trust was a certain James Riddle Hoffa. Tobin rushed back to the *Times* .

"Do you know Jimmy Hoffa's middle name," he asked the *Times* labor editor.

"Isn't it James R. Hoffa?" the editor replied.

"But what does the R. stand for?" Tobin asked, his excitement mounting.

Neither the labor writer nor the *Times* morgue had an answer. Finally, Washington bureau chief Bob Hartmann, after three days of searching, informed Tobin that the R. stood for Riddle.

Back at the county recorder's office Tobin copied down the names of the trustees from the deeds of trust of the Pension Fund. "Why those are mob names," one of the reporters told Tobin. There were names from the Kefauver investigations, names from news articles, names of organized crime figures from Los Angeles and throughout the country. The more Tobin probed the more he learned of a whole new world: kickbacks, finder's fees, and the laundering of funds.

At this point, McCulloch assigned Gene Blake to work with Tobin. With Blake's background in legal reporting and Tobin's newly discovered investigative skills, the two reporters became an effective team and began to compile a massive dossier on the use of the Teamster Pension Funds as a major conduit for the circulation of organized crime money. At one point Tobin drew up a memo containing eighty-five different story leads. One connection led to another with the Southeast/Southwest Pension Fund at the center of the web.

The first story broke on May 10, 1962. Tobin and Blake had interviewed Jimmy Hoffa on the phone for their first article. When the *Times* reporters asked the Teamster president about his relations with organized crime figure Moe Dalitz, Hoffa exploded, "Moe Dalitz is a respected citizen," he snapped at Tobin and Blake and abruptly terminated the interview. "I'm not going to talk any more about individuals," Hoffa said. "I'm not giving you any information for the grand jury."

While Tobin and Blake were unravelling their story, Attorney General Bobby Kennedy had convened a Federal grand jury to probe the affairs of the Teamster Pension Fund. In early 1962 while passing through Los Angeles, Kennedy was invited to a *Times* cocktail gathering with high *Times* executives. Frank McCulloch, unaware of the Justice Department investigation, approached the attorney general, and told him what the *Times* had uncovered. Kennedy, anxious about pretrial publicity, blew up. McCulloch went ahead and ran the series anyway, and used the grand jury probe to open the story.

Several stories—thirty in all—ran over the next fifteen months; the information seemed inexhaustible. Each story produced new leads and new information. McCulloch insisted that Blake and Tobin continue to probe and to produce. "I wanted to show that the *Times* was committed to this

kind of journalism and that it could happen here," McCulloch commented several years later.

Not everyone at the *Times* backed the investigations. Nick Williams
was confused and bored with the series, and night managing editor Frank
Haven was hostile to the whole idea. There was constant pressure to limit
or end the investigation. Haven, complaining that the paper was short on
staff, put Blake and Tobin back into the general assignment pool. When
the two reporters protested to McCulloch, he blew up and demanded they
get back on the Teamster Pension Fund story.

The *Times* management, aware of how much money was being spent,
finally put its foot down. In August 1963, when Tobin and Blake asked to
go to Miami to explore some of the Miami connections, they were refused
permission. This time Williams was firm: "The series is off," he told
McCulloch. "It's over." Defiant to the end, McCulloch ran three more
pieces from information which had already been gathered.

Though Blake and McCulloch speculated about outside pressure, for
Nick Williams, the termination of the story was a matter of journalistic
taste. The series, according to the *Times* editor, had gone on too long, was
no longer being read, and was not the kind of journalism with which he
felt comfortable.

Jack Tobin was furious about the decisions. The Florida connection
was leading straight towards LBJ's aide Bobby Baker and the biggest corruption story of the early sixties.

McCulloch tried to keep the spirits up and talked about training other
Times reporters to do the same kinds of investigations, but that idea was
vetoed as well. Tobin was sure that McCulloch's days were numbered.
Tobin himself was too impatient to wait for the end to come, so he quit,
telling McCulloch, "it won't be long before you'll be out, too."

When the attorney general's case against Jimmy Hoffa finally came to
trial in 1964, Blake's request to cover the proceeding was turned down. It
was a bitter irony to see the AP wire stories on the trial demonstrate how
the Blake/Tobin series, then more than a year old, had paralleled the attorney general's case. When Hoffa was finally convicted, Blake wrote a
sidebar on the Tobin/Blake stories and their role in the Hoffa affair, a bit-
tersweet reminder of the *Times* breakthrough in investigative reporting.

6. Civil Rights

Early in 1963, Frank McCulloch initiated two lengthy series on Mexican-Americans and blacks, written respectively by Ruben Salazar and
Paul Weeks. "It was a very significant set of articles," Weeks recalled.
"McCulloch had recognized that Northern cities should look in their
backyard rather than just covering the South. To me, the articles repre-

sented the new *Los Angeles Times*, a paper that gave me the free reign to go out and do the work for a story; the biggest story, I think, of the decade.''

Until the Weeks series, the *Times* had steered clear of any substantial coverage of the black community. "We were," Otis Chandler admitted in later years," a WASP paper." The *Times* still had no black reporters.

By 1960 it was getting a little difficult to avoid the issue. The black population in Los Angeles had mushroomed during and after World War II, and whole cities and communities, such as Watts and Compton had become predominantly black. During the periodic slumps of the late forties and fifties, the blacks were the first to enter the ranks of the unemployed. The collapse of the rail transit system in those years further exacerbated living conditions in the black communities.

Despite their numerous grievances, Los Angeles's black neighborhoods remained invisible communities for the *Times*.

One of the first groups to capture the community's frustrations was the Black Muslims. The Muslims created a powerful social identity involving black pride and nationalist rhetoric. The Muslim's critique of police intimidation of blacks immediately brought them into conflict with the LAPD. The *Times* backed the police department and denied the Muslim claim that racial motivations inspired police actions.

One day in late April 1962, a policeman stopped a black man outside of Muslim headquarters. Within moments, dozens of police had surrounded the building and raided the Muslim center with guns drawn. One Muslim was killed and eight other people, including two policemen, were wounded. " MUSLIMS RIOT : CULTIST KILLED , POLICEMAN SHOT ," ran the next day's *Times* headline in a page one spread. The Muslims were described as an "anti-white, anti-integration, anti-Christian cult which preaches 'without struggle there is no progress.' . . . " References to the Muslim dress style appeared in following editions of the paper. The repeated allusions to Muslim dress symbolized the nature of *Times* analysis of the organization as an alien and irrational cult. The *Times* stories ignored the widespread criticism of the police within the black community and, instead, focused on the Muslims as a hostile target for the next several days.

Important early civil rights events such as the February 2, 1960 action at the Woolworth's segregated lunch counter in Greenville, South Carolina—the first of the sit-ins—were not covered in the *Times*. But Frank McCulloch began to seek out ways to initiate coverage and saw his first major opportunity when Paul Weeks joined the *Times* in 1962.

Weeks had worked for the *Los Angeles Daily News* from 1946 to the day it folded in December 1954. He used to joke that it would be "the coldest day ever, the day I work for the Chandlers. Sure enough," Weeks laughed, "the day the *News* folded was the coldest day I could ever recall." Weeks was hired by the *Mirror*, and immediately hit it off with managing editor Ed Murray, who encouraged Weeks to do a series on the black community in 1955. When Murray was forced out in 1960, a despondent Weeks waited for the *Mirror* to die. Weeks was then picked up by the once-dreaded *Los Angeles Times*. He started out in the general assignment pool, but Frank McCulloch soon approached him about beginning a civil rights beat. Weeks happily accepted.

At first Weeks's contacts in the black community were sceptical. "There has never been any black coverage in the *Times*," they told him cautiously, but gradually they loosened up and started passing on some information. The picture they drew was of an economically depressed community seething with anger on the verge of a confrontation. Weeks described the situation to his superiors in a memo in 1963 and told them that a riot seemed likely. He never heard a word about it.

Weeks's coverage had its limits. Dealing with the civil rights movement at its most visible level, the *Times* reporter's contacts were the leaders of the established community organizations, not the people on the street. His reporting did not reach into the life of the community itself. "Coverage of hard-core problems was not available to me," Weeks recalled, "nor to any of the [white] daily newspapers at that time." In the eyes of the black community, the *Times* was the white establishment paper. Even as late as 1969 an academic survey found the *Times* the least trusted news medium in Los Angeles among blacks. The paper ranked lower than radio, television, and Hearst's *Herald-Examiner* .

Much of the information in Weeks' seminal 1963 series was not taken fully to heart by the *Times* editorial board. Simultaneous with Weeks's news stories, the paper ran editorials on various civil rights subjects. Though there was support for some of the goals of the moderate civil rights organizations such as the NAACP, the editorial board differed on significant specifics. For example, while Weeks wrote that "fair housing is of paramount importance" among blacks, the *Times* editorial board attacked the fair housing concept, warning of "the formidable dangers inherent in forced social reform at the expense of Constitutional integrity."

Many of the staff writers and editors at the *Times* shared Police Chief William Parker's feelings that "In overall race relations this community has done a magnificent job. We're afraid to tell the truth because it would prove this is the Garden of Eden." Some *Times* men displayed explicitly racist sentiments.

Weeks, who had rather tenuous relations with some of the higher editors beside McCulloch, was himself subject to harassment. In retrospect he minimizes his differences with the *Times* management. "You have to realize the context for all of this," Weeks said twelve years later. "The

Times today is a great newspaper, and these incidents are minimal when you look at the way the paper changed.''

By the summer of 1964, the first of the ''long hot summers,'' the *Times* had still not hired any black reporters, and McCulloch was gone. Weeks's coverage was redefined. He was assigned to the War on Poverty beat—an important story involving power struggles over control of federal funds—but the redefinition also meant the end of the civil rights beat. The *Times* management explained that it had to be dropped since the amount of coverage that Weeks had given civil rights was out of proportion.

Paul Weeks continued to get shuttled around at the *Times*. On August 9, 1965 he began his vacation. Two days later, at 7 P.M., a man was arrested on the corner of 103rd Street and Avalon Boulevard in the black community of south central Los Angeles. The incident escalated. The Watts Riots (or Watts Rebellion, as many in the black community called it) had begun.

The events in Watts would be a turning point for the *Times*. A changeover in the paper had begun, but it was change in fits and starts; one step forward and a stutter-step back. The dynamic at the paper was unclear; nobody quite knew just who was motivating whom. Had the Chandlers changed, or had events around them forced the issue?

CHAPTER 21

Many Monopolies

1. The Company Reaches Out

"Performance" and "visibility" were words that began to be heard by 1960 in the elevators and conference rooms, planning sessions and bull sessions, of the old gray building on Spring Street. They were the words of a new business era that thrived on expansion and had a passion for diversification. It was the beginning of the "go-go" decade, when the stock market climbed beyond the 1,000 mark; when small, obscure holding companies went after some of the largest and most distinguished industrial and financial corporations in the country; when the word "conglomerate" shook the foundations of Wall Street; and when the "get-rich-quick" strategy seemed to seize and feed the speculative spirit of the business entrepreneur. It was a decade that even affected the conservative Chandlers and witnessed the beginning of the end of the family-run newspaper in America.

McKinsey and Company had come, with their bright young executives eager to put Times Mirror on the corporate map. The Times Mirror McKinsey group was headed up by Jack Vance, an ambitious man, who was aggressive and pointed in his suggestions. Vance had Dorothy Chandler's backing, and with that security in hand, McKinsey was free to roam and pry into the affairs of the company, its management structure, the family holding companies, and even the individual portfolios of the various Chandlers.

Management consultants are not specialists as such—a group like McKinsey, for example, had few people with any large degree of expertise in the newspaper and banking fields—but they help size up a company's overall corporate performance, and make suggestions about its future directions. Often enough a consultant will apply fashionable concepts which are also likely to favor the needs of the people who hired them. From Dorothy and Norman Chandler's perspective, Times Mirror needed restructuring, partly to eliminate the potential and actual power of the Philip Chandler branch of the family, and partly to adopt to modern conditions and contemporary settings. By 1960 several old-line families, such as the Duponts and the Mellons, ran modern streamlined corporations which had high profit margins. The Chandlers had no intention of missing out. McKinsey was given the go-ahead to come up with plans to transform Times Mirror into a modern corporation.

The first step was to go public. In order to do so, a company needed to meet several specific requirements of the Securities and Exchange Commission. A public corporation needed outside directors—that is, people not connected to the company either in a management capacity or as major stockholders. Times Mirror already had a few outside directors—local bankers Harry Volk and Frank King—even before the McKinsey people arrived on the scene. A company also has to have a listing on a stock exchange and must subscribe to the rules of the SEC.

Going public enables a company to raise fresh capital by issuing new stock, and using that capital (and shares of company stock) to expand operations. Company assets increase as well as the value of the stock, giving the major stockholders a greater return on their investment in spite of a percentage reduction of their ownership of the company.

In 1960, Times Mirror was a privately held family-controlled corporation with the Chandler trusts controlling upwards of 60 percent of the stock. Many of the 1,700 stockholders were family relations, friends, or company personnel. Since the issuing of new stock could lower the percentage of stock controlled by the family under 50 percent, several family members argued against it. The divisions over the future direction for the company paralleled the family's political disputes. In this case the majority faction led by Dorothy Chandler was bolstered by McKinsey statistics. Family stock ownership could go as low as 25 percent, the family's advisors argued—50 percent was by no means a magic figure. If no single buyer emerged, the Chandler stock control would not be challenged.

The idea of greater dividends and more profits ultimately prevailed. In the winter of 1960 nearly six million new shares of Times Mirror stock were issued with 1.9 million shares held back for trading purposes. On May 27, 1964, five years after the McKinsey consultants had been hired, Times Mirror got its listing on the Big Board of the New York Stock Exchange. It was the first family newspaper company to go public. "The secret to success in expansive diversification," Norman Chandler, proudly standing on the floor of the exchange, was quoted that day, "is in advance planning and strong management. We worked closely with our accountants and management consultants in planning our program and have selected effective top executives."

The Times Mirror company had become a lot more than a prosperous newspaper. It had become a diversified corporate complex, a "synergistic company," as its managers called it in reference to "related diversification" instead of the unconnected buying of the conglomerates. Company officials argued forcefully that Times Mirror was a "communications company," with each new purchase having some relation to the whole.

Those first few years of expansion, however, put a strong accent on the diversification rather than the relatedness. Charles "Tex" Thornton, the whiz kid of Litton Industries—one of the first conglomerates—was brought onto the Times Mirror board in 1968, where he immediately took an important part in company decisions. McKinsey had consulted Litton in its expansion program and Thornton and Vance had a close working relationship. Though the framework for expansion had already been set in motion by what later came to be called *The McKinsey Report*, Thornton and Vance, along with Norman and Buff, worked out the guidelines for many of the suggestions adopted by the Board.

There were two key features to the McKinsey Report. Inspired by the opportunity to explore corporate management and the line of succession, McKinsey advocated bringing in a score of new high-level executives to guide the company through its expansion phase. As the company grew, new management slots had to be created in such areas as subsidiaries, heads of new divisions, and assistants in charge of acquisitions. Several new corporate personnel were hired through McKinsey recommendations and McKinsey people were placed in important advisory posts in the new subsidiaries and divisions. The heart of the corporate overhaul was an "acquisitions committee," which made decisions as to what companies Times Mirror ought to pursue. The committee included the three senior Chandler brothers—Norman, Philip, and Harrison; two old-time company officials, Dick Adams and Omar Johnson; Dorothy Chandler, who worked with the staff concerning questions of company "image"; and Robert Allan, Jr., hired on a McKinsey recommendation, who held the title "assistant to the President."

Allan, a former vice-president of an electrical switch gear company, did the legwork. He traveled around the country to seek out new properties for possible purchase. He had a great deal of leeway and could take his mandate in any one of a number of directions, though he still had to report to and implement the decisions of the majority stockholders.

The McKinsey Report's most important recommendation was to lessen the overall percentage of assets within the company which were dependent on newspapers. In 1960 the *Times* and the *Mirror* accounted for 75 percent of the company's assets—The *Times* alone responsible for 64 percent of the total assets and an even higher percentage of the company's profits. The report concluded that by 1980 Times Mirror newspaper holdings should account for no more than 25 percent of company assets. McKinsey, arguing that newspapers were not a growth industry, advised against any more newspaper purchases. "We set up a policy to bring in outside income not from newspapers," Robert Allan later wrote. "We felt in the long run that newspapers would have increased costs due to paper (timber), delivery problems and competition from TV or other new electronic news media."

The McKinsey people felt that the newspaper business in 1960 was in serious trouble. Most major dailies were either family-run newspapers or part of national chains like the Knight or Gannett organizations. The family paper was beset with problems over the line of succession and the rising capital outlays for new technological advances in the industry. Top-level executives were drawn from within family ranks and the second or third generation of publishers were frequently ill-equipped to deal with the economic and editorial complexities of their business. Nor was cash readily available to pay for the new plant machinery required by the shift in technology to offset production.

Newspapers were constantly dying and competition from television affected newspaper revenues. Whether the newspaper business could successfully readjust itself was unclear and it seemed like a risky investment to the McKinseyites. But Otis Chandler wanted to be a great newspaper publisher and was proud of the *Times*'s economic performance, even though the Chandlers' second paper was in financial trouble. The economic situation of the *Times*—and the *Mirror*—remained of central concern to the Chandlers, no matter how intriguing questions of diversification might be.

2. *"A Big Deal"*

At 11 A.M. on January 5, 1962, NormanChandler called together the staff of the *Los Angeles Mirror* . With tears in his eyes, Chandler told his employees that their paper would cease publication that day. "The *Mirror* was my dream," he said to the assembled workers, "but, unfortunately, the economics have proved to be such that my original concept has not worked out." That same day, the *Los Angeles Examiner* closed its doors, more than fifty years after a giant labor parade marched through the streets of Los Angeles to celebrate the first issue of the new paper. In one day Los Angeles's newspaper population had been cut in half; four competitors replaced by two monopolies—the morning *Times* and Hearst's afternoon *Herald-Examiner*.

By 1957 the Chandlers had decided that the *Mirror* no longer served their interests, and they began to bargain with Hearst. Within several months Otis Chandler issued a memorandum outlining various options the company could take: combining the *Times* and the *Mirror* into an all-day publication; folding the *Mirror* all together; or continuing the *Mirror* operation with its (tax-deductible) losses, to "keep Hearst off balance" and "singe the *Herald-Express*, or at least force an *Examiner/Herald-Express* combination."

The *Times* executives felt that the most advantageous deal would be to shut down the *Mirror* if the more profitable of the two Hearst papers, the *Examiner*, folded as well. Such a situation, *Times* treasurer Milton Day analyzed in 1960, "would load the whole future circulation pattern very heavily in favor of the *Times* morning and Sunday and probably, rather than increase competition in Los Angeles, would place the *Times* in such a dominant position that both the evening and Sunday Hearst papers would be in a very difficult competitive position."

The local Hearst newspaper executives were strongly opposed to any such deal. They felt it was a "bad deal" and would inevitably lead to *Times* monopoly. Morning papers always received the giant's share of classified advertising and are generally considered the prestige paper in town. To fold the *Examiner*, Hearst executives reasoned, would be like giving up the fight before even starting.

But by 1960 the pressure was on. Franklin Payne, the publisher of the *Examiner*, wrote to a high Hearst official in New York: "I have repeatedly said that the merchants in Los Angeles cannot and will not support four daily Los Angeles newspapers. . . . I am beginning to wonder," Payne wrote about the advertisers," if they can and will support more than two Los Angeles newspapers."

Killing newspapers was an old practice of the Hearst organization. In the 1920s Hearst shut down a number of his papers in order to reorganize his assets and juggle the market. The privately-held company, which included several newspapers and syndicated features, a magazine, and newsprint, book publishing, and real estate divisions, was still run by the Hearst family with some outside corporate managers. As a national organization, the Hearst empire demonstrated little or no loyalty to the needs of the communities its newspapers served, and every local editor and publisher still reported to the Hearst brothers and corporate headquarters. By 1961, with the local Los Angeles advertisers boxed into the corner and the Hearst organization about to embark on a major newspaper liquidation program, Payne's prediction was ready to come true.

Between 1957 and 1961 the Chandlers made several different offers to the Hearst organization, including the purchase of the evening *Herald-Express* for the figure of $5 million, and the simultaneous cessation of the *Mirror* and the *Examiner*. The latter proposal was Chandler's maximum option. By eliminating the *Examiner*, the Chandlers would achieve a morning monopoly, be rid of the stronger of the two Hearst papers, and shut down its own big loser the *Mirror*. By the fall of 1961 Hearst was willing to go along with Chandler's maximum and his own bottom line. One problem remained: to fold the *Mirror* and the *Examiner* simultaneously was a violation of the anti-trust laws which forbid two companies from knowingly engaging in actions designed to lessen competition. Hearst lawyer, James McInerney, was dispatched to see what he could do with the Justice Department.

On October 19, 1961, McInerney sent a letter to Attorney General Bobby Kennedy arguing that both the *Mirror* and the *Examiner* were "failing corporations" and ought to be exempted from antitrust regulation, so that they might terminate operations. About two weeks later an official from the Justice Department called back and told the Hearst lawyer the department could not legally approve the deal.

McInerney went to Washington and set up a meeting with Lee Loevinger, an attorney with the antitrust division of the Justice Department. Once again McInerney outlined his plans, but he didn't convince Loevinger, who saw the situation as two companies insuring themselves "against the possibility of somebody else coming in and buying up the failing ventures and thus providing competition." After McInerney argued that the Hearst company could lose a million dollars without such permission, Loevinger asked to see all the figures and facts in writing. McInerney replied that it would take too long to meet such a request and that the timing was crucial. The two lawyers reached an impasse.

Then Loevinger spoke up and casually mentioned that each corporation, if it had an unprofitable subsidiary, could "simply drop the unprofitable venture." McInerney likely saw in the remark a wink of the eye. Neither lawyer brought up the question of simultaneity, nor whether written permission from the Justice Department was needed, though such permission was standard operating procedure. The meeting had lasted only five minutes, but McInerney was convinced that Hearst and Chandler had their go ahead. A month later the *Mirror* and the *Examiner* closed their doors.

The day of the failure Congressman Emanuel Celler of the House Judiciary Committee issued a statement that the joint actions "exaggerate the most dangerous trend in this country: namely the curtailment of news communication." A UCLA study of audience reaction detected a great deal of dissatisfaction, not so much for the loss of those two particular papers but because of the concern over lack of competition. Pressure on Congress and the Justice Department led both bodies to undertake inquiries into the matter. A Congressional hearing began in 1963 and most of the congresspeople went out of their way to be friendly to the politically powerful newspaper publishers. Chairman of the antitrust committee, Democrat Emanuel Celler, contradicting earlier statements, commented toward the end of the hearings: "I don't like to see the law enforced just for the sake of enforcing the law and thereby create inequities and create wrong." Celler argued that though the Chandler/Hearst action was a technical violation of the law, it ought to be overlooked. The survival of a Hearst paper, according to the Judiciary chairman, was the ultimate criteria of fairness—a judgement made in the context of the still enormous political power of the Hearst press and its influence Election Day. The hearings ended without resolution. If anything, Congress was more willing to exempt newspapers from antitrust laws, a process which eventually culminated in the Failing Newspaper Act legislation of 1970.

While the failure of the two papers was a blessing for the *Times* —for the Hearst organization it was all downhill. Many of the best reporters from the *Examiner* went over to the *Times*. The *Herald-Express* had always been the shabbier of the two Hearst papers, and the combination somehow seemed to bring out the worst of each paper. Most important, the afternoon paper in the freeway-oriented suburbanized Los Angeles was not an attractive investment for the advertisers who strongly preferred the morning field with its home-delivery system and pinpoint demographics.

The Hearst motivation behind the agreement remains obscure. The Hearst organization did have other options. They could have maintained their two newspapers and attempted to upgrade their product. The Hearst papers were still committed to the traditions of Red-baiting and sensationalism, and the new *Herald-Examiner* occupied the worst of all Hearstian worlds. While the *Times* improved, the *Herald-Examiner* degenerated and frequently made the ten worst newspapers list. And Hearst continued to lose money on his paper.

The most significant option for Hearst would have been to sell either or both of his papers to another organization. New ownership might have led to an infusion of cash and editorial energy which, in turn, might have caused a serious challenge to *Times* dominance. But Hearst wasn't interested, and to this day persistent rumors circulate—though they've never been proved—which suggest a Chandler payoff of $1.3 million, Hearst's severance costs. Whatever the methods, the Chandlers had achieved monopoly status for their paper.

3. Supercity Monopoly

Otis Chandler's disagreements with Bob Allan and McKinsey about future purchases of newspaper properties formed the major conflict within Times Mirror in the early sixties. Otis complained that the McKinsey people didn't know the newspaper business the way the Chandlers did, and he insisted that Times Mirror management explore the possibility of acquiring other newspapers.

By 1960 and 1961 the success of the local suburban newspaper had come to the attention of conglomerators and newspaper owners alike. Southern California was an ideal location for such enterprises with its weak downtown and strong outlying suburban communities, which comprised the bulk of the three-county population. The department stores had helped the trend by setting up chain stores throughout the region and then advertising through the local press at rates often higher than the downtown dailies. The store owners felt that pinpoint advertising was more effective than the broader reach of the larger papers. Inadvertently, the merchants subsidized the smaller papers. There were more than seventy-five incorporated cities in the Southern California Basin and, thanks to the growth of the chains, many of the areas supported their own daily or weekly papers.

The Chandlers had always toyed with the notion of the Southern California basin as a supercity extending from Santa Barbara to San Diego. Until the sixties, the *Times* had run a page spread called "The Southland" which included news throughout the basin. As pinpoint advertising spread, the Chandlers tried their hand at zone editions—once- or twice-a-week inserts with local community news and a lot of ads. The zones were set up as an advertising medium, and never dealt with the problem of how to cover effectively the news in the townships and cities throughout the basin. Markets, not news coverage, concerned the corporate officials. Eventually, the *Times* had to contend with the suburban newspaper's competition for ads. The idea took root that the way to sew up markets was to expand into suburbia by buying up its newspapers. Acquisition executive Allan was given specific instructions to systematically inquire as to the availability of dozens of suburban papers in Southern California. A strategy emerged: the most effective purchase was the acquisition of a suburban monopoly. As Norman Chandler would later testify, each of these papers "had—well, in their respective markets they had what you might call a monopoly."

Allan got a fix on the *Santa Barbara News-Press* , the *Riverside Press-Enterprise*, the *Bakersfield Californian*, the *San Clemente Sun-Post*, the *Laguna Beach South Coast News* as well as papers in Pomona, Oxnard, and La Habra. Most of the papers' owners were not interested in selling, and resisted Times Mirror offers. But a few had second thoughts.

In 1961 Times Mirror made an offer for the Newport Beach and Costa Mesa *Globe Herald* and *Daily Pilot* which served the coastal and inland areas of western Orange County, near the Irvine Ranch. That winter, the Chandlers heard rumors that one of the national newspaper chains had also tendered an offer. Otis wrote to the publisher of the *Daily Pilot* and suggested that if they wanted to sell, they ought to keep the property in local hands. Times Mirror, after all, was mainstream Southern California. The plea worked; in January 1962 Times Mirror completed the purchase of the Orange County paper for $2.1 million, renaming it the *Orange Coast Daily Pilot*. Times Mirror had its suburban entry.

The biggest paper on the eastern rim of the basin was the *San Bernardino Sun*. The *Sun* was owned by the Guthries, one of the most powerful families in the San Bernadino/Riverside area. James K. Guthrie, the *Sun*'s publisher, was nearing ninety years old when the *Times* made its first offer to buy in 1961. The Guthries and Chandlers had been friendly for a number of years, and both families shared the booster ideology and expansionist goals for Southern California. The Chandlers had allowed the *Sun* to use a number of *Times* features over the years, though the *Times* normally exerted a strict control over their syndication rights.

The elder Guthrie was ready to retire and sell off his family interest. He wanted a favorable tax exchange to help his family's economic position with inheritance taxes after he died. Guthrie also wanted to avoid the possibility of family squabbles developing over control of the paper. His son-in-law (and major stockholder) John Lonergan agreed with the old man's estimate and wanted to explore all possible bids. Lonergan sought out a number of companies besides Times Mirror, including many out-of-state buyers, and weighed each offer carefully. Though Guthrie had sentimental ties to the Chandlers, Lonergan wanted the best deal.

The *Sun*, including both a morning and an afternoon paper in one of the major cities in the basin, was an attractive buy. The company yielded a 1962 profit of $483,000 and more than double that in 1964. After their first offer, Times Mirror executives continued to talk off and on with Guthrie and finally in 1964 came up with their strongest bid: $12.5 million.

But it wasn't strong enough. In the last week of May, the Pulitzer Company of St. Louis, publishers of a chain of newspapers including the *St. Louis Post-Dispatch*, offered the Guthries $15 million for the *Sun*. Their formal offer came on June 19 and the deal was to be consummated on Thursday, June 25. The elder Guthrie told his son to get on the Chandlers' tail, that the time to talk business was now, for in a few days it would be too late. On Saturday the twentieth, Guthrie's son Jimmy, who was a friend of Otis Chandler, called the *Times* publisher and told him: "If you are going to do something, you're going to have to do it [now]."

The next day, Otis, Norman, and Times Mirror lawyer Robert Erburu, took a Sunday drive out to San Bernardino. The Guthries told them that an equivalent offer had to be made then and there. The three Times Mirror men agreed and the papers were quickly drawn. The Chandlers proceeded without any authorization from their board of directors to match the Pulitzer offer. The deal was closed on Thursday, June 25, the day the Pulitzers were supposed to come to town.

This time the anti-trust division of the Justice Department took action. On March 5, 1965 the Justice Department, citing several sections of the Clayton and Sherman anti-trust laws, brought suit against Times Mirror, forbidding future newspaper purchases in the region and demanding that Times Mirror divest itself of the *Sun*.

The Justice Department suit contended that the *Sun* purchase diminished competition for advertising in the region, created a tendency toward higher ad rates, and lessened circulation competition. The Times Mirror defense, headed by Gibson, Dunn and Crutcher's senior partner Julian Van Kalinowski, argued that newspapers' real competition was radio and television and that further, whoever happened to own the newspaper made little difference as to its actual content.

On October 11, 1967, more than two years after the Justice Department had initiated suit, Federal Judge Warren B. Ferguson handed down his ruling. Ferguson noted that Guthrie's decision to sell was based on his friendship with Chandler and the Chandler economic relationship to San Bernardino County—Norman Chandler was on the board of directors of Kaiser Steel, the Sante Fe Railroad, and Safeway Stores, three of the largest corporations in the county—and that the effect of the sale was to further increase the tendency in Greater Los Angeles toward chain ownership of newspapers. The Judge concluded that the *Sun* purchase was a violation of Section 7 of the Clayton Antitrust act and ordered Times Mirror to divest itself of the company. The government's request to forbid further newspaper purchase by Times Mirror in Southern California was denied, but the effect of the ruling discouraged the Chandler super-city strategy. Times Mirror appealed the ruling to the Supreme Court, but in June 1968 the high court affirmed the decision. On December 10, 1968 Times Mirror made initial agreement with the Gannett newspaper chain to sell the *Sun* for $17,700,000, for a profit of more than $2.5 million. Times Mirror newspaper purchases were temporarily halted.

4. The Comprehensive Publisher

In those early hectic years of Times Mirror expansion, books, maps, slide rules, forest lands, and more all fell under the Times Mirror mantle. It all began in 1960, year one of Times Mirror diversification, when a couple of middle-brow book publishers, who couldn't stand each other, found a way to make a lot of money.

Kurt Enoch is a wiry man who grew up in the book business. His father owned several book and distribution companies in Weimar, Germany and Enoch became their general manager. After Hitler came to power, Enoch, a Jew, fled to France. He eventually came over to the United States in 1942, where he joined the American division of Penguin Books. He soon acquired a 40 percent interest in the American affiliate. With his background and training, he concerned himself with the business side, leaving editorial decisions to London.

The editor-in-chief of the American branch of Penguin was Victor Weybright, who had served with the U.S. Office of War Information in London during World War II. While in England, he came into contact with Allen Lane, the head of Penguin Books, who put him in charge of Penguin's American division. When Weybright arrived in New York he met Enoch and, as the *Wall Street Journal* put it, "began an association of mutual hostility that lasted for years." Enoch, the business operator, and Weybright, the would-be member of the literati, detested each other with a real passion, but an even stronger bond kept them together: their love of money and success.

Both Enoch and Weybright wanted independence and big profits. In 1947 they left Penguin to become joint owners and operators of a new company they called the New American Library (NAL). The company successfully established a large paperback market through its Mickey Spillane series and Ian Fleming's James Bond best-sellers. By 1960, NAL had become the second largest paperback house in the country.

But the more money the copublishers made, the more problems they ran into. NAL was a private corporation subject to a number of taxes Enoch and Weybright hoped to avoid. They approached an investment counselor who suggested that NAL merge with an existing company to solve the tax problems and provide a nice financial payoff for the NAL publishers. The counselor had been doing some business with Times Mirror and knew of the McKinsey Report and the upcoming diversification plans at Times Mirror. He suggested Enoch and Weybright explore the possibility of a deal.

The two publishers were soon off to Los Angeles. They met the Chandlers and were charmed by Norman and Buff. Conditions for a merger were discussed and the McKinsey group and Bob Allan were brought in to look over the company's books and performance. McKinsey was also satisfied. On June 2, 1960, merger terms were announced: Times Mirror would acquire New American Library in exchange for 416,000 shares of Times Mirror stock to be divided by Enoch and Weybright. It was the first big deal of the new regime at Times Mirror, and it made the business world take note.

The New American Library deal represented the first time a publishing house had been purchased by a company outside the publishing field. With the NAL purchase, Times Mirror executives began their expansion drive. McKinsey developed criteria to be used for future purchases in publishing which included how commercial and profitable was the publisher's backlist, whether there was a logic behind the company's line of products, and how it controlled distribution and costs. McKinsey had its own man in New York to evaluate publishing properties for possible Times Mirror bids. Within the year, the company picked up Four Aces Ltd., an English paperback house. Four Aces' name was changed to the New English Library and its operations were tied into the new publishing division of Times Mirror presided over by Enoch and Weybright.

In 1963 Times Mirror executives made their biggest move in purchasing World Publishing Company of Cleveland, Ohio, a major publisher of dictionaries and bibles with a trade list based in New York. The company was run by Ben Zevin, a specialist in the bible field. Zevin and his vice-president Bill Targ wanted World to remain in Cleveland, but Enoch wanted the entire operation to come to New York to integrate with NAL into a single "comprehensive publisher" of both cloth and paperback books. Enoch's ideas fit nicely into Jack Vance's notion of the integrated "synergistic" company with linkage of subsidiaries and assets. Enoch by now had become the favorite of the executives in Los Angeles, since he represented the business end of the publishing division, and, as Enoch put it, "It was mainly the business relationship that was important to Times Mirror."

In the early sixties McKinsey restructured the organizational flow chart at NAL, including the lines of authority. McKinsey's schema, placing Enoch's name above that of Weybright, reopened old wounds between the two, and exacerbated existing strains between Weybright and Jack Vance. In 1964 Weybright resigned and left full power within the division in the hands of his old antagonist. When he wrote his memoirs soon after, Weybright devoted some space to the Times Mirror takeover. The Times Mirror people struck Weybright as a graceless, tactless bunch of money-grubbers, not of the same class as the New York publishing world.

Yet the Chandlers represented the future—and the past and present reality—of the publishing business, whose goal had always been profitability. Times Mirror perhaps had not picked up the industry veneer, its tasteful economics. "Publishing is an egocentric organization," one McKinsey man commented. "Norman Chandler was probably the only nonegomaniac in publishing. Yet he was more likely representative of the modern publisher who doesn't also have to feed his ego, just his pocket-book.''

After New American Library, the expansion program took off, with purchases of a road map company (H.M. Gousha); an aeronautical charts corporation (Jeppesen and company); a maker of slide rules from Santa Barbara (Pickett Industries); a publisher of lawbooks and texts (Matthew Bender); and several paper mills and forest land acreage in Oregon, northern California, and Washington. All the newsprint subsidiaries were subsumed under the name Publisher's Paper Company, which had been set up after World War II in joint ownership with the *Deseret News* of the Mormon Church. In 1965 Times Mirror bought out the Mormon Church's interest for 300,000 shares of Times Mirror stock, making the Mormons the second largest stockholder (4.7 percent) after the Chandlers.

Times Mirror divested itself of its only broadcast property, KTTV, in 1963, as much for political reasons as business performance. KTTV's live airing of the Christian Anti-Communist Crusade seminars and the station management's failure to hold broadcaster George Putnam in rein did not endear the station to Otis Chandler. In 1963, Times Mirror sold KTTV to Metromedia for $10,390,000.

The forest products division grew the quickest. As the *Los Angeles Times* got thicker, it mowed down its own forests to provide the newsprint necessary for publication. Up to 75 percent of the tonnage consumed by the *Los Angeles Times* came from Publisher's Paper. The only reason the *Times* purchased 25 percent elsewhere was to protect itself against the dangers of disasters or strikes. Norman Chandler later told a group of security analysts that during World War II the *Times* had to scrounge around in order to find available newsprint sources and, as Chandler put it, ''they never wanted to be left in that position again where they were that vulnerable to outside pressures.'' By buying into the field, Times Mirror became the most protected of all newspapers, when newsprint prices went up.

The situation worked both ways. As the major *buyer* of newsprint the *Los Angeles Times* could also influence prices from that standpoint. In the early sixties the paper consumed upwards of 200,000 tons of newsprint annually, more than any other newspaper in the country—and up to 20 percent of all newsprint used in the entire eleven Western states. When a price *cut* occurred in 1964, one Times Mirror executive analyzed the company influence on the decision simply from ''the sheer volume of newsprint we [Times Mirror] use and the fact that we were casting about for a good price.'' Times Mirror could win either way from a price boost or a price cut, having losses in one division made up by profits in the other.

By 1965 the Times Mirror company had become the talk of *Business Week, Editor and Publisher*, and dozens of other business and trade publications; and the family was featured in the pages of *Look, Time* and *Newsweek*. There was much talk of the communications complex: a modern newspaper tied into computer terminals, microfilm libraries, and photo-offset composition. The Chandlers, however, were more tuned in to profit margins than technological fantasies. It was all right to talk of the future as long as present performance was up to financial expectations.

Times Mirror activity in the early sixties paralleled the tendency within corporate America toward the concentration of ownership, the widespread expansion of companies into areas outside their own market, and the specific movement toward monopoly. The new national Times Mirror company, a company of many monopolies, had become one of the communications industry's top ten.

CHAPTER 22

Weep No More

1. The Downtown Retreat

"These next few months are the key," *Times* city hall correspondent Carlton Williams confided to Mayor Norris Poulson in the winter of 1960. "If we don't win in '61, I'm out of a job too."

Norris Poulson had been mayor for eight years, the figurehead of the downtown business group and the *Times*, who had held sway without any serious challenge since the 1953 defeat of Fletcher Bowron. An accountant by training, Poulson had never been a wealthy man, and part of his attitude toward the businessmen/power-brokers was his class instinct in the face of the second- and third-generation elite that ran the city, an instinct to follow and serve, rather than lead or initiate. Poulson had acted on business needs and goals: Bunker Hill was undergoing redevelopment, and the Dodgers baseball team had come to Chavez Ravine. The downtown businessmen, content with their mayor, were determined to hold on to their power. Whatever misgivings they had about Poulson's lack of charisma as a candidate, they were satisfied with his performance. But the mayor was tired of the pressures of city hall. In the spring of 1960, he announced that he would not run for a third term.

Poulson's business backers saw disaster ahead without an incumbent candidate. A vacuum would be created, and the way left open to a candidate outside of business control. With Los Angeles in the midst of redevelopment plans with a major downtown project on the drawing boards, the fears about a Poulson withdrawal had turned into a panic. A meeting was called.

It was an extraordinarily hot, smoggy day August 11, 1960, when the twenty-five businessmen gathered together at the exclusive University Club. As Poulson was brought in, each of the men, from Lin Beebe to Charlie Jones of Richfield Oil, from Neil Petree to Asa Call, told the mayor, "Norrie, you've got to run." Poulson never did have the ability to say no, and the pressure was enormous. Within a matter of days the mayor consented; the businessmen and the *Times* had their candidate.

There didn't seem to be much opposition. Councilman Pat McGee came the closest to being a serious challenger. There were several candidates—even perennial campaigner Sam Yorty joined the race—but nobody thought the maverick Democrat Yorty, nor any of the other candidates, had much of a chance.

Sam Yorty was considered a classic political opportunist. He was elected to the California State Assembly in 1936 as a liberal-left, pro-New Deal Democrat. Having developed a reputation as something of a radical, Yorty tried to give leadership to the left-leaning Democrats in Sacramento. In 1938 he had attempted to get the backing of the recall forces as a mayoral candidate against Frank Shaw, but when the moderate forces objected, the more radical faction in the coalition dropped Yorty—a politician they never entirely trusted—for the conservative Fletcher Bowron.

The radicals had good reason to be suspicious. Within six months after the recall, Yorty became chairman of the newly formed state Un-American Activities Committee. The assemblyman turned on his former friends and, along with another former radical assemblyman, Jack Tenney, began an investigation of alleged Communist influence in the state Relief Administration.

Yorty's quest for power never let up. He failed to develop a substantial base within the Democratic party in spite of the financial support of conservative oil man Jack Elliot. Yorty's politics shifted around in the 1940s as he sought office for Congress, for U.S. Senate, for mayor of Los Angeles, and back to the assembly. In 1954, at the height of the Cold War, he got the Democratic nod against Republican Senator Tom Kuchel, and proceeded to red-bait the junior senator from California. The Republicans reciprocated with references to Yorty's past, and the race turned into one of California's ugliest elections. When Yorty tried to get the Democratic nomination for the senate in 1956, the liberal California Democratic Clubs, (CDC), who had no desire to see a repeat performance of 1954's mudslinging, successfully blocked his bid. Yorty bitterly attacked the CDC convention as "wired, packed, rigged, and stacked" and temporarily dropped out of political sight.

Yorty made the news again in 1960 with a pamphlet attack against John Kennedy entitled "I Cannot Take Kennedy." Kennedy, according to Yorty, could not govern fairly because he was a Catholic and a servant of

Big Labor and Big Business. Yorty defined his own position as a defense of the "little guy," a strange assortment of right-wing, antiestablishment populism and conservatism that would later mark the politics of such figures as Richard Nixon, George Wallace, and Ronald Reagan. The Kennedy pamphlet and Yorty's subsequent endorsement of Richard Nixon marked the final rupture in Yorty's relations with local Democrats. When Sam Yorty announced for the '61 election, nobody gave him a chance.

As the primary campaign got under way, the business group and mayor Poulson expected the customary crusading favoritism from the *Times*. Meetings at Perinos were attended by leading businessmen and campaign strategists such as PR man Herb Baus and *Times* city hall correspondent—and Poulson's informal campaign manager—Carlton Williams. Even Managing Editor Frank McCulloch, a newcomer to the local power scene, was obliged to come to a couple of meetings to hear the businessmen tell him what the *Times* was expected to do for its part in the campaign. McCulloch recalled one occasion when Poulson came running in an hour late. After apologies, the mayor was handed a list of campaign position papers. "Ah, so this is what I'm to run on," Poulson said out loud, still out of breath.

McCulloch made a lame effort at balanced coverage, but when Carlton Williams was assigned the overall election story, with orders coming from above, McCulloch got the message. "Carlton Williams," McCulloch observed, "was a hatchet man."

Though he was still in charge, Carlton Williams felt uneasy. He had never been challenged before at the *Times*, and he was certain that Nick Williams would not stand up for him in the family councils. With the family in turmoil, Williams was vulnerable. A Poulson victory would keep the city hall correspondent's enormous power intact, but a Poulson loss would possibly cause a forced retirement as his sixty-fifth birthday approached.

The primary campaign was not terribly spirited. Carlton Williams concentrated on plugging the incumbent and wrote up each new announcement of support while ignoring the opposition. Poulson's managers hoped the incumbency would be sufficient to put the Poulson vote over 50 percent in the primary, thus precluding a runoff. But a low turnout and Poulson's increasing unpopularity, stemming from the Chavez Ravine affair, kept his margin under 50 percent. Sam Yorty came in second, just barely ahead of Pat McGee.

Yorty and Poulson came out swinging the day after the primary. Yorty accused the mayor of being the tool of the downtown business establishment and the *Los Angeles Times*. He singled out Carlton Williams and questioned his unofficial status as campaign pundit, advisor, and strategist. Poulson, surprised at the vehemence of the Yorty attack, came back with charges about organized crime that Carlton Williams had helped to compile. Williams had access to police files on Yorty and had undertaken his own investigation concerning Yorty's link with garbage interests, the Teamsters, and Las Vegas money. What had been a quiet and mild campaign was turning into a raucous affair.

The Poulson camp was divided over campaign strategy. Herb Baus cautioned against the organized crime charges. Poulson had previously relied on the image of the incumbent above the fray who could count on a broad range of support. Yorty's disputes with the CDC and the 1960 Nixon endorsement helped Poulson receive the endorsement of the county Democratic party and the county federation of labor, both major liberal plums in the nonpartisan race. All the papers, especially the *Times*, backed the mayor. Yorty had literally nothing except a couple of television commentators.

By 1961 television had become an important political factor in electoral campaigns. Los Angeles television was dominated by one broadcaster: George Putnam of station KTTV, the nonnetwork independent then owned by the Chandlers. Putnam had developed an enormous following because of his deep bass voice, determined air, and occasional antiestablishment politics. Putnam's views paralleled those of Sam Yorty, and Putnam's program, "One Reporter's Opinion," became an ideal medium to promote Sam's campaign. Putnam's KTTV contract gave the TV commentator independence, even to the point of issuing anti-*Times* editorials. Although he had caused some anxieties during the Chavez Ravine affair, Putnam had never seriously strayed from the *Times* editorial point of view until 1961. But the KTTV anchorman disliked Norris Poulson, partly because of a personal falling-out between him and the mayor. When Putnam met Yorty, the two immediately hit it off, and the challenger had some backing at last.

The Yorty people arranged to have a paid television spectacular to be emceed by Putnam. When the first ad for the show appeared with Putnam's picture, a KTTV executive telephoned Norman Chandler to discuss what was happening. "If you want me to stop this, I can do it," the KTTV man told his boss. Chandler muttered an expletive. "The problem," the executive continued, "is that if we invoke some clause or other, it will also give ammunition to Yorty about censorship." The usually mild-manner Norman Chandler was livid. "Let that son-of-a-bitch do it," he hissed in a voice that startled the KTTV executive. The Yorty spectacular aired with Putnam as moderator, and the biggest theme of the evening was the Chandler family's hold over Norris Poulson.

During the campaign Poulson developed a severe case of laryngitis which was later analyzed as a form of throat cancer. As his voice weakened, Poulson found it difficult to speak at rallies and on radio and TV.

Some advisors thought he lacked the desire to win. Putnam made matters worse when night after night he invited the mayor to appear on his program to answer campaign charges. Poulson declined because of his illness, and each night Putnam would place an empty chair next to the podium and demand, in his stentorian voice, "Where is the mayor to answer these charges?" Finally, near the end of the campaign, Poulson decided to risk an appearance, but his hoarse voice and nervous manner produced an unmitigated disaster. The *Times* support, however, was as strong as ever. The paper carried daily news stories on Poulson endorsements, as well as the mayor's charges of corruption against his challenger.

In the last days of the campaign, Yorty took after the police commission and Police Chief Parker in a move to broaden his appeal to the black community from his existing base among the white lower-middle-class population of the San Fernando Valley. On Memorial Day, the Sunday before the election, an incident occurred that quite possibly provided the victory margin. When a young black man attempted to sneak onto a merry-go-round at Griffith Park he was stopped by a park guard, who started to rough him up. Within moments a large contingent of police arrived. A melee began, and dozens of blacks were injured, several hospitalized, and scores more arrested. The next day the papers were filled with headlines about the Griffith Park events. The black community saw the incident as one more example of police overreaction, which added fuel to candidate Yorty's contention that a change in police administration was needed.

Although the *Times* minimized the racial nature of the incident, many in the black community saw the episode as one more racial provocation. On Election Day, a substantial turnout in the black community combined with wide margins in the San Fernando Valley gave Yorty a 16,000 victory margin.

"There's Nothing Left But Hope," headlined the *Times* post-election editorial. "The threat is real," the editorial commented sadly, "The marching you hear is the retreat of what Mr. Yorty calls 'this vicious downtown clique that has long dominated City Hall' and the marching beat is thumped out on the tubs of the television performers. We love our city and we weep for it. Beyond that we can do nothing but watch and report—and hope that the voters will turn out next time."

When Norris Poulson and Carlton Williams retired soon after the election, an era was over.

2. Sam Yorty: Round Two

There is a political adage in Los Angeles that a Chandler doesn't care who's mayor as long as he gets to choose the police chief. At first, Yorty seemed defiant. "Out are such enemies as the 'downtown machine,' the present Police Commissioners, and Carlton Williams, the *Times* political writer," Yorty pledged the day after the election. But Yorty was cautious about Police Chief Parker. Though he had threatened to fire Parker on the day he took office, Yorty now spoke of "educating" his police chief. When it came time to make appointments, not only was Parker retained, but downtown business executive Neil Petree was asked to head up the Convention Center committee. Even Norman Chandler was approached to become chairman of the Community Redevelopment Agency, the powerful urban renewal body dealing with Bunker Hill and other development plans. Norman declined the new mayor's offer on grounds of conflict of interest—such an appointment could stir up a nest of charges about Chandler real estate holdings—and suggested as a suitable replacement Buff's second-in-command at the symphony, Z. Wayne Griffin. Within a matter of months, the champion of the little guy had made his peace with downtown.

For four years Mayor Sam built up his ties with his erstwhile business enemies. By the time the '65 election came around, Yorty had the complete support of the downtown business establishment. Yorty's main opponent was FDR's son Jimmy Roosevelt, then a liberal Democrat, who attacked the downtown plan and the Music Center/Bunker Hill project as a "ripoff."

The key to Yorty's *Times* support was its antagonism to Jimmy Roosevelt: "Roosevelt criticizes civic leaders," an April 2, 1965, editorial declared, "who successfully sought to rebuild Bunker Hill and who now champion a much-needed convention center exhibition hall in Elysian Park. He fails to appreciate the overall benefits of such projects, while resorting to the tired ruse of attacking 'special interests'. . . . Far from being a selfish clique, these are men and women with a keen sense of community welfare, who have participated wholeheartedly in the city's long-range improvement." With strong *Times* backing, solid campaign funds, and an opposition campaign that never got off the ground, Mayor Sam won a second term in office, polling over 50 percent of the vote in the primary.

There was, however, something different about the '65 election. Though editorial policy remained the same, the news coverage had changed. For the first time in its history, the *Times* covered a local mayoralty election with classically balanced stories. Political reporters Richard Bergholz and Paul Beck made straightforward presentations of the issues raised by both candidates with equivalent amounts of space given each candidate. This procedure had first been instituted three years earlier when Richard Nixon ran for governor of California and lost his way to the presidency.

* * *

3. Nixon's Last Stand

The '61 election between Poulson and Yorty was the last hurrah at the *Times* for "high power" journalism; no longer would *Times* reporters function as political power-brokers. Much of that journalism had been associated with its three leading exponents, Kyle Palmer, Chester "Chic" Hanson, and Carlton Williams. Six months after the election all three had retired. Although their replacements were not advocates of new journalism, they had little of the power and position of their predecessors.

Managing Editor McCulloch, responsible for political coverage, felt he could move in a different way in 1962. "A local race is one thing," he mused, "but a state election, though some interests are involved, is an entirely different matter."

The incumbent governor was Democrat Pat Brown. Brown called himself a political moderate and had cordial relations with the conservative wing of the party, led by fund-raiser/power-broker Eugene Wyman. The liberal strength within the party was centered in the CDC clubs, which had largely been responsible for the Democratic drive to power that culminated in Brown's election in 1958. The governor was wary of the CDC and they mistrusted him, but peace still reigned within the Democratic ranks.

Brown was friendly with the Chandlers. Dorothy Chandler had worked well with the governor while she sat on the board of regents, and the Chandlers were pleased with the support the governor had given to the state water project. Although the governor didn't expect an endorsement, he hoped the paper would tone down its support of the Republican candidate.

Less than three months after Nixon's narrow loss in 1960, *Times* columnist and Nixon intimate Jim Bassett had begun to speculate about Nixon's future. The former Nixon advisor theorized that if Nixon ran for governor in '62, he could run for president in 1968 after Kennedy's second term. As governor of the largest state in the country, Nixon would have a formidable political base for his run.

Former Governor Goodwin Knight also thought about running. When a Knight backer wrote to Norman Chandler about the Chandler position, Norman replied: "What Dick Nixon's decision will be, I do not know. Should he decide to be a candidate for Governor our newspapers would enthusiastically support him."

Like the *Times,* the old Nixon was getting a political facelift, an operation that began in the presidential race of 1960, continued in 1962, and finally succeeded in 1968. The "new Nixon" talked the language of political moderation. Although politically aware of the grass-roots strength of the Bircher right, the former vice-president was quick to support the

Times and condemn the Birchers in 1961. Nixon wished to shed the image of his Red-baiting past. He knew that although the right was strong within Republican ranks, the California electorate had become overwhelmingly Democratic and increasingly critical of anti-Communist politics. Nixon was faced with a contradiction: he was attacked from the right within his own party, but he also generated intense feelings about his past, particularly among Democrats who remembered what he had done to Helen Gahagan Douglas.

The Republican right found a candidate in Assemblyman Joe Shell, who, although not a Bircher himself, was generally supportive of Bircher politics. Nixon still had his old financial backers and important business allies, but Shell had many of the troops. When the primary results came in, Shell had pulled 40 percent of the vote. Nixon was in trouble.

The Nixon campaign counted on a lot of support from the *Times*. As the most powerful paper in the most populous county, with its traditional skill in turning election coverage into a crusade, the Nixon camp expected the *Times* to pull in the votes and keep the spirits high. What they didn't anticipate was the first major appearance in Los Angeles of the journalistic canons of objectivity.

Most newspapers, including the *Times,* ostensibly subscribed to the rules of objectivity, but several studies in the 1950s pointed out that the *Times* and dozens of other major dailies were heavily slanted toward the Republican candidates in their news coverage. By the early sixties, that practice was under increasing attack, and only the staunchest partisans, such as Knowland at the *Oakland Tribune* or Loeb at the *Manchester Union Leader,* continued the more blatant forms of favoritism.

In January 1962, when the *Mirror* and the *Examiner* folded, political reporters Richard Bergholz and Carl Greenberg were picked up to become the *Times*'s chief political writers. Dick Bergholz had built his reputation at the *Mirror,* where he had been free to analyze politics from a nonpartisan perspective. His counterpart at the *Examiner,* Carl Greenberg, was a political heavyweight—the closest thing to a Kyle Palmer the Hearst press ever had.

As the general election got under way, McCulloch insisted on taking a column-inch count of news copy to make sure that each candidate received the same amount of space—a far cry from the Republican bandwagon spirit four years earlier. Reporters Greenberg and Bergholz were systematically shuffled between the candidates to prevent either reporter from becoming too tied up with his source. Brown and Nixon position papers were compared and analyzed, and tough questions were reserved for both candidates. The new political coverage represented the first substantial separation in *Times* history between editorial policy and news judgment.

The Nixon camp was astounded. They were particularly irritated by Bergholz, who they thought went out of his way to attack Nixon. Several Nixon backers approached their old friend Norman Chandler and complained of *Times* coverage. "Talk to Otis," Norman replied.

Even the *Times* endorsement was milder than expected. Though the paper backed Nixon, it also had kind words for Brown: "On many of our State's tremendous problems," one editorial noted, "Republican Nixon and Democrat Brown are in general agreement regarding proper solutions."

On the day before the election, a *Times* editorial again remained neutral in its evaluation of Brown: "Our reasons for espousing Nixon's cause are primarily based on his own positive program rather than upon any marked deficiencies in the incumbent Governor Brown's performance since 1958."

As formerly crusading Republican organs throughout the state were giving free reign to the "objective style," the Nixon campaign began to turn toward television to reach a viewing audience, and bypassed the interpretation and analysis of inquisitive print journalists. The print media had become a Nixon bugaboo, especially the changing *Los Angeles Times.* "The Nixon people felt," McCulloch recalled, "that we had sent the *Times* down the primrose path."

By 1 A.M. on election night, incoming results pointed to a Nixon defeat. The former vice-president, facing the end of his career, sat in his room writing out a concession speech. His advisors decided to wait for more results before releasing it and urged the candidate to get some sleep. However, the irritable and harassed Nixon continued to stay up to watch the returns bring Pat Brown's victory margin to 400,000 votes.

Around seven in the morning, the Nixon aides concluded that a concession was in order but that the bedraggled Nixon should not be the one to make the announcement. Nixon agreed, but still wanted to congratulate his campaign workers, who were assembled in a room next to the pressroom. Nixon started shaking hands and thanking workers, and people began crying. It was an emotional scene. "Don't let them bluff you ever again," one campaign worker shouted, pointing to the pressroom.

Moments before, Herb Klein, Nixon's press secretary, had walked out to the pressroom to tell the reporters that Nixon would not appear. Just as Klein started to speak, Nixon suddenly appeared and, with the words "Good morning gentlemen," began one of the most bizarre statements of modern political history.

"I have no complaints about the press coverage," Nixon told the assembled reporters, and then proceeded to criticize the press bitterly: "I want that—I for once gentlemen—would appreciate if you would write what I say, in that respect. I think it's very important that you write it—in the lead—in the lead. Now I don't mean by that, incidentally, all of you. . . . One reporter, Carl Greenberg—he's the only reporter on the *Times* that fits this thing, who wrote every word that I said. He wrote it fairly. He wrote it objectively.''

The reference to Greenberg, Herb Klein later commented, was an indirect slap at Nixon's primary target Dick Bergholz. ''I don't mean that others didn't have a right to do it differently,'' Nixon went on, ''but Carl, despite whatever feelings he had, felt that he had an obligation to report the facts as he saw them.''

Nixon then took after the *Times.* ''I made a talk on television, a talk in which I made a flub—one of the few I make, not because I'm so good on television, but because I've done it a long time. I made a flub in which I said I was running for the governor of the United States. The *Los Angeles Times* dutifully reported that. Mr. Brown the last day made a flub,'' Nixon continued, ''a flub, incidentally, to the great credit of television, that was reported—I don't say this bitterly—in which he said, 'I hope everybody wins. Vote the straight Democratic ticket, including [Republican] Senator Kuchel.' I was glad to hear him say it, because I was for Kuchel all the way. The *Los Angeles Times* did not report it.''

The press corps sat in amazement as Nixon went on and on. ''I leave you gentlemen now,'' Nixon concluded, ''and you will write it. You will interpret it. That's your right. But as I leave you I want you to know—just think how much you're going to be missing. You won't have Nixon to kick around any more, because gentlemen, this is my last press conference, and it will be the one in which I have welcomed the opportunity to test wits with you.''

All hell broke loose after Nixon left the room. Carl Greenberg was mortified and immediately called his editor with an offer to resign on the spot. Bergholz, who had missed the press conference, hadn't realized what had happened when he strolled into the *Times* that morning. The city room was swarming with radio and television crews and other press. ''What's this all about?'' Bergholz asked in amazement. ''Who knows what was going on in his mind,'' he later mused, ''when he looked out into that room and maybe saw that bald head. . . .'' A balding Bergholz trailed off.

A few days after the election, Richard Nixon canceled his longtime subscription to the *Los Angeles Times.* ''What an unfortunate way for a man to close a political career—by a whimper,'' Dorothy Chandler wrote to a friend a month later.

4. Downstream with the Right

After the Nixon defeat, Republican circles were in disarray. In the fifties, with Knowland in the senate, Knight in the governor's chair, and Nixon in Washington, the power of the Republican financial donors was at its height. But the string of defeats that began with the '58 fiasco and culminated in Nixon's last press conference had also undermined the power of the financial backers. The Republican power-brokers were without a candidate, and Republican fortunes were at the lowest ebb in several decades. They had become the minority party.

The anti-Communist fervor and reactionary perspective that had once been so useful for winning elections now served to drive the Republicans only deeper into their minority status. But the Republican grass-roots workers would not tolerate any compromise. They wanted a national candidate they could call their own, someone who would stand up and fight against the intolerable leftward drift that seemed to be sweeping the country.

Barry Goldwater was no stranger to the readers of the *Los Angeles Times*. Since the changeover, the *Times* had run a Goldwater column on its op-ed page as part of its balancing act to provide all points of view. When the Arizona senator began to organize for the presidency, he already had a California base of Joe Shell campaign supporters, disheartened workers from the Nixon organization, and disgruntled *Los Angeles Times* readers.

The Arizona senator also had some money men. The Goldwater backers were new to the Republican power-brokering scene, though some had participated in Southern California upper-class affairs for a number of years. Oil men Henry Salvatori and Cy Rubel were both part of Southern California ruling circles but were relative newcomers to politics. Both were fervent anti-Communists and were surprised and disturbed at some of the political shifts that old friends like Dick Nixon and the Chandlers appeared to be making.

Goldwater's principal opponent for the nomination was Nelson Rockefeller. The New York governor had few troops but a lot of money. He began his California drive by hiring the political advertising agency Spencer-Roberts. The PR people found that many upper-class "luminaries," as they put it, were willing to lend their name to the Rockefeller cause. Leonard Firestone of the tire company (a minority stockholder in the Chandler Tejon Ranch), Justin Dart of Dart Industries, real estate man Bob Rowan, Senator Kuchel, and Otis Chandler's sister Camilla Spear all signed on as Rockefeller backers. The Goldwater people had control of the party rank and file and much of the organizational infrastructure. The Spencer-Roberts strategy for Rockefeller was to bypass the party machinery and go directly to Republican voters through a favorable press.

With the *Times*, the strategy paid off. Philip Chandler's political and financial backing of the Arizona senator did not help the Senator's cause at Times Mirror Square. The Goldwater forces thought, however, they still might get the *Times* endorsement because of Salvatori's connections with Dorothy Chandler. Salvatori's wife, Grace, a Woman-of-the-Year award recipient, was Dorothy Chandler's right-hand woman in the early years of the Music Center drive. When Henry Salvatori went to call on his friends at Times Mirror, he hoped for the best.

But there was never a doubt about the *Times* candidate. Everybody, according to editor Williams, including himself, Otis, Norman, and Dorothy Chandler, backed Rockefeller. Dorothy Chandler, especially, liked the New York governor and felt his brand of politics and style blended nicely with her view of the world.

On May 17, a couple of weeks before the primary, the *Times* endorsed Rockefeller. The paper praised both candidates as "earnest, outspoken and provocative campaigners," but questioned some of Goldwater's positions: "We tend to agree with Goldwater's broad objectives for the United States," the editorial cautiously commented, "but we cannot support a great many of the Senator's solutions to the specific issues before this country in domestic and foreign affairs." Rockefeller, the editorial went on, represented the "broad spectrum" of Republican thought.

But Goldwater narrowly won the California primary and rolled on to the convention with enough delegates to put him over the top. Rockefeller was booed, the press felt beseiged (Williams wrote that he and all the Chandlers "were very much alarmed and upset by the anti-press demonstration at the GOP Convention"), and Pat Brown spoke for many Democrats when he said of the San Francisco convention: "The stench of fascism was in the air in the Cow Palace." Some of the news coverage in the *Times* gave credence to the governor's views. "Is the Militant Right Trying to Seize Control of GOP?" headlined a May 24 Paul Beck news story, which quoted a Republican running for the assembly in Sacramento in the lead: "You don't realize how extreme these people are until you go downstream with them for awhile."

Right after Goldwater was nominated, Washington bureau chief Donovan approached editor Williams: "Why don't we take a gamble," Donovan said to his boss, "and assume that Goldwater is going to be beaten badly in November. I'll spend my time gathering material about the shape of the Republican Party and its future." Williams agreed, and Donovan set off on the road to talk to a number of Republican bigwigs and to research Republican fortunes dating back to the 1912 split between conservatives and progressives.

In the general election, the *Times* backed Goldwater against Lyndon Johnson. "At primary eve," Nick Williams later wrote, "we did, in an editorial, say that we would support Goldwater if he were nominated, but that we were strongly for Rockefeller. We believed that saying that did strengthen our message to Republican voters. And we did follow through, as we always had in the choice of President, by endorsing the Republican nominee." Otis Chandler, shortly after the election, characterized the Goldwater endorsement as "supporting the two party system rather than the candidate."

The day after the election, the Donovan series on the future of the Republican party ran and recouped some of the prestige the paper had lost with its Goldwater endorsement. Donovan theorized that a historical split between moderate and conservative factions of the Republican party had been responsible for many of the party's defeats, with the Goldwater debacle the latest and most compelling example. Donovan appealed to the moderates to regroup and take the leadership of the party without yielding to the right's extreme politics. "Stop Goldwater" politics were not enough, Donovan wrote. A positive program had to be issued that would recapture the imagination of the electorate.

On the ballot in the November '64 election was a statewide initiative designed to repeal the Rumford Fair Housing Act. The initiative, Proposition 14, prohibited the state from interfering with a person's "absolute discretion" in selling, leasing, or renting property—in effect, a license to refuse to sell or rent a house to a black family. Most newspapers in the state attacked the proposition, and many, including Governor Brown, felt that the vote would be interpreted by the black community as a referendum on racism. The *Times* backed the measure to its later shame, and although Goldwater went down to defeat in California, Proposition 14 passed by more than a two-to-one margin.

By 1965 the politics of the Chandlers remained strongly conservative. They were cold warriors in foreign policy and probusiness in social and economic matters. Yet their paper was being nudged, and, though wary and reluctant, the Chandler family began to adjust to the world of the 1960s.

Transition

1. McCulloch Departs

The first three years of the changeover of the *Los Angeles Times* had occurred in the framework of the optimism of the early sixties: the idea that peaceful change would gradually make its way throughout the land. But the country was in for some shocks: the Kennedy assassination, Vietnam escalation, violence in the inner cities and on the campuses. That peaceful optimism would dissolve almost overnight in the turbulence of events. By the fall of 1963, the *Los Angeles Times,* some said, had reached its limits for change.

The McCulloch/Haven division of day and night managing editor had turned into a real split over news judgment and principle. Dividing up the bureaus, desks, staff, and responsibilities was not very functional and added to the strain. The Hearst executives had used such a division to pit the two managing editors against each other in a competitive race to the top. Although Nick Williams knew about the Hearst precedent, he didn't have the same intentions. "The two men complemented each other," Nick Williams said of his appointments. "McCulloch was a first-class reportorial type and Haven was a desk man. They were put in apposition so that hopefully the product might be that much better than with just one managing editor." Instead of the best of both worlds, the *Times* got two hostile camps.

Nick Williams didn't care for conflict. He was constantly trying to mediate what seemed like totally irreconcilable points of view. But the *Times* editor was committed to transforming the paper, at least by eliminating

373

the outrageous practices of the past, and its more virulent reactionary politics. Williams was attracted to the sophistication of the *New York Times* and *New York Herald Tribune*. He wanted to make the *Times* more intellectually appealing and upgrade the product through the hiring of intellectually oriented specialists. Intrigued by intellectuals, Williams felt that they didn't mix with true conservatives. Although he was gradually moving to the left, his political history was *Times*-oriented Republicanism.

Williams was ultimately at the beck and call of the family, a "hired hand," as one staffer characterized it. Yet the *Times* editor was a cagey employee who learned over the years how to fend for his staff and support the changes they wanted. At the same time, Williams anticipated Chandler anxieties and often sharply criticized his assistants, especially McCulloch. With the Birchers on his right, and the numerous protest movements on his left, Nick Williams became the man of moderation, most at ease when the shouting and anger had subsided and civility and common sense prevailed. "Most of us, I feel sure by now," he commented in the mid-sixties, "are conservative about some things and liberal about others, or in transition about a whole raft of matters." "The essence of conservatism," he answered the *Times*'s right-wing critics, "is common sense." In those early years, while working toward gradual changes, Williams constantly found himself holding the whip against those causing trouble. He knew McCulloch was important to the process, but he often attacked his managing editor's decisions.

Once such attack centered around a story done by *Times* medical writer Harry Nelson. In the summer of 1962, Nelson stopped off in Saskatchewan to investigate a newly developed government-sponsored medical insurance plan—of special interest since the U.S. Congress was then in the midst of a bitter battle over President Kennedy's Medicare plan. When Nelson arrived in Saskatchewan, the opposition doctors had gone out on strike in an attempt to block the plan. Nelson's timely arrival gave him an important scoop. When he returned to Los Angeles, McCulloch asked him to do a piece on the strike for the Sunday opinion section. McCulloch told the *Times* reporter to write what he thought and not just whether the plan would work or how the doctors' strike might be resolved. "Write your opinion," McCulloch suggested. "Say what you think about the whole thing."

For Harry Nelson those were extraordinary words. *Times* reporters were not ordinarily encouraged to express their point of view, especially, as the case turned out, when those views contradicted the house position. *Times* editorials had always condemned any government participation in health-care systems, and Nelson knew that well, but at McCulloch's insistence, he decided not to hold back.

On July 8 Nelson's piece ran on page one of the opinion section under the heading NO RETREAT ON MEDICARE PATH. Nick Williams was out of town that week, and the article, in which Nelson contended that the step toward socialized medicine was "well worth taking," ran intact.

Pandemonium broke loose the next day. The County Medical Association sent several contingents to see Nick Williams and Norman Chandler. They asked for Nelson's head, but instead of criticizing Nelson, Nick Williams gave Frank McCulloch hell for first encouraging and then permitting the article to run. Williams wrote his own answer to Nelson's piece the following Sunday in an op-ed column with the head SOCIALIZED MEDICINE: A BITTER PILL. Williams tried to mollify angry readers by implying that the *Times* medical writer didn't really say what he said and was just describing the situation rather than taking a position.

The issue didn't subside. Letters continued to come in by the score, mostly from doctors who lashed out at the *Times* and Nelson. Nelson remained on staff and continued to report on medical affairs, and McCulloch held on to his post, although his position was a bit shakier, having absorbed the brunt of the criticism. Everyone wondered, including McCulloch himself, how long he would last. "I never did look back," McCulloch later recalled, "though I was always wondering when they would catch up to me."

One day that winter, Otis Chandler approached McCulloch about beginning a new Sunday magazine for the *Times*. McCulloch was unhappy with the idea. He told Chandler he didn't see the need for another Sunday supplement when all the other sections could use some beefing up, and he was skeptical about whether such a magazine could survive economically. McCulloch didn't want the extra responsibility, either. "I'm in the news business, not magazines," he complained.

As talk of the magazine increased, McCulloch knew the end had come. He would not tolerate having his job scrambled even further, so he finally wrote a letter of resignation and sent it to Otis and Nick Williams. Williams was out of the office that day, and Otis was engaged in consultations concerning the New American Library (NAL).

Later that afternoon Otis called McCulloch into his office. The husky *Times* publisher stood behind his desk, his hands spread-eagled, his face down, and McCulloch's letter directly in front of him. McCulloch couldn't tell whether the letter had been opened. Otis looked up and noticed his managing editor. Chandler asked McCulloch to take a two-week leave of absence. He wanted his employee, as a former Time-Life man, to help straighten out the difficulties at NAL. "You better read the letter, Otis," McCulloch told his boss, pointing to the envelope. Chandler sat down to read the letter and became very upset. When he finished, he paused, and then asked where McCulloch planned to go. "To Vietnam," McCulloch replied. "I've been offered a job as *Time* correspondent." For two weeks the publisher continued to act bewildered and refused to accept the resignation.

The old-timers breathed a sigh of relief when McCulloch departed. Their champion, Frank Haven, took over McCulloch's duties in the new, integrated post of managing editor. The McCulloch camp was dispirited and convinced that the paper would now go downhill. Who in high places, many of the staff wondered, would stick out his neck? Who would fight for the kind of independent journalism the *Times* so desparately needed? McCulloch had become a symbol. To some, it seemed the changeover had come to an end.

Just how far had the *Times* changed? The war in Vietnam was escalating, and the *Times* backed LBJ all the way. The paper lashed out at anti-war demonstrators in editorials that called for law and order on the campus. In May 1965 the *Times* endorsed Sam Yorty for reelection and discounted fears about the long, hot summer. This is not Alabama, nor is it Harlem, the paper assured its readers. There were no rat-infested tenements in sunny California; just single-tract houses and friendly people. It won't happen here, the Chandlers thought. But it did.

2. *"A Summer Carnival of Riot"*

About seven o'clock on the evening of August 11, just before sunset, a white policeman pulled over a car in the heart of a black neighborhood adjacent to Watts. The driver of the car, a twenty-one-year-old, unemployed black man named Marquette Frye, was given a sobriety test. A number of people gathered around, including Frye's mother and brother, who lived just down the block. More police showed up—all of them white. An argument ensued, and, within a matter of minutes, the entire Frye family was arrested. People from the community drifted toward the corner. The anger of the crowd perceptibly increased as several more people were taken off by the police. As word of the incident spread, hundreds of people began to gather in groups throughout the ghetto. The Watts Riots had begun.

The anger had been building for a long time. By 1965 the black population in Los Angeles had jumped to 650,000. Unemployment had become a chronic condition in Watts, especially after the recessions of 1957/58 and 1961/62. Since the death of the Big Red streetcars, the mass transit system serving Watts was completely inadequate. Those that held jobs often had to spend several hours a day on overcrowded, expensive buses in order to get to work. The de facto segregated schools of Watts and other black neighborhoods were the worst in the city. From 1963 to 1965 police violence in the ghetto had dramatically climbed. Sixty blacks had been killed by police, of whom twenty-seven were shot in the back or the side and twenty-five were unarmed.

Housing was another problem. Though the homes in Watts generally consisted of single-tract houses, symbolizing for the business community the difference between Los Angeles's black neighborhoods and the tenement ghettos back East, these houses, as one state-sponsored study reported, were "old and require constant maintenance in order to remain habitable." Two-thirds of the houses in Watts were owned by absentee landlords. Savings and loan institutions and other banks involved in mortgage financing practiced "redlining," that is, they refused to provide conventional loans in certain neighborhoods. There were so many documented social and economic grievances in the ghetto that in retrospect the only surprise about the events of August 11 was why they had not occurred earlier.

Ordinarily, when there was trouble in the ghetto, the *Times* desk men downplayed it, according to one *Times* staffer, "as a bunch of black jigaboos down there making trouble." When the first reports came in to the *Times* skeleton crew on the evening of August 11, the desk treated it as a routine matter and sent out some photographers and reporters. Shortly after midnight, when the police pulled out of the area, reporter Bob Jackson remembered being afraid. "The kids sensed that they had won," Jackson recalled. There was hostility toward the whites still in the area, including the *Times* newsmen. Suddenly, Timesman Phil Fradkin was struck in the shoulder by a huge rock and had to be rushed off to the hospital. The other *Times* staffers left with him. The kids continued to roam the streets that night, and the neighborhood became a battle zone.

The seven-paragraph story that appeared in the *Times* the next day—on page three—described the situation as a local disturbance. But by the second evening, August 12, it was unmistakably clear to *Times* editors that an event of major proportions was occurring. That night people gathered again throughout Watts. Within hours a fire broke out just a few blocks from the scene of the original arrest of Marquette Frye. By midnight the crowds were larger than those of the previous night's events, and people continued to group and regroup on through the morning. The city desk, worried about the attack against Phil Fradkin, did not want its white reporters out in the riot zone at night. Several photographers got flak suits, and the reporters stayed behind police lines.

The story was on page one now, although the coverage was cautious in its evaluation of the events. "The cause of the riot, first of its magnitude in Los Angeles, is indefinite," *Times* rewrite men Art Berman and Jack McCurdy wrote in the lead story about the events of Friday night. The story quoted Los Angeles Police Chief William Parker at length. Parker commented that he "did not consider it a race riot, since the rioters were all Negroes." The events in Watts, according to the chief, could be traced to the civil disobedience of the civil rights movement, when "people lose all respect for the law." The rioters, the chief concluded, were "people who gave vent to their emotions on a hot night when the temperature didn't get below 72 degrees."

The police chief's statements were not out of character. Parker had come to symbolize the conflict between the black community and the white establishment. When asked to describe how the riots started, Parker made his memorable remark: "One person threw a rock, and then, like monkeys in a zoo, others started throwing rocks."

The *Times*, which had previously supported the police chief, backed Parker's actions during the riots. A *Times* editorial on August 13, entitled "A Summer Carnival of Riot," went along with much of Parker's analysis: "A hot night, an area of simmering tension, a routine police arrest of a drunk driving suspect—and suddenly Los Angeles is faced with a full-scale riot and boastful threats of more to come. Police attempting to do their duty were interfered with, a mob quickly formed, rioting erupted. The area where all this took place has a predominantly Negro population. But there is no reason to believe that the outbreak was, in any real sense, a race riot.

"Explanations for this orgy of lawlessness are not hard to find," the editorial sternly continued. "It took place in an atmosphere where the potential for violence was high, in weather conditions conducive to outbreaks. The members of this largely-youthful mob were undoubtedly filled with a variety of discontents and grievances of long standing. The events of the evening provided the opportunity to give their discontents irrational expression."

Times news coverage in the next several days was little more than a rewrite of police handouts. The white journalists, forced to stay behind police lines, were accordingly dependent on police statistics and the police version of riot events. *Times* editors sent staff writers and photographers out during the day, when the violence subsided, to talk to South Central residents, but nobody believed a white reporter from the establishment paper could get an accurate picture of the mood of the community.

By the third day of the riots, Watts had become an international event, with reporters from all over the world arriving to describe the situation. The *Times* was the hometown paper and an important source of information, but the lack of any black reporters at the paper became a major embarrassment to *Times* management.

On Saturday, the third day of the riots, Bob Richardson, a twenty-four-year-old black *Times* ad salesman, walked into the city room with a proposition. Richardson, who lived in Watts, told the *Times* editors that he knew his way around the ghetto and could phone in reports each night. For the next several days, Richardson was the only *Times* reporter to wander on his own through Watts at night. "They're chanting Burn, baby, burn!" Richardson told the desk, and the rewrite men put together the most exciting copy to run in the paper.

Richardson had become the hero of the day because of his news reports. A grateful *Times* management promoted him, after the riots, to a full-fledged reporter. But Richardson's training and background had little to do with the realities of the *Times* city room. Within a matter of months, Richardson was arrested on a charge of breaking and entering, and the career of the *Times*'s black reporter came to an end.

The riots continued for more than five days. By early Tuesday, August 17, it was finally over. The National Guard patrolled the streets and South Central was a shambles. Thirty-four people, mostly Watts residents, had died, 1,032 people were injured, and 3,952 were arrested. There was $40 million in property damage. Many of the local white businesses had been set afire, although churches, schools, libraries, and private residences were untouched. The fires had not been limited to Watts; there were incidents throughout Southern California in San Diego, Pacoima, Pasadena, Monrovia, Long Beach, and San Pedro. It was the worst riot in the country's history.

Afterwards, tensions in Los Angeles remained at a breaking point. The day after peace had returned, the police surrounded and shot up Los Angeles's Muslim Mosque, firing between 500 and 1,000 rounds of ammunition before entering the temple. Fifty-nine Muslims were arrested, although three weeks later all charges were dismissed.

The riots profoundly affected the *Times*'s management and staff. Even Otis Chandler invoked self-criticism: "I think," Chandler was quoted soon after the riots, "all the media in Los Angeles, including the *Times*, were derelict in not exposing conditions in Watts. It's our job to send up warning flags."

The *Times* coverage, according to reporter Phil Fradkin, "was like answering a fire alarm." Aside from the Bob Richardson eyewitness accounts and the police blotter information, *Times* news stories were limited to once-removed background pieces—"Racial Unrest Laid to Negro Family Failure," "Area Appears Devoid of Community Leadership," "Two Psychiatrists See Anger, Anxiety, and Self-Hatred as Emotional Keys to Outbursts," for example. These complemented the occasional mood pieces, such as Chuck Hillinger's article on August 14, "Burning Buildings Symbolize Spirit of Hate Underlying Rioting."

The large-scale resources the *Times* threw into the coverage—what the paper called "comprehensive journalism"—could not substitute for the all-white complexion of the staff. After the riots had ended, *Times* editors sent a team, led by reporter Jack Jones, into the black neighborhoods to catalogue some of the social and economic reasons behind the community's anger. The Jones series, "The View from Watts," was printed in October, and won a Pulitzer Prize for the *Times*. It recouped some of the prestige lost during the events themselves.

Within a few days after the fires had died, Governor Pat Brown decided to appoint a commission to look into the Watts events. When UCLA Chancellor Franklin Murphy declined because of lack of time, Brown turned to John McCone, former head of the CIA and one of the leading members of the Southern California business establishment. Although two blacks were appointed to the commission, its three-person executive committee consisted of top members of the white establishment: McCone, Warren Christopher of the O'Melveny and Myers law firm, and the venerable Asa Call. The commission's staff director was Terence Lee, McCone's own private secretary. McCone also had veto power over staff appointments, effectively controlling the content of the staff findings. The executive committee made all the day-to-day decisions without informing other commission members and guided the commission's report to its final form.

The McCone findings, entitled "Violence in the City," pointed out few of the social and economic problems in the ghetto, and absolved Chief Parker, the city government, and the business establishment of any responsibility. "Put bluntly," one critic characterized the report, " 'Violence in the City' claimed that the rioters were marginal people and the riots meaningless outbursts." The commission minimized the extent of riot participation in the black community and advocated limited reforms. It backed the police department, criticized black civil rights leaders, and refused to consider the possibility that the riots were, as sociologist Robert Fogelson described them, "articulate protests against genuine grievances in the ghetto." The *Times* strongly endorsed the commission findings and broke precedent by printing the entire text in its news pages.

Black community activists criticized McCone investigators for largely ignoring first-hand accounts from blacks about conditions in the community. *Times* management, however, was sensitive to the charges concerning the white establishment's failure to heed the warnings from Watts, and over the next few years began to editorialize in favor of increased contact between blacks and the white establishment.

The riots, for both *Times* management and staff, were a traumatic event. No longer would Los Angeles just be the city of the warm sun, rolling hills, and ocean surf. Watts changed the terms of the local community identity. It changed the terms of *Times* urban coverage.

The full flavor of the 1960s—protests, political dislocations, the breakdown of the social consensus—hit the *Times* like a blast from a furnace. A "before and after" consciousness developed at the paper; Watts marked the point of departure.

CHAPTER 23

The Proverbial Snowball

1. "Kill the Messenger"

The first stage of changeover at the *Times*, marked by the periodic jumps and shifts embodied in the McCulloch/Haven clash, was over. Two camps had emerged: the old-timers who mistrusted McCulloch's brand of journalism, and those recently hired staff who were ready to make a complete break with the *Times*'s past. In those first years, the old-timers, still constituting a majority, had set limits to many of the changes.

After Watts a second stage of the changeover began. New staff, new attitudes, and new coverage took root. The people who worked at the paper now spoke of the new *Times*, the real *Times*, as if its origins dated back to 1960, not 1881. The early *Times* of land deals, Republican power-brokering, and red scares became a blur, an anecdote to tell over lunch.

"Our program to change the paper," Otis Chandler told the *Saturday Review*, "has become like the proverbial snowball rolling down the mountain. It keeps rolling faster." The new *Los Angeles Times* caught the attention of journalists throughout the nation, and the paper and its publisher were subject to dozens of favorable profiles in *Time*, *Newsweek*, the *Saturday Review*, *Business Week*, and *Los Angeles* magazine.

Much of the favorable commentary centered on the Washington bureau, headed by Bob Donovan. Based in Washington since the second world war, Donovan had contacts throughout the bureaucracy. He knew how decisions were made and implemented, and he could accurately pin down information from guarded sources. Often, when assigned a major story, he'd feign confusion and lack of knowledge on the subject and call

381

.cabinet officers or other high-level bureaucrats to plead with them to explain the story's background. The startled officials, touched by the wise old journalist's request, would carefully and thoroughly review the information and provide new leads, new ideas, and new scoops. The result would be an impressive article, bringing accolades to the bureau and respect for its staff.

The Donovan bureau was organized at a time when Washington journalism had just begun to change. The Washington press corps had lost some of its earlier naivete and tendency to puff up sources, but it still relied on manufactured news and inside contacts. "Most of the time," James Reston wrote in 1966, "reporters are in the distributing business, transmitting the accounts of what Presidents and Secretaries of State do onto the front pages and onto the top headlines."

In 1966 LBJ's administration, marked by escalation in Vietnam and the crumbling of the domestic consensus, developed an increasing need to stage-manage the news and manipulate opinion. "Seldom has information been a more jealously guarded commodity than it has been in Lyndon Johnson's Washington," *Times* staffers David Kraslow and Stuart Loory wrote in 1968. "He who has information has power. He who controls it keeps his power harnessed and working harmoniously for him."

One of the techniques of controlling the news flow utilized and improved upon by the Johnson administration was the "backgrounder." Under backgrounder rules a source passes on information only with the understanding that he or she not be identified, except in a disguised manner, such as a "high administration official" or a "usually reliable source." Unlike off the record statements, which supposedly forbid a journalist to use any of the information unless he or she later finds it from another source, backgrounders allow the reporter to use the information conveyed by quoting a "high source." Backgrounders enable government officials to express their opinions or give out information without being held accountable. The advantage of backgrounders for the reporter, as Washington Bureau Chief Alan Otten of the *Wall Street Journal* analyzed it, is that he "can appear to be on the inside, reporting matters on the 'highest authority.'" But, Otten warned, a reporter "has little time to check the facts independently and frequently can't alert his readers to the source's bias or motivation."

Johnson's secretary of State Dean Rusk and secretary of defense Robert McNamara each held once-a-week backgrounder sessions during which they frequently outlined their perspectives on the state of the war in Vietnam. The information would appear the next day, but without direct attribution.

As the war progressed, predictions from "high administration officials" frequently turned out to be inaccurate, and both Johnson's and the press's credibility began to suffer. *Times* reporters eventually began to question the veracity of the information they were receiving. "I remember one backgrounder in July 1965," Times staffer David Kraslow recalled, "after Maxwell Taylor had returned from one of those fact finding tours. Towards the end of the conference someone asked a 'throwaway' question to the effect, 'General, can you foresee the day when there will be 100,000 troops in Vietnam?' Taylor paused and responded, 'No, we'll never approach that figure. It shouldn't even be considered an outside limit.'" Kraslow always thought Taylor an honest and intelligent military man, but when the troop level passed 100,000 not much later, Kraslow began to doubt things he heard in Washington. "How," Kraslow asked himself, "could Taylor be so wrong?"

The problem, *Times* reporters felt, had to do with the man in the White House. Stuart Loory, *Times* White House correspondent in 1967, experienced the LBJ style at his first presidential interview. Loory had worked out an arrangement in which he would use direct quotes from LBJ only in the form "The President tells associates," a technique used by *Life* magazine correspondent Hugh Sidey, to disguise Sidey's regular, exclusive interviews with Johnson. The Sidey technique was a modified backgrounder: one could identify the president, but quotes would be one step removed by disguising the fact that they came from a direct interview. Johnson struck Loory as someone who wanted to be liked and "impress America's youth" but was fundamentally out of touch with what was going on around him. "With all this," Loory concluded in his front page article on LBJ, "the President is still perplexed about how to close the gap between the Oval Office and Main Street, between himself and the people."

The White House was angry with the story. They felt that Loory had violated the ground rule, even though Loory had kept to the "president tells associates" format. It was clear, White House aides claimed, that the information in the article came from a direct interview. Loory dismissed the criticism and felt that LBJ was primarily displeased by the tone of the story, which identified Johnson's own words and actions as the source of his credibility problems.

In retaliation for the article, LBJ aides began to freeze Loory out of the daily press routines. After the *Times* lodged a formal protest, George Christian, Johnson's press secretary, told Loory that normal press courtesies would be reinstituted, but all memoranda on the incident would be kept in Loory's "file." It was Loory's last one-on-one interview with the president.

The power of Washington officials to punish reporters was enormous, and most journalists were willing to play by the source's ground rules. "In Washington," national correspondent Jules Witcover wrote, "a reporter turns his back on the 'anonymous' source at his own peril. He either agrees to listen on a background basis or looks bad the next day when everybody else has the story.''

The question of attribution was one of several that produced friction between hometown editors and their Washington staff. The situation in Los Angeles was no exception. For the first couple of years, however, the Donovan bureau could hardly do any wrong. Donovan was aware of the *New York Times* western edition and knew his bosses in Los Angeles wanted a bureau that could "slug it out with the *New York Times*," as Donovan put it. The Los Angeles editors wanted a *Los Angeles Times*-bylined story, as opposed to a wire account, of even routine events such as press conferences or congressional votes. Staff articles almost always ran on page one, and Donovan's requests for more funds and a larger staff were largely met.

After the *New York Times* western edition folded, conditions began to change. By 1965 new instructions started to arrive from Los Angeles. More features, more background, more newsmagazine-type pieces, more material for the Sunday paper were requested from California. No longer worried about the *New York Times* competition, Los Angeles pushed the daily newsmagazine concept.

Though Nick Williams had decreed autonomy for Donovan, Managing Editor Haven—who had consolidated his position after McCulloch left—sought to step in and place the bureau under his jurisdiction. Haven increasingly came into conflict with David Kraslow, Donovan's news editor, who had charge of all the bureau's administrative matters.

In October 1966 Haven sent a memo to Washington asking for what the Los Angeles editors called nonduplicative material—stories not covered by the wires or the daily news flow. Haven wanted the bureau to be on alert for background pieces and feature articles and not worry about the day-to-day stuff.

The most difficult problem for both Washington and Los Angeles, however, continued to be the nature of the story itself. Vietnam dominated Washington news more and more, and it was hard to avoid questioning American policy. "The Administration would say one thing and then Vietnam correspondents would come back and say things that contradicted the White House position," *Times* staffer John Averill commented. As the war escalated, *Times* Washington copy began to express more skepticism towards government information.

Questions regarding the truth about the war were widely articulated, in part, by the growing antiwar movement. Teach-ins on college campuses, sit-ins at local draft boards, and massive demonstrations in the nation's capital challenged the government's misinformation. But McNamara continued to hold backgrounders, Westmoreland asked for more troops for "limited contingencies," and everyone in government promised a successful resolution. When the Tet offensive in February 1968 reached the central squares of Hue and Saigon, government credibility had virtually disappeared.

In the late spring of 1967, *Times* staffer Kraslow heard that a recent peace initiative had come apart when the United States had renewed the bombing of North Vietnam. After Kraslow related the intriguing story to White House correspondent Loory, the two compared notes and discovered that, in similar situations, public and private records concerning peace feelers were at variance. In numerous speeches Johnson had promised that the United States would go anyplace, anywhere, at anytime, in the search for peace. Kraslow and Loory decided that Johnson's statement ought to be checked out. The idea for a major investigation took root.

Kraslow and Loory both had contacts inside the government, but they realized that few of them would risk going on the record on such delicate subject matter. They would have to rely on leads that might end up nowhere, but the possibility of a major story involving government duplicity outweighed the risks. "It was," as Kraslow put it, "high risk journalism," involving large expenditures of time and money.

Kraslow and Loory received backing from Bob Donovan, who felt that the project was "the way the bureau ought to be going." But Frank Haven turned the proposal down. The managing editor didn't want two *Times* staffers spending so much time on just one story—especially such a long shot. The persistent Donovan eventually won approval for the project by sending Kraslow over Haven's head to Nick Williams.

Through the fall of '67 and the spring of '68, Kraslow and Loory spoke to career diplomats, intelligence officers, and disillusioned State Department employees, as well as official Washington, in their quest to "test the private record of Vietnam diplomacy against the public record." After eight months of research and 150,000 words of notes, the two reporters were able to chronicle the continuous rejection of possible negotiations from 1964 to Tet. "In the balance of forces in Washington," Kraslow and Loory discovered, "those who were urging the waging of an intense—if limited—war, far outweighed those in favor of seeking a negotiated, compromise peace."

The two journalists found that the lost opportunities for peace negotiations were consciously concealed from the press. Loory and Kraslow were told by a Johnson aide, as they probed one particular lead, that they would "never get the inside story." When the reporters asked why, the aide replied, "It makes our government look so bad." The comment was not for attribution.

On March 31, 1968 Lyndon Johnson announced that peace negotiations would begin in Paris. Four days later the first of the Kraslow and Loory stories appeared.

The series was a major journalistic triumph. It brought several honors, including the Polk and Clapper awards, to the authors. The articles were later published in book form under the title *The Secret Search for Peace in Vietnam* and quickly became a campus best-seller. "You won't find any surprises," Daniel Ellsberg later told the authors in comparing their work to the unpublished Pentagon Paper's volume on peace negotiations.

There was little joy among the deskmen in Los Angeles. "Things never sat well with Haven after that," Kraslow recalled. Haven was furious with the two reporters for going over his head to get approval.

In spite of the conflicts with Los Angeles and the deterioration of relations with official Washington, the Donovan bureau, in 1969, was at its peak. Journalism watchers praised the Donovan bureau—the *Times*'s entree into national journalism.

The Donovan bureau—and Washington journalism—had come a long way in the half dozen years since the Kennedy assassination, when the new *Times* bureau was first organized. The initial probing that had occurred during the Johnson years had severely strained a once comfortable relationship between reporter and government official. By 1969 Washington journalists constantly brought up the historical anecdote concerning the punishment meted out by Alexander the Great to those Greek messengers who brought bad news. "Kill the messenger," was Alexander's policy, when in fact it was the message and not the messenger that caused the problem.

2. A "Dangerous" Pen

While *Times* editorials during the Johnson years maintained a consistent proadministration position on the war in Vietnam, the attitude of the new *Times* cartoonist Paul Conrad changed from muted hawk to trenchant antiwar critic. Just as Loory and Kraslow questioned U.S. intentions with regard to negotiations, Conrad in a January 5, 1968, cartoon mocked LBJ claims. He placed Johnson at a lectern, speaking the lines "We were waiting for a signal from Hanoi," while kicking the curtain behind him at a figure under a blinking traffic signal whose outstretched hands held a telephone and an olive branch.

Sam Yorty was another Conrad target. When the mayor, who desired the post of secretary of defense, returned from Southeast Asia advocating escalation—including the possibility of nuclear attack—Conrad drew Yorty in a straightjacket holding a pointer toward a map of Vietnam with the caption "Secretary of Defense." The mayor sued—and lost.

When Nick Williams assumed the editor's post in 1958, Bruce Russell had been the *Times* cartoonist for more than a generation. Russell shared the reactionary and anti-Communist politics of the pre-1960 *Times* and continued to strike out at Fidel Castro, John Kennedy, and the New Frontier. When Russell died in 1963, a systematic search for his replacement began.

"Get us the best," Otis Chandler told his editor. Williams made inquiries about Herblock and Mauldin, considered the top two cartoonists in the business. Neither was available, so Williams concentrated on a second group of cartoonists who had begun to receive national attention. He narrowed the list to three names and came back to Chandler. The *Times* publisher asked his editor which of the three he preferred. "Paul Conrad," Williams immediately replied, "but let me warn you, he's going to cause us some trouble." When Chandler reiterated that he wanted the best, Williams sought out his man.

By the early 1960s, Paul Conrad, the cartoonist for the *Denver Post*, had secured a national reputation for his striking characterizations and critical perception of politicians. In 1964 he won the Pulitzer Prize. That year Williams convinced Conrad to come to the *Times*.

Conrad's cartoons created tensions between his superiors and the business community. One businessman, Union Oil president Fred Hartley was angry enough to sue the paper because of a Conrad cartoon. Conrad—in the midst of the winter 1973 energy crisis—drew a barren and shriveled Christmas tree with a Union/76 lightbulb on one branch and a "Merry Christmas from Fred Heartless" sign hanging from another branch. The caption read: "Federal Government diverts 500,000 barrels of Union crude oil from Southern California to Guam—news item."

"He's vicious," "vindictive," "dangerous," the old business and political elite said of Conrad. Many were willing to forgive the new Washington bureau, and some limited muckraking reporting, but a cartoonist was the symbol of the paper itself, old business friends complained to Norman Chandler. Not without reservations, the *Times* management refused to fire the new cartoonist. In 1967 a disclaimer was put on the masthead that disassociated the cartoons from the management's official point of view. Conrad called it the "Reagan disclaimer," since Reagan, a frequent Conrad target, took office just before the disclaimer was instituted.

"Conrad was always pushing on that barrier," Williams later mused, "and sometimes he'd pass it." In those cases, Williams scribbled a note—"I just don't like this one, Paul"—and a Conrad cartoon fell to the trash can. *Times* reporters told their friends, "If you think his cartoons are great, you should see the rejects." For many *Times* staffers, the cartoons became the best symbol of the new *Times*.

3. The Specialists

By the mid-sixties, changes at the *Times* took a variety of forms. A number of staff had been hired for new slots outside the traditional newspaper beats. They were specialists; journalists from a magazine background whose assignments focused on institutional settings within the society. The specialists gave the *Times* a more intellectual face and a more distinctive approach.

Times management was willing to pay much more—sometimes double the existing scale—in order to hire a specialist. Bill Trombley, the new higher education writer, was hired by the *Times* in 1964. Trombley, because of his beat, was wary of possible interference from Regent Dorothy Chandler. But despite other Regent complaints he was relatively independent from outside pressure and was able to define his coverage as he saw fit.

There were occasions when the *Times* writer tested the limits of his freedom. In December 1964, Edward Carter, chairman of Broadway Hale stores, major advertisers in northern and Southern California papers and then chairman of the Board of Regents, made a complicated deal with UCLA and its chancellor, Franklin Murphy, to acquire a Bel Air mansion with a lavish Japanese garden that lay adjacent to the UCLA campus. While Carter lived in the mansion, UCLA provided the upkeep of the garden, an expense of more than $30,000 a year. Carter also used the transaction as a tax deduction. "It was a noncontroversial, happy thing," Carter said of the deal. "It didn't occur to me it might become a source of embarrassment later."

In the fall of 1969, Trombley and Ron Moscovitz, education writer for the *San Francisco Chronicle*, almost simultaneously heard of the garden transaction. The two journalists, who had worked on stories together in the past, shared their information and divided up the work. They knew they were on to a sensitive story involving a major advertiser and a UCLA chancellor who had recently been hired as chairman of the board of the Times Mirror Company. Jeff Perlman, who worked for the UCLA *Daily Bruin* and was a stringer for the *Times*, also picked up on the information.

The *Bruin* broke the story on November 4, 1969. "It is questionable," an editorial in the same issued noted, "whether businessmen who sit on the Board of Regents should be able to use the University as an umbrella for their own financial interests, which is the effect of the Carter donation."

That morning Trombley walked into his city editor's office, armed with a copy of the *Bruin*. He argued that a *Times* failure to print his story would embarrass the paper. When metropolitan editor Bill Thomas showed the article to managing editor Haven, Haven exploded, saying he'd be damned if he'd run such a story. Nick Williams was called in. After Trombley reminded his editors about the *Bruin* article, Haven, Thomas, and Williams decided to let Trombley's story run but only after a meticulous review. Thomas did the editing, Haven worked up a head-line—DETAILS CONCERNING EDWARD CARTER GIFT OF GARDEN TO UCLA DISCLOSED—and Williams looked over everyone's shoulder. The three editors decided to place the story in the back of the paper, next to the Pix-ies cartoon on the second page of the second section.

Ron Moscovitz had an even harder time at the *Chronicle*. After Broad-way Hale owner Carter flew up to San Francisco to confront the *Chroni-cle* management, word seeped back to cityside that he threatened to with-draw his advertising if the story weren't changed. The next day, two days after the *Bruin* broke the story, Moscovitz's edited story ran. "It made Ed Carter look like a philanthropist," Moscovitz remarked about the final version.

Trombley was furious over the *Times* treatment of his story. He com-plained to staff writers, many of whom sympathized with his difficulties. But George Reasons, the official head of the *Times* investigative team, re-marked that he found it interesting that anything that embarrassing ran at all. Reasons' remarkable reaction, given his beat, exemplified the widely held belief among staffers that the tendency to anticipate an editor's re-jection and stop before even trying—rather than risk direct censorship—was the key problem at the paper.

4. *"Where the Action Is"*

The discussion of independence—of how extensively journalists are freed from traditional newspaper constraints—has usually been limited to the analysis of the section one news pages. The back of the paper, the newspaper's "software" sections—food, fashion, real estate, and en-tertainment, with their specialized audiences and targeted advertising markets—are rarely subjected to rigorous analysis or criticisms. Yet the problems are the same. The message of the government official ("don't alienate your source") is equivalent to an advertiser's warning ("don't bite the hand that feeds you"). Some of the most blatant journalistic sins have occurred in the back of the paper: news stories that are thinly dis-guised ad promos; articles keyed to ads that appear the same day; or rewrites of industry handouts. The tone of the overall coverage is almost always proindustry. The *Times* food editor in the 1940s and '50s, for ex-ample, considered herself a feature writer for the advertising department.

Since 1956 the *Times* has led all newspapers in number of ad lines and amount of advertising revenue. The thickest paper in the world, the *Los*

Angeles Times prints more pages on a daily basis than the *New York Times* or the *Chicago Tribune*. Most of the pages and most of those ads appear in the software sections.

The massive Sunday paper, with such ad-laden sections as Travel, Real Estate and *Home* magazine, greatly contributed to the overall profitability of the *Times* operation. In the early sixties, the female-oriented, upper-middle-class *Home*, a rotogravure section advertising home and decor products, generated annual revenues as high as $1.5 million. The magazine's success had caused Otis Chandler to wonder if a second rotogravure could duplicate *Home*'s profits by appealing to a different, male-oriented market.

Chandler, a great fan of *Playboy* magazine, was attracted to the notion of a Sunday supplement filled with sports, travel, recreational activity, some politics, and pictures of sexy women—a supplement that could, by the nature of its audience, pick up liquor, auto, tobacco, travel, and sports equipment ads.

In 1963, after Frank McCulloch quit rather than take on the new magazine, Chandler asked *Home* editor Jim Toland and ad manager Glen Peters to design a dummy issue and conduct a market survey for the new publication. The prototype issue had a bikini-clad surfer on the cover and the market survey pointed to the male-oriented ad base and possible national advertising. Other than its ability to create a new market, there was little thought or discussion concerning editorial purpose. "It was," the magazine's first editor remarked, "an economic decision from the start."

Marshall Lumsden was hired from the *Saturday Evening Post* to head up the project in 1965. Lumsden knew nothing of McCulloch's fight and departure, nor of the early plans for the magazine. Without specific instructions, Lumsden proceeded to develop his own concepts for it. He was attracted to the notion of covering California life-style and wanted to encourage controversial pieces in political, social, and cultural areas.

Life-style stories also appealed to Lumsden's immediate superior Jim Bellows, former editor of the *New York Herald Tribune*'s Sunday *New York Magazine*. When the *Tribune* folded in 1966, Williams hired Bellows as associate editor in charge of the special sections. The decision to hire Bellows was undoubtedly influenced by his experience with Sunday supplements. The software editor's main responsibility would be the new magazine, now named *West*.

"*West* magazine is WHERE THE ACTION IS!" Bellows wrote in a memo to Lumsden soon after coming to the *Times*. "That's the ad line. The Western area is where the action in this country is—we ought to be proud of it."

The first issue of *West* appeared on September 6, 1966. Early issues of *West*, with articles on a Vietnam critic, changes within the Mexican-

American community, the death penalty, and controversy over police confessions, did not conform to the management's conception of utilizing ad-related stories. "If Pan Am buys a $5,000 ad," *West*'s ad manager complained, "they don't want to hear about congestion in Hawaii." "What they wanted," Lumsden said of the *Times* editors, "was a Sunday magazine that wouldn't offend anyone, especially advertisers."

After *West*'s third issue, a Nick Williams memo to Lumsden asked "Where are the girls?" Williams insisted that "Any excuse for female skin, if it's decent, is useful." If *West* could touch the key bases, such as "sports, gals, booze," Williams told Lumsden, "then we'll be moving."

Williams argued in another memo that "nothing, brother, improves the appearance of a mag . . . more than lots and lots of beautiful expensive color ads."

In 1967, less than a year after *West* had begun, Bellows, Lumsden, Otis Chandler, sales vice-president Vance Stickell, and general manager Robert Nelson had a meeting. All urged Lumsden to put a greater emphasis on sports, entertainment, and travel material and to deemphasize analytic and controversial stories. The pressure had its effect. Articles appeared on motorcycles, Hawaiian vacation spots, campers, and men's fashions—material Lumsden characterized as "stuff that takes away from the credibility of a magazine."

"We were operating under so many limitations," associate editor Umberto Tosi remarked, "that it was like telling a guy to swim the Catalina Channel in a suit of armor. Every time you opened your mouth, down came a memo from Nick Williams or Bellows. The best part of the magazine was what we got away with."

For the Chandlers the magazine never performed up to economic expectation. In 1967, its first full year of operation, *West* lost $1 million. In 1968 it nearly broke even. In 1969 the magazine managed a little profit, but, with the Nixon recession in 1970, it went back into the red. Early in 1971 *West* editor Lumsden was fired, and a new man, Peter Bunzell, was brought in to give the magazine one last chance. *West* folded a year later.

5. Young Faces, Old Taboos

But while the memo wars were raging at *West*, a new mood was taking hold in the city room. The new young staff who joined the paper in 1965 and 1966 felt the effects of the riots, campus turmoil, and other turbulence outside the paper. By 1967 antiwar marches had grown from the tens of thousands to the hundreds of thousands, Eugene McCarthy was preparing to challenge a president, and a radical left, for the first time in twenty years, was criticizing the dominant institutions of society—including the press. An antiestablishment cultural movement had spread among young people, a post-war generation weaned on the breakdown of the nuclear family and the alienation of the fifties. American society was in a crisis.

In 1965, the *Times* metropolitan editor was Bill Thomas, who began his career on the news desk of the *Buffalo* (N.Y.) *Evening News*. In 1957 he was hired by the Chandler organization to do desk work for the *Mirror* and rose to become the *Mirror*'s city editor just before the paper folded.

Thomas came to the *Times* in January 1962 as metropolitan editor Hank Osborne's assistant. Osborne was of the old school, a classic generalist, committed to the daily coverage of hard news. Osborne couldn't adjust to the paper's new emphasis on magazine-style features and specialist take-outs. Thomas replaced Osborne as the instrument for change in the *Times* city room.

From 1962 to 1966, much of the praise for the new *Times* had shifted away from the metropolitan side of the paper, where Frank McCulloch had held sway, to Donovan's Washington bureau. Critics claimed that the *Times* practiced "Afghanistanism," a journalistic metaphor meaning that a story could get covered more easily if it happened in Afghanistan than if it happened locally. Media critic Bill Rivers wrote that the *Times* was not sufficiently sensitive to its environment and only got into important stories after the fact.

After Thomas became city editor, *Times* management, sensitive to criticism over its failure to cover the local scene, began to beef up the paper's local staff. By 1966 the *Times* had forty-seven reporters and twenty photographers on cityside, more than any other daily on the West Coast.

In the spring of 1966, Thomas assigned local general assignment reporter George Reasons to pursue a series of phone tips that came to the *Times* concerning possible corruption at the City Planning Department. For six months Reasons, a cautious and methodical worker, tracked down the information. His story exposed business ties between several city planning commissioners and San Fernando real estate developers.

After the appearance of the story—an important breakthrough for cityside—disgruntled city employees began to contact the paper to tell of other corruption. To follow up the deluge of new information, the *Times* set up its first investigative team since the killing of the Teamsters series in 1963.

The biggest corruption story uncovered by the investigations dealt with the city Harbor Commissions' awarding, without competitive bidding, of a $12 million building contract for a proposed World Trade Center.

The *Times* team discovered that the company which received the award was headed by city Human Relations Commissioner Keith Smith, and that two of the company's stockholders were Harbor commissioners. In addition, Smith owned 20,000 shares in a savings and loan association headed by the president of the Harbor Commission, Pietro di Carlo, and had a $26,000 personal loan out to a fourth Harbor commissioner.

Immediately after the story broke on October 18, 1967, Mayor Yorty sprang to the defense of his commissioners. What was wrong, the mayor rhetorically asked at a news conference the day after the story came out, with the fact that some of his appointees were businessmen who might have business with the people doing business with the city.

District Attorney Evelle Younger, a political ally and personal friend of Otis Chandler, worked closely with the *Times* reporters. A grand jury was called, centering on Smith and the four commissioners. Before any indictments were handed down, Pietro di Carlo was found dead near the San Pedro pier. Police ruled the matter death by accidental means, stating that Di Carlo had gone to the pier at 6 A.M. to meet a friend, had walked down the slippery pier, lost his footing, and fell into the water. The story became a sensation.

Three weeks later the five commissioners, including the deceased Di Carlo, were indicted. Two of the commissioners were found guilty and sent to prison for short terms. Yorty blasted the *Times* and claimed that pretrial publicity was responsible for the guilty verdicts. The mayor labeled the investigations a "smear," a political vendetta, because, as he later put it, "The *Times* couldn't run me, that's all."

The harbor series provided an ideal situation for Bill Thomas to launch his concept of investigative journalism with few risks and many potential rewards. The articles stilled the critics and raised the spirits of the staff and eventually brought the paper a Pulitzer Prize, the first for the new *Times* in the area of local investigations.

6. *"A Threat to Public Safety"*

After Watts, the *Times,* sensitive to charges of racial discrimination and anxious to keep on top of events in the black community, finally hired its first experienced black reporter, Ray Rogers. Rogers, whose major task was to make contacts and provide information, was hampered by the fact that many activists considered him a "sellout" who spied on the community for the "white establishment" paper.

In the late sixties the black movement was divided between two tendencies: The more conservative approach, "cultural nationalism," with its historical roots in the separatism of the Black Muslim and "Back to Africa" movements, emphasized an independent black culture, and the radical perspective; "revolutionary nationalism," which derived from the civil rights movement and the ghetto uprisings linked the need to change conditions in the black community to the need to change American society as a whole. The most prominent revolutionary nationalist group was the Black Panther Party.

As the Panthers grew and a state-of-siege mentality took hold of the Los Angeles Police Department, "the romance with all things black," as

Rogers put it, "came to an end." The *Times* management had become increasingly hostile to the Panthers, labeling them an "armed paramilitary group" that represented "in some degree, a threat to the public safety." The Panthers, according to one *Times* editorial, had repeatedly violated the law; therefore, "police not only have the right, but the duty to act."

On December 4, 1969, Black Panther leader Fred Hampton was shot to death in his bed during a massive police raid on the Panthers' Chicago headquarters. *Times* midwest bureau staffer Francis Ward, the only black reporter on the national staff, meticulously reconstructed the circumstances around the killing. The *Times* reporter wrote a cautious, well-balanced piece, presenting both Panther and police contentions, concluding that strong evidence pointed to police responsibility. The Hampton story was placed in the back of the paper on page twenty-three, despite the fact that the *New York Times* and several other papers played the shooting as a major, page one item.

Four days later Los Angeles police laid seige to local Panther headquarters. The *Times* story on the shootout, largely unsympathetic to the Panthers, appeared on page one. The next day, in a page one follow-up story—DISPUTE FLARES OVER WHO FIRED FIRST SHOT IN RAID ON PANTHERS—the paper continued to emphasize anti-Panther, propolice points of view. The article cited both police critics and defenders, but gave only ten paragraphs of space to the critics, and twenty-five to the police defense.

There were other indications, by the time of the Panther shootouts, that a backlash had developed at the *Times*. By 1969 metropolitan editor Thomas felt that the *Times* had been glutted with black-oriented stories and that it was necessary to cut back.

Tensions also surfaced cityside. Ray Rogers started to find "George Wallace for President" buttons on his desk. The question of police relations had become a substantive issue. During one of the Watts Summer Festivals, an incident occurred that led police to shoot a young black. *Times* reporter Linda Mathews was assigned to cover the stormy city council hearings which followed the incident. She handed in a classic, balanced article. But night city editor Glen Binford, with managing editor Haven's approval, cut the story by eliminating testimony that criticized the police. The edited propolice version exacerbated by the live public television coverage of the hearings was an embarrassment for Mathews.

Problems with the police were not limited to the black community. As the Vietnam war escalated, university protests mounted, and *Times* reporters were frequently dispatched to cover campus demonstrations. After the Cambodian invasion and the Kent State shootings in May 1970, massive, spontaneous demonstrations broke out at UCLA and scores of other schools throughout the country. After a state of emergency was called, hundreds of police entered UCLA and made sweeps up and down the campus. One of the *Times* reporters, Stan Williford, witnessed an incident in which a student walking across the quad with books in his hands was caught in a sweep and beaten savagely by two police, who took the student behind some bushes. Williford had seen nothing to provoke such a beating; the student was simply going to class.

Williford and other *Times* reporters phoned in many such stories, conveying a strong impression, backed with incidents, of police brutality. Metro editor Thomas was very dubious about the accusations against the police. When rewriteman Noel Greenwood brought up Williford's eyewitness account, Thomas brushed it aside; he told Greenwood that the police must have had a reason for going after the student and the reporters shouldn't judge anything unless they had all the information. Greenwood was forced to redo the story and limit it to the number of arrests, the fact of the state of emergency, and a description of the police actions as an effort to break up groups of demonstrators.

But Greenwood was determined to prove the *Times* reporters' version of the events. He received a list of civilian and police casualties from the UCLA Medical Center, compiled other eyewitness accounts of beatings and arrests, and picked up UCLA Chancellor Young's statement concerning the possibility of "very serious instances of excessive overreaction and overuse of force on the part of individual policemen." With the quote from a respectable source and the medical center statistics, Greenwood was able to produce a couple of follow-up stories that indicated "that police used unnecessary force and arrested persons indiscriminately." The *Times* editorial board, however, was not convinced and editorialized in favor of the police actions.

The rise of the protest movements and the impact of overall peer group influence contributed to the differences between the younger reporters and their editors. Mathews, whose friends included antiwar activists, began, soon after her hiring in 1966, to orient herself toward antiwar and antidraft coverage, an area largely ignored at the *Times* up to then. Most of her articles ran intact, but a few led to heated arguments with her boss. Mathews battled with the desk over the *Times*' use of the word "draft dodger" and insisted that "draft resister" be used instead. She also argued, late in 1967, that the presidential candidacy of Eugene McCarthy ought to be taken seriously and given coverage. Thomas countered that the *Times* shouldn't give impetus to a candidacy with "overblown" coverage.

The younger *Times* reporters, like Mathews, constituted a new minority at the paper and provided a link to an angry world outside the *Times*. Thomas was accessible to them but he rarely agreed with their point of view. He had a knack for cooling down his dissident staff and many maintained a grudging respect for him.

The Thomas style set the cityside tone in the late sixties. Unlike previ-

BANKS AND FINANCIAL INSTITUTIONS

Security Bank	(D)
Farmers & Merchants Bank	(D)
First National Bank of Niland	(C,D)
Mortgage Guarantee Corp.	(D)
Bond & Mortgage Insurance Corp.	(D)
First National Bank, Owensmouth	(C,D)
First National Bank, Van Nuys	(C,D)
Los Angeles First National Trust & Savings Bank	(D)
Los Angeles Investment Co.	(D)
Title Insurance & Trust Co.	(I)

REAL ESTATE, URBAN

San Fernando Mission Land Co.	(C,D)
Los Angeles Suburban Homes Co.	(C,D)
Rodeo Land & Water Co.	(I)
Beverly-Wilshire Investment Co.	(I)
Rancho Santa Anita	(C)
Central Investment Corp. (Biltmore Hotel)	(D,I)
Ambassador Hotel	(I)
Atherton Real Estate Corp.	(C)
The Palace Building (Orpheum Theatre)	(C)
Subway Terminal Corp.	(I)
California Hotel	(I)
Interurban Water Co.	(D,I)
Garden Foundation Inc.	(D,I)
Sherman and Clark Land Co.	(I)

AUTO, RUBBER, CONSTRUCTION

Western Construction Co.	(C,D)
L.A. Stone Co.	(I)
Southern California Rock & Gravel Co.	(I)

Goodyear Tire & Rubber	(D)
Major Highways Committee	(D)

FAMILY HOLDING COMPANIES

Chandis Securities	(C,D)
Chandotis	(C,D)
Chandler-Sherman Corp.	(C,D)
Southwest Co.	(C,D)
Southwest Land Co.	(C,D)

MEDIA INTERESTS

Times Mirror	(C,D)
Times Mirror Printing & Binding	(C,D)
Powell Publishing Co.	(D)
KHJ Radio	(C)
American Engraving Co.	(C,D)
L.D. Powell Law Book Co.	(D)
Pacific Coast Sales Book Co.	(D)
American Newspaper Publishers Association	(D)

AEROSPACE

Western Air Express	(D,I)
Transcontinental &Western Air Inc.	(D)
Pacific Zeppelin Transport Co.	(D)
Douglas Aircraft	(I)

OIL

Pico Oil Co.	(C)
Sherman Oil Co.	(C,D)
La Puente Oil Co.	(C)
Shell-Union Oil Co.	(D,I)
Union Oil of Delaware	(D,I)
Union Oil of California	(D)

AGRICULTURAL AND RURAL REAL ESTATE

Tejon Ranch	(C,D)
Big Conduit Land Co.	(C,D)
Colorado River Land Co.	(C,D)

ECONOMIC INTERESTS

California-Mexico
    Land & Cattle Co.   (C,D)
Imperial Valley Farm Lands
    Assn.   (C,D)
Rowland Land Co.   (C,D)
Signal Mountain Land &
    Water Co.   (C,D)
Carmel Cattle Co.   (C,D)
Ramona Acres Co.   (C,D)
Pioneer Pacific Worsted Co.   (C,D)
Vermejo Club (Bartlett Ranch)
    (C,D)
Sinaloa Land Co.   (I)
C.i.a. Jabonera del Pacific SCI   (D)

BOOSTER, BUSINESS, AND MANUFACTURING

Automobile Club   (D)
Community Development Assoc.
    (D)
California Chamber of Commerce
    (D)
Los Angeles Athletic Club   (C,D)
Merchant's & Manufacturing
    Assoc.   (D)
All Year Club   (D)
Central Business District
    Assoc.   (D)
Bond Great West Clothing Co.   (C)
La Hacienda Co.   (I)

SHIPPING

Los Angeles Steamship Co.   (C,D)
Los Angeles Shipping &
    Drydock Co.   (D,I)
Matson Navigation Co.   (I)

FOREST LAND

Esperanza Timber Co.   (D,I)
Crown Zellerbach Co.   (I)
Yosemite Park & Curry Co.   (D,I)

RAILROAD

Phoenix Railroad of Arizona   (C,D)
Ferro Carril Inter California
    Del Sur   (D)

EDUCATION AND CULTURE

California Institute of
    Technology   (D)
Stanford University   (D)
Pilgrimmage Theatre   (D,I)
Hollywood Bowl   (D)
Los Angeles Grand Opera
    Assoc.   (D)
Museum Patron's Assn. of
      Los Angeles Museum of
      History, Science & Art   (D)

KEY
C = Controlling Interest
D = Directorship
I = Investment

ous city editors, he seemed to flow with the period. Many of the staff appreciated him and his modernizing approach. Thomas pushed for change not so much on a political basis but through his greater emphasis on magazine-style feature writing.

He sat on top of a willing cityside news organization. He led a staff that had significantly changed from the *Times* of old, but the past was not completely shaken. There were still several taboos at the *Times*; some explicit, some a little more obscure, and a few overtly imposed. The *Times* ultimately served the needs of its owners, but those needs, by the late sixties, had become a little difficult to pin down.

CHAPTER 24

Politics In Flux

1. The Rise: Ronald Reagan

In 1965 the California Republicans were in a period of transition. The party's cohesiveness had broken down during the six years following the 1958 musical chairs campaign. The powerful individuals who had run Republican affairs since the days of Frank Merriam and Earl Warren had either died off or dropped out of politics, and a vacuum had developed. New financial strongmen, like local oil man Henry Salvatori, millionaire Ford auto dealer Holmes Tuttle, and Union Oil President Cy Rubel, emerged to take control of party affairs. The Salvatori/Tuttle/Rubel circle, known as the "millionaire's group," had begun to assume leadership of the California conservatives and the effective power within the state party apparatus. Others joined with the Salvatori group: Justin Dart of Dart Industries, the extraordinarily powerful Asa Call, Edward Mills, head of the Republican state central committee, and Leonard Firestone of the tire family.

The "millionaire's group" was initially a loose amalgam of right-wing money people who had been only on the fringes of electoral politics until the 1964 presidential campaign of Barry Goldwater. At the close of the 1964 race, the Republican campaign had produced a television special for Goldwater which featured former television actor Ronald Reagan speaking on the issues of the day. "The speech," as it came to be called, helped raise money and inject spirit into the last days of the losing campaign. Immediately after the election, the "millionaire's group" organized a "Friends of Ronald Reagan" committee and sent out thousands of letters asking for comments about a possible Reagan candidacy for governor in 1966. Satisfied with the response, the group drafted the former actor and prepared the most sophisticated media campaign in California history.

The Reaganites assembled a large team of public relations advisors, communications aides, and a psychological counseling organization to provide techniques of practical behavorial analysis. The public relations firm of Spencer-Roberts was hired to run the campaign and develop its overall look.

While the Reagan organization coalesced, the forces of incumbent Pat Brown, under attack from both the left and right wings within the Democratic Party, floundered. Sam Yorty opposed Brown in the Democratic primary, and criticized him for his failure to smash student protests and black rebellions. (To the surprise of many, Yorty polled 40 percent of the vote.) The largest grass-roots organization of Democrats, the CDC, also undercut the governor when it came out against the Vietnam War, despite the warnings of Brown and other mainstream Democrats. "Two terms is enough" became the slogan of many antiwar activists who refused to support the incumbent governor. Pat Brown, like Lyndon Johnson, was losing control.

In contrast, Ronald Reagan seemed to offer firmness and discipline in a chaotic period. His slogan, "the creative society," was both polished and vague. Reagan spoke over the heads of the press directly to the voters through the medium of television. The former actor's media charm and the deft hand of campaign manager Bill Roberts, combined with a growing uneasiness in the society over mainstream liberal solutions, increased Reagan's base beyond the old Goldwater right-wing constituency.

Though the *Times* had backed Goldwater in '64, it had also criticized the Republican right for its "head in the sand attitudes." Pat Brown was hopeful that the paper might be willing to change its pro-Republican stance, particularly if Reagan was the party's choice. Several months before the election, Brown approached Otis Chandler about the *Times*'s endorsement policy. The *Times* publisher told the governor that if Reagan won the June primary, the paper would refrain from issuing an endorsement in the general election. But on October 16, the *Times* endorsed Reagan. "California needs the drive and lift," the editorial noted, "which only a new management team can produce." On Sunday, November 6, two days before the election, the *Times* reiterated: "We continue to be impressed with Reagan's vigor and imagination as opposed to the manifest weariness of the Governor's approach to the immense problems of California." When Brown later asked Otis what had happened, the *Times* publisher replied that the decision had been made by members of the Chandler family—"the majority stockholders," as Otis coyly put it.

The *Times* endorsement was significant in that it helped undermine the extremist charge against Reagan which had become the cornerstone of the Brown campaign. If a changing *Times* could stomach Reagan, then so could that alienated block of voters searching for some "vigor and imagination" in their political choice.

Times news coverage of the election was in keeping with its new, objective style of shuffling reporters between candidates and providing equal space. Reagan aide Stuart Spencer felt that the *Times* reporters, as well as other journalists covering the campaign, stood somewhat in awe of Reagan's celebrity status, much in the same manner as the electorate. The press never successfully separated Reagan's image from campaign realities. On election day, Reagan swept to victory by an astounding margin of one million votes.

In its campaign endorsement, the *Times* had promised to "dissent where necessary," if Reagan were elected. The paper soon fulfilled that pledge. Even before his inauguration, the *Times* started to take issue with the new governor over his pronouncements concerning the state university system. Differences over the issue turned into a major policy clash.

By 1967 three distinct positions—radical, liberal, and conservative—had emerged with respect to the university. The radical perspective developed out of the growing political involvement among students which first crystallized during the Berkeley free speech movement in 1964. The students argued that the university had become merely a training ground for skilled labor, an institution that socialized young people to adapt to their future technical and professional jobs, one that provided a conduit for corporate and governmental research and development. A popular student pamphlet, "Who Rules the Multiversity," identified the corporate ties of the Board of Regents, including Dorothy Chandler.

The liberal position, represented by Board of Regents members Norton Simon and Fred Dutton and by university administrator Clark Kerr, agreed that the university was an essential part of a government/industry complex in its role of training the future technicians and managers of a corporate America. The liberals argued for large-scale budgets and government support of university programs. Though opposed to the student protests and in support of police intervention once the students went outside "regular channels," as in the free speech sit-in in 1964, they counseled a more tactful approach than the Reaganites.

Reagan gave leadership to the conservative regents. During his campaign, he had promised to "clean up the mess in Berkeley," and put an end to the "coddling of demonstrators." The conservatives, led by Reagan and Regent Edward Carter, tended to mistrust the corporate liberal analysis of the university and favored a stricter interpretation of the *in loco parentis* (the university as a substitute parent) function. They favored cutting the school budget and wanted to fire the leading exponent of the liberal "multiversity" perspective, UC Chancellor Clark Kerr.

Regent Dorothy Chandler tended to agree with the liberal position on issues, although she frequently acted as a mediator between the different factions. She fed stories to education writer Bill Trombley, who revealed the growing divisions in a series of page one stories. Editorially, the *Times* attacked both the radical students and the Reagan conservatives' "threat to higher education."

By 1968 the conservatives were a clear majority of the regents. Kerr was fired, a modified tuition was instituted, and Trombley's education stories became a serious bone of contention between the governor and the *Times*. That year Dorothy Chandler resigned from the Board of Regents, and the *Times* went into full opposition, criticizing the governor on other issues, such as budget cutbacks in the area of mental health.

Relations between Reagan and the Chandlers were further exacerbated after the *Times* management, on the heels of Reagan's 1966 victory, set up a new team of five full-time reporters in Sacramento. The paper's new bureau chief, Tom Goff, an old Sacramento hand who had come to the *Times* in 1964, immediately instituted the paper's new, independent, nonpartisan approach to change. But *Times* reporters still had difficulty trying to find the means to break through the Reagan veneer. The governor's frequent use of televised press conferences to explain policy initiatives frustrated print journalists, who wanted more depth than the image-oriented one-liners Reagan tossed out. Goff recalled how bureau reporters and Reagan aides became surly and argumentative at Reagan press briefings, which added to the already existing antagonisms between the *Times* and the Reagan administration. In spite of its differences, the *Times* management decided to back the governor for reelection in 1970. Reagan stayed in office, defeating Democratic challenger Jess Unruh by 400,000 votes.

2. The Resurrection: Richard Nixon

"Let us not be passive conspirators in the process of our own self-destruction," the *Times* warned its readers in the turbulent days of 1968. Vietnam, the campuses, the riots, the assassinations of Martin Luther King and Bobby Kennedy were all turning the country into a "threatened society" in the view of the *Times* management. The country appeared to be on the brink of a massive social confrontation.

Just ten weeks after Bobby Kennedy's death, the Democrats gathered in Chicago to select their Presidential candidate. "Everything is uptight at Armageddon," *Times* Chicago bureau chief Don Bruckner wrote the day before the convention began. Antiwar demonstrators had arrived by the thousands. They, and the antiwar convention delegates inside the amphitheater, felt under siege in Daley's Chicago and Lyndon Johnson's Democratic party.

As the convention got under way, the Chicago police broke up the protest activities. Demonstrators were gassed and clubbed, and several journalists were among the injured. "Newsmen who were beaten, and one who was threatened by the police," Bruckner wrote on August 27, "said the police attacked them without provocation." The actions outside had repercussions inside the convention hall. "Mayor Richard J. Daley's massive, uptight security measures," *Times* staffer Jack Nelson wrote, "have resulted in the manhandling of delegates, newsmen, and demonstrators and have brought angry cries from the Democratic Convention floor for him to end 'police-state terror.' "

A Paul Conrad cartoon depicted a policeman, labeled "Chicago Police," writing on a pad marked "Body Count," while another policeman waded into a crowd of sprawled bodies, some identified as "Press." The caption read, "Law and Order."

"There is certainly something both sad and frightening about the spectacle of armed guards and antipersonnel barriers in the the midst of a national political convention," the *Times* editorialized on August 27. "The arrangements seem to be almost a symbolic negation of a key part of our political process, inevitably if fatuously inviting comparison with the trappings associated with an uneasy totalitarian regime. Yet for all the glib comments," the editorial insisted, "the ugly fact remains that the security precautions are undoubtedly necessary." The *Times* management blamed both police and demonstrators for the violence.

The disjuncture between editorial calls for order and the reporters' observation of a "police riot" was widened with the arrests of two *Times* staffers. Linda Mathews came to Chicago during her vacation. On her request she was put back on salary and sent out on the streets to cover the events. On the third night of the convention, the most violent to date, Mathews found her way to a phone blocked by a police line. "Look lady, I don't care who you are. Nobody gets through," the cop in charge told Mathews when she asked to pass. The policeman refused to let her go by, even after she identified herself as press. When Mathews insisted on getting to the phone, she found herself pulled forty yards to a waiting paddywagon.

Times White House correspondent Stuart Loory, who had come to Chicago to write about Hubert Humphrey's nomination strategy, was arrested the next day. Loory had spent the first days of the convention writing inside the Hilton Hotel, while "the world was cracking up outside," as he put it. On the night of Humphrey's acceptance speech, Loory was sent out to follow the proceedings at Convention Hall. He tagged along on a

protest march to the amphitheater, but the marchers were stopped by police before they had gone more than a few blocks. When Loory tried to
continue on, crossing an "arrest line" established artificially by the police, as a representative of the press, he was immediately arrested. "It
was one of the few times I lost my reporter's objectivity," Loory later
commented.

"The old political warhorses, Humphrey and Nixon," Bob Donovan
wrote, "will be running in a different kind of America this fall." Nixon,
resurrected from his last press conference and keeping a low profile on
the war, had promised on the night of his nomination that he would "bring
us together." The Nixon strategy was, in essence, a media campaign that
included a package of slogans ("A Secret Plan for Peace," etc.), a series
of effective TV commercials, and maximum use of free television time.

The *Times* covered the campaign in its now traditional style of reporter
rotation and equivalent coverage. Analysis of campaign issues was handled in a strict, straightforward manner, without any attempt to interpret
the underlying media strategies. As Joe McGinnis documented in *The
Selling of the President*, the Nixon efforts neutralized a potentially critical
press. "If there was one feeling shared almost universally among the reporters who covered the Nixon campaign," Washington reporter Jules
Witcover wrote, "it was one of frustration—frustration that the machinery of the Nixon organization was so effective and seemingly so impene-
trable in its controlled use of traditional and media campaign tactics to in-
sulate the candidate and, often, to filter out the press."

Though the *Times*, throughout 1968, had worried about the state of
American society and the need for "true self-examination," the paper
finally endorsed Richard Nixon and welcomed the election results as the
Republican candidate came to power with 43 percent of the vote. *Times*
management seemed content: The hometown boy had finally made it to
the top.

3. The Disgrace: Sam Yorty

"We won't become a great city until our local officials develop a little
more sophistication—and indulge themselves in less small town name
calling," Otis Chandler remarked to a local reporter after a *Times* editorial criticized a Mayor Yorty Red-baiting attack against Governor Pat
Brown. But the image of the unsophisticated small town guy, used so
effectively against Mayor Poulson and his "downtown machine," was essential to Sam Yorty's strategy.

In 1965 Yorty had been supported for reelection by a united business
community, including the *Times*. The mayor maintained his business connections during his second term. Henry Salvatori of Ronald Reagan's

"millionaire club" was the mayor's top political adviser, and Yorty's financial backers included many of the region's major industrial and financial executives. Yorty's kitchen cabinet included corporate executives, financiers, and lawyers from such companies as Occidental Petroleum, Pacific Mutual Life Insurance Company, Southern California Edison, Thriftimart Stores, and Nixon's old law firm, Adams, Duque and Hazeltine.

The mayor, however, after carefully cultivating his folksy "Mayor Sam" image, did not want to be perceived as the candidate of big business. In spite of his probusiness connections and policies, which he tried to keep low key, the mayor attempted to create the impression that he was an underdog, outside the power structure.

Yorty was fashioning a new constituency of white suburban residents, who were fearful of the changes taking place in society, suspicious of both "Great Society" liberals and downtown business, and open to racial and anti-Communist appeals. Yorty invented stunts and gimmicks that might have seemed uncouth to the Chandlers but struck a chord among residents in areas like the San Fernando Valley. The mayor's appeal to the growing antiblack suburban constituency was strengthened by his blaming the Watts riots on left-wing agitators and his refusal to recognize or deal with the social and economic grievances in the ghetto.

Soon after the Watts riots, antagonisms between Yorty and the *Times* reemerged for the first time since 1961. The *Times* disliked Yorty's cultivation of his small town image and was angered by his Watts tactics. The paper was increasingly committed to a modern, liberal approach to the problems of the inner cities, and had modified its own previous position on many questions, such as open housing.

The incipient split became a full break when the *Times,* in the spring of 1967, began the first of several exposés of corruption in the Yorty administration. Yorty retaliated by blasting the *Times* on his own new ninety-minute local television talk show. Responding, in part, to Paul Conrad's biting cartoons, Yorty hired a cartoonist to make fun of Otis Chandler for the program. Conrad was amused by the TV cartoonist, but the *Times* publisher reacted angrily. The investigations and criticisms against the mayor multiplied in the pages of the *Times*.

The Chandler/Yorty dispute received national attention and upset local businessmen. Barker Brothers president Neil Petree tried to mediate. He went to Yorty, but the mayor just said "some very nasty things about the Chandlers and the *Times*," as Petree remembered it. Petree also had trouble understanding Otis Chandler's motivations: "I never knew why Otis Chandler and the *Times* were attacking Yorty so personally."

The feud helped the mayor a lot more than it hurt. By feeding off decades of anti-*Times*, anti-Chandler suspicions and hostilities, Yorty turned the paper's attacks around by claiming that the *Times* was out to get him. By the time he was up for reelection for his third term, Yorty, once again, had his downtown target.

Thirteen candidates entered the April 1, 1969, mayoralty primary, including Yorty, black City Councilman Tom Bradley, and Republican Congressman Alphonzo Bell. Yorty ran a low-key campaign for the primary, described by *Times* reporter Dick Bergholz as "lackluster." The *Times* endorsed Al Bell in the Primary. To everyone's surprise Tom Bradley placed first with 42 percent of the vote; Yorty came in second with 26 percent; TV announcer Baxter Ward was third; and Bell finished a poor fourth.

Within several days after the primary, the mayor organized a "truth squad" to demonstrate links between radicals and the Bradley campaign. The squad charged Bradley with membership in "an organization that is plotting to overthrow the government of the United States"; namely, the New Democratic Coalition (NDC) an antiwar reform coalition inside the Democratic party. The truth squad labeled NDC members "anarchists and revolutionaries."

Each time Bradley answered a Yorty charge, another one came up. The red-baiting continued throughout the campaign. When Yorty's squad discovered that one of Bradley's officials had once belonged to the Communist party, Bradley forces went on the defensive and eventually asked the campaign official to resign. A former blacklisted screenwriter, Dalton Trumbo—by 1969 a prestigious academy award winner—was asked not to use his house for a Bradley fund-raiser for fear of tainting the campaign. The Bradley forces, led by anxious liberals, were in complete disarray.

Yorty stayed on the offensive throughout the campaign. He accused the city councilman—a 20-year veteran of the LAPD—of being antipolice. The Yorty forces released leaflets claiming that Bradley's election would give rise to problack forces who would terrorize the white communities. Bradley officials were convinced that Yorty was also using covert tactics to frighten white voters: A bumper sticker with a clenched black fist on a red background and the slogan "Bradley Power" mysteriously surfaced in white neighborhoods, and San Fernando residents received calls late at night from the "Watts Committee for Bradley."

"The city of Los Angeles is approaching a choice at the polls that will determine the quality of its future for years to come," a *Times* editorial began, two days before the election. "The incumbent, Sam Yorty, has an eight-year record of bickering and weak leadership, racial divisiveness and clowning absenteeism on world-wide junkets, collusion and bribery among his appointed commissioners, and tirades against the agencies of justice in metropolitan Los Angeles. . . . The *Times* believes that the future of this city lies not in dividing into antagonistic factions those who will live in it in the coming decades, but Mayor Yorty has wilfully done that." Paul Conrad's cartoon that day showed three witches around a cauldron labeled "Fear." The caption read "We need Sam Yorty more than ever."

"Now more than ever." The campaign slogan for Sam Yorty in 1969 would become the campaign slogan for Richard Nixon's reelection in 1972. The Yorty/Nixon analogy is more than coincidence. Yorty and Nixon both defended individualism and competitive values underlying a strong probusiness policy. They appealed to the same set of social values and ideological perceptions. Their law-and-order style explained away the issues of racism and the war in Vietnam by attacking those who raised the issue in the first place.

Yorty and Nixon presented themselves as mainstream America. They attacked their opposition as "intellectual" or "elitist" or just plain different. Like Ronald Reagan, these law-and-order politicians used the same low-key, low-profile, media-oriented public relations approach, combined with scare tactics and accusations about the opposition in league with the devil's forces—be they students, blacks, or antiwar activists. By 1969 this politics was still on the rise. On election day, Yorty turned Bradley's lead around, and won with 53 percent of the vote.

Yorty's reelection deeply embarrassed the *Times* and its publisher. It was, as Al Bell had put it, a matter of "taste." Chandler wanted Los Angeles to be recognized as a modern and sophisticated city—home of the Music Center, the *Los Angeles Times*, and other institutions of prestige and culture. But "Mayor Sam's" reelection reaffirmed the nation's image of Los Angeles as the home of kooks and weirdos, a disgrace in the eyes of the new *Times*.

CHAPTER 25

Bigger Than a Breadbox

1. The "Financial Wizard"

"I'm an administrative kind of guy," Al Casey, the man who helped engineer much of the Times Mirror corporate expansion in the late 1960s, told *Forbes* magazine. To many businessmen Casey was also "something of a financial wizard."

Albert V. Casey, a Harvard Business School graduate, worked his way through the ranks of the Southern Pacific Company. In 1961 he was hired by the Railway Express Agency where he rose to the position of vice-president. Two years later Jack Vance's enticements brought him to Times Mirror. In 1966, at the age of forty-four, he became president of the company.

Casey took over Bob Allan's role as chief strategist and implementer of company acquisitions. Casey's strategy was two-fold. Through careful planning and research, the company would pick up a number of small- to medium-size companies in a broad range of information-oriented, technologically based fields. "By scattering our shots and buying small companies instead of a few giants," Casey told *Business Week* in 1970, "we have lessened our chances for catastrophe." In addition, the financially adept Casey set out to restructure the company's capital, debt, and stock situation.

Shortly before Times Mirror got its listing on the New York Stock Exchange, Casey wrote letters to dozens of top East Coast financial executives, with whom he had maintained ties, to ask for advice on "growth stocks." His request was a subtle means of interesting those potential buyers in the soon-to-be-public Times Mirror stock.

Early in 1965 Casey successfully guided the company through a $40 million bond offering and a $15.5 million offer of several hundred thousand shares of secondary stock. By creating new stock, Casey speeded up the process of Times Mirror expansion.

A cycle developed: the 1960s conglomerate cycle. The conglomerate, by purchasing a new company, would increase overall assets and become a more attractive investment, with a rise in stock value and greater appeal for future merger talks. It could then approach—and acquire—a second company and thus create another cycle of growth. Though the conglomerate would continue to grow, any one of the newly acquired companies might not show a profit. Buried within the conglomerate's annual growth rate increase, each subsidiary's performance would go unnoticed.

Casey's goal was to create a growth rate cycle of a 15 percent annual increase in the earnings per share value of Times Mirror stock by doubling income every five years—"a record that can be maintained," *Fortune* magazine commented, "only by dint of new acquisitions." Times Mirror executives went after companies that were related in any way to the "knowledge industry." "The Times Mirror approach," one company executive commented, "is to determine what kinds of information can be sold at an adequate profit . . . and then to enter such businesses that process such information."

From 1964 to 1969, Times Mirror acquired a maker of slide rules and scientific equipment, Year Book Medical Publishers, Harry N. Abrams Inc. (art books), Popular Science and Outdoor Life magazines, a company involved with teacher training aids, a company that produces audio-visual flight training manuals, a technical graphics firm, and five local cable TV systems.

Casey's assistants kept a list of product lines and companies directly or indirectly related to the information industries. The attractiveness of each company on the list was measured by what the Times Mirror executives called the PILE concept, which took into account the variables of population growth, income, leisure, and education.

Most of the acquisitions were paid with newly issued Times Mirror stock in amounts of approximately 100,000 shares per purchase. Though Times Mirror went into $50 million worth of long-term debt, its revenues increased from a 1963 figure of $175 million with $9.1 million in profits to $466 million revenues and $38.6 million profit in 1969.

The rise of Al Casey coincided with an expansion in the number of Times Mirror positions drawn from outside the family circles. While Norman, Buff, Otis, and Harrison Chandler (in charge of the Times Mirror

Press), as well as cousin Otis Booth (head of the forest products division) represented the family, more than a dozen top company executives were recruited from a range of corporations located outside Los Angeles. The most significant outsider was the new chairman of the board, Dr. Franklin Murphy, appointed in 1968 to replace Norman Chandler, who became chairman of the executive committee. Murphy, with Casey and Otis Chandler, was expected to provide overall strategic direction for the company.

2. The Corporate-minded Chancellor

Franklin Murphy, the son of Dr. Franklin E. Murphy and Cordelia Brown Murphy (the daughter of a wealthy banker/rancher/financier), was born and raised in Kansas City. After receiving his MD from the University of Pennsylvania, Murphy returned to Kansas City where he married Judith Harris, the daughter of the founder of the Lucky Tiger (hair tonic) Manufacturing Company.

In February 1948, at the age of thirty-two, Murphy was named dean of the Kansas University (KU) Medical School. Through effective lobbying at the state legislature, Dean Murphy was able to increase state funding of the school's medical center. Three years later the Board of Regents appointed Murphy KU chancellor, the youngest person to hold that position in university history. "I see the university as a corporation, one with two million stockholders," Murphy noted at the outset of his appointment. "The board of regents is the board of directors and I am the president."

The new chancellor soon put into practice his strong belief in the ties between the university and business. In August 1951 he became the first outside director of the Hallmark Corporation (makers of Hallmark cards), one of Kansas City's leading companies. He subsequently joined the boards of the Kress Foundation, Spencer Chemical Corporation, the First National Bank of Kansas City, Security Benefit Life Insurance Company, and the Topeka branch of the Carnegie Foundation. Murphy's corporate ties put him in contact with some of the most powerful businessmen in the country.

Murphy, who considered himself an Eisenhower Republican and who was constantly mentioned in Republican circles as a possible cabinet appointee, was a frequent guest at White House dinners. He was named chairman of the Study Commission on Federal Aid to Public Health in 1954, and a year later joined a committee which reviewed the federal security program for government employees. In 1959 Murphy was selected chairman of the Advisory Commission on Cultural Exchanges.

Despite the KU chancellor's attack in February 1960 on the Communist disclaimer in the loyalty oath required for National Defense Education Act loans—a position which made him popular with the students and faculty—Murphy's probusiness outlook kept him closely allied with most Kansas conservatives. His ability to raise funds through his corporate connections maintained the university standards at a sufficiently prestigious level and was crucial to his rise.

In the fall of 1959, Murphy made the acquaintance of conservative Democrat oil man Ed Pauley, a California regent who had come to Kansas for the opening of the Truman library. Impressed by Murphy, Pauley spoke to fellow regent Dorothy Chandler about the up-and-coming Kansas administrator. That winter, the UCLA chancellor's post became vacant. The Board of Regents created a search committee, chaired by regent Edward Carter, to draw up a list of candidates. Murphy's name came to Carter's attention, and like Chandler and Pauley, he was impressed. Murphy's approach toward a university/business alliance was looked upon favorably by the group, and on March 21, 1960, Franklin Murphy was designated the new UCLA chancellor.

Murphy's links to the business world became more extensive in his years at UCLA. He became a director of the Ford Motor company, the Bank of America, the McCall Corporation, the Carnegie Foundation, the Menninger Foundation, and the Ahmanson Foundation. He joined the board of agribusiness conglomerate Norton Simon Inc. and continued his Kansas associations with Hallmark and Kress. His government appointments included a position on the Board of Consultants of the National War College, as well as positions in the Institute of International Education and the Council of Higher Education in the American Republics.

In 1965 Murphy joined the board of the Times Mirror Company. Within the year he was selected to join the elite Committee of 25, a group of local businessmen who looked over the affairs of Los Angeles. His business benefactors, led by regents Ed Pauley and Dorothy Chandler, set up Franklin Murphy Associates, which funded various educational projects in the chancellor's name.

Franklin Murphy had become a prime example of the "corporate liberal." Universities, the UCLA chancellor stated in a 1965 speech at Loyola University, were essential components of the defense and business communities. Students attacked Murphy's notion of the university/government/business alliance and criticized the chancellor's outside corporate directorships.

Murphy also had differences with the right. When Ronald Reagan threatened to impose tuition and reduce university expenditures, Murphy attacked the governor: "I do not intend to preside at the liquidation or substantial erosion of the quality which fifty years of effort have built up," Murphy stated in 1967, "and I believe faculty members stand squarely behind me."

In the fall of 1967, Murphy began to think about leaving the university. Although he had traveled in the most powerful circles for years, Murphy had, by his own standards, only a modest salary and little income from investments. "He was ready," regent Ed Carter remarked, "to move into greener fields."

Murphy began to explore new job possibilities. He received offers from several large corporations and from the Johnson administration. Before he made a decision, he was approached by his friend Dorothy Chandler. "I almost fell off my chair," Murphy told *Fortune* magazine several months later, when Buff offered him the post of chairman of the board of Times Mirror. Frank King, an outside director of Times Mirror commented: "I believe that the family felt that Dr. Murphy could bring a public image and a broader respect perhaps outside of the family respect that is already there. He was a knowledgeable person. He would be a good public image."

The Times Mirror offer was a lucrative one: a large salary, which reached $350,000 a year by 1975; various company stock option plans and benefits; and the purchase, from the company, of a $600,000 home in Westwood at 4 percent interest with long-term payments, far below fair-market value. On February 16, 1968, Murphy announced his resignation from UCLA and his appointment at Times Mirror. "I find in the opportunity presented me by the Times Mirror company," Murphy noted in his resignation statement, "a new and extraordinary potential for personal satisfaction, for, as I view it, I will continue to serve the public interest in a different yet comparable way, since a great publishing company, like a great university, is ultimately in the business of communication and education."

The Murphy appointment brought substantial publicity to Times Mirror. A *Fortune* profile on the company was followed by a *Business Week* piece and dozens of articles in various trade publications. In a column he occasionally wrote for the *Saturday Review,* Murphy continued to espouse "pragmatic" politics while applauding "profit-minded management" and defining the national interest in terms of business objectives.

As Times Mirror chairman, Murphy became a top member of the establishment. He joined the local Central City Association (the old Downtown Businessmen's Association) and the national Intelligence Advisory Board (which oversees the activities of the CIA and other intelligence operations). A good friend of Bob Haldeman, Murphy was mentioned as a possible Nixon appointment to the number two position in the State Department.

By the mid-seventies, Murphy had become a symbol for several wary *Times* staffers of potential corporate interference. When powerful corporate or political figures wanted to criticize or kill a particular story, they would frequently bring it up with Murphy. Though Murphy publicly declared a hands-off attitude, he did intervene on occasion. When the feisty architecture writer John Pastier wrote a critical piece on a sculpture addition to the Murphy-backed County Art Museum, the Times Mirror chairman sent Pastier's supervisor a 2-page memo anticipating possible Pastier criticism. Although Pastier's piece was not edited, the memo had its impact. "It caused me later on to hesitate," Pastier commented, "and even pull back for a time. And if that happened to me, what's it going to do to people here who aren't as willing to write something that might be considered controversial?"

A memo might not change a specific news story, but it influences, in the long run, staff attitudes about their own independence. Franklin Murphy had become a wise choice for the Chandlers: A defender of the large corporation and the overall corporate ethos that profitability determines social value, he was Harry Chandler's modern face. With the appointment of Franklin Murphy, the company appeared to have put the final touches on its transformation from a family to a public corporation.

The new Al Casey/Franklin Murphy/Otis Chandler management team had their share of troubles. The book publishing subsidiaries, particularly World Publishing, were in deep trouble. Before its acquisition by Times Mirror in 1963, World had been primarily noted for its bibles and dictionaries.

Under Times Mirror a number of changes were immediately instituted. World was combined with and then separated from New American Library, as the company explored the possibility of developing a "comprehensive" unit with both cloth and paper operations. A decision was also made to produce more trade books and less encyclopedias and dictionaries. But World's dictionary division, which had been a solid money-maker, ran into increasing trouble under the Times Mirror ownership. There was constant tinkering and juggling, and decisions by World executives were often overruled or reworked by division head Martin Levin, who, in turn, was being scrutinized and double-guessed by Los Angeles. The changes ultimately demoralized the World staff.

By 1970, the original pre–Times Mirror World staff had completely departed, and the new management only made matters worse. In 1972 Levin was sent in for the the third time to supervise the declining company to no avail. The next year Times Mirror began the process of selling off, or discontinuing a substantial portion of the World operation, with a net loss of $5.2 million.

The World failure deflated the good PR the company had received during its previous ten years of expansion and diversification. Al Casey's glamour was fading. A vacuum developed over future directions. Murphy, oriented toward the public facade of the company, stayed aloof, and Otis Chandler, who was most concerned with the media end of the corporation, seemed most likely to step in. Chandler wanted to make his company bigger and more powerful than ever before with a major new acquisition, rather than follow Casey's small-company buying strategy. Chandler's way would prevail.

The Dallas Connection

James Floyd Chambers, Jr., former publisher of the *Dallas Times Herald* and a current member of the Times Mirror Board of Directors, has a sign on his desk which says "Money Talks Here." That's the story of Dallas.

Like Los Angeles, Dallas had none of the attributes of cities that developed in the nineteenth century: no waterways, no center of trade, and no major trails to lead people into the city. It was a frontier town with some cattle, some cotton, and an early legion of boosters.

Oil pushed Dallas development into "metroplex" proportions. In the twenties and thirties, Dallas began to supplant Tulsa as the major crossroads for oil men, as dozens of the wealthiest oil millionaires brought their money to the city.

The oil men, however, left the affairs of the city to the bankers, merchants, and newspaper owners, who had already informally held power for more than a generation. In 1937 the old elite decided to formalize their power through the Dallas Citizens Council, whose membership was limited to top Dallas executives like James Chambers. The Citizens Council created the Citizens Charter Association (CCA) as its political arm to screen and endorse candidates for the city council, and it set up a parallel organization for school board candidates. CCA endorsements meant campaign funds and became tantamount to election.

Chambers's background exemplified the crossover between the business world and the media. After working his way through the desk at local Dallas papers, Chambers became public relations director for the Chamber of Commerce in 1941 and for North American Aviation from 1942 to 1945. He returned to the news business in 1945 to become executive news director of the *Times Herald*.

The booster slogan "What is good for Dallas business is good for Dallas" has been the perspective of the *Dallas Times Herald* since it began under its first publisher, C.E. Gilbert, in 1888. Gilbert's paper went into receivership after the town's merchants broke with the publisher on a political issue. After passing through several hands, the paper was eventual-

TIMES MIRROR SUBSIDIARIES

NEWSPAPER DIVISION
Los Angeles Times
Dallas Times Herald
Newsday
Orange Coast Daily Pilot
Newspaper Enterprises Inc.
   of Texas
General Features Corporation
The Sporting News

NEWSPRINT and FOREST PRODUCTS DIVISION
Publishers Paper Company
Publishers Forest Products
   of Washington
Spaulding Pulp and Paper Company
Cladwood Company

BOOK PUBLISHING
New American Library
New American Library of Canada
New English Library
Harry N. Abrams, Inc.
Harry N. Abrams of Japan, Ltd.
Matthew Bender & Co.
C.V. Mosby Company
Year Book Medical Publishers
The Southwestern Company
Fuller & Dees Publishers
Fuller & Dees Marketing Group

BROADCASTING and CABLE
KDFW-TV (Dallas)
KTBC-TV (Austin)
(19 CABLE SYSTEMS)

Hill Tower Inc. (50 percent
   owned)
Long Island Cablevision
Orange County Cable Communi-
   cation Company
Palos Verdes Peninsula Cable
   Communication Company
Times Mirror Communication
   Company
Vista Cablevision
Carson Cable Television Company
   (80 percent owned)

INFORMATION SERVICES
Chartpak
Jeppeson and Company
Sanderson Licensing Company
H.M. Gousha Company
Plan Hold Corporation
Pickett Industries
Denoyer-Geppert

MAGAZINE PUBLISHING and PRINTING
Popular Science
Outdoor Life
Golf
Ski
Times-Mirror Press
American Community Publishers
Times Herald Printing Company

REAL ESTATE
Atherton Real Estate Co.
Starcraft Homes Inc.
Tejon Ranch (partially owned)

ly sold to Edwin Keist, who built up the afternoon paper's assets and established its place in the community. Under Keist, the paper became middle-of-the-road in politics (by Dallas terms), a promoter of the automobile, and supporter of the oil business. When Keist died in 1941, he bequeathed Times Herald stock to a small group of editorial employees led by chief editorial writer (and former cartoonist) Tom Gooch. "I don't want a bunch of goddamned bankers running the *Dallas Times Herald*," Keist had said of his will.

Gooch and his committee divided up the market with the more conservative *Dallas Morning News* and both were strong supporters of the business establishment.

In later years the spirit of cooperation between the two papers was extended into actual corporate links. In the 1960s, the Belo Corporation, owners of the *News* and the *Times Herald*, jointly formed the Hill Tower Corporation. After cable television began to be discussed in Dallas, Hill Tower filed for cable permits for all eighteen cities in the six counties east of the Dallas county line. In the same two-week period of time, Carter Publications, owners of the monopoly paper in sister city Fort Worth, filed for cable permits for all cities west of that same line. The three-company (Belo, Carter, and the *Times Herald*) triopoly not only controlled newspaper and cable operations, but also owned the three network-affiliated television stations in the Dallas/Fort Worth area.

After Tom Gooch retired, James Chambers consolidated his power within the organization. He became president of the company in 1960, and chairman of the board in 1972. Chambers's paper was content to simply boost its city. Although it gathered enough circulation and advertising revenue to make it a very good business, the paper provided mediocre news coverage. This kept its major stock owners, businessmen who had little to do with journalism except as a business, content. As Times Herald board member James Aston put it, second- or third-generation owners of a newspaper are usually not interested in the paper itself, but in the money they can get out of it.

After Judge Ferguson ruled that Times Mirror had to sell the *San Bernardino Sun*, the Chandlers began to look outside California for possible newspaper acquisitions. The company had been interested in the Texas market for some time. In the early sixties overtures were made to Oveta Culp Hobby for the *Houston Chronicle*, but she rejected the offer in order to keep her paper in Texas hands.

The Chandlers already had relations with some of the key men of Dallas; Norman Chandler's directorship at Dresser Industries brought him into contact with many of the top Dallas elite, and Otis Chandler was acquainted with *Times Herald* publisher Chambers. Ties between the business forces of Los Angeles and Dallas were brought closer when Carter-Hawley-Hale, headed by Chandler associate Edward Carter, purchased the giant Dallas department store Nieman-Marcus in 1969.

The Times Herald Company seemed an ideal acquisition for the Chandlers, with its monopoly status, local clout, and profitable newspaper and broadcast properties. In 1969 the two companies announced that merger talks had begun. Times Mirror offered 1.111 shares of new convertible preferred stock for each share of Times Herald stock. In order to do so, a special issue of 1.8 million shares of new Times Mirror stock had to be created. The deal was considered the richest in newspaper history; The *New York Times* estimated an eventual price tag of $90 million.

The *Times Herald* would be Times Mirror's largest subsidiary. The new property included the daily afternoon paper with a circulation of over 200,000; a big Sunday paper; radio stations KRLD AM & FM (subsequently sold because of FCC crossownership regulations); TV station KRLD, the CBS affiliate with the highest ratings of the five stations in the Dallas/Fort Worth area; two wholly owned subsidiaries, Newspaper Enterprises Inc. and Shopper Enterprises, publishers of advertising and newspaper circulars and supplements; 50 percent of the Hill Tower corporation; and various real estate holdings.

A big obstacle facing the deal was a suit, instituted in March 1968, by A.C. Greene, the most liberal of the editors in the *Times Herald* management. The suit contended that a recent Times Herald reclassification had vested control of the company in the hands of J.C. Chambers and his allies, including Times Herald director James Aston, through the creation of a special class of voting stock administered by the company's pension fund. The Republic National Bank acted as the pension fund's trustee. Aston was Republic's chairman and Chambers one of its directors. The bank was also a creditor of the Times Herald Company and had helped arrange the Times Mirror/Times Herald merger. The interlocks between Aston, Chambers and the Republic National Bank touched every aspect of the situation.

With Greene's suit threatening the merger, an out-of-court settlement was arranged. Greene retired in most comfortable means, no longer a Times Herald dissident. The deal went through in the summer of 1970, Aston and Chambers became members of the Times Mirror board of directors, and Times Mirror became a power in Dallas.

The Chandlers' new acquisition was not a quality newspaper, to say the least. For every one page of city news, there were four pages of sports. There was little reporting on state matters, most of the national news came from the wire services, and quotes for local stories invariably came from establishment figures. Editorials were generally bland and unfocused. "The Chandlers could never corrupt the personality of the *Dallas Times Herald*," Dallas journalist Bill Porterfield commented, "because it never had one." Although at the ceremonies in honor of the deal Otis Chandler vowed "no mediocrity," most observers adopted a wait-and-see attitude.

For the first couple of years under Times Mirror ownership, the *Times Herald* basically remained the same. A number of Times Mirror executives came out to Dallas, but major changes awaited the arrival of the new editor, an ambitious Texas newspaperman named Tom Johnson.

Johnson began his journalism career as a high school student covering sports for the *Macon Telegraph and News* in Georgia. During LBJ's tenure in the White House, he became an intern under White House press secretary Bill Moyers and rose through the ranks to become assistant to Moyer's replacement, George Christian. When Lyndon Johnson returned to Texas in 1969, he brought Tom Johnson along to serve as executive assistant in charge of LBJ's Texas Broadcasting Company. The following year Johnson, barely thirty years old, was elected executive vice-president of the company. He joined the board of directors of the City National Bank of Austin, headed up LBJ's Austin station KTBC, and participated in the town's business-dominated civic groups.

In 1970 the FCC ruled that LBJ's company had to either divest itself of KTBC or its cable interests. The former president decided to sell the Austin station and eventually negotiated a deal with Times Mirror. There was no formal provision involving Tom Johnson, but, according to an LBJ insider, young Tom made his own deal with the Times Herald and Times Mirror people. He would come to the *Times Herald* as editor with the understanding that he would advance to the position of publisher within three years; if he were not appointed, he'd move on at the end of that period. Johnson was formally made editor of the *Times Herald* in 1973.

As editor, he knew that to accomplish anything, he'd need money. A man of Nick Williams's heart, the skillful Georgian negotiated an across-the-board salary increase and raised women's wages to parity with men. The raise required such a cash outlay that it had to be prorated. The parent company had little to do with the paper except in money matters. Johnson reported directly to publisher James Chambers and, on at least one occasion, was able to go over his publisher's head to request funds. With the additional resources, Johnson began to expand the paper's coverage and hire new management. Within a year the *Times Herald* received a major face lift and by 1975—one year under his deadline—Tom Johnson was named publisher.

Typifying the political reaction to the Times Mirror takeover, County Commissioner Jim Tyson criticized the *Times Herald* after the paper did an exposé on unserved warrants: "It's a foreign newspaper with foreign people running it," the *Texas Monthly* quoted the commissioner. "They have foreign ideas. It's really the *Los Angeles Times*. Its people are imported from all over the country with views of foreign people."

Tom Johnson denied any influence from corporate headquarters. "Those who want to criticize us," Johnson told the *Dallas Journalism Review,* "would like to think the *Los Angeles Times* calls me every morning to tell me what editorial policy to have today. Of course that isn't true. I've not had a single call from Los Angeles suggesting I take any editorial stand or cover the news one way or the other. It's a phony issue."

One of the most significant changes at the *Times Herald* was its occasional foray into investigative journalism. A story on a bail-bond scandal was considered strong enough by many local journalists to have been censored in earlier days.

The major criticism of Johnson was that his liberalism and commitment to new journalism was slick at best and superficial at worst. With all its changes, the *Times Herald* still remained a partial extension of its former self. Certainly it had not become an antiestablishment paper. Of the ten city council seats up for election in 1975, the *Times Herald* backed only one non-CCA candidate, and sports coverage was still laid out on page two of the Saturday paper. Editorial board member Vivian Castleberry was still the only woman appointed to a high-level position since the Johnson changes. When a board vacancy came up, Castleberry recommended a woman she knew. The job went to a man. "You're representing the women very well," Castleberry was told privately—although publicly, the *Times Herald* argued that qualified women were hard to find.

The problems over racial questions are as severe as ever. In a city that is well on its way to becoming a black and brown majority, the *Times Herald* remains a thoroughly white newspaper both in coverage and employment. As of 1976 there was only one black reporter on staff, and although coverage of the black and Chicano communities has increased from the days of the old *Times Herald*, there is little in-depth, ongoing reporting about community developments. Johnson has said that the paper needs both women and minorities in order to bring their "special viewpoint" to the paper and give it more "soul."

Tom Johnson is an accessible man. He had tried to be both part of the establishment and in touch with the times. He had changed the *Times Herald*: increased state coverage, initiated investigations, upgraded Washington copy. In May, 1977, some of those speculations were realized when Johnson was appointed president of the *Los Angeles Times*, the second most powerful position under publisher Chandler. Johnson was possibly slated to become Times publisher if and when Otis Chandler replaced Franklin Murphy as Times Mirror chairman of the board.

Tom Johnson is still on his way up. Some had speculated that he might rise as high as vice-president of Times Mirror.

The *Times Herald* has been a profitable acquisition for the Chandlers. A protracted strike by the printing pressmen which began in 1974, and the loss of the daily circulation leadership to the *Morning News* have hurt, but the overall revenues continue to rise. If the relationship between an upgraded journalism and improved economic performance can be established, Dallas journalism will undoubtedly continue to change.

CHAPTER 26

The Odyssey of Ruben Salazar

"Rudy, Rudy, where are you?" *Times* assistant city editor Smokey Hale called out. "Guess what?" Hale said to Rudy Villasenor when he finally located the court reporter: "You won't be the only Mexican at the *Times*. We've just hired another one."

Ruben Salazar, a tall strapping man with long sideburns, a big smile, and an outward manner, was the new "Mexican" hired by the *Times*. As a child, he had immigrated to Texas with his family from Juarez, Mexico. After several newspaper jobs working on the beginner's beats of police reporter, rewrite, and general assignment, Salazar accepted a job at the *Los Angeles Herald-Express*. Three months later he arranged for an interview at the *Times* and was hired by Smokey Hale.

Salazar married a young Anglo woman who worked in the *Times* classified ad department, and they set up house in an Anglo neighborhood. "The only way to help the Mexican-American community is to be part of the American way of life," Salazar told others, insisting that he was not a Mexican-American reporter, just a guy doing a job.

Salazar took an immediate liking to *Times* managing editor Frank McCulloch and McCulloch's approach to journalism. McCulloch had some ideas about expanded coverage of the minority communities and asked Salazar to do a series on Mexican-Americans. McCulloch gave him the time to do background research and interviews, and after several weeks, Salazar put together a six-part series.

"No man can find a true expression for living who is ashamed of himself or his people," Salazar quoted Dr. George Sanchez, in his first article. The *Times* reporter analyzed the conditions of unemployment, housing, and education in the barrio, and the lack of political power among Mexican-Americans. "Politically," Salazar wrote in his fourth piece, "our Mexican-Americans are like a fighting bull—but a fighting bull made of paper." Without any real political cohesion, the community had no clout. Still, many Mexican-Americans were getting ahead. "Mexican-Americans can be found in almost every walk of life which spells the American dream," Salazar proudly wrote in his fifth article, undoubtedly including himself in the thought. In his final piece, Salazar analyzed "acculturation," the socio-economic intergration of Mexican-American with Anglo communities through the ending of de facto school and housing segregation. Until acculturation occurs, Salazar concluded, the Mexican-American community will remain subject to a paternalistic, "culturally deprived" attitude by academics and social workers wishing to "save" the community—a community trapped in the material reality of poverty, segregation, and isolation.

Salazar received a mixed reception on the six articles. Some in the Mexican-American community were critical and mistrustful of Salazar's analysis, but journalists praised the series and Salazar was awarded the state Gold Medal. McCulloch had several ideas concerning follow-up, but Nick Williams killed any sequel possibility.

Salazar got a chance to advance from cityside when a popular insurrection—led by followers of Juan Bosch—the first democratically elected president of the Dominican Republic, who had been overthrown by a 1963 right-wing military coup—broke out in the capital city of Santo Domingo. Soon after the rebellion began, Lyndon Johnson sent American marines "to prevent," as LBJ phrased it, "another Communist state in the hemisphere." With U.S. marines patrolling the streets, an uneasy truce held sway.

After the U.S. troops intervened, the *Times* sent Pentagon beat reporter Ted Sell to Santo Domingo. Sell realized that, unlike most "war" situations, both sides of the conflict could be covered. He asked Los Angeles to send a back-up man, and specifically requested Salazar because he spoke Spanish.

The situation was chaotic when Salazar arrived. The two *Times* reporters had only six minutes a day to use the phone to the States, and had to file their stories by talking to a recording machine in Los Angeles. Salazar and Sell decided to save time by dividing their assignment between the two zones: Sell, with his Pentagon contacts, covered the American military/Dominican junta side, and Salazar stayed with the rebels. Salazar's stories from behind the rebel lines were a major accomplishment and gave a far different picture from the official American military assessment. On May 13 Salazar turned in his first story from the rebel zone.

"I never had any anti-American feelings before," Salazar quoted a rebel leader, "but now I do."

"What about communism?" Salazar asked.

"Communism?" the rebel replied, "We don't know what it is. But every time a marine searches me, I think, 'I'm going to find out what communism is, and join them.' But what I actually want is just a return to our constitutional government. Why is that so hard for Americans to understand?"

Salazar did his best to explain those feelings, and in his next story, he interviewed those he called "man-in-the-street rebels" and "rebels by necessity." They are "fighting against hunger and tyranny," Salazar wrote, quoting another rebel soldier.

Salazar's dispatches made him a few enemies in the American compound, but the *Times* reporter returned to Los Angeles with respect and recognition. His Dominican exclusives were mentioned as Pulitzer Prize possibilities, and within a couple of months, he was assigned to a major position as the back-up man in the expanded Saigon bureau. "At last an appointment," Salazar crowed, "where nobody will say it's because I speak Spanish." On August 11, 1965, the day the Watts riots began, Ruben Salazar set sail for Southeast Asia.

Vietnam was *the* choice assignment. Convinced he had finally made it as a journalist, Salazar gained confidence. While in Vietnam, he was careful to keep his increasingly antiestablishment political feelings removed from his copy, but he wanted to go beyond the official military news, and looked for offbeat stories.

"One day," Salazar wrote about one such attempt, "I went to the small town of An Khe to look around. I was surprised to learn that the communists were 'selling communist propaganda' [an "underground paper, apparently printed in Hanoi," according to Salazar] under the nose of the 1st Cavalry." The division's information officer exploded about the story and sent a letter to the *Times*, warning them: "Use Salazar if you please, but keep him out of An Khe, because in this valley many people get shot. Us by them and them by us, and we don't know where he stands." The *Times* lodged a protest with the Pentagon, and an embarassed army gave Salazar the option to "send the officer back to the States or give him another chance." Salazar decided to let it ride.

When his one year tour of duty in Vietnam was completed, Salazar was assigned to head the Mexico City bureau, covering Mexico, Central America, and the Caribbean. When the Castro government extended invitations to several U.S. news organizations to cover two international gatherings in Havana, Salazar jumped at the chance. "Castro," Salazar confided in his journalist friends, "was the manifestation of the Latin American resistance to American domination."

Despite his attitudes about Castro and American policy in Vietnam, Salazar still kept aloof from politics. But more and more, Ruben Salazar was forced to face political issues. In the tumultuous period in Mexico before the 1968 Olympics, Salazar covered the student demonstrations. He was in the Plaza of the Three Cultures when police opened fire, killing several hundred Mexican students protesting the government's policy of spending money on the Games amid conditions of economic scarcity.

Though he had once rejected "Mexican-American" reporting, he now decided that he wanted to cover the barrio. The Chicano community had begun to develop a stronger, more coherent identity, and Salazar, like others in the community, was swept up in the events that created the emerging political and social solidarity of the urban Mexican-American.

In 1969 Salazar was an established journalist, with three tours of foreign duty and several journalism awards. He was offered university jobs, newspaper jobs, and positions in the broadcast media—the most attractive being the post of news director at Los Angeles's Spanish-speaking UHF TV station KMEX. In addition to a big jump in salary, the KMEX offer included a much greater chance to establish ties with the Mexican-American community. He took the KMEX news director job and immediately set out to cover the Chicano community. When Salazar gave notice to the *Times*, the paper's management, after some internal debate, offered him a weekly column on the op-ed page, and Salazar accepted, happy to have an opportunity to reach a mass white audience, as well as his KMEX outlet.

Salazar's TV coverage and *Times* column created more controversy than at any time in his twenty years in the business. His first *Times* column appeared on February 6, 1970, under the heading "Who is a Chicano? And What is it the Chicanos Want?" "A Chicano," Salazar wrote in his lead, "is a Mexican-American with a non-Anglo image of himself. He resents being told Columbus discovered America when the Chicano's ancestors, the Mayans and the Aztecs, founded highly sophisticated civilizations centuries before Spain financed the Italian explorer's trip to the 'New World.' Chicanos resent also Anglo pronouncements that Chicanos are 'culturally deprived' or that the fact that they speak Spanish is a 'problem.' Chicanos will tell you that their culture predates that of the Pilgrims and that Spanish was spoken in America before English, and so the 'problem' is not theirs but the Anglos who don't speak Spanish."

"The word 'Mexican,'" Salazar wrote in an April 17 column, "has been dragged through the mud of racism since the Anglos arrived in the Southwest." Salazar feared a political and social divergence between older traditionalist "Mexican-Americans," and younger "Chicano" activists that could hamper the all-encompassing need for community unity. "Chicanos and traditional-minded Mexican-Americans are suffering from the ever-present communications gap. Traditionalists, more concerned with the, to them, chafing terms like Chicano, are not really listening to what the activists are saying. And the activists forget that tradition is hard to kill.'' The search for unity was the most significant concern for Salazar in his writing in the *Times.*

The cry of Chicano power began to spread throughout the barrio during the winter and spring months of 1970. Students at Los Angeles's predominantly Chicano Roosevelt High School demonstrated and struck over unequal conditions at their school. Police were frequently called in at Roosevelt, and at one point more than a hundred students were arrested. KMEX filmed incidents of police beating the students, and some police officers entered the TV station in an attempt to keep the film off the air.

In July 1970 relations between the police and the community reached the breaking point. On July 16 four policemen charged into the room of a barrio apartment seeking a murder suspect. One of the cops spotted a "Latin type," as the officer later described him, closing the door of the apartment while the police swept through the hallway. The police shouted in English for the men to come out. When the door opened, one of the police opened fire. At the sound of the guns, five men inside scattered. Three policemen stationed outside the building shot one of the men trying to climb outside the back window. He died of forty buckshot wounds. Another of the five died of a gunshot wound in the heart. The suspect was nowhere to be found. There were no arms inside the apartment. None of the five men spoke a word of English. The police gunfire had been so severe that it ripped through the wall of an adjacent apartment, just a few feet from the crib of a ten-month-old child. The LAPD defended the attack and pointed out that the two men were "aliens," that is, they had entered the country illegally.

After the shooting, KMEX arranged for an interview with two of the survivors. The next morning, Salazar wrote in his *Times* column, "two policemen visited me to express their concern about the showing of the interviews. They did not question my right to run the interviews but warned about the 'impact' the interviews would have on the police department's image. Besides, they said, this kind of information could be dangerous in the minds of barrio people.''

When the district attorney returned indictments against some of the police officers involved, Salazar commented: "In matters of human rights, there is nothing more beautiful than to see the System work.'' But within two years, the policemen were cleared on a court technicality and granted six months' back pay.

Around the same time as the shooting, congressional testimony revealed that an informer for the LAPD had infiltrated "many of the barrio and ghetto organizations.'' The informant, Sergeant Robert J. Thoms, had spied on a range of organizations from the Black Panthers and Brown Berets to the Episcopal Diocese of Los Angeles. Salazar was infuriated by the way the police had lumped together all the community and political organizations into one catchall—subversive and violent—category. But the police strategy backfired. Radical and moderate organizations initiated community-wide coalitions against the police to protest discrimination in the barrio.

When a group called the Chicano Moratorium made plans for a demonstration against the war in Vietnam, it received support from a broad range of community organizations. The community was coming together: young and old, nationalist and integrationist, Chicano and Mexican-American. And Ruben Salazar had become the most visible proponent of that unity.

Other journalists were struck by the changes Salazar had gone through. Some of his colleagues at the *Times* had problems recognizing "good old Rube," as they had once called him. He would snap at reporters' apathy and was particularly irritated when the *Times* failed to give adequate coverage to events such as the demonstration against the war.

As the date for the antiwar demonstration neared, Salazar's excitement about the emerging coalition grew. He hoped that the demonstration organizers would be able to forge urban unity among the residents of the barrio, much as the farmworkers had established rural unity among transient laborers. Antiwar demonstrators were coming from all over the southwest: from Texas and the La Raza Unida Party, from New Mexico and the Allianza, and from Colorado and the Urban Justice League.

The morning of August 29, 1970, was sunny and warm, a beautiful day for a demonstration. It was an incredible success—25,000 people according to the demonstrators, 15,000 according to the police, took part, making it the largest nonwhite antiwar demonstration ever. "The scene was a peaceful one," Albert Herrara wrote.

Then, before speeches got under way, some sheriff's deputies, without warning, entered the park with billy clubs drawn. After the deputies' initial charge, some trouble broke out at a liquor store across the street. Bottles were thrown, and the deputies started spraying tear gas and shooting their guns into the air. The sheriff's sweep cleared the park and produced a major riot.

Salazar and his TV crew captured some of the action on film, and then retired several blocks away to the Silver Dollar Cafe. Outside the bar, sheriff's deputies Thomas Wilson and Manuel Lopez were told by a "man in a red vest," according to the sheriff's version of the events, that three armed men had entered the cafe. Wilson approached the bar, loaded his tear gas gun with a "Flite Rite" 12-inch projectile (he later testified he assumed he had loaded the gun with the much smaller "Tumbler" pellet), and looked through the curtain into the bar. Hearing the commotion outside, Salazar stood up from his seat and said, "Let's get out of here."

Wilson testified that he heard the words "get out of here" and sounds "like a chair falling over, or a stool slid backwards." Wilson thought the noise came from the same general area as the "get out of here" remark, so, as Wilson testified, he told everybody "to watch out, that I was going to fire into the bar. I then got ready. I was kneeling down at the east side of the doorway. I motioned for the deputy on the west side of the doorway to move back because I wanted to take up that space that he was standing in, and I jumped up and as I went up I fired the first round aiming in an upward angle."

The Flite Rite projectile, which bears a printed warning that it is not to be used in "crowd control," struck Ruben Salazar in the head. He died instantly. Wilson ran around the back just as a patrol car of sheriff's deputies pulled up. One of the deputies fired several more projectiles into the bar. Three people were killed that day in east Los Angeles.

The death of Salazar changed a riot into an international event. On October 5, a coroner's jury brought out a verdict of death caused at the hands of another person. But the vote was split, three of the seven jurors voted for a death by accidental means ruling. Nine days later District Attorney Evelle Younger decided not to indict Wilson or any of the other deputies. "It was obvious," Younger commented at a news conference, "that if three of the seven felt it was an accident, the likelihood is that at least one out of twelve jurors at a criminal trial would have thought it was an accident."

A *Times* editorial reserved its criticisms for Sheriff Peter Pitchess and his department for failing to find any "misconduct on the part of the deputies involved," and called for a grand jury investigation of the Sheriff's Department's procedures. The *Times,* however, made no criticims of Evelle Younger's failure to indict. "I don't know if that was because of Otis Chandler's friendship with Evelle Younger or whether they just went along with it," one of Salazar's reporter friends at the *Times* later commented.

Several months after the August 29 Vietnam moratorium, the name of Lincoln Park was changed to Salazar Park. Folksongs were written in honor of the *Times* journalist and a battle for Salazar's legacy began. The *Times* management reprinted several of Salazar's columns in a booklet which included Otis Chandler's funeral address but left out those Salazar columns that criticized the police. A *Times* reporter wrote a national magazine piece, characterizing Salazar as a "man in the middle," caught between his Anglo life-style and community pressures. Chicano activists recalled his attempts to unify the community.

Salazar's death closed out a decade; it was the culminating act in the evolution within the Chicano community. The 1960s had transformed an entire generation. Blacks, students, women, Indians, Asian-Americans, young workers, and Latinos (Mexican-Americans, Puerto Ricans, and other Latin Americans): each had challenged the system, demanded social and economic justice, and emerged with a new and positive identity. But all the basic problems that gave rise to the protests still remained.

Point/Counterpoint

As he approached his sixty-fifth birthday, Nick Williams prepared to retire. The decision concerning his replacement would reveal much about the future direction of the *Times*. As in most large commercial newspapers, such personnel changes constitute the real political decisions of the company. The publisher chooses his editor who in turn selects other editors and staff. Each appointment builds a framework for the politics and direction of the paper. The choice of editor—the person the publisher primarily relies on to work in accord with his or her social, political, and journalistic perspective—is thus pivotal. Although the battle over the selection of Nick Williams's replacement appeared to be fought in terms of personalities, the political future of the paper was at stake.

A number of candidates sought the job. For a while, the frontrunner seemed to be the editor of the editorial page, Jim Bassett, whose long service in the organization and strong ties to Republican party circles made him a likely candidate. But a heart attack in the sixties all but eliminated Bassett's chances. The Old Guard hoped the choice would be conservative-minded thirty-year veteran Frank Haven, but he never really figured prominently in the running. Many of the staff favored national editor Ed Guthman, but Guthman had been tagged as a Kennedy liberal, and his appointment would have undoubtedly caused a severe break between the Chandlers and the Los Angeles business establishment.

Metropolitan editor Bill Thomas seemed another strong candidate. Williams and Chandler had appreciated the job Thomas had done as metropolitan editor, and his appointment would not be unpopular inside the organization. But Thomas was unknown nationally, and Chandler, cognizant of the *Times*'s national stature, worried about the prestige factor. Chandler's thoughts turned instead to the man most responsible for the *Times*'s initial step into the world of national journalism: Robert Donovan.

Unlike most of the other candidates, Bob Donovan had no desire to be editor of the *Los Angeles Times* and had little idea that he was even being considered for the job. "There's not a grain of ambition in him," staffer Ron Ostrow commented; others in the bureau concurred.

Donovan and his staff were surprised when Otis Chandler came to Washington and offered his Washington chief the job. Donovan expressed reservations about his ability to manage such a large organization. He and his wife, Washington residents for more than twenty years, felt uncomfortable at the thought of a wrenching move to Los Angeles, a city they knew little about. But Chandler's insistence persuaded Donovan, reluctantly, to go along. The Washington man pulled up his stakes and came to Los Angeles for a period of gestation before the formal transfer of power.

Donovan spent his time in Los Angeles getting to know the organization, speaking to staff, and getting a feel for the paper. Respectful of Nick Williams's domain, he tried not to intrude until after the *Times* editor retired. Donovan, however, was a novice to high-level office politics, and some of his opponents felt he could be maneuvered out of the job. His lack of administrative skills, which Donovan himself had previously mentioned, was brought to Chandler's attention. His failure to take an active role in the editor's affairs, a result of his effort to keep out of Nick Williams's way, was interpreted as lack of drive, or, even worse, bureaucratic slow-wittedness. In addition, Martha Donovan's attitude about Los Angeles, which she considered slow-paced and lacking in intellectual ferment, grated on some of the Chandlers.

The whispering campaign that spread through the executive suites of the paper began to make Otis Chandler feel uncomfortable. In many ways Nick Williams had been more mediator than editor. He guided the family through the necessary changes, while still maintaining something of the manner of a hired hand. Like the Chandlers, he had little experience with a nationally oriented journalism, but he shared—and cultivated—Otis's ambitions to turn the *Times* into a high quality national newspaper.

Bob Donovan, on the other hand, was most definitely his own man. His background—the kind of background that would make the choice widely heralded around the country and increase the *Times* prestige—came into conflict with Chandler's image of an editor with whom he could feel socially and journalistically at home. Donovan, a man twenty years Otis Chandler's senior, with a vastly greater range of experience and knowledge of the world of journalism and national power than his publisher, would undoubtedly push the paper in the direction of greater analysis and investigation, a trend partially begun in the Frank McCulloch era but later skewered. "Otis had a vision of the *Times* being a national newspaper, of subduing its 'southland provincialism'," staffer Dick Dougherty commented on the Donovan choice, "but at some point they decided there were some limits to that national pretension."

Less than a year after his arrival in Los Angeles, Donovan was dropped, without consultation, and without ever formally assuming the editor's post. Instead, Chandler selected Bill Thomas and sent Donovan back to Washington, with the titular position of associate editor and the job of writing an occasional column. Nick Williams saw it as a decision of priorities, with local coverage needs outweighing the already beefed up national and international departments.

Donovan was "stunned," "almost speechless" when he heard the news, one staffer recalled. For some time after, Bob Donovan remained, in the words of his friends, "in a state of shock." He produced his occasional column, but, in spite of Chandler's statement that Donovan was really "going back to his first love, reporting," the column, as Donovan himself put it, became something of a "chore." Those of his old staff shook their heads in respect and admiration for the trials and staying power of their former boss. He had become a symbol of what the *Times* might have become.

The formal announcement of Bill Thomas's elevation to the post of editor was made on August 23, 1971. It was an uneasy time both at the paper and in the country. Faced with the Nixon recession and the continuing involvement in Vietnam, the nation was gripped by a strong sense of political, social, and economic malaise. Recession talk and worries about falling profit margins dominated the executive suites at the *Times* and other public corporations with newspaper subsidiaries. For the first time since the changeover, *Times* management spoke of editorial budget cutbacks. *West* magazine was about to be dropped, and the squeeze was on in the Washington bureau. Many on the *Times* staff took the Thomas appointment to mean that the Chandlers had, in effect, pulled in the reins.

Bill Thomas was a master of adjustment, sensitive to his environment and capable of taking on the coloration of those around him. As metropolitan editor, he had given the appearance of a man in charge, with his sleeves rolled up, accessible to his staff, and effective in keeping limits on experimentation. The editor, the publisher's man, was a lot more than a newspaperperson: he was part of the establishment. Putting his jacket back on, Bill Thomas became a new man of power and blended in perfectly with the Southern California establishment setting of his new job. Local staffers, who had once argued with and respected their city editor, now found Thomas distant and inaccessible. "I find it hard to understand just how enormously ambitious he's become," an up-and-coming desk man remarked of his boss.

Ultimately, the new editor represented a depoliticization of the paper. Thomas, like Otis Chandler, was a 1950s man. In many ways they were products of their generation: apolitical, ambitious, antiintellectual, optimistic. They were still celebrating the American Century. The Thomas appointment brought those attitudes back to the *Times* in a new, contemporary form.

The 1970s, however, were contradictory times. For some, like Bill Thomas and Otis Chandler, the period represented a throwback to the fifties, but for others it was a time of transition in a changing America. The Thomas/Donovan switch left some at the *Times* content, but it brought discouragement and an under-the-surface instability for others. A point/counterpoint had emerged for a paper without clear definition in an indefinite period: what some Angelenos called the *Times*'s permanent schizophrenia.

CHAPTER 27

Down and Up in Washington

1. Bureau Conflicts

"I don't think there'll be any more surprises," the Los Angeles-bound Bob Donovan told Washington staff regarding his replacement as Bureau Chief. He and other bureau members expected the position would go to Dave Kraslow, the bureau's news editor.

At the formal meeting to make the selection, attended by Donovan, Williams, national editor Ed Guthman, and managing editor Frank Haven, Haven spoke in strong opposition to a Kraslow appointment. The meeting, described as "brutal" by Donovan, lasted all morning without reaching a resolution. During a lunch break with Williams, Donovan expressed such a strong commitment in favor of his assistant that Williams decided to make the appointment. On returning from lunch, Williams announced that David Kraslow would be the new Washington bureau chief.

Kraslow, whose research into the world of secret diplomacy left him with an overriding interest in covert governmental activities and intelligence matters, seemed an appropriate leader for a Washington bureau faced with the secretiveness and duplicity of the Nixon administration. Kraslow hoped that the *Times* would be able to unravel the myriad activities of the intelligence agencies, national security advisor Henry Kissinger (with whom Kraslow felt a close relationship), and the Pentagon.

The previous tensions between the Donovan group and the Los Angeles editors turned into full-scale battle under the new bureau chief. Though Kraslow's primary antagonist was Frank Haven, many of the day-to-day squabbles involved national editor Ed Guthman. Guthman, a

Pulitzer Prize winner from the *Seattle Times,* who had previously served as Attorney General Robert Kennedy's press secretary, had come to the *Times* in 1965 to handle the growing number of national correspondents.

Many of the paper's former friends saw the appointment of Guthman, who they viewed as an extension of Kennedy politics, as a signal event in the liberalizing evolution of the *Times,* and several Nixon administration figures perceived Guthman—the "Kennedy loyalist," as Nixon's friend Bebe Rebozo put it—as the enemy within their hometown paper. Nixon fears about the Kennedys eventually placed Guthman, along with two other *Times* journalists, on Nixon's enemies list.

Under their new national editor, the *Times* went on to establish new bureaus in New York, San Francisco, Atlanta, Chicago, and Houston. Until the 1968 presidential election, Guthman had little to do with the Washington bureau. Despite a mutual commitment to maintain bureau independence from Washington officialdom, Guthman and Kraslow never developed a positive relationship. Their disputes could be traced back to the old debate on the proper focus for the Washington bureau, a debate that was endemic to nearly all Washington bureaus and their home-based management. The Los Angeles editors—Haven, Guthman, and later Bill Thomas—saw the problem as Los Angeles spending a great deal of money without getting the desired results. *Times* management, as part of its growing magazine-style orientation, wanted feature and background material, including stories for the new front page "non-dup" column, which highlighted story ideas not found in the daily news flow.

Another point of contention for the Los Angeles editors concerned coverage of the local California congressional delegation in Washington. The local management often perceived Donovan, Kraslow, and some of the other early members of the bureau, as "outsiders" who considered such coverage "menial." The Los Angeles editors wanted a lot more material that related to the interests of Angelenos.

"It ultimately came down to the fact," Guthman concluded, "that Kraslow was not listening, and the bureau was not producing the kind of quality coverage we wanted. They were not getting caliber material and in-depth stories."

Kraslow had a different interpretation of the conflict. He felt that many of the criticisms concerning performance since the Donovan days disguised the more substantial question of control. Kralsow interpreted the Los Angeles request to mean more frivolous copy. Ten cute features, as Kraslow saw it, could never make up for one probing analysis of the day-to-day practice of Washington politics.

The strain on Kraslow due to his conflict with Los Angeles began to tell. Washington staffers frequently overheard angry phone conversations between Kraslow and Guthman. Within a year of his appointment, the high-strung Kraslow suffered a mild heart attack that sent him to the hospital and kept him away from the office for several weeks.

In the spring of 1972, Bill Thomas and Otis Chandler came to Washington. On the first day of their visit, they complimented the bureau and minimized the conflicts. But the following day, Thomas told Kraslow that Los Angeles wanted a change. The *Times* editor offered Kraslow two choices: resignation without any public announcement or demotion to a general assignment slot. Kraslow, angry with the *Times's* desire for a "clean resignation," without bad publicity, decided to take the risk and openly resign.

Some of the conflicts, such as features versus daily coverage, have still not been completely resolved. Changes in wire service coverage have compounded the situation, as their trend toward more analytic and background pieces have obviated some earlier distinctions between *Times* copy and wire stories.

Kraslow and Guthman had been caught in the squeeze—Kraslow as the leader of the "outsiders," and Guthman as the national buffer between the desk and the bureau. The national editor had his own "credibility" problems with his more conservative superiors Thomas and Haven. To many in Los Angeles, Guthman was still the "glamour boy," the Kennedy man with a Pulitzer and a salary larger than anyone else behind the "glass row" that housed the desk men. By becoming the "heavy" in the conflict with Kraslow, Guthman was cut down to size. He had to make his corporate compromise in order to stay on and maintain a strong, high-quality national operation. In the process, though, the Washington bureau had begun to unravel, and even Guthman had had his fill, moving on in 1977 to join the *Philadelphia Inquirer.*

Despite the internal conflicts, the *Times* still had a premier Washington bureau. Its White House correspondent, Stuart Loory, had become one of the most heralded members of the Washington press corps. Loory's troubles with the White House, so prevalent during the LBJ days, increased in Richard Nixon's Washington. "Loory was biased against us," Nixon aide Herb Klein remarked about the *Times* White House correspondent, who also appeared on the administration's enemies list.

Early in 1970, Loory decided to assess various White House officials and advisors in a series of background profiles. Loory was particularly interested in Henry Kissinger, who had, soon after his appointment to Nixon's transition team in late 1968, granted the *Times* reporter an exclusive interview. The two men got on "famously," according to Loory. Kissinger admired Loory's work on the secret peace negotiations and referred to it in one of his own articles on Vietnam.

Loory arranged for an interview soon after the Cambodian invasion in May 1970. Kissinger was reluctant, but after a couple of sessions of relatively freewheeling give and take, assuming that Loory would write a general, academic-oriented, obscure piece on the shaping of foreign policy, the Nixon aide eased up.

Instead, Loory produced a straightforward article on the troubles facing the Kissinger foreign policy. The piece—"Kissinger Image Shows Signs of Wear and Tear"—appeared as a two-column page one spread on Sunday, July 5, 1970. "Like [Johnson's advisor Walt] Rostow two years ago, Kissinger has great problems," Loory wrote in his first paragraphs. "The plans he helped develop not only have not ended the Vietnam war, but some persons feel, they have helped widen it into the Indochina war. . . . In short, the patina is beginning to wear off the Kissinger mystique."

The Nixon advisor saw the paper while spending the July 4 weekend with the Nixon entourage at San Clemente. On his return to Washington the next day, Kissinger immediately telephoned bureau chief David Kraslow and asked to see him. When Kraslow arrived at the advisor's office a few minutes later, Kissinger, gesturing rapidly, exclaimed that he didn't care who the *Times* sent to cover him, as long as he never saw Stuart Loory again.

Kraslow told Loory about Kissinger's remarks later that afternoon.

At this point Bob Donovan intervened. Donovan pulled Kissinger aside at a dinner party and convinced him to reestablish relations with the White House correspondent. But, the diplomat insisted, there would have to be "a cooling off period between Stuart and myself."

Loory, however, still felt that Kissinger had gotten away with something. Sensitive to the power of political figures to dump on reporters at the slightest suggestion of critical news reports, Loory was determined to demonstrate his resolve not to be badgered or intimidated. Loory told reporter Joseph Kraft, then in the process of writing a piece about Kissinger, about the incident. Later that day, Loory received a call from Kissinger's deputy Alexander Haig, inquiring about the remarks to Kraft. The story had gotten back to Kissinger as Loory had hoped.

Loory continued to get into the hair of the Nixon administration. His writings on Nixon's Indochina policy cut through the rhetoric of "Vietnamization," and pointed out where and how administration policy represented an escalation rather than a "winding down" of the war. One month later, a Loory analysis of a Nixon policy statement also caused some trouble with Loory's superiors in Los Angeles.

In February 1971 Richard Nixon released his second State of the World address, a message which dealt exclusively with international affairs. In trying to find a lead for his story, Loory read through the message three times before discovering an obscure, but potentially significant, item. "Even if Hanoi were to negotiate genuinely about Vietnam," one section noted, "difficult issues remain concerning its neighbors: the removal of North Vietnamese and Viet Cong troops (from Laos and Cambodia), the securing of South Vietnamese borders, and the establishment of the Geneva agreements." Loory in his story on the State of the World added the parentheses "from Laos and Cambodia" as a logical extension of the meaning of the passage. A Kissinger briefing confirmed Loory's discovery.

Since LBJ's San Antonio formula on Vietnam negotiations a couple of years earlier did not mention North Vietnamese withdrawals from Laos and Cambodia, the State of the World message signified a subtle, though significant, hardening of the U.S. position. On February 26, under the headline NIXON ADOPTS TOUGHER LINE ON SETTLING WAR IN INDOCHINA, Loory wrote in his lead, "The increasing toughness of the American position on settlement of the Indochina war was made clear in President Nixon's second State of the World report." Loory analyzed the passages on Vietnam in that light and concluded that the increasing American aid and air assistance, along with the new negotiation position, might turn out to be a program to "perpetuate the war."

After the article ran, Ed Guthman and editor of the editorial pages Tony Day questioned the information in Loory's lead. In response to questions on the Laos and Cambodia withdrawals, Loory sent Los Angeles a transcript of the Kissinger press briefing and the proceedings of a follow-up Nixon press conference.

But Frank Haven was not convinced. "It is my conclusion," Haven wrote in a memo, "that we were in error, inadvertently perhaps, but still in error, in our report of the President's State of the World message. I have great respect for Loory's intuitive processes," Haven continued, "and it may be that he is foreseeing the future and is only putting it in the present tense. Maybe Nixon will up his price for withdrawal. But he didn't do it in the State of the World message. Normally I am overjoyed when the *Times* has an exclusive, but in this instance I'm a bit disturbed that the *Times* was the ONLY newspaper in the land that took the approach as we did, because I can't believe that some newspapers vehemently against the war editorially, would not have seized on this 'tougher' position in settling the war."

Loory was livid. The *Times* writer felt that the logic of Haven's statement about his ("perhaps") "inadvertent" error meant that, in other instances, Loory might have intentionally lied.

Once again, Loory defended himself in meticulous detail. "I am under the impression," Loory wrote in his reply, "that Los Angeles reporters are charged with the responsibility for reporting not only what the words say, but what they mean."

Loory's memo put an end to the affair, and he never heard another word about it from Los Angeles. But like David Kraslow, the once-praised Loory wondered how much of a future he had left at the *Times*.

Loory, thanks to the intervention of Bob Donovan, got approval for a leave of absence to follow up on extensive research on the American military machine. As his project got bigger, Loory asked for an extension of his leave. Management refused and conveyed the message that they didn't want any uncompleted projects hanging over his head when he returned. It was Loory's final straw. In the winter of 1971, Stuart Loory resigned ending one of the brightest and most independent careers in the short history of the new *Times*.

2. A Case of Analysis

Washington journalists, *Los Angeles Times* reporter Jules Witcover felt, were too dependent on government itself as a primary, if not exclusive, source of information, a dependency which undermined the press's ability to function independently and serve the public's interests. In a *Columbia Journalism Review* article in the winter of 1970, Witcover wrote that although journalists had done a professional job of reporting what the government said on an issue like the war in Vietnam, they failed to look into the validity and effectiveness of what the government said. Witcover, formerly a political writer for the Newhouse chain of Syracuse, had won national recognition and praise after his chronicle of Richard Nixon's remarkable comeback in *The Resurrection of Richard Nixon*. In 1969 his research for another book, on the little-known and written about career of Spiro Agnew, turned up data that later resurfaced in the Justice Department investigations of the vice-president. That same year Witcover was hired by *Times* bureau chief Kraslow; within a few months the new *Times* reporter convinced Kraslow to create a permanent national political correspondent's slot for him.

From the experience of several political campaigns, Witcover recognized that the press played an important political role by what it chose to cover and how it defined the issues. A journalist, Witcover felt, had to interpret and analyze, rather than just "report," in order to describe the real context of politics accurately. Witcover's notions immediately came into conflict with those of his editors in Los Angeles, and the Los Angeles desk frequently requested that Witcover change his lead to conform to *Times* standards. Los Angeles complained that Witcover's stories were too long and saw his failure to heed Los Angeles instructions as an indication of stubbornness. Bureau writers sympathized with Witcover, pointing out that length was never a consideration when the desk edited one of the light features written by one of Thomas's magazine-oriented stylists.

During the '72 elections, Witcover ran into constant problems with Los

Angeles. Two of his articles failed to run. One of the pieces dealt with Democratic presidential candidate George McGovern's attack on the press for its failure to expose Nixon's campaign strategy. Nixon had successfully avoided journalistic investigation and anlaysis by appearing as a noncandidate—the president—too preoccupied with matters of war and peace to be bothered by campaign questions. The tactic had left McGovern, the only active candidate open to press probing, at a disadvantage. Witcover wrote that McGovern's charges, though they might be self-serving, had a real basis which needed to be explored and analyzed.

He carefully prepared his article and showed it to other members of the Washington press corps before sending it in to Los Angeles. AP correspondent Walter Mears commented that with a little brushing up, the story could even run on the wires. The editors in Los Angeles, however, refused to run the article as a news story; they were only willing to print it as an opinion piece. After Witcover argued that analysis based on facts was essential to any news story, national editor Guthman told him that the story might run if Witcover rewrote the material to attribute the same points to a news source. Witcover replied that the function of analysis, as opposed to reporting, is to show that conclusions can be drawn from a given set of data. Both analysis and reporting, serving different functions, belonged in "news" stories. Witcover felt that his questions on the issue of Nixon's noncandidacy had been building momentum, and the article's analytic conclusions were timely and newsworthy. But his editors disagreed; the story didn't run.

The next day Nixon held a press conference, partly to answer criticism by other political reporters concerning his noncampaign. If Witcover's piece had run, it would have appeared the morning of the press conference and, Witcover felt, given the *Times* a major coup. Instead, embarrassed and angered by his treatment from Los Angeles, Witcover felt his future at the *Times* hung on a slender reed.

Two months after the election, on December 29, 1972, he wrote his analytic swansong, entitled "The Making of a Landslide," which described Nixon's "invisible campaign." The article exemplified the type of analytic reporting in which Witcover excelled. Three days later, on January 1, 1973, Witcover began a new job at the *Washington Post*. His departure might have been more a reflection of personality differences than a simple argument over journalistic methods. "I had a fair amount of undocumented analysis in my stories," staff writer Dick Dougherty recalled, "and I think they were just chipping away at Jules. Haven always resented those he considered 'hot-shot Easterners,' with their big salaries, and Jules clearly fit into that category."

The question of analysis in news stories did not get resolved at the *Times*. A double standard seemed to operate; the foreign correspondent, for instance, had broad freedom to interpret events without attribution. For a short period after Witcover left the paper, assistant managing editor George Cotliar came up with a compromise device in which articles with an analytic bent ran intact but under a headline kicker labeled "news analysis." Other desk men, however, disliked the device, and it was eliminated soon after. The narrow definition of analysis continued to dominate; hang your interpretation on a news source, don't intervene or draw conclusions on your own. The loss of Jules Witcover helped to transform that tendency into *Times* philosophy.

3. The Company Intervenes

In the spring of 1972, the *Times* management made a bad situation even worse when it replaced bureau chief Kraslow with John Lawrence, the paper's financial editor. Lawrence, an inordinately shy, yet ambitious journalist, had come to the *Times* from the San Francisco office of the *Wall Street Journal.* Although he helped expand the paper's financial coverage, Lawrence had no experience with the world of Washington politics.

Lawrence, like a classical "company man," began to anticipate management's intentions. The Washington staff immediately picked up Lawrence's attitude and felt his appointment might lead to an attempt to control the bureau.

Lawrence, who tended to be more conservative than other bureau members, began to mistrust some of their attitudes. He found it hard to believe staff contentions that Nixon aides frequently told lies and attempted to deceive the press.

Without any specific instructions about changing the bureau operation, Lawrence relied on signals, and he often gave them more significance than Los Angeles intended. A couple of weeks after his arrival, Lawrence was faced with the details of arrangements for the costly White House correspondents' dinner, an important Washington ritual attended by everyone in the government bureaucracy; bureau reporters, who were constantly bypassed by Washington officials who chose to pass their stories on to the *New York Times* and *Washington Post,* regarded the dinner as an excellent opportunity to establish contacts and help maintain a presence in Washington.

In reaction to Haven's comment that the days of big spending were over, the new bureau chief decided that to save costs only one small table would be set up. Many of the bureau staff were enraged, and several refused to go if others were excluded. The conflict brought the bureau squabble out into the open where it became a major item of Washington journalism gossip.

Lawrence's lack of experience and his support of Los Angeles's request for more non-dup features aggravated the growing conflict. "He was overinterested in packaging a story," one bureau staffer recalled, "and he never did understand Washington politics." Instead of asking for help, Lawrence turned inward and began to impose his authority in an arbitrary manner. Relations with nearly all of the bureau members were strained. "Kraslow had always been somewhat loud and boisterous, and Lawrence was just the opposite; quiet, withdrawn, inaccessible," staffer Bob Jackson remarked. "You'd be talking about something, maybe even talking about him, and then, all of a sudden, he'd appear behind you. He moved so quietly that he always took you by surprise. It would startle everybody." After a few months, Lawrence acquired the nickname "The Spook."

The *Times* was slow to get involved in Watergate coverage, by far the biggest story during Lawrence's tenure in Washington. The paper was frequently scooped by the *Washington Post* in 1972, but the *Times* bureau prided itself on its methodical care in verifying information. Although they applauded Woodward and Bernstein's efforts, bureau staffers tended to be more cautious about running certain unverified stories.

The *Times* did have one major exclusive before the '72 elections, when staffer Jack Nelson managed to secure an interview with Alfred Baldwin, the former FBI agent who had kept watch across the street during the Watergate break-in. Baldwin was to be a key government witness in the upcoming trial of the seven Watergate defendants.

When Nelson first attempted to speak to Baldwin, the witness wouldn't cooperate. In a "classic case of journalistic persistence," as colleague Ostrow recalled, Nelson literally camped outside Baldwin's door, insisting on the "public's right to know" and "America's interest" in getting out the story of Watergate. After several days of badgering, Baldwin finally agreed to talk.

During a five hour interview with Nelson and Ostrow, Baldwin told of involvement of unknown higher-ups and implied that Watergate was indeed a very big story. When the Justice Department learned of the interview, it threatened to withdraw Baldwin's immunity from prosecution and warned that he might be indicted if the *Times* story were published. That same afternoon, Judge John Sirica, on request from government attorneys, signed a court order prohibiting any witness from commenting on the case and warned that Baldwin would be cited for contempt if the story ran.

Times editors met that evening and decided to go ahead anyway. The Watergate exclusives appeared the next day with a page one summary by Nelson and Ostrow and Baldwin's own words, edited from a taped transcript, as an op-ed piece.

A couple of days later, government prosecutors informed Nelson and Ostrow that their notes and tapes of the Baldwin interview would be subpoenaed. Nelson and Ostrow were prepared to go to jail, but a high-level management meeting in Los Angeles which included Thomas, Haven, Guthman, and the *Time*'s lawyers—Chandler was out of town—decided to transfer possession of the material to John Lawrence, who, in a legal sense, was management's representative.

A short time later, government subpoenas ordered the *Times* to hand over all material concerning Baldwin. At the opening of the court session, Sirica ordered Lawrence to comply with the order or to be sent forthwith to jail. To the shock of everyone in the bureau, when Lawrence refused, he was immediately taken off to prison. For a brief moment, the entire Washington staff experienced solidarity with their imprisoned chief. *Times* lawyers managed to get Lawrence released a few hours later and immediately filed an appeal.

As everyone awaited the appeals court ruling over the next several days, Lawrence talked "bitterly about having to go back to jail," as one bureau staffer recalled, for a stand he saw as "quixotic." Lawrence's attitude caused all the old resentments to resurface, and what might have been a unifying act turned into yet another conflict.

As it turned out, Baldwin felt there was nothing to hide and was willing to turn over the material. Since their source no longer requested or desired protection, the *Times* management handed over the tapes and notes, and the contempt citation against Lawrence was withdrawn.

By summer of 1973, with Watergate dominating Washington news, the *Times* bureau swung into high gear. Ostrow, Nelson, Jackson, and later Paul Houston, were assigned to the story, although nearly everyone on the bureau staff chipped in. But relations with Lawrence stayed the same. The bureau chief grew to resemble a titular monarch, sitting off in his corner, occasionally writing an economics piece. Formal and informal staff meetings no longer occurred, and there was a complete breakdown of the little authority Lawrence had. Bill Thomas, on hearing grumblings from the bureau, was initially incredulous and reacted angrily to Lawrence's critics. "Look at the man's credentials," Thomas would say, "The Wall Street Journal . . . , the work on our financial section . . . , impeccable credentials." When staffers complained that Lawrence was eroding bureau morale, Thomas accused them of exaggerating.

Finally, Los Angeles got the message. In the fall of 1974, in a "face saving" solution, John Lawrence was sent back to the financial pages with a seat on the editorial board and the title of assistant managing editor in charge of economic news. The move occurred only a few weeks after the Nixon resignation. Both events produced a similar response from the bureau staff: relief that it was over.

In late October 1974, investigative reporter Jack Nelson became the new bureau chief. Nelson, who had come from the *Atlanta Constitution* to open up the *Times*'s first southern bureau in 1965, had secured a reputation as a tough and independent reporter, primarily from his long-standing investigation—and conflict—with the FBI.

Nelson, a one-time applicant for an FBI position, had worked closely with the agency in the early sixties when—following the 1964 murder of three civil rights workers in Mississippi—the FBI undertook a campaign against the Ku Klux Klan. But in the late sixties, Nelson's pursuit of a story of an FBI police gunfight with the Klan, which involved the death of a woman Klan member, created strains in his relations with the agency. Several months after the incident, an informant sold Nelson police documents concerning FBI and police complicity in the ambush. After Nelson broke the story with a page one article in the *Times,* furious FBI officials, complaining that the story might kill their informant program and "hurt innocent people," responded with talk of libel, and many of Nelson's long time FBI sources dried up. The agency launched a systematic campaign against the *Times* reporter, including leaking stories that Nelson had a drinking problem.

In September 1971 business manager of the *Los Angeles Times* Robert Nelson, a friend of a retired FBI official, met for three hours with FBI director J. Edgar Hoover and arranged for bureau chief Dave Kraslow to talk with the FBI head about the conflict. Hoover, seated behind a desk stacked with papers, told Kraslow that he knew Norman Chandler very well and thought very highly of him. Then, without pause, Hoover began to attack Jack Nelson for alleged activities as he read numerous FBI memos from his stack of papers. Insisting that Nelson and the *Times* were out to get him, the director made repeated references to alleged Nelson accusations that Hoover was a homosexual. An astounded Kraslow told the FBI director that Nelson would never have made such a charge, but Hoover continued to bring it up. After an hour and forty minutes, the session came to an end. Kraslow left in something of a daze.

By the mid-1970s, the bureau, transformed from the days of Bob Hartmann through the happy times of Bob Donovan, the tense conflicts involving Dave Kraslow, and the "cold war" with John Lawrence, had returned to a more temperate mood.

Washington reporters still, by and large, considered themselves "responsible" journalists—intelligent and influential figures with access to the most powerful people in the country. Their attitudes were often reflected in their tendency to act as advisors rather than adversaries. More than any other journalistic beat, the Washington press corps felt the pressure to work within the framework of the prevailing establishment.

"Responsibility," bureau reporter Paul Houston remarked, "is very subjective. Ultimately, therefore, the way to create balance is to have all views represented in a newspaper." Whose views, in what context, and who does the selecting are the crucial questions. A *Los Angeles Times* editor, a man of the establishment, who frequents the social milieu of the rich and powerful, has one idea of what constitutes an acceptable point of view. That editor might consider the poor or disenfranchised citizen's notion of a reasonable perspective a "crazy" viewpoint that has no place in "responsible journalism."

Washington journalism—buffeted by Vietnam, inspired by Watergate, but constantly influenced by the establishment norms that have historically determined its practice—remains in crisis. To LBJ and Nixon, the press was seen as a hostile force, too critical of administration policies. But, according to one study, that new, critical outlook stemmed not so much from a change in the political beliefs of Washington journalists as from their tendency to obtain more information, as in Watergate, from career bureaucrats and lower echelon officials who have started to move away from the given administration line; to rely, as Carl Bernstein put it, not just on the people who dictate the memos, but on those who type them as well.

Washington journalism has yet to indicate its full independence from the establishment. As the country changes and new challenges to established power emerge, Washington journalism—at the new *Times* and elsewhere—will likely face even greater conflicts.

CHAPTER 28

Eagle in Flight

1. Building a Base

The foreign correspondent has the prestige job in American journalism. The reporter who covers foreign affairs, one analyst noted, "is a cosmopolitan among cosmopolitans, a man in a gray flannel suit who ranks very high in the hierarchy of reporters." Foreign writers, more than other journalists, often serve as direct reflections of government policy. They have a great deal more flexibility in story selection and tone than their domestic counterparts and are allowed to interpret and editorialize in news copy at greater lengths. "The emphasis," *Times* correspondent Don Cook wrote, "is on putting a man in an assignment and expecting him to develop it with his own initiative and freedom and abilities to produce." Since the reader has practically no other alternative source of information, nor any other frame of reference to place the information, the selectivity factor, i.e., how the correspondent puts events in a context, leads the foreign correspondent to function fundamentally as a political journalist with an enormous power to influence readers.

When the Chandlers decided to upgrade the *Times,* foreign and Washington coverage were their two primary concerns. For more than fifteen years, Waldo Drake had run a one-man foreign bureau, initially based in China, then in Paris. His "Willy Loman" act, as he characterized it, would hardly do. With Drake ready to retire by 1960, Chandler and editor Williams used the opportunity to transform the coverage.

From a single bureau in Paris, the *Times* branched out to Rome, Bonn, London, Tokyo, and Latin America by 1964. Several of the foreign corre-

445

spondents hired in the 1960–64 period came from within the *Times* own ranks. In 1964 Williams hired *Business Week* writer and former Moscow correspondent for the UP Bob Gibson, initially to work as an editorial writer specializing in foreign affairs. Gibson was soon assigned to the recently created foreign editor's post, where he sought out new staff recruits with the kind of background and experience that could bring prestige to the paper. Although he made suggestions and recommendations as to whom to hire, final approval belonged to Williams and Chandler. "When Otis became convinced that it paid off in the cash register," Williams recalled of Chandler's fears about the costs of upgrading, "it became much easier to hire new staff."

With the number of bureaus eventually reaching seventeen, Gibson gathered together a foreign staff—correspondents such as Robert Elegant in Hong Kong, Jack Foisie in Saigon and later Bangkok, George MacArthur in Saigon, and Don Cook and Joe Alex Morris in Europe—most of whom came out of the strong anti-Communist traditions of the American foreign press corps. There were some exceptions: Stanley Meisler, a contributor to the *Nation* magazine, was hired as an Africa correspondent largely on the strength of his expertise in the field, and Bill Tuohy and Ruben Salazar, who both did tours in Vietnam before shifting to other bureaus, tended to write with a less jaundiced eye than their more conservative counterparts in the field.

The question of bias arises out of the greater degree of interpretive and selective freedom of the foreign correspondent. "One makes a subjective judgment ultimately," Gibson remarked, "but the analysis can be presented without prejudice. The *Times* relies on its own people and trusts them." Analysis without prejudice, according to the *Times* editor, is not "advocacy journalism." Gibson felt that to advocate was a denial of one's responsibility; the key for the *Times* was to have "responsible analysis by responsible people."

Under such a system of foreign coverage, the question of sources becomes extremely crucial. The real determinant of what constitutes a "legitimate" source is the correspondent's judgment and political framework. Some *Times* correspondents have explored alternative avenues of information. Staffer Jacques Leslie, who did a short stint in Vietnam in 1972/73, found that different sources came to him as soon as they sensed a receptive attitude. After several Leslie stories appeared, detailing corruption in the Thieu administration, a previously cautious and close-mouthed government official from the U.S. embassy sought out Leslie and began to feed him information and documents that led to some of Leslie's most significant Vietnam exclusives. The official would never have approached *Times* bureau chief George MacArthur, a hawk on the war with a close working relationship to high embassy officials.

2. Two Modes: Chile and China

On September 11, 1973, a military junta seized power in Chile, over-throwing the democratically elected Socialist President Salvador Allende. As later congressional testimony revealed, the CIA and the foreign policy agencies of the U.S. government had worked covertly for several years to weaken the Allende government through the subsidization of the opposition press, economic policies designed to create internal Chilean difficulties, massive financial support of anti-Allende political parties, and assassination plots against the commander of the armed forces, Reme Schneider, an advocate of the upholding of the constitution.

As some of the information about American efforts became public, largely through the 1972 investigation of IT&T, the *New York Times* and *Washington Post* pointed out the findings. But *Los Angeles Times* correspondent in Chile David Belnap ignored the story and focused instead on, as Belnap called it, the "politically totalitarian" nature of the Allende government.

Belnap's first story on the coup contained statements from the military junta attacking the Allende government and justifying its own actions. The junta became the exclusive source of information and interpretation for the *Times* correspondent. Air Force General Gustave Leigh provided Belnap with background material on such things as the number of casual-ties—estimates that were ten to twenty times lower than other figures, in-cluding those provided by the CIA.

While Belnap relied exclusively on the junta for information of the events in Chile, correspondents from other papers, such as the *New York Times, Washington Post,* and *Le Monde,* pointed to the advent of neo-fas-cism in the country. All political parties were banned, books were burned in the streets of Santiago, and thousands of political prisoners were held in the giant soccer stadium, awaiting execution or torture.

The correspondent for the French newspaper *Le Monde,* Phillipe La-breveux, put the reporting of Belnap and other like-minded U.S. journal-ists in perspective. "Anxious to polish their image, Chile's new military rulers have taken foreign journalists under their wing with lavish daily briefings and press conferences (often in their private houses), taking the reporters and bringing them back to their hotels before curfew," he wrote. "Try as they may, however," Labreveux added, "the Chilean mil-itary cannot camouflage the whole truth. The official tally of the victims of repression, while well short of the truth, continues to lengthen daily. . . . In short, repression continues at night under cover of the cur-few and all day."

Belnap put a different interpretation on the curfew and the state of mind prevailing in Chile. In a non-dup piece one month after the coup,

Belnap wrote that "the nightly curfew, imposed by military authorities in Chile's capital, has dramatically improved the quality of family life. The curfew has also narrowed the generation gap by compelling parents and children to stay together at home during most of the hours of darkness."

The Belnap dispatches were, according to foreign editor Gibson, an important determinant of the *Times* editorial position on the coup: "The army would have stayed out of politics if Allende had abandoned the more extreme elements of his socialist program," the *Times* commented in the first days after September 11. "The composition of the junta itself does offer, however, some hope that Chile eventually will find equilibrium."

The paper discounted talk of American participation in the events. "Inevitably the Marxists will charge," commented a September 18 editorial, "that the coup was stage-managed by the United States. Such intervention on Washington's part would not only be wrong, but stupid; we assume it didn't happen." Two years later a congressional report pointed to active American intervention in all the major events leading up to the September 11 action.

Foreign editor Gibson also strongly endorsed his South American correspondent, praising his insights, his backgrounder style, and his political insights.

In the same way, a *Los Angeles Times* reader was faced with a very partial view of China. Since 1965, *Times* coverage was carried out by Robert Elegant, author of three lengthy books on the Chinese revolution and contemporary conditions in China. Until late 1975 Elegant had never set foot inside the country. He was hired by the *Times* from *Newsweek* in 1965, in the period of wholesale expansion of the *Times* foreign staff. He quickly became a favorite of foreign editor Gibson, who admired Elegant's "China watcher" speculative analytic style, gossipy-oriented political chitchat, and strong impressionistic writing.

Elegant, who lived in a spacious house in Hong Kong and had numerous ties with the Chinese exile community in the British colony, felt a strong antagonism toward the Chinese revolution. His copy reflected his feelings about the Chinese government. From his very first dispatch on China for the *Times* in September 1965, Elegant's articles were a remarkable exercise in subjective "advocacy." "It's true that the act of selection is a decision all foreign correspondents make; and therefore each of us decides what's the truth and what one thinks is important," colleague Jacques Leslie remarked. "But Elegant's writing not only violates the classical canons of objectivity, . . . some of it borders on the outrageous."

Chinese leaders, Elegant wrote in one of his first *Times* articles, made "hysterical" attacks and used "wild language" in discussing U.S. aims in Vietnam. "Indeed," Elegant wrote on the occasion of the sixteenth anniversary of the Chinese revolution, "bitterness at a presumably hostile world began to drip from the tongues of China's leaders."

When the Chinese issued their political statement on the division of the world between the white "have" nations, including the United States and the Soviet Union, and the third world "have-not" and potentially revolutionary nations, Elegant characterized the analysis as a "strange melange of pulp-magazine science fiction, Nostradamus, and Karl Marx at his worst [which] is, inescapably, somewhat ludicrous." "Unfortunately," Elegant warned, "merriment must be tempered by the realization that the leaders of one of the world's major powers really believe such claptrap."

Through the late sixties, Elegant wrote about the war in Vietnam as intricately related to China and Chinese policies. "Peking is the prime mover of the war," Elegant wrote in an August 1966 opinion piece. "The United States is fighting to convince Peking that it cannot crush world capitalism through intensified guerilla war in Vietnam—or similar wars elsewhere."

Like other China watchers, Elegant was surprised by the magnitude of the events of the 1966 cultural revolution. But instead of providing information and analysis, Elegant provided exhortation. "A spectacle of mindless, indiscriminate terror rare on the annals of humanity has emerged from the rampages of adolescent Red Guards in China," Elegant wrote in his lead on September 22, 1966. The Hong Kong correspondent spoke of "China's new master, the ruthless generalissimo of guerillas, Lin Piao, [who] quite deliberately turned the youth of China into a scourge to terrorize and destroy his enemies and potential enemies."

"Before China was a problem," Elegant wrote in a September 18, 1966, piece, "she was an enigma—a land of oddly attired people practicing customs which bewildered outsiders. Except for those foreigners who were intrigued by her oddities—or her commercial possibilities—most of the world was content to allow China to remain an enigma." "Europe is grace, ease, comfort and sophistication," Elegant wrote in an earlier opinion piece, "and Asia is cruelty, discomfort, peril, naivete, and constant misunderstanding."

The China story, however, took on a different cast when Richard Nixon made his trip to Peking in 1972. China now became a different kind of news peg, with all the ingredients—the Great Wall, fantastic local color, and a long-standing mythology—of a spectacular affair. Recognizing the possibility that the anti-Communist, exile-oriented Elegant might not be accepted if and when China and the United States established relations,

Gibson hired Jacques Leslie, then a twenty-four-year-old antiwar-orient-
ed freelancer who spoke Chinese, as a possible standby to replace the
Hong Kong-based correspondent.

Although the Elegant style became an embarrassment to a number of
Times staffers, including a few of the foreign correspondents, Gibson
continued to defend his star correspondent. After the fall of the Thieu
government in April 1975, a "terribly depressed" Elegant, as he put it,
came back to the States for his annual return and medical checkup. Six
months later he was assigned a one-year "leave of absence"; Jacques
Leslie, his strongest critic on the foreign staff, was sent to take his place.

3. The Vietnam Mirror

During the years of changeover at the *Times*, Vietnam became the front
page story throughout America. It affected the values and beliefs of the
staff—in effect, their ideology—just as it affected every institution in
American society. The credibility of the *Times* stood or fell with the manner of its Vietnam coverage, and, like many of the newspapers and broadcast media, its credibility suffered.

As American involvement in Vietnam began to grow in the early sixties, Otis Chandler and Nick Williams toured Asia to judge the American
presence there for themselves. "In a nutshell," Williams wrote in April
1963 in the *Times* house organ, "here is what we concluded: the American
involvement in S.E. Asia, frightfully expensive in money and lives as it is,
is the only alternative to complete Communist domination all the way
south to Australia, and all the way north to Japan."

Soon after the Williams/Chandler trip, the paper organized its first
Asian bureau in Tokyo, headed by one of the paper's bright young stars,
Don Neff. Foreign editor Gibson felt Neff was an "excellent reporter,"
although they didn't always see eye to eye. After the Diem coup, Neff
spent a great deal of time in Saigon, trying to provide daily and background stories on the confusion and probable collapse of the Saigon government. Due to poor, frequently delayed communication out of Saigon,
Neff's dispatches were sometimes superseded by material from the wires.
When the *Times* correspondent discovered his stories had been substantially rewritten with the updated wire information, he insisted the foreign
desk couldn't "put those things under my byline." "Oh, yes we can,"
Los Angeles replied, and Neff decided to resign on the spot. The startled
Times editors didn't attempt to change his mind.

Neff's replacement, Jack Foisie, formally opened the paper's Saigon
bureau in 1965. Foisie, Secretary of State Dean Rusk's brother-in-law,
who had been hired from the *San Francisco Chronicle,* generally supported the American buildup in Vietnam and tended to have hawkish views on

the war. LBJ's perspective that the war effort was leading toward some kind of successful resolution—"the light at the end of the tunnel"—was frequently reinforced by the more conservative *Times* correspondents in Saigon.

While Foisie worked out of Saigon, *Times* backup correspondents, such as Ruben Salazar and Bill Tuohy, covered the troops from out in the field. Though not necessarily antiwar, many of the backup correspondents tended to have a more critical attitude toward the war effort. "It seems clear," Tuohy wrote shortly before the February 1968 Tet offensive, "that the allies are winning the battles. But are we winning the war? We are, in the view of most, making progress. But is it commensurate with the enormous expenditure of men, money and material?"

In February 1969 the *Times* editors decided to make Arthur Dommen, a one-time agronomy specialist and well-known expert on Laos and Foisie's top backup man in Indochina, the new bureau chief. Dommen became increasingly bitter about the antiwar tone of some of the foreign correspondents in the field. "The war was an extremely complex affair," Dommen said of his assignment, "not easy for a foreigner like myself to understand, and even more difficult for a correspondent to explain to the American reading public. The feeling of revulsion for the war was perhaps the most concrete evidence that the press failed in what I saw as its most important mission. In the end, very few people cared a whit about the American commitment to a sovereign government. The antiwar activists with their superficially plausible but palpably illogical arguments carried the field. It's small wonder."

The *Times* editorial change to an antiwar position in 1970 was a tremendous disappointment for Dommen, who saw it as an attempt to mollify the antiwar feelings of some *Times* staffers and the people in the peace movement. "It was the old story," Dommen remarked, "of the London *Times* and the appeasers of Hitler in the 1930s all over again."

Soon after the *Times* editorial, Dommen ran into problems with foreign editor Gibson. Dommen, president of the Foreign Correspondent's Association of Vietnam, in 1970 had suggested a twenty-four-hour work stoppage of all Indochina correspondents in order to focus attention on seventeen correspondents who were missing in action in Cambodia following the coup against Sihanouk and the American invasion. The proposal "hit the *Los Angeles Times* like a bomb, apparently," Dommen later remarked. A furious Gibson immediately sent off a telegram demoting Dommen from the bureau chief post and attacking him for "irresponsibility." Within a few months, Dommen, "with no regrets," decided to go back to the study of agronomy; he left the *Times* in the summer of 1971.

George MacArthur, a former AP Vietnam bureau chief and Dommen's backup man since 1969, became the new *Times* bureau chief. A strong hawk on the war, MacArthur was considered to have the best access to the CIA and other intelligence forces within the Saigon press corps. "If you wanted to know what the intelligence community was thinking," one Saigon correspondent said of MacArthur, "you read George. He had the best developed intelligence sources in Vietnam." MacArthur's girlfriend, Eva Kim, was Ambassador Ellsworth Bunker's private secretary (and later became Graham Martin's secretary when he replaced Bunker). Although Kim did not violate confidences, according to MacArthur, she undoubtedly increased his awareness of the ins and outs of the embassy.

Times coverage often reflected MacArthur's perspective. When Nixon invaded Cambodia in May 1970, MacArthur wrote of the Cambodian response. "President Nixon's official notice of intervention into Cambodia prompted much private relief in this capital Friday," MacArthur wrote in his lead. "A random sampling of Cambodian reaction was overwhelmingly favorable to the President's move." The military coverage of the Cambodian invasion, by William J. Coughlin, was straight Pentagon news.

Times advocacy became even more noticeable two years later in its coverage of the spring offensive of the Provisional Revolutionary Government (PRG) and the American counteroffensive—an expanded air war, and the mining of Haiphong Harbor. "Radio Hanoi," a May 11 news story reported, "which always wildly exaggerates such claims, said sixteen American jets were shot down. U.S. headquarters, which always withholds such information until search-and-rescue missions have been called off, made no immediate statement on American losses." News descriptions of military battles over the next several days were filled with strong editorial overtones. The National Liberation Front (NLF) or North Vietnamese Army "smashed," "hurled," or "spearheaded" their attacks with their "Russian built tanks" which came "churning out of the jungle"; whereas the U.S. or Saigon forces "defended," "held on," had "jets dropping bombs," with American planes "seeding" Haiphong Harbor with mines.

When Jacques Leslie was hired shortly after the 1972 escalations, he was sent to Vietnam for some training under George MacArthur's tutelage. Leslie had attended antiwar demonstrations and went to Vietnam opposed to the war. Gibson, although he liked Leslie and saw his rapid rise as a parallel to Gibson's own start in Korea twenty years earlier was nevertheless mistrustful of any potential advocacy on Leslie's part.

One of Leslie's first stories concerned the moral qualms expressed by several of the pilots who flew missions over North Vietnam, the first time such an attitude had been expressed publicly to a journalist. Leslie got an angry cable about the piece. "It was a biased story," Gibson complained. He later identified that article as the only one he could recall where his "analysis without prejudice" criteria were violated by a *Times* foreign correspondent. Gibson felt that Leslie ought to have interviewed all the pilots on the carrier, since, undoubtedly, many would have supported the war. Leslie wrote back to his boss that he thought it was an important point of view that ought to be expressed. But the decision had been made: the story was killed. A few months later, the American military command made naval carriers off limits to journalists.

In October 1972 Leslie and Veronique Decoudu of Agence France Presse contacted two members of the NLF to inquire about the possibility of going behind NLF lines. The NLF cadre liked the idea, but they had to wait until a cease-fire was arranged.

The day after the January 20, 1973, cease-fire, the group met again. The two NLF men warned that the Thieu government's police activity had dramatically increased, and an official NLF escort had to be delayed. Leslie and Decoudu, dismayed but determined to get their exclusive, decided to go out on their own.

The three-part series, which began on February 1, detailed life in the NLF village. Leslie described how the NLF operated an entire alternative government infrastructure. "Obviously, such a short, restricted visit provides no basis for drawing conclusions," Leslie wrote, "but it does invoke impressions and answers to obvious questions. Our trip, for instance, reinforced a notion that one Vietnam expert had tried to drill into me, that the government side relies on and draws strength from the populace's passivity, while the NLF requires constant activity of its supporters."

The Thieu government, displeased with the story, began to keep its eye on the enterprising reporter. With his new recognition, Leslie began to expand his Saigon contacts. While MacArthur continued to report from official military and intelligence sources, Leslie talked to American peace groups, such as the well-informed American Friends Service Committee, and to dissident bureaucrats within the embassy who told of government corruption. One Leslie story on the smuggling of brass finally caused the Thieu government to act. In the fall of 1973, Leslie was expelled from Vietnam.

When Leslie returned to the States, he asked his boss Gibson if he could write a farewell to Indochina piece for the opinion section of the Sunday paper. "What are you going to write?" Gibson asked his reporter. "That justice lies with the NLF," Leslie replied. Gibson refused the request.

After 1973, coverage of the war had reached a hiatus. With the American pullout and the return of the POWs, the war became invisible. In spite of the billions of dollars of continuing aid and major fighting between Thieu and the Provisional Revolutionary Government (PRG), Vietnam disappeared as a daily news item in the *Los Angeles Times*. Then, suddenly, in March 1975, PRG forces overran a town in the Central Highlands, and the great collapse of the Thieu government began to inexorably unfold. The paper, caught totally off guard, rushed in three correspondents to report the last days of the war.

The paper's inability to adequately cover the last months of the war jeopardized Gibson's position for a time. The coverage under MacArthur had created some discomfort among staff and editors because of the bureau chief's unequivocal, prohawk position—even after the American pullout. The last-minute shuffling-in of reporters only seemed to heighten the prior inability to analyze and give coherence to that most dramatic event in recent U.S. history.

After the fall of Saigon, a new mood quickly set in throughout the country, a mood expressed by Ford and Kissinger—and *Los Angeles Times* editorials. Let's not wallow in Vietnam, the President and his aides declared; America is still the mightiest nation in the land.

Times cartoonist Paul Conrad disagreed. "Our long national nightmare is over," ran the caption of a cartoon several days after the NLF entered Saigon. The picture depicted a peaceful, sleeping Ho Chi Minh. The *Times* cartoonist, who usually received bagfuls of mail after a controversial drawing, received little response for this one. "People were so drained by the war, and all its consequences," Conrad remarked, "that they really bought Ford's line that we should leave Vietnam behind."

The Ford policy of "no recriminations" meant, in effect, a policy of no self-criticism. "Our failure on Vietnam," Tom Wicker of the *New York Times* commented during the last years of the war, "is an indictment of the entire press corps. It was our greatest failure." Vietnam had become a mirror for American society. For the *Los Angeles Times*, the new *Los Angeles Times*, that mirror reflected the limits of its own change.

The *Los Angeles Times* has been and still is a strong anti-Communist newspaper. The recent practices of the daily newsmagazine, backgrounders, and the self-sufficient correspondent have all strengthened that tendency. Foreign copy has become a unique blend of apparently apolitical mood pieces and light features, explicit anti-Communist analysis, and occasional "balanced" coverage from the more liberal members of the team.

In spite of the extraordinary upheavals throughout the world, the foreign desk has been the slowest to change in the sixties and seventies. As the two worlds concept of the Cold War broke down into a myriad of national movements and "third world" alliances, the Cold War journalists, as ideological sycophants, began to lose their political base. Foreign coverage, once the strongest political bias within a newspaper, no longer appeared to have a center of gravity. Ideological copy in the post-Vietnam era, when a large segment of the American public no longer accepted the terms of the American intervention, could turn into an embarrassment. The crisis of foreign coverage today reflects the crisis of American foreign policy.

CHAPTER 29

The Soft Mood and Soft News

1. The Feature Writers

At cityside, the daily newsmagazine concept had become supreme. Several new young staff writers, such as Chuck Powers from the *Kansas City Star*, Al Martinez from the *Oakland Tribune*, Dave Lamb from the AP, and Dave Smith from the *Phoenix Republic*, whose strengths lay more with their writing style than their content had been sought out and hired. All the new feature-oriented writers were encouraged to develop their "style"—to write in an interesting, perhaps offbeat manner. Profiles of individuals or narratives of interesting events seemed well suited to the *Times*'s approach.

The feature writing tendency paralleled the "new journalism" concern with life-style, which attempted to analyze the changing quality of life in America. This more subjective writing tried to deal directly with experience—how people felt and how they perceived what was happening to them.

As it became more popular, the life-style concept veered away from its late sixties connection to politics and the counter-culture. By the early seventies, a noncritical apolitical wing to the new journalism had emerged, generating picaresque articles with portraits of sometimes unrelated fragments of reality, stories intended to describe a casual slice of life, with the selection criteria ultimately determined by the interests of the reporter and editor. As the feature approach became the predominant tendency, hard news items were frequently moved to the back of the paper, preempted by the long, stylized, life-style features.

456

The appointment of Mark Murphy to replace Bill Thomas as metropolitan editor had marked the first major step of the new overhaul. Murphy came to the *Times* in 1964, and he quickly advanced from desk job to desk job until he became Thomas's chief assistant. After three years he was promoted to city editor for the *Times*'s Orange County edition. But when Thomas advanced to editor, he brought his own man Murphy back to Los Angeles as the new metro editor. Murphy favored the Thomas approach toward feature writing, but he had little other strategic sense of the kind of coverage he wanted. He constantly told his writers to think of their audience, to write in an interesting manner so that the mainstream reader could stick with the text.

Good style replaced tightly edited copy as the criterion for a successful piece, and many of the staffers enjoyed the freedom to take days—or weeks—to file a feature. "You won't see the names of a lot of guys that Thomas hired in the paper everyday," Murphy remarked. "Maybe you'll see them once a month. But that one time at bat will be a home run." A 10,000-word and almost entirely unedited Dave Smith feature on an Arizona boy who had murdered some people in a beauty shop became, as one staffer ironically commented, "a kind of minor classic around the *Times*." "I felt like I was in heaven," Smith recalled, "with the kind of money I was spending and the amount of time I could take." But some of the copy editors grumbled about the length, and the nonfeature-oriented *Times* staff criticized this overriding tendency toward "soft" topics as a depoliticization of content. Any story that required complex and detailed analysis tended to be shunted aside in favor of one that lent itself to a looser prose form. Potentially controversial subjects were reworked in such a manner to either flatten out the information or change the emphasis to carry an interesting lead and easy reading matter.

Sometime in the fall of 1972, Mark Murphy approached staff writer Al Martinez, a newcomer to Los Angeles, with a story idea about the Committee of 100, an informal social organization of 100 powerful men. As Martinez began his research, he was mistakenly told by a Chamber of Commerce official that the committee had an executive structure called the Committee of 25. In fact, the two committees were entirely different organizations. Unlike the socially oriented committee of 100, which met monthly to hear speakers and socialize, the Committee of 25, consisting of some of the most powerful individuals in the city, functioned like an informal Council of Elders and dealt with the most significant issues affecting the region. Without taking formal positions as such or directly implementing actions, the committee, which gave a focus for a relatively diffuse regional class elite, gathered information and passed it on to the appropriate powers.

Nobody at the *Times* had heard of the Committee of 25, nor could Martinez find anything in the *Times* morgue. Political reporter Bill Boyarsky suggested Martinez start with Richard Nixon's reelection campaign contributors list. After calling several people on the list who refused to answer questions, Martinez finally reached Asa Call, Los Angeles's consummate man behind the scenes, who spoke freely of the committee. On Call's suggestion, the *Times* reporter contacted other members, such as Dr. Norman Topping, chancellor of U.S.C., and Dan Bryant of Bekins Industries. Martinez discovered that Norman Chandler and Franklin Murphy were also committee members, but he steered clear of his bosses. "If I had probed too hard into affairs involving *Times* management, I might have blown the story," Martinez recalled.

On December 3, 1972, Martinez's Committee of 25 story ran as a front page non-dup column. "There exists in Los Angeles," Martinez wrote in his lead, "an organization of rich and powerful men who have become what at least one of them regards as an 'informal instrument of government.' " Committee members, Martinez went on to write, insisted that they had no intention of controlling city affairs, but rather "desire to be better informed on civic issues and to offer suggestions at the right level to make this a better area in which to live." These men, Martinez wrote, "are not opposed to the subtleties of implied pressure, and believe that by nature of their influence and wealth they have a moral commitment to help shape the future of Los Angeles."

The Martinez piece came off as a light, casual description of a group of elderly men who held a modicum of implicit power. The most substantial piece of information in the piece was the sidebar which contained the committee's membership list. Martinez, struck with the fact that he could do such a story, felt he had done it the way he wanted; he had never intended the story to be, as he put it, an exposé.

Feedback regarding the piece was extraordinary. Calls flooded the *Times*, and some old-timers told Martinez that they couldn't remember any other story generating such interest. Martinez was asked to speak on college campuses and individual researchers called him, asking to look through his files. But Martinez, with no files and no experience at power structure research, had to brush off the inquiries.

Metropolitan editor Murphy had no intention of following up the story. It was, like other features, retired to the morgue, just one more interesting and unconnected news story.

The Committee of 25 feature exemplified the most effective method that an editor has in controlling the flow of news: the predictability of the way reporters cover stories. By assigning such a story to a reporter like Martinez, who was not inclined toward investigation or analysis, a Murphy or Thomas could help define the final product. An editor in an organization like the *Times*, which tries to measure up to nationally recognized journalistic standards, can ill afford to censor or chop up a story directly, although that ocasionally happens. But an editor can mold the direction of the paper without that intervention; that was precisely what Bill Thomas had begun to do with the 1970s *Times*.

Some writers, like Ray Hebert, internalized management perspectives. By the late fifties, Hebert had become a general urban troubleshooter for the paper, a "high power" involved in those areas most sensitive to family and corporate concerns.

Hebert was the most accessible *Times* staffer to the local business establishment. "I can still always talk to Ray," Barker Brothers president Neil Petree grudgingly admitted after criticizing the new, institutionalized *Times*. "I don't know if Hebert actually gets direct orders from the family or Franklin Murphy," a *Times* staffer remarked, "or if he just anticipates so well and has learned their signals so thoroughly that there's no need, but does it really matter? His articles are still the same." Hebert's failure to cover stories within his realm did not allow for other writers to fill in the gaps.

Other limitations, derived from the reporters' own anxieties, were generated by the de facto monopoly status of the *Times*. "I feel like I'm the lone voice in the region on a subject—and in fact I often am," environmental writer Larry Pryor commented about some of his air pollution coverage. "It gets uncomfortable from a journalist's point of view, and I feel like I'm out on a limb. What if I get something wrong?"

Management rarely needed to directly interfere with a writer, but a few instances did occur. Despite the staff's independence (an especially strong independence when compared to the more heavy-handed treatment at papers such as Hearst's *Herald-Examiner* or Knowland's *Oakland Tribune*). The control factors—the tendency toward self-censorship, the corporate ambience, off-limits topics, and staff insecurities—permeated the paper.

The below-the-surface anxiety at cityside in the 1970s was compounded by a strange blend of laziness, fragmentation, and individualism. There was no staff unity. Reporters rarely saw each other after work. Informal bull sessions, one bitter staff member commented, were dominated by talk of investments and mortgage payments. "Working for the *Times*," several staffers remarked, "is like working for an insurance company."

But most staff were satisfied with their working conditions and high pay. There was comfort from the security of the power embodied in the job; when a *Times* staffer left a message, it was invariably answered. In the old *Times*, that function was related to the chosen few, the "high powers" and surrogates who actively wielded that power as an extension of the family. In the new *Times*, even the lowly zone writer was recognized as a writer for the prestigious and powerful *Los Angeles Times*, the most important news medium in the West. Coupled with the freedom to work on long features—the life-style journalism of the seventies—this atmosphere created a studied casualness, an apparent comfort that was supposed to eliminate the enormous pressure of deadline journalism that once drove reporters to the bottle. The writer was now a worldly professional.

2. *"Without Union Interference"*

The reporters' basic satisfaction with their jobs complemented the *Times* management's hostility toward unions or independent organizations within its ranks. The Chandlers had fought early attempts by the Newspaper Guild to represent *Times* editorial workers in the 1930s. *Times* management quickly developed a policy of evading organizing attempts by keeping wages and other benefits at a higher scale than the Guild's, and salary increases paralleled or anticipated Guild decisions. Employees of the new *Times* were not prevented from joining the Guild, but those who belonged did not broadcast the fact. Most staff felt they were doing just as well or better without the Guild. To many reporters, working at the *Times* was a newspaperman's dream.

Union organizers in the pressroom felt they stood a better chance than their Guild counterparts. Previous attempts by the pressmen to organize during the Norman Chandler period had all met with total failure, but in the early 1960s the pressmen's union decided to try again. In an election held in February, 1962, the union won by a slight majority. When the ballots were counted, according to union organizer Bill Torrance, the pressroom superintendent fainted on the spot. Negotiations for a contract, however, did not come so quickly. Management, in what Torrance called a "cat and mouse game," held back from offering a package that would be acceptable to the union. Management objected to the union's presence and would only grant minimal concessions to keep up the appearance of bargaining.

Many of the pressroom workers were frustrated with the union's failure to secure a contract agreement after a year of negotiations, and a small group of pressmen began to organize for a decertification vote. Citing the loss of their yearly raise, the group sent out frequent circulars and posted charts comparing *Times* pay scales and benefits to those of union pressmen. "You have the finest group insurance. . . . You share in the company's profits," the decert group wrote, emphasizing that it was all "without union interference." "The union needs you. . . . You don't need them," leaflets urged.

In April 1963 the decert group filed for a decertification election with the National Labor Relations board (NLRB). Although the company was prohibited by law from making promises or discussing decertification with their workers, letters signed by Otis Chandler were frequently sent out to *Times* pressroom employees to keep workers up to date on the negotiations. Referring to union demands as "unreasonable, economically unrealistic, impractical, or not supported by convincing reasons," the *Times* publisher, after the decertification petition was filed with the NLRB, instructed company counsel to file a management petition in support of the new election, declaring in one letter, "We do not intend to hand the keys of this plant on a silver platter to the union." A few days later the union filed a charge with the NLRB that the *Times* had refused to bargain, but Chandler and the decert group denied the charges and accused the union of "stall tactics" to delay the election.

Over the next month, the decert group and management organized an intensive campaign for decertification. Chandler announced an upcoming annual pay increase and, through personnel manager Robert Flannes, informed the workers that the pressroom employees in the union's bargaining unit would not be covered by the raise. "Why are we the 'goats' for the rest of the shop?" the decertification group asked. "They are enjoying their raises while we, in the pressroom, suffer the lack of our raises." "Your future, and the future of every other *Times* employee, is tied directly to the success of the *Times*," Chandler wrote in another letter to the workers. The decertification group stressed the success of the company: "The *Times* has the *largest classified ad section in the Nation*. We are growing! As long as this Company is run without outside interference, it will continue to grow." You can't be loyal to "Our Company" and the union at the same time, they argued; VOTE "NO" posters hung from the rafters of the pressroom.

The union accused *Times* management of hiring new apprentices in an effort to pack the bargaining unit with pro-management employees in preparation for the decertification election. As the election neared, the county federation of labor unanimously adopted a resolution to try to get subscribers to boycott the *Times* as a "mass protest against the anti-union policy of the *Times* management." The decert group attacked the boycott as an example of the kind of union action that could end up forcing employees out of work. "What would happen if they got a contract?" the group asked, "Strikes, walk-outs, picket lines, no work, violence and all the other foul deeds that accompany such actions."

Two weeks before the election, two pressroom employees—union men—were arrested in what the *Times* called the "Times Bomb case." The two men were accused of having planted smoke bombs in the pressroom's air-conditioning system, resulting in the temporary evacuation of the building. "Evidently the union condones this action," a decert group memo to other pressmen noted, since the union had placed the two men in other shops after they were fired from the *Times*.

"Your 'NO' vote on June 27 will eliminate the endless campaign arguments, picket lines, and personal animosities which have existed in the Pressroom," Chandler wrote on June 25. At the election two days later, the union was voted out by a small majority.

The union, however, did not give up. A year later the pressmen's local won a new election for representation, capturing 190 out of 300 votes cast and becoming the bargaining unit for 450 of the company's 4,000 workers. This time the union was able to negotiate a contract, although the agreement fell short of what the organizers and the workers had wanted.

With union funds and energy concentrated on an unsuccessful protracted strike at the *Herald-Examiner*, the Los Angeles local had little time to devote to its unit at the *Times*, except to raise assessments and require members to do picket duty at the *Herald-Examiner*. As a result, dissatisfied *Times* workers, with the blessing of management, were successfully able to pull off another decertification campaign when the union contract ran out three years later.

Once again the *Times*—the only major newspaper daily in the country without a single bargaining unit in the entire plant—was without a union.

3. Desecrating the Temple

Since the days when Harry Chandler acquired his route monopolies, newspaper distribution has had a special place in *Times* history. As the *Times* grew in size and circulation, the company integrated the dealerships into its circulation department. But it also still maintained a leasing system for each route with an understanding that each dealer, in effect, controlled his or her own business as an independent entrepreneur. The paper used "the promise of independence as a lure to attract young men to become dealers," one longtime dealer recalled.

By keeping its dealers independent, the paper could avoid payroll taxes and general labor questions that would arise if the dealers had been legally considered *Times* employees. More important, the *Times* hoped to forestall any organization of its employees. "They wanted it both ways," one of the dealers complained. "They had us on a leash in terms of how much money we made or how we carved up our territories much as if we were their employees, but they also told us we were independent businessmen which meant that they didn't have to pay us other kinds of benefits in that situation."

Times dealers had several outstanding gripes: The paper's circulation department, by arbitrarily defining territories and subscription rates, controlled, in effect, overall circulation figures (which neighborhood received what volume of papers) and the amount each dealer would make. Many of the dealers thought that the circulation office wanted to maintain a maximum income level for each dealer, to prevent possible expansion or combination of dealerships.

In the 1940s several dealers had begun to talk of creating an organization of their own. The *Times* immediately let it be known that any dealer involved in organizing activities would be terminated. Each year around Christmas, the company invited dealers to the paper's executive dining room to hear a tape recording of Norman Chandler. "Although this was intended to be a Christmas message," one of the dealers recalled, "Mr. Chandler's remarks were invariably directed to the theme that the Times Mirror Company was unalterably opposed to any kind of organization of individuals who were associated with the Times Mirror Company." Chandler's remarks were carefully backed up by threats of dismissal from circulation executives who carefully monitored the dealers' activities. The threats effectively kept any dealer organization from getting off the ground through the forties and fifties.

In the spring of 1964, an open discussion was organized for dealers to hear professor John Van De Water of UCLA Law School speak on labor/management relations and the rights of dealers in relation to the *Times*.

Less than a month later, the three organizers of the Van De Water discussion were summoned to the office of *Times* circulation manager Jack Underwood. Underwood was a stern, theatrical man who scolded his employees to maintain discipline and company policy. When the dealers arrived in his office, Underwood stood quiet and motionless, facing a window with his back turned, for quite a while—almost five minutes according to one of the dealers. "We stood there feeling like dummies," one of the three recalled. Underwood then wheeled around and lit into them, calling them "gutless" for having arranged the discussion. "He pointed to several envelopes on his desk, stating that they were our termination notices and whether or not he would hand them to us depended on our immediate answers to his questions. . . . He told us what we had done could be likened to a 'big nigger' going into a beautiful temple for the purpose of desecrating it and tearing it down into the dirt." Underwood told the dealers that unless they instantly dissolved their association, he would fire them on the spot. The browbeaten men agreed.

Three days later Underwood called a special meeting of all *Times* dealers at Eaton's Restaurant. After everybody arrived, Underwood stood up and in an ominous voice ordered all the waitresses to leave the room and shut the doors behind them. "I feel like a dog who hasn't taken a crap in six months and I'm going to let it out," Underwood began. He then proceeded to lash out against the three dealers who had organized the Van De

Water meeting, calling them "ringleaders" and "scum" who were trying for their own selfish motives to usurp the policies of the *Los Angeles Times.* Only one dealer, Brian Bumpus, spoke in their defense. As a result of his remarks, Bumpus became a marked man, subjected to reprisals for several months and finally terminated a little more than a year later.

Bumpus's firing "scared the hell out of everybody," as Bob Cohen recalled, and the dealers unsuccessfully pleaded with management to take him back. The firing also stalled organizing attempts that might have been spurred on by the recently organized national dealer association (Association of American Independent News Dealers—AAIND), whose first convention was held in San Francisco in 1971. Several *Times* dealers wrote to the AAIND lawyer that they'd like to attend, but feared reprisals. Enclosing the anonymous note from the dealers, the lawyer then made inquiries to Otis Chandler, but he never received a response. *Times* management let it be known informally that they were opposed to any dealer attending the convention. The only employee that went was a company spy.

Six months later, *Times* dealers formed a local Southern California chapter of AAIND. Although the chapter wanted to represent the interests of the dealers and be able to state grievances, it rejected in its own bylaws all possible links to trade unionism, opposed strikes or boycotts, and did not wish to bargain collectively with management.

The new organization was nonetheless considered a threat by *Times* management. A few weeks after the local was formed, circulation manager Bert Tiffany, who had replaced Underwood, sent a letter to all *Times* dealers. "*The Los Angeles Times,*" Tiffany wrote, "is opposed to *Times* dealers becoming involved in this association. . . . Membership in this association could only result in a loss of much of the independence and freedom of action which you now enjoy."

Finally, one of the younger dealers, who had something of a reputation as a rebel, contacted the AAIND lawyer to initiate a suit under section 16 of the Clayton Act forbidding monopolistic practices concerning price and territory fixing. Other dealers, a little suspicious of the "longhair," met with him and, impressed with his courage and determination, also joined the suit.

The old tactics, *Times* management discovered, no longer worked. On October 13, 1975, as the suits slowly wound through the courts, the *Times* announced that the paper was abolishing its old "independent businessman" delivery system in favor of what it called a "delivery agent" system. The changeover to the new system, the company later revealed in its quarterly report, cost $5.2 million, including expenses resulting from termination of numerous dealerships. Dealers who had put their names on the lawsuit were the first to be fired; by January 1, 1976, every party to the lawsuit had been terminated. The dealers mobilized in face of the *Times* attacks. They issued leaflets, placed posters on buses, and demonstrated at the *Times*, demanding "Practice What You Editorialize."

On January 1, 1976, the new "delivery agent" system was instituted. The "independent businessman" facade, which had become an embarrassment for the paper, had ended. The long battle had changed the dealers: conservative, relatively well-to-do, surburban dwellers, they had believed in the system and the *Times* as well. "We're newspaper people," affirmed Bob Ash, who had been with the *Times* for thirty-seven years until his termination. "We defended the *Times*, we were proud of it. But somehow this paper has become too big, too powerful. They seem to have influence everywhere, wherever we turn. I'm beginning to understand how the younger generation feels about the establishment. I never would have believed it."

4. Self-Criticism?

With the development of the alternative press, press councils, and journalism reviews in the late sixties and early seventies, coverage and criticism of the press's performance began to grow. A number of newspapers around the country tentatively explored the possibility of providing their own institutional framework for media criticism. The *New York Times* created a media critic slot for one of its own staff, and the *Washington Post* set up an ombudsperson's job to air editorial grievances and facilitate internal criticism of the paper's performance.

The *Los Angeles times* had always been hostile to the idea of outside criticism of its operation. "If we are going to preserve our diversity," a *Times* editor responded to a *Columbia Journalism Review* query about the National Press Council, "our discipline has to remain self-discipline. Voluntary self-regulation [through the National Press Council] could slide pretty quickly to involuntary, imposed regulation." Otis Chandler insisted in a March 1976 speech that demands for access embodied in such regulatory institutions, must be resisted "with every ounce of individual and corporate strength."

After closely watching events at the other papers, editor Thomas decided to create a media slot at the *Times*. Although Bill Trombley was interested, Thomas chose general assignment reporter Dave Shaw, a Thomas favorite, for the spot. A loner at the *Times*, Shaw ultimately related best to his editors rather than his peers.

Shaw's only previous experience with media criticism came from his position as contributing editor, with environmental specialist and fellow *Times* reporter Larry Pryor, for *The Review of Southern California Journalism*, a local media review initiated in 1970 by journalism students and faculty at the University of California at Long Beach.

After their names appeared on the masthead for the first time, Shaw and Pryor began to feel pressure from *Times* management. Pryor's supervisor, George Cotliar, then managing editor of the Orange County edition, asked Pryor whether he felt uncomfortable writing for the journalism review while working for a large newspaper where, inevitably, he would come across things not meant for public consumption. Cotliar wondered if information meant for *Times* eyes only would end up in the other publication. Pryor acknowledged the conflict, and both he and Shaw eventually removed their names from the masthead.

Shaw, at first reluctant to take the assignment as the *Times* media writer, agreed after he and Thomas worked out what Shaw called his "preconditions." Shaw could write as infrequently as once a month, with no limits on copy length, and with little interference from the desk. Unlike other cityside writers, he would bypass the desk and report directly to Thomas. His extraordinarily lengthy stories became the envy—or scandal—of the paper.

Shaw did not want to cover day-to-day media events. His overall plan was to mix light and heavy stories: profiles on media personalities, trend pieces on phenomena such as political polls or the development of surburban papers; and light excursions, such as a look at the right-wing *Berkeley Gazette*. He considered himself completely independent from any management interference.

In a few of his pieces, Shaw obliquely referred to some internal conflicts at the *Times*, although the criticism appeared tacked on—unconnected statements to give balance to the overall article. Shaw's straight news account of the wild goose chase to locate Patty Hearst that sent two *Times* reporters half way around the world was, on the other hand, a quite successful attempt at describing an internal *Times* situation. The article, in its simple, unencumbered narrative form, captured the ludicrousness of the paper's attempt to come up with that ultimate scoop.

Shaw's *Times*-related remarks became the highlight of an internal memorandum from Otis Chandler to *Times* employees about the "increasing self-criticism at the *Times*." The paper, the publisher noted, had entered "the new era of honest self-appraisal," and the Shaw columns exemplified *Times* leadership in this "new journalistic direction." "In short," Chandler concluded, "we have been trying to give *Times* readers even more reasons to trust their newspaper."

Shaw represented the apparent new openness of the *Times*: its ability, as publisher Chandler saw it, to hold the mirror up to itself. The features, however, avoided the traditional questions of conflict of interest and censorship/self-censorship, and they shied away from ongoing coverage of the media industry as a whole. Although he made some criticisms of the *Times*, Shaw had an underlying bias that the thoughtful, provocative, and independent tendencies in the *Times* far outweighed the passing references to internal problems. "We are a great newspaper," Shaw defended his outlook, "and Bill Thomas is the best newspaperman I know."

5. The Women's Caucus

On August 26, 1970, the fiftieth anniversary of the passage of the woman's suffrage amendment, demonstrations signaling the growth of a new woman's movement took place throughout the country. Several thousand participants—women and men—marched through the streets of Los Angeles.

Although organizers from sponsoring groups had contacted the *Times* city desk, the desk ignored the calls and limited its predemonstration coverage to a single wire story on the day of the demonstration. "IT'S WOMEN'S DAY TODAY—WATCH IT BUB!" read the headline. "Marching to rallies, smashing coffee cups, dumping bras and cosmetics in trash cans and in some cases perhaps plopping the baby on the husband's office desk," the story began, "women from coast to coast will demonstrate for liberation today." Although the article mentioned plans for actions throughout the country and in California, no mention was made of the Los Angeles program.

The next day, the *Times* gave the local events front page coverage under the headline L.A. 'WOMEN'S LIB' MARCHERS GREETED BY CHEERS AND JEERS and a kicker "Not Exactly a Triumph." The article, written by Lee Dye, essentially belittled the event. Although Dye failed to mention the size of the demonstration or much about the content of the rally speeches, he did report that fifty antifeminist demonstrators had come to heckle under the leadership of "a striking thirty-two-year-old mother of seven who enjoys being female."

March organizers from the National Organization for Women (NOW) were furious at Dye's insulting coverage. Aware that the *Times* discriminated in its employment practices—one of the demonstration issues—they contacted a woman staffer at the paper to help gather inside information on male/female job breakdowns. The information pointed to a strong *prima facie* case of discrimination: no women executives, women excluded from production work, only one woman in the city room, only a few in the View section, and the vast majority of women employed in secretarial positions.

The NOW organizers asked their contacts at the *Los Angeles Times* if they would be willing to file a complaint with the Fair Employment Practices Commission (FEPC), but the *Times* women were hesitant. "It's not that I'd necessarily be fired," one reporter commented, "but if I got involved in something like this I'd probably get sent to the zones or some equivalent thing." The *Times* women were aware of the repression that had frequently met attempts to organize women inside other media organizations—the mass firings of women at *Newsweek* after initial organizing attempts, for instance. "After all," View staffers Ursula Vils and Jean Murphy remarked about the problems of organizing, "the *Times* is a monopoly and the only game in town."

The NOW women decided to proceed on their own. With information provided by *Times* staffers, NOW, along with the Los Angeles Women Journalist's Association, filed an FEPC claim of widespread discrimination against women and minorities. The FEPC report, issued in March 1973, noted "an underutilization of females and minorities": of officials and managers, 11.7 percent were women and 4 percent minorities; of professionals, 18.3 percent women and 4.8 percent minorities. Yet women made up 68.5 percent of the office and clerical pool, and minorities accounted for 67.9 percent of the *Times* service workers. Within the editorial departments, there were no blacks or women among officials, managers, or administrators. The FEPC suggested that the *Times* initiate an affirmative action program, and kept the investigation open.

While the FEPC probe was under way, seven women were hired to work cityside where Dorothy Townsend had previously been the only female reporter. The women in the View section, encouraged by the FEPC action and the growing women's movement in Los Angeles, also pressured the paper's management. The View women initially met as an informal group to discuss the "woman's image in the paper." They began to clip items with sexist overtones in their headlines or captions to send to the appropriate editor.

The group also discussed management attitudes. An article by View writer Betty Liddick on the problems of Barbara Rogers, a female dental hygienist who had to constantly fend off, as she put it, " 'the hand dangler, the fanny pincher, the leg grabber, and the bosom bumper' " in the dentist's office, was an interesting case in point. Liddick described Rogers' growing feminist consciousness, and Bill Thomas found the article one-sided. He sent a memo to Liddick's supervisor Jean Taylor, complaining of the lack of balance and the absence of the opposing male point of view.

A second FEPC report released in August 1974 commended *Times* management for improvements, but pointed out that large-scale discrimination still existed. Some of the apparent improvements, *Times* women staffers later discovered, were a result of the reclassification of job categories rather than real changes.

By the fall of 1974, the *Times* women were ready to create a formal organization (an earlier attempt had fallen apart when most of the staffers backed down, fearful of losing their jobs). In early September a dozen women from View and cityside got together after work, determined to form a caucus. At the gathering, the women discussed the numerous lawsuits against other newspapers across the country. They talked of the possibility of initiating a suit of their own and considered other approaches, such as filing an equal opportunity complaint or arranging for an affirmative action program.

The new *Los Angeles Times* women's caucus outlined a set of grievances on such topics as salary discrepancies, promotion, maternity leave, and the sexist content of the paper. Since the grievances also applied to Third World staff, the women considered including minorities in their caucus. The Third World men were supportive but cautious. "I wanted to be kept informed," Chicano Frank Del Omo recalled, "but I was worried that if it became a women and minorities caucus, that we'd get lost in the shuffle." Most of the other Third World men agreed, and although one or two came to a few of the meetings at the invitation of the caucus, it remained, in effect, a women's organization.

Another problem was whether or not to include noneditorial women. Women in the classified ad department, where discrimination was even more severe and blatant, had begun to meet on their own and approached the editorial women about consolidating into one overall organization. But the caucus decided to limit itself to editorial workers.

Women who worked in the zones—the once- or twice-a-week inserts that were published in the different regional areas of the city—were also excluded from the caucus. The zones had the worst conditions in the paper: the pay scale was much lower, discriminatory tactics were much more overt, and news decisions were more likely to have sexist overtones. The zone women, feeling a lot less stake in the *Times* system, and inclined to be more militant, were angry at the elitism in the caucus. But several caucus organizers from "downtown," who had come out of the zones and sympathized with their point of view, helped smooth over the conflict, and the zone staffers joined the new, unified Women's Editorial Caucus.

The caucus met with a feminist lawyer to discuss its status and decided to draw up a statement to circulate among the staff to develop support for the issues. The petition called for better career opportunities; the elimination of discriminatory practices, including anything that demeaned or degraded women or minorities; and immediate equal participation in *Times* decision-making processes.

The petition set out three initial goals: the development of an affirmative action program, preferential consideration for promotions and job openings (including job posting inside the organization and a job opportunity newsletter), and the elimination of "discriminatory treatment of women and minorities in headlines, copy, photographs, and captions."

More than a hundred people signed the petition, although some admitted they didn't agree with its objectives.

One of the caucus members recalled management's reactions. "They felt threatened," she said, "because we felt a certain amount of power in knowing that they anticipated and feared legal action." Recent law suits involving job discrimination at large corporations had resulted in multi-million-dollar awards to the women employees. "But," the woman added, "we didn't know how to use that power."

In the fall and winter of 1974, the women became more determined. That winter the caucus organized an informal session with editor Thomas. Although no specific agreements were made, Thomas gave the impression that goals such as the elimination of sexist headlines, the posting of jobs, and an increase in the hiring of women staff would be implemented.

In December 1974 the *Times* announced that View editor Jean Taylor would replace the departing Jim Bellows as associate editor in charge of the software sections. The Taylor appointment—the first time a woman editor joined upper management circles—was a high point for the caucus, which felt it had finally succeeded in getting management's attention.

But other changes were slow in coming. Headlines and news stories continued to reflect a male bias. Despite the lapses, the caucus felt that some of the more egregious examples of sexism had been eliminated. Five years after the August 26, 1970 NOW demonstration controversy— years of continual calls and pressure from local women's groups—the *Times* city desk assigned four women reporters to cover "Alice Doesn't" Day events organized by NOW. Their straightforward coverage was in marked contrast to Lee Dye's approach in 1970.

By the summer of 1975, the caucus had reached an impasse. It decided to drop the idea of legal action, and its meetings, reduced from once a week to less than once a month, had begun to center around outside speakers instead of discussions on internal *Times* matters. The group lacked leadership, and meetings became largely limited to women from the zones. The *Times* mood of privilege, comfort, and alienation had made its way to the caucus. When only four women showed up at a fall 1975 meeting, the women's caucus, barely a year old, temporarily disbanded.

Few of the basic problems had been resolved. Job posting had not been institutionalized, there were no women on the national staff, and it had taken two years to assign a woman to a foreign correspondent's post. Stories such as a Dave Smith profile on Bella Abzug or one on a Harold Robbins-sponsored beauty contest—considered derogatory to women by many feminists—continued to run in the paper.

But the *Times* women, particularly in cityside, felt they had achieved most of their goals. Many of the downtown women staffers felt an increased respect, or at least tolerance, from the male staff and editors. Some of the women, particularly those from the zones who tried to keep the caucus alive, felt this deceptive mood of the *Times* might ultimately have been responsible for caucus difficulties—"The Tender Trap of the Times," one of the staffers called it.

The existence of the group, itself a product of the growing women's movement, pushed the *Times* management in some minimal directions toward change. But the links between the women's movement and the *Times* women were not strong enough to continue providing the support and pressure that were necessary to keep that momentum. The caucus, narrowing its definition, excluded the most discriminated women from its organization and eventually lost the initiative that helped bring it together in the first place.

The caucus marked the first real attempt in the history of the paper, to talk about substantial changes from a staff point of view. While it existed, it created a sense of staff solidarity, at least among the women. Its difficulties pointed out the continuing strength of management in relation to staff. The real challenge to the *Times* and its policies, it seemed clear, lay not with its staff, but with the social movements that had initially precipitated changes at the paper.

6. The Other Side of Populism

Before her promotion to associate editor in charge of the software sections, Jean Taylor, hired by the *Times* in 1971 from the *Phoenix Republic*, had begun to transform the coverage of the software departments. Much in the same way Nick Williams tried to bridge the old and new *Times*, Taylor wanted to hold onto the "View" section's existing readership, primarily women, by keeping many of the traditional food, fashion, and society features while it expanded into new areas.

In place of the "women's section" format, Taylor envisioned a "humanist" section concerned with viewpoint, motivation, and human behavior—words that conveyed a discussion of life-style, that dealt in human terms with the lives of Angelenos.

"The section had a populist streak, " one-time View staffer Chuck Powers commented about the new format. Staff writers, encouraged to get into what Powers called "the texture of life," began to concentrate on personality profiles and descriptions of offbeat individuals and institutions. The articles were written as magazine-type pieces, and, according to one staffer, "they could be pulled out and placed intact in *Esquire*." Like *Esquire*, the View populism tended to reflect its distinctly white upper-middle-class constituency. For example, a series in early 1976 on "City People"—developed, according to Taylor's assistant Beverly

Beyette, to show "what the little people thought about their city," to have profiles on people "who ordinarily don't make the news"—limited itself almost entirely to white middle- and upper-class Angelenos with whom the writer and editor shared some affinity. A second series, "The Way We Are," began in May 1976 with articles on "Southern Californians and their diverse life styles," a concept along the same lines.

The influence of the women's movement had initially given View's life-style articles a social and political bent, but, once removed from that context, Jean Taylor's perspective, particularly as she rose within the organization, began to resemble Bill Thomas's notion of the new *Times* journalism. View populism by the mid-seventies had little room for social criticism. A key case in point involved the *Times* architecture critic John Pastier.

Pastier had come to the *Times* in 1970 as the first staff critic to cover architecture and the urban environment. "I slipped through the cracks," Pastier recalled, "but once I got in the *Times* could say they now had the full spectrum of opinion concerning real estate and architectural problems. Only it was really 90 percent real estate rewrites and 10 percent Pastier. It was the cheapest, simplest way for the *Times* real estate section to get rid of the curse of being tied into the real estate speculators."

Pastier's columns, which were transferred from real estate to op-ed and finally to the View section, concerned a wide range of architectural subjects, such as the problem of pedestrians in Los Angeles, "high" architecture and "pop" architecture, the Berkeley Traffic Plan, the architectural environment of "security systems," the city plans for Los Angeles and New York, alienation in cars, and Muzak in public places. Pastier analyzed the role of large architectural firms, major planning consultants, and top corporations who often worked together in the area of urban planning. His topics led him into controversial political and economic subjects, where he frequently found himself at odds with management.

Part of Pastier's difficulties stemmed from the ever-present shadow of Ray Hebert. When Pastier was first hired, he requested the title "urban design critic," but anything with the word "urban" sounded too close to Hebert's domain. *Times* management insisted on a narrower designation as a means of defining Pastier's role in terms of a limited "expertise" coverage. With his booster approach and intimate working relation with the downtown business establishment, Hebert sat on the opposite end of the spectrum from Pastier. By nature feisty and sharp-witted, the *Times* critic seemed out of place in the uncritical and guarded atmosphere of the *Times*.

In June 1975 Pastier was asked to do an article for the book review section on the possible relocation of the Los Angeles Central Library within the general downtown area—where Times Mirror owned substantial real estate. The move had been strongly promoted by *Times* editorials. " 'Peanut Politics' is a particularly apt phrase in the case of the Central Library," Pastier wrote, "since the city seems bent on building itself a classic white elephant. For all of downtown's apparent resurgence, manifested in half-empty office towers and splashy new shopping malls, it is clear that this district can never regain its prewar role as the hub of Los Angeles." Pastier criticized the notion that one central library could effectively serve Angelenos living in the decentralized communites of Southern California. After writing the article, Pastier was told by the book review editor that Jean Taylor had complained that the article was not appropriate for the book section. Taylor later commented that she thought the article duplicated another already-scheduled story for the book section. When Pastier rewrote it for his regular Monday column, Taylor hemmed and hawed. Although Pastier suggested taking out the more overtly political information, the decision had already been made that the library piece would not run.

Three months later Pastier was called into Taylor's office and told that he was fired. Taylor remarked that she'd been under pressure from Bill Thomas and Otis Chandler for nearly a year, but "it's not political," she told the staff writer. Pastier then went to see Bill Thomas, who blamed it on Pastier's copy; his writing, Thomas explained, was not the kind of writing they were looking for. He was, both Taylor and Thomas remarked, too philosophical, metaphysical, and futurist. The architecture critic later wondered why—if such dissatisfaction existed—they had previously given him an in-house award for his writing.

After the word got out, a group of architects and students held a demonstration outside the *Times* Building to protest the firing. They and critics of the downtown redevelopment plan raised the possibility that Pastier's voice had been silenced for political reasons, but the *Times* management strongly denied the implication. "There were philosophic differences concerning the thinking about what the beat should be," Taylor remarked about the firing. "What we wanted was quality of life type coverage, stories that talked more about how people used buildings, how buildings relate to people, but not the kinds of things that John got into with such questions as urban density or environmental factors. We wanted to get to the humanity involved; the man in the street."

Pastier's replacement, Art Seidenbaum, once considered a strong liberal voice during the changeover at the *Times* in the early sixties, became a prodowntown, probusiness-oriented observer of the buildings scene.

When Seidenbaum was first asked to take over the architecture critic's job, Bill Thomas assured him that Pastier's firing was not political. "If people got fired for political reasons in this place," Thomas told Seidenbaum, "then Martin Bernheimer would have been fired long ago." One week later *Times* music critic Bernheimer was on the brink of resigning.

Bernheimer was a respected and well-known critic for the *Saturday Review of Literature* when he was first approached by the *Times* in 1965. The newly opened Music Center and the Los Angeles Philharmonic, led by Buff's choice Zubin Mehta, attracted Bernheimer, since, he reasoned, Los Angeles seemed willing to support a serious effort at this most prestigious form of class culture. But the *Saturday Review* critic was also wary of Dorothy Chandler's enormous influence in Los Angeles's music world and feared possible interference.

Associate editor Leonard Riblet (then in charge of software) tried to convince the anxious Bernheimer that his independence was guaranteed. After many long-distance discussions, Riblet finally sent a wire: "If you'll protect Beethoven, we will protect Bernheimer."

In his new job, Bernheimer became a strong and consistent critic of Zubin Mehta and of many of the performances of the Los Angeles Philharmonic. Stories of Dorothy Chandler's rage at Bernheimer critiques abounded around the *Times*. A Bernheimer colleague recounted one incident when Dorothy Chandler returned from a trip in Europe and told the music critic when she ran into him at the *Times* that she had enjoyed her trip because she didn't have to read any Bernheimer reviews. Yet Bernheimer was insulated from the complaints that were directed toward Riblet, and Riblet's successor, Jim Bellows. Bellows recalled enormous pressures put on him from the music-oriented business establishment, many of whom wanted Bernheimer's head, and such pressures occasionally included angry remarks from a Chandler.

Bernheimer wrote of performances, not of institutions or the politics of culture. He was trained to be a critic of classical musical performance, not a reporter delving into the economic and political underpinnings of the world of music. In a modern newspaper, critics were not expected to simply boost performances and orchestras. The reading public had come to expect the kind of sharp and incisive statements in which Bernheimer excelled. The Chandlers, including the redoubtable Dorothy, decided early on to swallow their anger and accept the fact that such "negativity" on Bernheimer's part was the modern prerogative of newspaper criticism.

In the fall of 1975, Bernheimer became increasingly annoyed at the antics of some of the Music Center's box seat attendants—many of whom were members of Dorothy Chandler's Blue Ribbon 400 or Music Center founders. When the New York City Opera opened the Los Angeles opera season in November with a performance of "La Traviata," Bernheimer tagged a last line onto his review which commented on the outrageous behavior of the wealthy patrons who came for the $100-a-ticket benefit performance.

When Bernheimer handed in his copy to entertainment editor Charles Champlin, the *Times* editor complained about the last line and refused to run it the way Bernheimer had intended. Champlin told the music critic that if he really wanted to get into the question of people's behavior at concerts, it deserved an entire article rather than a throwaway line in a music review. Bernheimer agreed, and Champlin breathed a sigh of relief, "assuming, undoubtedly," one *Times* staffer remarked, "that Bernheimer would never follow through."

But the entertainment editor mistook the mood of his music critic. Bernheimer had had it with the upper-class music patrons. "It seemed to me," Bernheimer later commented, "that the people who finance culture are at the same time the least behaved at a performance, the least appreciative of the music."

Bernheimer handed in a new article, which elaborated on the "La Traviata" opening as a case in point, and left Los Angeles for a trip, assuming his piece would run in Sunday's *Calendar* while he was away. Instead, the story was withheld, stopped by Champlin and Jean Taylor. "It was an unfair piece," Taylor commented, "badly written and submitted too late (it was two weeks after the "La Traviata" opening) for reader interest. Our decision had nothing to do with music or music criticism."

Bernheimer disagreed. He returned to Los Angeles furious and demanding an explanation. "It was a nasty situation," Bernheimer remarked. He rejected the argument that the writing was bad: the only difference was the subject matter. It was the first time Bernheimer had ventured into what he called a "sociological story" instead of a performance piece. He threatened to have a showdown over the censorship.

Thomas, refusing to back down and run the story, stuck to Taylor's explanation that the argument was not over subject matter and offered Bernheimer the opportunity to write on such subjects in the future. "There are no holds barred here," Thomas told his music critic.

Bernheimer was faced with a choice—in effect, his bluff was called—resign or accept the story's rejection. Bernheimer stayed on and kept to his old performance-related subject matter.

Unlike the classical music scene, the movie industry was dominated by the publicist's maxim "I don't care what you print, as long as you spell my name right." Getting names and pictures in print was the name of the game in Hollywood.

In the early seventies, the *Times* hired several reporters to expand and upgrade entertainment coverage to include more investigation and analysis. These writers and the rest of the entertainment complex, which included the Sunday *Calendar* magazine, were still constantly deluged with information and story requests from the PR folks. "You always have to remember that you're a reporter and not part of the industry," former staffer Mary Murphy noted. That problem of distinction came into direct play in gossip columnist Joyce Haber's turbulent nine-year career at the *Times.*

When Hedda Hopper died in the early sixties, the *Times* management, in keeping with their upgrading effort, decided not to replace the *Times* gossip columnist. But entertainment editor Champlin and associate editor Jim Bellows felt that without Hopper's gossip the entertainment section had become too serious, too gray, and too sincere. Champlin and Bellows decided that a market still existed for a regular Hollywood column for personality profiles, trade information, and industry gossip.

Haber, the daughter of the vice-president of Philco International Corporation, began her career at *Time* magazine in December 1953 as a "clip girl" (clipping newspaper pieces). In 1963 she was transferred to Los Angeles as *Time*'s Hollywood reporter, where she was approached by editor Nick Williams and columnist Art Seidenbaum to do what Haber described as a part-time occasional "freewheeling column . . . which dealt with such subjects [as] 'Camp,' 'A&B Party Lists,' 'The Ten Most Attractive Men in the U.S.,' and 'The Nation's Most Sacred Cows.' "

The column, with its use of blind items (heavy-handed nonattributable news gossip shorts) and proindustry bias, generated controversy from the outset. In the fall of 1974, associate editor Bellows sent a detailed memo to Haber, which included some criticisms that had begun to make the rounds at the paper. After a Haber attack on *New Yorker* film critic Pauline Kael, *Times* editors ran a page of responses, which numbered 6 to 1 against Haber. A furious Haber sent a memo to Otis Chandler bitterly protesting the action. Haber leaked some of the criticisms against her column to *Daily News* gossip columnist Rex Reed and implied that she might be on her way out. Reed, and subsequently *Women's Wear Daily*, picked up on the story.

Once the battle had moved out into the open, Haber's position became more tenuous. "We felt," Champlin stated, "that the column had become inappropriate, in fact, generically so." The proliferation of TV talk shows and the new "people" magazines, as *Variety* magazine writer A.D. Murphy pointed out, had supplanted newspaper gossip columns. "There still is," Champlin insisted, "a market for names [gossip] but perhaps in a different context." Haber's column died in early October 1975.

Times editors decided to keep the trade gossip in the paper by spreading it out to several software writers who covered the Hollywood beat. The gossip column was dead but the trade news lived on.

* * *

The soft news feature approach of the new, mid-seventies, *Times*—with the Thomas/Murphy reign in the city room and Taylor/Champlin's software coverage—complemented the soft mood throughout the paper. Without competition, with little challenge from protest groups or social movements, with no unions or staff groupings, and with the enormous corporate and political power of the organization forming the backdrop for this new journalism, *Times* staff and *Times* editors became the contented link to an establishment world the paper had done much to create. Soft news at the *Times* was good news for the Chandlers and their friends.

CHAPTER 30

Management Ideologies

1. Two Editorials

In the first week of June 1970, the *Times* editorial board convened to discuss the issue of the Vietnam War. Unlike most editorial conferences, this one had a formal setting. Two positions were presented: that the *Times* should maintain its current position in favor of the war or that it should issue its first antiwar editorial. The prowar position was argued by foreign editor Bob Gibson, and the antiwar position by Anthony Day, the new editor of the editorial pages who had recently replaced the more hawkish Jim Bassett. The final say, as in all crucial editorial decisions, belonged to Otis Chandler.

The debate lasted for an hour and a half, "the longest editorial meeting I could ever remember," one of the participants recalled. When the discussion ended, a silence settled on the room. All eyes turned to Chandler, who had not spoken until then. Finally, the *Times* publisher declared that the *Times* would go antiwar.

On June 7, 1970, under the heading "Get Out of Vietnam NOW," the *Times* officially changed its position on the war. Chief editorial writer Lou Fleming called it "the most electrifying, courageous decision that I've ever seen." "The time has come," the editorial began, "for the United States to leave Vietnam, to leave it swiftly, wholly, and without equivocation." The editorial proposed that a specific date be set, perhaps eighteen months from then, in which all U.S. troops would be pulled out. The United States had done all it reasonably could do to support the Thieu government, the Times argued; and it was now up to the South Vietnamese Army (ARVN), stocked and supplied by American arms, to fight off the National Liberation Front.

The ultimate goal of American foreign policy, according to the editorial, was to defeat the Communists: "We shall be engaged against the Communist world one way or another all our lives," the editorial stated, "but in Southeast Asia we are engaged on the periphery of that world in a battle obscured by the elements of civil war and nationalism."

The new Vietnam position did not herald a change in the *Times*'s general foreign policy outlook. Through the early seventies, the paper, despite increasing domestic criticism of American foreign policy, maintained its staunch promilitary, interventionist perspective. "We are," one of the editorial writers coyly remarked, "conservative on issues of money and war, and liberal on the social issues." Although the *Times* management shared the Nixon "big stick" military preparedness and probusiness outlook, it disagreed with the administration's attitudes toward civil liberties, education, and welfare programs.

In the fall of 1972, while papers such as the *New York Times, Washington Post,* and *Boston Globe* geared up for an endorsement of the Democratic candidate, George McGovern, the *Times* position was unclear. The few anti-Nixon people on the editorial board—national editor Ed Guthman, editorial writer Phil Kerby, and op-ed editor Ken Reich—hoped at best for a nonendorsement of the Republican incumbent.

On October 15 the *Times* came out with its decision: "For the voter who seeks reasonable answers to the present problems," the editorial declared, "the choice in 1972 is clear. The *Times* recommends the reelection of President Nixon."

In its endorsement, The *Times* laid out a strong, unreconstructed view of the Cold War. "It is becoming an unfashionable cliche to say that world peace depends upon American power," the editorial argued, "but it is true. McGovern's defense cuts would, if put into effect, send to the nations of the world, especially to the Soviet Union, the message, unmistakeable and clear, that the United States was pulling back from the world as well as Vietnam. Such a signal could have the most dangerous consequences." "McGovern is weakest," the *Times* concluded, "where Mr. Nixon is strongest — in the perception of the nation's place in the world."

Ken Reich, a member of the editorial board, saw economics as a second major determinant of the Nixon endorsement. The *Times* management, according to Reich, might well have been operating out of self-interest, particularly in terms of possible tax reforms and other economic programs. "His changing prescriptions for problems," the *Times* editorial complained of McGovern's economics, "have largely ranged from the extreme to the vague. Taken as a whole, they suggest that he does not understand the intricate economic machine that produces the nation's wealth.''

Many of the new, younger staff were deeply disappointed at the Nixon endorsement. On assignment together the next morning, theater critic Dan Sullivan and photographer Tony Barnard talked about the editorial and came up with the idea of taking out a *Times* ad signed by staff who disagreed with the paper's endorsement. Sullivan recalled that there had been a similar move at the *New York Daily News*. On their return to the Times Mirror Building, the two immediately began to collect signatures and contributions for the ad. They soon realized that they couldn't raise the amount of money needed to place it, and, on the suggestion of one of the ad people, decided to submit their protest in the form of a letter to the editor. They warily approached the letters to the editor staff, who scoffed at any fears about censorship. The staff insisted that the letter would run intact.

One hundred and eighteen *Times* employees signed the "McGovern Letter,'' as it came to be known. More than half the petition signers were women. Several were noneditorial employees who felt a great deal more vulnerable than their counterparts in the newsroom. Many on the staff questioned the propriety of taking a political position and extended the argument to criticize any staff involvement in political organizations outside the paper. "Doesn't that undermine our credibility?'' reporter Bill Boyarsky remarked of the letter-signing. Other reporters pointed to the traditional distinction between editorial policy and news coverage.

Not one cityside reporter put his or her name on the statement. A number of staffers later recalled that they were "out of town''—practically depopulating the newsroom during the ten days signatures were collected.

The McGovern Letter appeared on November 1, 1972. "A newspaper is not a monolith,'' the letter began. "The undersigned employees of the *Los Angeles Times* differ with the *Times* endorsement of President Nixon. We plan to vote for Senator George McGovern.'' The paper was immediately swamped with letters over the issue. "I got twelve letters after the letter ran,'' music critic Martin Bernheimer recalled with pleasure, "and they all thanked me for signing.'' "We've been gloating ever since,'' remarked the organizer of the effort, theater critic Sullivan.

None of the signers were subject to reprisal, although word got back to the staff that Otis was displeased. "How can people read Bernheimer or [columnist Jack] Smith now that their bias is showing?'' Otis was heard asking on the cocktail circuit.

2. Shades of Gray

In the middle of the Watergate storm, on September 23, 1973—less than a year after the Nixon endorsement— the *Times* issued an editorial announcement that it would no longer endorse candidates for President, Governor, or Senator. The statement described how the *Times* had become a "comprehensive" newspaper which required professionalism, good judgment, and "above all, a sense of fairness." An editorial noted: "We are convinced by experience that progress in the social order has been achieved and will continue. We prefer trial and error to dogmatism, pragmatism to ideology." The paper, however, would continue to endorse local candidates and initiative measures where *Times* news coverage and editorial preference were practically the only source for information and opinion in a region-wide medium.

The new policy was, according to one editorial writer quoted in a March 1976 Dave Shaw article, "designed primarily to save the Chandler family the inevitable embarrassment of one day having to break a lifelong Republican tradition and endorse a Democrat for President or Governor." *Times* editors, however, denied to Shaw that tradition had anything to do with the decision.

A second aspect of the announcement involved the shifting of Paul Conrad's cartoons from the editorial page to the op-ed page. "Because the cartoon occupies a prominent position on the page where the institutional voice of the newspaper is expressed," the editorial noted, "the cartoon tends to color both the opinions expressed in these editorials, and the dispassionate news coverage we attempt to achieve. . . . It will come as no surprise to our readers to hear that sometimes Paul Conrad speaks for the *Times*, and sometimes not. As he is fond of saying, he works in black and white; the editorial writers work in shades of gray. . . . We believe that by displaying Conrad's cartoon on the opposite page, where many points of view not our own are given free play, we shall lessen the risk of confusing the voice of the *Times* with the pen of Paul Conrad."

"The *Times* developed a criteria about my work," Conrad commented about his editor Tony Day. "If it's within the bounds of taste and makes sense then they run it." One of Day's first applications of the taste criteria came during the trial of Charles Manson. After Richard Nixon uttered his famous "Manson is guilty" remark, a statement clearly prejudicial to the defendant, the *Times* ran the quote the next day as a banner headline. Manson whipped out a copy of the *Times* in court and held it up for the jurors to read. Soon after, Conrad produced a cartoon of Manson in the courtroom with a big button reading "Nixon's the One." Day refused to run the drawing, complaining that it was "inflammatory" and not in keeping with the *Times*'s taste criteria. Conrad disagreed.

In another discarded drawing, Conrad had Spiro Agnew urinating on several newspapers and magazines—identified as the *New York Times*, *Washington Post*, *Time*, *Newsweek*, etc.—with the caption reading "Leaks". Conrad, who insisted the taste qualification helped him overall, agreed that that was "a clear case of bad taste."

The cartoon that touched off the uproar that helped push Conrad off the editorial page portrayed H.R. Haldeman as a monstrous robot, with the caption "Son of Nixonsteen." Haldeman, whose parents were Chandler intimates, was vintage upper-class Southern California, was a good friend of Franklin Murphy, and had numerous ties to the local business establishment. "Son of Nixonsteen" touched off a systematic attack against the *Times* cartoonist, as evidenced by a letter-writing campaign and delegations of leading businessmen coming to see the *Times* management with the complaint that the "outrageous" *Times* cartoonist "had stepped out of bounds." Conrad's move came several weeks later, a "small victory," as one of the businessmen characterized it.

The Conrad move and the new nonendorsement policy pushed the paper further along in its quest for opinion based on the spirit of moderation. In another step in the same direction, the *Times* editors also began to change the op-ed page from its previous top-heavy political orientation to a new emphasis on personal experience.

Personal experience articles, like "life-style" journalism, could be a valuable means of providing outlets for points of view and ways of looking at the world for people that have no ordinary access to the mass media. But management's interpretation of "experience," coupled with the process of maintaining the "professional standards" of the paper, often flattened out and reduced any point of view to a proper middle-class norm. Like the news sections, the op-ed articles began to take on a single coloration: a *Times* style.

3. The Editorial Collegium

Tony Day is all Harvard. A major in nineteenth-century English literature and history, he immediately impressed all the *Times* editorial writers with his intellect and sophistication. Day came out from Philadelphia, where he had worked as Washington bureau chief of the *Philadelphia Inquirer*, to replace the aging Jim Bassett, who had been assigned to write an in-house version of the history of the *Los Angeles Times*.

Day's advice on changing *Times* policy on Vietnam put him clearly in the *Times* liberal camp, and he quickly established access to publisher Chandler. "I think Tony Day is sort of the ideological leader of the *Times*," conservative police chief Ed Davis remarked about the *Times* editor. "His very, very, super-liberal editorial positions are designed to traverse frontiers that aren't even attempted by many other papers, even though they might feel the same way."

Under Day the new *Times* moved further towards what editorial writer Phil Kerby called a "civilized and moderate newspaper." Yet Day refused to push certain limits that might have undermined his growing standing with publisher Chandler. When the paper endorsed Nixon in 1972, Day went along with the decision, though it tarnished his image with some staff members.

As editor of the editorial pages, Day had jurisdiction over the nine editorial writers—each of whom had broad areas of specialization and a variety of political points of view.

Every day at 9:20 A.M., the nine editorial writers met, with Day presiding, to discuss the issues that were likely to appear in future editorials. Day challenged his writers to make sure their reasoning was consistent and their logic clear; one writer compared the tone in the conference room to that of a professor leading a seminar of graduate students.

Despite the apparent ivory tower atmosphere the meeting was, in reality, a corporate service for the publisher and his editorial board, who ultimately made all the decisions. The writers, much as in any large bureaucratic organization, served as specialists.

At 10 A.M. the editorial board, consisting of the publisher, his editor (Bill Thomas), the managing editor, the foreign editor, editorial editor Day, a couple of assistant editors, and perhaps one or two editorial writers called in to discuss the subject of the day, would get together. "There's a kind of corporation feeling to the editorial board, like a meeting of the board of directors," Jean Taylor—the first woman in *Times* history to join the board— commented.

By the mid-seventies, the editorial page—a product of the paper's "modern" editorial board and staff—had become a fitting symbol of the new *Times*. With its premium on taste, balance, and responsibility, and its liberal social outlook, proexpansionist foreign policy, and corporate-based economic perspective, it most resembled the politics and methodology of the mid-seventies multi-national corporation. It was a new editiorial perspective for a paper that had come to maturity in the age of monopoly corporate power.

4. Watergate's "Cancerous Aftermath"

"We're opening up the pages [of the *Times*] to elements of society never before covered," Bill Thomas told *Fortune* magazine. "At the same time," Thomas continued, "we run the danger of closing out what used to be the Establishment voice. We don't listen enough to businessmen. The old Establishment voices aren't in the paper enough. Often we've put them in the same category that blacks occupied fifteen years ago."

Fortune's analysis of "The New Concerns of the Press" paralleled Bill Thomas's concerns. According to the magazine, the press changed in the 1960s and 1970s because of new readers; criticisms by students, antiwar protestors and blacks; and the new tendencies in journalism which called for more comprehensive coverage. The young reporters, the *Fortune* article asserted, deliberately "politicized" the news and ended the "sacred cow" tradition accorded powerful people. In the Watergate era, more and more politicians and businessmen became fair game for newspaper investigations and exposure. By the mid-seventies, *Fortune* declared, there had developed an "intense feeling among executives, in business and government, about what they see as its [the press's] systematic distrust of all established institutions. There is growing concern among these executives that the new journalism has made it hard for them to make their records and views known to the public *on their own terms* . . . . [our italics] The consequence, argue these executives, is that it has become increasingly difficult, if not impossible, to get the public's governmental and economic business done."

"Journalists," Otis Chandler told an audience of advertisers in March 1976, "are well-meaning but abysmally ignorant of how business and our capitalist, free-enterprise system work."

A post-Watergate backlash attitude, subscribed to by a number of business executives—including newspaper publishers and broadcasters—had surfaced. In a speech at the University of Kansas, Chandler talked of the country's "bad news." "This all may sound a bit corny or old hat for a newspaperman," Chandler remarked, "but I suggest that the newspapers of America hold a unique opportunity to turn the national mood of depression around to one of realism and eventually to one of pragmatic optimism. . . . I am not naive enough to believe, nor would I suggest, that printing only good news and patriotic slogans would bring the patients temperature back to normal. . . . I also am not suggesting we alter our course on legitimate investigative reporting or wrongdoing wherever it may occur. What I am saying is that the press, and I certainly do include newspapers, have gone bananas following Watergate. We seem to have lost our sense of balance, our sense of proportion."

"I was concerned long before Nixon resigned that the press was going to come out of Watergate with an inflated image of itself," Chandler stated a month earlier in an interview in the *Times* house organ, *Among Ourselves.* "They may now overreact. Everything Ford, Rockefeller and the others are doing is being looked at too skeptically, too negatively. It shouldn't be that way. I am not saying we should abandon our roles, but I do think we have gone too far with supercriticism. We are not giving people a chance to explain before getting after them."

The thrust of the message had to do much more with the incipient tendencies of younger journalists to probe and criticize once off-limit institutions and individuals rather than with actual antiestablishment tendencies in the paper as a whole. "Far from being too zealous," Washington bureau chief Jack Nelson insisted, "we're not zealous enough." "The ultimate responsibility of a reporter is to tell what's going on, and it is often negative," Nelson told *Among Ourselves*. "Our job is not to buoy the morale of our readers by not telling what is bad."

The major events of the last two decades—Vietnam and Watergate, racial conflict, student protest, the women's movement, and the emerging populist movements—threw the question of journalistic standards and performance into relief. It gave rise to alternative publications and to the notion of a press credibility gap. As a new generation of reporters became sensitive to the criticisms, different perspectives concerning the craft itself emerged: advocacy, critical analysis, first-person narrative, and the revival of muckraking in its new, popular "investigative journalism" form.

Yet much of the new "negative" information was not all that new for the antiestablishment groups and individuals. Revelations about the Vietnam War or Nixon's widespread and repressive efforts to eliminate his "enemies", had appeared in antiwar and underground papers long before the Pentagon Papers. Even when reporters substantiated radical "alternative source" claims, the information was sometimes held back until more "established" sources could make the story "legitimate."

While investigative news became a hot commodity in the 1970s, the exposes often were limited to governmental rather than corporate structures. As audiences eagerly awaited the latest "revelations," the owners of the press became increasingly anxious. Journalists got caught in the squeeze. They found themselves, on the one hand, pushed into the role of "public watchdog." But, on the other hand, they fell under heavy economic (investigative journalism loses money), social (the publisher's criteria of "responsibility"), and political (burn your sources and you burn yourself) constraints.

Ultimately, the battle lines for the press evolved around the self-definitions of publisher, editor, and reporter. In its editorial pages, the *Times* management had defended the "system" in its strongest terms. A February 1975 editorial, "In Defense of Business," declared: "There is a group at large in the political arena that equates profits with sin, free enterprise with evil, industry with exploitation. They conveniently forget that a profitable private sector benefits not only the Chamber of Commerce and the National Association of Manufacturers but every single citizen."

"The real conflict of interest at the *Times*, and at other papers—in fact, of the newspaper business," assistant metropolitan editor Noel Greenwood noted, "is that the publisher has a stake in the larger business and industrial establishment. The staff is constantly pulled back and forth: trying to act as a watchdog for the public; but, at the same time, developing that more 'realistic' sentiment that it's a job and they're practicing a trade as best they can under some very real constraints."

Journalists, particularly those at the *Times*, do not escape the institutional setting in which they operate. Reporters at the *Times*, largely isolated from each other and many of the communities they cover, have comfortable jobs and good salaries. They largely identify with those in power: with their life-style, their concerns about material benefits, and the notion that they, too, must be responsible people—advisors, in a sense, to "Presidents and Kings."

By the mid-seventies a coherent management ideology for the new *Times* had taken shape. It specified caution and structural limits to investigations and negative news, a defense of business and the capitalist system, and a liberal flexibility in matters of social outlook, such as civil liberties, education, race, and sex. The change was necessary because, as Chandler put it, "newspapers survive only if they adapt to their new audiences." It was, ultimately, a question of markets.

CHAPTER 31

Newsday: Times Mirror on the Island

1. Alicia and the Captain

"The business of a newspaper is to print the news and raise hell," Alicia Patterson loved to tell her staff, quoting the famous phrase of Chicago editor Wilbur Story. She wanted to have her paper, *Newsday*, the daily afternoon paper serving New York's Nassau and Suffolk counties in Long Island, try to live by that motto.

Alicia Patterson was one of three daughters of Joe Patterson, founder and first publisher of the *New York Daily News*, the world's largest circulation newspaper. Joe Patterson, who considered himself a Socialist, wanted to create a newspaper for working people, with large graphics and photographs, bold headlines, and sensational news stories—the standard fare of the tabloid press. By the end of the thirties, he began to shift political ground and turned the *News* in a reactionary direction.

Alicia Patterson loved the newspaper business. Up through the thirties, she worked for a number of years at the *News* as a $75 a week book reviewer. While her father moved to the right, she continued to support the New Deal and many of its liberal programs, and the two generations became increasingly alienated from each other.

During the depression, Alicia lived on Long Island with her husband, ex-Colgate star athlete, Joe Brooks, an insurance man who led the life of a party-going, wealthy sportsman. Bored with her life, Alicia left Brooks to marry Harry Guggenheim, of the wealthy mining family.

As Mrs. Guggenheim, Alicia continued to live on Long Island, then primarily composed of scattered small farms and the large baronial estates of the New York elite, who constituted the Island power structure. The Island had only one newspaper, the *Nassau Daily Review-Star,* a conservative, Republican paper aimed at the wealthy businessmen.

Alicia Patterson convinced Guggenheim to initiate a second Island newspaper. Harry, who would handle the business end of the paper, provided an initial investment of $750,000, and Alicia became the editor. The Guggenheim/Patterson paper, called *Newsday,* began publication in 1940 and printed out of a small office in Hempstead in Nassau County. Although Alicia was only given 49 percent of the stock to Harry's 51 percent, she maintained full editorial responsibility.

Alicia conceived the early *Newsday* as a more toned down and less brassy version of the *New York Daily News.* She wanted a tough and feisty tabloid, with big photos and hot leads, but a respectable amount of national news and political commentary. *Newsday* had a liberal editorial perspective and quickly attracted a lively staff that liked the easygoing independence at the paper.

After World War II, Long Island started to change and expand. Real estate speculators began to buy up land, subdivide it into small plots, and promote development. The Island's little townships became full-sized suburbs, and the Island pastoral scene was transformed into a ring of semiurban constellations. The consortium of developers, wealthy landowners, construction unions, and the county Republican party helped promote the idea of Island growth, with *Newsday,* which had become (after the *Review-Star* folded) the only news medium on the Island and, consequently, the only institution creating Island-wide consciousness, spurring on the development.

Newsday's circulation shot up from 25,000 to an astounding 300,000 within fifteen years. The paper became an incredible success, fat with ads—a secure monopoly in one of the fastest growing regions in the country.

But Alicia was not completely wedded to the idea of growth. The paper's first big break with the development forces came with its investigation into the construction empire of union head William C. De Koning. *Newday* staffers assigned to the story described a vast system of influence-peddling that the union boss maintained within the Island power structure. The story, under Helen Dudar's byline, won *Newsday* a Pulitzer Prize and helped send De Koning to jail. But it didn't stop the boom.

The Island continued to grow, and Alicia Patterson and *Newsday*'s reputation grew as well. In 1954 she made the cover of *Time,* portrayed as a no-holds-barred, two-fisted, heavy-drinking newspaper person.

"Editorial shakes the tree," was a frequent *Newsday* saying, and Patterson's staff fully appreciated their editor's independence and leadership. "*Newsday* was the best of all journalistic worlds," former *Newsday* managing editor Stan Opotowsky recalled. "All the profits were plowed back into the paper, which meant in practical terms that last-minute budget increases would be approved." With editorial autonomy legislated into the paper's operation, Patterson was literally the only commercial editor in the country who didn't have to worry constantly about business performance in order to justify editorial objectives.

When the popular Patterson became ill in 1963, the staff rented a helicopter to fly outside her window with the sign: "Get Well Miss P." But Alicia Patterson never recovered, and with her death the staff feared intervention from the right-wing anti-Communist publisher, Patterson's widower Harry Guggenheim.

The Captain, as Guggenheim was called, had occasionally fussed over what he considered some egregious editorial or news story. But whenever Guggenheim threw a storm, Alicia had always calmed her husband down and cautioned her staff to cool it for a few weeks until his anger passed.

After his wife died, Guggenheim alternated between embroiling himself in the paper and leaving it to his editorial staff to run. His main concern was trying to find a new editor. After his first two appointments failed, Guggenheim asked his friend Lyndon Johnson for advice. Johnson told Guggenheim he had just the man, a good Texas Democrat (then LBJ's press secretary), Bill Moyers. LBJ did not inform Guggenheim, however, that Moyers, who was about to resign as press secretary, had become a little too liberal for the conservative president. Guggenheim assumed Moyers was from good Texas conservative stock and immediately took a liking to the young journalist. He not only appointed Moyers to the editor's post, but promised the Texan a permanent future in the organization, with provisions to be written into the Captain's will.

For Moyers the situation was ideal. *Newsday* was a profitable, successful paper with a top quality staff and a monopoly status in the ninth largest metropolitan complex in America. The new editor wanted to maintain *Newsday*'s muckraking reputation and further upgrade the paper's quality by expanding national coverage and transforming the software section. The staff liked and appreciated Moyers. His initial impact as editor brought back the highpoints of the Patterson era, and his apparent sincerity reinforced the independent mood.

The Long Island Republican party had expected the conservative Guggenheim, after Patterson's death, to transform *Newsday* along lines more in keeping with the progrowth expansionism and conservative politics of its Republican politicians. Convinced that Moyers harbored political ambitions, perhaps with an eye to the U.S. Senate, Island power Joe Margiotta and friends tried to convince the Captain that he had made a bad mistake.

By the late 1960s, Guggenheim, ill and withdrawn, had come to the end of his patience with a paper—one of the most unique family operations in American journalism—he had never really understood.

2. The Sale

The Captain put out the word he wanted to sell. He received offers from Capital Cities Broadcasting, the Gannett publications, Time Inc., and the Newhouse chain. Several of the offers were quite substantial, but it seemed Guggenheim was not primarily interested in profit. Remembering his old friend Norman Chandler, with his impeccable Republican, conservative credentials, and aware that Chandler's company had undertaken a major expansion program, Guggenheim asked Norman if he was interested in making an offer. The Times Mirror bid, smaller than some of the others, was accepted by the Captain. On March 12, 1970, the *New York Times* broke the story about the intended purchase.

The announcement hit the staff like a bombshell. Within a matter of hours word had spread through the newsroom. Everyone believed that Moyers was through; Guggenheim, it turned out, had insisted on Moyers's removal as a condition for the sale. The staff, who knew little about their new owners and feared the worse, drew up a petition to send to Alicia Patterson's heirs, hoping they could, with their 49 percent of the stock, block the sale.

Times Mirror moved swiftly and efficiently to forestall any stock fight. They purchased Guggenheim's 51 percent for 500,000 shares of Times Mirror stock, with another 100,000 forthcoming and a $10-million cash outlay. Alicia's nephew, Joe Albright, tried to organize the minority stockholders, but all that resulted was the loss of his job as *Newsday*'s Washington bureau chief. Within the year, Times Mirror completed its purchase and bought out Patterson's heirs.

A few days after the sale, the staff held the first of many meetings. Many who spoke up anticipated a change in orientation. The new owners were expected to focus on profit and loss figures, which might affect editorial expenditures. Times Mirror, after all, was an outside owner concerned with the economic performance of its subsidiaries. With its right-wing heritage, antilabor reputation, and trademark as a rigid corporation, Times Mirror, many felt, spelled big trouble for *Newsday*.

Confusing and sometimes contradictory signals from Times Mirror heightened the staff's suspicions. On his first day at *Newsday*, Otis Chandler went around stiffly shaking everybody's hands; at that moment, the AP ticker announced that not one but two Pulitzer Prize awards had been awarded to Times Mirror's new subsidiary. Chandler praised the paper and promised autonomy. But just a few days later, according to a *New York Times* report, *Los Angeles Times* associate editor Jim Bellows hinted at the possibilities of a Republican publisher for *Newsday* and changes in the paper's editorial policy, particularly in relation to Vietnam and the Nixon administration.

The rumors pleased Long Island Republicans. Party chairman Margiotta, convinced that his pressure on the Captain had paid off, smugly expressed his belief to *Newsday* reporters that the Island would, at last, have a newspaper respecting the principles of free enterprise and anticommunism. When Moyers was dumped, the Republicans waited for the coup de grace—the appointment of a more favorably inclined publisher.

Within a couple of months, the Chandlers appointed ex-Kennedy speechwriter Bill Atwood, a preeminent member of the Democratic establishment, as the new *Newsday* publisher. Atwood, a former ambassador to Guinea and Kenya, had worked as editor-in-chief of *Look* magazine's Cowles publications. To Times Mirror he seemed ideal for the position. As a registered Democrat, he might cool down the fears of the staff, and, through his membership in the Foreign Policy Association, a powerful informal grouping of businessmen, politicians, and academics, he brought impeccable establishment credentials. Atwood's overall orientation, unperturbed by the potential problems related to the outside ownership question, indicated a strong concern for the corporate end of the job. The former *Look* editor, the Times Mirror executives reasoned, brought "administrative abilities" to the job.

When Atwood first spoke with Chandler about his party registration, Chandler noted that Times Mirror, hoping to calm the situation down, wanted to demonstrate to the staff its desire to have some continuity with *Newsday*'s past. With the announcement of Atwood's appointment on November 1, 1970, the corporate executives in Los Angeles held their breath and hoped for the best.

Atwood's first big job was to appoint a general manager, a new position created by Times Mirror. The Los Angeles executives wanted a *Newsday* equivalent of the *Los Angeles Times* general manager/business manager Bob Nelson, who had supervised the money-making functions of the *Times.* Chandler suggested Jim Grider, a Times Mirror employee since 1940, who had worked as a compositor, production man, and general manager of the Times-Mirror press.

When Grider arrived on the Island in April 1971, he was immediately perceived by the staff as the Times Mirror man inside *Newsday.* "Oh, they're sending in a vice-president in charge of autonomy," *Newsday* editor Dick Estrin remarked, referring to Chandler's well-known pledge for *Newsday* autonomy.

Under the new ownership, the divorce between business and editorial came to an end, as it undoubtedly would have with any outside ownership arrangement. Editors, by their own choice, began to call themselves "management" and organized their priorities around economic performance. Although Times Mirror had put forth the principle of subsidiary autonomy, it was a principle that only survived as long as there were profit margins.

The new *Newsday* management developed an executive committee which reflected the new economic priorities. Of the committee's six members, only one, the cautious and unassertive editor Dave Laventhol, strictly represented the editorial side of the paper. The other five members—Atwood, Grider, sales manager Dave Targe, the head of circulation, and the assistant to the publisher—worked almost exclusively in the business end. The executive committee met once a month to make overall decisions affecting the expenditure of funds and operation of the newspaper.

The management team also made conference calls to their superiors in Los Angeles to relate current decisions and keep them up to date on the paper's performance. Times Mirror was involved in all major financial decisions and played a direct role in format changes as well as the development of the Sunday paper. Far more important than any specific instruction coming from Los Angeles was the overall framework of decision-making that had developed out of the Times Mirror purchase.

Still, *Newsday* continued as one of the best newspapers in the country. Its reputation for local and national investigations and tough-minded independence in reporting local affairs continued into the Times Mirror era.

Soon after the purchase, the paper, following a tip, got involved in an extensive probe into the financial affairs of Richard Nixon's friend Bebe Rebozo. As *Newsday*'s investigative team began to make plans to go down to Florida to Rebozo territory in the summer of 1971, Atwood mentioned the idea to Otis Chandler. Chandler told the *Newsday* publisher he hoped they hit paydirt since a lot of money would have to be spent.

In October 1971 a six part series appeared, detailing Rebozo's activities and his ties to Nixon and former Senator George Smathers. The Rebozo series earned *Newsday* another Pulitzer Prize and a number of headaches from the Nixon administration. The paper's Washington bureau was harassed by the administration, kept out of "pool" arrangements, denied invitations to important affairs such as the President's trip to China the next spring, and generally snubbed by high government officials. Nixon aides, seeing a Kennedy plot extending from *Los Angeles Times* national editor Ed Guthman through former Kennedy speechwriter Bill Atwood, explored antitrust proceedings against Times Mirror because of the series. The *Newsday* management backed their staff and reprinted the series in pamphlet form, but held back on book publication on grounds that it would coincide with the 1972 presidential election.

On the local scene, reporters John Cummings and Drew Featherston uncovered a questionable land deal in Suffolk County involving the powerful Speaker of the State Assembly, Republican Perry Duryea. When Duryea got wind of the investigation, he telephoned Otis Chandler, ready to fly out to Los Angeles to confer. Duryea had already registered complaints outside the normal management channels on other *Newsday* stories: once through the chairman of Pan American Airways Juan Trippe (on whose board Otis Chandler sat) and another time through Nelson Rockefeller, who, in turn, contacted Franklin Murphy at Times Mirror. Chandler calmed Duryea down and suggested he talk to Atwood and Laventhol. The story ran and Duryea remained angry. Chandler's response pleased both staff and editors. Dave Laventhol characterized Chandler as a "rock" in his support of *Newsday*'s independence.

But that independence had its limits. What still counted, one staffer pointed out, was how the new management interpreted and used their independence. Even the Republicans realized that one need not phone Los Angeles to accomplish things at *Newsday*; sometimes, all that might be needed was a local toll-free call. Events centering around *Newsday*'s real estate columnist Jerry Morgan demonstrated that well.

Unlike his counterparts at other newspapers, including the *Los Angeles Times*, Morgan was consumer-oriented. His columns covered a lot of hard news and investigated the myriad practices of the Island real estate industry. In the booming, expanding Island, "real estate," as Morgan put it, "is politics." His articles, which included critiques of the title insurance charges levied by banks and savings and loans, and the informal arrangements of fixed brokerage fees for real estate groups, stepped on many toes. The real estate writer, widely respected by the staff, felt he had an important advantage at *Newsday* since the monopoly paper had the ability to "tell the advertisers to go screw themselves if they're unhappy," as Morgan put it.

In the summer of 1972, a seven-hour meeting took place between officials of the Long Island Board of Realtors and *Newsday* executives. "We very amicably discussed the situation," the realtor board's executive director Edward Boylan later commented. "We think we reached a degree of rapport that we're satisfied with now." *Newsday* agreed to call the realtor's group regularly on industry stories, "as a matter of courtesy," Boylan remarked, and "not because we're trying to slant them but just to check the accuracy of facts."

That August, Morgan's four-month-old column was shifted to the less prominent Saturday paper. Management wanted a new focus—straight reporting on soft industry news. Atwood complained that the earlier column had "accentuated the negative" and that some pieces were "exaggerated." When asked why they had waited four months before doing anything, Atwood astounded some of the staff by replying that he hadn't read the column before.

Morgan only became aware of the seven-hour marathon meeting from a real estate trade paper's oblique reference that the realtors had "gotten" Morgan. The real estate writer made some calls, found out about the meeting, and became even more determined to stick to his original kind of consumer-oriented, probing reporting. Morgan succeeded in maintaining those standards, but the affair contributed to the anxious mood throughout the paper.

In 1970 Times Mirror, as part of its expansion program, purchased several cable properties on Long Island and formed a subsidiary called Long Island CableVision. The group vice-president in charge of the cable properties, Philip Williams, also had direct supervision over the *Newsday* subsidiary.

Extensive cross-ownership of newspapers and cable subsidiaries already existed in New York state; other large media corporations such as the *New York Times* and Gannett had also purchased cable properties. Under a bill before the New York State Legislature for the creation of a state commission to regulate cable, such newspaper/cable cross-ownership would be limited.

Shortly before the legislature's vote on the bill, a *Newsday* Albany bureau staffer received a call from a *Newsday* executive, asking for Speaker Perry Duryea's private phone number. The Albany reporter, curious about the request, started poking around and quickly discovered that Times Mirror, as well as the other newspaper chains, were lobbying heavily to delete the cross-ownership provision. The reporter decided to do a story on the question and filed an article based on "unnamed legislative sources" who reported the "intense lobbying by newspaper owners," including Times Mirror.

Assemblyman Irwin Landes of Nassau County, on the instigation of the bureau reporter, read the *Newsday* story into the record and attacked the newspaper lobbying. As legislators rose to complain about the "pressure," the issue mushroomed, and the newspaper lobbyists had to put aside their efforts to delete the provision.

The tolerance level for censorship at *Newsday* was low and suspicions over outside intervention high. Many of the staff felt that their only protection was an independent organization of the staff to "mandate quality," as one staffer put it, and "legislate the ethics of noninterference."

3. One Big Union

Such a sentiment had existed since the first days following the Times Mirror purchase, when the idea of unionization was raised. *Newsday* journalists, suspicious of the Newspaper Guild's role during the New York City newspaper strike of 1963, initially looked to the United Auto Workers (UAW), with its progressive tradition and liberal political outlook, as an alternative to the guild. A representation election was held in the *Newsday* parking lot, which the UAW handily won.

Shortly after the vote, the UAW called off its organizing effort. UAW President Leonard Woodcock, then in delicate negotiations with the American Federation of Labor (AFL), didn't want the situation at *Newsday* to interfere with his talks with George Meany. Several staff theorized that the Newspaper Guild had pressured the AFL national leadership in order to forestall possible widespread raids from the massive UAW. When the guild made an attempt to win representation at *Newsday*, it was soundly voted down.

The rejection of the Newspaper Guild gave management a sense of security based on the feeling that staff discontent had no real organizational outlets. But, almost inadvertently, staff writer Ed Hershey and several others who had opposed the guild began to turn into organizers for still another union. For Hershey, an incident over *Newsday*'s installation of a security system at its Garden City plant precipitated the movement.

Newsday employees had been issued new security cards in order to prevent strangers from wandering onto the premises. The reporters noted that a security system undermined the loose and open environment at the paper and could cause a source, unable to enter the building for lack of a pass, to turn away. Hershey led a delegation in to see editor Laventhol, but the management insisted on keeping the system.

Sometime after the security dispute, George Tedeschi, *Newsday* local president of the International Printing and Graphics Communications Union (IPGCU), approached Ed Hershey to ask if he'd set up a meeting for him with some of the editorial staff. Unlike the *Los Angeles Times*, *Newsday* was not an open shop. Several units of the Printing Pressmens Union, which had recently changed its name to the IPGCU in order to expand its base beyond production units, had been established at *Newsday*. It was the same union that had attempted to organize the *Los Angeles Times* pressmen in the mid 1960s.

Tedeschi had developed a plant-wide strategy, representing a modified form of industrial unionism, which called for the creation of autonomous divisions within *Newsday*, each committed to support the other. The pressmen, photoengravers, and mailers had already been organized under this arrangement. But when Tedeschi began to sign up the photographers, the NLRB ruled that the photocrew could only be organized as part of a single division of all editorial workers. The *Newsday* managers, pleased with the NLRB ruling, were convinced that the blue-collar organizer would make little headway among the white-collar editorial professionals.

Hershey posted an anonymous announcement of the meeting on the *Newsday* bulletin board. Sixty people responded, including one individual later suspected of being a management plant. Tedeschi, who seemed serious and knowledgeable, was warmly received by the previously skeptical staffers. The drive was on; for the first time in newspaper history, a production union began to organize editorial employees.

Prior to the organizing drive, *Newsday* management, like other Times Mirror subsidiaries under pressure to keep profit margins stable during the hard times of the Nixon recession, had spoken of economic necessities and budgetary pressures. Using Nixon's phase one economic guidelines as justification, the *Newsday* executives had frozen wages, and conditions had remained tight for the next several months. But when the new organizing drive began, management began to change its approach. A 4 percent cost-of-living increase, which many staff assumed was aimed at the union effort, was instituted. But the move backfired; it caused some reluctant workers to recognize what the presence of the union might accomplish.

The management team took a head count. Individual staff members were brought in one at a time in an attempt to influence their vote by friendly persuasion, or "stroking."

The contest was a tight and bitter one. A great deal of antiunion sentiment still existed since the UAW affair, and several staff had misgivings about joining a production-related union. The union won, 149 to 144, but the vote was held up for a year and a half in management appeals to the NLRB. In January 1975 management dropped its appeal and defied the union to sign up a majority of the workers and come up with a negotiable contract.

The union had cause to worry. More than sixty workers, nearly all young, prounion staffers fed up with some of the paper's changes, had left *Newsday* since the vote. But the mood at *Newsday* had become more determined than ever. Within a couple of months, 260 of the 330 *Newsday* editorial workers had signed union cards. *Newsday* local 406 became the official bargaining agent of the editorial employees, the first union for Times Mirror editorial employees in its history.

By the time negotiations got under way in the summer of 1975, the division between management and staff seemed complete. The wage freeze was reinstituted. Los Angeles was kept informed of the state of the long and painstaking negotiations, and for a time a deadlock and possible strike seemed likely. But Times Mirror, reeling from an earlier strike in its forest division, which had hurt 1975 profit margins, found a second strike at the profitable *Newsday* a disagreeable prospect. The union, feeling that the long process of winning recognition and going through negotiations had drained a lot of staff energy, was also unwilling to push too hard. Although the compromise contract arrived at was not entirely to every-body's liking, both sides approved it. The union had become a *Newsday* fixture—for the time being.

4. *"Female PhD's . . . Are Usually Insane"*

In the spring of 1972, staff writer Annabelle Kerins began to send memos to editor Laventhol describing some of the problems women faced at *Newsday*. These included questions of salary and promotions, the kinds of stories women were assigned, and the overall attitude toward women in the newsroom. Kerins had done extensive research and backed her memos with numerous statistics. When an assignment she had re-quested went instead to a male writer, Kerins decided to take action. She drew up a petition about assignment policy which was signed by most of the women at the paper and became the initial stimulus for the develop-ment of the *Newsday* women's caucus.

The new group found an attorney who was working under a federal grant for employment discrimination cases. The group drew up a list of fourteen grievance areas including hiring, promotion, policy-making, types of assignments, placement of stories, bylines, captions, and types of headlines. The discrimination charges concerned nearly every aspect of the paper. The grievance list noted that women were often bypassed in the hiring process, that there were salary discriminations, and that women staffers were given titles often not commensurate with their experience and skills. Women were assigned less interesting and challenging stories, and all top level jobs, except for the women's page editor, were assigned to males. Only 6 of 330 circulation managers, 2 of 28 photographers, and one of 21 nonclerical workers in the art department, were women. Rela-tions with men, particularly male editors, were also a crucial element in the grievance.

The complaint quoted a 1970 interoffice employee evaluation of Kerins which noted that Kerins had "a nice pair of legs. She should be kept." Editor Laventhol had added to the memo the remark, "Let's look." Another memo from publisher Atwood about a woman with a doctorate degree who was attempting to get an article published in the paper stated that "Female PhD's . . . are usually insane."

On October 23, 1973, the caucus, through its lawyers, sent a letter to management stating that discrimination at *Newsday* was rampant and asked for a meeting between the caucus, the lawyers, and management. A month later the meeting took place. The caucus asked for parity in hiring and back pay, a grievance procedure, and job posting. Management, ac-cording to two of the caucus organizers, Sylvia Carter and Jerry Shana-han, told the caucus that the matter had to wait until the situation with the union was resolved. Caucus organizers saw the postponement tactic as a ploy to sow mistrust between the caucus and the union, but it didn't succeed. A large percentage of caucus members voted for the union which, in turn, backed the caucus demands.

In December 1973 the caucus filed formal charges with the Equal Employment Opportunities Commission. Management responded by stepping up its attacks on the group. The caucus complained that a February 1974 edict from management, which called for every staff person to fill out a revised evaluation form, was blamed on the caucus. Despite the attempt to cause a schism, relations between the men and women on staff grew stronger. A number of men began to perceive the women's complaints as parallel to their own feelings about the paper.

As the caucus grew, its leaders were sometimes harassed. "Some members of management have made disparaging and nasty remarks, indicating their displeasure at my involvement," caucus activist Jerry Shanahan stated in an affidavit. "Others have gone out of their way to ignore me. I have been isolated on the job and marked for no further career advancement." Although Shanahan was part of the Pulitzer team that produced the Rebozo investigation, as of 1976 she still sat on the copy desk working the early-bird shift.

In April 1974 *Newsday* management issued its own affirmative action plan. "Although *Newsday* is not required by law to adopt such a program," Bill Atwood wrote when the program policy was first announced, "I think we have a special responsibility to take the initiative in this area." Management insisted that it was "the most substantial plan of its kind in the country," but caucus leaders attacked the plan as a public relations job. Editors became more guarded in their remarks, and a few more female appointemnts were made, but the women complained that management's affirmative action program did not meet the problem in any substantial way. Many caucus demands—hiring requirements, pay scale, and internal procedures—were not even considered.

Six months after management issued its program, seventy-seven women staffers signed a resolution authorizing their lawyers to initiate a Title VII lawsuit on behalf of all editorial and noneditorial women at *Newsday*. The union joined as co-plaintiff. The suit asked for a permanent injuction to enforce equal pay for equal work, nondiscriminatory hiring and training procedures, posting of job notices, equal fringe benefits, pregnancy leaves, and an end to the harassment of the caucus and women staff.

It was one of the most comprehensive sex discrimination suits made against a media employer. Former managing editor Mel Opotowsky, himself a subject of some of the complaints from earlier years, labeled the suit and the documentation that went into it "extraordinary reporting." The brief was widely reprinted in women's publications, and women staffers at the *Los Angeles Times* circulated a copy in Los Angeles. It climaxed more than five years of caucus activity.

After the battles of 1971 to 1976, *Newsday*'s internal newsletter, "What's Going On," began to be called "Who's Going On," in reference to the frequent announcements of departing staffers. "I want to get out before the rest of the country finds out what's happened to *Newsday*," one staff writer remarked, reflecting a common sentiment.

Newsday, as established newspapers go, is a very good newspaper, rated by *Time* magazine as one of the ten best in the country. Its reporters are resilient and willing to go after the powers that be on the Island and throughout the country. But the staff is convinced the paper could be a whole lot better. They do not fear intervention to kill a story from the Times Mirror outside owners (though some misgivings on that score still remain) as much as they fear their local management, anticipating the needs of the parent company, running their paper like a corporation. Anxieties remain about content changes resulting in more positive and ad-related story ideas that tone down the old *Newsday* spirit.

The development of the union and the caucus—defensive in origin—has not led to a questioning of the fundamental structure and purpose of the corporate ownership of the paper. But it has projected the beginnings of an alternative simply by creating other sources of power with a different set of objectives.

As journalism continues to go through its post-Watergate changes, its function as a conduit for the establishment is increasingly challenged. With the development of alternative staff organizations, the situation at *Newsday* might be ripe for a modern-day interpretation of the old *Newsday* dream.

CHAPTER 32

The Agribusiness Interests

1. The Nader Report

In the summer of 1971, a Ralph Nader-connected task force of young lawyers and researchers issued an ambitious study on *The Politics of Land* in California. The analysis, on a subject at the very heart of power in the state, was long overdue.

The study contained critical material on a number of questions concerning land and water use in the state and the political tactics used by developers, big landholders, the water lobby, and the highway lobby. The book carried a key section on the history of the State Water Project, charts of campaign contributors for several important California politicians, a list of the holdings of the major land owners in different counties, a discussion of the role of corporations in political matters, and an overall analysis of the relationship between politics and land use.

Work on the report was greatly hampered by hostile landholding corporations who often refused to provide necessary information. Other omissions and inadequacies, plus its mechanistic approach to the link between politicians and the big agribusiness money, stemming from reliance on the data concerning campaign contributions, also hindered the report.

The public interest researchers had undertaken a topic largely ignored by the California news media. The group developed a wariness regarding attempts, particularly by the press, to attack and undermine the study's credibility. "The major newspapers in California's three largest cities—Los Angeles, San Francisco, and San Diego—along with their radio and television counterparts," the Nader researchers wrote, "have been long-standing and substantial investors in timberland, agricultural and ranch land, and recreational developments"—all areas touched on in the report. The Times Mirror Company's landholdings outranked all the other media interests.

The Nader group, though aware of the potential conflict of interest, realized that the *Los Angeles Times* was in many respects the only news medium in the state that could give the report adequate in-depth coverage. A comprehensive *Times* story was almost a prerequisite for significant press treatment in California, as it would boost the report in the eyes of assignment editors in radio and TV stations throughout the state. The researchers also knew they needed favorable *Times* treatment in order to offset the almost certain opposition from all the major politicians and corporate powers in the state.

As the report neared publication, the Nader people and several *Times* reporters sat down together—in an atmosphere of mistrust and suspicions—to go over the study. According to the Nader people, the *Times* reporters raised some criticisms of the report, but failed to provide a page-by-page critique as requested by the Naderites. The *Times* reporters recalled the situation differently. Environmental writer Phil Fradkin felt the Nader group's suspicions bordered on surliness, to the point where they were unwilling to hear any criticisms at all.

On August 27, 1971, the *Times* ran the first of several stories on the report, an unbylined article with the head: MOST OF CALIFORNIA HIT IN REPORT WRAP UP. A week later the paper devoted an entire page, with five separate news articles, to the story, and the editorial page carried a full-length evaluation of the task force material. "When consumer advocate Ralph Nader's task force was deep in its study of California land usage last summer," *Times* writer Ray Hebert began in the lead story, "Robert Fellmeth, the project's director explained, 'We're sticking our nose into everyone else's business.' Now that the report has been released, it's clear what Fellmeth meant. He was referring to the twenty million people in California. Few have come off untouched by the denunciation of California's land-use practices. The report points a finger at most Californians—either directly, by association, by implication through their own ignorance, or by the plain fact that they are residents of the state."

Although the four other articles were more even-handed than Hebert's—environmental writer Phil Fradkin's "Monied Interests Held Real Villain, But Report Lacks Nitty-Gritty Conservation Data" or political reporter Bill Boyarsky's "The Raiders Look at Land Lobbyists: No New Information," for example—they were equally as critical of the report as Hebert.

The *Times* reporters were piqued because the task force—cocky and brash out-of-towners, fresh out of law school—had undertaken a project that properly belonged in the pages of the *Times*. For fifteen years, highway lobby or land-use issues—most of the areas within *The Politics of Land*—had primarily been covered by Ray Hebert, whose articles were decidedly proindustry and prodeveloper. *Times* sensitivities concerning that earlier coverage provided an ironic contrast to the reporters' and editors' charge that the Naderites had failed to turn up new information.

The *Times* editorial on the task force study declared that the report "indulges throughout in the sweeping charge, the undocumented allegation, the reckless assertion." Like the reporters, the management was at once defensive and aggressive, denying the potential conflict-of-interest charge against itself, and claiming the same goals as the Nader movement. The editorial, backed by Hebert's attack and the Fradkin/Boyarsky/Houston criticisms, served to question the credibility of the analysis and dismiss the overall importance of the report.

2. Family Ranches

Times reporters knew that agribusiness interests were a substantial part of Chandler/Times Mirror holdings. The *Times* writers could hardly be censored, since they rarely pursued the subject. When they did, the story resembled more a corporate hand-out than a tough, probing story.

Coverage of the opening of Interstate Highway 5 between Los Angeles and San Francisco in 1972 is a good example. The major four-lane interstate used the old Tehachapi/Tejon Pass route, which passed over Tejon Ranch lands, causing ranch revenues from commercial rents to more than double from 1971 to 1973. Since the California Division of Highways, shortly before the advent of the winter 1973 energy crisis, predicted increased vehicle traffic over the route for the future, the ranch planned to develop another Tejon-owned interchange.

In the midst of the 1973/74 energy crisis, *Times* reporter Ray Hebert did a background story on the new interstate and its effect on the lands adjoining it. Under the title "Interstate 5—It Has Brought A Boom to San Joaquin Valley," Hebert wrote a glowing, positive news commentary on the highway. Hebert hardly touched on the energy crisis and its impact on highways and development.

The interstate development was a major boon for the Tejon Ranch. Leasing policies—which substantially benefited from the new highway—had become a major source of income for the ranch since the Depression years. Ranch plots first began to be divided among oil developers, such as Standard of California, Union Oil, Texaco, British-American Oil Company, and Hancock Oil Company, after oil was discovered on the ranch in the late 1930s. By the fifties, 450 producing oil wells operated on the ranch, grossing $1.5 million for the company. Substantial oil leasing arrangements continued into the 1970s. Land was also leased out for crop diversification; cotton, alfalfa, and potato crops were developed. The ranch spent $1.4 million in 1973 to acquire the Waterman-Loomis Company, a producer of alfalfa seeds.

The ranch had also become a key part of the infrastructure of power in Kern County, where it had allied itself with the other major agribusiness interests such as Tenneco, to influence the county Board of Supervisors and take a major role in the Kern County Water Agency. By the 1970s the Tejon Ranch—the fourth largest landowner in the state and one of the biggest income-producing components of the Chandler fortune—had become Big Business.

The Chandler family also tied into another powerful and profitable agribusiness company in California. In 1952 Norman Chandler's sister Ruth became, on the death of her second husband, James Boswell, the chairman of the board and major stock owner of the James G. Boswell Company, the seventh largest landowner in the state. First organized in 1925, two years after James acquired some farmland in the San Joaquin Valley in central California, the company had steadily expanded. By the 1930s Boswell, already one of the largest cotton producers in the country, had become the major landowner in Tulare and Kings counties.

After Ruth Chandler Williamson Boswell assumed the post of chairman of the board and became the major stock owner, the J.G. Boswell Company purchased: 65,000 acres of land in Fresno County and northern California, the Tulare Lake Land Company, a major realtor in Tulare County; 49 per cent of the stock of Del Webb Development company, a subsidiary of the Del Webb interests (owners of the Flamingo Hotel in Las Vegas and other properties), which developed the "Sun City" suburban community out of some of Boswell's Arizona land; 175,000 acres of leased land and 200,000 acres of fee land in central Oregon; the Ted Smith Aircraft Company; a 50 per cent share of Reybos, the personally owned investment company of Robert Reynolds, the president of California's Golden West Broadcasters; a 6 per cent share in Southern Pacific Properties, owner of hotels and housing units in the Fiji Islands; and 100,000 acres in New South Wales, Australia.

Boswell received $837,000 from the Australian government as a tax stimulus to encourage its cotton production; at the same time, it obtained a $4-million subsidy from the U.S. Agricultural Stabilization and Conservation Service not to grow cotton on its U.S. properties. The U.S. subsidy was supposed to protect U.S. prices on the world market by preventing overproduction—prices undermined by Boswell's Australian cotton production. By the early 1970s, the J.G. Boswell Company received more subsidies than any other agribusiness property in the country. U.S. Senate hearings on the conditions of rural farm workers in the United States in 1971 and 1972 frequently cited the Boswell Company as an example of how large agribusiness interests are given favored treatment by the government. Sixty percent of Kings County residents (mostly migrant farm workers) received welfare, but the Boswell Company, which collected $4.5 million worth of federal subsidies for its King County properties, was the biggest welfare recipient of them all. Total subsidies, paid at rates as high as $1,000 an acre, amounted to $3.3 million in 1966 and $5 million in 1970.

The company also participated in the Westlands Water District, a combine of the major landowners in the San Joaquin Valley which played a major role in federal and state water and land questions. For years the Westlands district was able to deflect the implementation of the 160-acre law, which limited federally reclaimed water to farms under 160 acres. And water, for Boswell, the Tejon Ranch, and other agribusiness interests, was their number one concern.

3. The State Water Project

"If you don't have the water, you won't need it." This William Mulholland truism, implying that future water supply provided the impetus for future growth, had become the operative ideology of the Southern California business establishment. In spite of massive problems in housing, transportation, air pollution, and unemployment, generated by the post-World War II boom, the Southern California establishment still dreamed of unending growth. Many spoke of a Southern California population of 18 million by 1975; one 1961 prediction in the *Times* foresaw 22 million within the decade. Population guessing was a favorite pastime of the *Times*, with much of the optimistic forecasting based on the availability of a future water supply.

By the early 1950s, the Feather River, north of Sacramento, had emerged as the agribusiness and water lobby's favorite choice for California's future water distribution system. "The idea of moving the Feather River out of its own watershed began as the brainchild of the big San Joaquin Valley landowners: the corporate farms, land management farms, railroads with huge acreages," Erwin Cooper wrote in *Aqueduct Empire*.

The agribusiness farms, based on irrigated farming, needed the water available from the Federal Bureau of Reclamation. The agency's 160-acre size limitation prevented large landowners from receiving the cheap, re-claimed waters. The agribusiness companies hoped that, by having the state government operate a water distribution system, they could do away with the 160-acre provision.

Plans that had developed under the Republican administration of Good-win Knight received their final push under Democrat Pat Brown. Like his one-time conservative opponents, Brown strongly backed the notion of expansion and development. Unlike the conservatives, however, Brown saw both the trade unions and the government as essential components of the growth matrix. The conservative Southern California establishment had, since the days of the New Deal, rejected such a concept of public sector/private sector alliance, but by 1960—led by the *Times* and the wa-ter lobby—that perspective had begun to be accepted.

Brown's politics equated more population with more money and jobs, with the government underwriting the entire development. As a prowater, progrowth incumbent, Brown received praise from the *Los Angeles Times*. He also had the support of the large landowners in the state who wanted a State Water Project; a number of trade unions especially the construction unions, who looked forward to the building of a several-hun-dred-mile aqueduct; and Southern California businessmen wedded to the promise of future water supplies spurring future growth.

In 1959 Brown and his allies in the state legislature helped push through legislation to create a State Water Project to take the Feather River water through the San Joaquin Valley into Southern California. To get the sup-port of the large rural landowner-backed northern California legislators, Brown sided with conservative forces to beat back proposed amendments to establish a state version of the 160-acre limitation for water use. The governor's fight for the State Water Project, according to Brown himself, was the key reason for the fair and balanced campaign coverage of his reelection against Richard Nixon.

A measure to approve the $1.75 billion estimated for the State Water Project was put on the 1960 ballot. Los Angeles Mayor Norris Poulson became the Southern California chairman for the initiative, and the *Times* gave it full editorial backing. The two biggest financial contributors to the support campaign came from the Southern Pacific and the Tejon Ranch.

The 1960 campaign also saw the first significant manifestation of an en-vironmental perspective which questioned the disrupting of land and wa-ter patterns in the state in order to stimulate development and subdivi-sion. *San Francisco Chronicle* editor Scott Newhall and some other northern Californians opposed the measure, criticizing the Southern Cali-fornia penchant for population boosting.

By the end of the campaign, the issue of financing stood out as the most controversial aspect of the entire plan. Two outside consulting firms were brought in to investigate and give an appraisal. One report tended to favor the project, and the other stayed neutral, but both questioned the accuracy of the financial projections because of failure to take inflation into account. One team of consultants even suggested postponing the entire project.

The *Los Angeles Times* and *San Francisco Chronicle* chose to emphasize different aspects of the report. Squeaking through by a few thousand votes, the initiative measure divided along regional lines, but as the construction on California's newest water project got under way—with the Tejon Ranch subsidiary, the Arvin Rock Company furnishing materials for the aqueduct construction—more and more voices began to question the once unquestionable development ethic. The *Times* continued to maintain its prodevelopment posture through support of the State Water Project. It editorially denied any connection between its position and Tejon ranch interests.

4. The Ranch Moves into Real Estate

In the mid 1960s, the California Legislature passed another important piece of legislation concerning rural land use called the Williamson Act. The measure provided for a tax break for landowners who signed an agreement with the state to use their land solely for agricultural purposes. To receive the tax break, the landowner had to keep the land agricultural for at least ten years. If the landowner decided to subdivide his land, he'd lose the tax break.

The Tejon Ranch, still primarily devoted to agricultural practices and oil leasing, signed its first contract under the Williamson Act in February 1968. A battle between those committed to the ranch as an agricultural operation and those who wanted to get involved in real estate development had already begun. The disagreement led to a major corporate shake-up resulting in the resignation of the president of the company, William Moore. The new management team gave wide latitude to its real estate division.

In August 1971 the Tejon Ranch approached the supervisors with a request to cancel the ten-year agreement. The ranch management planned to create a recreational community out of 8,000 acres of uninhabited Tejon property. When one of the local Bakersfield environmental organizations learned of the Tejon agenda item, its representative went to the meeting to ask for a postponement in order to study the proposed request. The supervisors turned the group down and approved the cancellation on the spot.

But the environmentalists were not to be put off. In 1972 the California Supreme court handed down the Friends of Mammoth decision, which called for the inclusion of Environmental Impact Reports (EIR) on any new development projects, with the appropriate public body having the power to halt any project that was deemed especially harmful to the environment.

Tejon hired consulting firm James D. Roberts to prepare its EIR. Their results minimized any potentially detrimental effects, but a local group, the Project Land Use Task Force, hired another firm, Systems Management Inc., whose report criticized the Tejon project. The Systems Management study noted, among other things, a scarcity of water in the Tehachapis—one of the reasons why the area had not previously supported a major development effort. The Tejon developers, on discovering that water from the State Water Project, which they had hoped to use for the development, was unsuitable for drinking, had proposed that the limited Tehachapis water be used and then replenished by California aqueduct water. But the System's Management people argued that the alkalinity of the aqueduct water might permanently damage the existing Tehachapi supply.

Despite these and other objections in the Systems Management EIR, the Kern supervisors once again upheld the Tejon's plans. But prior to a formal hearing to implement the plan, a discovery was made that the recreational community would be situated right on top of a major earthquake fault. The supervisors postponed the development and brought in an advisor from the Naval Weapon Center to look over the situation. After the Naval expert presented a plan to shift the development outside the fault line, the plan was approved for a third time. A hearing took place the next month in August 1973, and, over the objections of the local environmentalists, lasted only thirty minutes.

The environmentalists' objections were outlined in a detailed *Project Land Use Report,* which was presented to the Kern County Planning Commission. "The proposed Tejon Ranch project is a classic 'premature subdivision,'" the report argued, "a land project that is not near heavily populated areas, in a setting that is presently pastoral or agricultural in use. Such land is cheap for development that capitalizes on existing natural resources and caters to a limited market of purchasers who do not reside in the area at this time. It is the parcelling of land without a demand for its existence, and without relation to the needs of the community at large for primary housing. We have had too much of this type of land division in Kern County already. *It is time to say—No More.*"

A court ruling in the winter of 1973 concerning another development scheme near the Tehachapis halted the Tejon project once again. The rul-

ing specified that land in the Cuddy Valley, adjacent to the Tejon property, could not be developed without an EIR taking into account how water
use also affected the entire area bordering the development. A new EIR
had to be prepared. The Tejon development was postponed—this time for
good—but the battle over the future of the Tehachapis was far from over.

To the readers of the *Los Angeles Times,* the fight in the Tehachapis
could just as well have been in Afghanistan. There were no editorials
about the matter, no environmental specialists to do background pieces
on the question, and only occasional one-paragraph blurbs or condensed
Tejon press releases in the real estate section. *Times* environmental writers were hesitant to inquire directly into the situation.

But *Times* reporters didn't always stay away from controversial matters involving agribusiness interests. In 1975 and 1976, general assignment
reporter Bob Jones did a couple of stories on the Westlands Water District and the 160-acre law, and detailed the various maneuvers of different
San Joaquin Valley agribusiness companies. The role of the Boswell company, however, was not brought up.

By the mid-1970s, with the environmental movement under full-scale
attack by coalitions of unions and corporations trying to revive the booster ethic of unlimited development, *Times* coverage of land and water use
became even more crucial to the public's perception of environmental issues. Although *Times* writers made tentative forays into agribusiness and
water issues—once considered off limits—large areas still lay unexplored.
Mindful of their paychecks, the hesitant *Times* reporters stood between a
development-minded corporation and an emergent environmental consciousness.

For the first time in Los Angeles history, population began to decrease,
and the trend promised to continue. The Southern California nexus of
boosterism and development had suffered its first defeats, and Angelenos
began to show concern about the philosophy of unlimited expansion.
"The limitations imposed by the air resource alone are so severe," one
environmentalist noted, "that any planning for the region which anticipates a population in excess of 14 million resource customers—living as
they do today—is gullible at best and criminal at worst."

In 1972 the *Times,* looking for a middle ground position, bitterly attacked an environmental initiative proposal which called for major controls over expansion and development, but backed the more modest
coastline initiative which created a commission to supervise development
projects along the California coastline.

For the first time in its history, the *Times* talked in more hushed and
guarded tones. A May 1973 *Times* editorial said: "Population expansion,
with attendant smog and transportation difficulties, looms large in the

minds of ecologists. . . . Such growth must not be allowed to go uncontrolled. There must be proper planning and zoning controls at the local level.''

An unthinkable position just a few years earlier was now hesitatingly put forward by the *Times*. But development plans still proceeded, in some areas as chaotically as in the early Harry Chandler-influenced days of Southern California expansion. The *Times* ignored those expansion-minded company's plans in news coverage and editorials, but continued to take their full-page ads.

CHAPTER 33

The GeoTek Affair

1. Burke's Idea

In 1964 Otis Chandler was a very wealthy man. Much of the family fortune was tied up in the enormous Chandler Trust #2, the trust fund set up by Harry Chandler in 1936 to insure a single voting unit for all the Chandlers. Otis had also inherited some money from his mother's fund, the Buffum trust, and, as a young man, had built up a little portfolio of his own of stocks and other investments. His wife also had some inherited money, the Brant trust, derived from the Title Insurance fortune that grandfather Otto Brant had put together in the days of the San Fernando Valley land syndicates.

Some of Chandler's friends thus found it a bit disconcerting that Otis and Missie seemed constantly strapped for funds. "She'd always be complaining about their money problems," one of Missie's friends recalled of the early sixties, "and I never could understand it."

Otis and Marilyn had large expenses: a new house in San Marino, Otis's overseas big-game-hunting jaunts, his Duesenberg. They had the money, but little of it was available as ready cash. Otis's $60,000-a-year salary was handsome, but most of his other assets, tied up in the stocks and trusts, were largely inherited wealth. The ambitious Chandler wanted to be recognized for his own accomplishments and contribution to the family fortunes. He was open to suggestions.

Chandler had a very close friend from Stanford days, a co-member of the school's track and field team, Jack Burke. Burke was not a rich man. After Stanford, he became an investment counselor and had worked for a time at Paine, Webber, and Pierce, one of the largest brokerage houses in the country, where he developed some interest in the oil business.

Burke decided to create an oil exploration and drilling company, using capital raised through the investments of wealthy individuals. The oil business had quickly become one of the most lucrative and attractive investments of the time. Besides possible high profits, an oil exploration and drilling company could provide a tax shelter for the wealthy investor. Internal Revenue Service provisions in the early 1960s—which were later amended—allowed a deductible oil "depletion allowance" of 22 percent of the revenues produced from oil operations.

Burke was well aware of the situation and strongly emphasized this aspect as he built up his company. "A person whose taxable income is $50,000 will find that a $10,000 investment . . . will have an after tax cost of only $4,950. . . . In other words, 51 cents on the dollar is actual tax savings," a company promotional brochure advised.

By 1964 Burke had organized a series of related corporate partnerships where investors could put their funds. The accumulated capital was then invested by Burke in various explorations. Twenty-two different corporate entities, collectively known as the GeoTek companies, had emerged.

Burke's immediate problem was to figure out how to attract wealthy investors. Even if he overcame the obstacle of securing appointments with corporate figures, Burke had to convince them why this tax shelter was more compelling than countless others.

Burke needed someone who could provide entry, and he immediately turned to his old friend. Within months after the first of the GeoTek partnerships had been organized, Otis Chandler took a crucial role in Jack Burke's new company. In many ways it was similar to the role his father had played in the Emmet and Chandler insurance firm: opening the doors by using his powerful name to attract the money.

Beginning in 1964 Chandler systematically began to write and telephone wealthy friends and associates to tell them about the new oil-drilling tax shelter and why it was a worthwhile investment. Chandler personally contacted corporate executives, politicians, and other well-known personalities. These included Art Linkletter, Jack Kent Cooke (owner of the Los Angeles Lakers basketball team and Los Angeles Kings hockey franchise), Jack Drown (one of the earliest Nixon backers and one-time head of the Nixon foundation), Evelle Younger (at that time Los Angeles district attorney), several influential Democrats such as the Wymans and the Carters, family relations such as cousin Otis Booth and brother-in-law Kellogg Spear, and corporate heads of the Republic Corporation, General Precision company, Western Air Lines, Golden West Broadcasters, the Union Bank, Motion Pictures International, TRW, Title Insurance and Trust Company, and even associates in his own Times Mirror Company.

In some instances Chandler arranged to have a potential investor meet Jack Burke in the executive suites of the *Los Angeles Times* building.

Chandler's name became so intimately associated with the GeoTek enterprise that one investor even sent his check by mistake to Chandler directly instead of to the GeoTek offices in San Francisco. Investors told other investors that "Chandler's in it" and that for many was enough.

Otis's help did not go unrewarded. At the end of 1965, Burke told his friend, as Chandler's lawyer Robert Warren described it, that "he was paying sums to other individuals who were making similar introductions and that he desired to pay Mr. Chandler as well." Such payment, a "finder's fee," frequently used by companies to encourage their sales force to solicit more clients or investors, was, and is, subject to legal restriction. Securities laws require the finder to inform potential investors of the finder's own interest in the matter, but prosecution for violations are rare.

For his solicitations Burke paid Chandler 2 percent of the $460,000 that Chandler helped bring into GeoTek up through December 1965. Starting in 1966 Burke raised the figure to 5 percent of the $2 million more that Chandler raised for the GeoTek entities. All told, Chandler received finder's fees amounting to $109,000.

Burke also passed on $373,000 worth of promotional stock in the company to the helpful Chandler, to add to the $248,000 that Chandler had invested. The *Times* publisher calculated an overall profit return of anywhere from $700,000 to $1,500,000 or more, on basically no investment since the tax shelter savings, one SEC accountant estimated, plus the $109,000 in finder's fees, likely approximated the $248,000 of Chandler's own money.

Chandler's long-range plans were complemented by a number of short-term deals that Burke arranged for his friend. In 1967 Chandler and Burke, each putting in $16,000 in a speculative investment for an oil exploration site in Nicaragua, created the C-B partnership. C-B had a 12 percent share in the Nicaraguan property, with other shares owned by ARCO, McCulloch Oil, and the Signal companies. A year before any drilling took place—before there were any definite indications of the presence of oil—Chandler and Burke concluded a second deal, drawn up by Chandler's lawyers from Gibson, Dunn, and Crutcher, whereby Burke agreed to pay Chandler $33,000—more than double what Chandler had paid in.

In addition, Chandler maintained a 1 percent interest in the venture. "The [1 percent] interest reserved by Mr. Chandler is a royalty which is 'off the top' and expense free," Burke's lawyer wrote to Chandler's lawyer. If Burke were to later sell the C-B interest and receive a profit over and above the price he paid for Chandler's share, "the excess," Burke's lawyer continued, "will be given to Mr. Chandler." It was, in effect, a $17,000 gift with a possible promise of more to come if the drilling proved successful.

Another deal, in 1967, continued the no-loss-possible profit-making relationship between Burke and Chandler. After stock in the Apache Oil Company, in which they had each invested $73,000, started to drop, Burke bought out Chandler's share for the $73,000, in spite of the stock's loss in value.

The Chandler/Burke relationship was strewn with favors and gifts. In 1966 Burke bought a new Mercury station wagon for Chandler and provided a Standard Oil credit card for his and his family's use; in 1969 Burke replaced the Mercury with a new Pontiac with all repair bills and related expenses sent to Burke.

As the two men spent more and more time together, the name GeoTek (or one of its myriad partnerships or secondary corporations) increasingly appeared in Otis Chandler's cash receipts book under the category "Oil Royalties." Although members of the family felt somewhat uncomfortable with the relationship, and Missie complained to friends that she disliked and mistrusted the oil operator, other Chandler friends, including District Attorney Younger, got on well with the hustling Burke. By the late 1960s, Burke's talk seemed to have most everybody convinced that GeoTek was a very good thing.

2. The Scam

For Jack Burke the project had become a good thing in more ways than one. What Chandler helped bring in through investor funds, Burke took out by way of transactions between himself and GeoTek. The GeoTek president set up a number of dummy corporations in the name of his brother, Robert Burke. In one instance, according to Robert Burke's testimony, one of the dummy companies, the Island Oil Corporation, bought an oil property for $14,000 and then sold it to GeoTek for $65,000. Robert Burke, Island Oil's president, withdrew the money from Island's checking account and transferred it to Jack's personal account.

In another transaction, Jack Burke purchased an oil property in his own name. After its production had substantially declined, Burke sold the property to GeoTek at a profit for himself of $960,000. Burke's $260,000 worth of debts from the property were also assumed by GeoTek.

Burke also created a no-loss situation for himself out of the same Nicaragua deal in which he had paid off Chandler. After purchasing Chandler's share, Burke—on paper—sold the entire Nicaraguan property back to GeoTek at a profit for himself, but without notifying any third parties about the transaction until after it became clear that the expensive ex-

ploratory drilling had failed to strike oil. If the drilling had been successful, the SEC claimed, Burke could have torn up the documents of transfer
and kept the successful property in his own name.

Unlike some of the ingenious fund-juggling scams of the late 1960s and
early 70s—such as Equity Funding or Home Stake Productions—the Geo-
Tek arrangements were relatively straightforward—"like using a meat
cleaver to chop up parsley," one securities analyst noted.

Burke, however, knew he had a powerful backer in Otis Chandler.
Chandler, after all, was in a position to detect the frauds involved in the
Nicaraguan deal and other situations—and Burke undoubtedly felt confident that he could head off any problem if it arose. But Burke's blatant
juggling of the books was sensed by other investors, who started to complain. Some expressed their fears to Chandler who had encouraged them
to invest in the first place, but the *Times* publisher assured them of his
confidence in his college buddy.

Otis's brother-in-law, Kellogg Spear, a descendant of one of the oldest
blue-blood families in Southern California, numbered among the skeptical
investors whom Chandler had interested in the new oil company. Spear,
grandson of mining man Emerson Spear, had married Otis's sister Camilla in the late 1940s, and was one of a circle of Chandler intimates, having
been Otis's best man at Chandler's wedding in 1951.

When Spear first raised questions about GeoTek, Chandler brushed
them aside and denied he was receiving any finder's fees or promotional
stock. "I think I made a point," Spear later testified, "of calling him and
telling him I would not call anybody [for GeoTek] and that I also made
reference to the fact that I hoped he wasn't receiving any fees because
this would be very poor, and he got very incensed and said emphatically
that he was not."

Spear invested $10,000 in 1965, another $30,000 in 1966, and later
another $19,000 for which Chandler received his finder's fee percentage.
By the late 1960s Spear became suspicious about the lack of dividends on
his investment, but when he tried to question his brother-in-law about it,
Chandler became angry. It was, as Spear put it, "a touchy situation." "I
think that Otis' pride had a lot to do with it," Spear tried to explain, "the
fact that I would question any decision that he had made or make any
judgments he took offense at."

Spear, who had contacted his own oil expert from the Howard Hughes
organization to look into the situation, was not the only person to make
inquiries. "What's happening?" Evelle Younger asked Spear one day
about the GeoTek situation, for complaints from several other investors
had begun to filter their way to the district attorney's office where Younger, himself a recipient of Burke generosity, sat in office.

Otis Chandler had introduced Younger to the ubiquitous Burke sometime in 1965, and the two men had worked out a situation similar to the Chandler/Burke win/no-loss arrangements. Younger put up a $16,500 investment in GeoTek through two interest-free loans he had received from a campaign backer. Several months before the note came due, the district attorney and GeoTek president worked out an arrangement whereby Burke picked up Younger's debt. Younger didn't have to pay anything back at all unless his GeoTek investment "produced sufficient revenues to liquidate the note," as Younger himself described it. In effect, Younger had a cost-free $16,500 investment.

In exchange, Younger provided the oil promoter with a list of several names, including campaign contributors, personal friends, and wealthy individuals who might be interested in GeoTek. The list included Buzzi Bavasi of the Los Angeles Dodgers baseball team, H.R. Haldeman, Superior Court Judge Philip Newman, several top corporate executives, and Younger's cousin, attorney Kenneth Younger.

As the head of the prosecutor's office, which might be called in to examine any criminal wrongdoing on Burke's part, Younger, far from establishing an arms-length relationship, continued his ties with Burke and ignored the increasing complaints about GeoTek. The GeoTek president was invited to a Younger dinner party in late 1967 and joined ten other Younger backers in fronting a $55,000 loan to Younger's candidacy for the 1970 attorney general's race. As late as March 1971, Younger was still asking favors from the Burke brothers.

A number of investors continued to complain. Investor Ed Rees, the president of Flying Tiger Airlines, had begun to examine systematically GeoTek's corporate reports and financial statements, and immediately noticed a number of discrepancies in the documents. Rees and several other disgruntled investors demanded an audience with Burke or the chance to be bought out by the GeoTek president, but Burke dismissed their requests.

At one point Rees forwarded the material to another GeoTek investor, Times Mirror counsel Julian Van Kalinowski, in the hope that the Gibson Dunn lawyer might look into it. Instead of responding to Rees, Van Kalinowski and *Times* general manager Robert Nelson—another Chandler-solicited GeoTek investor—arranged with Burke to buy back their shares. Burke offered the Chandler associates the amount of their initial investment minus whatever money they saved from the tax break, plus 25 percent of the difference. Burke urged Nelson and Van Kalinowski to take advantage of this "unusual offer."

To Ed Rees and others who had no special ties to Otis Chandler, Burke turned a deaf ear. Finally, a couple of investors, sensing nowhere else to turn, wrote to the California Division of Corporations to intervene in the affair.

In 1967 Governor Ronald Reagan had appointed Robert Volk to head the California Department of Corporations, a state agency with specific powers to regulate how companies solicit investors. Volk, another Stanford graduate, was a longtime acquaintance of Otis Chandler's. His father Harry Volk, chairman of the powerful Union Bank—sixth largest in the state—had sat on the Times Mirror Board of Directors for twenty years, one of its first two outside directors. When Robert returned to the family business as president of Unionamerica, the corporate spin-off from the Union Bank, he invited Otis Chandler to sit on the Unionamerica board. Young Volk also casually knew Stanford graduate Jack Burke.

Shortly after Volk became California corporations commissioner, he received a visit from Burke and Burke's Gibson, Dunn, and Crutcher lawyers—the same law firm which represented the *Times* and the Chandlers. Burke protested that a GeoTek permit had been unduly delayed; soon after the meeting, the permit was issued.

Even before the Burke visit, the corporations commissioner had started to receive GeoTek investor complaints, some of which pinpointed specific areas of irregularities. The commission office became entwined between the angry investors, who wanted an open hearing on the subject, and GeoTek executives. Volk's office wrote back and forth, trying to find a way to avoid conflict. Although a letter from GeoTek attorney Bob Rose to Burke referred to the "power and rapport you have with Volk," Volk later denied the existence of any such relationship. No hearings, however, took place, and GeoTek received its permits during Volk's two-year tenure in office.

After Volk resigned to go work at Unionamerica in 1969, his replacement scheduled a hearing. The investors who showed up spoke harshly about the GeoTek operation and Burke's dealings. Although Evelle Younger's cousin Kenneth Younger observed the hearings, the D.A.'s office, like the corporation commission, did not institute any action.

A week before the hearing, Otis Chandler wrote to his friend and business associate Simon Ramo, vice-president of the aerospace firm TRW and a director of Times Mirror and Unionamerica, that "after carefully reviewing Jack Burke's new fund," he had agreed to join its board of directors. "I think it has great potential," Chandler wrote. "I would hope that you would agree to go on the board also. I think that between the two of us we could keep Jack's feet to the fire."

Chandler hoped to stem investor discontent by finding a way for those who were complaining to sell their GeoTek interest or, as Chandler later put it, "to stay in or cash out." Chandler formulated a plan to get GeoTek listed on a stock exchange in order to go public, thus making it easier for investors to cash out by selling their shares directly through the stock market. Previously, investors had to go through a cumbersome process involving numerous difficulties.

In 1970 merger negotiations got under way between GeoTek and the Pacific Oil and Gas Corporation, an inactive company which had a listing on the Pacific Coast Stock Exchange. Chandler and Ramo joined the GeoTek Board of Directors, to meet outside directorship requirements, and a proxy statement for shareholder ratification was filed with the Securities and Exchange Commission in order to get approval for the merger.

In the summer and fall of 1969, before the merger was arranged, Chandler's lawyer Dan Frost of Gibson, Dunn, and Crutcher drew up an indemnification agreement between Chandler and Burke, which provided that Burke insure Chandler against any claims that might later be made against Chandler in his capacity as GeoTek director. Such an arrangement is neither unusual nor illegal; many outside directors, being liable for acts of malfeasance—acts that they performed or acts they should have known about—protect themselves with such agreements. But, as in the case of the finder's fees, failure to disclose the arrangement is illegal. Chandler, who had drawn up the agreement between himself and Burke personally, rather than with GeoTek, never disclosed the indemnification in any of the GeoTek filings for the SEC.

Before the company went public, Frost also wanted Chandler to receive the promotional shares of GeoTek stock that Burke had promised the *Times* publisher. "As I have told you several times, I am very anxious from a tax standpoint to have Otis' promotional shares issued as soon as possible," Frost wrote to Burke in June 1969. "Obviously the closer we get to registration and public sale, the greater the value that might be attributed to these shares." Chandler received the free stock soon after.

As the company was about to go public in 1971, Burke offered yet even more stock to the Chandlers, but this time placed it in Chandler's wife's name. As part of the merger procedures, GeoTek filed a statement with the SEC, listing all the stock received by outside directors since they became directors. Chandler, failing to include the gift to his wife, listed none. As the last details of the merger fell in place, Chandler and Burke went off on their last big-game-hunting expedition to Outer Mongolia.

Chandler arranged to have Gibson, Dunn senior partner Francis Wheat, a former SEC commissioner, brought in to help secure SEC approval for the GeoTek merger. But it was too late. In November 1971 the SEC, one of whose Los Angeles staff members had previously been in touch with investor Ed Rees, issued an order of investigation. Two months later formal interviews began.

Shortly before Jack Burke was scheduled to appear, he informed Chandler and other GeoTek officials that he would tell the SEC of his affairs, including the numerous transactions with the dummy corporations. Under advice from the company's attorney, Burke resigned from GeoTek. Chandler, upset and disheartened, made a formal break with his longtime friend.

In March 1972 Chandler, represented by a full battery of Gibson, Dunn lawyers, appeared before the SEC for the first time. During the hearing, Chandler and his lawyers realized that the SEC had broadened its investigations to include the finder's fees, the Nicaraguan deal, and the indemnification agreement, as well as the overall character of the Burke/Chandler relationship. "We submit," Chandler's lawyers wrote to the SEC investigators, "that it would be harsh to hold Mr. Chandler, a man without experience in the securities field, to a standard of disclosure higher than that which seems to have satisfied the office of the California Commissioner of Corporations." The Chandler defense argued, in effect, that if the California Division of Corporations (and the Los Angeles district attorney) had not done anything, then why should the SEC? But the local SEC, which feared both the Chandler clout and potential political pressure from Washington, still continued to pursue the matter.

3. Enter the Press

In July 1972 a reporter for the *Wall Street Journal* got wind of the GeoTek investigation and several aspects of Chandler and Younger's participation—although not the existence of Chandler's finder's fees. On July 24 GeoTek official Ed Beckwith sent a confidential memo to Otis Chandler and Simon Ramo informing them of the *Journal's* activity. "The most critical question he has asked me," Beckwith wrote of his interview with the *Journal* reporter, "is why Ramo, Chandler and I would have become involved with Burke in 1969 and 1970 [the GeoTek board relationship]. My answer was that we thought we were starting to build a new operating company in a technically based and vital arena; i.e., discovery and production of energy at a time when the national shortage was increasingly apparent." The *Journal* reporter, Beckwith noted, had scheduled another interview with him for August 8.

On August 4 Otis Chandler returned his finder's fees and promotional stock to the company. When the *Journal* reporter called him up later that week the *Times* publisher said he had done nothing wrong and specifically denied receiving any finder's fees. "I had no reason," Chandler remarked, "to suspect Jack of any dishonesty or self-dealing. Jack Burke was—and I use the word 'was' very carefully and knowingly—up to February one of my oldest and closest friends."

On August 11, 1972, the *Journal* broke the story with a page one head: WEALTHY ACQUAINTANCES OF CALIFORNIA PUBLISHER EVIDENTLY LOST

BUNDLE; OTIS CHANDLER 'OPENED DOORS' FOR COLLEGE PAL WHO RAN OIL FUND, SEC NOW PROBES. The *Journal* piece detailed the Chandler/ Burke friendship, some of the questionable practices of GeoTek, and Evelle Younger's connection to the entire affair.

Shortly after the article appeared, Younger called a press conference in his defense and denied any wrongdoing or conflict of interest. Younger acknowledged the $16,500 investment, but stated that as D.A. or attorney general, he failed to receive any complaints or requests for action. With the *New York Times* picking up on the story, the threat of a scandal of major proportions loomed large.

On the day the *Journal* story broke, *Los Angeles Times* financial editor Rob Wood was assigned to write a *Times* story. Wood saw assistant managing editors, managing editor Haven, editor Bill Thomas and publisher Chandler about the piece. In an hour-and-a-half talk, Chandler told the young financial editor how he had been deceived by his old friend and had become involved in the oil company. Toward the end of the interview, the *Times* publisher initiated discussion on the finder's fees, stating he had received these fees from Jack Burke, but had since returned them to the company. Chandler did not mention that he had only returned the fees one week earlier, after learning of the *Wall Street Journal* probe. Wood, unaware that Chandler had specifically denied receiving the fees to the *Wall Street Journal*, included in a paragraph near the end of the article the "exclusive" information about the fees in his story. When the *Times* was later criticized for its GeoTek coverage, Wood proudly pointed to the fact that he had first publicly revealed the information about the fees.

Times staff, who read the *Journal* article and the *Times* story that appeared the following day, couldn't understand why the wealthy Chandler would get involved in an affair that included something so apparently piddling as a car and credit card. Even the $109,000 from the finder's fees and the $373,000 from the promotional stock was not considered all that substantial. A theory began to make the rounds at the paper; many staff concluded that he had been taken by his old college chum. The publication of court documents that included Chandler memoranda pointing out that the *Times* publisher, by his own estimates, stood to gain at least $700,000, did not dissuade most of the staff.

While Wood and *Times* editors boasted about the paper's coverage, pointing to the number of spot stories as proof that the paper went out of its way to cover the affair, a couple of reporters whose copy got severely chopped asked to be removed from any further GeoTek assignments and to have their bylines taken off the reworked stories. Most *Times* staff, however, defended the paper. "We might have even gone overboard in coverage," one editor remarked, noting, "we leaned over backwards to cover the story because it was Chandler."

4. The Election

Evelle Younger decided to run for reelection as the incumbent attorney general rather than expose himself to the gubernatorial race, which he had been considering for several months. His GeoTek troubles did not deter major contributions from a large cross section of the Southern California business elite. Asa Call; Otis Chandler's sister Camilla Spear; Gibson, Dunn and Crutcher senior partner William French Smith; GeoTek director Simon Ramo; and former California commissioner Robert Volk were among those who contributed. In his well-financed campaign, Younger became the most heavily backed candidate of the business establishment for statewide office in 1974.

Before the June primary, the *Times* endorsed Younger for the June election, and, at the same time, for the general election in November. "No attorney general in recent history has had better qualifications than Younger," the *Times* commented. "The attorney general is the people's lawyer. Younger has been an excellent one."

Former Los Angeles police commissioner Bill Norris, a partner in the powerful Tuttle and Taylor law firm, opposed Younger in the general election. Norris made GeoTek his number one issue, but he proved to be a weak and ineffective candidate.

The *Times* did much to lessen Norris's impact in the state. It gave only perfunctory coverage to Norris's GeoTek charges, had no detailed analysis, frequently buried stories in the back of the first section, and was occasionally mocking in tone. Assignment selections for GeoTek stories shuttled around "like a game of Russian roulette," as one *Times* staffer put it. "When we hear something like GeoTek in a political race," *Times* staffer Frank Del Omo commented shortly after the campaign, "we usually go all out to check the story; in fact we blanket it to make sure we've left nothing unturned, but we didn't do that at all with GeoTek."

"The mood was, 'who the hell wants to cover that story?'" another *Times* political reporter noted. "After all, it's not as sexy as the Governor's race. Everybody was a little conscious of the relationship between Younger and Chandler, though I don't think it affected the coverage as such. Nobody got any orders, but then again everybody knew who paid the checks. Our natural reaction was to not make trouble."

A month before the election, the *Sacramento Bee*—published by C.K. McClatchy, whose mother once sat on the state Board of Trustees with candidate Norris—ran the first major investigative GeoTek story to appear in a California daily. McClatchy assigned his top investigative reporter Denny Walsh to the story. Walsh wrote about the possible cover-up, dating from Younger's days as Los Angeles district attorney, and about the three-way ties between Younger, Chandler, and Burke. Deep in the story, a passage noted Chandler's failure to disclose the finder's fees and its possible violation of state law, which would have made Chandler subject to criminal prosecution by the attorney general.

When Otis Chandler found out about the story, he immediately telephoned *Bee* publisher McClatchy, another Stanford graduate and acquaintance of Chandler's. Chandler complained about alleged inaccuracies, particularly the item about the violation of state law. The *Times* publisher told McClatchy that he had spoken over the situation with his lawyers and decided not to sue; a strong and clear message that thoughts of libel were in the air. When the nervous *Bee* publisher asked his reporters to check out Chandler's charge, they discovered that the law mentioned in the article had been replaced by a superseding law. But the new law's language on the question of finder's fees was identical to the previous one. The error, to stretch the word, was highly technical.

With the exception of the *Bee*, listener-sponsored radio station KPFK Pacifica, and the alternative *San Francsico Bay Guardian* newspaper, coverage by the media was virtually nonexistent. Like most stock frauds, the GeoTek story was difficult to understand without detailed investigation and analysis. Most news media in California looked to the *Times* to provide leadership in such coverage. Though the *Times* carried a sufficient quantity of articles, they were mostly done in circumspect wire style, without any attempt to get to the substance of the issue.

Evelle Younger easily won reelection. Less than a month after the November 1974 race, the *Times* speculated about Younger's chances for a gubernatorial try in 1978.

5. The Trial

On May 17, 1973, after nearly two years of formal investigation, the SEC handed down civil indictments in the GeoTek case. Charges were filed against Jack and Bob Burke (Jack was charged with various counts of fraud and conspiracy to commit fraud); the GeoTek lawyers and treasurer of the firm; the company's accountants, Arthur Young and Company; and Otis Chandler. Chandler's charges were based on several violations of federal securities law, including failure to notify and file information to the SEC under its disclosure requirements.

As the SEC indictments were civil charges, no criminal penalties were involved. The SEC requested an injunction—a legal admonition against all the indictees not to break the securities law again. "Though injunctions only technically prohibit further illegal activities," SEC regional administrator Gerald Boeltz commented, "they can hamper a person trying to reenter the securities industry." More important, a guilty verdict in an SEC indictment reflected on a person's standing, particularly if the executive was in an area of public visibility. The impact of indictment and prosecution, with all the attendant press coverage and publicity, could be substantial.

"What is going to determine the ultimate thing," business executive and family friend Ernest Loebbecke noted, summarizing the concern and questions of many of Chandler's friends and establishment associates, "is whether or not Otis' position when this lawsuit is over is upheld or whether it develops a Watergate type of thing that he knew Burke was doing a shady deal. . . . If it comes out that he did know then I think it could be damaging to Otis in his position as publisher of the paper."

The civil indictments also foreshadowed possible criminal charges. "The standard practice," according to SEC coordinator Boeltz, "is for the SEC to make recommendations on who is to be prosecuted." In the case of GeoTek, those recommendations were forwarded to the U.S. attorney's office in San Francisco in the summer and fall of 1973. For a number of months, the SEC sent memos, set up conferences, and made its findings available to the U.S. attorney, Nixon appointee James Browning. Finally, in November 1973, just before the statute of limitations ran out, a federal grand jury was impaneled to look into the matter.

When Chandler was called before the grand jury in early 1974, he was asked about Burke's 1972 telephone call, when the GeoTek president revealed his troubles. But Chandler was not asked about the finder's fees, the promotional stock, or any of the other activities with possible criminal implications. The U.S. attorney's failure to delve into those subjects was so clear-cut that grand jurors later stated that they were unaware that Chandler was even considered as a possible candidate for indictment. SEC investigators were furious that the criminal statutes corresponding to the civil charges had not been used. Failure to inform the buyer of the existence of a finder's fee, for example, is a violation of Section 17A of the Federal Securities Law. Nearly identical statutes exist in California law. The SEC staff had been convinced of the futility of expecting state prosecutions under Evelle Younger, but the attitude of the U.S. attorney's office surprised them. When indictments were handed down in March 1974, they were limited to Jack and Bob Burke and a few second-level officers of GeoTek. Otis Chandler was to be a witness for the prosecution.

The criminal case against Jack Burke seemed cut and dried. Burke's brother Robert agreed to turn state's evidence and testify about the juggling of funds—almost $30 million had been invested—and the use of the dummy corporations. Otis Chandler testified early in the trial, stating that he was "shocked and terribly upset" when Burke called him up in February 1972 and told him of some of his financial manipulations. "I told him," Chandler testified, "this was a terrible blow and that I didn't know what the future held for our business relationship or for our personal relationship." Burke's attorney, John MacInnis, treated the *Times* publisher gingerly and failed to probe into any matters of substance concerning Chandler's own activities. All three parties—prosecutor, defense attorney, and judge—demonstrated considerable respect and cordiality for the *Times* publisher.

Toward the end of Burke's trial the U.S. attorney's office, which had presented its case poorly, presented a compromise proposal: of the sixteen counts against Burke, the prosecutor agreed to drop fifteen if Burke pled guilty to the charge of filing false documents with the SEC. In early 1975 Burke was sentenced by U.S. District Judge William Sweigert—a one-time political advisor to Earl Warren with substantial ties to California Republican party circles dating back to the 1940s when Kyle Palmer held sway—to ten to thirty months. Burke served time and was released in the spring of 1976.

The SEC trial was tentatively scheduled for June 1975 in Sweigert's court. Chandler retained three lawyers from Gibson, Dunn and Crutcher, and another three from the powerful San Francisco firm of Sullivan, Jones and Archer. Senior Gibson, Dunn partner Robert Warren served as chief counsel. From the outset Warren attempted to narrow and restrict the SEC probe. Chandler's lawyers constantly criticized the SEC for political motivations; they protested when SEC lawyers attempted to subpoena Chandler's cash receipts journal, income tax records, and other financial information; and they introduced a pretrial motion to allow the defense to examine all SEC memoranda or internal documents on the case to locate possible prejudice or political motivation. Sweigert, who had become increasingly unsympathetic to the SEC arguments, ruled in favor of the Chandler motion.

By this point in the case, the local SEC lawyers and investigators had developed a bad case of paranoia. Chandler seemed everywhere: in his connections to Evelle Younger, the state Corporations Commission, U.S. attorneys, and district judges. But the SEC still had a strong case. The local team told journalists that they would go to trial and refuse to settle out of court, no matter what.

Chandler was enormously concerned about the consequences of the case. The Federal Communications Commission had already advised that Chandler could not participate in the management of a TV station that Times Mirror had purchased in Austin, Texas, until the GeoTek case was resolved. In the fall of 1974, the Gibson, Dunn lawyers informed the SEC that Chandler had resigned from all of his directorships—Union Bank, Pan American, the Associated Press, all except Times Mirror—implying good faith on the *Times* publisher's part.

After Sweigert ruled in favor of Chandler's motion to go through the

SEC files, some of the SEC higher-ups in Washington began to have second thoughts about continuing the case. Sweigert's ruling, the Washington officials told the local staff, was a terrible precedent for the SEC and could hamper future cases. Washington agreed to go as far as the appeals court on the motion and then take a second look.

The local SEC staff also received what they considered an "informal message" from the magistrate in the case, Judge Owen Woodruffe, who suggested that if the case against Chandler came to trial, the SEC would lose. The SEC staff interpreted the message as possible signals coming directly from Sweigert. When the appeals court ruled in Chandler's favor to allow his lawyers to review the SEC papers, the SEC, which for two years had insisted that it would follow the prosecution out to the very end, decided to settle out of court.

On March 17, 1975, Otis Chandler agreed to drop his motion in exchange for an SEC acknowledgement "that it did not and does not claim that Otis Chandler intentionally violated any securities law." The SEC/Chandler settlement put a halt to informal discussions within the State Assembly Judiciary Committee, which had tentatively explored the possibility of holding Watergate-type hearings into the entire affair. GeoTek ended up costing Chandler a lot more money that he got out of it, but he was effectively able with his enormous resources to prevent both civil and criminal prosecutions. Chandler's long personal nightmare was over.

But the GeoTek affair had taken its toll on the *Times*. Those reporters who read the *Wall Street Journal* and were less inclined to believe the in-house arguments were dismayed about the entire event. The affair undoubtedly undermined some of the prestige the paper had carefully built up over more than fifteen years, and politicians—themselves frequent *Times* targets—delighted in reminding *Times* reporters "What about Geo-Tek!" Most of the staff, though, supported the paper's coverage and were more than willing to believe Chandler's protestations of innocence and deception. "Why would he do that for a credit card?" was still the word.

Like much else concerning the *Los Angeles Times*, the issue largely died after the SEC settlement, and never received the kind of national exposure and attention that a similar issue at the *Washington Post* or *New York Times* might have received. Its most important effect in the end was the fact that it had no effect.

CHAPTER 34

Who Rules Los Angeles?

"I think the *Times* is the only thing in Los Angeles that brings cohesion to the entire area," Otis Chandler told the *Times* house organ in March 1975. "Even more than the mayor, the City Council, the Board of Supervisors. It is the only thing that tells you what is happening every day and what might happen. It is a tremendous force."

The new *Times* was less blatant than its ancestor in wielding that force. Rather than attempting to stand supreme, as it did in the era of Kyle Palmer and Carlton Williams, the *Times* shared with and complemented the various economic and political power centers in the region. Power, in its newer, more far-reaching and integrated forms, was becoming institutionalized.

1. Ruling the County

Until the early 1970s, the county Board of Supervisors, made up of five elected supervisors, each representing a different district within the county's vast geographical boundaries, worked closely and harmoniously with *Times* management. The board, with both administrative and legislative duties, controlled a budget of up to $3 billion a year. "The only equivalent of so much power concentrated in such a few hands in a local setting has been Daley's Chicago," one supervisor's assistant remarked.

As in Daley's Chicago, political favoritism, development schemes, and corruption among the supervisors, dubbed the "Five Little Kings," was widespread. Many of the commissions and agencies set up by the board were chaired by executives of the county's largest corporations, who were especially concerned with several county functions such as tax assessments and zoning decisions. Real estate speculators and promoters also successfully dealt with supervisors to get zoning changes and expand the perimeter of suburbanization.

The *Times* had its own interests as well. From the late 1950s through the 60s, the construction of the multi-million-dollar Music Center, with half the funds provided by a "lease-lease-back" arrangement with the county, was the single most important county project of concern to the *Times* and much of the business establishment. The supervisors gladly went along with the arrangement and held the assumption—until the advent of the new decade—that *Times* reporters would find county scandals and probes into supervisor decisions largely off limits.

By the early 1970s, *Times* political reporters assigned to county stories to supplement *Times* county reporter Ray Zeman's coverage smarted from criticisms of the *Times* taboo. The election of television newscaster Baxter Ward to the Board of Supervisors in 1972 helped open up some of those restricted areas.

Baxter Ward, a short, serious-looking man with a craggy face and a deep bass voice, began his Los Angeles career as a television broadcaster in the 1950s. Without any particular liberal or conservative ideology other than hostility to the big powers that ran the town, Ward developed a reputation as something of an anticorruption, antiestablishment character. No friend of the *Times*, he had attacked the Chavez Ravine development in the late fifties and provided an outlet for criticism of city hall reporter Carlton Williams.

When Ward announced his intentions to run against incumbent supervisor Warren Dorn, neither Dorn nor Dorn's conservative backers took Ward's effort seriously. Ward had already failed in an earlier political attempt, finishing third in the 1969 mayoralty race. But by 1972 a strong antiincumbent, antisupervisor sentiment had begun to build in Los Angeles County. Ward issued a series of charges against Dorn. Though the *Times* backed Dorn in both the primary and the general election, *Times* political reporter Bill Boyarsky gave ample space to the Ward charges. In a close election, Ward defeated the incumbent.

Within a few months, Ward put together an investigative staff of assistants to look into the myriad forms of county corruption. Ward's staff checked out incidents of favoritism and potential criminal activities in the sheriff's, D.A.'s, and county marshal's offices and conflicts of interest involving other supervisors.

The former television newscaster was adept at using the media to develop public awareness of his charges. In the face of hostile law enforcement agencies who were unwilling to initiate prosecutions around the investigations—which frequently centered on the law enforcement agencies themselves—Ward used his broadcast experience to present succinctly the substance of his charges. At first the *Times* covered the Ward charges; there was a six-to-eight month "honeymoon period," as Ward characterized it, when *Times* reporters maintained friendly ties, and the paper ran a favorable portrait of Ward's staff investigators. As the charges and conflicts between Ward and other county officials heated up, the *Times* appeared to move in to provide major coverage.

Ward's biggest fight was with the sheriff of Los Angeles County, Peter Pitchess. A former FBI agent and chief special agent for Richfield Oil Company, Pitchess, head of the sheriff's department since 1958, was one of the most powerful politicians in Southern California. Pitchess kept a low profile in office, receiving favorable press coverage and major financial backing from the most powerful businessmen in town. While in office, Pitchess invested in land deals with some of these business friends and became a wealthy man.

"I was close to them in earlier days," the sheriff remarked about the *Times*, "and I had personal relations with them." The *Times* endorsed Pitchess each election, even though the sheriff, an enthusiastic Goldwater backer in 1964, appeared to be far more conservative than the new, more liberal *Times*.

By the time Baxter Ward came to power, the sheriff, backed by the most powerful businessmen and a favorable press which helped him maintain his effective, low-profile image, had reached the pinnacle of his power. Baxter Ward and Peter Pitchess had never been allies. As a TV newscaster, Ward initiated live coverage of the hearings into the death of Ruben Salazar, killed by one of Pitchess's deputies. The hearings put Pitchess's department into the public spotlight for the first time, and attacks by citizen groups over the conduct of the office increased over the next several months.

Ward, as supervisor, was less interested in the community protests than in the possibility of corruption and conflict of interest. Ward's investigators began to piece together an informal substructure of power involving major business interests, large law firms who often brokered the deals, several of the supervisors, and the major county offices such as the district attorney and the sheriff. The interrelations were extensive: the most powerful corporate executives and lawyers, for example, were the major donors to the county officials' campaigns and ran the incumbents' finance committees and fund-raising efforts. Even those incumbents who ran without significant opposition, such as sheriff Pitchess in 1974, still received substantial contributions from the heads of the top corporate firms.

Ward's investigators' accidental discovery of a land swap involving the Southern Pacific Railroad and the West Hollywood sheriff's station led to an extensive probe of the sheriff's affairs, including research into the arrest and subsequent release and destruction of the arrest records of the daughter of a prominent public official. "Our efforts," Ward wrote the county grand jury, "have uncovered so many contradictions, demonstrably false statements and major investigative oversights that the suspicion that officials of both the Sheriff's Department and the District Attorney's Office have been involved in a conspiracy to obstruct justice is inescapable."

Ward's investigations into the sheriff's affairs snowballed by the fall of 1974, and *Times* reporters did a couple of follow-up investigations on their own, stemming from the Ward charges. The *Times* investigative team, headed by George Reasons, also began to look into the sheriff's financial affairs and extensive land holdings, a great deal of which had been acquired while in office. The paper had the workings of its most substantial investigative story since the Sam Yorty days.

Pitchess and his business allies besieged the *Times* with phone calls and visits. The sheriff told his former golf partner Bill Thomas that he wasn't exercising control "over this new breed of reporter." Otis and Thomas "just wouldn't accept responsibility for what was going on in their paper," the sheriff stormed, and his business allies began to put on the pressure.

Although the *Times* had largely kept its investigations off the front page—the display usually given a major *Times* expose—metropolitan editor Murphy had assigned the story on a continuous basis. Even that became a bit too extensive for editor Thomas, who asked Murphy whether he wasn't doing too much. At the height of the Ward corruption charges, the *Times* editors assigned Jerry Cohen, an old-timer with close ties to law enforcement circles, to do a Pitchess profile. " PITCHESS: HIGH MARKS AS SHERIFF," headlined the highly favorable Cohen story. "The sheriff's office under Pitchess' command has been afflicted by few scandals," Cohen noted, "and the few embarrassments that have occurred almost always have been revealed by the sheriff himself. The latter tactic has suggested to voters that he is a man able to clean his own house."

The *Times* investigations were terminated by the spring of 1975. "The decision to bury the story," one of the editors involved in the investigation remarked, "was a decision by Bill Thomas." Metropolitan editor Murphy told his reporters the probe was killed because "no crime was involved."

By 1976 the *Times* had made Ward their number one local enemy. When the supervisor proposed his "Sunset Coast" rapid transit line as a measure for the June 1976 ballot, the *Times*, which just two years earlier had supported Proposition A, another rail transit ballot initiative, blasted the Sunset Coast proposal. Although there were differences—Proposition

A would have exclusively served downtown via a Wilshire Boulevard subway—Ward's Sunset Coast system incorporated many of the earlier proposal's features. But the *Times*, through its news coverage and editorials, took after Ward's initiative in a tone reminiscent of an earlier era.

County government, following revelations about the sheriff's office, nursing home conditions, corruption in the county marshal's office, and scandal in the Public Administrator-Public Guardian Department, among others, was in turmoil. D.A. Busch identified the problem as a Ward-induced "government by accusation." In the fall of 1974, establishment circles began to try to pick up the pieces. "You mark my words," Asa Call exclaimed in a November 1974 interview, "within six months county government will begin to change." Several days later, County Bar association President Warren Christopher presented a proposal to the Haynes Foundation (whose board encompassed some of the leading members of the establishment). Christopher suggested that the foundation fund a commission to study Los Angeles county government to see if limited reform proposals, such as the creation of a county mayor and expansion of the number of supervisors, might alleviate the crisis situation. The Haynes group agreed, and on February 20, 1975, announced—with front page coverage and a lead editorial in the *Times* —the creation of a Public Commission on County Government.

Although the *Times* had opposed reforms in the past, it gave the commission its unqualified support, with frequent and favorable news stories and strong editorial backing. Commission staff met constantly with *Times* reporters and editorial writers, going over, in great detail, the points the commission wanted to emphasize.

When the commission issued its report, which included the two reforms, Baxter Ward, now in the ironic position of defending the old "Five Little Kings" system, became the commission's strongest attacker. "The establishment is still as strong as ever," Ward complained, linking the commission to the establishment's attempt to maintain hegemony in the county.

The commission's reform proposals, placed on the November 1976 ballot, left Angelenos with the choice of a corrupt and dysfunctional status quo versus a limited reform that did little to make decision-making structures more accessible to the community. The proposal lost by a wide margin.

"Out of my experience," one of Ward's investigators remarked, "I'd say there were three powers in the county. First, there are the Asa Call types, the fat cats. Then there's the group that for years centered around the sheriff, the D.A. and some of the supervisors. They're the second power. And then there's the *Times*, off in its own corner, occasionally flexing its muscles, but never really acting in opposition to the others. Together those forces for years ran county government; and," the staffer paused, "as much as I hate to say it, they still do."

2. Running the City

City Councilman Tom Bradley, in his second bid for mayor of Los Angeles, had a better strategy. He hired a new public relations firm, kept a low profile on his candidacy, and often referred to his twenty-year history on the police force. Sam Yorty backers assumed that Tom Bradley had become a *Los Angeles Times* man and an instrument in the paper's quest to get back in to city hall. But it wasn't the *Times* but the mayor himself who was responsible for Bradley's success.

The Occidental Oil controversy was the first thorn in Yorty's attempt to win a fourth term as mayor. The large oil company had wanted to acquire land from the city through a land swap, and, despite resistance from local residents, Yorty favored the deal. Opponents discovered and publicized the fact that Occidental president Armand Hammer had given Yorty a $10,000 gift in the form of a shrine for the mayor's deceased mother in Ireland and that Occidental had supplied its corporate aircraft for Yorty campaign trips in 1970 and 1972, as well as private trips.

Second, Yorty's famous jaunts out of the city rankled many Los Angeles voters, and the *Times* was quick to use the issue with headlines such as: OUT OF TOWN 372 DAYS IN 43 MONTHS, YORTY REVEALS.

The *Times*, though, didn't take after the mayor with quite the same editorial crusading spirit it had brought to the 1969 election. "I think they realized they violated an old saying by Confucious: 'Never heat the furnace of your adversary so hot that you singe yourself,'" Yorty explained. "And I think they realized they'd overdone it in '69 and they modified a little in '73. And used their news columns more to hurt me."

By 1973 the right-wing pseudopopulism tactics of racism and anticommunism no longer produced the instant response from an alienated white lower-middle-class constituency. Nixon was in trouble in Washington, Reagan was a lame duck governor in Sacramento, and Sam Yorty, in his twenty-first campaign, was on his way out. Yorty challenger Tom Bradley rolled up 55 percent of the vote and became the most powerful black politician in America.

The new mayor came to power with significant support among liberal, proenvironmental, and minority constituencies, and many of Bradley's initial commission appointments reflected those interests. Bradley's forces had pulled together the most substantial progressive coalition in the city since the 1938 recall. A strong hope developed among those progressive friends and backers that a new spirit would emanate out of city hall.

The business establishment was not necessarily hostile to the new mayor. Although most of the downtown business forces had backed Yorty for his fourth term, many, such as Neil Petree, felt that the dispute with the *Times* and the continuing story of corruption might have impaired Yorty's ability to function effectively. As Bradley seemed receptive to business, the ties quickly developed. Two senior corporate executives, one from the Security Bank and the other from Prudential Life Insurance, were "loaned" to the city administration for $1 a year to advise on economic matters, and several ad hoc committees outside the formal commission arrangements were set up to advise and set policy on substantial matters.

Of the myriad interconnected problems that faced the new Bradley administration, the issue of most concern to the large corporations and the *Times* was the question of downtown development, an issue that had preoccupied the local establishment since the days of the Greater Los Angeles Plans Inc. and the Bunker Hill fight.

Major downtown expansion following the eviction of the nearly 6,000 residents of Bunker Hill in the 1960s included the construction of large, plush skyscrapers—the ARCO Towers, the United California Bank building, the Security Pacific complex, and the upper-class residential Bunker Hill Towers—as well as the Music Center. To make way for the new buildings, the bulldozers pushed Los Angeles's poor ethnic neighborhoods outside the downtown rim: Chicano to the west and north, Asian to the northeast, black to the south of downtown. The Community Redevelopment Agency (CRA), chaired since its inception by corporate allies, served as the instrument for all this redevelopment. The CRA, which had the power to condemn existing neighborhoods and spend money and formulate plans at its own discretion, worked in tandem with downtown's business objectives.

But downtown, in spite of its facelift, was, as *Forbes* magazine put it, "an artificial heart." The new skyscrapers were not filled with tenants, business and residential patterns were still decentralized, and the upper-class apartment boxes were not renting.

In the late 1960s, the downtown businessmen's association, renamed the Central City Association (CCA), decided, after a series of discussions initiated by Franklin Murphy, to once again actively involve itself in the planning and development of downtown Los Angeles. William J. Bird, vice-president of Kaiser Industries, was selected to head up the new CCA-organized Committee for Central City Planning (CCCP) Inc. Composed of twenty-two executives from the largest downtown businesses, the CCCP read like a who's who of business power in Los Angeles. It included the top executives of the major department stores (Silverwoods, J. W. Robinson, Bullock's, and Broadway-Hale); banks (Security Pacific, UCB, Union, Bank of America, and Crocker); insurance companies (Pacific Mutual Life Insurance, Prudential, and Occidental); oil companies (ARCO and Standard Oil); the phone and gas companies; downtown corporations (Dillingham, Neil Petree's Barker Brothers, and Kaiser Industries); and Franklin Murphy of Times Mirror.

In 1969, with the encouragement of the Yorty administration and the help of City Councilman Gilbert Lindsay, the CCA/CCCP convinced the city council to grant a $250,000 matching fund (the other $250,000 to be raised by the CCA) to initiate a planning study for downtown, with CCCP supervising the preparation of the plan.

The city politicians, many desirous of *Times* support and unwilling to offend the major business powers in the city, okayed the extraordinary arrangement, despite the obvious conflict of interest. According to CCCP chairman Bird, the twenty-two businessmen in the group were the most logical group to work on the plan because, as Bird put it, they "have the most to gain."

In April 1972 the plan, entitled "Central City Los Angeles: 1972–1990" was completed and ceremoniously presented at the Dorothy Chandler Pavillion of the Music Center. The 113–page document presented a highly detailed sketch of the type of development envisioned by the downtown businessmen.

To finance the plan, the CCCP forces advocated a "tax increment" method. Under such a system of funding, a portion of the county's tax revenues would be diverted to the CRA for use within the redevelopment area. The tax base within the redeveloped area—in this case, downtown—would be frozen; the county would only receive the tax revenue based on the assessed value of the property as of the date the project was created. Any taxes generated by increases in property values would go directly to the CRA to fund the redevelopment. Since the basic purpose of such redevelopment would be to upgrade property within the plan area, it would be a virtual certainty that substantial increases in property values would occur. This method would deprive the city and county, whose operating expenses would continue to rise, of the increase in revenue for such things as schools and hospitals, and therefore that burden would have to be shifted onto the rest of the taxpayers.

Opponents of the plan called it a "tax ripoff" to subsidize downtown interests at the expense of the overall region, but defenders of redevelopment insisted that help for downtown was help for everyone.

The *Times,* in editorial and news coverage, gave the downtown plan its strongest backing. "Any city—and especially a city as spread out as Los Angeles—is as healthy as the sum of its parts," the *Times* editorialized in the summer of 1975. "This is one reason why downtown redevelopment must go forward."

Times management assigned urban troubleshooter Ray Hebert to cover the downtown story. Herbert, who had followed the redevelopment issue from the 1950s, had given extensive and favorable coverage when the CCA unveiled its initial efforts in 1969. The issue heated up in the summer of 1975, as Hebert continued to cover the story from a proplan bias. When the Board of Supervisors held hearings on the plan, complete with critical testimony from the tax assessor, Hebert failed to provide coverage. When the supervisors decided to join a legal suit blocking the plan, a short squib appeared back on page 28 of the paper—two days after the action had occurred.

Staffer John Pastier's troubles at the *Times* might have had some relation to the paper's downtown interests and its position on the plan. The architecture critic wrote a piece critical of the downtown plan in 1972, one month after the CCA plan was released but before it had received any significant public scruitny. After the story ran, Pastier recalled, editorial page editor Tony Day informed Pastier that Franklin Murphy had sent a critical memo on the piece. "Pastier had a deadly combination," a *Times* writer commented. "He could analyze the urban planning aspect of the redevelopment story, but he also had the ability to understand the economics of it. He was clearly a threat to the downtown powers."

The *Times*—and Times Mirror Company—were part of that downtown power. Franklin Murphy sat on the executive committee of the CCCP, Times ad manager Vance Stickell was on the CCA Board of Directors, and Times Mirror and the Chandler family had substantial downtown real estate holdings. According to the conservative figures of the tax assessor's office, Times Mirror alone had $63.2 million worth of holdings in a concentrated downtown area within the scope of the downtown plan.

As the only major newspaper in the region, the *Times* was the primary medium capable of providing in-depth coverage and analysis of the plan. Yet through its holdings and the activities of its corporate executives, a major conflict of interest existed—a conflict fully borne out by editorial backing, news coverage, and staff shake-ups. As critics of the plan began to focus on the *Times*, the paper replied with an editorial asserting that "The *Times* has long supported the downtown plan. Redevelopment will not give this newspaper or its parent company—or anyone else—one cent of the tax advantage."

Times sensitivities increased when conservative Democrat Allen Robbins made indications of challenging Tom Bradley in 1977 and threatened to use the issue of the "downtown machine" that Sam Yorty had once made popular. Robbins and others began to inquire into *Times* coverage and *Times* holdings; but the attacks did not hold back the paper. The

Times and the united business community went all out in support of the mayor, who won reelection with about 60 percent of the vote.

Although the city council approved the plan in the summer of 1975, it continued to receive widespread criticism. After Bradley and the council created a blue-ribbon advisory committee to review the plan to help offset the attacks, the *Times* called for the critics to "cool it." Popular mistrust of the plan prevailed, the paper implied, because the project was complicated, and therefore easily misunderstood and distorted. But for CCA executive director Dan Waters, the question was relatively simple: would government maintain its current "partnership" with business, or would it become a hostile, antibusiness force?

Many former Bradley backers began to develop strong reservations about the mayor's new allies. Bradley had not only fully supported the downtown plan, but had made a strong embrace of the entire business establishment. In the years between 1974 and 1976, executives from Los Angeles's major corporations—who had given little financial support to earlier Bradley campaigns—became Bradley's largest financial donors to help absorb the considerable debt the mayor had accumulated from the '73 campaign. A major fund-raising dinner held for Bradley in 1975 was co-hosted by Asa Call and MCA business executive Lew Wasserman. Former Yorty campaign manager Henry Salvatori contributed $1500 to Bradley's reelection in 1977 to add to the thousands given by right-wing business types. "The morality of so many conservative business leaders seems to melt when money comes into the picture," a right-wing anti-*Times* public official declared. "Whoever becomes mayor, even though they hated him and fought against him, all of a sudden they exploit him and use him and join him."

In 1975 the mayor lined up with ARCO, the *Los Angeles Times*, and the business-oriented managers of the Department of Water and Power against a utility reform coalition. The reformers wanted to reverse the current utility rates under which large energy users, such as big corporations paid lower rates. The reform proposal, which aimed to conserve energy and aid low-income consumers by charging them lower rates, directly affected the *Times*, the twenty-first-largest user in Southern California. If the *Times* paid the rates charged individual consumers, it would have to pay approximately $720,000 more a year.

The mayor influenced his liberal backers on the city council to vote the coalition's rate reversal proposal down. In July 1975, while hearings on the utilities rate structure were under way before the Public Utilities Commission, the *Times* editorialized—under the heading UTILITIES: NO PLACE FOR WELFARE—against the utility reform.

Midway through Bradley's term, J. Paul Getty offered to donate his huge house in the exclusive Hancock Park section of town—not far from where Dorothy Chandler lived—to the city to be used as the mayor's residence. The building symbolized the mayor's move up into a previously denied exclusive social world. The *Times* strongly supported the move. The old Los Angeles slogan that once in office, even the most critical challenger will make his peace with the powers that be—a truism valid for Sam Yorty—had become Tom Bradley's truth as well.

3. Controlling the Police

In the northeastern edge of downtown Los Angeles, a block and a half away from the *Times* Building, stands a tall, massive glass structure— "The Glass House," some call it—which is the home of the Los Angeles Police Department. Inside the office of Police Chief Ed Davis are his plaques, mementos, and carefully arranged magazines, including the right-wing publication *American Opinion.*

From the outset of his appointment in 1969, the conservative Davis, a former lobbyist for the police organization, had a complex and turbulent relationship with the *Times* and its management. Davis was a frequent guest at *Times* luncheons. "Oh, I'd have lunch with Otis every three or four months with his editorial board," Davis noted, complaining that "the trouble with Otis is that he'd never let you finish a meal. He serves the best meals. . . . But he makes you start working from your salad right on. He'll sit there and eat, and the rest of them will eat, and they'll say 'Right Ed, what do you think of this, what do you think of that,' and you'll never get the chance to finish anything."

But divisions between the *Times* and the chief existed, too. *Times* reporters, often caught in the middle of conflicts between the police and the black, brown, and student communities, more and more began to view clashes involving the LAPD from the point of view of the victim.

The chief viewed the paper's shift in news and editorial perspective as intolerable. Davis, a classic Southern California rightist, was strongly opposed to the *Times*'s liberal positions on social questions such as reduced penalties for marijuana, hand gun control, and support on civil liberties positions. His politics were cast in the mold of anticommunism and the Cold War, compounded by a measure of antagonism toward wealthy liberals. He was the little guy who had worked his way through the ranks in conflict with the head of a fourth-generation family who had been handed his power through family succession. Davis described Chandler as a rich boy out of touch, aloof and incapable of really understanding the environment around him. "He's used to the raw use of power, almost the abrasive use of power. . . . I hate to say Father forgive him for he knows not what he's doing—but in effect that's the way it is, because he's out of touch with mankind. Yet he has this terrible power."

Although *Times* police reporter Bill Hazlett, who was criticized by several *Times* reporters as "more cop than reporter," worked well with and was frequently praised by the chief, Davis was convinced that the *Times* was out to get him through its news columns. After Bradley took office, *Times* editors sent in a couple of outside reporters to cover certain police activities above and beyond Hazlett's routine coverage. In 1975 *Times* management assigned political reporter Ken Reich, whom Davis called "a full-time hit man," to cover the chief.

Davis developed a perspective that the way to survive in Los Angeles politically was to develop an independent political base, to be free of the need for the support, or at least the neutrality, of the *Los Angeles Times*. As the *Times* attacks on the chief increased, Davis created a media strategy that he hoped might feed off the popular resentment of the *Times*. He became a media celebrity, holding raucous press conferences and developing catchy one-line remarks, such as "Bar your doors, buy a police dog, call us when we're available and pray" and "Now is the time to prevent letting swimming-pool Communists and sophisticated Bolsheviks who have worked this sort of thing around the world, who always avoid arrest, from making victims of Mexican-Americans as prison fodder." Davis's humorous media performances were designed to bypass the influential *Times* by talking directly to his audience through television, magazine profiles, or even the wires.

The strategy worked. Although the Bradley administration was hostile to the chief and his tough law-and-order stance, it felt politically incapable of dumping him for fear of popular outcry. Although he generally steered clear of political endorsements, Davis cultivated relationships with Bradley opponents, such as conservative Allen Robbins. The chief kept his own counsel on politics and concentrated on taking after the *Times* and its social liberalism. In the fall of 1975, he sent a letter to the editor, canceling his *Times* subscription and accusing the paper of "constantly attempting to condition us to a dramatic new set of moral values, as is well attested to through the assigned staff reports, the articles you print and your strong editorial support of homosexuality, marijuana, and many many other forms of behavior recently proscribed in our country. You are the Paul Revere of the oncoming avalanche of libertine behavior. . . . The soul of your paper." Davis concluded, "is sick."

The Davis attacks, however, were a perfect foil for the *Times* management. With the increasing criticism of the cozy *Times* relationship with the Bradley administration and the conflict of interest over the downtown plan, the paper could point to its fight with the police chief as an example of how it was a hard-hitting news medium which took on powerful public officials. Reminiscent, in many ways, of the fight with Yorty, Davis used every opportunity to chip away at the *Times*, to cultivate what he considered to be a David and Goliath situation.

Although Davis represented many of the attitudes of the disenfranchised right, appearing, for example, as a guest speaker at a John Birch Society function, he also had a fair share of power. He had every opportunity to test out his anticoddling thesis, and the LAPD became as controversial and despised in the ghettos and on campuses as in the days of Bill Parker. The "Crazy Ed" designation, from *Rolling Stone,* took on a double meaning: "Crazy Ed," the controversial media star, and "Crazy Ed," whose officers came in shooting first and asked questions later.

Davis did not cultivate relations with corporate executives and the downtown elite to the same extent as some of his counterparts, like Sheriff Pitchess. He was incapable of reconciling the marriage of the liberals inside the Bradley administration—"all kinds of ideological freaks out on the left," Davis characterized them—with the conservative business establishment. The *Los Angeles Times,* according to the chief, was the most extreme example of that type of self-serving establishment interest.

The *Times*/Davis war ultimately was a battle in the political and media arenas, rather than a conflict over Davis's police performance. "Ed Davis," Chandler said in a television interview "is a good cop." Standing outside the war were those people in the community—the victims—who were still looking for the redress of their grievances.

4. From the Family to the Corporation

Power was passing into new hands. By the 1960s the Asa Calls and the Chandlers began to be eclipsed, not by other individuals, but by entities such as ARCO, the Times Mirror Company, and Standard of California. Like the transition from Harry Chandler's family empire to the corporate power of Norman and Otis's Times Mirror Company, the shape of power in Los Angeles changed from the family and its representatives to the corporation and its executives. The corporation of 1970s America, with vast resources at its disposal and the ability to influence its market as well as people's minds, had become the single most widespread and important individual unit of power. Corporations advertised messages, contributed to political campaigns, and acquired property. Corporate executives became cabinet officers and other high government officials, sat on private foundations and commissions, supported candidates, and exercised local power in their role as media-identified "civic leaders." Corporations drafted individual executives to serve in "civic" matters.

* * *

538

THE TIMES MIRROR BOARD OF DIRECTORS

NAME	OFFICER	OTHER DIRECTORSHIPS
Franklin Murphy	Times Mirror Kress Foundation	Bank of America Ford Motor Company Norton Simon Inc. Hallmark Cards
Otis Chandler Milton H. Day	Times Mirror Newsday Inc. Times Mirror	American Newspaper Publishing Co. Orange Coast Publishing Co. Times Herald Printing Co.
Robert Erburu	Times Mirror Pfaffinger Foundation Times Mirror Foundation	Unionamerica Inc. YMCA of Metropolitan Los Angeles U.S. Chamber of Commerce
Gwendolyn Garland Babcock (Chandler family)	W.M. Garland & Co.	
Warren B. Williamson (Chandler family)	Crowell, Weedon & Co.	
Walter B. Gerken	Pacific Mutual Life Insurance Company	
James W. Aston	Republic National Bank Republic of Texas Corp.	American Airlines Lone Star Steel *Dallas Times Herald* Neuhoff Brothers Packers Hoblitzelle Foundation General Portland Inc. Group Hospital Service
Peter Bing	Bing Foundation	
Albert V. Casey	American Airlines Pacific American Income	Bank of California Shares Inc. CIT Financial Pacific Insurance Corp. YMCA of Metropolitan Los Angeles
James F. Chambers	Times Herald Printing Co. Scottish Hospital	Republic National Bank Republic of Texas Corp. Associated Press Hart, Schaffner & Marx Dallas Symphony Orchestra Presbyterian Hospital of Dallas
F. Daniel Frost	Gibson, Dunn & Crutcher (law firm)	Avery Products Tejon Ranch Ralph M. Parsons Co. Rohr Corp.
Simon Ramo	TRW	Union Bancorp.

The establishment doesn't care about political parties; what they care about is performance," Baxter Ward remarked, as the once rock-ribbed Republican Southern California ruling group learned to accommodate Democrats in power. The corporations didn't take chances. The Southern California based Northrop Corporation, for example, funded both Democrats and Republicans. Northrop also gave out the services of its corporate aircraft (for Ronald Reagan, among others) and its company hunting lodge; it eventually developed a secret fund of nearly a third of a million dollars to disburse to various candidates.

Corporate executives have been connected to all aspects of local activities. In 1976, for example, Times Mirror's Franklin Murphy and ad manager Vance Stickell were involved in the downtown Central City Association; group vice-president Charles Schneider was a director of the Music Center Operating Committee and president of the board of governors of Buff's Performing Arts Council; Franklin Murphy sat on the United Crusade Corporate Campaign team and on the board of trustees of the Los Angeles County Art Museum; *Times* business manager Robert Nelson was chairman of the Los Angeles Better Business Bureau; Times Mirror president Robert Erburu had a position on the Los Angeles Committee of Foreign Relations and was a director of the metropolitan Los Angeles YMCA; and so on. The corporate talent pool became the "larger pool" that Title Insurance's Ernst Loebbecke saw as necessary to maintain leadership and power in an expanding region.

The *Los Angeles Times*, the Chandler family, and the Times Mirror Company are today a unit of power within several centers of power in the Southern California region. That power is institutionalized and complex; it's no longer a simple case of a phone call and a round of golf to get things done. The phone calls and the golf games still exist—and still lead to decisions—but there is also an entire infrastructure of boards and commissions and organizations. The faces of those who rule Los Angeles have changed, but the corporate names and the interests concerned have remained the same. And on everybody's list of power is a Chandler—or a Murphy—or an Erburu, or a . . .

"Thinking Big": A Conclusion

"We like to talk of big things in Southern California, just as we like to do big things," Norman Chandler wrote on the occasion of the *Los Angeles Times*'s seventy-eighth anniversary in 1959. "Doing things the big way has always been the Southern California way—the big things the *Times* has helped you do in the past, such as bringing water to the city from the Owens River and winning the fight for a free harbor at San Pedro, the greatest manmade harbor in the world. And the big things that you will do in the future to solve our smog problem, our water problem, our rubbish and sewer problems. This is going to be the greatest state in the Union. And Los Angeles, we believe, is going to be its greatest city. All of us have to plan on the big scale, as we always have."

That message was the same for four generations of *Times* publishers. Harrison Gray Otis, Harry Chandler, Norman Chandler, and Otis Chandler had each seen their dreams for Los Angeles's expansion realized. General Otis's influence took shape with the first great real estate booms as he profited, with his son-in-law, from the subdivisions around Los Angeles. Harry Chandler, whose economic fortunes were based on those real estate developments, went on to direct and benefit from the business boom of the 1920s. Norman Chandler witnessed the population explosion and industrial development after World War II. And Otis Chandler came to power during the last period of expansion in the prosperous days of Vietnam and the Great Society.

As Southern California spread, tearing up the land, terracing the mountains, moving rivers hundreds of miles, and transforming farmland into tract houses, an enormous number of new problems—"big" problems,

541

the *Times* admitted—emerged. Pollution crept over the basin, a condition that many experts attributed to the growth matrix of the region; the subdivisions in the hills created annual quick-spreading brush fires and mudslides; and freeway congestion awaited commuters forced to take automobiles in the face of a deteriorating rapid transit system.

Despite the problems, Otis Chandler's new *Los Angeles Times* continued the "thinking big" philosophy. The new *Times* continued to be, since the days of Harrison Gray Otis, the thickest paper in the world, with more newsprint consumed—300,000 tons plus a year—than any of its big East Coast counterparts.

The new *Times* described growth's consequences but applauded the growth cycle, taking full-page ads for the latest subdivision scheme while adopting a modern-sounding editorial judgment in favor of limited controls. Yet even that modern perspective was tempered by the paper's hostility to any essential challenge to the oil/energy/growth combines.

William Mullholland's vision, William May Garland's projection of the great population boom, and the *Los Angeles Times* Midwinter all shared the notion that nature—and people—could be manipulated and redefined in the interest of profit and growth. That was essentially the American dream, and Los Angeles became the foremost American city fulfilling the country's expectations and fantasies. "A modern Canaan, a land flowing with milk and honey," the *Times* had called it. Los Angeles became the first city where the new settlements were almost entirely American. "Los Angeles, it should be understood, is not a mere city," Morrow Mayo wrote forty years ago. "On the contrary, it is, and has been since 1888, a commodity; something to be advertised and sold to the people of the United States like automobiles, cigarettes, and mouth washes."

The booms and promotions led Angelenos always to look forward to the future: the past had no identity except as a contrast for future things to come. There was no real continuity, no traditions; in the apparently free and open social setting, the new immigrants dreamed of making it big. "I do not mean to say that everybody in Southern California is rich— but everybody expects to be rich tomorrow," Charles Dudley Warner wrote of the city.

Even up to 1960, the census reported, Angelenos who lived in their city for less than five years far outnumbered the more settled residents. Southern California became a land without roots, a land of future expectations, as each new generation of immigrants moved in unaware of the struggles of those who came before.

There had been many struggles in the region, struggles that went to the heart of regional identity. Socialists and trade unionists had fought against the link between boosterism, the open shop, and water-feeding-growth policies; EPIC had protested the system of idle factories and fallow land while people went hungry; Asians, Mexicans, and blacks wondered why this city could not be considered theirs; movements of the 1960s challenged the crux of the growth/profits relationship and called for a different and more equal quality of life in Los Angeles, in America, and the world.

The *Times*—adopting the eagle as its symbol, as it celebrated the American chauvinism of Los Angeles—fought against those who challenged its influence and control over information in the region. But the *Times* of General Otis ànd the Chandlers defeated its opponents and continued projecting its labor policies and racial appeals—an ideology of Americanism based on the twin symbols of business and the boom. Under a multitude of banners—the Better America Federation, the American Plan, the "White Spot" of America—the Chandler-sponsored identities helped shape Los Angeles for many years.

The *Times* provided the primary "historical" identity for Los Angeles—the continuity of wealth and power—as the "class paper" most responsible for the establishment's point of view. The *Times* was always conscious of its history, filled with anniversary issues, special series on the fight for the open shop or the quest for new water supplies, and defining the *Times* and Los Angeles as intertwinable parts. It asked rhetorically in its seventy-fifth anniversary edition: "Has any newspaper ever played a greater role in the development of a region?" "To tell the story of Southern California is to tell the story of the *Times*," the paper proudly proclaimed. "The two fit like pages in a book."

The *Times* of today continues that tradition, its new methods in tune to a changing world. "It's not that the *Times* uses its power blatantly all the time," one reporter said of his paper. "But it's so big, and its monopoly influence is so widespread, that the power is working at all times. It's like a big clumsy oaf who is constantly brushing into things and knocking them over."

Newspapers often gave definition to their communities' and the country's dominant ideologies. The development of the monopoly press, tied to the larger world of business through its corporate parents, is now complete: no new major metropolitan daily has been initiated in the last twenty-five years, and existing operations have been centralized in fewer and fewer hands.

Like the corporation itself, the modern newspaper is under attack for its composition, operation, and objectives. That attack takes on several forms: from Third World and women's groups that complain of the white male middle-class bias and employee practices; from the range of radical and citizen's groups that criticize the establishment, probusiness bias of the media; to the journalists themselves, who develop alternative notions of performance and goals, sometimes in contradiction to the goals of the owners.

In turn, the monopoly press in the 1970s has developed new methods of control in the newsroom and a different, nonpartisan image of itself in the social and political arena. The battles are the same, although some of the individuals have become institutionalized.

"It all comes together in the *Times*," the paper's latest promotional slogan notes. It does come together: the definition of Southern California history; the control of Los Angeles; the future of journalism.

Like Los Angeles, the paper is troubled, trying to shake off an uneasy feeling that things are somehow out of control. The booster ethic, it seems, has run its course. The Bill Thomas/Otis Chandler *Los Angeles Times* can be interpreted as a holding action, a transitional team that complements the transitional mood of the 1970s. As one reporter remarked, "They might rule Los Angeles, but do they have complete control over it?" It comes down to a question of power, and power is what the *Times* has always been about.

That power is rooted in four generations. Its origins go back to the old days when old man Otis and his shrewd young son-in-law saw the way to make a buck by boosting, expanding, subdividing, annexing, boosting, expanding, and on and on. Beneath that *Times*-defined history of power lies a half-hidden opposition that dates back to the days when Socialists cried out against the real estate conspiracy that was engulfing their city. That opposition has periodically reached the hearts and minds of the residents of Los Angeles and today has the capacity to link up with the writers and workers at the *Times* itself.

"History is a nightmare," James Joyce wrote. But history is also an awakening, an awareness of roots and the real conflicts that few have learned to integrate as part of their lives. History derives its power from those who have learned to use it. As Angelenos attempt to redefine their city, they learn to see and recognize their past. The present is history, and the future awaits history's battles.

A Note on Our Methods

"A serious writer who seriously undertakes an unauthorized book-length study of a corporation is probably slightly mad," financial writer John Brooks once remarked. We began such an undertaking on the *Los Angeles Times*, the Chandlers, and the Times-Mirror Company nearly five years ago.

The "we" in those first months was a group of about a dozen journalists, photographers, and other people who had toyed with the idea of establishing a new alternative newspaper in Los Angeles. Our shared interests eventually led some of us to look into the history, influence, and present status of the number one newspaper in the state and its powerful owners. Although just two of us pursued the idea to its final form, we had invaluable help from a number of people, particularly: Eleanor Osgood who did the research and legwork for the "All for San Pedro" chapter and other related material; and Marilyn Good, who did the research and writing on the *Dallas Times Herald* and *Times-Mirror*'s other Texas properties.

A great deal of our research combined methods that are commonly described as "investigative" with the more traditional approach of the historian combing through existing archival and other primary and secondary sources. The scope of our subject was incredibly vast.

Our investigative efforts carried us to County Recorder's Grantor/Grantee Indexes (for property transactions), the tax assessor's rolls, the Superior and Federal Courts, the Probate Index, and other governmental agencies such as the Securities and Exchange Commission and the California Division of Corporations.

Our historical research took us to presidential papers, newspapers, several foundations and special collections throughout California, as well as to the federal government files in the National Archives in Washington, D.C. We were also aided by several people and organizations which offered us their own scrapbooks and private collections of letters, clippings, and other material.

We interviewed over three hundred people, including *Times* reporters and editors; Chandler associates, friends, and a few family members; Times Mirror officials; former governors, mayors, and other politicians; businessmen; and other direct participants. We also attempted to set up a cooperative relationship with the Chandlers and Times Mirror. Unfortunately, as most "unauthorized" historians and journalists have discovered, cooperation by those who are not used to public exposure is rarely granted if the subject of the research fears any possibility of criticism. Otis Chandler, Franklin Murphy, and other high corporate officials refused to be interviewed and denied us access to the *Times* morgue, which has been generally available to researchers and other journalists.

The deeper we got into the research, the more our methods and our subject matter tended to blend. We began to integrate "journalism" methods into our historical research and analysis, and "history" into the descriptions of the state of journalism and the nature of power in Los Angeles today.

Our special thanks go to Dr. Oral Hendricks and the staff of the Sherman Foundation; the Special Collections and Public Affairs Libraries at UCLA; Patricia Palmer and the Manuscripts Division at Stanford University; the Bancroft Library at Berkeley; the Huntington Library; the central branch of the Los Angeles Public Library; the National Archives, particularly the staff of the Records of the Department of Justice; the archives at the Los Angeles Chamber of Commerce; the Los Angeles Typographical Union Local #174; the Social Science Research Library in Los Angeles; Title Insurance and Trust Company; the County Recorder's Office in Los Angeles and Imperial County; the Federal Records Center of Southern California; the Los Angeles County Clerk's Office; and the Los Angeles and San Francisco offices of the Securities and Exchange Commission.

We would also like to thank Howard Bray and the Fund for Investigative Journalism for their invaluable research grant, our friends and colleagues who shared our vision and encouraged our efforts, and those inside and outside the *Times* whose help was crucial to the whole undertaking.

We began this project with the idea that Los Angeles—and every other city in the country—needed an alternative newspaper and alternative sources of information. Five years later we feel even stronger that such an alternative is needed. We hope this book begins to provide a view of history, journalism, and power that makes that possibility more accessible. Information, as four generations of *Los Angeles Times* owners have understood, is power.

BIBLIOGRAPHY

This bibliography is an abridged version of our sources. Only those materials and interviews of primary reference to each chapter are listed. Some interviews have not been listed, including several that were done on a "not for attribution" or "background" basis. We have also limited any mention of our extensive material gathered from Los Angeles newspapers and periodicals, particularly the *Times* .

PART I

"A Great Big Boom"

Cleland, Robert Glass. *The Cattle on a Thousand Hills*. San Marino: Huntington Library, 1951.

Dumke, Glenn. *The Boom of the Eighties*. San Marino: Huntington Library, 1966.

Guinn, James. *A History of California and an Extended History of Los Angeles*. Los Angeles: Historic Record, 1915.

Hutchinson, W. H. *Oil, Land, and Politics: The California Career of Thomas Robert Bard*. Norman, Oklahoma: University of Oklahoma Press, 1965.

Langsdorf, William Bell, Jr. "The Real Estate Boom of 1887 in Southern California." Masters thesis, Los Angeles: Occidental College, 1932.

Matson, Clarence. *Building a World Gateway* . Los Angeles: Pacific Era, 1945.

Nadeau, Remi. *City-Makers*. Costa Mesa: Trans-Anglo Books, 1965.

Newmark, Harris. *Sixty Years in Southern California*. New York: Houghton Mifflin, 1930.

Romer, Margaret. "The Story of Los Angeles" Part III and IV. *Journal of the West*, April and July, 1963.

Splitter, Henry Winfred. "Newspapers of Los Angeles: The First Fifty Years, 1851–1900." *Journal of the West*, October 1963.

Willard, Charles D. *A History of the Chamber of Commerce of Los Angeles, California*. Los Angeles: Kingsley-Barnes & Neuner, 1899.

Workman, Boyle. *The City that Grew*. Los Angeles: Southland Publishing, 1936.

Chapter 1: " Destined To Do Big Things "

Ainsworth, Edward M. *History of the Los Angeles Times*. Los Angeles: Times-Mirror, 1958.

Bard, Thomas R. Papers. Correspondence between Otis and Bard. San Marino: Huntington Library.
Beck, Warren, and Williams, David. *California: A History of the Golden State*. New York: Doubleday, 1972.
Bingham, Edwin R. *Charles F. Lummis — Editor of the Southwest*. San Marino: Huntington Library, 1955.
Bonnelli, William G. *Billion Dollar Black-Jack*. Beverly Hills: Civic Research Press, 1954.
Burdette, Robert J. Papers. Correspondence between Otis and Burdette. San Marino: Huntington Library.
Chandler, Marion Otis. "Basic Americanism Placed First in Battle of Press." *Editor and Publisher*, July 27, 1946.
Chapin, Lon. *Thirty Years in Pasadena*. Vol. 2. Los Angeles: Southwest Publishing, 1929.
Chaput, Donald. "From Publisher to General Harrison Gray Otis." *Terra*, Spring 1974.
Clodious, Albert. "The Quest for Good Government in Los Angeles, 1890–1910." PhD. dissertation. Claremont: Claremont College, 1953.
Cobre, Sidney. *The Development of American Journalism*. Dubuque, Iowa: William O. Brown, 1969.
Daniels, Roger, and Olin, Spencer C., Jr., eds. *Racism in California: A Reader in the History of Oppression*. New York: Macmillan, 1972.
"Defenders of the Union." *Overland Monthly*, July 1896.
Ford, John Anson. *Thirty Explosive Years in Los Angeles County*. San Marino: Huntington Library, 1961.
Freedom (Manila newspaper). April 4, 1897.
"General Otis: Storm Center of the Unpacific Coast." *Current Literature*, January 1912.
Gordon, Dudley. *Charles F. Lummis: Crusader in Corduroy*. Los Angeles: Cultural Assets Press, 1972.
Haynes, John Randolph. "Opposition of Harrison Gray Otis and the Times." Los Angeles: Unpublished manuscript.
———. Papers. Los Angeles: UCLA Public Affairs Library.
Hine, Robert V. *William Andrews Spalding: Los Angeles Newspaperman*. San Marino: Huntington Library, 1961.
Hutchinson, W. H. *Oil, Land, and Politics: The California Career of Thomas Robert Bard*. Norman, Oklahoma: University of Oklahoma Press, 1965.
Hynd, Alan. *In Pursuit*. Camden, N.J.: Thomas Nelson & Sons, 1968.
Illustrated History of Los Angeles County. Chicago: Lewis, 1889.
Los Angeles Public Library (Main Branch). "Ancestry of H. G. Otis" file.
Los Angeles Typographical Union, Local #174. *Mr. Otis and the Los Angeles "Times"*. Los Angeles Typographical Union, 1915.
Lummis, Charles. "One of the Old Guard." *Land of Sunshine*, January 1900.
———. "Memories of Thirty-Seven Years." Gordon, op. cit.
Marietta [Ohio] *Daily Times*, July 7, 1957.
Markham, Henry H. Papers. Correspondence between Otis and Markham. San Marino: Huntington Library.
Mayo, Morow. *Los Angeles*. New York: Alfred A. Knopf, 1933.
McKinley, William. Papers. Correspondence between McKinley and Otis. Washington, D.C.: Library of Congress, Manuscript Division.
Miller, Richard Connolly. "Otis and His Times: The Career of Harrison Gray Otis of California." PhD dissertation. University of California, Berkeley, 1961.
Millis, Walter. *The Martial Spirit*. Cambridge, Mass.: Riverside Press, 1931.

Mosher, Leroy. *The Stranded Bugle and Other Poems and Prose*. Los Angeles: Times-Mirror, 1905.

Murphy, William S. "Walker to the Land of Sunshine." *Los Angeles Times*. February 1, 1976.

Nadeau, Remi. *Los Angeles, from Mission to Modern City*. New York: Longmans, Green & Co., 1960.

National Archives, Old Military Records Section. "H. G. Otis, Military Record in the Spanish-American War, 1898, and in the Filipino Rebellion, 1899." Also Otis' Civil War Record. Washington, D.C.

Newmark, Harris. *Sixty Years in Southern California*. New York: Houghton Mifflin, 1930.

Newmark, Marco. *Jottings in Southern California History*. Los Angeles: Ward Ritchie, 1955.

Osborne, Henry Z. "Business Reasons Why Action Should Be Taken in the Los Angeles Newspaper Matter." February 2, 1899. Los Angeles: UCLA Special Collections.

————. Papers. Los Angeles: UCLA Special Collections.

Otis, E. S. *Phillipine Islands, Military Governor Annual Report*. Washington, D.C.: Government Printing Office, 1899.

Otis, Harrison Gray. "Address to the Los Angeles County Teacher's Institute." Los Angeles: Times-Mirror, March 28, 1898.

————. "A Letter from Harrison Gray Otis." Times-Mirror, 1917.

————. "Los Angeles: A Sketch." *Sunset*, January 1910.

————. "Milestones." *Los Angeles Times*, October 11, 1943.

Palmer, Frederick. "Otistown of the Open Shop." *Hampton's Magazine*, January 1911.

"Personal Glimpses: Harrison Gray Otis." *Literary Digest*, August 18, 1917.

Roosevelt, Theodore. Papers. Correspondence between Otis and Roosevelt. Washington, D.C.: Library of Congress, Manuscripts Division.

Rosecrans, William S. Papers. Los Angeles: UCLA Special Collections.

San Francisco Call, May 1, 1898 and May 9, 1908.

"Santa Monica and the Los Angeles Times." *Overland Monthly*, July 1896.

Sinclair, Upton. *The Brass Check*. Pasadena: Published by author, 1920.

Spalding, William A. *History of Los Angeles City and County*. Vol. 3. Los Angeles: J. R. Finnel & Sons, 1931.

Splitter, Henry Winfred. "Newspapers of Los Angeles: The First Fifty Years, 1851–1900." *Journal of the West*, October 1963.

St. John, Adela Rogers. *Final Verdict*. Garden City, New York: Doubleday, 1962.

Storke, Thomas. *California Editor*. Santa Barbara: News-Press Publishing, 1958.

Taft, William Howard. Papers. Correspondence between Otis and Taft. Washington D.C.: Library of Congress, Manuscripts Division.

"Those Tireless Chandlers." *Newsweek*, April 30, 1956.

"Walrus of Moron-Land." *American Mercury*, February 1928.

Waterman, R. W. Papers. Correspondence between Waterman and Henry Boyce. Berkeley: Bancroft Library.

White, Stephen. Papers. Palo Alto: Stanford University Library.

Wolfe, Frank. Testimony in *Final Report and Testimony Submitted by the Commission on Industrial Relations*. Vol. 6. Washington, D.C.: Government Printing Office, 1916.

Workman, Boyle. *The City that Grew*. Los Angeles: Southland Publishing, 1936.

Chapter 2: "Stand Fast, Stand Firm, Stand Sure, Stand True"

American Federationist. January–December 1903.

Bonnett, Clarence. *Employer Associations in the United States.* New York: Macmillan, 1922.

Carlson, Oliver. *A Mirror for Californians.* New York: Bobbs-Merrill, 1941.

Caughey, John. *California.* New York: Prentice-Hall, 1940.

Coleman, McAllister. *Eugene Debs, a Man Unafraid.* Indianapolis: Greenburg Publishers, 1930.

Commons, J. R. *A History of Labour.* Vol. 2. New York: Macmillan, 1921.

Cross, Ira. *A History of the Labor Movement in California.* Berkeley: University of California Press, 1935.

Debs, Eugene. "The Los Angeles Times—Who Committed That Crime?" San Francisco: 1910. San Marino: Huntington Library.

Dixon, Marion. "The History of the Los Angeles Central Labor Council." Masters thesis. University of California, Berkeley, 1929.

Faulkner, Harold Underwood. *The Quest for Social Justice 1898–1914.* New York: Macmillan, 1931.

Final Report and Testimony Submitted by the Commission on Industrial Relations. Vol 6, "The Open and Closed Shop Controversy in Los Angeles." Washington, D.C.: Government Printing Office, 1916.

Flannery, Helen. "The Labor Movement in Los Angeles 1880–1903." Masters thesis. University of California, Berkeley, 1929.

Foner, Philip S. *History of the Labor Movement in the United States.* Vol. 3. New York: International Publishers, 1965.

Frank, H.W. "The Merchants and Manufacturers' Association." *Land of Sunshine,* April 1897.

Haynes, John R. Papers. Los Angeles: UCLA Public Affairs Library.

Hine, Robert V. *William Andrews Spalding: Los Angeles Newspaperman.* San Marino: Huntington Library, 1961.

Holman, Alfred. "In the Calcium Light, Harrison Otis and his Fight for the Open Shop." *Overland Monthly,* March 1908.

Hopkins, Jerome. *Our Lawless Police.* New York: Viking Press, 1931.

International Brotherhood of Teamsters. Untitled labor history of Los Angeles. 1952.

Jacobson, Pauline. *The Struggles of Organized Labor in Los Angeles.* Los Angeles: Central Labor and Building Trades Councils. n.d.

Knight, Robert E. Lee. *Industrial Relations in the San Francisco Bay Area, 1900–1918.* Berkeley: University of California Press, 1960.

Los Angeles Times, *The Forty-Year War for a Free City: History of the Open Shop in Los Angeles.* Los Angeles: Times-Mirror, 1929.

———. "The Los Angeles Times: A Plain Statement of the Bedrock Facts and Unanswerable Reasons Sustaining the Attitude of the Times and its Owners Toward Labor during the past 6 Years." Times-Mirror, 1896.

———. "The Story of the Distinct Victory over Militant and Despotic Trades-Unionism Won by the Los Angeles Times in a Sixteen Years Battle Showing the Virtue of Standing Fast." Times-Mirror, 1907.

———. "The Truth: Concerning the Attitude of the Los Angeles Times Toward Labor." Times-Mirror, 1892.

Los Angeles Typographical Union Local #174. *Minutes,* 1875–1910.

————. *The Los Angeles Times Fight and Some Pertinent History.* August 12, 1909.

————. *Mr. Otis and the Los Angeles "Times."* Los Angeles: Los Angeles Typographical Union, 1915.

————. *100 Years of Organized Labor: Los Angeles 1875–1975.* Los Angeles: Los Angeles Typographical Union, 1975.

Markham, Henry H. Papers. San Marino: Huntington Library.

McKinley, William. Papers. Washington, D.C.: Library of Congress.

McWilliams, Carey. *Southern California Country: An Island on the Land.* New York: Duell, Sloan and Pearce, 1946.

Miller, Richard Connolly. "Otis and his Times: The Career of Harrison Gray Otis of California." PhD dissertation. University of California, Berkeley, 1961.

Otis, Harrison Gray. "A Long Wining Fight Against the Closed Shop." *World's Work,* December 1907.

Palmer, Frederick. "Otistown of the Open Shop." *Hampton's Magazine,* January 1911.

Pardee, George. Papers. Berkeley: Bancroft Library.

Perlman, Selig, and Taft, Philip. *History of Labor in the United States.* New York: Macmillan, 1935.

Perry, Louis B., and Perry, Richard S. *A. History of the Los Angeles Labor Movement, 1911–1941.* Los Angeles: University of California Press, 1963.

Pomeroy, Eltweed. "Really Masters." *Arena,* January 1905.

Proceedings of the American Federation of Labor. 1896 through 1909.

Roosevelt, Theodore. Papers. Correspondence between Otis and Roosevelt. Washington, D.C.: Library of Congress.

Searing, Richard Cole. "The McNamara Case: Its Causes and Effects." Masters thesis. University of California, Berkeley, 1952.

Stimson, Grace. *The Rise of the Labor Movement in Los Angeles.* Los Angeles: University of California Press, 1955.

Stockton, Frank. *The Closed Shop in American Trade Unions.* Baltimore: Johns Hopkins Press, 1911.

Tracy, George A., ed. *History of the Typographical Union.* Indianapolis: International Typographical Union, 1913.

Warne, Colston E., ed. *The Pullman Boycott of 1894.* Boston: D.C. Heath, 1964.

Wolf, Jerome. "The Los Angeles Times, Labor, and the Open Shop." Masters thesis. University of Southern California, 1961.

Chapter 3: "All For San Pedro"

Baisden, Richard Norman. "Labor Unions in Los Angeles Politics." PhD dissertation. Chicago: University of Chicago, 1958.

Barsness, R. C. "Railroads and Los Angeles." *Southern California Quarterly,* December 1965.

Clodius, Albert. "The Quest for Good Government in Los Angeles, 1890–1910." PhD dissertation. Claremont: Claremont College, 1953.

Cole, Cornelius. Papers. Los Angeles: UCLA Special Collections.

Conmy, Peter Thomas. *Stephen Mallory White.* San Francisco: Delores Press, 1956.

Dobie, Edith. *The Political Career of Stephen Mallory White.* Stanford: Stanford University Press, 1927.

Grassman, Curtis. "The Los Angeles Free Harbor Controversy and the Creation of a Progressive Coalition." *Southern California Quarterly,* Winter 1973.

Harrison, Benjamin. *Fortune Favors the Brave.* Los Angeles: Ward Ritchie Press, 1953.

Harrison, Benjamin. Papers. Correspondence between Otis and Harrison. Washington, D.C.: Library of Congress, Manuscripts Division.

Hawgood, H. "An Outer and Inner Deep Water Harbor at San Pedro." *Engineers and Architects Associates Proceedings of Southern California,* April 1895.

Hinckley, T. C. "George Osgoodby and the 'Murchison' Letter." *Pacific Historical Review,* November 1958.

Hutchinson, W. H. *Oil, Land, and Politics: The California Career of Thomas Robert Bard.* Norman, Oklahoma: University of Oklahoma Press, 1965.

Investor. Vol. 2. 1894 and 1896.

Jacques, Janice. "The Political Reform Movement in Los Angeles 1900–1910." Masters thesis. Claremont: Claremont College, 1948.

Land of Sunshine, December 1900.

Lewis, Oscar. *The Big Four: The Story of Huntington, Stanford, Hopkins, and Crocker, and of the Building of the Central Pacific.* New York: Knopf, 1938.

Los Angeles Chamber of Commerce. *Minutes of the Boards of Directors.*

Ludwig, Ella. *History of the Harbor District of Los Angeles.* Los Angeles: Historic Record, 1928.

Markham, Henry H. Papers. San Marino: Huntington Library.

Matson, Clarence. *Building a World Gateway: The Story of Los Angeles Harbor.* Los Angeles: Pacific Era, 1945.

McWilliams, Carey. *California: The Great Exception.* New York: A. A. Wyn, 1949.

Merritt, George. "Story of the 'Murchison Letter' as Remembered by George Merritt." Unpublished manuscript. Berkeley: Bancroft Library.

Miller, Richard Connolly. "Otis and his Times: The Career of Harrison Gray Otis of California." PhD dissertation. University of California, Berkeley, 1961.

Mowry, George E. *The California Progressives.* Chicago: Quadrangle, 1963.

Older, Fremont. *My Own Story.* New York: Macmillian, 1926.

Olin, Spencer C. Jr. *California's Prodigal Sons.* Los Angeles: University of California Press, 1968.

Rosecrans, William S. Papers. Los Angeles: UCLA Special Collections.

Rowell, Chester. Papers. Especially Rowell to Mark Sullivan, May 27, 1910. Berkeley: Bancroft Library.

Santa Monica Evening Outlook, January–June, 1892.

Stimson, Marshall. "A Short History of Los Angeles Harbor." *Historical Society of Southern California,* March 1945.

White, Stephen M. Papers. Palo Alto: Stanford University Library, Manuscripts Division.

Willard, Charles Dwight. *Free Harbor Contest at Los Angeles.* Los Angeles: Kingsley-Barnes and Neuner, 1899.

———. *History of the Chamber of Commerce.* Los Angeles: Kingsley-Barnes & Neuner, 1899.

———. "How Secretary Alger Treated Our Harbor." *Pacific Outlook,* July 17, 1909.

Williams, R. Hal. *The Democratic Party and California Politics 1880–1896.* Stanford: Stanford University Press, 1973.

Chapter 4: "The Pestiferous Reformers"

Alice Rose Collection. Palo Alto: Stanford University Library: Manuscripts Division.

Baisden, Richard Norman. "Labor Unions in Los Angeles Politics." PhD dissertation. Chicago: University of Chicago, 1958.

Bard, Thomas R. Papers. San Marino: Huntington Library.

Bean, Walton. *Boss Ruef's San Francisco. The Story of the Union Labor Party, Big Business, and the Graft Prosecution.* Berkeley: University of California Press, 1952.

Beck, Warren, and Williams, David. *California: A History of the Golden State.* Garden City, New York: Doubleday, 1972.

Bird, Frederick L., and Ryan, Frances M. *The Recall of Public Officers.* New York: Macmillan, 1930.

Burns, William. *The Masked War.* New York: Arno Press, 1969.

Campbell, Kemper. "The Reminiscences of Kemper Campbell." Oral history. University of California, Berkeley, 1954.

Clodius, Albert. "The Quest for Good Government in Los Angeles, 1890–1910." PhD dissertation. Claremont: Claremont College, 1953.

Crouch, Winston W. *The Initiative and Referendum in California.* Los Angeles: The Haynes Foundation, 1950.

Delmatier, Royce D. *The Rumble of California Politics.* New York: John Wiley & Sons, 1970.

Farrelly, David, and Hinderaker, Ivan. *Politics in California.* New York: Ronald Press, 1951.

Haynes, John R. Papers. Los Angeles: UCLA Public Affairs Library.

Hichborn, Franklin. *Story of the Session of the California Legislature of 1911.* San Francisco: James H. Barry, 1911.

Hill, Gladwyn. *Dancing Bear: An Inside Look at California Politics.* Cleveland and New York: World, 1968.

Hutchinson, W. H. "Prologue to Reform: The California Anti-Railroad Republicans, 1899–1905." *Southern California Quarterly,* September 1962.

Jacques, Janice. "The Political Reform Movement in Los Angeles 1900–1910." Masters thesis. Claremont: Claremont College, 1948.

Layne, J. Gregg. "The Lincoln-Roosevelt League: Its Origin and Accomplishments." *Historical Society of Southern California Quarterly,* September 1943.

Lissner, Meyer. Papers. Stanford: Stanford University Library.

Los Angeles Typographical Union, Local #174. *Minutes.*

———. *Mr. Otis and the Los Angeles Times.* Los Angeles Typographical Union, 1915.

Mowry, George E. *The California Progressives.* Chicago: Quadrangle, 1963.

Norris, Frank. *The Octopus.* New York: Doubleday, 1901.

Olin, Spencer C. Jr. *California's Prodigal Sons.* Berkeley: University of California Press, 1968.

Pacific Outlook, April-July, 1909.

Pardee, George. Papers. Berkeley: Bancroft Library.

———. "The Political Reminiscences of Dr. George Pardee." Unpublished manuscript. Stanford: Stanford University Library.

Phillips, Herbert L. *Big Wayward Girl: An Informal Political History of California.* Garden City, New York: Doubleday, 1968.

Rogin, Michael, and Shover, John. *Political Change in California: Critical Elections and Social Movements 1890–1966.* Westport, Connecticut: Greenwood, 1970.

Rowell, Chester. Papers. Berkeley: Bancroft Library.
Scharrenberg, Paul. "Reminiscences." Oral history. University of California, Berkeley, 1954.
Sjoquiest, Arthur. "From Posses to Professionals: A History of the Los Angeles Police Department." Masters thesis. California State, Los Angeles, 1972.
Steffens, Lincoln. *The Autobiography of Lincoln Steffens*. New York: Harcourt, Brace, and World, 1958.
Stimson, Marshall. Papers. San Marino: Huntington Library.
Taft, William Howard. Papers. Correspondence between Otis and Taft. Washington, D.C.: Library of Congress, Manuscripts Division.
Willard, Charles D. Papers. San Marino: Huntington Library.
Woods, Joseph. "The Progressives and the Police: Urban Reform and the Professionalism of the Los Angeles Police." PhD dissertation. UCLA, 1973.

Chapter 5: The Bombing of the Times Building

Adamic, Louis. *Dynamite: The Story of Class Violence in America*. New York: Harper & Row, 1960.
Adams, Graham Jr. *Age of Industrial Violence 1910–1915*. New York: Columbia University Press, 1966.
Baker, Robert Munson. "Why the McNamaras Pleaded Guilty to the Bombing of the Los Angeles Times." Masters thesis. University of California, Berkeley, 1937.
Blake, Gene. "Attorney Oscar Lawler at 84." *Los Angeles Times*, January 19, 1959.
Burns, William. *The Masked War*. New York: Arno Press, 1969.
Caesar, Gene. *Incredible Detective*. Englewood Cliffs, New Jersey: Prentice-Hall, 1968.
California State Federation of Labor. "The Times: A Morgue of Human Character." Four-page broadside. November, 1910.
Caughey, John. *California*. New York: Prentice-Hall, 1940.
Cleland, Robert G. *California in Our Time*. New York: Knopf, 1947.
Cohn, Alfred, and Chisholm, Joe. *Take the Witness*. New York, N.Y.: Frederick A. Stokes, 1934.
Darrow, Clarence. *The Story of My Life*. New York: Scribner's, 1932.
Davis, Le Compte. Papers. Los Angeles: UCLA Special Collections.
Debs, Eugene. "The Los Angeles Times—Who Committed That Crime." Broadside. San Francisco: 1910.
———. "The McNamara Case and the Labor Movement." *International Socialist Review*, January 1912.
Dixon, Marion. "The History of the Los Angeles Central Labor Council." Masters thesis. University of California, Berkeley, 1929.
Final Report and Testimony Submitted by the Commission on Industrial Relations. Vol 6. Government Printing Office, 1916.
Ford, Patrick H., ed. *The Darrow Bribery Trial*. Whittier: Western Printing Co., 1956.
Gompers, Samuel. "The McNamara Case: Murder is Murder" *American Federationist*. June 1911.
———. "Gompers Speaks for Labor." *American Federationist*. March 1912.
———. "The Man Higher-up Outcry." *American Federationist*, February 1912.
———. "The McNamara Case II." *American Federationist*, July 1911.
———. "The Organized Assault Against the Rights and the Leaders of the American Working man." *McClure's Magazine*, February 1912.

————. "President's Report." *American Federationist,* December 1911 and January 1912.

————*Seventy Years of Life and Labour.* New York: E. P. Dutton, 1925.

"Gompers and Burns on Unionism and Dynamite." *McClure's Magazine,* February 1912.

————. "That Asinine Canard: 'Gompers Desecrated the National Flag.'" *American Federationist,* February 1912.

Hynd, Alan. *In Pursuit.* Camden, New Jersey: Thomas Nelson & Sons, 1968.

Johnson, Hiram. Papers. Especially McNamara File. Berkeley: Bancroft Library.

Knight, Robert E. Lee. *Industrial Relations in the San Francisco Bay Area, 1900–1918.* Berkeley: University of California Press, 1960.

"Labor's Repudiation of the Dynamiter." *The Literary Digest,* December 16, 1911.

"Larger Bearings of the McNamara Case." *Survey,* December 30, 1911.

Lawler, Oscar. "The Bombing of the Los Angeles Times: A Personal Reminiscence." *Claremont Quarterly,* Spring 1958.

————. "Oscar Lawler, L.A. Attorney." Oral history. UCLA, 1962.

Lissner, Meyer. Papers. Especially McNamara File. Palo Alto: Stanford University Library.

Los Angeles Times. *For Nation-Wide Free Industries.* Los Angeles: Times-Mirror. December 4, 1912.

————. *The Forty-Year War for a Free City: History of the Open Shop in Los Angeles.* Los Angeles: Times-Mirror, 1929.

Mayo, Morrow. *Los Angeles.* New York: Knopf, 1933.

McManigal, Ortie E. *The National Dynamite Plot.* Los Angeles: The Neale Co., 1913.

McWilliams, Carey. *Southern California Country: An Island on the Land.* New York: Duell, Sloan and Pearce, 1946.

Mooney, Thomas. Papers. Letters of J. B. McNamara. Berkeley: Bancroft Library.

"Murder is Murder." *American Federationist,* May 1912.

O'Higgens, Harvey J. "The Dynamiters: A Great Case of Detective William J. Burns." *McClure's Magazine,* August 1911.

Older, Fremont. Papers. Berkeley: Bancroft Library.

Pacific Outlook, December 3, 1910.

Palmer, Frederick. "Otistown of the Open Shop." *Hampton's Magazine,* January, 1911.

Perry, Louis B., and Perry, Richard S. *A History of the Los Angeles Labor Movement, 1911–1941.* Berkeley: University of California Press, 1963.

"Persons in the Foreground: Detective Burns and his Psychological Method." *Current Literature,* June 1911.

Proceedings of the American Federation of Labor. 1910–1912.

"The Progress of the World." *American Review of Reviews,* January 1912.

"A Review of the World." *Current Literature.* June and November 1911 and January 1912.

Riley, Frank. "The City's Changing Newspaper." *Los Angeles,* July 1966.

Robinson, William W. *Bombs and Bribery.* Los Angeles: Dawson's, 1969.

————. *Lawyers of Los Angeles.* Los Angeles: Ward Ritchie, 1959.

Rolle, Andrew F. *California: A History.* New York: Thomas Y. Crown, 1963.

Roosevelt, Theodore. "Mr. Gompers, General Otis, and the Dynamite Charges." *California Outlook,* June 24, 1911.

Scott, Joseph. Letter to Curt J. Hyans, September 6, 1950. Berkeley: Bancroft Library.

Searing, Richard Cole. "The McNamara Case: Its Causes and Effects." Masters thesis. University of California, Berkeley, 1952.

"Sense and Hysteria on the McNamara Affair." *The Nation,* January 11, 1912.

Sherman, Moses H. Papers. Corona Del Mar: Sherman Foundation.

Shoaf, George H. "Notebook of an Old-timer—Clarence Darrow and the McNamara Case." *American Socialist,* December 1957.

Steffens, Lincoln. *The Autobiography of Lincoln Steffens.* New York: Harcourt, Brace & World, 1958.

———. "An Experiment in Good Will." *Survey,* December 30, 1911.

———. "The Gospel of Jesus Christ Brought about the Pleas and Acceptance." *Los Angeles Tribune,* December 2, 1911.

St. John, Adela Rogers. *Final Verdict.* Garden City, New York: Doubleday, 1962.

Stone, Irving. *Clarence Darrow for the Defense.* New York: Bantam, 1958.

Taft, Philip. *Labor Politics American Style: The California State Federation of Labor.* Cambridge, Mass.: Harvard University Press, 1968.

Taft, William Howard. Papers. Washington, D.C.: Library of Congress.

"Third Perch." *Time,* July 15, 1935.

Tichenor, Henry M. *A Wave of Horror.* St. Louis: National Rip-Saw Publishing, 1912.

United States Department of Justice. Correspondence. File 15677. Washington, D.C.: National Archives.

United States Department of Justice. Documents. Bell, California: Federal Records Center.

United States v. Frank Ryan, et al. Court Transcripts. San Marino: Huntington Library.

Weinberg, Arthur, ed. *Attorney for the Damned.* New York: Simon and Schuster, 1957.

Weinstein, James. *The Corporate Ideal in the Liberal State.* Boston: Beacon, 1969.

Chapter 6: The Battle Goes On

Alice Rose Collection. Stanford University Library.

Brissenden, Paul F. *The IWW: A Study of American Syndicalism.* New York: Russell & Russell, 1920.

Burdette, Robert J. Papers. San Marino: Huntington Library.

Davenport, Frederick M. "Did Hughes Snub Johnson?" *The American Political Science Review,* April 1949.

Davenport, Robert. "Weird Note for the Vox Populi: The L.A. Municipal News." *California Historical Society Quarterly,* March 1965.

Dubofsky, Melvyn. *We Shall Be All: A History of the IWW.* Chicago: Quadrangle, 1969.

Final Report and Testimony Submitted by the Commission on Industrial Relations. Vol. 6. Government Printing Office, 1916.

The Industrial Worker. March-June 1912.

Johnson, Hiram. Papers. Berkeley: Bancroft Library.

Keesling, Francis. Papers. Palo Alto: Stanford University Library, Manuscripts Division.

Kornbluh, Joyce L., ed. *Rebel Voices.* Ann Arbor: University of Michigan Press, 1964.

"A Letter from Harrison Gray Otis." Copy in Lissner Papers. Palo Alto: Stanford University Library, Manuscripts Division.

Lincoln, A. "My Dear Governor." *California Historical Quarterly*, September, 1959.

Lissner, Meyer. Papers. Palo Alto: Stanford University Library, Manuscripts Division.

McWilliams, Carey. "The City that Wanted the Truth." *Pacific Spectator*, Spring 1949.

Miller, Grace. "The I.W.W. Free Speech Fight: San Diego, 1912." *Southern California Quarterly*, Fall 1972.

Mowry, George E. *The California Progressives*. Chicago: Quadrangle, 1963.

Olin, Spencer C. Jr. *California's Prodigal Sons*. Berkeley: University of California Press, 1968.

"Otis Opposed to Social and Economic Betterment." *Los Angeles Express*, June 17, 1911.

"Otis' Program of Murder: 'Quickly, Surely, Silently.' " *American Federationist*, February 1912.

Pinchot, Amos R. E. *History of the Progressive Party 1912–1916*. New York: New York University, 1958.

Renshaw, Patrick. *The Wobblies*. Garden City, New York: Doubleday, 1967.

Richmond, Al. "The San Diego Free Speech Fight." Unpublished manuscript.

Rowell, Chester. Papers. Berkeley: Bancroft Library.

San Diego I.W.W. *The History of the San Diego Free Speech Fight*. Chicago: May 1973.

Sherman, Moses H. Papers. Corona Del Mar: Sherman Foundation.

Sinclair, Upton. *The Brass Check*. Pasadena: Published by author, 1920.

Taft, William Howard. Papers. Washington, D.C.: Library of Congress.

Weintraub, Hyman. "I.W.W. in California: 1906–1931." Masters thesis. UCLA, 1947.

PART II

" *The Richest Man In Southern California* "

Arkell, William J. *Old Friends and Some Acquaintances*. Los Angeles: Published by author, 1927.

Carlson, Oliver. *A Mirror for Californians*. New York: Bobbs-Merrill, 1941.

Chandler, Harry. "Harry Chandler, 'Oldest Employee,' Has Seen the City Transformed." *Los Angeles Times*, December 4, 1941.

Chandler, Marion Otis. "Basic Americanism Placed First in Battle of Press." *Editor and Publisher*, July 27, 1946.

"Chandler Makes Dreams Come True." *New York Times*, April 22, 1928.

Crowe, Earle. *Men of El Tejon*. Los Angeles: Ward Ritchie Press, 1957.

Currier, Stanley P., and Clement, Edgar. *History of Landaff, New Hampshire*. Littleton, New Hampshire: Published by authors, 1966.

Dumke, Glenn S., and Grenier, Judson A. "Harry Chandler." *Dictionary of American Biography*. Supplement Three, 1941–1945.

"Effectively Transplanted New Englander." *Saturday Evening Post*, June 5, 1926.

Ford, John Anson. *Thirty Explosive Years in L.A. County*. San Marino: Huntington Library, 1961.

Hart, Jack Robert. "The Information Empire": Interviews with Norman and Dorothy Chandler. PhD dissertation. Madison, Wisconsin: University of Wisconsin, 1975.
Haynes, John R. Papers. Los Angeles: UCLA Public Affairs Library.
Municipal League. *Bulletin,* October 1923.
Palmer, Edwin O. *History of Hollywood.* Published by author, 1938.
Sherman, Moses H. Papers. Corona Del Mar: Sherman Foundation.
Shippey, Lee. *Luckiest Man Alive.* Los Angeles: Westernlore Press, 1959.
"The Story of Harry Chandler." *Los Angeles Record,* March 4, 1934.
Taylor, Frank J. "It Costs $1,000 to Have Lunch with Harry Chandler." *Saturday Evening Post,* December 16, 1939.
Taylor, Ken. "Harry Chandler's Crowded 50 Years." *Editor and Publisher.* August 15, 1936.
INTERVIEWS: Herbert Allen, John Anson Ford, Whitney Williams.

Chapter 7: The Owens Valley Water War

Annual Report of the Board of Water Commissioners. Los Angeles, 1901/1902.
"The Aqueduct and the Water." *California Outlook,* October 19, 1912.
Board of Public Service Commissioners. *Complete Report on Construction of the Los Angeles Aqueduct.* Los Angeles, 1916.
Chalfant, W. A. *The Story of Inyo.* Published by the author, 1922.
Cifarelli, Anthony. "The Owens River Aqueduct and the Los Angeles Times." Masters thesis. UCLA, 1969.
Clary, W. W. *History of the Law Firm of O'Melveny and Myers, 1885–1965.* Published privately, 1966.
Daughters of the American Revolution. *The Valley of San Fernando.* D.A.R., 1924.
Dillon, Richard. *Heroes and Humbugs.* Garden City, New York: Doubleday, 1970.
First Annual Report of the Chief Engineer of the Los Angeles Aqueduct to the Board of Public Works. Los Angeles: March 15, 1907.
Fogelson, Richard M. *The Fragmented Metropolis: Los Angeles, 1850–1930.* Cambridge, Mass.: Harvard University Press, 1967.
Hichborn, Franklin. Papers. Los Angeles: UCLA Public Affairs Library.
Leavitt, Jacqueline. "Option Lost: Opportunities Remaining: A Preliminary Study of Water and Land Planning in the Los Angeles Region." UCLA School of Architecture and Planning, 1973.
Lillard, Richard S. *Eden in Jeopardy.* New York: Knopf, 1966.
Lippincott, J. B. "William Mulholland." *Civil Engineering,* February and March, 1912.
Mayo, Morrow. *Los Angeles.* New York: Knopf, 1933.
McClure, W.F. Letter of Transmittal and Report. California Senate. Sacramento: 1925.
McWilliams, Carey. *Southern California.* Santa Barbara: Peregrine, 1973.
Nadeau, Remi. *The Water Seekers.* New York: Doubleday, 1950.
Nash, Gerald D. *The American West in the Twentieth Century.* Englewood Cliffs, New Jersey: Prentice-Hall, 1973.
Ostrom, Vincent. *Water and Politics.* Los Angeles: Haynes Foundation, 1953.
———. *Water Supply.* Los Angeles: Haynes Foundation, 1953.
Pardee, George. Papers. Berkeley: Bancroft Library.
People's Aqueduct Investigation Board, *Report on the Los Angeles Aqueduct.* Especially testimonies of E. T. Earl, J. M. Eliot, John J. Fay, Fred Johnson,

J. B. Lippincott, Henry Lowenthal, and W. B. Matthews. 7 volumes, 1912: Only known copy at the Los Angeles Public Library.

Robinson, W. W. *The Story of San Fernando*. Los Angeles: Title Insurance and Trust, 1967.

Sherman, Moses H. Papers. Corona Del Mar: Sherman Foundation.

"Statement of the People of Owens Valley in Relation to the Proposed Diversion of the Waters of Owens River to the City of Los Angeles." 1905. Pardee Papers. Berkeley: Bancroft Library.

"A Theft in Water." *Inyo Magazine*. September 1908–January 1909.

Water Commissioners' *Report for Year Ending November 30, 1905*. Los Angeles; 1906.

Whitley, Hobart J. Papers. Especially the L. A. Suburban Homes Sale Book. Los Angeles: UCLA Special Collections.

Wood, Richard Coke. *The Owens Valley and the Los Angeles Water Controversy*. Stockton: Pacific Center for Western Historical Studies, 1973.

Workman, Boyle. *The City That Grew*. Los Angeles: Southland Publishing, 1936.

Chapter 8: The Empire Builder

Armitage, Merle. *Success is No Accident*. Yucca Valley: Manzanita Press, 1959.

Beaton, Kendall. *Enterprise in Oil*. New York: Appleton Century Crofts, 1957.

Campbell, Joyce. "Mountain Memories." *The Mountain Enterprise*, February 22 and March 1, 1974.

Clary, W. W. *History of the Law Firm of O'Melveny and Myers, 1885–1965*. Published privately, 1966.

Cottrell, Edwin A., and Helen L. *Characteristics of the Metropolis*. Los Angeles: Haynes Foundation, 1952.

Crowe, Earle. *Men of El Tejon*. Los Angeles: Ward Ritchie Press, 1957.

Eberle, Gordon, S. *Arcadia: City of the Santa Anita*. Claremont: Saunders Press, 1953.

Final Report and Testimony Submitted by the Commission on Industrial Relations. Especially testimony of Edwin Janss. Vol. 6. Washington, D.C.: Government Printing Office, 1916.

Finney, Guy. *Angel City in Turmoil*. Los Angeles: Amer Press, 1945.

"Flight Plan for Tomorrow." Los Angeles: Douglas Aircraft, 1962.

Gray, Francine du Plessix. *Hawaii*. New York: Vintage, 1973.

Harmer, Ruth. "Yosemite: Slum in the Sun." *Frontier*, October 1955.

Haynes, John R. Papers. Especially "Sale of Times Building" folder. Los Angeles: UCLA Public Affairs Library.

Hays, Will H. *The Memoirs of Will H. Hays*. Garden City, New York: Doubleday, 1955.

Henry, Bill. Papers. Los Angeles: Occidental College.

"Image of Leadership: Chandler of the Los Angeles Times." *Printers' Ink* September 18, 1959.

James, Marquis, and James, Bessie R. *Biography of a Bank*. New York: Harper & Row, 1954.

Johnson, Hiram. Papers. Berkeley: Bancroft Library.

Keller, Henry. Papers. Los Angeles: UCLA Special Collections.

Kidner, Frank I., and Neff, Philip. *Los Angeles: The Economic Outlook*. Los Angeles: Haynes Foundation, 1946.

Los Angeles County Recorder. Grantor/Grantee Indexes for 1886–1950 for Harry Chandler, Chandis Securities, Chandler-Sherman Corporation, Harrison Gray Otis, Rancho Santa Anita (1936), Times-Mirror.

Merrill, James M. "A History of the Los Angeles Steamship Company." Masters thesis. Claremont: Claremont College, 1948.

Moody's Industrial Manual. 1901–1944.

O'Melveny, Henry W.O.K. Diaries. San Marino: Huntington Library.

Palmer, Edwin O. *History of Hollywood.* Published by author, 1938.

Robinson, W.W. *The Story of Kern County.* Los Angeles: Title Insurance & Trust, 1961.

Samish, Artie. *The Secret Boss of California.* New York: Crown, 1971.

Sherman, Moses H. Papers. Corona Del Mar: Sherman Foundation.

Shotliff, Don. "San Pedro Harbor of L.A. Harbor." *Historical Society of Southern California,* Summer 1972.

Southern California Business. September 1924 and June 1926.

Sterling, Christine. *Olvera Street.* Los Angeles: Old Mission Printing, 1933.

Swanberg, W. A. *Citizen Hearst.* New York: Charles Scribner's Sons, 1961.

Taylor, Frank J. "It Costs $1,000 to have Lunch with Harry Chandler." *Saturday Evening Post.* December 16, 1939.

Taylor, J.F., and Welty, E. M. *Black Bonanza.* New York: McGraw-Hill, 1956.

United States Department of Justice. Correspondence. Title Land Insurance and the Tejon Indians. Washington, D.C.: National Archives.

United States House of Representatives. "Hearings Before the Select Committee to Inquire into Operations, Policies and Affairs of the U.S. Shipping Board." Washington, D.C.: 68th Congress, 1st session, Part F.

The Vermejo Club: Its Purposes and Properties. Vermejo Club, 1927. Available at Sherman Foundation, Corona del Mar.

Walker's Directory, 1910–1944.

Weaver, John D. *El Pueblo Grande.* Los Angeles: Ward Ritchie, 1973.

Werner, M. R. *Privileged Characters.* New York: Robert McBride & Co., 1935.

Yeomans, Patricia Henry. *Behind the Headlines with Bill Henry.* Los Angeles: Ward Ritchie, 1972.

INTERVIEWS: Tony Araujo, Ralph Kreiser, Ernest Loebbecke, Phil Scheuer, Whitney Williams.

Chapter 9: Intervention In Mexico

Armstrong, Leroy, and Denny, J.O. *Financial California.* San Francisco: Coast Banker Publishing Co., 1916.

Blaisdell, Lowell. *The Desert Revolution: Baja California, 1911.* Madison, Wisconsin: University of Wisconsin Press, 1962.

———. "Harry Chandler and Mexican Border Intrigue 1914–1917." *Pacific Historical Review,* November 1966.

Boyle, Walter F. (American Consul). "Political Connections of the Governor of Lower California." Washington, D.C.: National Archives. April 24, 1919.

Calexico Chronicle, December 1914–March 1915.

Callahan, James Morton. *American Foreign Policy in Mexican Relations.* New York: Macmillan, 1932.

Carr, Harry. "The Conquest of Mexico." *Sunset,* September 1916.

———. "The Kingdom of Cantu: Why Lower California Is the Oasis of Perfect Peace in Bloody Mexico." *Sunset,* April 1917.

Chamberlin, Eugene Keith. "Mexican Colonization Versus American Interests in Lower California." *Pacific Historical Review,* February 1951.

———. "United States Interests in Lower California." PhD dissertation. University of California, Berkeley, 1949.

Chandler, Harry. "Imperial Valley's Most Essential Need Is a Flood Control and

Storage Dam in the Colorado River." Corona Del Mar: Sherman Foundation, n.d.

————. *Mexico: The New Melting Pot.* Los Angeles: Times-Mirror, 1926.

————. "The Other Side of the Question." Colorado River Land Co. n.d.

————. "To the Members of the Imperial Valley Farm Lands Association." November 10, 1915.

Cooper, Erwin. *Aqueduct Empire.* California: Arthur Clarke, 1968.

Crowe, Earle. *Men of El Tejon.* Los Angeles: Ward Ritchie, 1957.

Dulles, W. F. *Yesterday in Mexico: A Chronicle of the Revolution 1919–1936.* Austin: University of Texas Press, 1961.

Goldstein, Robert A. "The California Press and the World War." Masters thesis. Palo Alto: Stanford University, 1953.

Hendricks, William Oral. "Guillermo Andrade and Land Development in the Mexican Colorado River Delta, 1874–1905." PhD dissertation, USC, 1967.

Hoover, Herbert. Papers. Especially correspondence with Chandler. Westport, Iowa: Hoover Presidential Library.

Hundley, Norris. *Dividing the Waters: A Century of Controversy Between the United States and Mexico.* Berkeley: University of California Press, 1966.

Imperial Valley County Recorder's Office. Grantee/Grantor Index.

Industrial Worker, June and July 1911.

Johnson, Hiram. Papers. Berkeley: Bancroft Library.

Kenny, Robert. Papers. Berkeley: Bancroft Library.

Linholm, Earl. "A Study of the Agrarian Revolution of Mexico." Masters thesis. USC, 1937.

Martinez, Pablo L. *A History of Lower California.* Mexico, City: D.F., 1960.

McWilliams, Carey. "The Colorado Is Sovereign." *The Nation*, April 9, 1949.

Morrison, Margaret Darsie. "Charles Robinson Rockwood: Developer of the Imperial Valley." *Southern California Quarterly*, December 1962.

Olson, Reuel Leslie. *The Colorado River Compact.* Los Angeles: Published by author, 1926.

Packard, Walter. *Land and Politics in California, Greece, and Latin America.* Oral history. University of California, Berkeley, 1970.

Sherman, Moses H. Papers. Corona Del Mar: Sherman Foundation.

Simpson, Lesley Bird. *Many Mexicos.* Los Angeles: University of California, 1966.

Stowe, Noel J., ed. "Pioneering Land Development in the Californias: An Interview with David Otto Brant." *California Historical Society Quarterly*, March, June, and September 1968.

Stuart, Gordon. *When the Sands of the Desert Grew Gold.* Pacific Palisades: Published by author, 1961.

Taft, William Howard. Papers. Washington, D.C.: Library of Congress.

Tannebaum, Frank. *Mexico: The Struggle for Peace and Bread.* New York: Knopf, 1962.

————. *Peace by Revolution: Mexico after 1910.* New York: Columbia University Press, 1933.

United States Department of Justice. Correspondence. Files #90755 and 90755-I. Washington, D.C.: National Archives.

United States of America v. Balthazar Aviles, et al. Bell, California: Federal Records Center.

Weintraub, Hyman. "The IWW in California, 1905–1931." Masters thesis. UCLA, 1947.

Whitley, Hobart J. Papers. Los Angeles: UCLA Special Collections.

Chapter 10: The Red Menace

Arnold, Ralph. "Laying Foundation Stones." *Historical Society of Southern California*, September 1955.

Bernstein, Irving. *The Lean Years*. Baltimore: Penguin, 1960

Better America Federation. *Newsletter*, June–September 1920.

Boyer, Richard, and Morais, Herbert. *Labor's Untold Story*. New York: United Electrical, Radio & Machine Workers of America, 1970.

Carr, William Jarvis. "The Memoirs of William Jarvis Carr." Oral history. UCLA, 1959

Delmatier, Royce T. *The Rumble of California Politics*. New York: John Wiley, 1970.

Dickson, E. A. Papers. Los Angeles: UCLA Special Collections.

Edson, Katherine Philips. Papers. Los Angeles: UCLA Special Collections.

Feuerlicht, Roberta Strauss. *America's Reign of Terror*. New York: Random House, 1971.

Finney, Guy. *The Los Angeles Bubble*. Los Angeles: Milton Forbes, 1929.

Haynes, John R. Papers. Los Angeles: UCLA Public Affairs Library.

Hoover, Herbert. Papers. Westport, Iowa: Hoover Presidential Library.

Kenny, Bob. "My First Forty Years in California Politics." Oral history. UCLA, 1964.

Levin, Murray B. *Political Hysteria in America*. New York: Basic Books, 1971.

Lissner, Meyer. Papers. Palo Alto: Stanford University Library.

Los Angeles Chamber of Commerce. *Board Meeting Minutes*, April 12, 1923.

Los Angeles Record, March 1923 and 1924.

Los Angeles Times. The Forty-Year War for a Free City: History of the Open Shop in Los Angeles. Los Angeles: Times-Mirror, 1929.

McHenry, Dean. "The Pattern of California Politics." *The Western Political Quarterly*, March 1948.

McWilliams, Carey. *Southern California Country: An Island on the Land*. New York: Duell, Sloan and Pearce, 1946.

Mowry, George E. *The California Progressives*. Chicago: Quadrangle, 1963.

Municipal League. *Bulletin*. January 19–22, 1924.

Murray, Robert K. *Red Scare: A Study in National Hysteria, 1919–1920*. Minneapolis: University of Minnesota Press, 1955.

Parry, Albert. "Washington B. Vanderlip: The Khan of Kamchatka." *Pacific Historical Review*, August 1948.

People's World. Series on Los Angeles history. January–May 1938.

Perry, Louis B., and Perry, Richard S. *A History of the Los Angeles Labor Movement, 1911–1941*. Berkeley: University of California Press, 1963.

Phillips, Herbert L. *Big Wayward Girl: An Informal Political History of California*. Garden City, New York: Doubleday, 1968.

Reed, Mary. "San Pedro." *The Nation*, July 29, 1924.

Seldes, George. *Lords of the Press*. New York: Julian Messner, 1938.

Sherman, Moses H. Papers. Corona Del Mar: Sherman Foundation.

Sinclair, Upton. "Upton Sinclair Defends the Law." *The Nation*, June 6, 1923.

Stoker, Charles. *Thicker'n Thieves*. Santa Monica: Sidereal Company, 1951.

Story, Harold. "Memoirs." Oral history. UCLA, 1967.

Taft, Clinton J. *Fifteen Years on Freedom's Front*. Los Angeles: American Civil Liberties Union, 1939.

United States Congress, Senate Committee on Education and Labor. *Violations of Free Speech and Rights of Labor: Hearings of the Committee on Education and Labor*. Washington, D.C.: Government Printing Office, 1940.

Van Valen, Nelson. "The I.W.W. in the Los Angeles Area, 1919–1923." Masters thesis. Claremont: Claremont College, 1951.

Weintraub, Hyman. "The IWW in California, 1906–1931." Masters thesis. UCLA, 1947.

West, George. "After Liberalism Failed." *The Nation*, May 30, 1923.

Woods, Joseph. "The Progressives and the Police: Urban Reform and the Professionalism of the Los Angeles Police." PhD dissertation. UCLA, 1973.

INTERVIEWS: Elmer Bromley, Bob Kenny.

Chapter 11: The EPIC Challenge

Anderson, Dewey, and Davidson, Person. *Ballots and the Democratic Class Struggle*. Stanford: Stanford University Press, 1943.

Baisden, Richard Norman. "Labor Unions in Los Angeles Politics." PhD dissertation. Chicago: University of Chicago, 1958.

Borough, Reuben. "Reuben Borough and California Reform Movements." Oral history. UCLA, 1968.

Burdette, Robert J. Papers. San Marino: Huntington Library.

Chandler, Harry. "Viewpoint of Southern California." *Review of Reviews*, March 1936.

"The EPIC of Upton Sinclair." *The Nation*, October 31, 1934.

Hopkins, Jerome. *Our Lawless Police*. New York: Viking Press, 1931.

Los Angeles Chamber of Commerce. *Minutes*, November 2, 1934.

McIntosh, Clarence F. "Upton Sinclair and the EPIC Movement, 1933–1936." PhD dissertation. Palo Alto: Stanford University, 1955.

McWilliams, Carey. *Southern California*. Santa Barbara: Peregrine, 1973.

Pringle, Henry. "Yes, Mr. Mayer, Part II." *The New Yorker*, April 4, 1936.

Rogin, Michael, and Shover, John. *Political Change in California: Critical Elections and Social Movements—1890–1966*. Westport, Connecticut: Greenwood, 1970.

Shaw, Joseph. Papers. Los Angeles: UCLA Special Collections.

Sinclair, Upton. *Depression Island*. Los Angeles: End Poverty League, 1934.

———. *I, Candidate for Governor, and How I Got Licked*. Los Angeles: End Poverty League, 1934.

———. *I, Governor of California and How I Ended Poverty*. Los Angeles: End Poverty League, 1934.

———. "Immediate EPIC." Los Angeles: End Poverty League, 1934.

———. *The Autobiography of Upton Sinclair*. New York: Harcourt, Brace, Jovanovich, 1962.

Sloane, Melvin. "The Press Against Upton Sinclair." Masters thesis. UCLA, 1968.

Taft, Clinton. *Fifteen Years on Freedom's Front*. Los Angeles: American Civil Liberties Union, 1939.

United States Congress. Senate. *Congressional Record* (Harry Chandler on Unemployment). March 2, 1932.

INTERVIEWS: Eleanor Bogaygian, Madeleine Borough, Asa Call, Bob Kenny.

Chapter 12: "A New Deal For Los Angeles "

Allhoff, Fred, and McKinney, Dwight F. "The Lid Off Los Angeles" *Liberty*, November 11–December 16, 1939.

Auerbach, Jerold S. *Labor and Liberty: The La Follette Committee and the New Deal*. New York: Bobbs-Merrill, 1966.

Baisden, Richard Norman. "Labor Unions in Los Angeles Politics." PhD dissertation. Chicago: University of Chicago, 1958.

Barrett, Edward, Jr. *The Tenney Committee: Legislative Investigation of Subversive Activities in California*. Ithaca, New York: Cornell University Press, 1951.

Bonelli, William G. *Billion Dollar Blackjack*. Beverly Hills: Civic Research Press, 1954.

Borough, Reuben. "Reuben Borough and California Reform Movements." Oral history. UCLA, 1968.

Burke, Robert. *Olson's New Deal for California*. Berkeley: University of California Press, 1953.

Caplan, Jerry Saul. "The Civic Committee in the Recall of Mayor Frank Shaw." Masters thesis. UCLA, 1947.

Carlson, Oliver. *A Mirror for Californians*. New York: Bobbs-Merrill, 1941.

Chamberlain, Ernest R. "Buron Fitts." Unpublished manuscript. Los Angeles: UCLA Special Collections.

———. "The Civic Committee of Los Angeles." Unpublished manuscript. Los Angeles: UCLA Special Collections.

Clinton, Clifford. Papers. Los Angeles: UCLA Special Collections.

Creel, George. "Unholy City." *Collier's*, September 2, 1939.

Finney, Guy. *Angel City in Turmoil*. Los Angeles: Amer Press, 1945.

Halberg, June E. "The Fitts-Palmer Campaign for District Attorney in Los Angeles County." Masters thesis. UCLA, 1940.

International Brotherhood of Teamsters. Untitled Los Angeles labor history, 1952.

Leader, Len. "Los Angeles and the Great Depression." PhD dissertation. UCLA, 1972.

Perry, Louis B. "A Survey of the Labor Movement in Los Angeles, 1933–1939." PhD dissertation, UCLA, 1950.

———, and Perry, Richard S. *A History of the Los Angeles Labor Movement, 1911–1941*. Berkeley: University of California Press; 1963.

Riznik, Joseph, "California Racket Buster." *The American Magazine*, June 1938.

Schneider, Betty V. H., and Siegel, Abraham. *Industrial Relations in the Pacific Coast Longshore Industry*. Berkeley: University of California Institute of Industrial Relations, 1968.

Shaw, Joseph. Papers. Los Angeles: UCLA Special Collections.

Shoup, Paul. Papers. Palo Alto: Stanford University Library.

Stoker, Charles. *Thicker'n Thieves*. Santa Monica: Sidereal Company, 1951.

United States Congress. Senate Committee on Education and Labor. *Violations of Free Speech and Rights of Labor: Hearings of the Committee on Education and Labor*. Washington, D.C.: Government Printing Office, 1940.

Woods, Joseph. "The Progressives and the Police: Urban Reform and the Professionalism of the Los Angeles Police." PhD dissertation. UCLA, 1973.

INTERVIEWS: John Anson Ford, Don Healy, Bob Kenny, Ellis Patterson.

Chapter 13: Crime Waves, High Powers, And Union "Gorillas"

Arnold, Ralph. "Laying Foundation Stones." *Historical Society of Southern California*, September 1955.

Benson, Ivan. "The Los Angeles Times Contempt Case." *Journalism Quarterly*, March 1939.

Bridges v. California/Times Mirror v. Superior Court of California. 314 U.S. 252 (1941).

"California's Seven Old Men Unpack Their Case Load." *Fortnight*, February 4, 1949.

Carlson, Oliver. *A Mirror for Californians*. New York: Bobbs-Merrill, 1941.

Dickson, E. A. Papers. Los Angeles: UCLA Special Collections.

Haynes, John R. Papers. Los Angeles: UCLA Public Affairs Library.

Hoover, Herbert. Papers. Westport, Iowa: Hoover Presidential Library.

Mavity, Nancy Barr. *Sister Aimee*. Garden City, New York: Doubleday, 1931.

McCarthy, John Russell. "Los Angeles' Bad, Bad Boy." *Westways*, February 1934.

Municipal League. *Bulletin: Light on Your City's Affairs*. September-November 1924.

Rosten, Leo. *The Washington Correspondents*. New York: Harcourt, Brace, 1935.

Sherman, Moses H. Papers. Especially Robert Armstrong File. Corona Del Mar: Sherman Foundation.

Shippey, Lee. *Luckiest Man Alive*. Los Angeles: Westernlore Press, 1959.

Sinclair, Upton. *The Brass Check*. Pasadena: Published by author, 1920.

Stewart, Kenneth, and Tebbel, John. *Makers of Modern Journalism*. Englewood Cliffs, New Jersey: Prentice-Hall, 1952.

Stossenberg, Dorothy. "Twenty-five Years of Women's Pages in Los Angeles." Masters thesis. UCLA, 1950.

Thomas, Lately. *Storming Heaven*. New York: William Morrow, 1970.

Turner, Timothy G. *Bullets, Bottles, and Gardenias*. Los Angeles: Southwest Press, 1935.

Vanderbilt, Cornelius, Jr. *Farewell to Fifth Avenue*. New York: Simon & Schuster, 1935.

Yeomans, Patricia Henry. *Behind the Headlines with Bill Henry*. Los Angeles: Ward Ritchie Press, 1972.

INTERVIEWS AND CORRESPONDENCE: John Aiso, Nick Avila, Nadine Bickmore, Al Blanchard, Elmer Bromley, Asa Call, Herbert Dillon, Waldo Drake, Bill Dredge, Robert Finch, Robert Hartmann, Kent Redwine, Phil Scheuer, Don Shannon, Taylor Trumbo, Rudy Villasenor, Bob Will, Alan Williams, Mrs. Carlton Williams, Al Wirin, Paul Zimmerman.

PART III

"Principles Don't Change"

Among Ourselves (in-House *Los Angeles Times* Publication). November, 1973.

Barnett, Chris. "An Interview with Dorothy Chandler." *PSA California*, November 1974.

"Building the Pavilions of Culture." *Time*, Dec. 18, 1964.

Chandler, Dorothy. Remarks at "Amazing Women of Dallas" luncheon, sponsored by Nieman-Marcus, September 29, 1966.

———. Statement in *Hearings before a Subcommittee of the Committee of Education and Labor*, House of Representatives, U.S. Congress, January 20, 1956.

Current Biography. 1958 Yearbook.

Domhoff, G. William. *Bohemian Grove and Other Retreats*. New York: Harper & Row, 1973.

Gross, Leonard. "Soul of the Center." *Westways*, February 1975.

Hart, Jack Robert. "The Information Empire: A History of the *Los Angeles Times* From the Era of Personal Journalism to the Advent of the Multi-Media Communications Company." PhD dissertation. Madison, Wisconsin: University of Wisconsin, 1975.

"Image of Leadership." *Printer's Ink*, September 18, 1959.

Los Angeles Chamber of Commerce. *Minutes of the Board of Directors, 1930–1939*.

Los Angeles County Clerk. Probate Index. Especially Frederick Warren Williamson Probate, 215805, 1942.

Los Angeles County Recorder. Grantor/Grantee Index. Especially Deed 2928, 1965: Norman Chandler.

"Los Angeles Society." *Town and Country*. May 1974.

May Goodan v. Earle Crowe. Los Angeles Superior Court C67875, 1973. Especially Chandler Trust Agreement, July 26, 1935.

Maynard, Paul. "The Exciting Story of Buffums." *Orange County Illustrated*, October 1967.

"New World." *Time*, July 18, 1957.

Neylan, John Francis. Papers. Berkeley: Bancroft Library.

"Norman Chandler: Heir to an Empire." *Look*, May 27, 1947.

Poinsettia. Hollywood High School Yearbook, 1917.

Standard and Poor's Directory of Executives. 1950–1973.

Storke, Thomas. Papers. Berkeley: Bancroft Library.

"Those Tireless Chandlers." *Newsweek*, April 30, 1956.

United States v. Times Mirror 65–366–F. United States District Court Central District, California. Especially Norman Chandler deposition, December 17, 1965.

Van Der Zee, John. *The Greatest Men's Party on Earth*. New York: Harcourt Brace Jovanovich, 1974.

INTERVIEWS: Herbert Allen, Tony Araujo, Daniel Bryant, Richard Buffum, Asa Call, Z. Wayne Griffin, Robert Hartmann, Preston Hotchkis, Frank King, Ernest Loebbecke, John R. Mage, Neil Petree, Victor Weybright, Paul Zimmerman.

Chapter 14: Big Red Dies

Automobile Club of Southern California. *Digest of Minutes of the Board of Directors*. 1900–1924.

Bowron, Fletcher. Papers. San Marino: Huntington Library. Papers. Los Angeles: UCLA Special Collections.

Brilliant, Ashley. "Some Aspects of Mass Motorization in Southern California." *Southern California Quarterly*, June 1965.

Clary, William W. *History of the Law Firm of O'Melveny & Myers*. Los Angeles: Privately printed, 1966.

Dickson, Edward. Papers. Los Angeles: UCLA Special Collections.

Doty, Robert, and Levine, Leonard. *Profile of an Air Pollution Controversy*. Los Angeles: Clean Air Now, 1974.

Hendricks, William O. *M. H. Sherman: A Pioneer Developer of the Pacific Southwest*. Corona Del Mar: Sherman Foundation, 1971.

Hilton, George W., and Due, John F. *The Electric Interurban Railways in America*. Palo Alto: Stanford University Press, 1960.

Keller, Henry W. Papers. Los Angeles: UCLA Special Collections.
Los Angeles Herald-Express. October 21–29, 1947.
Mathison, Richard R. *Three Cars in Every Garage*. Garden City, New York: Doubleday, 1968.
Moody's Industrials. 1918–1950.
Moody's Utilities. 1948–1951.
Post, Robert C. "The Fair Fare Fight." *Southern California Quarterly*, September 1970.
Report of the Executive Committee of the Activities of the Major Highways Committee Since November 4, 1924. Los Angeles: UCLA Special Collections.
Robbins, George W. and Tilton, L. Deming. *Los Angeles: Preface to a Master Plan*. Los Angeles: Pacific Southwest Academy, 1941.
Sherman, Moses. Papers. Corona del Mar: Sherman Foundation.
"Smog Kills." Pamphlet: Los Angeles: People's Lobby, 1974.
Snell, Bradford. *American Ground Transport*. Presented to the Subcommittee on Anti-trust and Monopoly, U.S. Senate. February 26, 1974.
Stuart, Frank. "Smog Circus in L.A." *Frontier*, December 1954.
"The Automobile Club and Population Growth: A View From a Los Angeles Realtor." Los Angeles: Los Angeles Realty Board, 1925.
Who's Who In California. 1950.
Interviews: Robert Doty, Joyce Koupal, Ernest Loebbecke, Neil Petree, Larry Pryor, Hugh Wilkins.

Chapter 15: Running City Hall

Adler, Pat. *The Bunker Hill Story*. Glendale, California: La Siesta Press, 1963.
Arnebergh, Roger. *Statement Before Assembly Committee on Government Efficiency and Economy*. California State Assembly. May 15, 1958.
Baisden, Richard N. "Labor Unions in Los Angeles Politics." PhD dissertation. Chicago: University of Chicago, 1958.
Borough, Reuben. Oral history. Los Angeles: UCLA Special Collections, 1968.
Chamberlain, Ernest. "The Civic Committee of Los Angeles." Los Angeles: UCLA Special Collections.
Clinton, Clifford. Papers. Los Angeles: UCLA Special Collections.
Committee Against Socialist Housing. *Campaign Leaders Handbook*, 1952.
Freedman, Leonard. "Group Opposition to Public Housing." PhD dissertation. Los Angeles: UCLA, 1959.
Marine, Gene. "Bunker Hill." *Frontier*, August 1959.
Poulson, Norris. Oral history. Los Angeles: UCLA Special Collections, 1966.
Poulson, Norris. "The Untold Story of Chavez Ravine." *Los Angeles*, April, 1962.
Rigby, George. *Los Angeles City Administrative Officer: The Leask Years 1951–1961*. Los Angeles: Privately printed, 1974.
Roybal, Edward. Papers. Los Angeles: UCLA Special Collections.
Roybal, Edward. *Statement to Legislative Hearing*. Los Angeles City Council, May 16, 1958.
Sjoquist, Arthur W. "From Posses to Professionals: A History of the Los Angeles Police Department." Masters thesis. California State University, Los Angeles, 1972.
Town Hall Meeting. *The Dodgers Referendum Issue*. Los Angeles: April, 1958.
Wentz, Walter. "The Los Angeles Newspaper Guild." Masters thesis. Claremont: Claremont College, 1940.
Who's Who in California. 1958.
Wilkinson, Frank. "And Now the Bill Comes Due." *Frontier*, October 1965.

INTERVIEWS: Joseph Aidlin, Herbert Baus, Madeleine Borough, Asa Call, George Cronk, Edward Davis, Ernest Debs, John Gibson, Samuel Leask, Jr., Norris Poulson, Stuart Spencer, Philip Watson, Frank Wilkinson, Alan Williams, Mrs. Carlton Williams, Rosalind Wyman.

Chapter 16: Republican Fortunes

Barrett, Edward L., Jr. *The Tenney Committee*. Ithaca: Cornell University Press, 1951.

Blumberg, Nathan B. *One Party Press?* Lincoln: University of Nebraska Press, 1954.

Burke, Robert E. *Olson's New Deal for California*. Berkeley: University of California Press, 1953.

Carney, Francis. *The Rise of the Democratic Clubs in California*. New York: Henry Holt, 1958.

Faries, McIntyre. Oral history. Los Angeles: UCLA Special Collections.

Graves, Richard. Oral history. Los Angeles: UCLA Special Collections.

Greenstone, David J. *Labor in American Politics*. New York: Alfred A. Knopf, 1969.

Harvey, Richard. *Earl Warren: Governor of California*. New York: Exposition Press, 1969.

Katcher, Leo. *Earl Warren: A Political Biography*. New York: McGraw-Hill, 1967.

Kenny, Robert W. Oral history. Los Angeles: UCLA Special Collections.

Knight, Goodwin. Papers. Palo Alto: Stanford University.

McWilliams, Carey. "Government by Whitaker and Baxter." *New Republic*, May, June 1951.

——. "Warren of California." *New Republic*. October 18, 1943.

Phillips, Herbert. *Big Wayward Girl*. New York: Doubleday, 1968.

Rogin, Michael Paul, and Shover, John L. *Political Change in California*. Westport, Connecticut: Greenwood, 1970.

Rowse, Arthur Edward. *Slanted News: A Case Study of the Nixon and Stevenson Fund Stories*. Boston: Beacon Press, 1957.

Scoggins, Verne. Oral history. Los Angeles: UCLA Special Collections.

Stevenson, Janet. "The Undiminished Man." Unpublished manuscript. 1975.

Storke, Thomas. Papers. Berkeley: Bancroft Library.

Tuttle, Frederick Jr. "The California Democrats 1953–1966." PhD dissertation. UCLA, 1975.

White, Theodore. *Breach of Faith*. New York: Atheneum, 1975.

Willburn, James R. "Social and Economic Aspects of the Aircraft Industry in Metropolitan Los Angeles During World War II." PhD dissertation. UCLA, 1971.

Williams, Lance M. "Press Coverage of the Nixon/Douglas Senate Race, 1950." Masters thesis. University of California, Berkeley, 1974.

INTERVIEWS: Pat Brown, Asa Call, Frederick Chase, Charles Ducommun, Howard Edgerton, Robert Finch, John Anson Ford, Alfred Gittleson, Robert Hartmann, Leo Katcher, Robert W. Kenny, Herbert Klein, Virginia Knight, Carey McWilliams, Ellis Patterson, Don Shannon, Thomas Webster, Alan Williams.

Chapter 17: Winning the Poker Game

Bonelli, William G. *Billion Dollar Blackjack*. Beverly Hills: Civic Research Press, 1954.

Conlon, Timothy J. "The Death of the Los Angeles Mirror." Masters thesis. Palo Alto: Stanford University, 1962.

Cottrell, Edwin A. and Jones, Helen L. *Metropolitan Los Angeles: A study in Integration. I: Characteristics of the Metropolis.* Los Angeles: Haynes Foundation. 1952.

Current Biography. Yearbook, 1958.

Editor and Publisher. January 5, 1948; October 9, 1948; July 16, 1949; October 15, 1949; December 25, 1954; February 12, 1955; December 29, 1956; February 2, 1957; November 16, 1957; November 1, 1958; August 13, 1960.

Friedman, Ralph. "Booming California." *Frontier*, April 1957.

Hensher, Alan. "No News Today." *Journalism Quarterly*, Winter 1970.

Scott, Paul T. "The Mass Media in Los Angeles Since the Rise of Television." *Journalism Quarterly*, Spring 1954.

Scully, Frank. "Billion Dollar Blackjack." *Frontier*, October 1954.

Stocker, Joseph. "Sex, Crime, and Slaughter." *American Mercury*, January, 1953.

"The Undiscovered City." *Fortune*, June 1949.

United States v. Times Mirror, 65-366-F. United States District Court, Central District California. 1967.

INTERVIEWS AND CORRESPONDENCE: Mahlon Arnett, Julie Byrne, Robert Chandler, Dorothy Coleman, Ernest Debs, Art Goldberg, Leo Katcher, J. Edward Murray, Vern Partlow, Frank Rice, Arelo Sederberg, James Seyster, Jack Tobin, Paul Weeks, Art White.

Chapter 18: Cold War Journalism

Benson, Ivan. "Los Angeles Times Contempt Case." *Journalism Quarterly*, March 1939.

Burton, Bernard. Testimony. *Hearings Before the Committee on Un-American Activities Committee.* United States House of Representatives, September 2 & 3, 1958.

Chandler, Harry. *Testimony. Hearings Before the Committee on Immigration and Naturalization, House of Representatives.* 71st Congress, 2nd Session.

Daniels, Roger. "The Politics of Prejudice." PhD dissertation. Los Angeles: UCLA, 1960.

Editor and Publisher. December 15, 1956; December 29, 1956; October 18, 1958.

Fitzgerald, Robin. "The Mexican-American in the Los Angeles Area: 1920–1950." PhD dissertation. Costa Mesa: USC, 1961.

Griffith, Beatrice. *American Me.* Boston: Houghton Mifflin, 1948.

Grodzins, Morton. *Americans Betrayed: Politics and the Japanese Evacuation.* Chicago: University of Chicago Press, 1949.

Hoover, Herbert. Papers. Westport, Iowa: Hoover Presidential Library.

Jones, Solomon J. "The Government Riots of Los Angeles." Masters thesis. UCLA, 1969.

McWilliams, Carey. *North From Mexico.* Westport, Connecticut: Greenwood Press, 1968.

———. *Prejudice.* Boston: Little, Brown, 1944.

———. "The Zoot Suit Riots." *New Republic*, June 21, 1943.

Myer, Dillon S. *Uprooted Americans: The Japanese-Americans and the War Relocation Authority During World War II.* Tucson: University of Arizona Press, 1971.

Poulson, Norris. Oral history. Los Angeles: UCLA Special Collections, 1966.

INTERVIEWS AND CORRESPONDENCE: Nadine Mason Bickmore, Glen Binford, Gene Blake, Al Blanchard, Herbert Brin, Tom Cameron, Waldo Drake, William Dredge, Albert Goldberg, Richard Hannah, Robert Hartmann, Richard Mathison, Clark Roberts, Ted Sell, Don Shannon, Cecil Smith, Taylor Trumbo, Rudy Villasenor, Leonard Wibberly, Robert Will, Nick Williams.

Chapter 19: The Politics of Culture

Barnett, Chris. "An Interview with Dorothy Chandler." *PSA California*, November, 1974.

"Building the Pavilions of Culture." *Time*, December 18, 1964.

Chandler, Dorothy. "A Dream Comes True." *Junior League News*, February, 1960.

Clary, William W. *A History of the Law Firm of O'Melveny & Myers*. Los Angeles: Privately printed, 1966.

Davenport, Charles. "The Music Center and Mrs. Chandler." *Los Angeles*, May 1962.

————. "You and the Music Center." *Junior League News*, May 1961.

Gross, Leonard. "Soul of the Center." *Westways*, February, 1975.

Hopper, Hedda, and Brough, James. *The Whole Truth and Nothing But*. New York: Doubleday, 1963.

"Los Angeles Society." *Town and Country*, May 1974.

"Pride and the Power." *Women's Wear Daily*, March 18, 1975.

"That Cultural Curtain." *The Nation*, February 4, 1956.

"An Interview with Igor Stravinsky." *The New York Review of Books*, January 3, 1965.

Knight, Arthur. "Bloom in the Cultural Desert." *Saturday Review*, December 26, 1964.

Toland, James, ed. *The Music Center Story*. Los Angeles: Music Center Foundation, 1974.

INTERVIEWS: Mahlon Arnett, Richard Buffum, Asa Call, Victor Carter, Charles Ducommun, John Anson Ford, Albert Goldberg, George Gose, George Kuyper, Neil Petree, S. Mark Taper, Thomas Webster, Rosalind Wyman.

PART IV

Most Likely to Succeed

Aronson, James. *The Press and the Cold War*. Indianapolis: Bobbs-Merrill, 1970.

Chandler, Otis. "A Publisher's View of Credibility." in *Politics and the Press*, Richard Lee, ed. Washington, D.C.: Acropolis Books, 1970.

————. "Why a Newspaper in an Electronic Era?" Speech before the Lovejoy Convocation at Colby College, Waterville, Maine, November 10, 1966.

"Changing Times." *Time*, April 25, 1960.

Current Biography. Yearbook, 1968.

"How to Build an Empire." *Newsweek*, January 2, 1967.

"L.A.'s Mighty Chandlers." *Look*, September 25, 1962.

"L.A. Times Revises its Image." *Business Week*, November 19, 1960.

McKinsey & Co. *"Planning Executive Organization Succession, Times Mirror Company."* Memorandum to Norman Chandler, June 11, 1958.

SEC v. GeoTek C-73-0819-WTS. United States District Court, Northern District California. Especially Otis Chandler Deposition, March 23, 1972.

Standard and Poor's Directory of Executives, 1965–1977.

"Survey of the L.A. Market." *Printer's Ink*, November 13, 1959.

United States v. Times Mirror, 65-366-F. United States District Court, Central District California. Especially Otis Chandler Deposition December 20, 1965.

INTERVIEWS: Asa Call, Z. Wayne Griffin, Frank King, Frank McCulloch, Neil Petree, Norris Poulson, Art White, Nick Williams, Paul Zimmerman.

Chapter 20: Taking Off

Bell, Alphonzo. "A Look at Union Pension Funds." Congressional Record reprint. 87th Congress, House of Representatives, 2nd Session.

Chandler, Otis. KNXT interview (Channel 2 Los Angeles), October 13–17, 1975.

Hart, Jack R. "The Information Empire. A History of the Los Angeles Times From the Era of Personal Journalism to the Advent of the Multi-Media Communications Company." PhD dissertation. Madison, Wisconsin: University of Wisconsin, 1975.

Johnson, Paula, Sears, David O., and McConahay, John. "Black Invisibility, the Press, and the Los Angeles Riot." *American Journal of Sociology*, January 1971.

"L.A. Times' Goals Defined by Year's Moves." *Editor and Publisher*, December 2, 1961.

Lincoln, C. Eric. *The Black Muslims in America*. Boston: Beacon Press, 1973.

"New York Times Out West." *Columbia Journalism Review*, Winter 1963.

Sheridan, Walter. *The Fall and Rise of Jimmy Hoffa*. New York: Saturday Review Press, 1972.

Storke, Thomas. Papers. Berkeley: Bancroft Library.

Talese, Gay. *The Kingdom and the Power*. New York: Bantam, 1970.

Times Mirror Company. *Minutes of the Regular Meeting of the Board of Directors*, 1961–1962.

"Troubled Times." *Business Week*, January 11, 1964.

United States v. Times Mirror 65-366-F. United States District Court, Central District, California.

"Violence in the City." *A Report by the Governor's Commission on the Los Angeles Riots*. The McCone Commission, 1965.

INTERVIEWS AND CORRESPONDENCE: Mahlon Arnett, John Averill, Gene Blake, Edward Carter, Robert J. Donovan, Robert Hartmann, Gladwyn Hill, Don Irwin, Dr. Granville Knight, David Kraslow, Frank McCulloch, Don Neff, Ron Ostrow, Morrie Ryskind, Don Shannon, Paul Talbert, Jack Tobin, Paul Veblen, Paul Weeks, Nick Williams.

Chapter 21: Many Monopolies

Chandler, Otis. Speech Before Los Angeles Financial Analysts. *Wall Street Transcript*, April 14, 1968.

"Changes Implement Acquisition Program." *Editor and Publisher*, May 7, 1960.

Conlon, Timothy. "The Death of the *Los Angeles Mirror*." Masters thesis. Stanford University, 1962.

"Death in the Cityroom." *CBS Reports*, January 25, 1962.

Fuller, Edmund. "Book Publisher Offers Warning to the Trade." *Wall Street Journal*, October 24, 1967.
Gordon, Mitchell. "The Chandlers of Los Angeles." *Nieman Reports*, June 1965.
Gottlieb, Bob. "Does the Herald-Examiner Have a Future?" *Los Angeles*, February, 1977.
Guttman, Daniel and Willner, Barry. *The Shadow Government*. New York: Pantheon, 1976.
Hearings on Concentration of Ownership in the News Media Before Anti-Trust Subcommittee of the Judiciary, House of Representatives, March 13–15, April 9, 1963.
"Los Angeles Times Revises Its Image." *Business Week*, November 19, 1960.
Lyle, Jack. "Audience Impact of a Double Newspaper Merger." *Journalism Quarterly*, Spring 1962.
Magazine of Wall Street, June 6, 1970 (126:22).
Moody's Industrials. 1960–1976.
"Publishing Giant Takes a Big Step." *Business Week*, March 14, 1964.
"Senators Get Documents Revealing L.A. Dailies Pact." *Advertising Age*, April 22, 1968.
Standard and Poor's Directory of Executives and Corporations. 1960–1977.
"Start the Presses." *Barron's*, September 12, 1966.
Targ, William. *Indecent Pleasures*. New York: Macmillan, 1975.
"Times Mirror Analyzes Prospects in Modern Newspaper Industry." *Barron's*, July 9, 1973.
"Times Mirror Publishing Stock Analysis." *Wall Street Transcript*, May 7, 1973.
United States v. Times Mirror, 65-366-F. United States District Court, Central District California. Especially depositions of Robert Allan, Milton Day, Otis Chandler, Nick Williams.
Weybright, Victor. *The Making of a Publisher*. New York: Reynal & Co., 1966.
INTERVIEWS AND CORRESPONDENCE: Mahlon Arnett, Robert Chandler, Kurt Enoch, Frank King, Stan Leppard, J. Edward Murray, Victor Weybright.

Chapter 22: Weep No More

Baus, Herbert and Ross, William. *Politics Battle Plan*. Garden City, New York: Doubleday, 1968.
Bollens, John and Geyer, Grant. *Yorty: The Politics of a Constant Candidate*. Pacific Palisades: Palisades Publishers, 1973.
Curtis, Christopher. "What Makes Sammy Run." *Los Angeles Free Press*, May 25, 1973.
Donovan, Robert J. *The Future of the Republican Party*. New York: New American Library, 1965.
Hill, Gladwyn. *Dancing Bear*. New York: World, 1968.
Knight, Goodwin. Papers. Palo Alto: Stanford University.
Mayo, Charles. "The Mass Media and Campaign Strategy in a Mayoralty Campaign." *Journalism Quarterly*, Summer 1964.
Peterson, Harry. "A Study of the 1962 California Gubernatorial Campaign as Reported in the Press of the State." Masters thesis. University of California, Berkeley, 1963.
Phillips, Herbert. *Big Wayward Girl*. Garden City, New York: Doubleday, 1968.
Riley, Frank. "The Changing Direction of the Times." *Los Angeles*, June 1966.
Storke, Thomas. Papers. Berkeley: Bancroft Library.
"The Untold Story of Nixon and the Press." *U.S. News and World Report*, November 26, 1962.

Williams, Carlton. Papers. Los Angeles: Private Collection.
Wills, Gary. *Nixon Agonistes*. New York: New American Library, 1971.
Yorty, Samuel. "Why I Cannot Take Kennedy." Pamphlet. Los Angeles, 1960.
INTERVIEWS: Herbert Baus, Richard Bergholz, Pat Brown, Asa Call, Robert Donovan, Howard Edgerton, Robert Finch, Alfred Gittleson, Donald Healey, Don Irwin, Herbert Klein, Frank McCulloch, Neil Petree, Norris Poulson, Stuart Spencer, Alan Williams, Nick Williams, Samuel Yorty.

Transition

Cohen, Jerry and Murphy, William. *Burn, Baby, Burn*. New York: E. P. Dutton, 1966.
Conot, Robert. *Rivers of Blood, Years of Darkness*. New York: Bantam, 1967.
Crump, Spencer. *Black Riot in Los Angeles*. Los Angeles: Trans-Anglo Books, 1966.
Fogelson, Robert. *The Los Angeles Riots*. New York: Arno Press, 1969.
Jacobs, Paul. *Prelude to Riot*. New York: Random House, 1967.
Lyle, Jack. *The Black American and the Press*. Los Angeles: Ward Ritchie, 1968.
Riley, Frank. "The Changing Direction of the Times." *Los Angeles*, June 1966.
"Violence in the City." *A Report by the Governor's Commission on the Los Angeles Riots*. The McCone Commission, 1965.
Williams, Nick. "America's Third Force: The Watchdog Press." In *The Responsibility of the Press*, Gerald Gross, ed. New York: Fleet Press, 1966.
INTERVIEWS AND CORRESPONDENCE: Art Berman, Gene Blake, Asa Call, Robert Donovan, Philip Fradkin, Robert Jackson, Frank McCulloch, Harry Nelson, Ray Rogers, Paul Weeks, Nick Williams.

Chapter 23: The Proverbial Snowball

Bart, Peter. "New Look at the Times." *Saturday Review*, June 12, 1965.
Blanchard, Robert. *Congress and the News Media*. New York: Hastings House, 1974.
Carroll, Donald, "Paul Conrad: The Pen That Needles." *Coast*, March 1974.
Editor and Publisher. February 6, 1971.
Hart, Jack. "The Information Empire." PhD dissertation. Madison, Wisconsin: University of Wisconsin, 1975.
Kerby, Phil. "Most Likely to Succeed." *The Nation*, January 15, 1968.
———. "Nose for Corruption." *The Nation*, November 6, 1967.
Kraslow, David and Loory, Stuart. *The Secret Search for Peace in Vietnam*. New York: Random House, 1968.
Otten, Alan. "Background Briefings in the Capitol Are Used for Both Good and Ill." *Wall Street Journal*, April 10, 1968.
Reston, James. *The Artillery of the Press*. New York: Harper & Row, 1966.
Rivers, William. "New Winds in the South." *Saturday Review*, September 23, 1967.
Ross, Rob. "Waste, Westward Woe." *UCLA Bruin*, February 10, 1972.
Sigal, Leon. *Reporters and Officials*. Lexington, Mass.: D.C. Heath, 1973.
Vier, Gene. "The Decline (and Fall) of West." *LA*, September 30, 1972.
Wakeland, Jeanie R. "How the West Was Lost." Masters thesis. Eugene: University of Oregon, 1974.
Witcover, Jules. "Washington, The News Explosion." *Columbia Journalism Review*, Spring 1969.

————. "Washington Letter." *Columbia Journalism Review*, Spring 1968.
INTERVIEWS: Rudy Abramson, John Averill, James Bellows, Art Berman, Glen Binford, Dennis Britton, Peter Bunzell, Paul Conrad, Ed Davis, Robert Donovan, Howard Edgerton, Ron Einstoss, John Gibson, Noel Greenwood, Z. Wayne Griffin, Edward Guthman, Paul Houston, Frank Interlandi, Don Irwin, Robert Jackson, David Kraslow, Ernest Loebbecke, Stuart Loory, Marshall Lumsden, Linda Mathews, Ron Moscovitz, Jack Nelson, Ronald Ostrow, Peter Pitchess, Ray Rogers, Art Seidenbaum, Doug Shuit, William Trombley, Francis Ward, Nick Williams, Stanley Williford, Samuel Yorty.

Chapter 24: Politics in Flux

Baus, Herbert and Ross, William. *Politics Battle Plan*. Garden City, New York: Doubleday, 1968.
Bollens, John and Geyer, Grant. *Yorty: Politics of a Constant Candidate*. Pacific Palisades: Palisades Publishers, 1973.
Boyarsky, Bill. *The Rise of Ronald Reagan*. New York: Random House, 1968.
Bradley, Thomas. Papers. Los Angeles: Private Collection.
Cannon, Lou. *Ronnie and Jess*. Garden City, New York: Doubleday, 1969.
Curtis, Christopher. "What Makes Sammy Run." *Los Angeles Free Press*, May 25, 1973.
Draper, Ann and Draper, Hal. *Who Runs The Multiversity?* Berkeley: Independent Socialists, 1965.
Lewis, Joseph. *What Makes Reagan Run?* New York: McGraw-Hill, 1968.
McGinnis, Joseph. *The Selling of the President*. New York: Trident Press, 1969.
Turner, William. *Power on the Right*. San Francisco: Ramparts Press, 1971.
Witcover, Jules. "Focusing on Nixon." *Columbia Journalism Review*, Winter 1968-1969.
————. "The Press and Chicago." *Columbia Journalism Review*, Fall 1968.
————. *The Resurrection of Richard Nixon*. New York: Putnam's, 1970.
"Yortytoons." *Newsweek*, February 12, 1968.
INTERVIEWS: Pat Brown, D. J. R. Bruckner, Asa Call, Edward Carter, Paul Conrad, Howard Edgerton, Tom Goff, Edward Guthman, Don Irwin, Stuart Loory, Linda Mathews, Neil Petree, Ray Rogers, Stuart Spencer, William Trombley, Samuel Yorty.

Chapter 25: Bigger than a Breadbox

Casey, Albert. "Group Publishers Weigh Expansion." *Editor and Publisher*, December 29, 1973.
————. *Speech Before Investment Analysts of Chicago. Wall Street Transcript*, December 31, 1973.
"Defining Monopoly." *Newsweek*, October 23, 1969.
"Is Now the Hour." Al Casey profile. *Forbes*, March 1, 1974.
Kidder, Peabody & Co. *Research Information: Times Mirror*. July 27, 1970.
"L.A. Times." *Business Week*, November 20, 1971.
Magazine of Wall Street, June 6, 1970.
Mecklin, John. "Times Mirror's Ambitious Acquirers." *Fortune*, September 1, 1968.
Moody's Industrials. 1965–1976.
Murphy, Franklin. Papers. Lawrence: University of Kansas.

———. "Address to the Shareholders." Times Mirror Annual Meeting, 1975.
———. "Presentation to Security Analysts of San Francisco." *Wall Street Transcript*, May 19, 1975.
———. "Yardsticks for a New Era." *Saturday Review*, September 21, 1970.
Ridgeway, James. *The Closed Corporation*. New York: Random House, 1968.
"Start the Presses." *Barron's*, September 12, 1966. Also December 26, 1970.
"They Found Newspapers Best After All." *Business Week*, December 26,1970.
"Times Mirror Analyzes Prospects." *Barron's*, July 9, 1973.
Times Mirror. Annual Reports 1965–1976; 10K Reports 1968–1976; Prospectus 1969–1975.
INTERVIEWS: Edward Carter, Frank King, John Pastier, William Van Patten.

The Dallas Connection

Broadcasting. February 9, 1974; February 18, 1974.
Gepfert, Kenneth. "The Texas Statehouse Press." Masters thesis. University of Texas, Austin, 1971.
A. C. Greene v. James Chambers, et al. CA-3-2515-C. United States District Court, Northern District of Texas, Dallas Division.
Holley, Steven. "The Dallas Morning News and the Image of Dallas the Decade After the Kennedy Assassination." Masters thesis. University of Texas, Austin, 1974.
Leslie, Warren. *Dallas, Public and Private*. New York: Grossman, 1964.
Maranto, Samuel. "A History of Dallas Newspapers." Masters thesis. University of Texas, Austin, 1971.
Rogers, John. *The Lusty Texans of Dallas*. Dallas: Cookesbury Book Store, 1965.
Smith, Griffin. "Deadline in Dallas." *Texas Monthly*, June 1974.
Standard and Poor's Directory of Executives. 1977.
Thometz, Carol Estes. *The Decision Makers*. Dallas: Southern Methodist University Press, 1963.
Times Herald Printing Company. Proxy Statement, December 5, 1969.
Westmoreland, Reginald. "A History of the Dallas Times Herald." PhD dissertation. University of Missouri, Columbia, 1961.
Who's Who in America. 1976–1977.
INTERVIEWS AND CORRESPONDENCE: James Aston, Vivian Castleberry, A. C. Greene, Carolyn Jackson, Lady Bird Johnson, Tom Johnson, J. C. Kellam, Felix McKnight, Bob Mann, James Maxwell, Dave McNeeley, David Montgomery, Marian O'Brien, Darwin Payne, Bill Porterfield, John Schoellkopf, Griffin Smith Jr., Lou Sterrett, Dorothy Stuck, Sara Lee Tiede, James Turner.

Chapter 26: The Odyssey of Ruben Salazar

"Chicano Columnist." *Newsweek*, January 22, 1970.
Drummond, William. "The Death of the Man in the Middle." *Esquire*, April, 1972.
Herrera, Albert. "The National Chicano Moratorium and the Death of Ruben Salazar." In *The Chicanos*, Ed Ludwig and Tamis Santibanez, eds. Baltimore: Penguin, 1971.
Salazar, Ruben. "A Major Misunderstanding." In *The Eight Ball*. Los Angeles Press Club, 1966.
———. *A Selection of Columns. Los Angeles Times* reprint. n.d.
INTERVIEWS AND CORRESPONDENCE: Nick Avilla, Frank Del Omo, Ron Einstoss,

Paul Finch, Robert Gibson, Frank McCulloch, Ray Rogers, Sally Salazar, Ted Sell, Rudy Villasenor, Baxter Ward, Nick Williams.

Point/Counter-Point

INTERVIEWS AND CORRESPONDENCE: Rudy Abramson, James Bellows, Dennis Britton, Robert Jackson, David Kraslow, Stuart Loory, Ron Ostrow, Nick Williams.

Chapter 27: Down and Up in Washington

Clancy, Paul. "The Bureau and the Bureaus." *The Quill*, February and March, 1976.
Crouse, Timothy. *The Boys on the Bus*. New York: Random House, 1973.
Davis, Jim, and Carter, George. "L.A. Times: Retrenching in Washington." *Review of Southern California Journalism*, April 1973.
Kraslow, David. Memo of meeting with J. Edgar Hoover. October 13, 1971.
Latham, Aaron. "How Glomar Really Surfaced." *New York*, April 7, 1975.
Loory, Stuart. *Defeated: Inside America's Military Machine*. New York: Random House, 1973.
Nelson, Jack. "An Interview with Jack Nelson." In *CBS Reports, "Inside the FBI."* January 26, 1976.
———, and Ostrow, Ron. *The FBI and the Berrigans*. New York: Coward, McCann and Geoghegan, 1972.
Powledge, Fred. *The Engineering of Restraint*. Washington, D.C.: Public Affairs Press, 1971.
Thomas, William. "Warts and All, Our Cause is Your Cause." *Los Angeles Times*, December 24, 1972.
"Times Bureau in Washington Loses Another." *LA*, January, 1973.
Witcover, Jules. "Two Weeks That Shook the Press." *Columbia Journalism Review*, September-October 1971.
———. "Where Washington Reporting Failed." *Columbia Journalism Review*, Winter 1970–1971.
INTERVIEWS AND CORRESPONDENCE: Rudy Abramson, John Averill, Dennis Britton, D. J. R. Bruckner, Marlene Cimons, Don Cook, Robert Donovan, Richard Dougherty, William Farr, Edward Guthman, Paul Houston, Don Irwin, Robert Jackson, Herbert Klein, David Kraslow, Stuart Loory, Linda Mathews, Mark Murphy, Jack Nelson, Ron Ostrow, Nick Williams.

Chapter 28: Eagle in Flight

Cohen, Bernard. *The Press and Foreign Policy*. Princeton: Princeton University Press, 1963.
INTERVIEWS AND CORRESPONDENCE: Don Cook, Arthur Dommen, Waldo Drake, Robert Gibson, David Lamb, Jacques Leslie, Stanley Meisler, Donald Neff, Don Shannon, Sterling Slappey, Nick Williams.

Chapter 29: The Soft Mood and Soft News

Arnold, William D. et al v. Bert Tiffany et al. Civil Action 73-9312-HP. United States District Court, Central District, California.

California Fair Employment Practices Commission. *Investigation of the Los Angeles Times*. March 1973. "Progress Report" April 1974.

Chandler, Otis. Speech before the Ad Club of Los Angeles. March 31, 1976.

Hart, Jack. "The Information Empire." PhD dissertation. University of Wisconsin, Madison, 1975.

Hearings Before the Subcommittee on Antitrust and Monopoly of the Committee on the Judiciary, United States Senate. *On S. 408*, Part 2, May 12, 1975.

International Printing and Graphics Communications Union. Papers. Los Angeles.

Kushner, Sam. "Why Not the Times." *The Review of Southern California Journalism*, May 1974.

Los Angeles Times Women's Editorial Caucus. *Initial Goals; Suggested Action; Additional Goals for Future Dialog*. Los Angeles, October 1974.

McKinsey, Floyd et al. v. Times Mirror. Civil Action 73-946-EC. United States District Court, Central District California.

Morris, Monica B. "Newspapers and the New Feminists: Black Out as Social Control." *Journalism Quarterly*, Spring 1973.

Murphy, Art. "Time, Not Times Overran Haber." *Variety*, October 17, 1975.

"Pride Makes Editorial Department Go." *Among Ourselves* (in-house publication). June 1974.

Times Mirror Company. *Annual Report*, 1970–1976. *10K Statement* 1975–1976.

Wenz, Walter. "The Los Angeles Newspaper Guild." Masters thesis. Claremont College, 1940.

Wolt, Irene and Good, Marilyn. "The Times Versus the Newspaper Guild." *The Review of Southern California Journalism*, May 1974.

INTERVIEWS AND CORRESPONDENCE: George Alexander, Robert Ash, Beverly Beyette, James Bellows, Cheryl Bensten, Martin Bernheimer, Harry Bernstein, Glen Binford, Gene Blake, Bill Boyarsky, Daniel Bryant, Charles Champlin, Marlene Cimons, Robert Cohen, Frank Del Omo, Lee Dye, Albert Goldberg, Art Goldberg, Noel Greenwood, Robert Harlow, Lee Harris, Gregg Kilday, Beth Ann Krier, Lynn Lilliston, Jack McCurdy, Al Martinez, Charles McGuire, Jean Murphy, Mark Murphy, Mary Murphy, Harry Nelson, John Pastier, Neil Petree, Charles Powers, Larry Pryor, Lionel Rolfe, Art Seidenbaum, David Shaw, Doug Shuit, Cecil Smith, Dave Smith, Daniel Sullivan, Jean Taylor, Kevin Thomas, William Torrance, William Trombley, Ursula Vils, Wayne Warga, Nick Williams, Narda Zacchino.

Chapter 30: Management Ideologies

Carroll, Donald. "Paul Conrad: The Pen That Needles." *Coast*, March 1974.

Chandler, Otis. "Chandler Says 'America Not Going Down Drain.'" *Among Ourselves* (in house publication). June 1975.

———. "Otis Chandler Answers Some Questions." *Among Ourselves*. March 1975.

———. Speech before the Ad Club of Los Angeles. March 31, 1976.

———. Speech before the Sigma Delta Chi National Convention. November 13, 1975.

Conrad, Paul. *The King and Us*. Los Angeles: Clymer Publications, 1974.

Emery, Mike. "How the Times Picked Dick." *The Review of Southern California Journalism*, December 1972.

Gottlieb, Bob, and Kaye, Jeffrey. "Missy Chandler: Howard Hughes' Secret Connection at the Times." *Los Angeles*, May 1976.

"The New Concerns of the Press." *Fortune*, April 1975.

Thomas, William. "The Press: Is It Biased Against the Establishment?" *Los Angeles Times*, March 30, 1975.

INTERVIEWS: Martin Bernheimer, Peter Bunzell, Paul Conrad, Edward Davis, Lou Fleming, Robert Gibson, Z. Wayne Griffin, Ernest Loebbecke, John Pastier, Kenneth Reich, Sharon Rosenhause, Dan Sullivan, Jean Taylor, Rob Wood.

Chapter 31: Newsday: Times Mirror on the Island

"Affirmative Action: A Policy for Newsday." *Inside Newsday*, October 23, 1973.

"Alicia in Wonderland." *Time*, September 13, 1954.

Altshul, Jack. "Pulitzer Prizes in our Past." *Inside Newsday*, May 14, 1974.

Aronson, Harvey. "The Captain and the Kid." *New York*, March 30, 1970.

"Atwood Named Publisher of Newsday." *Advertising Age*, September 7, 1970.

"Captain Bails Out." *Newsweek*, April 27, 1970.

Caro, Robert. *The Power Broker*. New York: Alfred A. Knopf, 1975.

Carter, Sylvia et al. v. Newsday Inc. 75-Civ-52 (JRB). United States District Court, Eastern District New York.

Lomask, Milton. *Seed Money: The Guggenheim Story*. New York: Farrar, Straus, 1964.

Moody's Industrials. 1970–1973.

"No Comment: Purchase of Newsday." *Time*, March 23, 1970.

Patterson, Alicia. Special Issue Devoted to Alicia Patterson. *Inside Newsday*, April 1975.

Tebbel, John. *An American Dynasty*. Garden City, New York: Doubleday, 1947.

Times Mirror Company. *10K Statement*. 1970–1976.

Welles, Chris. "Newsday: Will the Times Make It Just Another Fat Tabloid?" *The Review of Southern California Journalism*, April 1973.

Wise, David. *The Politics of Lying*. New York: Random House, 1973.

INTERVIEWS: James Atwood, Hal Burton, Sylvia Carter, Kenneth Crowe, Peter Goodman, Edward Hershey, Bruce Lambert, David Laventhol, Edward Lowe, Jerry Morgan, Mel Opotowsky, Mike Quinn, Russel Sackett, Geraldine Shanahan, Ernest Volkman.

Chapter 32: The Agribusiness Interests

Ackerman, Adolph. *Final Report on the Feather River-Southern California Aqueduct*, October 20, 1960.

Boyle, Robert, Graves, John, and Watkins, T. H. *The Water Hustlers*. San Francisco: Sierra Club, 1971.

Cooper, Erwin. *Aqueduct Empire*. Glendale: Arthur H. Clark, 1968.

"Farmworkers in Rural America 1971–1972. *Hearings Before the Subcommittee on Migratory Labor of the Committee on Land and Public Welfare*. United States Senate, 92nd Congress.

Fellmeth, Robert. *The Politics of Land*. New York: Grossman, 1973.

Finance. Article on the Tejon Ranch. October, 1970.

James G. Boswell Company. Joint Proxy and Information Statement, May 25, 1973. Also "Application for Qualification of Securities." File 301 3442. Department of Corporations, State of California.

James G. Boswell Foundation. 990PF Report. United States Internal Revenue Service.

Kern County Recorder. Grantor/Grantee Index, 1970–1976.
Kuttner, Bob. "Covering Up in California." *MORE*, November 1971.
Los Angeles County Recorder. Grantor/Grantee Index, 1970–1976.
Milliman, J. W. *Economic Problems of the Metropolitan Water District of Southern California*. Western Economic Association, August 1957.
Project Land Use. *Request for Disapproval of the Proposed 'Tejon Ranch Lake' Development Project*, Bakersfield: March 5, 1973. Also *Task Force Study*, December 4, 1972, submitted to Kern County Planning Commission.
Systems Management, Inc. *Report on Tejon Ranch Lake Development*, 1972.
Tejon Agricultural Partners. *Prospectus*, 1972.
Tejon Ranch Company. *Annual Report*, 1968–1976; *10K Statement*, 1969–1976.
INTERVIEWS: Pat Brown, Ransom Chase, Robert Fellmeth, Philip Fradkin, Paul Houston, Robert Jones, Joy Lane, Ernest Loebbecke, Linda Mathews, Scott Newhall, John Pastier, Larry Pryor, Richard Richards, Alan Williams.

Chapter 33: The GeoTek Affair

Edmund H. Shea, Jr. et al v. John P. Burke et al. C-73-0899-RFP. United States District Court, Northern District, California.
GeoTek Resources Fund. Papers. Division of Corporations, State of California.
Gottlieb, Bob, and Shapiro, Eric. "Otis Chandler and the GeoTek Affair." *Coast*, April 1975.
Los Angeles County Recorder Grantor/Grantee Index, 1964-1972.
Securities and Exchange Commission v. GeoTek Resources Fund et al. No. C-73-0819-WTS. United States District Court, Northern District, California. Especially affidavits and depositions of Otis Chandler, Kellogg Speer, Jacob Swartz, Donald Winton; Also "Record and Distribution of Cash Received" (Otis Chandler's Cash Receipts Book).
Stern, Philip. *The Rape of the Taxpayer*. New York: Random House, 1972.
INTERVIEWS: Gerald Boeltz, Asa Call, Victor Carter, Ernest Loebbecke, C. K. McClatchy, Kellogg Spear, H. Van Dyke Johns, Robert Volk, Rob Wood, Rosalind Wyman.

Chapter 34: Who Rules Los Angeles?

Boyarsky, Bill, and Boyarsky, Nancy. *Backroom Politics*. Los Angeles: J. P. Tarcher, 1974.
Central City Association. *Annual Report*, 1974-1975.
Drummond, William. "There is More to Chief Davis Than Meets the Ear." *Los Angeles Times*, August 15, 1971.
Gottlieb, Bob. "Is This the Tom Bradley We Elected?" *Los Angeles*, March 1977.
———. "Mr. Christopher Goes to Washington." *Los Angeles*, May 1977.
"Los Angeles: City With an Artificial Heart." *Forbes*, October 1, 1973.
Los Angeles County Tax Assessor. 1974-1976 Tax Rolls.
Marcuse, Peter. "Mass Transit for the Few: Lessons from Los Angeles." UCLA School of Architecture and Urban Planning, 1975.
Meyers, Robert. "The Downtown Plan Faces Open Rebellion." *Los Angeles*, December 1975.
Public Commission on County Government. *Staff Working Paper: The Principal Law Enforcement Agencies of Los Angeles County Government*. Los Angeles: 1976.
———. *To Serve Seven Million*. Los Angeles: 1976.

Silverbook: Los Angeles Central City Proposed Plan, 1972–1990. Los Angeles, Department of City Planning, 1972.

Socialist Media Group. *Who Rules Los Angeles?* Los Angeles: 1975.

Solomon, Shirley. "All Rigged Up." *Coast*, April 1972.

Stump, Al. "Ed Davis: America's Toughest Cop." *True*, January 1975.

Ward, Baxter. *Cancel the Booking and Destroy the Records: A Case Analysis.* Presented to Members of the Los Angeles County Grand Jury, March 28, 1975.

INTERVIEWS: Jonathan Beatty, Hal Bernson, Dorothy Blake, Bill Boyarsky, Tom Bradley, Lance Brisson, Daniel Bryant, Asa Call, Edward Carter, Victor Carter, Edward Davis, Ernest Debs, C. Edward Dilkes, Lee Dye, John Anson Ford, John Gibson, Thomas Hession, Hal Holker, Robert Karp, Harold Katz, Robert Kholos, Oscar Lawlor Jr., Gilbert Lindsay, Ernest Loebbecke, Peter Marcuse, Mark Murphy, John Pastier, John W. O'Melveny, Neil Petree, Peter Pitchess, Kenneth Reich, Doug Shuit, Maynard Toll, Daniel Topping, Daniel Waters, Philip Watson, Samuel Yorty.

Index

LEWIS AND CLARK COLLEGE
PORTLAND, OREGON 9

Lewis and Clark College - Watzek Library
PN4899.L64 L6625 1977   wmain
Gottlieb, Robert/Thinking big : the stor

3 5209 00348 3563